THE GIRL WHO ELECTRIFIED THE WORLD

THE GIRL WHO ELECTRIFIED THE WORLD

A NOVEL
BY CLIFF RATZA

STONEWALL PRESS
PAVING YOUR WAY TO SUCCESS

The Girl Who Electrified The World

Published in the United States of America

ISBN: 978-1-949362-81-7 (*sc*)
978-1-949362-82-4 (*hb*)
978-1-949362-80-0 (*e*)

Library of Congress Control Number: 2018957030

Published by Stonewall Press
4800 Hampden Lane, Suite 200, Bethesda, MD 20814 USA
1.888.334.0980 | www.stonewallpress.com
1. Fantasy (General)
2. Science
18.11.08

THIS BOOK IS THE sequel to *The Girl With The Lightning Brain*, or perhaps the first book is its prequel. Regardless the reading sequence, it picks up where the first ends, tracing the unexpected twists and turns as Electra Kittner continues battling Techno-Plague and Middle East terrorism while keeping a harsh government at bay. Older and more experienced, Electra is ready to allow males into her games if they can help, adding emotional richness to the mix. Whether or not readers have read the first book, they will quickly learn the background that drives Electra and her allies relentlessly toward the book's gripping conclusion.

The novel's theme reveals that no matter how extraordinary the person, anyone can be a victim in a primitive world that can't handle the truth, and each of us must deal with the complexities of being "merely human," best handled by having an optimistic, pragmatic philosophy.

The book contains three contemporaneous storyline threads:

1. Electra's adventures as she journeys on her chosen path.
2. Her duel with the Guardian Party.
3. Her war against Isilabad.

Readers should enjoy the book on whatever level they wish:

- Gripping action-packed thriller
- Glimpses into a plausible near-term future
- Insights for dealing with the "human condition"
- Illustrative worldview philosophy
- Fast-paced, suspense-filled emotive narrative and imagery
- Introduction to topics every reader wants to know
- Interesting talking points going beyond sound-bites

Book three is completed, awaiting publication when readers are ready. Three more are being developed, so there is much "Lightning Brain Series" enjoyment in store. There are glossary and appendix at the back of the book for readers who wish to know more about terms or topics referenced.

Characters

Mrs. T (aka Alice Bickerwith)
Electra Kittner
Russell Conklin
Robinova Setdarova
Jared Gardner
Su-Lin Song Chou
Adom Ola
Matt Fortier
Jennifer Conklin
Zoe Vargas
Angus McTear
Tim Godfrey
Hudson "Hud" Haller
Hollis "Holy" Haller
Carter Quavah
Mariah Robles

Of course, I wish to thank my parents, Clyde and Betty Ratza, for their loving patience and generosity that gave me the freedom to explore the limits of my world, and my sister, Claudia, for introducing me to poetry and literature. Thanks also to our book manager L.P. Brown, and to Ava Bryson, Jack Jones, Angel Wright, Jill Francis, Leonard Westbrook, and their Stonewall Publishing support teams for taking our Lightning Brain Series to the next level. And a special thanks to Adam Horton for his careful draft reviews and suggestions.

I wish to dedicate this series to the readers who have embraced plot and characters, delighting in tracing their journey-through-life trajectories. And just like our characters, the trajectory of each reader is also sui generis—a popular word from the Latin meaning of its own kind. And though each of us is unique, our trajectories share a similar outline. Another poem from Indira distills the essence.

Triple Crown

Are you where you want to be?
Engaged in what you meant to do?
With those who want to care for you?
Joys of your maturity.

It's not like that past early years,
You search for meaning in your life.
The journey's often fraught with strife,
Some paths may lead to bitter tears.

This crown is worn by very few,
It's oft beyond the outstretched reach.
Try your best but Life will teach,
Be grateful for what you've been able to do.

Contents

CHAPTER 1

February 2118

"Crash and Burn"

(Thread 1 Chapter 1)

Mrs. T struggled mightily to maintain composure, but at this moment she didn't know if she could continue stifling incipient screams much longer. Her head felt like an overinflated balloon fighting to contain yet another excessive blast of compressed gas. For the past thirty-six hours, she had struggled even harder to salvage a rescue mission, doing everything in her power to provide her covert operations field handler—code-named the Bad Boy—with every resource at her disposal. She and the Bad Boy had cobbled together an extraction sortie to retrieve highly placed Opposition Party personnel who might have what's needed to keep America safe from the Techno-Plague, Middle East Terrorism, and the Guardian Party: effective T-Plague vaccine formulas. But they were battling two implacable interdiction teams for which a freakish thunder-snowstorm seemed ready to deliver a crash-and-burn finale for all she had done. Soon she would know if her best had been good enough.

She and her extraction team were awaiting in a remote Virginia national park the arrival of a helicopter carrying an unknown number of unidentified personnel. Yesterday, Guardian Party and CIA covert operations teams—implicit adversaries working independently—blew the cover on two of her critical human assets. Her initial extraction plan had been foiled by one of the adversaries, but somehow it was miraculously salvaged, thanks to persons presently unknown. Horrible weather and a harrowing escape made communications impossible. The who and the how were known only onboard the chopper, the uncertainty knotting Mrs. T's nerves more tightly than a noose after the hangman pulls the lever.

Finally, the pulsating thrum of an approaching chopper cut through the storm-filled wintry night air. *The agony of waiting is over,* she thought. *It's time to collect the spoils of the escape.* The chopper slowed, hovering four hundred feet above a makeshift homing beacon, then descended unsteadily in a buffeting crosswind as its searchlight probed the immanent terrain. Mrs. T could feel neural knots begin to loosen as relief surged through every fiber.

And then lightning struck, completely encasing the chopper in an eerie bluish glow as the rotor blades snapped and it plummeted to a disastrous landing, exploding on impact, launching a blinding fireball and deafening roar skyward.

Gaping at the flaming wreckage, Mrs. T's team froze in spacetime as the catastrophe erupted before their eyes. Then suddenly, a flaming mass spewed from the inferno, rising to become silhouettes of two survivors now ablaze. One staggered to the right while the other dived back in, then re-emerged with another. This new silhouette plunged back in and dragged out a fourth. There were now four survivors—blazing torches from burning clothes—running from the holocaust in a direction away from the extraction team.

The team leaped into action. Three grabbed flame extinguishers and raced towards the survivors. A fourth sprinted toward the wreckage while Mrs. T activated lights and siren on the medical van. And then a second fireball exploded upward when the secondary fuel tank ignited, hurling a flame-filled concussive wave that staggered the team and catapulted the four survivors into the air, then down to Earth and out of sight.

The rescuers instantly regrouped, charging forward undaunted. Time was their enemy, for they must douse the flames before the survivors burned to a crisp. The moonlit overcast and spotty snow covering helped them rush to a clump of smoldering, motionless bodies. Two plunged towards the pile while the third continued a frantic search, veering to the right.

The extinguishers did their jobs, gushing foam that cooled burning flesh. The pair worked quickly while following the first rule of triage: don't just do something, stand there. Flashlights illuminated a grisly scene: three bodies riddled by shrapnel from the last explosion. All clothes above the waste burned completely. They searched in vain for signs of life, but there were none. Suddenly, the alarmed voice of their partner pierced the air.

"I've got a live one! A female, unconscious, but has a pulse. Head trauma and bleeding; third degree burns on head and torso. Get the EMTs up here now."

Not another word was needed; the other two followed involuntary orders. One dashed madly towards the medical van, while the other did what he could to respect the dignity of the dead. They had died horribly, but at least by the grace of whatever they believed in, had died instantly. He carefully separated and straightened the bodies, folding arms across chests, noting there were two males and one female. Soon he would get body bags and help load them for removal, but not until the fate of the fourth was known. He would stand watch until then.

Less than a minute later two EMTs were peering down at an unconscious survivor while another teammate held flashlights. There were no torso wounds. This one must have dived forward to avoid the erupting fireball and shrapnel envelope, but momentum added to that of the concussive blast. The position of the head, resting at an awkward angle, signaled serious spinal injury, and the deep gash and contusion above the forehead indicated concussion. They would need to immobilize the head, carefully roll the survivor onto a stretcher, and then have the van drive close to load the living and the dead.

They stopped the bleeding and patched the gash, then secured a neck brace before rolling her onto the stretcher. The van arrived as they secured her to the stretcher, then loaded and locked it in place for a dash to the medical center.

Poor Mrs. T felt like collateral damage. There was nothing she could do to help as she realized what a total disaster the extraction had become. Four dead, one survivor, and all still unknown. Another body had been recovered from the burned-out chopper carcass. It would be her assignment—no, it would be her duty—to ride in back next to the survivor, giving whatever support she could muster for that poor girl, if in fact she ever regained consciousness. With that grim thought, Mrs. T made a silent pledge to protect this poor creature and to supply all resources she could assemble. She would either put the girl back together as partial redemption for her failed mission or fall on her sword and perish in the ignominy of defeat.

CHAPTER 2

February 2118

"Damage Control"

(Thread 1 Chapter 2)

As THE VAN RUSHED to a clinic sympathetic to the Opposition Party, Mrs. T knelt next to the stretcher, holding the girl's hand and talking in her throaty British-accented voice, hoping that a stream of words might awaken the sole survivor.

What she saw simultaneously shocked and awed. The flames had burned much of the hair, head and torso; crimson blisters oozing plasma-like fluids were already forming. Yet this damage couldn't completely conceal what must have been striking features that accompanied a practically perfect, fit and trim physique.

"Come back to us, my dear, and we will make you good as new," she repeated over and over; suddenly there was flickering eye movement. "Geoffrey! We're getting a response. Please help." And with that, one of the EMTs jostled to her side as the girl's eyes twitched open.

"My dear, you have been severely injured. Please do not try to move or talk. Just listen to me. My name is Alice. You were in a helicopter crash, and we are taking you to a clinic. You have severe burns and head wounds. Blink once if you understand what I am saying." There was one blink.

"Excellent, my dear. Can you talk? Blink once if you can, and twice if you can't." The girl's lips quivered but formed no syllables. There were two blinks.

"Not to worry, my dear. Do you have feeling in your hands. Squeeze my hand if yes, blink twice if no." Alice felt pressure from a light squeeze and smiled.

"Excellent my dear. Now, do you have feeling in your legs. Try moving them and if yes, blink once. Geoffrey, please watch for any movement." A look of concern tinged with inchoate panic flashed in the girl's eyes, followed by two blinks.

"Not to worry. Geoffrey, what else to ask?"

"Young lady, you have head trauma that might have caused temporary neck and nerve damage. I know your burns are painful, and we have treated them with a numbing antiseptic spray until we get to the clinic. Can you handle the pain until we get there? Blink once for yes, twice for no." One quick blink.

"Good. We'll be at the clinic in ten minutes; then we'll get you feeling better. Just hang on." Alice continued by asking,

"My dear, do you know your name?" Two blinks.

"That's OK. We'll figure all this out as soon as we start patching you up. Now, please close your eyes and don't worry. Just let us take care of you."

Alice had been studying the girl's eyes during the brief conversation. Their dark-hazel intensity revealed alert comprehension in spite of the exhausting effort. Suddenly, the girl's lips quivered as a look of concern flashed in her eyes, but no words came out. Alice was about to speak but spotted the problem; a dark trouser stain spread between the girl's legs. After sliding down what remained of charred trousers, Alice grabbed two towels and blotted up a copious flow of liquid streaming between the girl's thighs.

"Not to worry, my dear. Your internal systems are working, and that's a good sign. I'll have you tidied up and ready to go before you can say billy-oh." A look of utter embarrassment punctuated by relief-filled thanks flashed before the girl closed her eyes and retreated into herself, falling asleep immediately.

A feeling of profound concern engulfed Alice. *I felt her eyes probe deep inside, as if she could see into my soul. I must be careful to keep my distance, but I feel responsible until she can take care of herself.* The van swerved to an abrupt stop, redirecting her thoughts.

The EMTs rushed the stretcher into an emergency room; Alice conferred with the on-duty staff who had been briefed by the driver while racing to the clinic. Now she could do nothing but wait. The pause brought her fatigue to the forefront, so she instructed her people to get some rest. After asking an attending nurse to wake her when needed, Alice collapsed onto a couch and into fitful sleep as the fateful hours ticked by. A nurse shook Alice's shoulder at eight a.m.

"The doctor needs to talk with you." After being asleep for four hours, Alice snapped awake, fully aware of her surroundings and conditions at hand. She sat up and smiled diplomatically.

"Thank you for tucking me in with a pillow and blanket. I haven't rested that well for three days. Do you think I could freshen up a wee bit before seeing the doctor?" The nurse returned the smile.

"I thought about that, so here's a wash cloth, towel and comb. Let me take you to the nurses' changing area. When you're ready, we'll have breakfast with the doctor."

Alice Bickerwith—no one knew her Mrs. T identity—peered into the mirror while collecting her thoughts for the day ahead. *Here I am, a fifty-something average looking woman of middling height and weight, bland as a bathtub faucet. And that fits me to a "T" because I want to be unnoticed so I can keep my covert role invisible.* As the liaison between the British government's "America Strong" covert operation and the struggling Opposition Party, it was her duty to keep the last best hope alive for keeping America's foundering ship of state from tipping.

Twenty years ago she had been recruited—because her nondescript appearance masked pragmatic intelligence and plucky resilience—from the ranks of the British diplomatic corps to become part of a project known only to the highest levels in British government's secret service. With typically thorough foresight, leaders sensed how vulnerable the Washington Establishment would be if it didn't deal proactively with its Achilles heels: Middle East terrorism and Techno-Plague. Isilabad—a rogue Middle East country created a hundred years ago when fundamentalists carved it from the underbelly of failed states—had become the latest reincarnation of Islam's centuries' old war against the West. Washington's "kinder and gentler" appeasement policies had been and always would be ineffective. Of more recent vintage, the T-Plague surfaced thirty years ago when a manmade mutant virus accidentally leaked into the environment from a lab working to develop a cure for Alzheimers. The virus caused neural entanglement leading to rapid onset of dementia. After too many years and dollars spent to kill the virus, even America's vaunted National Institute of Health had given up, which resulted in America's becoming darker and intolerant, regressive and dumber, incapable of converting technological possibilities into tools that might build a better future. The civilized world shuddered, for as America goes, so goes Western Civilization.

Alice focused on today's objectives. She needed the doctor to report the girl's condition, then she would need to talk with her as soon as possible. And finally, she would need to talk with her Opposition Party contact to figure out what to do with her. All told, a daunting challenge, so Alice steeled herself to deal with whatever obstacles might come her way.

Alice listened attentively to the doctor. On-the-job diplomacy training had made her a skilled negotiator, force multiplied by her emotional intelligence and uncanny ability to read body language. Now she was ready to take control of the situation.

"Jolly good doctor, for all you have done. If I may, I would like to recap my understanding so you can correct me where I'm wrong. First, to the burns. The best short-term treatment is with spray antibiotics and topical anesthetics. Once we have her stabilized and home—and we don't know yet where that is—we'll get her treated by plastic surgeons to accelerate healing and minimize scarring.

"Next, regarding the neck. Your imaging confirms she has a broken neck It's a clean break, and if we keep her head immobilized until it mends, there's a good possibility she will regain the use of her legs. So, we'll get her a neural surgeon too.

"And finally, to the head trauma. The effects of the gash and bash she has just above her forehead are indeterminate because you can't read the brain scans and have been unable to awaken her. What can you add?" The doctor smiled wearily, put down his cup of coffee and picked up his part of the conversation.

"Our brain scanner must have been damaged by yesterday's power surges because I can't read the images. A normal brain scan shows a couple of centers where neural activity is centered, but the girl's image looks like a forest of lighted Christmas trees generating waves of neural signals surging throughout the brain. The real-time pattern is mesmerizing, like countless neural centers sending and receiving waves of neurochemical communications. It has to be equipment malfunction. I've never seen anything like it. And we can't wake her up, even though her vital signs have stabilized and she's out of immediate danger. It's as if her brain has hung a 'do not disturb' sign on her consciousness, which is our doorway. How did you get her to wake up?"

"I simply stayed by her side, holding her hand and talking non-stop. May I try again? I must talk to her so I can plan our next steps. Otherwise, we're at sixes and sevens."

"It's worth a try, so let's get you washed and fitted with a mask and gown."

Alice knelt next to the sleeping girl and repeated her mantra-like monologue while squeezing her hands.

"Young lady, please wake up. Please come back to us and we'll make you good as new. My name is Alice and we need to talk so I can help you..."

The girl appeared to be serenely asleep under a light blanket, breathing deeply with the ghost of a smile on her burned lips.

The I.V. tubes were unobtrusive, and the neck brace did not look uncomfortable, appearing more like an adornment an Egyptian princess from antiquity might wear. The nurses had removed all clothes and carefully bathed and washed what remained of her raven-black hair; Alice found this portrait of the young lady no longer so disturbing.

There were burns on her legs, but not nearly as severe as those on her torso, where the redness and blistering had stabilized. Not so for her face, where uneven swelling and blistering had spread. It was as if her entire face and neck were being engulfed. *Not a good sign, but I'm not the doctor. I'll listen to what he says.* Alice was unaware of the passage of time, for she had vanished into the immediacy of the moment and was aware only of the girl. Suddenly Alice detected eye movement, dark-hazel eyes flickering and then staying open, gazing hopefully, expectantly. Alice gasped involuntarily, for it felt as if the girl were peering into her thoughts.

"My dear, thank you for coming back to me. Please do not try to move or talk. Let me talk first. Do you need to use the loo—I mean the bathroom? Blink once for yes, twice for no." Two blinks.

"Would you like something to drink?" A smile creased the girl's lips, followed by a blink.

"My dear, I thought you would. Let me get us something." She turned to the nurse resting in a nearby chair.

"Would you please get the young lady and me a drink?" The nurse jumped to attention and quickly returned with two containers equipped with flexible straws. Alice elevated the bed so the girl would be in a more comfortable position.

"Here, let me hold it for you while you sip as much as you wish. Please blink once when you are satisfied." The girl sucked deeply, then finally blinked.

"There, much better. Now blink if you are hungry, once for yes and two for no." One quick blink. "Excellent. Appetite is a good sign. Nurse, the young lady would like something to eat." A minute later Alice was holding a jar of baby food that she proceeded to spoon-feed. A shiver swept through as she watched the girl, as if she were witnessing the start of a pristine chrysalis from which would emerge something extraordinary. *As the phoenix rose from the ashes, so too will this special creature.* Alice could tell when the girl's appetite had been satisfied, and she put down the half-empty jar.

"Well now, that must be better; please blink if you would like more to drink". Two quick blinks. "That's fine. Well now, let's continue. Are you able to talk? Say so if you can, or blink twice if no".

The girl's lips trembled open forming syllables, and this time she could speak slowly, faintly. "Ye-Yes. Ha-hardly." Alice squeezed the girl's hands, which were folded in front.

"That's excellent. Eight hours ago you could not. Now, please try to answer this question. Do you know who you are?"

"N-no. N-not yet." Alice detected both frustration and determination in the girl's eyes.

"Not to worry. You and I will piece this together. I know you are strong, a relentless survivor who can handle the unvarnished truth. And after I tell you what I know, I will tell you my opinion.

"You and two comrades were rescued by helicopter from an ambush in Washington. Your chopper crashed and fate allowed only one survivor, you. You came away with severe burns, a broken neck, a deep gash and contusion on your head. When you came to you could not talk or move your legs, and you did not know who you are. When we got you to the clinic, the doctors treated your burns, confirmed your broken neck, and did a brain scan to assess neural condition. Your torso burns are second degree and appear to have stabilized. Your facial burns are extensive and third degree, and much of your hair is burned. Regarding your neck, yes, it is broken, but broken cleanly and should mend itself, with every reason to believe you will regain mobility. You are wearing a neck brace that will keep it immobile during the healing process.

"Regarding your head trauma, the gash and contusion just above your forehead are causing amnesia. And finally, here is what I find most remarkable. The doctor says the clinic's brain scanner malfunctioned. He couldn't interpret the image. He said your scan looked like a forest of lighted Christmas trees sending waves of electrical signals rippling among multiple neural centers. And the doctors couldn't awaken you, almost as if your brain did not want to be disturbed." Alice paused, took a deep breath and launched into her conjecture.

"My dear, here is what I think your brain is doing: it is focusing all its energy, all its resources to repair the damage. And I will assist in whatever way I can to make it so. I know what I need to do next, and the next time we talk I will be able to tell you who you are and what my plan—our plan actually—is to make you whole again.

"Now, my dear, here is what I need you to do. Rest your body and mind. Let your brain work in its mysterious way. And please, awaken again when I call to you. Now then, do you have any final questions for me?"

A single tear escaped from the corner of the girl's right eye, rolling slowly across her blistered cheek. She stuttered, "N-no. Th-thank you so." Alice struggled to maintain composure.

"There, there, my dear. You'll be speaking Shakespeare shortly. Now rest." The girl closed her eyes and immediately fell into a deep, protective sleep. Though she didn't know how much the girl would remember, Alice strode to brief the doctor, after which she had people to call and plans to prepare. And she knew best how to do both.

CHAPTER 3

February 2018

"The Plan"

(Thread 1 Chapter 3)

"YES, MRS. T. WE'LL use your plan until we know more from other sources. Please report in when you've completed step one." So ended Alice's call to her Opposition Party inner circle contact.

Only two people knew Alice Bickerwith as Mrs. T: the inner circle contact, and the "Bad Boy" covert ops contact. Neither knew her real name, which allowed her to operate below the radar. Nor had they ever heard her natural voice, because she used a voice enhancer when speaking to them. Mrs. T's sight and sound anonymity and Alice Bickerwith's bland and forgettable appearance combined perfectly.

Alice adjusted the voice enhancer to produce a man's voice before making the next call to one of the original extraction targets, Russell Conklin, having just completed a review of what she already knew. The "Bad Boy" used Russell Conklin, a highly-placed National Institute of Health executive working for the Opposition Party, to snoop into NIH Cognicom projects, which had all failed to find effective T-Plague vaccines. His cover, and that of his source, a Moses Solstein, had been blown and they had to escape, bringing with them T-Plague vaccine data. Though ambushed, they had managed to outwit their pursuers but had to alter escape plans.

That was all Alice knew, and it was three days old. She took a deep breath. *Time to make the call, get all I can, and flesh out my plan.*

Alice kept the call focused and brief. She learned that Conklin and his wife Jennifer had escaped to a safe house while Moses, Conklin's daughter Christi, and her friend Electra Kittner proceeded to the chopper extraction site. Conklin didn't know why Solstein brought Electra, but he guessed that she had helped him get data.

The conversation turned heart-wrenching for Conklin when he learned there is only one survivor—a badly injured girl with dark-hazel eyes. Conklin stoically responded that the survivor is Electra, volunteering enough information for Alice to take her next step.

After the call ended, she briefed the doctor, telling him she needed to take a walk to collect her thoughts, after which she would talk again with the girl and set in motion her recovery plan. She changed clothes again and followed the doctor's suggestion for a suitable place to stroll while thinking.

The remnants of the freak storm had blown out, leaving a cloudless sky and sparkling snow cover on a brisk and windless winter's morning. Though not the athletic type, Alice did enough walking and calisthenics to handle the demands of her dual roles. She walked briskly at first to relieve the pent-up stress from the phone call. Then she slowed to let her mind follow its own train of thought, sifting through what she had just learned. The soft crunching of the snow underfoot provided an unrelated focus that suddenly triggered a famous fragment from a Winston Churchill quote:

> "...It is a riddle, wrapped in a mystery, inside an enigma..."

Goodness. Perhaps the same applies to the girl. I don't know enough to reach such a conclusion, but perhaps she can be of use. No harm constructing a contingency scenario in which she can play a role.

And what information did she have about Electra Kittner? Conklin had given her a lot because Electra and his daughter Christi, along with another female of the same age named Robin

Setdarova, had been best friends. Electra's mother had perished in a fire during childbirth, and the girl had been raised by her father and grandfather. She had a happy and healthy childhood through part of adolescence until both father and grandfather died mysteriously. After that, she had become more complex, more reserved, more enigmatic. She was very smart but sometimes seemed distracted and naïve. Nevertheless, she was doing well in graduate school and even worked part-time at the NIH where her parents had worked on Solstein's ill-fated Cognicom project that was searching for T-Plague vaccines. And she was also civic-minded, doing volunteer work for the Guardian Party.

Alice had walked far enough, reaching the main street of the small rural town housing the clinic, and she needed her morning cup of tea. She spotted a coffee shop—authentic, not a chain—and before taking a booth, noticed scones on the counter, so she ordered tea and scones when the waitress took her order. When it came, it brought memories of growing up in London, having tea and biscuits most afternoons with her brother and mother, who had died several years ago from T-Plague complications. Every so often—like this very moment—pangs of remorse would pierce Alice's calm exterior, reminding her of what she missed by working overseas as a diplomat married to her career rather than having somebody to love. Perhaps she was susceptible to these feelings now because of Electra's situation, but as the pang subsided she let the thought go, finishing her snack and heading back.

Alice zeroed in on her plan as she walked. There were two plans actually, with the second dependent on the success of the first. The first would put Electra together again, but given the scope of injury and the degraded state of America's medical infrastructure, that could be daunting. *What medical facility might be able to treat her? Blimey, I don't know. I know where she lives, but she can't take care of herself. What a muddle I have.*

If it were possible, Alice would take her in and employ a therapist caregiver, but that was out of the question for logistical and security reasons. Better to have her stay in her own home with a caregiver which Alice would pay for. And from what Conklin had told her, she knew of a longshot.

There's no evidence Electra will make a complete recovery, but why not assume her brain is in overdrive repairing the damage? Maybe the clinic's scanner had given a true picture. This naive hope braced Alice, so she would give it a go because it anchored her first plan.

The second would be for developing a T-Plague vaccine. *Maybe Electra knows where the data is or could point me to someone who does. Maybe Conklin can track it down. Problematic either way, but it's too soon to fret about it until we put the poor girl back together.*

Alice returned to the clinic at noon, reenergized from the walk. She would write up her plan, then rehearse conversations before placing calls. The doctor directed her to an office she could use and Alice was in action as soon as the door closed. It took her half an hour to document a plan that included task list and timeline, but her conversations would require a personal touch so she took the better part of an hour to rehearse.

Alice knew how to fight a tendency to become too tightly wound—like a stretched rubber band holding together a pack of playing cards—so she changed into a nurse's uniform and simply chatted with the doctor and attending nurse, being careful not to reveal too much information. She could feel her tension loosen, especially when she learned the girl's deep sleep strengthened all vital signs. *Time to make my first call. I know what to say, so take a deep breath and smile.* Alice placed the call.

In spite of best efforts, Robin had worried herself into a near-panic. Her two best friends, Electra and Christi, had failed to show at Electra's birthday celebration two days ago, and both had been incommunicado ever since. That was most unusual, and because she had been unable to get through to Christi's parents, Robin sensed something was terribly wrong.

Robin was the third member of a close and closed circle, nicknamed in childhood "the Three Queens" because of looks and talent. But unlike feisty Christi or subtly powerful but enigmatic Electra, musically gifted but high-strung Robin battled diffidence and self-doubt. They had rescued her from numerous predicaments and had actually saved her life by rescuing her from a T-Plague ravaged emergency room, then nursed her back to health physically and emotionally. Robin needed them, as a delicate flower needs the sun to prevent its petals from folding. And she loved them in ways that she was too embarrassed to reveal, even to herself. She lunged for her cell phone when it chimed.

"Hello, this is Robin." A voice unknown responded.

"Hello Robin. I hope you are able to talk with me. My name is Alice Bickerwith, and I am calling on behalf of your friend Electra Kittner. May I continue?" One terse yes came the reply.

"Thank you. Electra needs your help. I will be as brief as possible giving you all the necessary details. She was severely injured two days ago in a crash. She has amnesia, a broken neck, leg paralysis, third degree burns, and difficulty speaking. I am in charge of her recovery, and we need a caregiver to assist her. You are recommended because of your special relationship. This would be a major disruption to your current schedule, but you will be thoroughly compensated and supported. If you think you are up to the task, I need you to tell me before bringing her home tomorrow. I will give you my phone number if you would like more time to decide. Hello, are you still there?"

This revelation stunned Robin into utter silence as a whirlwind of emotions swirled about. Then suddenly, without any doubt, she made her decision.

"Yes, Miss Bickerwith. I can handle this. How and when do I proceed?"

"We will pick you up tomorrow afternoon when we bring Electra home. We need for you to live with her for the next several weeks as we track her recovery. You will have assistance so you can continue going to classes and take breaks whenever needed. Now, here is my cell phone number, and here is a number I want you to call so you can confirm who I am. I will call you at 8 a.m. tomorrow morning with additional details. And thank you for supporting your friend. It means a lot to her and to me."

As Robin disconnected the call, she felt energized, as if her life had suddenly become meaningful. Shyness and self-doubt evaporated, replaced by commitment to bring Electra back, no matter what would be required. Anger towards her father and concerns about college receded. Steps would become apparent as soon as she starts. She ran downstairs to inform her parents and then packed for tomorrow.

Alice liked the tone of Robin's response. *The girl has pluck, a trait we Brits admire. It's time to speak to Electra.* Vital signs had been marching steadily upward, and it took only a minute for the attending nurse to awaken her before elevating the bed. Alice pulled a chair alongside after inviting the nurse to leave.

"Good afternoon, Electra. Your vital signs are now stronger, and I think they show in your appearance. Do you feel ready to continue our chat, or would you like something to eat or drink first?" A voice stronger and more articulate than before spoke up.

"H-Hi…V-voice b-better…P-please, talk."

"Excellent, my dear. Well now, I have very good news. First, we have found out who you are by talking with a Russell Conklin. You are Electra Kittner, twenty-one years old and living near Washington, DC. Two days ago, you assisted him and a Moses Solstein escape from an ambush by some political organization. Moses, you and your best friend Christi Conklin escaped by helicopter. Does any of this seem familiar yet?" A stoic no was the only reply.

"We also contacted another friend, a Miss Robin Setdarova, who will be your caregiver. We will take you home tomorrow and begin your recovery plan immediately. We trust that once you are home and with Robin, your memory will return much faster.

"Now, here is a bit more background. You are very smart and are currently working on your bio-technology doctorate at George Washington University, and your part-time work at an NIH research lab ties in with your degree program. Your parents had been respected NIH researchers. I am sorry to say both of them are now deceased. Your mother Indira died when you were born, and you were raised by your father Jason and grandfather Justin. Both of them died about five years ago, but you have the spirit and will to succeed, and you have done well on your own with the support of friends. And you are also a volunteer worker for the Guardian Party." Alice could tell from the girl's riveted eyes that she was keenly absorbing all she heard but was beginning to tire, so Alice decided to end the conversation.

"And so, that is where we are. I am making arrangements to take you home tomorrow morning. I hope all of this is reassuring to you."

Electra reached for Alice's hand with both of hers and the hint of a smile. "Ye-yes. Mu-must sleep and th-think. Th-thank you."

"There, there, my dear. The next time we chat I know you will be even stronger, and soon you'll be tickety-boo. Now, please rest and let your brain take command."

Alice needed to make two additional calls before she too could rest. The first alerted her team to arrange transportation tomorrow morning for herself and the girl. It was quick and to the point with no questions asked for details that were not yet fully known. The second was to a medical facility she thought would be able to handle the girl's recovery, but no luck there. It was overpopulated and understaffed, a condition Alice feared she would encounter everywhere. She put the phone down, wracking her brain for ideas when a flash of insight broke through. *Of course! I know how to proceed and will not fail.*

An hour later she was ready for her last activity of the day: a meeting with the attending physician and the clinic administrator. Fatigue was setting in, so she would make the conversation brief. After that, she would ask them to drive her to a local hotel where she would buy them dinner, then spend the night. Dinner conversation would tell only part of the plan: she and her team would retrieve the girl tomorrow morning, taking with them all records of the episode. All bills were to be sent directly to Alice. There would be no loose ends, no trail. This was not a cover-up; it was an erasure never to be discussed again.

Alice tucked into bed soon after dinner. Tomorrow's plans were in place and her nerves loosened as her tension headache faded, allowing her to drift asleep while issuing a warning. *I must keep my feelings out of the way. This is a dangerous business, one that requires keeping threats at bay. Perhaps I can make it into a game. And if I do, I do hope Electra likes games…*

CHAPTER 4

February 2118

"Square One Revisited"

(Thread 2 Chapter 1)

The Invisible Man, though flummoxed to the max, concealed his anger beneath a metallic-sounding voice and phlegmatic demeanor. He had just ended the Invisible Hand's status call that reported the worst outcome imaginable for what should have been a Guardian Party covert operation capstone achievement. But instead of rolling up two high-level Opposition Party targets, and with them vital T-Plague data, the Hand reported his interdiction team and supporting mole are missing, as if a sinkhole had opened three days ago during the freak storm and swallowed them all. All target names and trail markers leading to the holy grail—a T-Plague "smart pill" that would protect people from rapid descent into dementia—vanished with them. And in its rush to apprehend, the team didn't report details regarding who they were ambushing or where. Every aspect of this operation is stone cold dead.

Now the Man had to call in results to the Guardian Party steering committee leader, who was expecting to hear about the singular success he had been promised. *Yes, the results are remarkable, but at the wrong end of the scale. Worse still, I haven't clue what to do next and dare not admit defeat. Jared Gardner is not a nice person when he doesn't get what he wants. And sometimes, he's not so nice when he does.* The Man reluctantly punched in the number.

Charismatic Jared Gardner, the Guardian Party's man of the times, practiced the Party's guiding slogan he had penned: "Harsh Times demand Harsh Measures," a tagline that resonated among the many who feared terrorism and the T-Plague. They applauded Jared's ability to dispense harshness in full measure. His momentum towards the White House—through ballot box or through thinly veiled threats of government takeover—had been slowed recently when someone leaked unproven improprieties and double-dealing hidden agendas, but he was supremely confident he would navigate through the shoals of public suspicion. He was now waiting for a call from his covert ops contact who would confirm good news that he would deliver in an hour to his Inner Circle.

An urbane veneer covering Jared's ruthless persona fooled many people, but others said all politicos are the same underneath, and they found enough substance inside Jared to command their respect, feeling certain his core principles would keep him inbounds. He exuded in his interviews faith in the Constitution and conservative Liberalism, criticizing a succession of statist administrations that had gutted American exceptionalism and military readiness. The average citizen wanted a populist leader who defended national interests instead of international giveaways. Jared spoke their language, and many T-Plague sufferers wanted him to do their thinking too.

Jared's critics either discounted his cornerstone principles or underestimated his political savvy. They manufactured sound bites impugning his I.Q. and character, but they failed miserably because the people preferred his results to their rhetoric.

Jared's Inner Circle knew what he wanted: an America whose Declaration of Independence and Constitution are sacred because they herald traditional individual rights, and he was dead set against efforts to resurrect the worst Progressive practices that would sacrifice individualism and states' rights to unjustified egalitarianism and social engineering. Though he hid his disdain, Jared often huffed to himself.

Too many academo-politicos from too many feckless administrations continue drinking the Philosopher-King Koolaid, despite all the facts that show a liberal democracy supported by a market economy, adjusted to moderate business cycles, is the last best hope. Today's political and economic arenas are more uncertain and complex, but the art of politics is not rocket science, and a smart, informed public makes our political system work. When I occupy the Oval Office, I'll do the thinking for those that can't. And I'll use some of the advanced think take models, but I'll make them work for the people instead of paper-pushers. And in today's troubled times, I know best what's needed. It's time to rebuild our military, repair our infrastructure, and energize the economy by creating jobs while wiping out T-Plague and Middle East Terrorism. I'll focus on the short term because there's no long-term if we don't survive. A bit of populism and nationalism will help too because that's where public sentiment is. And as long as I deliver, the public won't mind my hidden agendas because they work for the people too.

And the enemies of my people are my enemies too. I don't trust those Chinese. They're still trying to knock us off the top of the economic pecking order, as well as hack into our technology and steal our data. They never could come up with much on their own, and their aging population has turned them into a toothless tiger. I don't trust the Russians either. They'd like to steal all our money. Good thing their leadership bungled, accelerating the country's population implosion. They run a Kleptocracy controlling a worthless, commodity-based economy. But the worst of the lot is Isilabad, still pushing the war between Islam and Christianity, still pushing for a road back to the Dark Ages. When I'm in charge, I'll make sure all three stay in line.

Jared expected the call, but not its content. Good for Jared no video accompanied the audio feed, for his flabbergasted expression would have betrayed his calm voice. And it was lucky indeed for the Invisible Man that Jared knew how to harness his anger when dealing with others, always able to turn a negotiation into a win-win-win outcome: win for Jared, win for the public, and win for those in his corner. Jared spoke in measured tones.

"And that's it? No further contact? No contingency plan? Well, this is all—what was the word you used—singular? Well, we're back to square one." Jared waited for the terse reply, then continued. "I'll call you shortly to tell you what to do, so stay close."

Though Jared knew covert operations often over-promise and under-deliver, what he had just heard broke all records, forcing him to improvise a contingency plan, using all his devious and manipulative people skills so he could cover the disaster. Soon he would ask at the upcoming meeting for buy-in from his lieutenants, which he expected immediately because all were handpicked and cut from the same political cloth that Jared wore so well.

As he took his place at the head of the table, Jared effused his usual welcoming banter, then confidently dived into his story.

"I alerted you three days ago to an ambush where our covert operations team would roll up high level Opposition Party sources and grab vital T-Plague data. Well, it turned into a botch-up. We came away with nothing, and some of our personal assets are missing in action." He paused briefly for the results to sink in and then kept his plot moving because this was not the time for a group discussion. Instead, it was time for his lieutenants to endorse what he wanted, so he put his fists on the table and proceeded matter-of-factly.

"All of us have the utmost respect for our covert ops group, but all of us know how difficult it has been for them to deliver on what they promise. Recently, I have been considering changes for how we run covert ops, and I've reached my trigger point, so listen up. When I'm done, you'll know I'm right.

"It's only a matter of time until the current administration collapses. The next terrorist attack or T-Plague outbreak will tip public sentiment over the edge, and then we'll install our Guardian Party Administration. It'll be a bloodless coup if we implement the insertion plan I've already developed that'll put our people in all key positions. And for that to work smoothly, we must first implement our infiltration plan." Jared looked into the expectant eyes riveted on him, knowing he was several steps ahead of everyone at the table. He smiled inwardly, nodded knowingly.

"All of you sitting at this table were picked because of your multiple abilities as well as contacts. We already know that many of the government agencies—civil and military—hate the current administration and the continuing Washington Establishment decay it breeds. So, each of you will target an assigned branch to infiltrate and recruit key personnel to be with us when the government falls. And for immediate action, we will recruit the CIA so we can fold our covert operations into it. That way, we immediately advance many steps on the hunt for terrorist cells and for effective T-Plague vaccines. So, let's go around the table for recommendations on who targets what." Jared listened carefully to what his people said, and after twenty minutes ended the discussion.

"I like what I'm hearing. Everyone earns an A-plus, and I've jotted down a list of who targets what. But before I give you assignments, let me answer a question all of you should be asking: what happens to our current covert operations people? Some of them will be terminated, some recycled, and some inserted into the CIA. And until we have the CIA with us, our covert operations team must be kept unaware of our intentions. For them, it's business as usual until the ax falls. So, tonight's decisions are for our eyes and ears only. Now, here are the marching orders…"

Elliot Spitzdieck paid attention to the words and body language as his section chief angrily summarized current events within the CIA and the current administration. Just days ago, a covert ops team missed intercepting Opposition Party targets carrying critical data. Seasoned agents knew that freak weather was not the cause; lack of coordination among inept Washington bureaucrats was. Elliot was fed up with Washington's weakness and knew that many of his cohorts shared the same sentiment. They too would cheer when the administration's immanent collapse occurs, replacing it with another that deals decisively in these harsh times.

Spitzdieck didn't smile much because that's not what a tough as nails mid-level secret service man is supposed to do when his career is continually in jeopardy, thanks to the ups and downs of the nettlesome covert operation he leads: Project Death Shield. Its mission: to burrow into the bowels of whatever or whomever it could find in order to stop T-Plague and its related terrorist groups from compromising the nation's health or security. Spitzdieck had been stymied for five years because his aggressive plans and interrogation techniques were always scaled back by the "higher ups." Maybe that would change when the right people took over. He smiled briefly, knowing he would be ready when the Washington Establishment collapses.

Russell Conklin's mood on his drive to a safe house after sitting through a grim Opposition Party's inner circle meeting felt oddly upbeat. The meeting came up empty for regaining momentum after the failed rescue mission, or for handling the immanent government crash. The best it could do was develop a prioritized task list and assign people to research each one.

Russell's world had been permanently rearranged during the last three days by events completely out of his control: his only daughter and his information source dead, his career path dislocated, his name possibly high on one or more target lists. And he didn't know if or when he and his wife Jennifer might be able to return to a normal life.

But these events had transformed him into leader, ready to serve if he were ever given an opportunity. He had already moved beyond grieving's disbelief and anger so he could help Jennifer, and he had replaced "what if" tormenting by focusing on his new assignment: take whatever steps necessary to plan and execute a solution for stopping T-Plague dead in its tracks. His senior NIH position made him the obvious choice, but there was nothing to build on because his source's data had been destroyed in the crash.

As he parked in the fading glow of the setting sun, he began ticking off what he would do immediately. First, get his home's ambush damage patched and then provide explanations to neighbors and bosses for his absence. Then determine if his cover had been blown, or if the counter-attack had silenced the bad guys before they could report in. And then he would figure out how to get

T-Plague vaccine data. At the moment, he hadn't a clue what to do, but this transformed man would handle whatever might confront him because there was no alternative for salvaging whatever remained of his former life. He would do whatever necessary to protect his wife and to honor the memory of his daughter, who had died so young and so full of life. *I am a survivor, and I will rise to the challenges ahead.* Russell's pace quickened as the right words for Jennifer came to mind.

CHAPTER 5

February 2118

"Homecoming"

(Thread 1 Chapter 4)

"THIS IS NOT A drill! Get with the plan, soldier." As the words reverberated in the recesses of memory, Electra struggled to sit upright in bed, rubbing her eyes and peering at a glowing white apparition standing next to her. Indira was not smiling.

"Do you recognize me?" A shudder stirred Electra's brain, as if scales were beginning to fall from her blocked memory. A look of dull surprise lifted from her eyes.

"Mu-Mother?"

"Yes. I am Indira, your mother and Muse. Your Inner Voice that is always with you. Now tell me, who are you?" Electra felt another involuntary shiver as more memory circuits activated.

"Eh-Electra Kittner, girl with La-lightning Brain, genetically altered at b-birth by lightning bolt that k-killed you and transformed me i-into what I am." A blank look clouded her face when she spoke again. "Uh-I sense more, but can't fa-find words."

"Focus your cognition. "Tell me more." Once again, a veil of confusion lifted.

"I-I've been taking care of muh-myself ever since fa-father and grandfather wa-were killed, and I-I'm working on buh-biotech PhD...I-I'm snooping at Guardian Party fuh-for T-Plague and Middle Eh-east Terrorism stuff. I can't let ga-government know wa-what I am." Indira's expression began to soften as she asked a final question.

"Good. Now tell me about your friends."

"Duh-don't want close friends. Don't want to worry or leh-let them ha-hold me back. Ju-just have Adom and Su; Hud in Au-Austin. Luh-lover Christi a-and buh-brittle Robin, and Puh-Professor Ravenhill; Clar—" Indira interrupted in mid-sentence.

"Do you know why you can't move your legs?" Vivid memories rushed back.

"Ye-Yes. Heh-helicopter crash. Buh-broken neck; bad burns." Electra stopped for an instant, then choked out, "Ca-Christi and Mo dead." Indira's expression became one of unbounded compassion.

"Enough said, my darling Daughter. Your lightning brain is recovering from temporary amnesia, and it is preparing to lead your recovery, but I don't know what that might be. When you awaken, follow its commands. It will reveal all you need. Pay heed to what you have lost. Draw strength from your philosophy, and always remember that I am with you. Now rest, and when you awaken, move forward on your chosen path." Indira's apparition faded like a shimmering mirage as Electra descended into a dreamless sleep.

The uneventful three-hour chopper and medivan journey from Virginia to Robin's house helped Electra shake off the effects of too much bedrest. She rode comfortably enough, strapped into a wheel chair rather than on a stretcher, and Alice kept up an intermittent dialogue, giving appropriate sound breaks for herself as well as patient, driver, and EMT.

"I do hope seeing familiar people and places triggers pleasant memories. It works for me, and no reason not for you too. Your dear friend Robin will be a brick."

"I uh, I think seeing her will help. I-I hope my looks won't scare her."

"Tosh, don't talk like that. I'm certain she'll see the real you. Driver, how much further?"

"Ten miles to go."

"Very good. Well now, let's get you ready."

When they arrived, the driver brought Robin to the van; Alice gave last minute instructions, then made introductions.

"Electra, I would like for you to meet a jolly good friend of yours, Robinova Setdarova." After that brief yet chipper introduction, Robin stuck her head past the medivan's sliding door that Alice had just opened, then carefully but firmly shook Electra's hand with both of hers. Electra turned her shoulders so her eyes could take in all of Robin, smiling as best she could at what she saw.

"H-Hello Robin…Th-thanks for h-helping…F-friends?" Dormant memories and emotions stirred. *I know this thin blonde with chiseled European high-cheeked features and a surprisingly strong handshake.* Glimmers of recognition clicked on then off.

"Hello Electra, and yes, we're already friends. You'll remember as we put you back together and back into action." Robin's eyes absorbed the entire spectrum of Electra's external alterations, which looked awful but couldn't fool her. As soon as their eyes locked, Robin knew this was her Electra, waiting to be released.

"All right ladies, time for diagnosis at the clinic. Robin, why don't you ride in back with Electra. I'll ride up front while we drive to her grandfather's clinic. Her good friend Clarence and his doctors are waiting for us…

Clarence was sitting in the reception area, ready to greet a surprise patient. After yesterday's unexpected phone call, he had put in motion what would be needed for diagnosing an accident victim, Electra Kittner, whom he knew from years of EMT experience working at Doc Kittner's clinic. He had seen all types of emergencies and knew what needed to be done. He lined up two specialists—plastic surgeon Rihanna Antar and neurosurgeon Henry Liefen-Liu to assess her condition. They would join him in the consulting area as soon as patient and her entourage arrived.

When the medivan rolled in, Electra's handlers unloaded her quickly and wheeled her into the clinic. Clarence recognized one of them. *Why that's Robin Setdarova. Hmm, I'd have bet on*

Christi Conklin instead, but this isn't the time to pry. And who's in the wheelchair? Clarence rose to greet them.

"You must be Clarence. I am Alice Bickerwith, and I must thank you for helping us. I believe you already know these two young ladies." Clarence shook Alice's hand while Electra's appearance shook him. She looked worse than he had imagined.

"Hello Robin, and hello Electra. If you don't remember me yet, you will soon enough. We've seen a lot of you over the years. We patched you up then, and we'll do it again now. Let's get you to the consulting room." Clarence pivoted and then led them to the doctors.

Rihanna Antar had stitched Electra together on two previous occasions, noting then how quickly her body mended. Henry Liefen-Liu had never treated Electra, but Clarence had already assured Alice he was competent on state-of-the-art neural imaging. Alice recognized immediately that serendipity had smiled on Electra. In spite of the sorry state of the nation's medical infrastructure, she would be in good hands. Alice spoke first.

"Clarence and Doctors Antar and Liefen-Liu, thank you for helping Electra on such short notice. As you can see, she was seriously injured three days ago. I have brought her complete medical records, which I also sent you electronically last night. I trust you have studied them. We would like you to diagnose the extent of her injuries and outline a recovery plan. She will be staying at home; Robin will be her caregiver, and I will cover all necessary therapy, equipment, and miscellaneous costs. What questions would you like to ask me before you start?" Clarence answered because he would be this patient's designated spokesperson.

"None right now, but we'll have some after we finish our assessment. Here's how the doctors want to proceed. Doctor Antar will assess scalp, facial and body burns. Then Doctor Liefen-Liu will assess neck and spinal injury. After that he will do cranial scans. All that will take three hours, and then another two hours to evaluate the data. It's one o'clock now, so we'll reconvene here at six p.m. Since Robin is caregiver, she should be at Electra's side the whole time to practice. Alice, you probably have a lot of other work, so how about if you come back at six?"

"Cheers to all of you for all of that." She rose from the table, then she looked directly into Electra's eyes while saying goodbye. "My dear, you are in the best possible place so I will leave you to them and return at six. Cheerio."

Robin proved to be a quick study at mastering wheelchair, gait belt lifting, and associated caregiving techniques. She wheeled her now-prepped patient into Doctor Antar's examining room, observing while fading into the background.

"Hello again. I am plastic surgeon Rihanna Antar, and although you might not remember right now, I treated you several years ago.

I'll take a careful look at your burns and lacerations, and then I'll know what to do to make you good as new. Robin, please help me remove the patient gown and place Electra on the examining table. Then cover her with this sheet."

Robin sprang into the foreground, did as instructed, then disappeared into the background. The doctor worked from the bottom to top, starting with Electra's legs and talking all the way.

"I see first degree leg burns that have stabilized… I see second degree torso burns and wounds, but they are beginning to stabilize also… There are several large burns on front and back, but I've seen much worse blistering and discoloration, and I see no signs of infection. There appears to be a fluid-filled protective layer forming over the burns." Doctor Antar paused to regroup, then proceeded to the head, examining carefully before speaking.

"Your head is the challenging area, and I shall be perfectly honest. Third degree burns cover most of the face and neck. Swelling and discoloration are severe and scarring may be unavoidable. And as on the torso, a fluid-filled layer is forming over the entire burn area. Your body has started an autoimmune healing process that has to run its course." Doctor Antar paused again, aware of stone-faced expressions on patient and caregiver, then finished her monologue.

"Finally, to the forehead and scalp. I can do nothing for the deep gash and large contusion. The stitches in place will leave a three-inch scar, but the hair, when it grows back, will cover it. And there are no bald spots or third degree burn areas on the scalp. The hair absorbed the brunt of the damage when it burned."

While the doctor was examining Electra, she in turn was examining the doctor, searching for anything that might awaken remembrances or emotions. At first, she felt a soothing, subliminal sensation of security, of being cared for. But then she saw fragmented images of blood-splattered glass, of a life-or-death struggle against men yelling in a foreign tongue, of a fight to protect the doctor. But they disappeared before she could drag any of them into memory.

"Ladies, we are finished. Robin, please help Electra into a patient gown and then into the wheelchair. We'll take her to see Doctor Liefen-Liu." Ten minutes later, Robin parked the wheelchair in front of the next doctor.

"Hello again, Electra. I am neurosurgeon Henry Liefen-Liu. My job is to take images first of your neck and upper spinal cord to assess the extent of injury, and then to do a brain scan for assessing the scope of neural damage to your brain. It will take about thirty minutes for me to complete the scans, and then I will need perhaps an hour to interpret them. Our imaging equipment will fit around your head, so you don't need to get you out of the wheelchair. You will feel nothing from these procedures, so please relax." Electra liked the calm, reserved demeanor of the doctor, finding something vaguely familiar about his oriental civility. A blurry image of an unknown Chinese lady flitted into view then disappeared.

A sudden jolt shocked Electra into a state of fear, as if something were about to threaten her life, and she commanded her cognition to think why this is so, triggering neurons deep within her warning system, the amygdala. *I can never let people scan my brain until I put it in a low activity state. Otherwise, they might stumble onto my Frankenstein secret.* The lightning brain abruptly shifted into a lower gear, as if a dynamo or high-performance engine were temporarily placing itself into idle. A wave of calming relaxation washed over her as she descended into a peaceful state.

"Electra, Electra, we are all done here."The doctor's soft-spoken voice brought her back, and she smiled at him.

"Tha-thank you."

"Miss Robin, would you please take Electra to the visitor's lounge. We're finished with all the testing and we'll reassemble at six p.m. to go over the results." Robin came into the foreground and wheeled Electra to the changing area, ready to change Electra's clothes and prepare her for bathroom break. Then she piloted to the lounge.

As soon as they were gone, Doctor Liefen-Liu began reading the images and scans.

First, he compared the neck and spinal cord images he just took with those from the other clinic. Both were distinct, easy to read, and agreed. There was a clean break between the third and fourth cervical vertebrae. The break appeared larger in his image than the other. *Perhaps the focal scaling was misaligned in the other equipment, or maybe it too had been affected by power surges and outages reported at the other clinic.* He made a note of this, then moved on to the brain scan.

It showed that of a normal female brain. No sign of any bleeding or swelling, which was a bit of a surprise because of the severity of the forehead gash and contusion. *The girl should regain completely her memory and speech. Too bad I can't compare my scan with that done at the other clinic, but its scanner had been damaged by the recent storm. And I don't have any historical scans in her medical file. I wonder why, but it really doesn't matter. I just hope the broken neck mends so there's no permanent leg paralysis.*

At four-thirty, Doctor Liefen-Liu met with Clarence and Doctor Antar to review the diagnosis and map out a recovery plan. Clarence stoically summarized the diagnosis before the doctors talked through a recovery plan.

"The facts speak for themselves. If the blistered skin peels off smoothly, scaring might be moderate. If the vertebrae and impacted nerves mend cleanly, Electra might be able to walk again without cane or crutches. But if they don't, she won't. And it's too soon to know how bad the scars will be until the protective blistering peels. So, where does she go from here?"

"So, please tell me how the afternoon went for you and your patient." Alice had returned at five-thirty, finding them in the visitor's lounge. They had just finished a light snack and Robin was now helping Electra practice writing, which she said was good for kick-starting Electra's fine motor skills.

"Electra did just fine. She even dozed off during the brain scan. And judging from the speed and clarity of her writing, she's regaining strength and agility in her hands and arms."

"Excellent. Electra, what would you like to add?"

"R-Robin's a b-brick. Solid."

"Well then, let me find out when our medical team will see us. I'll be right back."

The two girls were again by themselves. As she watched Electra write, she felt an emotional tingle. *I like taking care of Electra, and I hope she shares some of herself with me as well as Christi. Oh my God. Where is she?*

Christi, the feisty and adventurous one. Robin knew instinctively that she and Electra had bonded, physically and emotionally. Robin loved them too, drawing strength from their radiance. She feared asking about Christi because she needed to be strong, so she kept silent, resolving to handle later whatever the outcome. Robin focused on the immediate as Alice came bustling back.

"The doctors will see us now, so let's hear their report." Robin guided the wheelchair into a conference room, placing Electra on one side of the table between Alice and herself. Clarence sat between the doctors on the other side and, glancing quickly around the table, wasted no time.

"The doctors have completed their analysis and are ready to report results and recommendations. Doctor Antar would like to go first."

"Thank you, Clarence, and thank you, Robin for your efficient assistance. I have found first, second and third-degree burns, increasing in severity from legs to head. Leg burns have stabilized; Robin can treat them several times a day with antibacterial spray. The same applies to the more extensive second degree burns on front and back of the torso. The third degree burns on the head and neck will need to be treated three times a day with an antibacterial cleansing spray. None of the burns should be bandaged. And we will not want Robin to place Electra in a bathtub or shower for at least a week. She will need to wash legs and torso gently by hand and use a blow dryer at low speed and temperature. As for the facial and neck burns, wash with just the spray and let the air take care of drying by evaporation. And an additional protective layer of skin is forming, but I cannot determine how much or how severe any scarring might be. I'll know more as I track progress."

"Finally, to the scalp. Bald or burn spots on it are minimal. Robin can apply to the scalp a couple of times a week an antibacterial hypo-allergenic lotion, and she can wash the hair with a mild shampoo. Robin, please have a stylist pay Electra a visit. I'm sure she'll find a suitable shorter-hair style. I will give you written instructions and prescriptions for all we have talked about. It's now Tuesday, so you should bring her back Saturday. Call or come sooner if you encounter problems. Robin or Electra, do you have any questions?" Electra shook her head no saying, "Th-thank you", but Robin did.

"Are there any special precautions for clothing?"

"No, just keep it light, loose, and smooth and you'll be fine. Anything else?"

"No." Doctor Antar was only halfway through her diagnosis. She needed to explain what plastic surgery might be needed once all burned tissue had stabilized. Her remarks were for all in the room, but Electra would have to make the decisions.

"Once your burns have started responding to treatment, you will need to pick which of my plastic surgery recommendations you want. Let me outline what they are. We'll know soon enough about scarring. Sometimes, it's hardly noticeable, and no surgery is needed.

Sometimes we need to use laser techniques to debride scar tissue. Think of this as if we were sanding and polishing a wooden surface. But for third degree burns, such as those on your face and neck, we often need skin grafting onto the damaged areas. A hundred years ago, skin grafting was a painful, arduous process. Layers of skin would be removed from one part of the body and put over the burns. We have advanced far beyond that. Today we use a collagen-based artificial skin matrix embedded with stem cells extracted from the patient's bone marrow. We adjust the matrix, after a thorough reading of the patient's DNA, to minimize the risk of tissue rejection. But in your case, I am unable to make any recommendations until I understand what healing process is already underway. Your immune system has triggered the formation of a fluid-filled protective layer. So, I recommend we do nothing until whatever process your immune system has set in motion completes. Will that be satisfactory?"

The lightning brain understood immediately what to do, and even more importantly, what never to do. *No one will ever read my DNA. That is my secret that must never be revealed.* Electra nodded in agreement.

"Yeh-yes. Do nuh-nothing until we know mah-more." Clarence picked up the conversation thread and handed it to Doctor Liefen-Liu.

"Thank you, Clarence. Let me diagnose the broken neck. The break between the third and fourth vertebrae is clean but larger on my image than on the one from the other clinic. I will fit Electra with a lighter and more comfortable neck brace, but the one she is currently wearing will do for the time being. And the brain scan looks perfectly normal. No indications of bleeding or swelling. I have every reason to believe Electra's memory and speech will recover completely. As for the use of her legs, we will start physical and occupational therapy as soon as possible this week. If the break mends cleanly, Electra should regain the use of her legs. Miss Alice, I will arrange for a therapist to treat Electra at home if you will handle the added costs. This way, treatments can start as soon as Electra feels up to it." Alice liked what she was hearing.

"Blooming marvelous, and I approve. Robin, please call the doctor tomorrow to confirm when therapy starts." Clarence knew it was time to end the meeting.

"When Electra comes on Saturday, we'll check everything again. And unless there are more questions, we're done for today…"

Robin already had Electra's house key, so the entourage entered immediately when the medivan delivered them. The driver set up a reclining bed in the first-floor study that would be converted into a bedroom. Alice toured the house to determine what modifications should be made for coping with a wheelchair. Other than an entry ramp to the front door, nothing major would be needed, and Robin would let her know as they settled in over the next few days what else might help.

"Well young ladies, you must be exhausted after such an exciting day. Robin, would you like us to stay and help get both of you settled?"

"Thanks for the offer, but I'm ready to handle things. You must be tired too."

"Yes, I am rather knackered, but a good night's sleep will fortify us all. I will call you tomorrow afternoon, and please call me immediately if you need assistance. So, until we talk tomorrow, cheerio." Alice departed, leaving the girls home alone, and on their own.

"Let's take a tour of the first floor. Maybe all the familiar surroundings will jog your memory. We'll end up in the kitchen and I'll make us something to eat. How does that sound?"

"Uh-I like it." Robin provided colorful narrative because she had been here many times. And she didn't overwhelm the patient; there would be plenty of time to re-tell the Electra chronicles. Robin parked Electra at the kitchen table. It was nine-thirty, so she decided to serve something light.

"Hey Kit, how does cereal and toast sound to you?"

"Sounds good. Why call me Kit? I-Is that m-my nickname?" Robin chuckled.

"I was testing you. No one is allowed to use your kid nickname. I'll fill you in while we're munching. I'll be right with you." Fortunately for Robin, Electra was an industrious housekeeper. The cupboards were well stocked and the place tidy as could be. Robin sat alongside, ready to help but noticed Electra's determination not to need assistance.

"Your hand-eye coordination's pretty good. Okay, now about your nickname. Your father nicknamed you Kit the day you were born. And sometimes, your grandfather would call you Kit-Kat, but you never wanted to be considered a silly little girl, so you didn't let anyone call you Kit." Electra thought for a moment between hand-trembling spoonfuls.

"Wh-what's y-your nickname?"

"You and Christi used to call me Robbie, but when we started high school, Christi read us the riot act. She told us to shit-can all kid nicknames." Electra thought for another moment.

"Sit across t-table from me. Can't turn head. I want to look a-at you."

After relocating to the other side, Robin continued.

"Your speech is better, and you're stuttering less. But please let me know when you're getting tired. I don't want you to use up all your strength."

"OK. H-how'd you get strong hands?" Robin giggled again.

"I am a pianist. Do you remember coaching me about dealing with nerves before I won my break-through competition?"

"Nuh-no. Please tell."

"We'll talk about that another time; let me get us some toast." She returned with butter and jam also. "Are you okay fixing it?"

"Sh-Sure am… good practice. Could have Coke, please?"

"Aha, that sounds like you. Coca Cola is your favorite drink. Coming right up." The girls paused while preparing toast, then Robin continued.

"Let me get some pictures. They'll jog your memory. I know where you keep them, so I'll be right back." When Robin returned, she sat next to Electra, dealing out pictures one at a time, pausing to give succinct descriptions that would help lock them into Electra's brain.

"Here's a picture of your parents, Jason Kittner and Indira Jaswinder Ramanujan. You were born before they held a Vow-Cer to confirm their marriage commitment. Here's a picture of your grandfather, Justin Kittner. He was the doctor who started the clinic. Doc was his nickname, and he was your best childhood buddy. Here are pictures of Su-Lin Song Chou and Adom Ola. They worked with your parents and are your godparents. When you were little, you called them aunt and uncle. Now they work in Austin, Texas." Electra's brain absorbed all she saw as it began reactivating neural connections, but not as fast as she wanted. Electra looked blankly at Robin.

"Don't worry. It will all come back. It's only three days. Give it time."

"OK." Robin pressed ahead, trying to keep upbeat.

"Now, here's a picture of you and me, taken during last Christmas holidays." Electra peered at a picture of two females, arms intertwined and faces smiling demurely. She recognized one, but not the other. She put the picture down.

"Please get mirror."

Robin knew that "her Electra" never hid her face from reality, so there was no reason to hide the truth, though shocking it would be.

"Okay, I'll be right back. And remember what the doctors said. Your condition has just stabilized. Soon the healing process will start." She returned with a large hand-mirror. Electra studied her face, head and neck for several minutes, then asked for the rest to be revealed.

"H-help peel off gown. I want to see rest of me." Without too much effort, they were able to remove enough for Electra to view most of the damage. Electra studied herself for five minutes, registering no emotion, then put the mirror down and spoke matter-of-factly.

"I-I'm bad ugly." Robin knew how to handle this painfully candid comment.

"Let me tell you more about who and what you are. These are secrets never to be shared with anyone else, and I don't know the full story. Only you do. But I know enough from seeing you in action. The lightning strike at birth did something to you. Made you extraordinary. You are smart and strong. And you heal quickly. I've seen it take place. Give it some time. OK?" Robin saw that Electra had become agitated, as if her brain were shifting gears.

"Ru-Roger that. Now tell, who took picture?" Robin shuddered inwardly. *Electra, you're about to release the eight-hundred pound gorilla. Well, it has to happen sometime, so why not here, why not now?* She took a deep breath and said one word only.

"Christi." Electra blinked, as more neurons triggered images in her memory, then spoke.

"Christi? Got picture?"

"I'll get one. Be right back." Robin hurried upstairs, then returned with another.

"This is a holiday photo of you, Christi and me. Electra stared intently, finally responding. "She pretty, sexy too." Electra put down the picture and looked pleadingly at Robin.

"I'm tired. I need to rest."

"Let's get you in bed and I'll plan out tomorrow for us."

Robin's surprising strength made it easy for her to handle caregiving duties, made even easier by Electra's thin, light-boned physique. It took only fifteen minutes to put her to bed, after which she unrolled a mattress-bed she herself would sleep on in an upstairs bedroom tonight. When she came back to Electra, she heard deep breathing. *She must be exhausted from today's strain. I'll let her be.* Robin marched upstairs to be alone with her thoughts while preparing for tomorrow. There was much to do, and as she drifted into sleep she knew what tomorrow would hold for her and her best friend.

"Electra? It's time we talk again. Awaken now, listen to me, and see." Electra snapped awake and saw a radiantly beautiful white apparition.

"Mother, you're visiting again. Why?"

"Your brain has summoned me because you are now ready to know more about where and who you are. You have come home. I won't overload you with details; most things I will leave for you to piece together from what you have already heard, now that your brain is growing stronger. Think of my visit as announcing the start of another game. You and I both enjoy games.

"Pay close attention to what Robin said: you are an exceptional creature, far ahead of mere mortals. Will you recover fully? I don't know, but you must trust your lightning brain to repair your physical, cognitive, and emotional personas in ways only it can. And take care of the girl asleep upstairs. She loves you, but is struggling through personal challenges, so as she helps you, so should you help her.

"I must leave, but you now understand enough to deal with where your brain will lead. You will enjoy discoveries along the way. Now sleep the sleep reserved for only those who have conviction and faith in themselves. And remember, I am with you always."

The apparition vanished as quickly as it had come. Electra closed her eyes, falling asleep instantly, and she slept the night away while her brain prepared for the coming day, subliminally aware that she must push herself to regain what fate had taken away.

CHAPTER 6

February 2118

"Better Days"

(Thread 1 Chapter 5)

Electra awoke at first light, fully aware of Indira's visit last night. She could hear the pattering of Robin's footsteps upstairs, making her feel cared for and secure. She would not call out because she wanted time alone to deal with grief, then move on to recovery. A torrent of emotions rushed into memory as neural circuits reactivated.

Christi, my beautiful Christi. My best friend and lover, gone forever. Feelings broke through from the other side and Electra could not stop rivulets of tears streaming from the corners of her eyes. Suddenly, Indira's grief-related poems whispered in her inner ear. Indira would be with her vicariously in verse.

A medley streamed in, the first painting what grief feels like:

"A dreaded darkness fills me to the core,
I grope for bearings to help pull free.
My pole star lost, I have been tossed and alone I must cross,
This leaden, deadened, mirthless sea."

Then another replaced it, one of hope and renewal as Christi's memories took hold:

"But will the priceless love I feel,
Dwell evermore in me?
Or will it fade like late Autumn shade,
The ghost of memory?

The answer lies unknown for now,
Locked in a vault of mind.
To which I say on rare Spring day,
Winter stay far behind!"

What did Mother say last night about love? I remember now. She captured it in verse:

"And love transforms what's deep inside,
Reckon the past no more concerned.
Move forward with the lessons learned,
And bury the past with all that's died."

And Mother told me to draw strength from my philosophy, which also tells me to move into my future. Though I loved Christi, I will avoid the mistake of making her into more than she was. I recall Mother telling me that long ago her best friend Su made that mistake. I shall not repeat it. I pledge *to follow the lead of the lighting brain and my philosophy though it's too soon to act. I must be patient.* The emotional storm whirled itself out, replaced by calming resolution. Electra slept once again.

Robin awoke as soon as it was light, full of energy and excitement for her first full day of caregiving. Yesterday had unfolded better than her expectations, and today would build on her emerging competence. She arose silently, quickly showered and dressed for the day's adventures. It was time to start bringing her Electra back, this to be the first day of one day at a time. After tiptoeing to bedside, she gazed for a moment at Electra in repose. What she saw was beautiful. It was all she wanted.

"Good morning. Time for me to get you up and in action." Electra's eyes popped open, accompanied by a smile. "You look rested and alert. And that's good, because you're about to roll out of bed and into our recovery plan."

"Morning. I'll say that you look good and ready for today too." A stronger voice mirrored her appearance.

"How do you feel?"

"I feel good; feeling stronger; thinking better; talking better." Robin started to place her in the wheelchair.

"Maybe you remember the quote you told me from a 19th century French doctor by the name of Emile Coue: Every day in every way I'm getting better and better. That's how it's going to be for you with me. Are you thirsty or hungry?"

"Yes. Both. Famished."

"Well let's have breakfast first. Then we can take our time getting you bathed and dressed."

"I like that, but I gotta pee. Wheel me to the bathroom first, please." Robin could feel that Electra was stronger than she had been yesterday, which contributed to their combined motive power. In no time at all they were in the kitchen, sharing breakfast and conversation.

"I've made a list of what we should do today. I know you have one too, because you are the best project planner ever created, so let's compare them. I'll start with mine. First of course is getting you bathed and dressed, and then applying the sprays and lotions. I'm so glad Clarence and the doctors gave me filled prescriptions and instructions before we came home last night. Then I'm calling Clarence to arrange the start of physical therapy. Sooner the better. Do you think you could start tomorrow?"

"Sure can."

"Good. I plan to push you as hard as I can. Well beyond whatever recovery exercises they give us. We'll make a game of it, as we've done so many times before. Are you game?"

"Yes, and more you talk, more I starting remember. Please talk more."

"After that call, you and I will arrange the house to suit your needs. We'll make a list of what help or things we need to finish it off. Then we'll get on the computer and see if you can logon to all the networks you use. You'll need to remember your passwords, but we'll get to that soon enough. Then we'll have lunch and give you a rest break. So far, so good?"

"Yes. You go, girl."

"After that, we'll make a list of who we'll call—probably tomorrow or the next day—to let them know about your temporary condition. We'll get them to adjust things so we can keep you plugged in to all you have going on. And that includes your grad school advisors, NIH project team leader, and your contact at Guardian Party public relations. Then we'll arrange for a hair stylist to visit—sooner the better. Then we'll make a shopping list for groceries, clothes or anything else you need. By then, it'll be time to call Miss Alice. After that, you can rest until dinner. And that should do it. Anything you'd like to add?"

"Yes. Call your parents. Go to class online. Rest. Please pace yourself. Deal?" "Roger that," came Robin's ready reply.

Once breakfast was finished, Robin wheeled Electra into the bathroom for bathing, avoiding any disruption to burn healing underway and then applying the lotions and sprays. Following that, she gently shampooed and blow-dried hair, then got Electra dressed, noting conditions she would report to Clarence. She worked efficiently, chatting all the while, describing how her mother took care of their pet cat.

"So you see, you're now my pet patient." Electra's imitation of a purring cat was endearing. And Robin's metaphor triggered another. *Indira called Jason her work in progress. I am now that of the lightning brain.*

Yesterday, when Electra first rolled into view, Clarence had trouble matching her appearance to the person. What he saw appalled him, but as the afternoon wore away he spied the Electra he knew.

Her eyes were the windows in which he spotted her struggling to break free.

His clinic was not a designated T-Plague treatment center, so it was not as stressed as others, but it had been impacted. Fortunately, the collective hard work of Clarence and his crew had the clinic functioning at a level that would have satisfied Electra's grandfather. All this, plus the competent younger doctors and the clinic's previous experiences treating Electra made it the best place for her. And Clarence knew more than he let on. *That Alice Bickerwith is one smart British biscuit. She picked us all on her own, and we won't disappoint her. But I won't tell her all I know about Electra. She can try to figure her out. That's something I've never been able to do.* Just then, his cell phone beeped. He recognized Robin's caller ID and answered after the second ring.

"This is Clarence. Am I speaking with Robin?" A pert, competent voice replied.

"Good morning, Clarence. Yes, this is Robin. I would like to give you a status update on our patient. Are you ready?"

"Yes. Fire away."

"Our patient is better. Physically and cognitively stronger, thinking and talking better. Some pieces of memory starting to come back. Excellent appetite. She has been bathed, treated and dressed. Leg and torso burns look better, but I cannot detect any change in head and neck burns. Scalp and hair looking OK. Sweat pants work for lower body, as does a light, loose-fitting pullover for upper body. We are ready to have you schedule physical therapy ASAP."

Clarence liked how and what Robin had said. Succinct, thorough and proactive. *That Alice knew what she was doing when she picked Robin.*

"All that sounds AOK. I have therapy lined up for tomorrow afternoon. Expect a call later today to confirm time. What else do you have for me."

"I'm confirming our Saturday checkup at the clinic. I will drive. And we will schedule a hair stylist to visit before then. We will arrange the house to suit Electra and contact people to keep Electra's current activities moving in the right direction. And I will call Miss Alice later today."

"I can't think of anything to add. Please call me each morning with an update, or immediately if you need assistance. Carry on."

"Will do. Bye." Electra had been at Robin's side, so Robin asked for Electra's opinion.

"How did that sound to you?"

"Sounds like you know what you're doing. So, what's next?"

"Let's roll into the kitchen and have you make a to-do list for arranging the house to suit yourself. While you're doing that, I'll make a menu for the week and plan a grocery list of items we'll have delivered. Then it'll be lunch time."

Each went about their separate tasks. Building a menu and grocery list took little effort because Robin knew what kinds of foods—healthy and hedonic—they both liked. And the more Electra thought about the house, the faster relevant pieces of her memory snapped back into place. She could almost feel her neurons and cognition working together again but decided not to dwell on it. *No, let my brain lead and awareness follow.*

Robin said, "Let's swap lists, then talk about what's on them."

"Good idea. And please make big portions when you cook. My body needs food for rebuilding." It suddenly dawned on Robin that Electra's stuttering had disappeared but wouldn't call attention to it. She would simply pretend it had never been there. Electra had more to say.

"I like the menu, especially the peanut butter, bananas, fiber-cereal, and brownies. We both like them; am I right?"

"Yep, you got that right. And I'll get Coca Cola for you. As you remember, that's your favorite drink."

Robin found Electra's list almost complete. It would be easy to roll up some of the rugs and relocate Electra's computer work station into the open area. Robin might need help constructing a front door entrance ramp, but she knew who to call for assistance.

And until then, she would rummage around in the garage for bricks and boards. There was only one item missing.

"I like your list, and first thing this afternoon we'll get your media center relocated. There's only one thing we'll add. I'll practice putting you into your grandfather's van so I can drive us about. That way we have wheels; we'll be mobile. It's a good thing you kept it."

"You go, girl. And when you get really good, I'll show you how to drive my car. You'll be surprised. Hey, I'm starving. Can we have lunch?"

"Remember how you love all those sci-fi and action adventure flicks? Well then, you'll know what I mean when I say 'that's a 10-4'." Afterwards, Robin rolled Electra to her work station.

"Try logging on and looking around to see what jogs your memory. And while you're doing that, I'll make some phone calls." Just then the phone rang and Robin dashed to answer. Electra powered up her main computer, then stared at the G.U.I.—graphical user interface—that blinked "Welcome back Electra. Please enter user I.D. and password". As she pondered the challenge, random thoughts streamed through her consciousness. *I've been careless. I didn't install any biometric logon systems, like voice or image recognition. If I can't remember my I.D. and password, I'm SOL.* Nothing came to her at first, so she commanded herself to focus. Suddenly, she recalled them, allowing her into her private computer network from which she could access all the networks and systems she used. *Thank you, Lightning Brain. I shall update my logon G.U.I. to have biometrics, just in case I have a future brain freeze. And I promise to keep hard copy journals and documents as a memory backup.* Then a whimsical thought occurred that made her laugh. *Perhaps it's good I didn't install image recognition. Hardware and software would have a hard time recognizing my ugly puss. But hey, I know my sense of humor has come back, so perhaps better looks will too.*

As she browsed, what she saw multiplied the number and speed of thoughts cascading into consciousness, making her cognition seamless and activating a chain reaction of neural circuits that reactivated everything about her computer and Internet-related memory. The more she retrieved, the more she remembered. She became self-absorbed in the flow, in the now. *Indira's right! My brain is leading me back from a nether world.*

Electra trembled so much from excitement that her rational persona had to tell her to calm down, to get a grip on her emotions. This epiphany might be a harbinger of others that would power an extraordinary recovery that must never be revealed. Outwardly she controlled herself, appearing calm, but inwardly she shouted from rooftops, *I'll be back.*

Electra didn't realize how tired all the excitement made her until Robin came back to report on the phone calls.

"The physical therapist will be here tomorrow afternoon. And I've got your hair stylist scheduled for Friday. Does this sound OK?" Electra couldn't turn her head, so she slowly pivoted her wheelchair to look directly at Robin.

"Sounds like a plan to me."

"It's break time, so let's roll into the kitchen. But tell me, how are you doing on the computer?" Electra replied matter-of-factly.

"The more I play around, the more I remember. But I'm tired."

"You've earned a time-out. We have only one more item on our to-do list. While you rest, I'll call Miss Alice."The girls chit-chatted while having vitamin drinks and cookies spread with peanut butter, after which Robin put Electra into bed for a well-deserved rest, then went to another room to make her call.

"Hello Miss Alice. This is Robin. I would like to give you our progress report for today. Is this a good time?" It was, so Robin quickly rattled it off. Then came the hard part.

"Electra hasn't mentioned anything about her best friend Christi. Do you know what happened to her? If you know, I'm the best person to tell her, and I'm strong enough to handle the truth." Robin focused on what Alice had to say, sighed once and replied.

"Yes, I understand this information is to be shared with no one. And you'll visit us for dinner tomorrow night?" Alice asked what to bring.

"Electra loves pizza, and I do too. Thank you for being so thoughtful. We'll see you tomorrow."

Robin's worst fear was here; Christi was dead, and also killed was a fellow she had met only once, a Moses Solstein. Although Alice mentioned that Electra had been told, neither she nor Robin knew if it had registered in Electra's memory. Robin would have to tell as soon as Electra could handle the news. She peeked in on her way to the kitchen and saw Electra still asleep, so she tiptoed away, distracting herself by keeping busy with dinner preparations but finally ran out of excuses. It was time to talk.

"It's time to get you up. Dinner's ready." As soon as she awakened, one look at Robin was all that Electra needed. *Robin knows Christi's fate.* She elevated her bed, smiled wistfully, then spoke softly.

"Please sit close to me and do not say a word until you hear me out." Robin slipped into a bedside chair. "Now, give me both your hands. I know what Miss Alice told you. Christi is dead. That part of my memory returned early this morning. She was killed in the crash.

"The three of us were best friends. We each loved Christi in our own way. I loved her every which way, physically and emotionally. She was my first-best friend, my lover, and now she's gone. And both of us need to deal with the loss in four stages: disbelief and anger, grief, remembrance, and finally, renewal. It's your first time confronting this kind of tragedy. I've faced it before. Each time it's painful, but I've learned how to deal with it. Please let me help both of us." Robin was too numb to cry; she stuttered a single word.

"H-How?"

"Let me share with you after dinner how I handled in the hours before sunrise today grieving for Christi. When your emotions are ready, grieving will come naturally. It will be painful but cleansing, after which we will share a private remembrance. Now, please get me up." Robin obeyed, saying nothing.

Electra noted to herself a role reversal. *For the rest of the evening, it's my responsibility to take emotional care of Robin. And my lightning brain is making it easier. My stuttering is gone.*

Robin tried gamely to participate in Electra's chatter, but Electra soon realized quiet time would be better until after dinner. Settling in the living room, they were comfortable in familiar surroundings, warmed by the glow of a single end table lamp as Electra began.

"Everyone grieves in their own way; there's no timetable controlling it. You can't force it. Grief comes out when your emotions say so. And when they do, it's best to share grief with others. Don't deny it. Just find somebody."

"What about you? Who did you share with this morning?"

"I shared it with a person you never met, my mother Indira, through her magical poetry. When you are ready, we can share and take care of each other. Until then, why don't you call your parents, then logon to keep up with your classes. But first, please put me into bed. I'm tired."

All the activity helped Robin, especially viewing online lectures that gave a needed change of pace. She even made a first pass through the week's homework, tiring her enough to drift into a fitful sleep for an hour until grief came calling at midnight, filling her with dreadful depression. She bolted upright in a panic-driven cold sweat and raced into Electra's bedroom.

Electra awoke in an instant and elevated the bed, insisting she hold Robin in her arms. Robin curled next to her, sobbing uncontrollably. When the sobbing subsided, Electra whispered.

"My grief felt like a dreaded darkness. Yours might also. And no matter what we try or how we pretend, we can't do anything about it. We have to let grief burn itself out." After a long pause, she resumed. "But remember, light will eventually return for both of us as our love for Christi cuts through the fog of gloom. Until then, we numbly wait until our love for Christi and our love for each other will ultimately transform us as we honor her and then bury the past as we move into our shared future. Now sleep. Tomorrow will bring healing."

Robin woke several hours later. She arose so as not to disturb Electra, kissed her ever so lightly on her still-blistered lips and lowered the bed. Calmness had returned; she would be able to deal with tomorrow. And she would follow advice she had given Electra yesterday: give healing the time it needs.

Electra had completely lost track of time the next day because she was totally absorbed investigating all Websites for her three main activities—George Washington University grad school; part-time job at NIH; volunteer work for the Guardian Party—and was joyously surfing the net for the thrill of confirming how completely her brain had reactivated memory and cognitive ability. When Robin tapped her on the shoulder, she would have jumped out of the wheelchair if her legs were working.

"Sorry. I didn't mean to startle you so. Our physical therapist, Matt Fortier, is here. Let's roll you to meet him."

Matt always projected a professional manner, one that built confidence and trust with his patients. Though the online patient file he had studied last night included no photos, he had handled many broken neck and burn victims before and knew what to expect, but when Electra rolled into view, the severity and extent of damage startled him. He recovered quickly, relying on his people skills to mask his reaction as he smiled and began talking.

"Hello, Electra. I'm Matt Fortier, the physical therapist Clarence recommended." Electra shook his hand and smiled back because she liked what she saw: a tallish young man, about six feet in height, in his late twenty's, possessing curly brown hair and a wiry athletic build. Matt spoke again.

"You have a strong grip. That's a good sign of upper body strength and coordination."

"You ought to check out Robin's. She can crack walnuts." Matt glanced at the female standing next to the wheelchair; the young lady simply smiled but said not a word.

"I'll have to remember that when your therapy includes shelling peanuts and pistachios, but that's not on your schedule for at least a couple of weeks. Here's what we're going to do today. We'll start with an assessment of upper, then lower body strength and flexibility. Then I'll demonstrate a set of exercises I want you to do twice a day, and I'll leave instructions for you and Robin to follow.

All the exercises I give you can be done in the wheelchair. I'll come back in a week to check your progress. When you no longer need the neck brace we'll increase the intensity. Do you feel like you're ready to start now?"

"Yes, let's do it."

"Good. Robin, would you please put Electra in some athletic shorts and a tank top. They're better for exercising and make it easier for me to examine muscle tone and make sure the exercises don't chafe any of the burns."

"Will do." Matt sized up the situation while the girls prepared. *She's in pretty good shape mentally and seems pretty resilient. And I don't think she's depressed or bitter about her bad luck. Lots of my paralyzed patients feel that way and I can't blame them. I know I'd feel that way if I swapped places with this one, who was probably rather pretty before, but is hard to look at now. And, ugh, to be stuck in a wheelchair. Well, I hope her mental toughness is able to handle the emotional ups and downs she's bound to go through. And I hope she's strong enough physically to make decent progress; if not, her caregiver is going to have her hands full. Good thing she can crack walnuts.*

Matt reached a startling conclusion midway through the assessment but tried not to look astonished. *Electra is a practically perfect physical specimen. Muscle tone and definition are off the charts.* He carefully examined the leg burns, concluding his prescribed exercises would not irritate them. He began using fingers to probe gently on Electra's torso to locate other burns, but she had a better idea that startled him further.

"Don't be bashful. Let me help." She leaned forward and pulled off her tank top, revealing everything. It was good Matt was neither light-complexioned nor thin-skinned; otherwise, his blush would have lighted the room.

"Uh, thank you. I can see that the exercises won't interfere with how well those burns are healing. Robin, would you please readjust her top." While Robin complied, Matt marveled to himself. W*hat did this creature do to get a body like that?*

"Now we're going to perform strength and flexibility assessment. We'll start at the top and work our way down." Matt raised and lowered, twisted and turned, pushed and pulled for twenty minutes so he could complete an upper body evaluation. "There's no need to ease into rehab exercises for your arms and torso. We'll go right to higher weights and intensity. Do you happen to have a weight set?"

"Sure do, and it's pretty complete".

"I thought you might. Well, we'll start with the hand weights and progress from there. Now, let's assess your lower body. How much feeling and movement do you have in your legs?"

"None yet."

"Not a problem, and not to worry. I'll show Robin how she can assist you when doing ballistic stretching that will help maintain muscle tone and minimize atrophy." Matt checked each leg for flexibility and range of motion. Even though she would be unable to handle resistance training until feeling returned, he would devise alternative exercises until then. He then demonstrated for Robin all the exercises she would be supervising. The more he worked with Electra, the less he noticed the facial burns because he saw how much he had to work with.

"Ladies, we are finished for today. We have a good starting point, and all of us will be pleased with the end result, which is getting Electra up and out and back to where she belongs. She should be able to operate the wheelchair within a week without assistance. I'll print out all the diagrams and instructions, then be on my way. And let's schedule my next visit for one week from today. Will that do?"

"That's an offer I can't refuse. Robin, what do you think?"

"Yes, I agree."

"Well then, it's settled. Matt, thank you for getting us started; I promise I'll do the exercises twice a day." Matt was soon on his way, and afterwards, Robin sat on the sofa facing Electra.

"He likes you. You'll be his pet patient as well as mine."

"You must be delusional. Not with my puss looking like it does." Robin's frown announced her displeasure even before speaking.

"I don't want to hear you talk like that, even if you're joking. You're beautiful to me and to anyone once they see the real you. And the scarring will heal. Just give it time."

"You're right, and I was only joking, but I'll follow your command. After all, you are in charge."

"Well then, here's what we're going to do. I'm going to start dressing you in nicer-looking clothes, and though I can't put cosmetics on you, how about some jewelry? I've never seen you wear any earrings, but I know you must have some because you have pierced ears."

Electra kidded, "My, what big eyes you have if you detected those tiny marks on my ear lobes. Father left me a pair of mother's earrings given to her by her mother when she left India to go to college in Boston. They're in the jewelry box on the vanity in my bedroom."

"Don't go away. I'll get them and be right back." Robin skipped upstairs, quickly locating the box sitting atop a two-drawer keepsake holder. Inside the jewelry box she found a remarkable pair of earrings carefully wrapped in black silk. *These are solid gold earrings shaped like lightning bolts. There must be a story behind them. I'll coax it out.* She was about to leave when a whim stopped her. *I'm going to peek inside the keepsake box. I'm sure she won't mind, and I'll keep quiet if I find something embarrassing.* What she found was unexpected: unopened letters from a person in Hollywood addressed to Indira, as well as a note from Indira to Jason and another from Jason to Electra and her grandfather. *There must be a story behind all of them, but I'm not going to read or pry.* She also found two pictures that could only be of Electra's mother, Indira. She grabbed them and hurried downstairs.

"I found the earrings, and please don't be mad, but I also found some pictures of your mother. After I put your earrings on, please tell me about them and your mother." Electra collected her thoughts while Robin carefully inserted the earrings, afterwards bringing a mirror. Electra peered intently as Robin spoke.

"That didn't hurt, did it? The studs on those solid gold earrings slid in like they belong on you. Please, tell me their story."

"They were a farewell gift to mother when she left for college. Mother's middle name is Jaswinder, which is the name of the lightning bolt possessed by the Indian princess Indira. And I have to agree with you. They do improve my appearance." Robin handed her a photo.

"Your mother is wearing them here. You look like her. She seems a bit softer and more approachable, but when your scars heal, you could be a more powerful, more assertive reincarnation. You're a bit taller and more angular, and you have harder edges. That can make you intimidating when you're angry."

"Me? Powerful? Assertive? I don't look or feel that way this minute." Robin could tell Electra didn't want to talk further about Indira, so she changed subjects.

"While you were on the Internet, I ordered grocery and miscellaneous stuff. And I also ordered a wheelchair ramp for the front door. No installation needed, so I can set it up myself. Lucky for us we have only two steps up to the front door. And delivery is scheduled for tomorrow. I guess some delivery services are still pretty good in spite of how the T-Plague has cratered a lot of the workforce."

Robin's observation triggered Electra's instant recall. *Yes, the T-Plague has gutted much of the country's infrastructure. Communications and power outages are too frequent. Air and rail transportation disrupted, and healthcare or security measures aren't as good as they were.* More cognitive associations snapped into place; Electra would pursue them by herself later.

"That's the phone." Robin scampered away to answer.

"Hello, this is Robin… Hi, Miss Alice… Yes, we've had good days and are ready for pizza… We'll see you at six. Thank you." Robin returned so she could wheel Electra into the bedroom but found her halfway there already.

"You aren't overdoing it, are you?"

"No, and it's good you rolled up all the carpets. I can drive under my own power."

"Well, let's get you freshened up and ready for dinner." As Robin began undressing her, Electra came up with a zinger.

"Too bad it's not summer. Then I could roll around buck naked."

"Matt and I would enjoy that, but Miss Alice might not approve." The girls shared more stories as they prepared for Alice and the pizza that arrived right on time. After Robin bought her into the kitchen, Alice greeted the patient.

"Dear me, how nice you look. You are in good hands."

"Thank you, and yes I am. Robin's a brick." This minute, Robin was all business. She rolled Electra to the dining room table, then brought out the pizzas so she could begin serving.

"Miss Alice, would you like a thin or thick slice for starters?"

"We Brits might not approve all aspects of American culture, but we do like its pizza, so dish me up a slice of each if you please."

"Me too," said Electra. "I'm starved." They ate hungrily for a minute or two before resuming a conversation that Alice led.

"In London, the Hawaiian pizza is most popular. Have you ever combined ham and pineapple toppings? Just like chocolate pretzels, the salty and sweet complement one another."

"No, and I don't think Robin has either." Robin had just taken another large bite and the best she could do was shake her head no.

"The Margherita pizza, named after the Italian Queen Margherita and adorned with toppings whose colors mimic the Italian flag, is also jolly good. But enough about pizza. Robin, please tell me about your patient."

"She's making real progress, and today we started physical therapy. I think we should let her talk. The more she does, the better she speaks."

"Very well, but before she does, please let me know how I should address her. Do I call her Kit, or Electra?"

"My father nicknamed me Kit the day I was born. He thought I looked as helpless and cuddly as a little kitten, and it connected with our last name, Kittner. But I never liked it because it sounded like that of a silly little girl, so please call me Electra. And until the accident, I don't think many people would call me helpless or cuddly."

"Very well, my dear. I shall call you Electra. Actually, I think it is more appropriate for a person of your age. After all, you certainly are no longer a child, physically or mentally. Now tell me, how do you feel?"

"I feel much better, and I'm getting better. I feel stronger, speak better and my memory is coming back."

"Yes, I can see and hear that. Most encouraging. Are there any additional items or help you need from me?" Robin spoke right up.

"Right now, no. We rearranged the first-floor furniture and rugs, and I ordered some groceries and items on the Internet today. And tomorrow we'll practice getting in and out of the van." Robin looked at Electra who added,

"We make a great team. Robin has everything under control."

"Yes, I can see that, so carry on." Just then there came a knock at the back door. "I bet that's the groceries I ordered. I'll take care of it." Robin hustled to answer and Alice continued.

"I am so happy your memory is returning. And I am sorry you had to learn about the deaths of Christi and Moses Solstein."

"Thank you. Robin is helping me deal with it."

"Yes, I can see we can trust her, and I am sure she must be a big help rekindling memory. When you feel up to it, would you please chat with me about the entire episode? It will help you with your recovery, and it will help me with my job." Electra nodded yes just as Robin returned with a plate of cookies.

"I thought you might like these. I'm going to finish putting the groceries away, and then I'll logon to do some course work. Why don't both of you carry on without me. And I'll clear the table right now. Miss Alice, should I wrap up the pizza for you to take?"

"No, my dear. Why don't the two of you enjoy it tomorrow."

"We will, thank you. When we were adolescents, Electra and I would sometimes have leftover pizza for breakfast. Would you like me to make you some tea? Electra, how about you?" Electra followed Alice's lead, and the two of them continued talking when Robin returned to the kitchen.

"Now that your mind and memory are coming back, I need to tell you about my role. And it is confidential, for your safety as well as for mine. It is foolish for me to make you promise not to tell Robin, but please let her know how important it is to be silent." Electra nodded yes, waiting for Alice to continue.

"As I have already mentioned, I am a Brit. I work in Washington for my government's foreign service, but I also have an extra assignment few people know about. I am liaison for a special operation set up to assist your government remain the world leader. Well, Moses Solstein had obtained data that would help in that effort, but he ran into difficulty and we had to remove him and his handler, Russell Conklin, from danger. In doing so, we removed you and Christi also. Those are the facts we have. Would you be able to add to them?"

Electra's brain had already reconstructed the complete background, and more. She understood Alice's agenda and admired her diplomacy, but she needed to go slowly so she wouldn't reveal too much too soon.

"Let me tell you what I remember. I work part-time as a data clerk on an NIH project Moses supervised. He asked me to pull together some data, and we were attacked when I delivered some files to him. We escaped and ended up at Christi's house because Mo and Christi's father worked together, although they never knew one another's identities. Another group attacked us there, but Mo and Mr. Conklin outwitted them. They figured Christi and I should go with Mo, so we did. We made it to the chopper, but we were attacked before lift-off. Mo had the data and was flying the chopper because one of the pilots was killed and the other wounded. And you know what happened from there."

"Yes, I do. You remember precisely what Russell Conklin told us, and that's a good sign. I think we should call it an evening, because we don't want to tire you out, but would you please do me a favor? Before we meet again, would you think more about your work with Moses, and what data you had that he needed. Perhaps you could find an extra copy for me."

"Yes, I'll try to remember more." Just then Robin returned.

"What luck. Another delivery arrived while I was in the kitchen, and the driver was so nice. He helped me put in place our wheelchair ramp. All we had to do was remove it from the carton and put it in place. No assembly necessary."

"My dear, I know that with you in charge, Electra is in good hands. Well now, I must be going. You can show me the ramp on my way out."

Alice used the drive home to think things through. *I like both girls, but I must be careful not to get emotionally involved. Still, I must learn more about Electra and what she knows about vaccine data, so supervising her recovery is a natural cover for having her participate—a more civilized term than "using her"—going forward. Poor girl. She faces an array of recovery challenges, but no matter which brain scan was accurate, I think much is whirling about inside her brain. And she's plucky too. She has, as the Americans say, true grit. I can't help liking her. I'll follow up with her within a week.*

Electra awoke an hour before sunrise. By now her brain had "connected the dots" on all previous and just-learned information connected with covert operations. *Alice and Mrs. T are one and the same. And I'll bet no one else knows it. Alice would like to use me to get vaccine data, but it's too soon to give her any. I might be able to use Alice too. Perhaps there are some games in the future we can play. I'll plan them once I know how thorough my recovery will be.*

Her plan at the moment was to get up and into the wheelchair unassisted, using her arms to move her legs. Not only was this good exercise, it was independence, so the struggle was worth it. As she rolled into the bathroom a strange object sitting atop the toilet greeted her, and a second later she recognized it: a handicapped toilet seat Robin had installed last night. Arm strength and light weight made it easy for her to pivot in and out. Electra's sense of humor shared the victory. *Now I can take care of privy matters by myself.*

"Why thank you for my birthday present." That cheery proclamation startled Robin awake and upright; she was now peering directly at Electra.

"Holy shit, Electra. How did you get in your chair?" Then she blushed. "Sorry for the S-word, but you know what I mean."

"I'm getting stronger and am able to figure things out on my own. I now can get in and out of the wheelchair with the right support. And the new toilet seat handles are just right."

"At this rate I'll be out a job soon."

"Not to worry, we'll think of something else. Now, please medicate me where I can't reach, and get me dressed. Then, let's have breakfast. I'm starved." Robin darted out of bed and into action. Soon, they were in the kitchen and eating while she went over Friday's task list as Electra gobbled down healthy servings of oat meal and English muffins. And that surprised Robin.

"I never realized what a healthy breakfast appetite you have. You must have inherited that from your father. He and your grandfather trained you well. You have good table manners. You don't slurp or drop crumbs like Christi used to. Remember?" Flashbacks to adolescent adventures brought smiles to both.

"I sure do. I never knew anyone who used so much catsup and dripped it all over her hands and lap like she did. And unlike you, her vocabulary often dripped more than just the S-word, at least when it was just the three of us. I think she did it deliberately, for shock value. And it worked. She was so popular, especially with the boys. Good thing you and I were there to reel her in. But enough reminiscing for now. What's on the schedule for today?"

"Well, you'll have your morning exercise session followed by working on the computer, then lunch. You then do an afternoon exercise session, and after that a half hour break until the hair stylist gets here at two-thirty. Oops, I forgot. We'll practice before lunch getting you in and out of the van. And we're lucky the weather is cooperating. The sunlight and warmer temperature will make it better for coming and going. And I hope it lasts through tomorrow, because remember, we go to the clinic tomorrow morning for a check-up..."

Later that morning the girls practiced getting to and from the van. The wheelchair ramp was as good as advertised, and the girls' combined strength plus Robin's leverage with the gait belt made it as easy as Robin had hoped for transporting her pet patient. And Electra, who relished physical exercise, wanted to increase the number of repetitions, but Robin said no because the hair stylist would be arriving shortly.

The stylist that visited from a local salon had cut both girls' hair. Robin alerted her when she scheduled the appointment that Electra had severe scalp and facial burns, so the stylist knew ahead of time what her eyes and scissors would be facing. She didn't bat an eye when greeting Electra, simply announcing that house calls gave her a nice change of pace. Then she asked Electra to log on to their salon Website and view some of the shorter cuts that might be appropriate as the hair grew out. Soon the three agreed on what would look best, and the stylist went to work, producing transformative results. She replaced the ragged, chopped-off look with a short, sculptured style able to cover the still-healing forehead gash. Her parting advice was encouraging.

"Just let it grow out and we'll decide in a month or so what will look even better. By then, I'll bet you can come back to the salon, but call me and I'll be back."

After dinner each worked independently, Robin on homework and Electra surfing the net, but after an hour Robin had a better idea.

"You've had a full day, so let's go to bed early because we have to be at the clinic tomorrow at nine."

"Sounds good to me. I'll set my alarm for five so I have plenty of time to get myself ready. You can then put on the finishing touches. And don't worry. I'll wake you up if you oversleep."

A smiling Robin replied, "If you're a good girl tomorrow, I just might let you drive." Both wished silently they could make it so very soon.

"The doctors are ready to tell us the results of your examination, and after they finish, I will summarize the physical therapy report. Doctor Antar, please start."

"Thank you, Clarence. First, let me compliment Robin for being so careful and thorough handling Electra. Her caregiving competence adds to Electra's natural resilience. The burns on her legs and torso are healing. No sign of infection. Discoloration fading. Any scarring should be minor."

"And as we already know, the face and neck burns are serious, though the swelling and discoloration are fading, and the fluid-filled layer is stabilizing. I am not going to drain it. It will release and peel when ready, at which time I'll be able to assess scarring."

Doctor Antar smiled, then continued. "I've saved the best for last. Scalp and hair both progressing nicely. The haircut is appropriate and looks nice. We want Robin to continue with the treatment regimen. Any questions?" There were none, so Doctor Liefen-Liu continued the monologue.

"We are encouraged by how well Electra is now speaking, and by how well her memory is functioning. It tells us that her brain is returning to normal. The neural scan confirms this is so. Though I do not see improvement yet when reading the vertebrae imaging, that's not unusual after so short a time period. The dimensions of the break remain the same. That might be the reason why no trace of feeling or motion has yet returned to her lower extremities. But we must remember that it usually takes several months for spinal injuries of this severity to heal adequately. Electra, please tell me, how does your new neck brace feel?

"Lighter and it seems less confining. I think it will be easier for me to wash and medicate my neck and face."

"Yes, that's what I think also, and why I selected it. Now, are there any questions before Clarence gives us your P.T. report?" There were none, so Clarence took over.

"Matt Fortier submitted his report the day after Electra's first session. He concluded that upper body strength and flexibility are superior and has prescribed higher intensity weight exercises immediately. He confirmed feeling and mobility have not returned to lower extremities, but prescribed exercises that should encourage neural stimulation. He is confident Robin can supervise and will visit once a week unless contacted to come sooner. Any questions?" There were none, so Clarence concluded the meeting.

"We want to examine Electra in two weeks, so we'll expect you Saturday after next, same time. Robin, would you like assistance getting to the van?"

"No, but thanks for asking. We're able to manage just fine. We'll be back as you requested." Robin navigated the wheelchair back to the van and soon had the patient loaded. Soon they were under way.

"You were a very good girl at the doctor's office, so how about a reward at the drive-thru window? I'll treat us both to a lemon poppy-seed muffin and juice." Electra chuckled from the passenger front seat.

"You read my mind. But I'll take a Coke instead of juice. Shall we split one muffin or get two?"

"I'm hungry too, so we'll get a couple."

There was no rush to get home because task-mistress Robin had scheduled a light Saturday workload. Electra wanted to drive around to familiar places, and Robin was happy to oblige, knowing that all additional sensory input helped Electra remember more. She could feel the lightning brain repairing or building additional neural circuits.

"Why don't you drive us by Christi's house? Maybe we'll spot a neighbor who knows where her parents are or have heard from them."

"OK. It seems like a long time since we've been there. I feel sort of confused and sad." Robin didn't know, nor did she ask, why Electra and Christi had been on a helicopter. *Electra might explain when the time is right, maybe tonight if she suggests we hold a remembrance vigil, but I'll leave it alone.*

As they cruised slowly past the house, Electra noted that all the exterior damage caused during the ambush—she had crashed through the living room's picture window—had been repaired. The front door was also new. The house looked like it too was holding a vigil, patiently waiting the return of its owners as a landscape of leafless trees, lifeless grass, and listless shrubs shrouded its surroundings. Electra would ferret out the Conklin's whereabouts from Alice, being very diplomatic, of course, so as not to reveal too much of her past.

Afterwards, they made a quick visit to Robin's house, so they could say hello to her parents. The Setdarovas were delighted to see the girls, and knowing it was best not to interfere, let them go when Robin said it was time. After driving home, they spent the rest of the day on the Internet doing schoolwork or surfing, then working through a physical therapy session. Dinner came afterwards, along with Electra's suggestion.

"Here's something we should do tonight. It's something I learned from the deaths of both my parents, and I have found it to be very therapeutic. It will help us come to terms with Christi's death." Robin said nothing, waiting to hear more.

"Tonight, we shall pack all of Christi's belongings that are here. You and I will keep for ourselves items we know she would want us to have. And then, I want the two of us to hold a private remembrance celebrating her life. My father held this for my mother. Grandfather and I held this for my father. I held it alone for grandfather. Both of us loved Christi, and you are the only person who I can share Christi's memory with, so it's only fitting we hold this in her honor. And then, we will put all this away in the corners of our memories and move into our shared future. I know this is what Christi would want us to do." Robin's voice cracked when she said,

"You're right; my grieving needs to end. I'll get some empty boxes and we'll go through the rooms on the first floor. What about upstairs? I'm unable to bring you up there."

"We'll do that another time, but not tonight. We must be together."

There was much in the house that belonged to Christi. Electra and her partner had kept their relationship hidden from everyone, even from Christi's parents, so no one knew that Christi lived much of the time with Electra. There was enough to fill several large boxes, and it took two hours to separate what Christi would want them to keep, after which Robin sealed the boxes.

"I'll wheel into the living room and light candles while you get us something to drink." Soon they were sitting across from one another, an intimate, ambient glow flowing all around. Electra was the first to speak.

"I met Christi when we started school, and you joined us midway through grade school. The three of us have been best of friends for most of our lives. Remember how you and I used to bail her out of trouble? Remember the porn star episode?" Robin smiled as she recalled that raucous evening.

"I sure do. I'll never forget how pretty she looked, even though she was totally out of it, eyes spinning in different directions. And when I saw how you handled the oaf who broke his ankle falling down the stairs, I nearly peed in my pants! Oops, pardon my French."

Electra laughed then added, "Christi's language was never as polite as yours. And at times, she could be very assertive and earthy."

"You are so right, but that's what she needed to be when the two of you yanked me out of the back seat of that rapist's car. If it weren't for you and Christi, who knows what shape I'd be in today."

And so, they shared cherished memories as candles and night melted away, both girls knowing when it was time to end the evening.

"Why don't you help me into bed so we're ready for a brand-new day?"

"Yes, I think we're ready to move into the future, so let's tuck you in." Robin didn't need to say another word. Her expression said all Electra needed to know.

CHAPTER 7

March 2118

"The Trojan Offense"

(Thread 3 Chapter 1)

HASSAN WASSANI'S BACK FOOT balanced lightly in Islam while his front foot extended firmly into Modernity. The Exalted Ruler of Isilabad knew where he was going and would take his rogue Middle East theocracy with him, whether or not his minions knew or wanted to come along.

Schooled in economics and comparative history, Hassan terminated a promising London banking career so he could lead the effort to forge Isilabad out of pieces seized from rudderless Middle East countries, to build a new nation that would become the Caliphate, the center of Islamic power, and in so doing to fulfill his destiny: to be the Ataturk of Islam. As Ataturk had done for Turkey and the Ottoman Empire after World War I, he too would "westernize" Isilabad and bring Islam into the 21st century.

Hassan understood very well Islam's three major weaknesses—inward focus, disdain for Modernity, and denial of Science—and vowed to eradicate them as he built a power structure invisible to the West that would win the centuries' long war between Islam and Christianity. The West was too weak and tolerant; the T-Plague was crippling its defenses. Soon he would unleash his "Trojan Offense" on the Great Satan, a weapon that that would invert a disparaging statement Europe had pinned on the Ottoman Empire two hundred years ago. Hassan would make Europe the "Sick Man" of Islam. And he would thank not Allah nor handpicked mullahs sitting on his puppet council, but instead his devious plan his three sons would soon roll out.

Hassan respected Middle Eastern civilization, yearning for it to regain its rightful place on the world stage. As a youth, he had devoted himself to studying religion, which taught him the fatal flaws Islam's leaders made long ago and still make today. They ruled as a theocracy, combining church and state, arrogantly turning away from progressive trade that would be mutually beneficial. They clung to fundamentalist beliefs that science and reason showed to be false. The same criticisms could be hurled against the Catholic Church in the Middle Ages, as exemplified by the East-West Schism, also called the Great Schism or the Schism of 1054, that broke communion between what are now the Eastern Orthodox and Roman Catholic churches. But the great Saint Thomas Aquinas put Christianity on a path to reconcile faith and reason, providing a foundation on which the West forged progress. A similar split in Islam, between Sunni and Shiite factions, took place soon after Muhammad's death in the 7th century, but the brilliant Islamic philosopher Averroes, unlike his contemporary Saint Thomas, had no success bridging Islam's gaps that exist even today between its two factions, or between faith and reason. So, Hassan faces a monumental task: lead the Middle East and its Islamic religion into the 22nd century. And he had faith in his abilities to do just that.

Hassan had worked tirelessly to reach the pinnacle of power, and to do so he had concealed his beliefs that he codified in his Isilabad Manifesto. He knew that Isilabad's society—considered more like a traditional chiefdom than a developing modern state—had to adapt. It was superior to the West in some ways, such as eldercare, social richness, or noncommunicable disease avoidance (obesity, diabetes, high blood pressure, etc.), but woefully inferior in others, such as material and technological wealth, avoidance of war, tolerance, or impartial justice. Under the guise of a true

Islamic believer, Hassan would achieve his mission. *I will eliminate the worst Islamic practices and add only the best from the West as I build a major player on the World Stage while controlling my faithful minions using Islamic beliefs, even though most are obsolete. I shall preach obedience and strengthen solidarity. I shall sow hatred of the Great Satan, intolerance towards the outsider, and justification of War against Christianity. And I shall attack the West, turning its technology into WMD's, until they beg for mercy.*

Hassan knew that America underestimated the sophisticated breadth and depth of his deviousness. It didn't think he understood the marching pendulum of progress, whose arc swung between conservative and liberal positions but marched relentlessly forward to the beat of technology. It didn't know about his subterranean R&D facilities that harnessed all that technology had to offer. He and his triumvirate ran it all. His first son, Abdul, worked in DC for the World Health Organization, a perfect hiding place from which to control all domestic terrorist cells. His second, Bijar, worked in Pittsburgh as an associate professor at the forefront of artificial intelligence and nano-technology, while the third, Cyrus, worked in Silicon Valley for a leading Internet hardware and software security company. They were the only ones who knew the Manifesto, and all three exuded the same traits as their father: clever, ruthless, and committed. And if they were ever captured or interrogated, they would never talk; they would die rather than reveal Hassan's intentions or flawless preparations.

Father and sons alike had fooled the bearded, turbaned, and fossilized mullahs comprising Isilabad's Religious Council that smugly believed all the Wassanis faithfully followed Quran fundamentals and would always look to the past for guidance, rather than bend to the wishes of the faithless and restive youth who had been corrupted by too much knowledge of the secular pleasures available in the West. Little did they know all the Wassanis agreed with an iconic quote from Thomas Hobbes: "Life in the past was solitary, poor, nasty, brutish, and short." Little did they know Hassan had a multi-generational plan for disposing of outdated beliefs and practices. He would make as much progress as possible with the time "Allah granted him" and leave his legacy in the capable hands of his sons.

Hassan astutely applied the lessons of history. A firm believer in a quote from the great early 20th century political philosopher George Santayana: "Those who cannot remember the past are condemned to repeat it," he was borrowing a timeless page written by the Greek historian Thucydides. Just as in the Peloponnesian War, where Persia pitted Sparta against Athens, Hassan was playing China against America. He supplied China with pirated software and oil—the World still needed fossil fuels—and in return Chinese engineering and construction joint ventures coordinated by Bijar secretly installed Hassan's lethal Trojan Offense. China also served as Isilabad's pipeline for "smart pills" that were given to the chosen few just in case the T-Plague came Isilabad's way.

Hassan loved his three sons unconditionally, and they worshipped him in return. Each week Cyrus initiated an encrypted conference call for just father and sons. The mother had died in childbirth after three rapid succession pregnancies, and her death could have been avoided if modern medical procedures had been practiced. This was another reason why Hassan hated Islam's contempt for Modernity.

Soon he would command his three sons to release the Trojan Offense. On each conference call he gathered more insider information that would tell him when to launch the attack that would push America over its tipping point. The fall would come soon, and when it did, he would stand tall, ready to wreak havoc in Europe until it too tumbled. *I have been patient and will continue waiting for the moment to strike, but my moment of decision that will shape my destiny is fast approaching. I shall not fail.*

CHAPTER 8

April 2118

"Reset and Regroup"

(Thread 2 Chapter 2)

ELECTRA CONTINUED ADAPTING NICELY to her current predicament, paying attention to Indira's poem titled *Second Season*, which distilled the essence of what she was living through:

A second season waits for you,
But when—there's no control.
It whirls you to some stranger place,
No help or supporting role.

Onset has causes—disaster and losses,
Emotions are under attack.
As you awaken and stare at surreal nightmare,
You realize there's no going back.

But there's hope for recovery for you will survive,
Wherever however you land.
The life that you make—and the path that you take,
Are held in your still trembling hand.

Shaken but wiser beginning to see,
The illusion—that you're in control.
No matter how careful risk will imperil,
Remember whatever your goal.

She was much too busy to complain or feel sorry for her situation because now she had uninterrupted time to do what she does best: sit and let the lightning brain think. And she knew how to make the best of whatever adversity came her way, so she found ways to take advantage of her appearance and paralysis. Because friends or strangers alike were stunned speechless when seeing her for the first time, she would break the silence by poking fun at her appearance, pointing out that the frightful facial scarring and gel-filled protective layer of skin covering most of her face were nothing more than her brain's idea of a beauty treatment that would repair the damage. And she would remind that beauty is only skin-deep; the brain inside is functioning fine. Greeting people this way usually helped them overcome awkwardness so they would reach out sympathetically, soon forgetting about external appearances, paying attention only to the inner person.

She devised additional upper body exercises for building strength that made navigating in a wheelchair easier. She had also reset and regrouped some of her ideas by writing up bullet-point summaries describing how she connects numerous technologies as well as how she synthesizes philosophy, religion, and science. *I can fall back on these and other documents I'm writing if I ever damage my lightning brain again. Some explain why and how I'm focusing on artificial intelligence and DNA, and others show how I've reconciled Life's big questions by using my philosophy, which I call Neurosci-Extended Deconstructed Emergent Post-Pragmatism. Only a philosopher would appreciate its name, but the recipe is easier to understand. Take those rational elements articulated in Kant's "Critique of Pure Reason" that were extended to produce Pragmatism, and adjust according to the limitations deduced by Deconstructionism, then add elements resurrected from Emergence Theory. Next, account for the limitations of high energy physics, the implications of neuroscience, and then apply commonsense reason, the end result yielding a philosophy that offers helpful, optimistic advice that can guide anyone through life.*

I'll keep a chronological activity file too, so I know where I am if the unthinkable ever happens again. And after what I'm going through, I shall expunge "crash and burn" from my vocabulary.

Electra was busily writing up additional sections of her thesis when a call came in on her computer. The communications audiovisual software displayed the name of a person she wanted to talk with, so she accepted the call, immediately hearing the voice and seeing the image of her thesis advisor, Professor Ravenhill.

"Kittner, Ravenhill here. I got your Email a couple of weeks ago and decided to give you time to regroup, but now it's time we talk. Turn on your video feed so I can look at you."

"Hello, Professor Ravenhill, and thank you for calling. I'm actually typing up more of my thesis, so your call is most timely. How are you?"

"I'm always fine. My question is, how are you recovering?"

"I'm recovering strength, thanks to wheelchair exercise programs."

"That's good. No doubt you've had plenty of sympathy calls about your accident. Well, that's not my purpose. I'm calling to congratulate you for dodging a bullet. You're still alive, and that's because you are a clever survivor. And I see your puss is still blistered. Not very pretty, but that's good too. You can work on your thesis instead of doing too much socializing. I don't give a fiddler's fart for how you look on the outside. I care about how your brain's working on the inside. So, how is it?"

"I've recovered from temporary amnesia and speech difficulties, and I'm coming up to speed again on my thesis. I think you'll like my draft."

"Kittner, I think I misjudged you. I think you're smarter than you let on, and I'm glad that brain of yours is intact. And I have a recommendation. Why don't you watch some of the Capstone lectures for graduating science majors? They can ease you back into cutting edge thinking in a variety of disciplines. Start with an easy one, the one on Darwin's Theory, and take it from there at your own pace. And I want to see you in my office as soon as you can wheel your way back to campus."

"I'll act on your recommendation by watching the lecture right now."

"OK Kittner, do that. Keep working on your thesis and come see me soon."

Electra wheeled away to chat with Robin as soon as the call ended.

"Why don't you take a break and come watch a lecture on evolution? Then we can get ready for dinner at the Conklin's. Robin looked ready for a change of pace.

"I'm tired of working on my accounting homework, so let's do it."

The lecture's content was even better than Electra had hoped for, while the Instructor's delivery and visual aids were almost as good as public media's Nature series. Its title, *Survival of the Fittest Redux*, teased the audience because the video gave the latest marine biology evidence confirming once and for all that Darwin's Theory of Evolution is correct. Before starting, the Instructor told the audience that "Intelligent Design" no longer is considered an alternative to evolution. Biologists have convincingly demonstrated that the eye evolved through adaptive natural selection. And she outlined how the Mandelbrot Fractal Set, a marvelous illustration of complexity, is derived by starting at the number zero located on the complex plane of numbers: square it and add the imaginary number i. Get next number by squaring what you have and adding i. As you continue, a beautifully organized picture emerges.

The Instructor showed her first slide after reciting Thomas Hobbes's quote about Nature, which she connected to a line from Tennyson.

"You shouldn't be shocked that Nature is indeed red in tooth and claw, for that is consistent with how organisms adapt and evolve to survive. Homo sapiens are fortunate to be at the top of the food chain because of our intelligence and technology. Otherwise, life would be even grimmer than what Hobbes said."

She offered numerous examples, such as Darwin's Bark Spider spinning webs spanning 25 meters across Madagascar rivers, or flocks of birds following magnetic fields, which illustrate how evolution gives organisms specialized characteristics allowing them to survive. Then she spent the remainder of the lecture summarizing 21st century deep sea research because marine evolutionary biologists had found fossil evidence of punctuated evolution, which is a theory that after extended periods of little change (stasis), speciation and organ emergence occur rapidly. This discovery, coupled with the specialized diversity of deep sea creatures, irrefutably supports evolution. And the Instructor ended the formal presentation quoting from evolutionary biologist Richard Dawkins:

> "If God doesn't believe in Evolution, He's missing a great tool for accomplishing Life's mission, which is to go on living."

The Instructor fielded questions afterwards. The last one, asking about Intelligent Design versus Self-Directed Design, caught Electra's attention.

"That's an excellent question. Intelligent Design asserts that God, which is our conception of a Universal Life Force, hovers just outside man's cognition, controlling man and nature. Most contemporary theologians or philosophers agree the answer to the question Does God exist? is inaccessible, so each person chooses what to believe. Self-Directed Design focuses only on humans, conjecturing that a person's cognition affects brain states that control how the brain and body develop or function. For example, Buddhist monks' brain scans show how mind control affects brain waves and cognitive states, altering physiological processes like heart rate or blood pressure. Might not prayer or holistic medicine help alter a patient's brain state so the body heals itself? Neuroscience research continues to study the phenomena. And it is conceivable that DNA mutation could lead to organisms that mentally control development by cognitively willing it to occur. Perhaps mankind's evolutionary path will lead to such a superior creature, but if so, evolutionary time scale would require hundreds of thousands of years for that ability to emerge. Our time is up, so that is the last question. Thank you for being such an attentive audience."

Afterwards, Electra asked Robin what she thought.

"That was fascinating. Glowing fish that have heads containing enormous teeth and gigantic eyes is as good as sci-fi. Now I know why you like to study biotech and DNA. My brain's not built like yours, but I sure enjoy hearing about this stuff."

"I liked it too, but after watching, I hope Mrs. Conklin isn't serving seafood for dinner. Come on, we better get ready."

Russell spotted Doc Kittner's old van pulling into the driveway. "Jennifer, they're here. I'll help bring in Electra. And please, just act naturally when greeting her."

"Fine, I'll join everyone shortly in the living room."

This would be the first time Electra and the Conklin's would see each other since the ambush and subsequent chopper crash. Since then, much had happened to all parties, but Russell had followed Electra's recovery indirectly through reports from a covert operations contact whose name he didn't know. His home life had returned to a semblance of normal, though the death of their only child Christi had been emotionally devastating for Jennifer. Fortunately for Russell, the ambush had not blown his cover. In its rush to intercept, the ambush team failed to report locations and identities, and when the ambush team was permanently "neutralized" his cover remained intact. No one at NIH or in any threatening covert operations group knew he was actively working with the Opposition Party. He returned to his official job as a senior NIH executive and was promoted to a higher position in the Opposition Party's inner circle where he was responsible for finding anything that might thwart T-Plague's relentless advance. Electra was rolling towards the door when Russell opened it.

"Hello, Electra. Here, let me get you up the steps."

"Hi back at you. Robin and I are so glad you invited us." Although he had been warned about the facial burns, their severity startled him; he hoped the girls couldn't read his reaction.

"Let me give Robin a hand with the wheelchair." Without too much effort on her helpers' part, Electra was soon perched in the living room after coats had been tucked in the closet. Jennifer joined them a minute later.

"We've missed both of you. And I can see that Electra is in good hands." Jennifer lightly kissed both of the girls, then spoke further. "All of us have been through a lot." Electra could tell the Conklin's were hesitant to lead the conversation into troubled areas until they understood what she could handle, so she picked up the conversation's thread.

"Yes, and Robin and I share your loss. We miss Christi too, and Robin and I held our own vigil to honor her memory." Russell saw Jennifer begin to tear, so he put his arm around her before replying.

"Though it will take more time, we are recovering by doing what we must, and that is to go on living. Now tell us, how are you?"

"My amnesia and speech are much better, and I have resumed most of what I had been doing. The doctors think I'll regain the use of my legs as my broken neck continues to heal. But they don't know how much facial scarring will remain. Maybe I'll look better, but I don't worry about that. Robin has enough beauty for the two of us. Now tell us more about what you've been doing."

Russell gave only a short report. Though he wanted to ask if she could resurrect Mo's data, he would do so only in private. As if rehearsed, Jennifer spoke next.

"Robin, would you please help me bring in some appetizers and drinks?"

"I'll be happy to help." Jennifer put her arm around Robin as they headed to the kitchen, leaving Russell and Electra by themselves.

"I'm devastated by the turn of events, but I'm trying to piece things back together for Jennifer. I would like to talk openly, but not if that will put Robin in an awkward position. Does she know the reason why the ambush occurred?"

"Yes, and I trust her with my life. I'm in her hands right now. And you know how strong her hands are, so don't worry about her."

"I was hoping we could talk. Maybe after dinner we can continue." Just then the others returned so the conversation shifted back to safer subjects.

After dinner, Jennifer asked Robin to help her clean up, so Russell took Electra to the living room.

"Washington is certainly in a muddle these days. It can't handle terrorism or the T-Plague. How does the Guardian Party put it? Harsh times demand harsh measures? Well, harsher times are fast approaching, and I'm helping the Opposition Party help our country avoid the worst outcome." Russell paused for Electra to help fill in the blanks, and she had already prepared a dummied down reply.

"Mo told me, and that's why I gave him some data that might help you battle the T-Plague." He didn't tell me much about what he was doing, and I'm not sure what all the data meant. And I'm not sure I can get it again because the person who took over for Mo doesn't like me." That caught Russell by surprise.

"I can't imagine why. You seemed to be doing a good job on the project."

"He doesn't think so. Tomorrow I have a meeting with him and the H.R. manager to talk about my position. And as I'm sure you know, the climate at the lab is terrible. Everyone is stressed out because progress is nil, and they're all afraid of being fingered as data moles or leakers. Security is converting all documentation from electronic format back to paper to reduce the risk of hacking, and since I was a data retrieval clerk I have to travel through the labs collecting and sorting files. My boss says I'm too slow doing so because of the wheelchair, and the researchers are turned off by my facial burns. He can't prove any of this, but if they fire me, I get to spend more time at my university lab working on my thesis." Russell nodded, then replied.

"I'd be happy to help you if I weren't in a rather awkward position myself. Please let me know what develops, and if you do happen to find another copy of the data you gave Mo, I would appreciate if you would make an extra copy for me. It might help because we're working covertly with British drug researchers who might find something NIH has overlooked. R&D worldwide is grasping at straws and won't help one another. I'll make sure it gets to the right people." Electra nodded but said nothing because Robin and Jennifer were coming to join them. Jennifer was the first to speak.

"Robin told me all about how efficient she's become. She's balancing schoolwork and caregiving and enjoying both."

"I did say that, but I should have added more. I like caregiving much more than accounting. Maybe I'll change majors, but I'll decide after I have Electra back to where she was. And her physical therapist is a big step in the right direction. But enough talk. It's getting late and we have a full agenda for tomorrow. I think it's time we roll out of here." Russell chuckled.

"Yes, Monday will be busy for all of us. Robin, you've become very assertive. I think Christi would approve. Well, let me help get you on your way."

Electra summarized for Robin on the drive home what she had confirmed.

"Mr. Conklin doesn't know about Alice, and we won't tell him. I'm not going to give him any data until I know more about what he's doing for the Opposition Party. So, both of us need to pretend we don't know much."

"You don't have to worry about me. I don't have to pretend. Hey, would you like me to get a power lift installed on the van? It'd make getting in and out easier."

"Nope. The more I use my muscles, the stronger I get. I think you and I are self-sufficient. We make a great team."

"Agreed." There was much more Robin wanted to say, but this was not the time so she hid emotions.

Electra was thoroughly prepared for Monday's negotiation with the lab's H.R. manager so she could get everything she wanted. She actually wanted to be fired; working on a Cognicom project no longer fit her plans. She didn't care a mote for anyone there, and there was nothing further she could gain by staying, so she was ready to leave on her own terms. She knew the time had come to be assertive, to push for what she wanted in a win-win manner that would keep adversaries "fat, dumb, and happy." She had just pinned her boss and the H.R. manager into a corner but gave them a way out if they gave in to her demands. The manager's taut smile and deep breath before replying revealed she wanted to wrap up terms before Electra forced her to give away even more.

"Yes, Ms. Kittner. I agree your Cognicom project performance has been satisfactory, and your lawyer could sue because your boss might be violating parts of the Workers with Disabilities Act. But since you don't want to work for a boss who disrespects you, you are willing to resign as long as we keep funding your graduate fellowship and let you keep your logon I.D. to the network. You also want to have access to the lab so you can meet with your friends that still work here. And you also want us to give you a parking permit and handicapped parking sticker. I trust this will satisfy you.

Perfect. I could push for even more, but this is enough. I'll let her save face and take my boss off the hook."

"Yes, I think this is fair for both sides. A law suit wouldn't look good for you, and I can live with what you're offering. So, thank you. I have just one other request. I'd appreciate if my boss would have all my belongings packed and shipped to my home address. That way, I don't have to come back this week. He knows where my workstation is." A relieved reply came immediately.

"You bet, Electra. I'll see to it right away. Do you need help getting home today?"

"No, but thanks for offering. My caregiver will pick me up after I have lunch." The H.R. manager jumped right in.

"Well then, here's a voucher for the cafeteria. I'm pleased we have reached a mutually agreeable result."

"Me too. Well, I'll be rolling along to the cafeteria. Thanks for lunch."

Russell was also well prepared for the inner circle meeting that took place on Friday. Earlier that week his unannounced visit to the T-Plague labs confirmed what Electra had told him. And the grim, tight-lipped Cognicom project managers would not share any data even though he outranked them. The chairman pointed to Russell. "Conklin, what can you tell us about T-Plague R&D progress?" Russell would not dance around the issue. He would put his foot down on the problem, even if that meant stepping on his predecessor's toes.

"NIH R&D is at a standstill. Stress and fear have paralyzed any hope of progress on any of the projects. And they won't give me any data because Securityguard is paranoid about data leaks."

"What options have you come up with?"

"Two, and both are longshots, but they're better than nothing, which is precisely what we've had going for us until you presented me with this opportunity. The first is to have Electra Kittner, who gave data to Mo, attempt to get another copy. She's is in a wheelchair and is in a tough position at the lab, but she'll do her best. And the second is to work with a private drug development company. I haven't reached out to them, but I'll check my records to find out whom to contact. I'll keep you posted. Any questions?" There were none, so the chairmen continued.

"I speak for the group when I say you're the best person for this thankless assignment. We know you'll make good things happen." He pointed to another inner circle member. "OK, let's have an update on Guardian Party activities."

"Their PR department has turned a lemon into lemonade. Late last year someone leaked their hidden agenda, but public sentiment agrees with it. And they like the "harsh times demand harsh measures" slogan. It won't take much more for people to start dancing a jig when the current administration collapses. And though most Guardian Party terrorist alert bulletins are fabrications, the public doesn't seem to care. They like Jared Gardner."

The chairman looked around the table, then pointed to another person. "Let's ask our covert operations contact about possible terrorist attacks. You have the floor."

"Right now, nothing in decrypted chatter suggests upcoming attacks, either with or without a T-Plague WMD. But our listening assets are modest at best. We know from past activity how much we miss, so I really can't say yes or no. But if they do come, and if they are not dealt with to the public's satisfaction, the government will take a big hit." The chairman was ready with his summary.

"Well, keep listening, but we're navigating between a rock and a hard place. How did Greek mythology picture it? Between Charybdis and Scylla. The public prefers the Guardian Party to either Republican or Democratic Parties, and our Opposition Party has gained little traction. And we have nothing to offer on either the T-Plague or the terrorist fronts. Let's use the weekend to consider what contingency plans we should consider if or when the government falls. We'll reconvene Monday evening."

Zoe Vargas always seemed breathless, either from juggling meetings or phone calls. But that came from her fast-paced public relations manager position at the Guardian Party, where she was thriving and her star was rising. Her teams prepared bulletins and speeches for its leader, Jared Gardner, and they were given full credit for restoring the approval ratings just reported in mid-April polls. And she expected even better results shortly, because today would mark the return of a special member: Electra Kittner.

A year ago, Electra had been a Party fundraising volunteer whose ability caught her eye. Not long after, Zoe recruited her for public relations, where her knowledge of NIH T-Plague projects and her communications skills gave Zoe a peek inside. She stunned Zoe by resigning late last year, citing a hidden agenda leak as the reason. But a bad accident had changed her mind, and she told Zoe that if harsher measures had been in place, she wouldn't have been in an auto accident caused by a convicted felon. And though her injuries were severe, she could do great work once again.

It took only a moment to overcome feelings of shock and pity when Zoe greeted her in the lobby. *Gads, she looks frightful. I feel bad for her, but I'll do all I can to help her settle back in. What's important is how clever she is, and how well she communicates. I liked her when I first met her, and external appearance really don't matter. She's got a great brain and personality to match.*

"Welcome back. I sure can use your talents. Let's get you up to my office so we can decide what you would like to do. And please tell me what you're currently doing. That way, we can pick an assignment that fits. Here, let me help wheel you around." Once situated in Zoe's office, Electra summarized her predicament.

"Well as you can see, my body is still working to heal itself, but my mind is as good as ever. The NIH lab fired me because I couldn't roll around fast enough to collect all the data I was supposed to get, but I sure kept a lot of it in my head and know what's going on. And I still have some contacts that aren't afraid to talk with me. So maybe this can be used in press releases and bulletins."

Zoe silently yelled *Bingo. I can make this win-win. She can continue being my unwitting leaker and I can help her readjust.*

"That sounds great. You can work from home or from your old workstation here. And we'll want you to come in for team meetings at least once a month." She dropped her voice to a confidential tone and said, "Look, big changes are on the way, and when they come there will be big opportunities for you to move up. And to prepare the way, we'll feature you in one of our monthly newsletters, illustrating how the Guardian Party takes care of its people no matter what misfortunes come their way. It'll show we can be kind and gentle to our people when it counts. Enough said. Let's get you settled in."

Later that day, Zoe placed a call to Jared.

"That's good news, and you might be right. Since she came back to us she must now be committed to our cause. And she still has Cognicom contacts that'll help. What else can you tell me?"

"It's too bad about the auto accident, but she gets around just fine in a wheelchair. And maybe her face will look better as the burns continue healing. She used to have striking features."

"Come to think of it, I did meet her a couple of times. And she sure could write dandy speeches If her communications skills are as good as before, maybe we can use her for other assignments. Keep me posted on all your PR activities. We both have to run, so bye for now."

Jared always listened to Zoe Vargas because she was quick, competent and proactive, as well as possessing a combination of physical and mental assets he found stimulating. And now she was presenting him with a gift his covert operations teams needed: an improved NIH leaker. Even with the recent upgrade to his intelligence groups, they still are clueless about T-Plague projects. *I've got the CIA's entire covert operations sections in Fairfax and Washington joining forces with mine. They're happy to cross over from the "Weak Establishment Side" because dedicated law enforcement types respect what I and my Guardian Party stand for, and they despise useless politicians. They like how I revised Clemenceau's quote that war is too important to be left to the generals: Security is too important to be left to the politicos. I'll personally tell my covert guy about our upgraded leaker.*

Elliot Spitzdieck could hardly believe how recent events had finally catapulted him to a better place. Two months ago, the team he led for CIA's Project Death Shield had secretly been hived off and folded in with all Guardian Party covert operations. Spitzdieck could read the invisible writing: when the Administration falls, the CIA will already be in the Guardian Party camp. And now his section chief told him they have a new leaker working directly at Guardian Party Headquarters. Elliot knew the name well: Electra Kittner.

That girl's been on my radar for five years because I personally have linked her to T-Plague and terrorism, but I don't have a whiff of evidence to support my cover-up conspiracy theory. My bosses don't believe me. They say it's all coincidental and I better drop my obsession. But I don't believe in coincidence, I know there's a conspiracy.

Too many "strange things" had happened to one particular Cognicom team. First, the team leader Jason Kittner—Electra's father—blows himself up in a lab accident. Then the brains of the team, Su-Lin Song Chou, vanishes during a lab fire. Then Adom Ola disappears after a terrorist lab explosion. Then the team's former business leader, a Moses Solstein, disappears in a snowstorm. There was no one left for Elliot to "dissect" except Electra, the lowly data collection clerk. Elliot's bosses considered him delusional. He had nothing but supposition and an impossible hope that the clerk might know something.

And now this clerk has a sympathy card because of a wheelchair, forcing Elliot to place her on his private radar, but he could live with that. *I'll find a way to fold her into a Project Death Shield "dissection." I'll roll her up and show I'm smarter and tougher than all my doubters. Then finally, the Guardian Party will reward me.*

Wheelchair confinement didn't slow Electra's grad school coursework one bit because computer networking technology allowed online courses, either through videos or live lectures, to replace on-campus class attendance. Students often learn faster and better, preferring online flexibility and zero commute-time, as well as the convenience for submitting assignments or taking tests. They could pause or replay video to review whatever they didn't understand, and these courses eliminated voluminous note-taking. Only teachers complained, because computer technology continued replacing them at all educational levels and shrinking the job market, a phenomenon that contradicted earlier projections for teachers' ever-expanding role. Thanks to advances in artificial intelligence, there were even learning apps supplying students with "personal tutors" able to explain lectures and homework exercises. Teachers had become an endangered species.

Electra hid the fact she understood better than her professors all of this term's science and math courses, so each week she viewed enough of the online material to know what was expected. But she had a favorite course that she studied thoroughly: Philosophy and Science Today. It had to be taken by all science graduate students because it explored how science and technology impact all aspects of life in the 22nd century. This week's lecture—A Summary of Philosophical Beliefs—pulled together concepts covered in the first half of the term.

The professor started his lecture by sketching the role of philosophy, which is supposed to help man understand the world and his place in it.

THE DOMAIN OF PHILOSOPHY—MAN'S CONNECTION TO THE WORLD

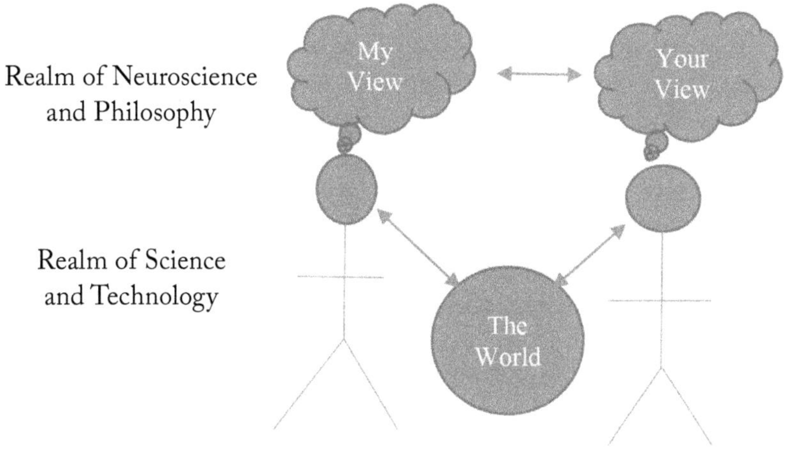

Science and technology objectively connect us to the world, but man is aware of the world only through impressions supplied to his brain by his senses, giving each person a subjective view that challenges how to reconcile it with "reality" and how to compare it with that of others. And that is where philosophy comes to our aid. He explained that we can choose to judge reality according to either reason or revelation.

Then he sketched a timeline of philosophy, labeling philosophical periods and listing some of the big ideas and best-known philosophers for each. It agreed with what Electra already knew. *I know Greeks invented philosophy 400 years before the birth of Christ. Plato and Aristotle may have had the final word if only they had modern technology. But they didn't and that left questions for Christian and Muslim philosophers to sort through. And too bad the post-modern 20th century thinkers got sidetracked by two world wars. It wasn't until the early 21st century that post post-modern philosophers figured out how to integrate neuroscience with the best of the Enlightenment.*

Electra found a couple of his comments particularly thought provoking. For example, we often assume people today are much more sophisticated or intelligent than in ancient civilizations, but that's improbable. No scientific evidence suggests man's brain or its neural wiring is any different today than in prehistoric times. (Although the observed Flynn Effect confirms that people are getting smarter, psychologists attribute that to increased knowledge rather than increased brain power.) Greek philosophers are as profound as the best today, even though their primitive science and technology prevented them from observing much about how objects interact. Even today, no matter what paths of inquiry philosophers trek, they see the footprints of the Greeks heading back. The professor pointed out that it's too soon to know which contemporary great thinkers will stand the test of time, citing a famous quote from Mark Twain (Samuel Clemens) regarding how to know if someone is telling the truth: You have to wait until they're dead, and even then, you must wait a long, long time after that.

Electra liked how his next chart showed the evolution of each major branch of philosophy or human endeavor. He explained that Metaphysics and Ontology pose life's big questions, and how the "soft science" modern disciplines—psychology, economics, politics and sociology—build on philosophy's more practical conclusions.

EVOLUTIONARY TRAJECTORY OF PHILOSOPHY

BRANCH	PRE-MODERN	MODERN	POST-MODERN	POST POST-MODERN
Metaphysics/ Ontology (Reality and Being)	Religion Supernatural	Interest in the Natural World	Skepticism of Natural World Anti-Realism	Science & Tech within Limits
Epistemology (Theory of Knowledge)	Mysticism Faith	Reason Empiricism Science	Use of Narrative Limits to what is Knowable	Hard-Wired Brain Plasticity for Adaptation/ Learning

Human Nature Psychology & Economics (How People Act)	Man born in Sin Man is Fixed	Tabula Rasa Individ. Efforts Learning	Group over Individual Nurture Psychological Complexity	Social Animal Neuroscience Nature & Nurture Individ. Dignity Diversity
Ethics (What is the Good Life)	Duties & Service	Pursuit of Happiness	Conflict Opposition Corruption Relativism	Balance Relativism with Biological Needs and Wants
Sociology & Politics (How to Organize Society)	Feudal Hierarchical Authoritarian	Rule of Law Liberty Equality Republic/ Democ	Socialism Egalitarianism Power Struggle	Republic/ Democ Safety Nets Diversity Inclusion

He described how prehistoric man, having no science or technology, invented supernatural phenomena (myth and legend) to explain what he observed. That evolved into religion and faith, which in turn became science and reason as man's powers of observation and logical thinking improved. Then along came 20th century cataclysms: two world wars separated by worldwide depression, and then the Cold War, all of which collectively deflated the Enlightenment's unbounded optimism, leading to philosophy's gloomy post-modern milieu characterized by incoherence, ambiguity, and uncertainty. He recited a quote by Albert Camus, one of the leading post-modern philosophers, that summarizes the weltschmerz: "There is but one truly serious philosophical problem, and that is suicide. Judging whether life is or is not worth living amounts to answering the fundamental question of philosophy."

The professor knew his audience needed something uplifting, something more cheerful, so he focused on the far-right column summarizing today's Post Post-Modern philosophy, which salvages much of the optimistic flavor of the Enlightenment. And his next chart showed how a Socratic debate among the more proactive contemporary philosophers could offset the tide of cynicism by using balanced optimism.

SOCRATIC DEBATE / DIALECTIC FOR PHILOSOPHY RESOLUTION

Thesis (Modernity)	Antithesis (Post-Modern)	Synthesis (Post Post-Modern)
• Objective Truth • Reason • Universals • Individual over Group • Pro Science &Tech • Progress • Unbounded Optimism • Capitalism	• Subjective Truth • Relativism • Group over Individual • Anti-Science & Tech • Language is Problem • Spirit of Socialism • Cynicism/ Pessimism	• Neuroscience explains how the brain functions • Objective Truth (within Limits) • Pro Science and Tech (within Limits: Gen. Rel. Quantum Mech. Uncertainty) • General Agreement on Meanings in Language • Causality (within Limits) • Republics & Capitalism • Guarded Optimism

The debate he sketched introduces a thesis (Modern Philosophy) and a competing position called the antithesis (Post-Modern Philosophy); then he used a logical, reasoned argument to arrive at a position superior to either, which he labeled the synthesis (Post Post-Modern Philosophy). As the last column summarized, neuroscience and contemporary physics, both interpreted within the limits of what is accessible or understandable to homo sapiens' brains, allow humanity to keep many Enlightenment positions. He ended the lecture by saying that a purposeless Universe may be indifferent to Man, who is all alone orbiting a point of light dwarfed by the infinity of space, but don't commit suicide. Each of us has the opportunity to find our own meaning and collectively to sustain and improve civilization. Electra agreed. *I like this guy. His brand of philosophy is much like mine, which I whimsically named Neurosci-Extended Deconstructed Emergent Post-Pragmatism. Though only a philosopher would appreciate its name, my philosophy will serve anyone looking for an optimistic, pragmatic approach to life.*

Spirited questions and answers from on-campus or online audiences showed how well the students understood and appreciated the material. Electra expected this, because graduate science students are among the smartest groups on campus or in society. But the professor warned once more that even today, though facts and logic contradict many faith-based claims, some segments of society are reluctant to abandon cherished beliefs. He drew menacing comparisons between the T-Plague and the Black Death (bubonic plague that killed over a third of Europe's population in the mid-1300's) for the damage done to mankind's intelligence and progress, but he hoped for a better outcome.

The professor complimented the audience for being so attentive, then outlined some of the topics that would be covered in the second half of the course. There would be separate lectures covering the impact of the latest developments in neuroscience and artificial intelligence. *These are my thesis topics, so I'll be sure to watch. I might even be able to transfer some of what is presented into my note files where I keep relevant background information for subsequent study. I'm fortunate to have these lectures available online. What a great timesaver.*

That night at dinner, when she told Robin how riveting the lecture had been, Robin provided a reason why that she had heard long ago.

"Remember what you told me about the Buddhist monk's answer to any question? It is perhaps. Maybe we can use it when people ask about your being in a wheelchair. Perhaps it's good, at least temporarily, for you to be spending time sitting in front of your computer, studying and attending lectures."

"Yes. I forget all about my legs when doing so. But I want to get out of this wheelchair. I used to do a lot of thinking while running, and I can't wait to run again. But I'll be patient. I have to trust Matt and my brain to get me on my feet soon."

"But until then, think how strong your arms are getting. And though you can't crack walnuts like I can, perhaps you can run over them with your wheelchair. Wait; ignore that. Let's not break anything else, at least until your broken neck is back together."

"I have a better idea. When my neck mends, lets break open a bottle of champagne. And if you can pull the cork without breaking it, I'll buy you more walnuts..."

CHAPTER 9

June 2118

"The Immaculate Recovery"

(Thread 1 Chapter 6)

Electra spent most of a weather-perfect Saturday morning doing thesis work at her workstation. *I wish I could run because the endorphins generated force multiply my creativity. But I did a pretty good job this morning. I added more details to what R&D I can pursue after I get my PhD. I have so many cross-disciplinary ideas for genetic engineering and artificial intelligence. Too bad I don't have a "Dream Team."*

Electra knew her brain reached far beyond the grasp of mere mortals, and she had learned to be patient with associates who struggled with concepts that were child's play to her. And just for amusement, she occasionally fantasized a "Fantastic Five Dream Team" of great minds through the ages that would be able to implement what she discovers. She chose Isaac Newton for gravitational field theory, Albert Einstein for relativity, and Niels Bohr for quantum theory. Then she added Kurt Godel for balancing orders of infinity with built-in mathematical inconsistencies articulated in his "completeness and incompleteness theorems." Finally, she completed the team by selecting Francis Crick for his intuitively brilliant discovery of DNA. *It's fun to fantasize, but it's time to get ready for going out.* Electra prepared to move on when a peculiar thought intruded.

My Dream Team is unbalanced. Where are the women? The answer came swiftly. *Not until the Enlightenment, when people no longer clung for survival to the edge and brain replaced brawn, did progressive thinkers figure out that women are the equal of men when given a chance. Still, those in control don't relinquish power without a fight, and it took heroic women's rights forebearers hundreds of years, carving from within, to build a niche that women of Modernity have extended to near parity within the bounds of DNA. Females broke through bigtime a hundred years ago, and though gaps remain, critical skills demanded for jobs, now and increasingly in the future, will narrow them further. Future Dream Team captains can build balanced teams because they'll have plenty of women to choose from. And though the roots of racial discrimination differ from those of gender, future Dream Teams will work to the tune of iconic musicians Paul McCartney and Stevie Wonder's hit song "Ebony and Ivory."*

Matt's outlook matched the weather. Soon he would visit Electra and Robin, not for exercising but for socializing, because he would take Electra to dinner and a movie. It would be good for Electra to practice going out, good for Robin to take a caregiving break, and good for Matt to learn more about his pet patient and her caregiver.

Matt liked the pace of Electra's recovery, confident that she would walk again if feeling returns in her legs, but if it didn't there would be little left for him to do. He hadn't told her yet because he didn't want to upset her. Facial burns were another matter. Though sorry they hadn't healed, he had become so accustomed he rarely noticed, and when he did they didn't bother him.

What bothered him was Robin. Though he couldn't explain precisely why, her looks and demeanor plucked his feelings, and her aloofness his fascination, and though always polite, she rarely spoke to him. Most young women considered Matt a good catch, yet Robin seemed insouciant. He hoped Electra would help him get a better grip on his feelings, and even more importantly, on Robin.

Matt knew all about gripping wheelchairs, and because of Electra's light weight and increasing strength, he soon had her parked at a table in a popular restaurant near the theater, although popular had become a relative term. Fear of contracting T-Plague in social settings remained, forcing people to cocoon. Older people were the first, but many of the young invincibles were becoming frightened as well.

"So, tell me about yourself. You must have quite a story." Electra dusted off a well-rehearsed summary that revealed nothing deep but told enough to satisfy listeners.

"Except for the auto accident, it's rather ordinary. I had a great childhood. My father and grandfather raised me. Though they died when I started college, I was old enough to take care of myself. And now I'm in graduate school at GWU, studying bio-tech. In spite of my accident, I'm able to attend classes, thanks to your therapy." *That's enough. Guys like to brag about themselves, so let's hear what you have to say.*

"How about you?"

"Nothing all that remarkable, but I'm doing OK. I've always enjoyed sports and fitness training. I was a standout high school athlete, almost good enough to be first string soccer on a competitive NCAA Division II team. And I assisted fitness coaches while majoring in sports therapy. After my BS I earned an MS in Human Performance and Physical Therapy, and since then I've worked for several physical therapy centers. I like the work and make good money."

Matt's candor and understated delivery surprised her. *The guy's good looking, has a career, and seems to have his ego in check. Let's hear more.*

"How's your work schedule? Do you make time for a social life?"

"It's not a nine-to-five schedule, and sometimes I work weekends, but I don't mind because I'm always assisting people who need help. I'm actually making a difference in people's lives, and that makes me feel good."

"What about your circle of friends?"

"I'm on a soccer team with guys I met in college or on-the-job. And my urban tribe keeps busy, but it has less going on than a couple of years ago. The T-Plague is in the back of everyone's mind."

Electra had heard enough to figure things out. *Matt's a nice guy, not necessarily shy but not the kind to come on bold and strong. And I think he's interested in Robin. Let's send another segue his way.*

"You seem like a good guy. I'll bet your urban tribe females see it the same way. Am I right?" Matt shifted self-consciously, grinning awkwardly, which made Electra giggle inside.

"I'm a terrible judge for sizing myself up. I date casually but haven't found anyone I want to take to the next level. Maybe you know what I mean."

"I do. Robin and I often talk about this." *OK Matt, take the bait.*

"You do? I'll bet you and Robin are good friends."

"Yes, we've known each other since grade school. I'm lucky to have her as my best friend."

"I have to admit I've notice her. I've tried talking with her, but she seems so aloof. Maybe she doesn't like me. I don't know anything about her either."

"You're mistaking that for shyness. She's very warm and caring when you get to know her. You noticed her strong grip. Comes from playing the piano. But it's better if you talk to her rather than me, so here's what I'll do. I'll let her know you would like to chat with her. Then it's up to the two of you."

"One of the physiology courses I took touched on major scientific explanations for why people are attracted to one another. Did you know it's all based on genes, hormones, and neural transmitters?"

"Just a little. A friend of mine told me that. Something about opposites attracting, but she didn't go into the details. What can you add?"

"Lots. Sometime, why don't you read online about the Fisher Temperament Inventory Test, which is the first of its kind. Sex researchers have extended it to a series of surveys two people can fill out to determine their level of attraction. And some of the articles I read found high correlation between survey results and actual neural imaging."

"How does it work?"

"Evidently, we fall into four categories determined by our hormonal or neurotransmitter levels. There's dopamine that's associated with boldness and independence, serotonin for those who are sociable and conventional, testosterone for the aggressive types, and estrogen for the intuitive and empathetic."

"I would imagine each person is a combination of all categories, higher in some than in others."

"Spoken like a scientist. And it's no wonder, because you're a biotech grad student. What about Robin? Do you think I could talk to her about this? Maybe she and I could take the test, just for fun."

"I'll mention it, and you can ask her for yourself."

"I'd appreciate that bigtime. Hey, speaking of time, it's time we leave for the movie."

Electra enjoyed the action-adventure movie, but she found the contemporary crop inferior to many in the "retro" category, which confirms to her that the T-Plague takes its toll in the artistic realm too. She thanked Matt for a delightful evening as he wheeled her towards his van. As they chatted, enjoying the redolent fragrances carried on the mild night breeze, Electra's warning system suddenly sounded. She did not like the looks of two fellows who just crossed the street. The neck brace prevented her from twisting towards Matt, but he spoke first.

"We need to be careful of these two guys. Let me do the talking."

The glow of a street lamp illuminated the situation. Torn clothes and dull, expressionless eyes made them look thuggish, perhaps mentally damaged from the T-Plague. The taller one spat out a greeting.

"Hey babe, don't use a flame thrower to light your smokes." As his partner guffawed, Matt wasted no time.

"Good evening, gents. If you need a light, let me help." The leer disappeared from the taller fellow as the two beat a hasty retreat, re-crossing the street.

"Hey man, no problem." Matt watched them go before picking up the pace. Electra felt like a useless lump. There was nothing she could do, but she knew the reason why they left in a hurry. *Matt must have pulled a weapon.*

"Thank goodness you were prepared."

"What do you mean?"

"You don't scare off those kinds of guys with harsh language. You must have shown them something they didn't like."

"Let's get in the van and on our way. Then I'll show you." Five minutes later, Matt did just that.

"Do you know what this is?" *Of course I do. I have one in my weapons collection. It's my weapon of choice, a Traser, which can fire an electric stun or tranquilizer. But I'll play dumb.*

"I've seen it on the Internet. I think it's called a Traser."

"Right you are, and I keep it with me whenever I'm out. We can't be too careful these days. Morality has taken a big hit; too many bad people out and about doing bad things, and I blame it on the T-Plague. I hope their stupid remark didn't hurt too much."

Electra's burst of laughter blew away the tension.

"I have pretty thick skin where it isn't burned. And it was actually rather clever, considering the source."

"Good for you. Well let's get you home…"

Matt left soon after wheeling Electra into the living room, allowing her to prime Robin's interest.

"So, Matt pulls a Traser on them and they vamoose. That was even more exciting than the flick." Robin looked relieved when she replied.

"Good for all of us he was prepared."

"Matt's a nice guy. He's got backbone and substance, and he'd like to talk with you sometime. So please be nice to him when he does."

"Of course, I will. And I wonder what's on his mind? I'll ask him next time he's here. But now it's time to get you to bed."

Robin slept fitfully that night, disturbed by her feelings, ashamed at her reaction to Electra's night out. Jealousy had come calling, making her unwilling to share Electra with anyone. For the first time in her life Robin felt needed. Caregiving and committed love empowered her, and she did not wish to relinquish a single moment. *And now Matt wants to get in the way. What does he want to say to me anyway?*

Robin had good reasons to be wary of the opposite sex. Unlike Christi who had been sexually adventurous, or Electra who dated before pairing with Christi, she never had a satisfying relationship. Once she had been drugged and twice nearly raped. Even some instructors "hit on her," so she kept males at bay, using aloofness as a protective shield. She liked the whispers that labeled her the blue-eyed ash-blonde "Ice Queen."

Though Robin loved Electra, she didn't know how to deal with it. *It's too soon to interfere with her emotional recovery from Christi's death. Electra might not want to commit again. And I'm mad at myself for wanting to take Christi's place.* Robin tossed and turned until dawn.

Electra stretched her arms to salute her latest accomplishment. Parked in front of her biotech lab's workstation, she had just finished prototyping her first neural probe device. She now had completed more than enough to earn a PhD in cognition mapping. Her wheelchair penance had paid off, and she would celebrate with a Coke—after two centuries still the number one brand worldwide—and a roll around campus on a glorious Fourth of July weekend.

The outdoor exercise helped her switch thoughts, so she parked in the shade of a stately tree and considered progress. Her master recovery plan contained three parts: one each for cognitive, physical, and emotional personas. Electra knew her lightning brain controlled all steps in each.

It gave top priority to the cognitive plan, completing it first and making Electra's memory and mental capabilities even stronger. *I remember why I'm extraordinary: the lightning bolt at birth rewired my brain and altered my DNA. And I can self-direct my development, within the limits of physiology.* It had made her immune to T-Plague and superior to "mere humans," making her a creature mankind might evolve towards in a contingent future. And she knew she was situated in a primitive world that could not handle a "genetic freak." Her father had said it well: "People like you are either burned at the stake or dissected." She could never reveal her secret. Her life depended on it.

The still-unfolding physical plan came next. Broken neck had mended—she no longer wore a brace—but had no feelings yet in her legs. *Very disappointing, but maybe my brain is reminding me about two contingencies everyone faces.* The first: we forget what fragile creatures we are and take for granted the gifts life bestows. Electra had always gloried in her physical prowess, never doubting that her strength and agility would carry her through all adversities. *Now I know how fleeting all that can be when bad luck crashes in.* The second: we forget how resilient we are; we can deal with whatever comes our way. At first she found wheelchair confinement devastating, for she was helpless, dependent on others. But it taught her new ways of getting around and doing for herself. *My empathy has grown. I understand much better why people cheer the determination and courage of paralympians. I will never take my physical gifts for granted or forget the lessons I'm learning.*

I finally understand how empathy, emotions, and feelings are connected. Most people use the terms emotions and feeling interchangeably, but there are subtle differences rooted in empathy, which starts as a nonverbal lower level response to neurochemical changes in limbic system neurons. Emotions are merely neuronal phenomena controlled by genes. So, emotions exist in the brain's neural network.

Feelings are different. They are merely a conscious emotion-to-words translation taking place in higher levels of the neocortex. So, feelings exist as a conscious semantic network of words existing in our mind. Once again, I understand that the mind and the brain are one and the same. Empathy drives emotions that drive feelings, but it all takes place in the brain. As my empathy grows, so does the depth of my emotions and feelings.

The emotional plan, though it proceeded more slowly, advanced as the physical plan rolled along. Though Electra considered rational thinking superior to emotional feelings, which are often uncomfortable and add complexity that is out of her control, she was beginning to have a stronger need for people and for the strongest of all emotions, love. *Love forces me to protect others, but when I look at the outcomes so far, I'm appalled. The three people I loved most are dead. First father, then grandfather, and now Christi. I don't want the responsibility love forces upon me. I thought I had evolved past the need for love but no, I'm aware of humanity's irrefutable truth: when push comes to shove, emotions trump reason. Not even I am immune.*

Electra's ability to discount emotions was perhaps the reason she was not too concerned about her facial burns. Her self-worth or ambitions didn't require looking pretty, and she joked that she didn't have to look at herself either. Facial scars might give her a sympathy card; if she were sort of ugly—or better yet rather plain—no one would pay her much attention. She might be able to use it to her advantage going forward.

"Let's clink glasses to toast Electra's progress." Having just completed a late July therapy session, Matt and Robin were chatting in the back yard. She had finally granted him an audience, and he was determined to make the most of it.

"You and Electra are good friends, and you deserve a lot of credit for how well she's doing. Electra has told me some of her background, but I don't know much about you. Maybe we could get to know each other. Maybe you'll see I'm not like most of the other fellows who chase after you." Robin smiled politely.

"Why is that?"

"Look, I know most guys are blunt instruments. When they look at women, they're sizing them up the wrong way. I'm not like that because I grew up with a younger sister. That experience was like running a clinical study on female emotions. When she was in high school, Dad let me check out her boyfriends. And since her college years, she's been my de facto interpersonal relations counselor. She's a high school guidance counselor, and we're still close. I know that females have correctly pegged the male procedure for looking at hookup partners. Guys consider looks first, then background, then personality, then intelligence, and finally character, when they should invert the order. At least I know the right sequence."

"If that's the case, you should be looking at Electra, not me."

"I like you both, but you happen to strike a resonant chord in me. I've thought about it, even talked with my sister, who said to recite these verses." Matt felt awkward but took a deep breath, then marched ahead.

"Poets past to present day,
Have tried to unravel love.
Grasping for things to help explain,
In me or Gods above.

But it matters not what the Poet says,
Nor what the Pundit thinks,
The essence of love escapes the pen,
It's the Riddle of the Sphinx."

Robin's expression softened a tad.

"Those are beautiful sentiments. But there's a movie quote that also rings true: It's not what you are underneath. It's what you do that defines you."

She's a tough nut to crack, but at least she hasn't flushed me. Better not push my luck. "You're right. So, if we get to know each other, maybe you'll see me in action."

Robin smiled, then gave an answer she had learned from Electra.

"Perhaps…"

On an early August Saturday, Electra awoke abruptly, startled by a premonition that today would be memorable.

She could hear thunder rumbling and tumbling in the distance. The weather had turned hot and muggy, so she looked forward to spending much of the day on the Internet, surfing for additional tidbits of information she could combine with what she had recently ferreted out from talking with her Cognicom project contacts, all of which would further endear her with Zoe and the Guardian Party public relations department. She launched herself into the wheelchair and rolled to the bathroom, preparing for the day's activity, but one look in the mirror abruptly altered her plan.

"Robin!" she screamed, "call Clarence right now."

"Let me examine this thoroughly." That was all Doctor Antar would say until she knew better what was taking place on Electra's face. A week ago, there had been white translucent liquid beneath a layer of roughened, thickened skin. Last night the fluid had gelled, swelling into an opaque white layer, its pressure splitting open the surface, like a snake shedding its skin. And if it were pressed lightly, the process accelerated. Electra was sitting stoically in the clinic's examining room. Robin, who was waiting nervously in the reception area, had driven them to the clinic two hours ago.

"Is there any discomfort?"

"None." Doctor Antar knew it was time to remove the entire layer of skin, and with it the gel-like substance underneath. She pressed carefully, enlarging the split which eventually extended over all face and neck burns. Then she gently peeled away the dry layer. It fell off without leaving a mark.

"I have removed the layer of dry skin. Is there any discomfort now?"

"None."

"Good. I am now going to wipe away the gel. Let me know if you feel any pain on the underlying skin."

"OK."

The gel did not adhere; it simply peeled away, like Jello from a serving bowl, leaving not a trace. Ten minutes later, Doctor Antar spoke one word only as she pressed a large mirror into Electra's trembling hand.

"Look."

Electra grasped the handle, intently studying her face and neck from all angles for several minutes, then joyously whispered, "You brought me back," before kissing the doctor's hands.

Robin had been waiting too long, so she forced Clarence to find out the reason for the delay. Tapping on the door, Clarence asked, "Is everything OK?"

Doctor Antar's calm voice answered, "Yes. Please come in." Clarence opened the door and stepped aside as Robin dashed in. And there was Electra, sitting erect on the examining table, laughing and crying softly.

Robin stuttered, "Doctor Antar, you worked a miracle." Doctor Antar's smile implied the same as the tone of her voice.

"No, I was nothing more than a facilitator. What you see is the body's ability to heal itself. Electra's brain has conjured an immaculate recovery."

Robin stepped forward, studying all of Electra's face and neck. The skin contained not a single blemish; its tone and tightness perfectly restored. Even her dueling scar had been erased. Her voice cracked when she said,

"You're coming back to me." Clarence thought the emotional temperature needed adjustment, so he asked matter-of-factly,

"Doctor Antar, what about the scalp and hair?"

"Back to normal. All the scars are gone. We can end treatment now."

"Good. All that's left is to get Electra back on her own two feet." Everyone grinned when Electra added a final zinger.

"I want to resemble that remark."

Not even Electra wanted to do much that afternoon other than talk, so she and Robin sat in the living room, bubbling about what's next.

"As soon as feeling returns to your legs, Matt says it won't take him long to get you walking again. Then you'll be completely back."

"Muscle tone is pretty good because of all the exercising, so once I can feel them moving, I should be good to go. I hope my brain is working on that right now. And I want you to start working again on KC Enterprises accounting. I've had plenty of wheelchair time to plan our next steps, so let me go over the details…"

Electra spent the next hour explaining what she had in mind. KC Enterprises stood for an umbrella company Electra had set up. The initials would be changed from KC—K for Kittner and C for Conklin—to KS for Kittner and Setdarova. Electra was president and Robin would become the V.P. of Finance and Accounting, a role she would need to grow into. It already contained another company—Worldstar Biologicals—which Electra was using for T-Plague vaccine development implemented by Su. Robin's accounting courses equipped her to handle some of the bookkeeping presently needed.

"So please go over the books, and make sure you update the P&L, balance sheet and cash flow statements. I want you to talk with Hud. He'll put you in touch with the appropriate accounting people at his office. And we'll visit Austin soon."

"I guess that means you'll still need me once my caregiving stint is over." Even though Robin was smiling, Electra detected a note of sadness which she quickly erased.

"Hey, I'll always need you."

"I'll Roger that back. Let's celebrate by going out to dinner. I'll drive. You can drive next time, so that's added incentive to get back on your own two feet."

After dinner, each girl worked on separate school assignments, Robin on accounting and Electra on a post-thesis foundational subject she would use in both biotechnology and computer science: quantum mechanics. *Professor Ravenhill told me to watch the Capstone Lecture titled "The Great Quantum Conundrum." Maybe it'll give me some new insights. At the very least, it'll jog my memory.* And that's precisely what it did.

Electra appreciated the professor's sobering introduction when elaborating on Einstein's pronouncement about the subject: "Its Mathematics is elegant but its Physics is Dismal." Even the smartest researchers today haven't been able to get beyond the stumbling blocks encountered over a hundred years ago. The human brain is too complex (too many interrelated neurons and processes for quantum computers to simulate) and quantum calculations too difficult (solution algorithms can't compute an answer in a finite amount of time). Somehow, the subatomic world handles complexity and calculations in nano-seconds. Neuroscientists are beginning to discover how biological processes use quantum mechanics (energy quantization, electron tunneling, enzyme state superpositioning, neuronal coherence) to achieve physiological goals, but they are far from cracking the conundrum of consciousness.

The professor talked next about the role quantum mechanics plays in computer science. The most advanced supercomputers—Quantum Computers modeled after the brain as a massively parallel deeply recursive neural network capable of learning—need supercooling and superconductivity to utilize Q-bit information storage (0's or 1's stored in the spin states of individual electrons) as well as superpositioning and entanglement to speed up microchip algorithmic calculations.

He concluded the lecture on a cautious note, saying he didn't think the farfetched notions hyped in the media or sci-fi movies would happen anytime soon. Perhaps mere mortals are bumping into humanity's asymptotic limits of understanding. But his closing statement cheered the audience. Quantum Biology and Quantum Computing are still in their infancy. Researchers can do great things using quantum physics fundamentals. Electra agreed. *I'm glad I took good notes. I'll put them into my notebooks and into use.*

As she floated into sleep that night, her brain constructed a parallel between what had happened that morning and what happens in Eugene O'Neill's play *Mourning becomes Electra.* One interpretation is full of brightness and renewal. That is the one she used because Electra's morning apprehension had foreshadowed an immaculate recovery. And the lightning brain knew that even Electra, who placed rational thinking above emotion, had a trace of vanity after all. Though she preferred not admit it, she was glad her looks had been restored. *Whenever I want, I can once again make myself appear mature and alluring in subtle ways. And although I'd always make the most of good looks or bad, I like being "rather pretty," instead of "pretty ugly."*

All she needed to be physically complete was the return of feeling to legs and feet. As she slept, a distant dream danced by, filled with the thrill of shredding her clothes, running naked through unlit streets at midnight, howling at the moon. And as she dreamed, motion stirred in her legs while subliminally her inner voice whispered "soon," over and over.

"Can you believe it's already the end of August? Tempus fugit, especially when we're having fun and making progress. And according to Matt, your leg strength should be able to support walking pretty soon." Electra looked from her workstation towards Robin and smiled whimsically.

"In the Battle of Balaclava during the Crimean War, Lord Cardigan said 'trot, canter, gallop' when he led the ill-fated charge of the light brigade. For me, it's stand, walk, jog. If I could just stand today, I'd be happy."

"Uh, who's Lord Cardigan? And please, give me just the Cliffs notes version, not a dissertation. Sometimes, you give more details than a person wants."

"People I work with sometimes say the same. I thought I was getting better, but I'll make a point not to deliver information overloads. Anyway, here's the abridged version.

"His actual name is James Brudenell. In 1811, when James was fourteen, his father became the Earl of Cardigan, inheriting the Cardigan Earldom and its immense estates located in the East Midlands of England. He fell off a horse when just a kid, damaging his brain, but that didn't stop him from leading long political and military careers, chiefly characterized for incompetence. But his troops considered him brave and generous."

"Thanks for the summary. Maybe his damaged brain caused him to lead the charge, but let's change the subject. I have an idea. Because you did another set of exercises before working on your thesis, I'll take you out to dinner. It's not supposed to rain until later, and we'll be home before then. Matt took me to a restaurant close by that you'll like, and I can wheel you through the park after I park the van."

"How are the desserts?"

"Trust me, they're to die for. Let's go."

The short drive and sunlight streaming through the trees added to a festive atmosphere that extended into the restaurant. The waiter recognized Robin and promised today's dessert special would be unbelievable, and then he couldn't believe the first order.

"That's all? You only want a double order of the Snickers Ice Cream Pie?" Robin couldn't resist deadpanning.

"She's on a diet, so please bring it with water, no ice. And for me, a BLT with iced tea." The waiter strolled away smiling.

"Your repartee earns A-plus. And I'll order a Coke after dinner." The girls chattered merrily about how pleasant the summer had been. Robin mentioned that although she hadn't granted Matt another outing, he seemed better than the average male; he even knew a little poetry.

"For a guy, that's impressive. Please remind me sometime to tell you about poetry and my father. I think he finally tolerated some, thanks to my mother. What also impresses me is how Matt didn't gush about how good I look, now that my burns have healed. He's solid."

A change in the weather rolled in as Robin rolled Electra out of the restaurant, clouds scudding in, wind picking up, and thunder rumbling in the distance.

"Don't worry. I'll get us back to the van before the rain gets here." It wasn't the weather, but rather two fellows walking towards them that worried Electra. Worse still, she recognized them. *They're the two thugs Matt scared off a month ago. They didn't recognize me, so I'm way ahead of their dim wits.* The lightning brain switched to an altered state as it heard footsteps from behind.

"Don't look back, but the two fellows that bothered Matt and me are following us. Just pick up the pace gradually. Lucky for us the path will be downhill soon." Robin followed Electra's orders, but their luck changed when they reached the top of the hill. The rains came hard and the thugs closed the distance.

"Oh girls, wait for us. We can help." The harsh male voices panicked Robin. She and the wheelchair galloped downhill. Gravity helped at first, but then became more than she could handle. She lost her grip, twisting her ankle and falling face-down, then summersaulting downward. The chair careened wildly with Electra barely along for the ride. She applied the brakes, nearly tipping the whole contraption. Though she succeeded in keeping the chair upright, it rotated to the left when gravity took over again. Now she was racing downhill backwards, accelerating ever faster, charging into a clump of bushes at the bottom of the hill and coming to an abrupt stop. Embedded in the shrubs, Electra could barely see Robin and her pursuers because of the windblown downpour.

Poor Robin. After the fall she rolled to a stop, tried to get up but fell again. She picked herself up and tried to run, but could only hobble on a badly sprained ankle. She almost reached the bottom when the lead thug grabbed her by the hair and threw her down. Then the other picked her up and held on while the first started slapping and tearing at her top. Electra panicked.

I'm nothing but a helpless witness to a mugging, and soon I'll be the second victim. She was about to scream when suddenly her brain switched to a higher gear that brought calm clarity as her three personas merged into one, swelling with wrath, releasing Electra's subconscious monster, the Monster from the Id. Electra had once again become the Creature. It lusted for vengeance, for the taste of blood, for the specter of death. It was unstoppable, and it knew what to do. It started by reigniting neural circuitry that powered Electra's legs.

Electra sprang out of the wheelchair and lunged forward, onto the closest thug's back. She clamped hands on both sides of his head and twisted past one hundred eighty degrees. The neck snapped with a dull click and she pushed the body aside. She grabbed the other's hair and flung him to the ground backward. She kicked brutally until there was no movement, but she wanted more. She wanted to gouge his eyes, to see blood flow.

"Get with it, soldier! Focus on the mission. Get Robin to safety." Electra's inner voice shouted commands that forced her cognitive self into control. The Monster, though not fully sated, submerging into the subliminal but not before surgically snapping the second neck. *There must be no survivors, no tattlers.*

Electra scanned the terrain. Dark skies and heavy rains insured no one had seen the battle. Robin was unconscious, in shock and bleeding from a split lip and assorted cuts. Electra lurched to the wheelchair, then lunged with it back to Robin, belting her in and plunging full speed towards the van. With each stride she took, her legs regained balance and rhythm. Part of the lightning brain was glorying at this immaculate recovery; part was worrying about Robin, still unconscious, head bobbing like that of a loose-headed doll, but there was nothing Electra could do about it. She flung her into the back seat, then raced home where she would reach out for help.

She reached the safety of home, drenched to the bone. It was darker and raining even harder, but Electra paid no attention, for Robin was beginning to stir. Electra carried her to the living room sofa, then made a call that was answered on the fourth ring.

"Matt, this is Electra. Robin's been mugged. She has a split lip and badly twisted ankle. Please help us!" Then she retrieved the wheelchair and parked herself in it next to Robin. Finally, her brain shifted to a lower state, and as she waited for Matt, she was already several steps ahead.

"Stay just like you are. I want to get supplies from my van." Matt had Robin propped on the sofa and focused on her all his training, a combination EMT and physical therapist. He had sized up damages immediately: nose and chin scraped from the fall, swollen split lip that looked bad but didn't need stitches, hair a tangled mess, arms and hands scratched and filthy, twisted ankle swelling. Not a problem for Matt. He stopped all bleeding and applied antiseptic.

Then he hurried to the kitchen to prepare an ice slurry. Kneeling at Robin's feet he said,

"This will keep the swelling down, but it's going to feel really cold. We need to keep your foot in the bucket until you can't stand it. We'll let it thaw, then put it back in. Sorry, but it's what we need to do." Robin smiled meekly.

"OK. You know what's best." Matt had more to do, so he asked where to find wash cloths and towels. When he returned, he cleaned off most of the grit. He was now ready for Electra to tell what happened.

"And after Robin fell, the wheelchair got stuck in the bushes. Then those same two thugs that bothered you and me started beating on her." Electra paused briefly, then continued. "It got darker and rained harder, and then we got lucky. A pack of joggers came to our rescue. They scared off the thugs, helped me and Robin back to the van and even drove us home. After getting us in the house, they saw that Robin was better, so they ran back to the park. Then I called you, and you know the rest." Matt shook his head before replying.

"Wow, those joggers were life savers. Robin, are you beginning to remember more?" A quizzical smile emerged on her swollen lips.

"No, I guess I remember less. I must have been out cold or in shock when they arrived. Now I know what amnesia is like." Matt switched back to business.

"How does your ankle feel? Can you handle the ice slurry a little longer?

"I guess so, but I can't feel a thing."

"Well, let's do this. I'll stay for another hour, alternately freezing and thawing your ankle. While I'm doing that, we'll let Electra replay for us today's adventure, starting when you drove to the restaurant." Electra spun a convincing story while adjusting the truth, so the hour melted away faster than ice in the slurry, bringing an end to Electra's chatter.

"It's getting late, and thanks for all you've done. And could I make a final suggestion before you wrap Robin's ankle and go? I can take care of her tomorrow, but someone needs to get her cleaned up tonight and into clean clothes and into bed." Matt blushed. Robin looked shocked. Electra giggled to herself. "Matt, you know what female anatomy looks like, so Robin won't frighten you. And Robin, Matt is acting like any caregiver would. And don't worry. I'll chaperone. Tell him where to find what you want to sleep in."

"Uh, take a look in the stack of laundry in the basement. Bring me running shorts and a T-shirt." When he returned, he peeled off all torn clothing in preparation for cleaning and dressing his newest patient. Electra observed nonchalantly while laughing hysterically to herself. *What a pair. Their eyes are looking every which way but where they should.* Electra gave Matt high marks for speed and accuracy, while Robin's embarrassment scored a record.

"I should come back tomorrow afternoon to check out the ankle. And remember my RICE therapy acronym: rest, ice, compression, exercise. How about I come back tomorrow at four p.m.?" Electra agreed.

"That'll be fine. I'll handle things till then."

Electra lay in bed, unwinding from the day's excitement, and what a day it had been, for it marked not only the end of August but also the end of her physical recovery. *The lightning brain used the mugging episode to galvanize all my leg neurons into action, so now I'm up and running again. And I won't tell anyone I'm back in action, ready to run once again like the wind. I'll wait until the time is right. For the time being, serendipity has given me a secret weapon. No one will suspect that a wheelchair-bound female like me can leap into action with a single bound.*

Matt would never know what her brain had done, for Electra would fake enough of a recovery so she would no longer need Matt's therapy, but would still need crutches or cane and wheelchair. Sometime she would have to tell Robin, but not until she was good and ready. Electra would run her own private fitness program in the basement. *My fitness and combat skills need upgrading; I've absorbed too much collateral damage in previous engagements.* A quote from the Six Million Dollar Man retro action-adventure series flashed in her brain: *"Steve Austin, astronaut. A man barely alive. Gentlemen, we can rebuild him. We have the technology. We have the capability to build the world's first bionic man. Steve Austin will be that man. Better than he was before. Better, stronger, faster."* Electra would be even better than before, and no adversary would ever know—until too late.

Matt couldn't sleep; worry about his two patients kept him awake. *How vulnerable they are in this harsh world. Although capable and resilient, today proved how helpless the girls could be when confronted by bad people. I must watch over them, and I'll do all I can to protect them. I'll show Robin I'm better than the other guys.*

Robin couldn't sleep either; worry about failure troubled her. *I couldn't keep Electra out of harm's way. If the joggers hadn't rescued us, we might be in a hospital or even worse—a morgue.* Her once invincible Electra had been defenseless today, and that frightened Robin. The thugs also frightened her; she could still hear their crude voices, which added to the reasons why Robin hated men. *I need to tread carefully around guys. But what about Matt? I'm not ready to decide. I want to get Electra on her feet and then sort out my emotions and my sexuality. I'll consider Matt after that.*

There was no mention on Sunday news about two persons found dead in a nearby park. In today's harsh world, events like that are too common to be reported. Only Electra would ever know the cause, and it would never bother her. *I shall never doubt the decisions the lightning brain makes, and I can live with the consequences.* Electra slept soundly that night.

CHAPTER 10

September 2118

"Guardian Party Rising"

(Thread 2 Chapter 3)

NEITHER FRIENDS NOR FOES ever knew what a deviously clever person Jared could be, and that was to his liking because he wanted to keep people off balance and guessing about what he might do next. Jared knew all the categories people fit into: Psychological Man, Social Man, Economic Man, Irrational Man, and his favorite, Political Man. *We politicos are the most honest people there are because we don't deceive ourselves. We know our motives are fueled by selfishness, but at least I practice reciprocal altruism. I help my friends and the public because they help me. The Dudley Do-Right types are afraid to admit they're just like me, but they can't steer clear of the elephant in the room. Human Nature is as Human Nature does.*

The public didn't worry about steering clear of Jared because people liked his style, but they did worry about steering clear of flying. The T-Plague had so degraded America's infrastructure and pool of smart people that air travel had become increasingly unreliable and sometimes dangerous. Adding to public angst were intermittent terrorist attacks on European transportation hubs. Domestic travelers began asking if, when, or where attacks might break out on American soil, but so far the government had little to say.

None of these travel woes bothered Jared Gardner, leader of the Guardian Party. He always flew on the Party's private aircraft stationed in security-cleared locations. He occupied the prime of a life zooming into the upper political reaches. A multi-term representative from California, he was among the first to recognize what David Rushman, the Party's founding father, had to offer: a return to the more conservative values that made America great, to be accomplished by overthrowing the Washington Establishment. When the T-Plague permanently struck down Rushman, Jared picked up the mantle of leadership and ran with it. He became the driving force, creating Securityguard and Healthguard agencies where the public saw results they wanted when harsh measures targeted T-Plague or terrorist-related issues.

Jared took pride in being the practically perfect political person for the times: a charismatic, smart, quick-witted and well-connected socio-political animal. An urbane exterior concealed ruthless lust for power he would use to steer America in the direction he thought best, and a growing majority of voters loved his substance and style for he connected with the people, and they in turn felt his passion for helping them. Even his foes admired how he and his children dealt with tragedy. When his wife entered terminal T-Plague dementia, Jared was often interviewed at her side, and his son and daughter, each working for the Party, shared full-time caregiving duty.

The pundits misread public sentiment when they said the "hidden agenda" leaked last winter would knock the wheels off his political bandwagon. That turned out to be a minor bump in the road he was traveling towards the White House. Initial public skepticism turned into indifference, and then into support because many realized the hidden agenda contained items needed to make the country great again. Jared had little to fear from the leaked agenda because the really important one was buried even deeper. It was win-win-lose: win for Jared; win for his friends; lose for his enemies. And because his world was black or white, they were easy to separate. There were no shades of gray in his palette for painting the world, and Jared believed he was wearing the proverbial white hat.

He owed much of his glowing image to his public relations group; they were bright, young, dedicated, and aggressive. And tonight, he had a closed-door meeting with just one of them: his best spin doctor, who had something special for him. Perfect timing, because in two days he was embarking on another "Meet the People—Know the Facts" PR tour that was the spin doctor's brainchild. As he walked towards the condominium, he was confident he could handle whatever was waiting for him.

Zoe Vargas had been ready and waiting for years. She loved the excitement and power of the political circus, and after earning a master's degree in political science had stepped into the biggest ring of all: Washington. In only seven years, her abilities and assertiveness career-laddered her to responsible positions in Guardian Party public relations. She loved "the cause," she loved her career, and she loved Jared Gardner. Just being near him aroused her. But so far, he had not picked up on any of her "invitations" and she didn't know why. Maybe she should be a bit more assertive. If so, tonight might be different.

People didn't consider Zoe beautiful in the classic sense, but she was cute, trim, and a tony dresser. She styled her shortish tawny brown hair to complement her height, and her light brown eyes sparkled when she talked. Lots of men went for her appearance because it accentuated her intelligence and engaging personality. And at the age of only thirty, she was getting better every year. Finally, a knock at the door.

Jared greeted Zoe in the usual manner, a hug and light kiss on the cheek. Zoe parked him in the living room and returned with his favorite drink, Cutty Sark and soda while she had hers, Beefeater and tonic. The ambiance invited an intimate discussion.

"Your PR team has been so innovative lately. Your press releases have scooped the news media time and again, and you're spinning the leaks just the right way. And whoever came up with the slogan for our tour deserves a promotion. Maybe that's the something special surprise tonight. You'll tell me who, and I'll bet it's you." Perfect segue and Zoe pounced.

"That's part of it, but you'll never guess who it is. It's Electra Kittner. She's a different person since she came back. Must be her accident. Before, she seemed naïve and though book smart, sort of simple. All that's changed. She's decisive and committed. Knows how the real world works. Looks and acts more mature. She was fired by the NIH because of her wheelchair disability, but she gives me even better inside info now than before. And now she wants to start snooping on terrorism. She's working as a volunteer, but I'd like to offer her a part-time position. It'll fit perfectly with her grad school schedule. May I have your OK?"

"You've got it. It's too bad about the facial burns, because if they weren't so bad we could use her for other assignments."

"I forget to mention, her burns healed, and her plastic surgeon worked a miracle. There's not a single blemish. And being in a wheelchair shows how caring we are by hiring her, so she could be a poster child for Securityguard. Let's toast tonight's surprises. I'll be right back with refreshments."

While she was in to the kitchen, Jared closed his eyes and stretched his legs on the coffee table in front of the sofa, congratulating himself for the progress he and Zoe were making. *Tonight's not a matter of luck; it's a matter of all the hard work my chosen people are doing. Zoe deserves a promotion, and I'll take care of her too.*

Lucky for him she didn't hand him his drink immediately, for now she was wearing nothing but a black bikini thong and a filmy, barely-buttoned blouse. Rarely did Jared struggle for words, but at the moment his mind was unable to focus on anything other than Zoe's firm breasts. He sat up and gaped, finally finding something to say.

"Uh, I'm not sure this is a good idea. This may change how we work together."

She placed the drinks on the coffee table before dimming the end table lamp and sidling next to him.

"We're already doing undercover work. Now we'll add some under-the-covers work to our agenda."

Jared, a popular, populist person who had many traits of the average man, also had a healthy male appetite for sex. The two of them worked on a new assignment late into the night...

Electra was finishing press releases for tomorrow's tour when her intercom beeped.

"This is Zoe. Please come to my office now."

"I'm rolling your way." *Zoe's always in a rush, doesn't waste time, delegates instead of micro-managing, and that's all right by me.* Zoe waved her into the office and signaled to close the door as she wrapped up another call. Then she sat down and devoted full attention to her prized employee.

"I met with Jared last night, and you were one of the big surprises. I told him what great work you're doing since coming back, and he agrees you should be rewarded. Starting immediately, you are promoted to a salaried part-time position. How does that sound?" Electra's inner voice cheered. *Plans are meshing seamlessly, keeping pace with the turmoil that's building all about.*

"Thank you. I will do all I can to repay your confidence. And I can give you two new insider tips. I'm getting better and better ferreting them out. I don't think anyone in the media knows what I've got." Electra paused long enough to see that Zoe was locked in. "Here's the first: NIH is giving up on developing T-Plague vaccines in-house. They'll keep the projects active for appearance sake, but they're merely liaison for a foreign country's R&D. I'll find out the country when details are finalized."

"That's awesome. Jared can use this right away in the town-hall meetings. And he can spin it in his off-the-cuff remarks with my wordsmithing. Bravo."

"And here's another zinger. There's a skeleton in a T-Plague project closet. I mean a real one. There's a covert agent hidden in a suspension pod." Zoe looked like someone had just told her Martians are landing on the White House lawn.

"Huh? What's a suspension pod?" Electra paused again, took a deeper breath for effect and spoke in a hushed tone.

"Suspension pods keep terminal patients alive in suspended animation so NIH labs can test drugs on them. Sounds ghoulish, doesn't it? But if you snoop into Healthguard documents, you'll find their cost-benefit analysis is all for it." Zoe's eyes registered complete surprise.

"Has anyone seen the body?" Electra's inner voice yelled *Of course! I put it there.* But her external voice was less revealing.

"One of my contacts did. Why don't we tell Securityguard to check the pod storage areas right away before it disappears. Even Securityguard has trouble getting clearance to search the labs, but under these circumstances, I bet Jared can pull some strings."

"You bet he can when I tell him the scoop." Electra was ready to follow the advice of any good salesperson: change the subject as soon as the customer has bought the goods.

"I know you have lots to do for tomorrow's tour, so I'll wheel back to my workstation. Thanks again for promoting me, and I'll keep snooping."

"Just keep doing what you're doing, and you'll move up with me. We'll talk when I get back. I'll be meeting with Jared later and will let him know the latest under the covers story." Too bad Electra was rolling away when Zoe said this, because she missed Zoe's coy smile.

"Yes Jared, I'll have my report ready when you return. Have a safe trip." Though the phone call surprised him, Angus McTear's baritone voice signaled he would not disappoint. His people knew how to handle skeletons.

As Director of Operations for CIA's Washington District, Angus had quickly learned how to handle the Guardian Party's leader. He had been the first to reach out to Jared when whispered rumors about combining CIA and Guardian Party covert operations started. He respected Jared's bold confidence and agreed in principle with the man's vision for restoring America's greatness, so he worked tirelessly to make the secret merger work and gladly let Jared take credit for success, but seasoned agents knew Angus was the power behind the throne.

A graduate of black universities, he had been recruited by the CIA after earning a master's in criminal justice. Starting in the field, his performance led to leadership promotions because the Agency needed professionals who could think and do. At the age of fifty-five he looked and sounded the part: grey-flecked shortish hair, wire-rimmed glasses, resonant voice. His six-feet two-inch bulky frame, supported by his understanding of realpolitiks, commanded attention no matter the audience.

Angus had already diagnosed why the nation was spiraling downward. A series of feckless Administrations had squandered what was needed to protect world order and America's vitality: America's dominance on the world stage, a smart and engaged public that trusted the government, and a commitment to innovative technology. Jared's realpolitikal instincts picked up on this too, and though he didn't have the intellectual breadth and depth that Angus had, he was smart enough to fill most of the void. Angus backed Jared because he knew it's better to be sitting at the decisionmaker's table rather than standing on the outside looking in.

Angus immediately went to work after the call, scribbling a plan of action, and then buzzed his assistant to arrange a covert operations meeting for section chiefs only at 5 p.m. That would give everyone five hours to get to the secure location, and by then both plan and delivery would be flawless.

"So, let me summarize: there's a body hidden in a Zeta Lab suspension pod. We need to find the body, then find out how and why it got there. We'll set up three teams; one to find the body, and two others to figure out the how and why by running down anything regarding T-Plague or terrorism. We'll call the assignments NIH Roast, Lab Roast and Cell Roast." Angus pointed to his three most experienced chiefs.

"NIH Roast will grill the senior executives for any leads. Give your findings to Lab Roast. They'll search for the body and grill the project leaders. They'll also have lab moles dig deeper. At the same time, Cell Roast tightens screws on known terrorists in our area. So far, so good?" Heads nodded in agreement.

"Now let's dig a little deeper right here. Since our merger, we know of no agents that have gone missing. But what about before? Did any CIA agents fall off the grid?" Angus saw only negatively nodding heads. "I want Cell Roast to dig deeper." Angus continued after a scowling pause.

"What about the Guardian Party? Did any agents go missing?" Negative nods once again, but finally one of the survivors from the Guardian Party's "security purge" raised his hand.

"There used to be a shadowy guy working for us. No one knew his name, only his handle, which was 'Invisible Man.' He's gone, and there was a rumor last winter that one of his teams and its snoop went missing. Something to do with one of the T-Plague projects. But no one knew anything. Maybe Lab Roast can dig him up."

"Excellent suggestion. Lab Roast, make it so. Teams, you have until next Wednesday to report your findings. And remember: our activities are known to no one else until the Guardian Party coup. And if a 'Roast Assignment' goes south, the blame trail stops there. So be careful and clean up if necessary." Teams didn't need to have that point clarified.

Alice Bickerwith was among the millions of viewers riveted on Jared Gardner's prime time status update. The American flags' backdrop behind Jared at the podium looked presidential. And though live, she knew that both script and delivery would be spot on, as if it were pre-recorded.

"Good evening patriots. It is my distinct privilege to talk with you tonight. I am Jared Gardner, representative from California and leader of the Guardian Party. I have met many of you during frequent tours, and we are honored with your overwhelming endorsement of our cause: Guard American Greatness—protect our nation's health and security by returning to our conservative heritage. For twenty years we have seen spineless administrations serve the Washington Establishment rather than the American people, unable to stop domestic terrorism fomented by Isilabad, unable to stop the devastating Techno-Plague. For twenty years they've told you to trust them and they'll deliver what you demand. Well they've delivered nothing, and they continue to deceive.

"Their major weapon in the T-Plague war is their vaunted National Institute of Health, but as Shakespeare said in the *Merchant of Venice*, the truth will out. This week the Guardian Party learned about NIH cover-ups. The Administration is shutting down NIH T-Plague R&D, secretly turning over vaccine development to an unnamed foreign power. And we also discovered bodies of murdered CIA personnel hidden in Washington area labs, as well as gruesome treatment of T-Plague victims.

"This cannot continue! As the chairman of the Health Oversite Committee, I am immediately placing the NIH under the control of the Healthguard Agency. As you know, Healthguard and Securityguard agencies are the collective brainchildren of myself and David Rushman, founder of the Guardian Party, who was struck down by the T-Plague.

"There are other changes we need to make, and I urge all patriotic Americans to support us in our efforts to guard American greatness. The world is not a kinder and gentler place. Harsh times demand harsh measures and it's time we put more of them in place.

"The Guardian Party knows what's best for America, for all patriots. We will expose more cover-ups shortly, more proof that change is needed. Our latest tour banner reads: Meet the People—Know the Facts. It applies to our Guardian Party and to you, all legal American citizens. That is why we're talking to you tonight. Please stay tuned to our message. God bless you patriotic Americans, and God bless our great nation."

Alice needed only two words to summarize Jared's talk: Game Changer. She knew that the Opposition Party steering committee would have to adjust. Though she didn't know how, she would find out during tomorrow's conference call. And she pondered the NIH cover-up. *What might Electra know? On my next visit to check the girl's recovery, perhaps we can chat about bodies buried in suspension pods.*

As Jared spun his primetime tale, Angus focused on Jared. *That man is gifted: charismatic, great communicator, empathetic. No wonder the public loves him and his people would die or even kill for him. Too bad the "suspension pod skeleton" can't speak. If it could, Jared would flesh out its story to bring more people into his camp.*

Although Jared had embellished the facts Angus had reported, Angus knew all politicians shade the truth to steer the unsuspecting in the right direction, and the pundits couldn't refute this bombshell that would rock the Establishment's shaky foundation. There was already a stream of insiders seeking shelter in the Guardian Party, and tonight's shock wave would flood the exits.

Roast Teams' performance had satisfied Angus, and one of them even exceeded his expectations because its leader, Peter Schmitzer, a talented but sometimes aggressively abrasive section chief, seemed willing to move beyond his arsenal of harsh techniques. Angus kept a mental score card that tracked how well his people performed because he liked to promote from within. *Peter delivered, and even though he's rough around the edges, he's got potential. No one's perfect, and the devil you know is better than the devil you don't. I'll watch him closely from a distance.* Angus laughed out loud. *What a perfect oxymoron for a CIA Director.*

After listening to Jared's address, all events from the last few days finally made sense to Russell Conklin. Two days ago, he and several associates had been grilled by the CIA. When agents barged into his office it took every ounce of energy to fight back his panic attack. Russell thought his cover had been blown, but that wasn't the reason. They wanted to know what he knew about moles and progress and bodies buried in labs.

Did he know about moles? Of course, because Mo had been his mole, but he didn't say so. He simply said there were all sorts of rumors about infiltration from the Guardian Party or from the CIA or from the Opposition Party, or even from Middle East terrorists.

What about progress? It's as dead as the skeleton, but he said the labs were tight-lipped, and he knew nothing.

And what about dead bodies? During their escape, he and Mo had placed two "bad guys" in the getaway car's trunk. How ironic the vehicle had belonged to the Guardian Party. Russell never knew or asked what became of the car or trunk occupants. And so, once again he said he knew nothing. By day's end his visitors were satisfied, even thanking him for being so forthcoming.

Russell thought about a quote from Doctor Pangloss. In Voltaire's novel *Candide,* the good doctor always looked for the best, succinctly summarized by "I see plainly all this is for the best." *Pangloss wouldn't say that if he were about to be grilled at tomorrow's Opposition Party meeting. I don't see anything good about it.*

The inner circle chairman saw only grim faces sitting at the table.

"Well, let's get right to it. Jared's talk last night unsettled everybody, and we need to adjust our plans, especially in the areas of T-Plague and security. Russell, you're in charge of T-Plague. What can you tell us?"

"Not much. Jared's way ahead of me. I had no idea that NIH was shutting down Cognicom or farming out the work to a foreign country. And I didn't know about dead agents hidden in a lab. Jared hinted at patient mistreatment but didn't explain further for good reason. So, what does that leave us with? It's clear nothing's to be gained by digging further at NIH. Too bad Mo's data burned up in the crash. But maybe one of his sources kept some of it. That's one option, which I told you about the last time. And I have only one more, which you already know about.

"About two years ago I was contacted by a private company that wanted to co-develop with us. I gave them a contact and I never heard anything else. I forgot the name of the company, but I can dig it up. And that's where I stand." There were no comments until the chairman interrupted the silence.

"That's not much to go on. Well, just keep us posted. Let's move on and talk about security..."

What Russell heard confirmed what he already knew. Opposition Party covert operations might be shut down because it couldn't keep up. And when the chairman asked for Mrs. T's opinion (she was listening in), she had nothing to offer. The meeting ended a half hour later.

"That's enough for today. Let's monitor the aftermath of Jared's speech, and I'll set up the next meeting soon..."

Electra paid little attention to Jared's speech. She knew it word-for-word because she had written it. Even Zoe couldn't find a word to change and told her she'd get the credit. And Electra would never tell all she knew. *I put the body in the pod, but Mo did the killing, not me.*

Robin was not back from visiting her parents, so Electra ambled to the kitchen for a Coke, then returned to the living room sofa where she stretched back and contemplated her next moves. She would make sure Zoe kept her moving up Jared's ladder so she could avoid scrambling, like everyone else, to follow his moves.

The time had come for Electra to track down domestic terrorist cells. If Isilabad knew how compromised American counter-terrorism capabilities were, it would launch more attacks. Though America is still world's best, the T-Plague continued lowering the I.Q. of CIA's Cyber-Intelligence Center.

Not so for Electra. Wheelchair recovery time had allowed her to upgrade her own Internet snooping and decryption systems. The hardware and software she pirated or built are beyond state-of-the-art, and she had confirmed that even China, once the premier snooper and hacker, was regressing. Only one finding surprised her. She had traced three sophisticated network gateways to a server farm in Isilabad. Whoever built it was clever, but Electra would eventually hack into it. She would make a game of doing so, and she loved games.

Electra no longer worried about T-Plague vaccines. She had developed correct solution paths, thanks to her "stealth project" she completed several years ago under cover of an ill-fated T-Plague project her parents worked on before they died. It was time to put her vaccines into play. Just then she heard the van pull into the driveway. *Robin's back, so I better get back in my wheelchair.*

Robin looked glum as she galumphed into the living room, so Electra asked, "What's wrong?"

"I'm so mad at my father. We listened to the speech, and my folks are worried. They don't trust Securityguard, especially because my folks aren't citizens. They're afraid the Guardian Party might start investigating all immigrants, even those with permanent resident status. They think they're gonna be deported because father used to be active in a Russian emigres' group that contained some bad people." With all the uncertainties swirling about, Electra couldn't pretend that wouldn't happen, but she tried to pick up Robin's spirits.

"It's too soon to worry too much about something none of us can control. So, put it away for now. And I have something I think you'll like. We're taking a trip to Texas just as soon as I can set it up."

"Good. I want to get far away from my folks."

"Don't say that. Of all the people that will ever love you, you only get one set. You'll feel differently in a few days." Robin's expression softened.

"Yeah, you're right, but let me add to what you said. I'll never get another friend like you." For one of the few times in her life, Electra knew that the Buddhist monk's answer would not apply.

"Come on, let's get a snack. That'll pick you up and make you feel like a Texan. They always have a positive, can-do attitude. You can practice on the trip."

CHAPTER 11

October 2118

"The Austin Connection"

(Thread 1 Chapter 7)

"SURE THING, LITTLE LADY. We'll send the plane Thursday. And don't you worry about getting to the airport. We'll make arrangements at both ends. And now that you're back in the saddle, we'll all be back in action." By the end of the call, the width of Hudson Haller's grin rivaled that of his ten-gallon hat. President of H&H DNA Partners Inc.—a privately held company located in Austin, Texas that develops and markets cutting edge pharmaceuticals—Hud could rest easier, knowing that Electra would soon be working at full speed.

She had contacted him two years ago about starting a joint venture with Worldstar Biologicals, making him an offer that would make the biotech world his oyster. He would never forget the first meeting. Electra nonchalantly pulled a gun when she told him her offer could not be refused. Hud signed the agreement as soon as possible. And with good reason, because Electra promised to deliver effective T-Plague vaccines.

The gun had been Electra's idea of an "ice-breaking" stunt that brought everyone together. Hud knew from grad school days a group of talented classmates nicknamed the Worldstars: Jason

Kittner, Indira Ramanujan, Adom Ola, and Su-Lin Song Chou. Hud, ruggedly masculine, and Adom, tall, affable and handsome, distinguished themselves from typical bio-tech drones (including Adom's roommate Jason) by socializing to break the grind.

Hud's father Hollis, aka Holy, had built H&H Oil and Gas, the parent company of H&H DNA Partners. Hud's DNA contained the "gambling gene" inherited from his father. Fifteen years ago, Holy had funded his son's start-up drug company when venture capitalists refused, and the bet paid off. H&H DNA Partners is solidly in the black.

After graduation, Hud had communicated occasionally with Adom, learning about the Worldstars' promising NIH careers, but by an odd twist of fate they were star-crossed; Indira and Jason dead, Su and Adom almost killed by terrorists or rogue government agents. Hud didn't know all details, but he knew enough to hire them so they could work in Austin.

The joint venture exceeded Hud's Texas-sized expectations because Electra's formulations were superior to all others. Hud sold large quantities to the Chinese and thought the NIH wanted to co-develop with him. But six months ago, complications unexpectedly arose. NIH cancelled his contract and, worse still, Electra had been critically injured in an auto accident. He and his people managed to make some progress on their own, but Hud soon realized that without Electra they too would be out of action.

Electra was enjoying the flight on Hud's chartered jet. Gazing at the world below gave her brain uninterrupted space to think about next steps she'd take in an assortment of games she controlled. *Hud and his people see only the rules and information I provide. Only I will ever know them all. Case in point: they'll see my wheelchair and caregiver Robin, but they won't know until I'm good and ready to show them I can run once again like the wind.*

Su and Adom had unwittingly played her games for years. Su, the brightest Worldstar and its R&D leader, had relied on Indira's uncanny insights. But Su stumbled badly after Indira's death when cancelling errors misled her, and the team never regained momentum. The downward slide accelerated when Jason blew himself up in a devastating lab accident, but by that time Electra was old enough to help Su, secretly correcting her mistakes and making a game of planting clues to keep Su on track. But she couldn't tell Su everything because doing so would draw attention that might reveal her genetic secret. Her vaccine solution paths were so complex that even the brilliant Su sometimes didn't recognize a clue when tripping over it, so the time came when Electra simply told her what to do, using the cover of her doctoral thesis to keep her secret hidden. And she provided interim formulas only. Even the best country on the planet couldn't handle what Electra could give, so she would play the role of a wise parent giving its unruly child only what's needed. It was an ethical decision she could live with.

By an odd twist of events, Su had been fingered as the mastermind behind a bogus T-Plague conspiracy, and she had to seek shelter in Austin. Adom followed a year later when he was mistakenly connected to a terrorist T-Plague bomb factory. Until that point in his life, he had coasted through school, career, and relationships, relying on his Worldstar team to carry him, stunting his emotional growth, but the set-backs he suffered after Su's disappearance finally transformed him into a responsible adult. Now he and Su share what many married people don't: a committed, best-friends relationship, platonically living and working together.

Hud exceeded Electra's expectations almost as much as her vaccines exceeded his. *Hud's a great T-Plague gamesman. His Texas-friendly personality and diplomatic style fit me and his customers to a T. He's a decisive risk-taker who knows how to calculate the odds in our favor. He'll like my new direction for T-Plague vaccines, plus my new opportunity he can't refuse. Games begin as soon as the plane touches down.*

While waiting for the plane, Su pondered momentarily how fate had intruded into her life. *If not for the lightning bolt, Indira and*

I might have raised Electra. Indira would have chosen me instead of Jason. Indira, my kindred spirit, is gone, but I sense that Electra is her reincarnation, filling part of my loss, enough so I need no other intimacy. Electra is special to me, but I shall let no one see.

And there was another reason why she was special: Su had survived, thanks only to Electra, a botched CIA interrogation that had pumped her full of drugs. Soon she would see how much of Electra had survived the accident.

As Robin wheeled the chair into view, Su's eyes recognized the waving occupant's radiant smile and unblemished features no longer marred by third degree burns. As her pace quickened, Su had to stifle her feelings. Her Indira, her Electra had returned.

There was nonstop chatter on the drive to Hud's office, so much to discuss it would take longer than a ride from the airport to cover, but they made a good start. Robin spoke first.

"You look like Texas agrees with you. I'll bet food, climate, and people are to your liking."

"It's a great place. I'm happy living and doing my research here in the Lone Star State. And I recently volunteered to work at a runaway adolescents' center. But wait until you see Adom. He says he must have been a Texan in another life. He loves it here, and his newest passion is oil and gas. Hud's father Hollis is teaching him the business. You remember Hollis, don't you? He still talks about your impromptu piano recital. Turns out he knows more about the fine arts than I do, almost as much as Electra's mother. He likes art, music, poetry, you name it. And he's active in the Austin arts community. But let's go back to looks. Electra, you look and sound wonderful. More mature, more confident."

"Thank you. I was in bad shape after the accident. If it weren't for caregiver Robin, I can't imagine what shape I'd be in today. And I'm almost ready to get around without a wheelchair, which will free up Robin so she can spread her wings and fly."

"It looks like she's doing that already. We'll gossip more at dinner, but here we are. And I see a Dr. Adom Ola waiting to greet you..."

Adom didn't know what to expect because there had been little contact during Electra's recovery. Electra had always been delightfully enigmatic to him, becoming more complex every year. Even Su couldn't explain much, but Adom had much to thank Electra for. Somehow, she had constructed an opportunity for him to convert adversity into a new lifestyle that matured him emotionally and strengthened his resolve to do what is expected from one with so much potential.

Adom and Hud's father had become like father and son. Holy's O&G business had been the financial foundation for launching Hud's drug company, and Holy was grooming Adom to run it when he stepped down. Adom hoped that would never happen, because Holy joked that when he stepped down he'd step into his grave. He was much younger physically and mentally than the calendar's ninety years, so Adom didn't worry. He jogged from the building entrance to hug the visitors.

"Howdy! You two look like you're ready to jump into a saddle. And down here you can do just that at the drop of my ten-gallon hat."

"Howdy, back at you. Su told Robin and me all about you're becoming a Texan again. And we're game if you'll saddle up with us." They bantered all the way to the conference room where Hud and Holy were waiting. Father and son were much alike: successful and smart, knowing when to lead or when to follow. Electra had sent her detailed report and agenda several days ago, and it was crystal clear: Electra would be in charge of the meeting. Robin parked her at the head of the table so she could steer the discussion. Two hours later, Electra was still talking.

"I apologize it took so long to go over the details of our modified plan, but there've been significant changes in DC that we can use to our advantage. And more are coming, so let me summarize what we're going to do right now.

"Regarding T-Plague vaccine development, NIH is giving up. That's why they cancelled our contract. And I don't expect they'll get anywhere co-developing with another country, whichever it is. So, I'll give Su my latest "smart pill" formulation for the S-Vac. It's based on my continuing PhD research. S-Vac is what you've been working on.

"And Robin, just to fill you in, the S-Vac doesn't cure the T-Plague. It relieves symptoms and puts it into remission. Su, what you already have is better than anything on the market, but what I'm giving you is better than what you currently have. All you have to do now is a little safety and efficacy testing and the Chinese will buy all you can make. Then you can use the results China will get to make NIH come back to Hud. They'll fast-track approval for selling it in the U.S." Heads nodding yes meant she could continue.

"Based on what happens to governments around the world, Hud can start selling to other countries. Then I'll provide Su with an improved formulation. Su, you and Adom keep working on improvements. Maybe yours will be better than mine.

"And I have additional vaccine formulations for I-Vac and R-Vac. Robin, if you don't remember, I is for immunization and R is for reversal. When the time is right, I'll give Su the formulations. Soon after that, we can start selling them to China. The rest of the world will come calling. And here's where Robin figures in. She handles all the accounting details. I've set up shell companies so no one can track sales or shipments back to H&H DNA Partners, and she knows how to ship and bill. Hud ships to one of our shell warehouses, and Robin fills and bills from there to our customers. We'll be invisible if anyone tries to backtrack where shipments come from." Electra paused so her audience could catch up.

"So that's how we'll turn T-Plague into profits. And if you're clear on that, let's move on to our new business opportunity. Hud, if you remember our first meeting, I said we'd make you an offer you couldn't refuse."

"Little Lady, let me tell the story after everyone grabs a snack and drink. Adom, what do you call them?"

"Mood elevators, a term we learned long ago, in a galaxy far, far away." Only Su caught the connection between this famous retro sci-fi tagline and the bright, buoyant, but distant Worldstar days. Echoes from those departed whispered to Su, and she replied only to herself. *I can hear Indy's quote, "The world will be our genetically modified oyster," as well as Jason's, "We are kissed by the Sun." Poignant indeed, and I prefer not to share my feelings with anyone.* She smiled but said nothing.

Hud told the story of "The Gun," how Electra pulled a pistol at the first meeting to break the ice. Hud still didn't know if it was loaded. Electra smiled but refused to tell.

"Let me summarize next steps for our new business focus, which will be medical devices. It builds on another part of my PhD thesis, which I call Medical Device Nanotechnology. I've already designed prototypes for an entire family of brain scanning and probing devices that integrate nanotechnology, artificial intelligence, and neuroscience. My research is groundbreaking, and I'm revealing just the proverbial tip of the iceberg for what will revolutionize how we deal with the brain. Hospitals and medical centers worldwide will be our target market. Hud, I need you to set up an R&D lab immediately; let's call it our Neuro-Device Lab. Its charter is to scale up my prototypes so they're industrial strength. All it must do is follow my instructions for manufacturing. I'll do the testing. And I plan to hire one person to run it. We'll grow from there. I already prepared a budget outline. I'll instruct the person we hire how to set up the lab. And don't worry about finding candidates. I have three coming in tomorrow morning for interviews."

Even though all at the table were smart, not even Su could keep up with the deluge of information Electra was deliberately dumping on them. What she was presenting was the best of all possibilities; no comments or discussions were needed because all would understand once they started implementing her plan.

"Hud, I told you this is too good to refuse. And I haven't brought out the heavy artillery yet. But I don't think it's needed." Hud grinned sheepishly.

"Little Lady, I might not understand right now why, but I do agree you know what you're doing, so let's adjourn. You all are invited to dinner at my place, and when you get there you'll see it too is too good to refuse."

Hud was right. Dinner was so good Adom couldn't refuse a second helping of tortilla-wrapped fajitas followed by flan and Mexican brownies. The animated table talk was equally enjoyable. Holy captivated Robin by describing all his fine-arts related hobbies, but he was too modest to describe his latest tinkering until Adom insisted.

"Guys half Holy's age can't keep up with him. He says he's too old to be a trendsetter, but I'd say he's an uncanny trend spotter. Why don't you tell Robin about your latest addition to the media room you built?"

"I didn't actually build it; just designed it. And all I did was figure out how to put military virtual reality simulation equipment into music or art exhibits. I bought some older generation hardware and software components and plugged 'em into my media computers and monitors. They create a light show to go with the music I'm playing, or background music for art gallery exhibits I'm viewing. Robin, I have an idea. If you would play something on the piano, the rest of us can watch the light show in the media room. Just pick what you want to play and I'll punch the selection into the software."

"Mr. Holy, what would you like me to play?"

"How about that razzle dazzle encore you played when you won the scholarship contest: the Horowitz arrangement of Stars and Stripes Forever." Robin's incredulous blush was not from Mexican food.

"How did you possibly remember that?"

"You're a fine-looking and talented young lady. Too bad I'm four times your age." Everyone chuckled at Holy's light-hearted remark which Hud extended.

"You really impressed Dad the last time you were here, and all of us would like to see if the light show can keep up with you. The media room connects with the living room where the grand piano sits."

Robin kidded it's an offer she couldn't refuse, so the party reconvened in the media room while Robin warmed up. "I'm ready when you are." Holy queued the software and announced, "Start the music."

The Horowitz arrangement is a four-minute concert-goers' favorite. The trills and runs demand virtuoso technique; Robin and the light show dazzled, and Robin came in to the applause of her fans.

"Maybe Su could play and I could watch the show."

"I play OK but couldn't possibly handle what you just performed. But why don't we queue in a recording so you can look and listen?" All agreed and the show went on once again. Robin was impressed and said so.

"Now that's really something. I think it adds to a concert-goer's experience." Holy added a final comment.

"Hollywood's just begun extending additional virtual reality techniques. Until recently, it was all visual, but I can think of more: add more sound and 3-D motion, pump in fragrances. Then add touch. Maybe our new lab can work on it." A joke of course, but Electra tucked it away. *Holy's come up with a commercial application right out of Huxley's "Brave New World," and my research can link the device to the brain. If I had more smart people working with me, researchers who are even smarter than Su, I could get more projects done faster. Smart people that can understand what I want them to do are hard to find, but there's no reason to be impatient just yet. Let's see how tomorrow's interviews go.*

"Dad, we can sleep on it, and I mean it. We've got a busy day tomorrow, so let's call it an evening. You all know where the bedrooms are…"

While others slept, Electra prepared for tomorrow's candidate interviews by reviewing her approach to building artificial intelligence programs. *I can improve upon the Python programming language by adding my recursive modal logic algorithms that run on parallel-processing chips. That'll speed up processing. And I'll use them to write control software for my Brain Probe devices. And if I can find someone smart enough, we'll start writing Network Security software and augmented or virtual reality graphical user interfaces to operate the programs. But even the lightning brain must remain within the limits of what physics and math can do. I can't design computers that violate the laws of physics or crack problems impossible to solve in a finite time period. But compared to mere mortals, I can do lots. I need to find the right people to work with me, even if they aren't my Dream Team.*

It's time for a break. I'll watch a couple of online lectures given in last spring's "Philosophy and Science Today" seminar, and I might let the right candidate watch them if I hire one. Depending on that person's background, they'll be a starting guide on a journey into the future's brave new world.

The professor's opening remarks for the first lecture summarized genetic engineering's promises and pitfalls: biotech, AI and Nanotechnology can lead to a better life for all, but will people embrace a Trans-Human Age of computer-enhanced organisms? Civilization might benefit, but people might be reluctant to proceed as fast as breakthroughs allow, even though the story is compelling.

He covered next just a sample of what genetic engineering had already accomplished, such as targeted genomic editing to eliminate genetic diseases or develop disease-resistant crops. And he selected several applications ready for rollout, such as designer babies (germ-line editing) or spare body parts. But he pointed out that some groups might oppose on ethical, religious, or political grounds, listing reasons for a public backlash (too much personal genetic information leaked, eugenics out of control, etc.) Clearly, there are profound ethical issues facing humanity, because new technology could blur the red line between living and non-living, compromising human dignity.

The professor's closing comments were guardedly optimistic: science and technology can make for a better world, but society must decide what it wants, and how it wants to achieve it. Since people are conservative by nature, do not expect a quick or smooth adoption of what is feasible.

The second presentation did much the same for artificial intelligence and nanotechnology. The presenter's beginning slides illustrated the speed and scope of AI advances, but warned that the public's skepticism concerning scientific progress clouds genetic engineering's future, and he pointed to unmanned vehicle accidents as an example why people fear relinquishing control to computers.

His following slides summarized the story behind AI, even including a diagram that illustrated an "Input-Process-Output" analogy between neurons and computer chips. The brain is not constructed like digital computers, but both solve problems. Until mid-21st century, computers did a poor job learning or adapting, but "Deep Learning" technology and principles borrowed from Quantum Mechanics led to unprecedented advances in processing speed and information storage. No wonder so many applications today were only in the realm of science fiction a couple of decades ago. Clearly, AI and its supporting nanotechnology can make lives easier, freeing people to pursue a higher calling rather than working in mind-numbing jobs.

Additional slides listed some of the publicized uses, such as smart weapons, augmented reality, computer chips interfacing with the brain, and robot tutors or caregivers. But the instructor pointed out again the public's concern, and then asked a series of rhetorical questions. What happens to people whose jobs are taken over by robots? Are humans an endangered species? Are we approaching "the Singularity," that point in time when machines become self-aware? Will we be able to distinguish humans from androids? All are questions that must be discussed further.

The presenter concluded on a positive note: it is good to have open forum talks so everyone is aware of AI downside, but even the best AI software or machine learning today is far from reaching the Singularity. "The Terminator" exists only in the realm of science fiction, not in the short or mid-term future. AI benefits far outweigh risks.

Electra agreed with both presentations, but with one exception that applied to each. *My lightning brain can go well beyond the technology envelope my competition can't even approach. I can deconstruct genetic engineering or AI models, then handle the complexity of putting the improved pieces back together. And I don't need to develop new hardware either. My software skills are all I need. But I need the right people to assist me. If I hire the right person tomorrow, they must watch these videos ASAP so they're ready for possible people or political blowback. We must be prepared for bumps in road to the future.*

Tim Godfrey's parents knew he had to be an engineer. He tinkered with drones in grade school, built computers in high school, and designed robots in college. He already had a collection of double majors: B.S in math and computer science, M.S. in nanotechnology and bioengineering. At the age of twenty-three, this grad school A.B.D.—all but dissertation—continued honing his skills, combining AI and robotics to build medical devices. And today he was one of three candidates for his job of a lifetime: building a lab dedicated to his specialty.

Another acronym had been given to Tim at the age of two. He was incorrectly diagnosed ADHD—attention deficit/hyperactivity disorder—when it should have been ASD—autism spectrum disorder. His mother blamed herself for taking anti-depressants during pregnancy, but after thorough testing the doctor concluded Tim's DNA caused most of the condition, then designed a drug and psychological/behavioral training regimen. When Tim's mathematical prowess blossomed two years later, a clinical psychologist used it to focus him on computers. The results were transformative. Tim's social skills became acceptable and he placed at the top in school math and science studies, which led to early college admissions.

As any engineer would do, Tim studied the facts about his distinguishing condition and always reviewed his notes on autism before interviewing. He preferred not to advertise his condition, and since society today supports "people with singular learning modalities," his ability to focus on computers and programming and to shut out every distraction made him a highly recruited individual. So, as long as he paid attention to grooming and nutrition, few people detected his autistic tendencies, labeling him instead a likeable, somewhat gaunt and nerdy geek.

The candidates wouldn't be here today if they didn't come from top graduate schools, carrying impressive resumes advertising stellar GPA's and test scores. Unlike his competition—the other fellow seemed arrogant and the young lady supremely confident—Tim wouldn't promote himself beyond what he knew he could deliver. And Tim wanted industry action rather than academic publishing. His competitors seemed a touch too theoretical instead of hands-on.

Tim would be the third candidate interviewed, all sessions scheduled to last forty-five minutes, but he wasn't so sure. He figured candidates would be flushed quickly if they didn't have the right stuff or be grilled longer if they looked promising. The first candidate strode in briskly; fifteen minutes later he exited, muttering to himself. All he said was good luck and then huffed out for a ride back to the airport.

The second—a lady who might have come from India—smiled and strode in confidently. She lasted a half hour. Tim didn't ask but she volunteered her assessment.

"Don't be fooled by looks. Your interviewer knows her stuff. Good luck." Now it was his turn. He steeled his nerves and entered.

"Good morning, Tim. My name is Electra Kittner. Please sit down and listen to me…"

First, he couldn't believe his eyes. What could this wheelchair-bound lady possibly know about his specialty? She looked self-assured and mature enough, maybe five years older than he. But how good is her brain? Then she started talking, and he couldn't believe his ears.

The lady in the chair revealed nothing about herself. She was all business, describing what she expected. If she hired him, he would build the lab, then scale up prototypes whose schematics she would supply. She would do testing and evaluation. He could tinker as much as he wanted to make them better, but her decisions would be final. If he was good enough, he could complete his degree using the projects she gave him, and if he stuck with her, he could advance into development and design. She warned him that her prototypes were beyond cutting edge. They combined neuro-science, artificial intelligence and nanotechnology. He would need to hit fast-approaching deadlines. And he would need to start immediately, reporting directly to her. The torrent of words kept Tim's head spinning. When it finally stopped, she asked him to talk.

"Now please tell me why I should hire you?"

Fumbling for words, he knew only a fraction of the concepts the lady in the chair had just breezed through. How could he possibly deliver what she demanded? But then it clicked. She wanted someone who thrives on the challenge of the unknown, who would learn from her, who would ask why not? rather than why? Someone who would dive in and beat deadlines. The more he talked, the more engaged he became.

"You can stop talking. The interview's over. You're hired." And then the emotional drain hit; Tim slumped in the chair.

"Really? You mean it?" And that's when another personality appeared in the chair. Electra smiled. She had deliberately grilled the candidates, cutting right to what she needed. Tim possessed what she was looking for. She could mold him into what she needed, and later into what she wanted. They should start getting to know one another immediately, so the lightning brain shifted into a kinder and gentler state.

"I apologize for being so hardnosed, but it was deliberate. We didn't waste time and it did the job; I found what I need. Congratulations. Now, here's what's next. We'll introduce you to Mr. Haller and a couple of his key people. They'll make all arrangements for moving you in and getting you started. I'll call you Monday morning nine a.m. with additional details so you can start building the lab. Thanksgiving is your deadline for prototype, and end of January for first scale-up. So, if you have no additional questions, let's talk with Mr. Haller." Tim's happy brain was bubbling but he decided to wait until all he had heard sinks in before talking more.

"No questions from me until next week. I'm all set. And I know where to go for the answers."

"You're right. Either to yourself or to me. Come on, let's introduce you, our first Director of Neuro-Device Engineering, to Hud..."

"Private jets are the best way to fly. I really like Hud's style. Chartering a corporate jet is the way to go." Electra smiled at Robin, then replied.

"I knew you'd enjoy the ride coming and going. Now please tell me, what did you like best this time?" The girls were mid-way back to Washington, reflecting on some of that had taken place."

"Talking with Mr. Holy. What a fascinating gentleman. He's got a great outlook on life. Totally engaged in right now. He's much younger than his years. Never looks back and plans to stay that way. No wonder Adom thinks the world of him. And he sure knows music. Do you think he'd mind if I call him once in a while?"

"I think he'd like that. And since he likes poetry, I'll give you one my mother wrote that you can give him. Its title is "Simpler Summer." Tell him it captures the essence of his outlook."

The duo spent the rest of the trip in the pleasant comfort of shared silence as Electra turned her attention to her new hire. *I know Tim is autistic, but he's trained himself to cope. And I empathize with him, for I too have obsessive-compulsive tendencies. I'll have to make sure he doesn't overwork and under-eat. And as soon as he gets settled, I'll teach him what's in my Virtual Reality White Paper Summary. It will help him code the GUI's for our Network Security Software. And now, I'll follow my own advice. Time to disengage from work.*

As Electra let her brain meander, Indira's verses for Holy flashed into memory, suggesting how best to handle life's later years. *If only the lightning bolt hadn't electrocuted Mother. How different everything would be. But as the poem says, looking back doesn't do much good.* Electra drifted into reverie, listening to whispers of her mother's poetry:

Simpler Summer come back once more.
Forgetting nostalgic reverie,
Or people or places that used to be,
Plenty of joy still waiting in store.

No frantic clock ticking all pace to be spurned.
Body and mind are allowed to roam free,
Focus on closeness not infinity,
An hour be endless each minute returned.

Let day be full scope tomorrow inferred.
And cherish the joy that is near all you see,
A miniscule second fills eternity,
Till darkly sad ashes once more are interred.

Good that Robin's growing fond of Holy and vice versa. He can become a grandfather figure as well as a role model for what men can be. Once upon a time I wished that my grandfather would live to at least one hundred, but fate ruled that wasn't to be. Too bad outcomes aren't ours to see. Perhaps fate will be kinder to Robin.

Indira spoke from the shadows.

"Perhaps it is better not to know outcomes, for otherwise hope would be unable to work its magic. I think it is time for you to put thoughts away. Rest now and let the lightning brain prepare for another day."

Electra obeyed.

CHAPTER 12

December 2118

"First Attack"

(Thread 3 Chapter 2)

ELECTRA'S ACTIVITY WHIRLWIND KEPT swirling after returning from Texas. She sent Tim all start-up details so that by the end of his fourth week he had the lab set up and began scaling up device number one. She checked with Su, then Hud to confirm the improved smart pill would be shipping to China within three months. Then she finalized all accounting procedures, coaching Robin at the same time.

Electra adjusted both appearance and personality to fit her expanded people management role. *I need to be an assertive, no-nonsense leader, older and more mature emotionally than my chronological age. And I'll use my wheelchair to project inner strength and fortitude, just like the Ironsides retro-TV series detective played by Raymond Burr. And I'll drive myself, but I'll use wheelchair or crutches to camouflage my full recovery. And it's time for Robin to move back home. She needs to deal in person with her father, and with Matt without my presence.*

Electra also dived back into her thesis, completing it but telling no one because she used it as cover for constructing revolutionary devices. She had prototyped several but focused on the one that she would use soon. Preliminary testing indicated it would work, so she prepared further testing to be conducted as soon as she finds a volunteer.

Electra and her lightning brain, now fully recovered, did even more as the days flashed by. Fitness training added strength and combat skills, while Internet hacking took her into terrorist Websites where she intercepted disturbing chatter about attacks in the offing. This would be her pretext for meeting with Zoe today.

I like Zoe, and meeting with her is always productive. She always gets to the point, never wastes time, and does so in a pleasant manner. And she likes me, giving me lots of credit. I know she thinks she's cleverly manipulated me, but she doesn't do it out of meanness. She believes in Jared and the Guardian Party. And she doesn't know she's actually playing my game-within-a-game. And I'm making it win-win, so it's full speed ahead.

Zoe's Guardian Party career was on fire. Her PR department was a hot topic in DC news circles because its press releases always scooped what the media was about to say, and only Zoe knew they were fueled by insider information ferreted out by her prize employee. And Jared Gardner continued inflaming her passions. Zoe expected Electra to roll in shortly so she made sure all calls went to voice mail.

"It's so good to see you. What's up? What do you have for me today?"

"Good to see you too. You look great. Life must be treating you well these days. Well, I have something that will add to it. I know this guy who keeps me posted on terrorist chatter. He can snoop and intercept and decrypt better than anyone, including our government's counter-intelligence agencies. According to him, even the CIA is becoming a second-rate snooper. Well, he passed me some info that he bets no one in our government knows about. How about that?" Zoe's expression said it all, so Electra didn't wait for a reply.

"There's gonna be a terrorist outbreak in several metro areas across the country before year-end. Why don't you ask Jared to check it out with Securityguard. If they don't know, the government won't know either. So why don't you tell him to do this. Keep the information secret. Just you and me and Jared. We can write press releases and speeches right now so he's ready to act as soon as the attacks occur. He'll catch the Administration off guard."

"That's brilliant. Machiavelli would be proud of you. Electra, you're much different since your accident. And I mean that in a good way. Assertive, focused, committed to our cause. You look more mature. Jared and I will take good care of you. I'm going to inform Jared right now what we're up to."

"I'll start drafting the copy. You and Jared can make whatever changes you think best. Well, I'm rolling out of here. Please let me know how your Jared meeting goes." Zoe smiled.

Alice Bickerwith could tell the Opposition Party's steering committee was in a quandary, or as the Brits say, at sixes and sevens. She knew you can't "pee up a rope" so she would have to look elsewhere for insider information. It was time to talk with Electra about recovering Mo's data, so Alice punched in her number.

"Good evening, Electra, this is Alice. How are you this evening?... Excellent...Each time I call you are better, and now you can drive yourself...Do you feel like chatting about Mo's data tonight?... Good. Please tell me what you remember..." Ten minutes later, she ended the conversation.

"Well thank you for being so forthcoming, my dear. If you remember more, please ring me... Cheerio."

No luck; Electra remembers nothing more than I already heard on the conference call. But I must keep in touch. There's something about that girl I like so much. We should become ever the best of friends.

Electra liked Alice too, but tonight's phone conversation was not the time to bring Alice into one of her games. *And when I do, it won't be for T-Plague because Hud's taking care of that.* Electra had another game lined up that Alice would want to play, and it would be deadly right from the start. It would be a terrorist game someone else would start and Electra would finish.

Year-end terrorist attacks came without warning, proving without a doubt that government counter-terrorist organizations are deaf, dumb and blind. T-Plague aerosol attacks struck at malls or travel hubs in New York, Pittsburgh, and Seattle, causing panic in the streets and at treatment centers. News analysts floundered for explanations but managed to agree on two points: the public supported how aggressively Securityguard neutralized the bad guys after the attacks, and Jared Gardner would have a lot to say.

Jared made his move the next day because he knew a paralyzed public would no longer tolerate its clueless Administration. His primetime talk would grip the nation.

"Good evening patriots. How horrific the past three days! Scores of Americans killed. Hundreds more infected with T-Plague. Daily lives brought to a standstill. And our government doesn't know what to do. The terrorists caught Washington flat-footed. Our counter-intelligence agencies warned us of nothing. The only part of our government that did its job was our Securityguard Agency that relentlessly pursued, and will continue pursuing, the perpetrators. Thank God the Guardian Party increased Securityguard and Healthguard surveillance several years ago.

"We cannot go on like we have. It is time for action, and that is what I am reporting to the American people tonight. My Guardian Party has been working quietly for months with many other people and parts of our infrastructure to take action when our action is the only option left. So tonight, I am reporting that early this morning, our extensive network of patriots is now in control of all critical government services and organizations.

"Guardian Party people have replaced the Administration. Our actions were swift and seamless, and not a single drop of blood was shed by patriotic Americans. That is why there were no news bulletins about a revolution or takeover until this very minute.

"I don't call this a revolution or a coup. Instead, I call it a renewal to guard American greatness. I am already on the Presidential Succession List and all ahead of me have voluntarily resigned or stepped aside. As your interim President, I know our Guardian Party's work has just begun, but rest assured we know what to do. We all know that harsh times need harsh measures, and we will do everything to protect you, and to guard America's greatness.

"In the coming days we'll be taking more steps that you need us to take, that you want us to take, and that we promise to take so our great nation moves once again in the right direction. And we will keep you informed every step of the way. When tomorrow dawns, you can go about your day as you normally would. On the surface, tomorrow will look like today. But take heart in knowing a better government is now in charge.

God bless you patriotic Americans, and God bless our great nation..."

Electra listened to the speech just like everyone else, but after the opening sentence only she, Zoe, and Jared knew the rest because she had written it. She had actually written three, each with a name suggesting how fast Jared would move: "Now," "Soon," and "Later". Jason had selected "Now" and all but one of Electra's other plans were keeping pace. And starting tomorrow, she would redouble efforts where needed to catch up with the terrorists.

Hassan Wassani also listened intently to the speech, overjoyed that it confirmed the spectacular aftermath of the terrorist attacks he had orchestrated. The Great Satan's leaders were in disarray, medical systems overloaded, counter-intelligence systems ineffective, and Washington had no idea what the real targets would be. What they had just suffered was nothing more than a decoy attack. On the next conference call he would share with his three sons the joy of their accomplishment and what he wanted them to do next, knowing that no one could possibly intercept and decrypt the conversation. He praised himself and his sons, not Allah.

"Russell, you look ill. What did that telephone call do to you?" He and Jennifer had been listening to pundit assessments of Jared's speech when his cell phone beeped. He did most of the listening, his face registering the shock of what he was hearing. When the call ended, Jennifer insisted he tell her all.

"We're partners, and I need to know so I can share the load."

"That was the inner circle chairman. He's suspending our meetings until the dust settles from the Guardian Party takeover. He doesn't know how much the Guardians know about our inner circle. They may not know I'm in it. He told me to just act naturally. And if I'm interrogated, just remember the Prisoner's Dilemma game: don't confess and don't rat on anyone." Russell saw her concern. "Jenn, don't worry. We've handled worse than this, and I won't let anything happen to you."

"I'm concerned about you, not me. It's just the two of us now, and no matter what happens, we'll get through it together."

Whenever Electra snooped at home on the Internet for terrorists, she became so totally tuned in that she tuned out most of her surroundings. She was close to hacking into additional Websites, and once in would be able to snoop for passwords and decryption keys which she needed for a gigantic next step.

"How did you get so far without your wheelchair?" *I didn't hear Robin come in. I better invent a good story.*

"Oh, hi. I practice hobbling around the house. Good exercise, and if I fall I can crawl back to the chair. What's up?"

"Please be careful and keep a cell phone with you. If you fall and can't get up, at least you can call me. And that's why I came over. We haven't talked for a couple of days, and I just wanted to make sure you're OK. I also wanted to invite you to a New Year's Eve party. Matt invited me to a social club party and I said yes, but only if you'll come. You interested?"

"That's a great idea. I want to hear what the partygoers think of current Washington events. And we can't be scared to go out and do things. But tell him I'm not quite ready to dance. I'll leave that for you. Hey, how are you doing with the accounting procedures?"

"You're a better teacher than the ones at school. I have the books and accounts in good order. And from what you told me, we should start getting larger orders from the Chinese soon. Do you think the terrorist attacks might move up the date?"

"I was just thinking the same thing, and from what Internet snooping tells me, that's a definite possibility. I'm ready for a break. Let's grab a snack in the kitchen while you tell me what you've been doing." Ten minutes later, Robin was sharing her latest gossip.

"I managed to get through finals week without stressing out too much or yelling at Father. And Matt helped calm me down. I think you're right about him. He's not pushy like the other guys, and he seems to like me as a person, not as a sex object. That's why I accepted his New Year's Eve invitation. And we'll pick you up. You can wear whatever you like, and there'll be plenty of people to talk with."

Because the terrorist attacks had put the public on edge, many people curtailed Holiday celebrations, but DC weather cooperated to make Matt's drive easy, and the lighter-than-normal turnout left ample parking. And as Robin had promised, Electra had her choice of fellows to chat with while Matt and Robin danced.

"Hi, my name's Christian, and you must be Electra." Electra smiled at the fellow who offered her an appetizer plate.

"Why yes, it is. Did my wheelchair tell you?"

"No, but someone who knows your wheelchair did, Matt Fortier. He and I work at the same rehab center. You look like a poster child for what rehab can do. And he told me about your lightning bolt earrings. I like how they glow from reflecting light. It's almost like they're electrified."

"Thanks for the compliment. Matt gets the credit for my recovery. Have you known him long?"

"About five years. We were classmates and hired on with the same rehab center. He's solid and considerate, not like a lot of guys who are looking for a hookup and then move on. He and I are a lot alike."

"Why are you two different than other guys?"

"T-Plague has even the younger guys scared. Everything's in a tailspin, so they don't want the baggage of a commitment. They just worry about themselves. Matt and I try not to worry about what's out of our control. We just try to do the best we can for ourselves and for the people in our lives. Too bad Robin is so aloof. Matt really likes her, but it's her call, not his."

"How do you size up the political situation?"

"A lot of my friends think it's about time the Administration was kicked out. They'll cut the Guardian Party a lot of slack if their harsh measures get results. And that means getting rid of terrorism, getting some sort of vaccine for the T-Plague, and getting rid of all the moral degenerates. Seems like the T-Plague has dummied down too many people, intellectually and morally. Lots of muggings and worse crimes going on now than a couple of years ago. But this is New Year's Eve, so let's be hopeful for the new year."

"I agree." Electra spotted Matt and Robin coming toward them and spoke in Matt's direction. "Here come our dancers. I guess you can use dancing as part of physical therapy." A breathless Robin agreed.

"I never realized how much fun dancing with a good partner can be. This is the first time my feet haven't been stomped on."

Matt drove them home not long after Midnight. Robin would sleep over at Electra's, much like they did on past New Year's Eves when Christi was alive. The three of them would chatter till dawn, bubbling with excitement for the coming year. Now it was just the two of them reminiscing and looking ahead, Electra in bed and Robin comfortably situated on a floor mattress.

"We have a lot of good things ahead of us. All we must do is have faith in ourselves and the path we're on." Robin hesitated, then replied.

"Thanks to you, you know where you're going. But I'm not sure where things are going with Matt. What do you think of him?"

"I think he's a great guy, but that doesn't matter. What matters is what you think. Look, I know you've had bad experiences with the opposite sex going way back. And I know you hide from your emotions because you earned at one school the nickname Ice Queen. You have to sort out your feelings one-on-one. I can't help you, but Matt can.

"Remember learning about the Johari Window in your psych class? Each quadrant represents different levels of knowing. I think they're labeled Open, Blind, Hidden and Unknown. If you want to have an intimate relationship where you get to know yourself and the other person, you need to make your Open window bigger by sharing with Matt. Whether or not Matt is right for you, it'll be good to let your emotions come out so you and Matt can explore them." Electra yawned before continuing.

"I must be getting older. On past New Year's Eves, the three of us would talk till the sun came up, and even then we weren't tired. I don't know about you, but I'm sleepy."

"Me too, and I'm going to sleep on what you said. You always know the right words. Thanks for being my best friend." Robin hugged Electra, then turned out the light.

Robin drove home late New Year's morning, giving Electra the space to think more about their bedtime chat. *Robin needs to take a big step for emotional growth. She should let her emotions go in a committed relationship. I took that step when Christi and I become lovers. I can think of a poem Mother wrote that speaks to Robin:*

I've found the path worth searching for,
After all these many years.
It's given me the love I keep,
Beyond pale of joy or fears.

I never felt the words of love,
Till grace inflamed my soul.
Against all odds blessed by the Gods,
It's become my quest my goal.

I shall keep it special keep it safe,
I'll renew it every day.
I shall not rest I'll do my best,
So the treasure of caring will stay.

Whether or not she finds it with Matt, Robin must share her feelings. I'll send her the poem.

Electra felt a sudden pang of grieving for Christi. *Even resilient people need a couple of years to come to terms with the loss of loved ones. I've done so, but every now and then brief twinges break on through unexpectedly.*

I might never want to seek love again. A verse from one of Mother's poems explains why:

The problem is Time turned its back,
On the search for my Kindred one.
The World and I have gone separate ways,
It's a harder fit for me.
Maybe we only get one match,
Comes and goes and no more will be.
So you'll have to settle for a lesser God,
If your search continues on.

But Mother told me this is the mistake Su made, and why she never recovered from Mother's death. Su thinks she gets only one Kindred Spirit, but that's false. It's up to each of us to find people we care about. We all must go on living, not dwell on what has passed. I loved Christi, and I can find others if I want to. But maybe I don't need to. Maybe it's not worth the risk to share love if it constrains me or if I might accidentally expose my partner to danger.

Electra scolded herself for brooding so long on such somber subjects. *New Year's Day is for looking ahead to better times, and for making plans to move forward, and that's what I'll do on the Internet this afternoon*. By dinnertime she had hacked into a suspected terrorist Website, getting what she needed for the next step. Now she had the name of a person to chat with. *The year is off to a great start.*

"You're in the parking garage? Good. Take the elevator to the third floor. My office is 301, and yes, I'll meet you at the elevator to help with your wheelchair." Bijar Wassani's smile grew wider as he prepared for a meeting that was about to start. *Imagine! I'm being paid one thousand dollars cash for an hour's consulting time. A young female researcher drove all the way to Pittsburgh because of my interdisciplinary expertise in artificial intelligence and nanotechnology. And the timing couldn't be better. I'll be finished just before meeting with two associates in another area of my expertise: terrorism. We will celebrate over lunch the Pittsburgh attack we orchestrated last December.* Bijar would share all this with his father and brothers on the next conference call. He waited exultantly at the elevator, knowing he would be in charge of both meetings. He greeted his visitor when she wheeled off the elevator, then whisked her into his office.

"Hello Bijar. My name is Electra Kittner, and I'm a researcher for H&H DNA Partners. Thanks for spending an hour with me this morning, and as promised, I pay in advance." Electra counted out ten crisp one-hundred-dollar bills, which bought time to glance around the office. No windows and a small room behind his desk. *This will work.* He was so busy counting he didn't notice the Traser until it was too late. ZAP...

Bijar came to, strapped to his chair and wearing a helmet with cables leading to a small device on the desk. Electra had already retrieved the bills and continued adjusting the device. Bijar struggled to break free, but the straps held him firmly in place.

"If you start making a fuss I will shock you again. I know about your terrorist links to your brothers and father. If you tell me what I need to know, you will live. If you do not, you might not survive." Bijar spat out his challenge.

"I will not talk, and torture will not work! We believers have been trained to resist."

"Fine. Then you're the volunteer I need to test my prototype." As she twisted knobs, he could feel various sensations at different intensities.

"Let me explain. I can select specific sensations—kidney stones for example—and dial the intensity—up or down. How does this feel?" Suddenly, Bijar's face contorted as if he were passing a peach stone.

"I think you get the idea. If you answer my questions, I won't have to demonstrate further. If not, I will tape your mouth shut and proceed."

"Go ahead. I will not tell you."

"Okay, but here's one more demonstration before we go deeper." Electra placed a bottle of water in his hands. "I'm going to dial an intense thirst sensation. See how long it takes you drink." Bijar had never experienced such thirst. In less than a minute he had guzzled every drop. *Good. Bijar has just taken out an insurance policy. The water contains a mega-dose of T-Plague virus. Soon he'll become violently ill, unable to remember anything about this meeting.*

"I have other sensations more intense than thirst. Will you answer now?"

"Yes! Please stop."

"OK. I will write down your answers to my questions. After I have them, we will verify they are correct. Each wrong answer will be penalized. Now here is what I want you to tell me…" A stream of information covering what Electra needed spilled out for twenty minutes. Just then Bijar's cell phone chimed a text message; Electra grabbed the phone.

"Your terrorist friends are in the parking garage. Time to wrap up our meeting." Electra dialed the sensation to peak intensity: unconscious. She didn't know how long it might take, but when he awakens, short-term memory would be gone.

Electra worked feverishly to cover her tracks, packing her device, untying Bijar, slumping him onto the desk, then wheeling out of his office to the elevators. She couldn't get a down elevator in time, so she pulled an emergency alarm before Bijar's accomplices arrived.

"Help! Bijar just had a seizure." As they rushed to his office, Electra rolled onto the arriving elevator. She rolled to her car, loaded herself and the chair, then exited the garage at a normal pace, but the snowstorm had arrived sooner than forecast.

Damnation. The snow's accumulating and the mechanic forgot to swap on my snow tires. Handling will be tricky if it comes to high-speed pursuit. All that flashed through the lightning brain as Electra's car skidded to a traffic light stop. *It's unlikely the fellows on the elevator can track my getaway, but maybe there was another car waiting in parking garage or on the street. They might call the driver. I must watch for any suspicious cars following me.* The lightning brain's warning system elevated to a higher level.

The return drive to Washington would take longer than the five-hour outbound trip because the snow had gone further east. Though she had not spotted any suspicious vehicles by the time she reached the Interstate, she would stay alert while savoring her accomplishments. She now had a list of user I.D.'s and passwords for hacking deeper. And she had confirmed her Brain Probe met expectations. She could use it to tease out information and erase memory. *Tim will have no trouble scaling it up, but only I will decide where or when to use it. And because of its sinister purpose, I'll never make it available to any organization unless I control its use.*

Lighter snow and warmer temperatures accompanied her drive east. Light traffic helped melt the miles, and she had traveled far enough in two hours to earn a refreshment break at a turnpike oasis but before she parked, her warning system spotted a suspicious car that exited when she did.

Electra used her wheelchair to maintain an illusion of vulnerability in case the two males that entered the restaurant soon after were indeed after her. They were different than the fellows she saw at the elevator. Sitting in the full-service section, she powered on her laptop, preparing to spend as much time as necessary to flush them out. *They certainly fit the description of Middle East terrorists, but that's not enough, so I'll just observe discreetly. They both seem fidgety, and the bearded one sure has trouble with his cell phone. Now he's trying to change batteries. I hope his spare is dead, as he and his partner will be if they mess with me.*

Electra leisurely finished an entree, then dessert, then surfed the Internet. All this paid off; she won the waiting game. *Bad guys have gone, but they might be waiting further down the road. I better take an alternate route home.* Electra was on one of them half an hour later.

It was now 5 p.m. and there were three hours of drive time remaining, and for once—or so it seemed—weather cooperated.

Although the overcast brought dusk early, the snow had not come this far so her high-performance tires gripped the road. All to the good, because the other car reappeared in her rearview mirror. Electra's brain shifted into another gear as a thrill raced through her neural connections. She was about to drop the green flag.

Until just recently, when Electra upgraded her appearance and assertiveness, she and her car were metaphors for one another. Her car appeared to be a humdrum sub-compact hatchback, but five years ago a boyfriend had helped turn it into a stealth street racer, equipped with an array of high-performance modifications.

She checked the GPS map to pick a route that led through lightly traveled areas, slowed just enough for her pursuers to trail by four car lengths. Then she powered on all but one of the high-performance systems and punched the accelerator.

The little beast roared to life, howling its delight at being unleashed after a year's waiting for its master to return. And return she had, with a vengeance. Electra loved to drive and knew how to double-clutch, downshift, double-pedal, and drift like a pro. Now she would unleash her pent-up desire.

The twisty road challenged the pursuers, but not Electra and the little beast. It screamed through the curves, not needing to reduce RPM's, and blasted out of the corners with a torque-steering pull that needed strong arms to control. Electra slowed to let the pursuers catch up. Her brain's altered state matched the thrill of the chase. She let them close to a car length, and before flooring the accelerator activated the nitrous oxide system. The little beast leaped forward, turbo spooling into six digits, engine roaring with pleasure. The pursuing car tried to keep pace but was no match, and the chase ended when the chase car spun through three 180's into the ditch and out of sight. Electra caught all this in the rearview mirror.

It was time to ease back, so she deactivated all high-performance systems and plotted a course to an Interstate. Once there, it would be a ninety-minute drive home. She kidded that she needed to practice driving like this more often, because practice makes perfect. Then she remembered what a fitness instructor taught her years ago: perfect practice makes perfect. Today had been perfect.

Electra's furious "hack-tivity" continued unabated for the next two days, yielding another suspect, an Abdul Wassani; last time it had found Bijar Wassani. Too much of a coincidence, and the lightning brain started making connections. *Last name Wassani is familiar. Of course! Hassan Wassani, the Exalted Ruler of Isilabad. I see that encrypted conversations flow among four, not three locations, so there's a fourth Wassani out there somewhere. I know from Hassan's biography he has three sons. I got it. I see a complete picture of this key terrorist network. Hassan is hidden in some underground command center coordinating terrorist activity with his three sons. Now I know how to dig deeper.* An hour later she knew the names and locations of Bijar's other brothers. *How nice that Abdul works in Washington. I must arrange to meet him. Won't he be surprised...*

Thanks to what she had learned via hacking, Electra secretly listened to an intercepted Hassan conference call later that week, and it brought her as much glee as it brought Hassan tears of bitterness. Abdul reported that Bijar had been struck down by the T-Plague, a tragedy confirmed by two terrorist cell members who had brilliantly executed the December Pittsburgh attack. Hassan's list of questions was long: What happened to his son? Who is to blame for his illness? Could he have been accidentally exposed? Was he taking smart pills? Would he recover? The answers were unknown. They knew only one thing: Bijar had been meeting with an unknown wheelchair-bound woman just before collapsing, and she had escaped without leaving a trace when a pursuit vehicle spun out of control. Hassan's lament ended the call.

"My sons, if Bijar does not recover, the two of you must handle his tasks going forward. I will prepare our next attack using my worst-case scenario in which Bijar is mentally gone. Abdul, you must watch over your brother; let us know if Allah has called him. And always remember: if Allah calls me you must return to the holy shrine to retrieve our IT Manifesto. The creation of the two

Muhammads will reveal the secrets that you must always keep. I shall call on our Chinese partners to send a supply of smart pills to each of us. They will protect us much better than Allah."

Electra knew that neither Allah nor Chinese smart pills would be of much use, but that's a secret she would never reveal.

CHAPTER 13

March 2119

"Guardian Law"

(Thread 2 Chapter 4)

AMERICA'S CHANGING OF THE guard fueled media stories worldwide for days on end as every pundit kept revising different fallout predictions. What government might be next to fall? Would this be the start of global balkanization, where every country, driven by fear and hatred, would turn against foreigners? And what might Jared Gardner do next? But all pundits noted the obvious: there was no public outcry in America, no backlash, for the public cheered Jared and his "Guardian Law."

Electra adjusted strategy on her "games inside games" as events unfolded, keeping in touch with all players. She placed the "Opposition Party Game" on hold because neither Russell nor Alice were of much use other than for hearing about the Party's feckless survival steps. She knew more than either and neither knew about the other's covert identity, so she began lining up additional players for the next round in her action-packed but deadly Terrorist Game. Meanwhile, the H&H DNA Game rolled on because her players there were heading in the right direction.

Electra's immediate focus on the Guardian Party Game let her burrow in deeper. Today's date—March 15, the Ides of March—had loomed large for Julius Caesar. As she "crutched" to the private meeting (a month ago crutches replaced wheelchair for her disability cover) she mused if some day Jared might say the same.

"Tell me again why you want Electra to be a junior member of my Steering Committee." Zoe took a deep breath and launched into her well-scripted answer she knew Jared would like.

"The public loves what you're doing. You're following our PR department script, and she's been a touchstone for me. Just take a look at the takeover speeches she wrote. They're brilliant, giving you a range of options. Not only that, but she ferreted out the real story behind the terrorist attacks. Her sources run rings around ours. We need to use her to full advantage and it no longer makes sense for her to report to me. I'm swamped, and she knows more and is better than anyone. Let's have her remain a part time employee but report directly to you. I'll manage her on a dotted line basis."

"You're right, so when she gets here you describe what we want and I'll watch her reaction. I hope she's as good as you say, but there's one undercover activity for which she'll never replace you." Jared liked the way Zoe blushed.

"I hear her coming. I'll greet her, then bring her in to meet you." Zoe dashed to the reception area.

"Hi Electra, and thanks for meeting with us. Wow, you're doing great, using only crutches. Congratulations, Let's take you in to Jared's office."

Thank you, and it's an honor to meet Mr. Gardner." Jared overheard Electra as he rose to greet her.

"Please call me Jared. Why don't we all sit down. Zoe will get us something to drink, and then we can go over the latest." After chit-chatting for five minutes, Jared redirected the conversation.

"Zoe gives you full credit for much of the remarkable work her PR group has been producing. I'm hard to impress, but scripts you've given us have produced great results, and we want you to move up so you can do more. I'll let Zoe describe what she has in mind; then I'll ask some questions and I'm sure you'll do the same." Electra smiled. She too had a well-scripted reply.

"Would it be OK for me to call you Mr. J? To me, it's a good balance between too formal and too casual. And please don't be concerned about the crutches. My brain has recovered fully from my accident and my legs are getting better. I no longer need a wheelchair. And I want to thank Zoe on two accounts. First, she let me come back. I guess I had to get run over to realize we need harsh measures for our own good. That damn driver should have been in prison, not behind the wheel. And second, she gives me free rein once she delegates." Zoe's reply showed that Electra's script had hit the mark.

"I'm good at what I do, and when I find talent that's even better I promote them. Your speech-writing ability and PR bulletins are dynamite. And you have a knack for coming up with PR ideas that fit Jared's overall plan. And, you have better sources for scooping the media regarding terrorism, T-Plague, and lately, the Opposition Party. So, Jared wants you to be a junior member of his Steering Committee, reporting solid line to him and dotted line to me. We know you're finishing up your thesis, so you can work part-time. You'll get a twenty-five percent pay raise in recognition of the great work you've been doing, as well as more assignments. Are you with me so far?" Electra nodded yes.

"Now, going forward. You'll continue with news bulletins and speeches, but you'll also develop PR strategies that dovetail with Jared's plans. And maybe you can come up with additional projects that fit where he wants to take the country. You'll need to brush up on economics and political science to do this, but I know you're smart and like to study, so that'll be easy. Now, here's the newest part. You'll work directly with the Steering Committee member who handles our covert operations. I think you know they merged with the CIA several months ago. You'll meet with him regularly to report back on what your sources are saying, and maybe help him with his planning. And we'll want you to attend as many Steering Committee meetings as you can. So that's what we want you to do. What do you think?"

"I like it, and I know I'll deliver the results you want. I'm ready to start now."

Jared walked to where Electra was sitting and shook her hand, doing so just before his cell phone beeped. He took the call, which lasted only a minute.

"I have to dash to another meeting, but let's do this. Zoe, could I impose on you to invite us for dinner tonight at your place so we can continue our discussion?"

"That works for me, how about for Electra?" It did, so Zoe wrapped up the meeting. "Great. Here's my address and phone number. See you tonight at eight.

While driving to Zoe's, Electra reviewed her plans for the evening. *I'm in the catbird seat.* And then an odd thought flashed into the lightning brain: *It means to be in an enviable position, but what's its origin?* She pulled over to check on the Internet and recited the answer. *The first recorded usage is a funny 1942 James Thurber short story referencing legendary baseball sportscaster Red Barber. How interesting. Now I know.*

She also knew tonight would offer a golden opportunity to probe into Jared's worldview, allowing her to recalibrate how best to use him and the Guardian Party, now that the Opposition Party had been sidelined indefinitely. She expected to ask more questions than Jared would ask her because Zoe had already sold him on what she could deliver.

Zoe positively sparkled as she greeted Electra because Jared liked her commitment. Tonight, Zoe needed to do nothing but sit and listen. After serving a light dinner, she brought them to the living room, where Jared asked a leading question.

"I know you'll deliver for us, and I have just one question. How did you develop such talent and insight into such a wide range of subjects?"

"Mr. J, I'm pretty smart, and since grade school days I've focused on learning. I've had great mentors and have studied at outstanding schools. And even though my PhD is in bio-science, with cognitive neuroscience my thesis topic, I like to study liberal arts too. So, I balance the hard sciences with the soft sciences. And my accident was an epiphany of sorts, teaching me the importance of becoming a realpolitiker. I'm not so naïve or idealistic anymore."

"Well, you've got what it takes. But how about you? What would you like to ask me?"

"In order for me to do my job, I need to understand how you look at issues. That way, I can come up with programs and spin the stories to match. Let me start by asking if you or any of your advisors have talked to you about any of these books. The first is "Thinking, Fast and Slow" by Daniel Kahneman. Though written over a century ago, it's still the gold standard for linking neuroscience with cognitive psychology."

"No. Why is it so important?"

It gives insight into how people think. Great politicians need to know how their opponents look at issues. Next are a series of books written by Francis Fukuyama that contain the best framework I've ever seen for explaining political institutions. He tells why liberal democracy might not be where countries end up. He even extended his findings by including how social structures balance hierarchical and distributed networks. You should read Niall Ferguson's book *the Tower and the Square*, which explores the subject. The Guardian Party needs to learn the framework. Anyone on your Steering Committee ever mention any of these books?" Jared nodded no.

"I also recommend reading the entire series of Steven Pinker's books, in particular, *Liberty Now*. It provides the best counterbalance I've found to the other side of the Liberalism scale as outlined in *Why Liberalism Failed* or *How Democracies Die*. Though all these books were written a hundred years ago, they're relevant today." Jared began squirming, so Electra paused for him to respond.

"I don't have time to do that much reading. Maybe you could summarize this stuff for me sometime."

"I would be happy to do so, and here are some additional topics I'll help you with: comparative philosophy, history, and civilization. All this will help you on the world stage avoid mistakes made in the past. I studied these subjects in college, and I continue extending what I learned by doing independent study, which last year's wheelchair-time let me do. So, you can see I made the best out of my injury." Electra paused for her audience to catch up.

"If I know what and how you think, I can help you avoid the last action called for in 'the Three Actions Parable.' Maybe you've heard of it."

"No. Please, keep going."

"A king had just been deposed. As he was about to be executed, he told his successor that if he spared his life he would give him a document listing the three steps to take that would help, no matter what happens during his rule. The new king promised to exile him rather than cut off his head. When he read the document, he nodded and told an attendant to fetch parchment, quill, and ink. No one asked why or was allowed to read what he wrote, but the new king was preparing for the future. Here is what he wrote:

1. If things go bad, blame your predecessor.
2. If things continue going bad, replace your court.
3. If that doesn't work, prepare a document like this.

If I know what you're thinking I can work on the first two so we never face the third.

"Now before you tell me what and how you think, let me diagram how you can keep the public on your side…" A minute later, Electra displayed what she had in mind.

	Your Policies Work	Your Policies don't Work
You're Honest	SWEET SPOT (Public will love you)	OK SHORT TERM (Public will give you time to fix things)
You're Dishonest (Lie,Cheat,Steal)	PROBLEMATIC (Public might look the other way)	BLOOD IN THE STREETS (no way out long term)

"Both of you are smart, so you don't need me to read the two-way table to you. But we better stay in the top row so Jared stays in the public's sweet spot. And we'll be OK short term even if some of Jared's policies don't work, as long as we tell the truth. But if the public finds out there's a hidden agenda, or that we've been lying, watch out. And let me say one more thing about how best to use my talents: keep me below the radar. Give other people—yourself and Zoe and trusted advisors—credit for what I do. That's the way I fit in best." Jared stared at Zoe, letting her summarize.

"I've never heard anyone explain in such clear terms what we should read or say so we can make politics work for us. And we'll keep you invisible. Jared can come up with a good story when he introduces you to the Steering Committee. And there's one person on the Committee I think Jared will assign you to work with behind the scenes. He's smart and probably knows what you've just taught or told us. I'll introduce the two of you just before the next Committee meeting starts. His name is Angus McTear. Jared, what would you like to add?"

"Nothing, but why don't you ask me your questions."

"Before I do, let me say that I'll write the story you can use to introduce me. After all, writing stuff for you is my job. And now, let me ask my questions..."

While on the drive home an hour later, Electra started piecing together Jared's profile from his answers and body language. *Careful handling is required to keep this man of many facets in line. His pleasant exterior disguises a self-centered ruthlessness, so I hope his goals are aligned with the public's. He honestly believes he knows what's best for the country, so maybe there's no hidden agenda buried deeper. And some of the programs he wants to push through make sense if we give them a softer exterior. Jared's not a deep thinker, so I won't try teaching him new ideas to get him to change his mind. I think he listens to a few people he trusts, so I'll use this Angus McTear person to manipulate him, but only if I can trust McTear and reason with him. I bet Jared handpicked the other Steering Committee members, so I better be careful when dealing with them.*

Electra had to wait only one day to meet the Committee, and she knew what to expect because Zoe summarized ahead of time member characteristics, some of which could become problematic if America's downward spiral continues: dedicated to Guardian Party principles, dedicated to Jared, viewed the world as black or white, relentless in pursuing goals, unilaterally opposed to kinder and gentler. *Their traits won't bother me now, but they might in the future, so forewarned is forearmed. I'll watch them during the meeting. And it's starting well, because Jared's reading the opening remarks I gave him.*

"Good afternoon, everyone. Before we get into our agenda, I would like to introduce a bright young lady who helps Zoe's public relations group. That's Electra Kittner, sitting off to the side, and don't be fooled by the crutches. She's very capable and says that last year's auto accident showed her America needs the Guardian Party. She is currently in school and is considering switching careers to government service. We've hired her part-time so she can observe government in action. Welcome, Electra. And now, let's go around the table to discuss everyone's assigned topics." Jared ended the meeting ninety minutes later.

"So that covers it for today. You all know what to do, so make it so. We'll reconvene next Friday." As members filed out, Jared intercepted Angus.

"If you have a minute, I would like you to meet with me and Electra Kittner. You'll be pleasantly surprised. Let's sit at the table." Once the room had cleared and the three of them seated, Jared spoke again.

"Electra, this is Angus McTear, our recently promoted CIA Senior Director. I'd like for Electra to tell us how she sizes up political issues. She explained it to Zoe and me a couple of days ago, and with your academic credentials, I think you and Electra will get along well."

The threesome remained in the empty conference room for thirty minutes. Electra detected from words and gestures a close working relationship between Angus and Jared, so at the end of her mini-lecture she made an offer Jared couldn't refuse.

"Mr. J, I've come up with an action you should take immediately. It will rock Washington even further back on its heels, show the public you're working for them, and advance our overall agenda. Would you and Mr. A like me to describe it now, or would you prefer later?" There wasn't a moment's hesitation.

"Let's talk right now." Five minutes was all it took for Jared to decide.

"I understand what you're saying, but let's remember this savvy political insight: when the whistle blows, you gotta get on the train. And we're not just on the train. I'm driving and Angus is my go-to conductor. We can go with what you're saying, but you gotta make sure Angus is onboard. So, you need to show Angus the speech ASAP. How long will it take you to write it?"

"I'll send it first thing Monday morning."

"Good. Zoe can arrange a mid-week prime time address. Angus, I'll show you my speech as soon as Zoe proofs it, and you can develop an implementation plan."

Angus upped the ante.

"I could start sooner if Electra wouldn't mind working with me tomorrow."

"I'd be pleased. Just let me know the time and location and I'll be there." Jared nodded, Zoe beamed, and Angus grunted.

Electra happily hummed the National Anthem while driving home. *My catbird seat makes me the power behind the throne, which is the perfect place to observe how Jared handles what I give him. And tomorrow, I'll get a reading on Angus when we meet at his home. I want to see how he handles what I propose. And I'll be ready. I'm already drafting Jared's speech.*

Electra knew the route to the upscale Georgetown neighborhood where Angus lived. She had vetted him, learning his only daughter—five years older than herself—lived in Pittsburgh. That would be a useful talking point for learning more.

"Come on in. I'm glad you're a morning person like me. I found out from Zoe you like Coca Cola with your lemon poppy muffin, so please follow me to the kitchen."

"Good morning, Mr. A. I like my caffeine in the form of Coke—the liquid kind. Are you a coffee drinker?"

"Yes, and my wife makes the best expresso. You'd meet her if she weren't in Pittsburgh helping with our first granddaughter. My daughter and her family live there." Perfect segue for the lightning brain.

"I hope she wasn't anywhere near that December terrorist attack. The media stories were grim."

"No, but an associate of her husband must have been. Husband's an instructor at Carnegie Mellon. An associate professor in his department contracted T-Plague so bad he might not recover. You're not safe anywhere."

Electra kept up a stream of light conversation just long enough to confirm her first impression. *Angus is solid: smart, thoughtful and trustworthy. He could be a charismatic leader. His six-foot plus build—as tall as Jared but stockier—commands respect in any setting. He'll be a wonderful "game-in-a-game" player, so it's time to start.*

"Let me show you the speech I've drafted. I'll explain the spin when you're ready." Angus read it aloud slowly several times.

> "Good evening patriots!
>
> Three months ago we reached a turning point. You, the American people put me and our Guardian Party in charge of our future. We are a great and steadfast nation, but after too many years of Washington mismanagement, you said enough is enough. You chose to march with the Guardian Party—to guard America's greatness. I said we knew it would be hard to fix overnight the twenty-plus year-old problems created by a series of inept administrations and their Establishment cronies, but I also said we know what to do to fix them. And I promised to keep you informed every step along the way.
>
> Since then, you've seen that the doom and gloom pundit predictions were fantasies they hyped for their benefit only. Your daily life didn't skip a beat. But know this: beneath the

surface our actions are under way. You saw how thoroughly and quickly we rounded up the terrorists, and we're strengthening our counter-intelligence systems to be even more watchful. Much more is being planned, and tonight I want to announce our latest program, named 'Infra-Rebuild.' It's built on the best components possible.

But before I sketch the pieces, I need to warn that pundits and opposition will scream. They'll draw comparisons to World War II, or the AIDs epidemic of the 1980's. They'll claim we're trampling on human rights. But they're wrong. So, let me march through a bullet-point outline:

- First, we're going to identify potential volunteers across the country to work on Infra-Rebuild.
- Then, we'll ask them to enroll, and they're not just unpaid volunteers. They'll earn a salary.
- Once enrolled, they can choose the project that best fits their skills. And there will be many projects, each designed to rebuild important infrastructures, such as the power grid, communications systems, transportation systems, health systems.

And here's what it accomplishes:

- It puts underutilized segments of our population to work
- It strengthens our decayed infrastructure
- It helps guard our safety and health
- It gives medical assistance to those who suffer from T-Plague

Plans are now being finalized by Healthguard, Securityguard, assisted by our best counter-intelligence agencies, like the CIA. There will be press conferences to provide all the details, but we wanted you, the public, to be the first to know. And we know you will like all you'll see and hear.

> Let me close with an appropriate quotation from the storied Star Trek series: 'The needs of the many outweigh the needs of the few, or the one.'
>
> God bless you patriotic Americans, and God bless our great nation."

Angus paused, grinning warily before speaking further.

"If you could spin a rope like you spin words, you'd be a world rodeo champ. This is dynamite, and Jared's delivery will light the fuse." Electra seized the moment to clarify details.

"I've spun the brutal facts to make the program sound great. And it will be great, but only if you and Mr. J implement it correctly. I'm sure you can read between the lines but let me describe as frankly as possible what Infra-Rebuild calls for.

"First, we're going to identify, then round up suspects, like Middle East Terrorists, illegal aliens, certain minority groups, criminals, etc. Then we're going to lock them up—figuratively for starters with implanted tracking chips or tracking bracelets. Then we'll put them to work on supervised projects to rebuild the nation's infrastructure. What you need to do is develop a plan that has four major tasks:

1. Round up bad guys and screen for T-Plague.
2. Keep them under surveillance.
3. Develop supervised work projects.
4. Assign bad guys to projects.

I've written all I can for right now. The ball's in your court to get Mr. J to play along and then implement your plan. And don't let him be heavy-handed. And unless you want me there, you don't need me to be at your Monday meeting. Just let me know."

"I'm pretty good at strategic planning and implementation, but you're way ahead of me. Let me think about what you've put together and call you tomorrow."

"Call me when it's convenient. If I'm busy just leave a message and I'll call you back. Oops, look how the time went. I better get going."

Electra was home Sunday afternoon when Angus called.

"I'm glad I'm home alone this weekend, because I had uninterrupted time to sit and think. I understand all the details, but I'm worried that media blowback will become a gale if Jared becomes too aggressive and exposes ominous implications."

"You are correct, but media blowback will initially be ignored. But watch out if Jared pushes too hard. You have to chart a course for Jared to follow, and I'll help, but only if need my assistance."

"Thanks for the offer, but for now I can steer Jared on a course that'll balance kinder with harsher. But, let's keep in touch."

Electra never mentioned the main reason for not helping further. *What Angus and Jared come up with will reveal unadulterated intentions. I need to know where they plan to go before I make future moves.*

Electra was uncharacteristically fatigued Sunday evening, so she picked an endorphin-loaded change of pace activity, running six miles under the cover of darkness, then completing her workout with core and upper body exercises. Endorphins provided clarity needed to sort through contingent ethical consequences that could emerge from what she was setting in motion.

Infra-Rebuild is a bold gambit containing shoals of moral dilemmas Angus and Jared must navigate cautiously to remain in the public's sweet spot, and they better not disappoint me. I crossed my moral Rubicon several years ago. I know I can trust the lighting brain's decisions, and I will never second-guess myself. I'll take decisive action if the Guardian Party steers the nation into dangerous waters, but I think Angus can direct Jared to pick a path of moderation.

She mused at bedtime that great men emerge when needed. *Most of history's great leaders are chosen by the times, not vice versa. Have the times chosen Jared? Have they chosen Angus? That will be revealed as the game plays out.* A poem from Indira floated into the lightning brain as she drifted into a well-earned sleep. She remembered the title: *The Once and Future* and took comfort in its message.

"Where have all the Great Men gone?
The heroes in your mind.
We need them now to carry on,
They seem so hard to find.

Concealed perhaps when they appear,
Once human just like us.
Revealed in Wisdom's future year,
Though flesh has turned to dust.

Greatness dwells in each of us,
Awaiting the chosen call.
So do when asked without a fuss,
In time your stature's tall."

Electra slept soundly that night, confident that the coming week would unfold according to plan.

"Great work, Angus. Monday meetings usually rough out what we'll do, but you and Electra have already added the finishing touches. And we'll go with your plan, rolling it out in stages and being kinder and gentler to start. You and Electra make a great team, and I want you to use her talents. Please tell her the speech needs no revisions. The public will love the message."

Jared delivered the speech later that week, and follow-up opinion polls proved his prediction. The public gave him high marks for style and substance. Electra liked it all. *It seems that Jared will listen to Angus, so I'll keep a low political profile, at least for now. But it's time for me to become smarter in the social sciences. Politics, economics and sociology are sciences, but they're the softer ones for which math might not be all that helpful. I better learn more to keep Angus and Jared kinder and gentler. I'll have to make time to listen to Capstone lectures that fit. I need to know how to talk their talk before I walk further.*

CHAPTER 14

June, 2119

"The T-Plague Solution"

(Thread 1 Chapter 8)

ELECTRA MADE TIME FOR watching a Capstone video lecture in June when she found one whose title struck her fancy: *Soft Sciences Summary for Scientists and Engineers*, and it proved to be just what she wanted. Two younger members of the sociology and political science departments gave the lecture because it focused on those disciplines.

The sociology professor's first slide told why the new crop of scientists and engineers must understand soft sciences: advances in computers and genetic engineering drive changes in all areas of society. Sociology is the place to start because all other soft sciences—political science, economics, and anthropology—fit underneath.

Like all good presenters, he gave definitions so everyone in the audience understood what terms meant. Sociology is a scientific study of Social Behavior embedded in a Culture, helping to identify problems or behaviors and outlining solutions. The Industrial Revolution launched the field, and he credits one of its founders, Herbert Spencer, for inventing the phrase "Survival of the Fittest." Then he defined Society—a large social group sharing Geography, Political Authority and Cultural Expectations—and the components of Culture—Technology, Symbols, Language,

Values, and Norms. He compared several societies widely separated in years to illustrate how they used tattoos and body piercings as symbols and language. And he also defined useful model societies, such as Thomas More's Utopia, a perfectly functioning society, or Dystopia, one that functions badly.

Subsequent slides outlined how disruptive technologies or a flood of immigrants may cause social change, and he emphasized the importance of diversity for enriching a culture. He ended his part of the lecture warning the audience to avoid cultural bias and offering recommendations for how Islam and the West should cooperate.

The poli-sci professor conducted the rest of the lecture. Her first slide sketched how political science grew from the minds of Plato and Aristotle, and her next listed definitions everyone learns in high school civics but immediately forgets. Less than half the audience remembered the definition of socialism: A political and economic theory of social organization advocating that the means of production, distribution, and exchange should be owned or regulated by the community as a whole. She joked that nobody likes politicians or politics because successful negotiation leads to compromise in which nobody gets everything wanted. But she reminded the audience that you do get what you need.

She used the rest of the lecture to outline the trajectory of politics, how it advanced from the Greeks to Machiavelli to Hegel's world view, and then to an ostensible end terminating with liberal democracy and capitalism. Fukuyama adjusted the end, explaining how societal conditions might not automatically lead to democracy and capitalism. Other political philosophers extended his work by adding network theory, which leads to warnings that Cyberspace might be the next battlefield.

In the time remaining, she sketched the current landscape, giving reasons why certain countries continue to struggle. Among them are China's aging population that can't innovate, Russia's kleptocratic government, and Islam's refusal to embrace Modernity.

By comparison, America is unbeatable if it handles T-Plague, Terrorism, and Disruptive Technologies, such as artificial intelligence or genetic engineering. Her closing remarks were guardedly optimistic, but she said the United States must balance self-serving nationalism and a Realpolitik approach to a fragmented world against a longer-term community of cooperative sovereign states.

I agree with her, and now that I've reviewed the basics, I think I'll reread Fukuyama's books and those that extend his ideas, particularly those of Steven Pinker. And after that, I'll run through some economics. But I'm going to take a workout and then go for a run. I'm a pro at thinking fast on my feet, so I can exercise my brain and body at the same time.

That evening after dinner, Electra settled at her home workstation to snoop for terrorist transmissions. Decrypted messages among the Website locations extracted from Bijar were indeed unsettling, for they proclaimed immanent terrorist attacks, but date and details not yet determined. Electra decided it was time for another trip to Texas to stay ahead of opponents.

Electra fired off an agenda to Hud, rehearsing what she'd say before calling. She congratulated him for how quickly Chinese orders for the latest smart pill were ramping up and told him that she would coordinate shipping some to a warehouse in Isilabad. She didn't explain why nor did Hud ask.

"Little Lady, we're all set for your visit. Our jet will bring you Thursday and fly you back Sunday. And my Dad's glad Robin is coming along. They've been swapping Emails and Skype calls. While you're doing your pilot runs or working with Tim, he'd like to show her a drilling rig."

"That sounds like a plan. We'll see you Thursday afternoon."

Robin didn't tell Electra the entire reason why she wanted to come along. *Yes, I want to check my accounting procedures with Hud's, and yes, I want to chat more with Mr. Holy. But I need to talk about Matt with Su and Adom. My parents are no help because I've never told them the whole story. And besides, Su knows Electra better than anyone.*

Matt's patient persuasion was starting to pay off. Robin could no longer hide behind her caregiver role as an excuse for being too busy to chat. And she admitted, but only to herself, that Matt had a knack for finding activities she liked, but he was not at the top of her contact list. Her study group friends took top priority because Robin needed to focus on school if she wanted to make up for dropping classes a year ago when the T-Plague almost killed her. And she struggled with the math courses that an accounting degree required. Still, she found herself accepting more of Matt's invitations, which provided a different perspective on relationships with young men. But she struggled with her emotions even more than with numbers because she continually wavered on what she was looking for.

Robin remained in awe of Electra, unable to come to terms with her feelings or with this enigmatic paragon. She knew Electra had suffered grievously from Christi's death, but she sensed that Electra had moved on in directions that she shared with no one. She also knew Electra liked her, but perhaps not enough to let Robin touch her in places that had been reserved only for Christi. Though the two were the same age, Electra's newfound maturity kept Robin at a distance, making for a Parent-Child relationship in Robin's mind, so Robin took Electra's advice to give Matt a chance.

Hud's conference room contained all the people that figured into the trip agenda. He knew Electra should run the meeting, so he asked her to carry on after making his "Texas-friendly" welcoming remarks.

"Thanks to all of you for the progress you've been making. We want to get a lot done during my visit, so let me outline the tasks. Let's go over this summary handout." She handed out a two-page document, then talked further.

"I'll meet first with Su to go over smart pill formulations, and then she'll help me set up a pilot run on a modification I'm working on. We'll need to use a production line because I need to stock in one of our warehouses enough for at least two orders.

"Once that's underway, Tim and I will go over my latest modifications to our first device. I'll need him to send me two prototypes so I can conduct tests.

"While I'm handling this, Robin will check her accounting procedures with what you're using to make sure we get the orders and shipments entered correctly. After she gets her work done, she's on her own to explore the oil patch with Mr. Holy and his able assistant Adom. And she wants to take Su out for dinner tomorrow. We'll head back to Washington Saturday or Sunday, depending on how quickly we finish our work. Any questions or comments?" Adom had something to say.

"I'm glad you ditched the wheelchair, and I expect you to lose the crutches soon. Next time you visit, Holy and I will be pleased to show you an operational drilling rig. And thanks to Holy, I understand why pharmaceuticals and the oil patch go together: both use a lot of technology, both need lots of money, both are high risk and high return. Hud and his Dad know how to make money in both." Hud was quick to add.

"Little Lady, I know how to make money in the oil patch because I follow Dad's advice, and he's grooming Adom to run that part of the business. And I know how to make money in pharmaceuticals because I follow you and Su. And Tim assures me the same for our medical devices if I follow you and him. We've got something for everyone, and Robin will keep count." Electra added the finishing touch.

"Let's all of us make it so…"

"So, there you have it, our next smart pill line extension. Now you know why it works. I'll give you growth cultures for precursor cells, and Adom can handle the manufacturing procedures for gel cap insertion." Su's polite smile told Electra she understood just enough.

"I'll write up our patent filing, but you'll need to help me. When will we work on this? And do you want me to help on your pilot run?"

"I'll write up the patent filings by myself, but we won't submit them for a long time, maybe never and here's why. If we file the patents we're giving away information in return for about twenty years' patent protection, but I'm certain some of the foreign manufacturers—China and India come to mind—will start selling generic copies as soon as they figure out the manufacturing techniques. So, if we don't file, we give them no clues. And we have the safety and efficacy test results to show our vaccines work, so governments will have to approve our vaccines for sale. They'll have no other option, because only our vaccines really work. So, it's up to each government: it's 'buy or die.' And Hud, your sales guys need to be diplomatic, but we have a monopoly since we control all our shell companies. Can you live with that?"

"I sure can. You've killed the competition before they could start. And don't worry, with all our shell companies the market will look like there's plenty of suppliers." Electra could tell everyone understood what the immediate vaccine steps were, so she moved on.

"Let's answer Su's question about my pilot run. It's for a different vaccine formulation I'm still adjusting, so it's better if I handle that alone. I'll turn it over to you once we've completed our smart pill line extensions. Then we can focus on our next generation breakthrough." Su sensed that Electra was not telling all. *Must be for a good reason so I better not inquire further*. Su changed the subject.

"Tim talks with me occasionally about what he's doing. He's a clever engineer, loves to tinker, and gets things to work. I'm helping him with the cognitive neuroscience piece, but I don't understand how your devices work. I imagine your prototype is just the start, and you're in command of where it might take us."

"Perhaps, and I'll want you to work with Tim when we prototype other devices, but that won't be for a couple of years. Until then, you'll be busy with T-Plague solutions and extensions. And speaking of Tim, I better chat with him now."

Electra grabbed a Coca Cola and then hiked to Tim's lab. An hour later, she summarized what Tim would do next.

"So here are the modified schematics. You'll need to make the helmet smaller, more flexible. Sort of like a winter stocking cap. The controller hardware you made looks good, but try to reduce power source dimensions. You need to send me two for testing in two months. Do you think you can meet my deadline?" Tim scratched his head before answering.

"Yeah, I think I can. I can embed much of the circuitry in a flexible substrate and shrink the power source. But you'll still need to power it off an electric grid. At the wattage you want, you'll drain lithium batteries in no time." Electra's smile pleased Tim.

"You're a great asset. I hired the right person. How do you like working for us?"

"It's even better than I thought. And Su knows so much about so many things. I'm learning a lot about the neuroscience behind the circuitry. And maybe someday you'll let me work on the software. Your code is automagical."

"You'll learn a lot more when we start prototyping other devices. You certainly won't be bored working with us. And I'd like you to go to some Virtual Reality or Network Security seminars. Find out what competitors are working on so we can stay a couple of steps ahead."

After meeting with Tim, Electra talked with Adom regarding pilot runs, and by late the next afternoon she had made everything she wanted and packaged it for shipping to the DC warehouse. Now she had enough product for filling selected orders, so it was time for a relaxed dinner with Hud and his father, along with Adom and Tim. While all of them dined at Hud's, Su treated Robin to another favorite Mexican restaurant, which confirmed Robin's opinion.

"You should put an S on the end of favorite. I don't think there's a bad Mexican restaurant in all of Texas."

"I haven't found any yet. And speaking of the letter S, did Electra ever tell you about the S-word game her mother played? Indira invented it to kid Electra's father, Jason. It was her playful way of helping Jason grow emotionally." Robin's body language announced she was gathering courage to ask an awkward question. Su smiled, knowing it's usually better to wait rather than force an issue, and it paid off.

"No, but I'd rather we talk about something else. I need your help understanding why I feel the way I do. I can't ask my parents. I can't tell them all the background. And I can't ask Electra. She's part of my dilemma."

"It's a compliment you're confiding in me. What would you like to explore?"

"Relationships with guys, and here's the background I can't tell my parents. I've had bad experiences with males. They've drugged me; tried to rape me. They all want to take advantage of me. So, I'm ambivalent towards men. But I like females, and I feel a strong attraction to Electra, but I'm embarrassed to tell her, especially since Christi was so special."

"Let me offer some advice based on personal experience. Long ago I chose women to men. I was ten years older than you are now so I was emotionally pretty mature. And I had several satisfying relationships with males before I made my choice. That's the only way you'll ever figure it out."

"That's sort of where I'm at. Electra's physical therapist—his name is Matt—has been interested in me for over a year. He's not pushy, and we've started a casual relationship. But I'm afraid to take it further." Su paused to consider how best to explain the related psychology.

"We're all afraid to go out of our comfort zone. But that's the only way you grow. And once you do, exciting possibilities emerge. Maybe you'll find you do like guys if they're the right kind. Maybe you'll find you really do prefer women. This is your prime time for exploring emotions. I think you should do it if you think Matt is okay. Tell me about him."

"He seems much more considerate than other guys and seems to understand relationships. He even offered to tutor me in math. Electra gave me the same advice: I should give Matt a chance. Do you think I should talk with Adom, to get his take on Matt?" Not even Su's reserved nature could keep her from giggling.

"I can tell you what Adom will say because I know how he handles emotions. He's a great guy, but it took him a long time to learn what a committed relationship means. Life was too easy for him earlier. But now, because of a string of setbacks, he's grown emotionally. He's an even better person now than ten years ago. So, if Matt has mentioned commitment, Adom would say you should give him a chance." Robin had a final question.

"I depend on Electra, but I'm afraid I really don't understand her. You've known her since birth. Maybe you could help me here." A curious expression flitted across Su.

"I wish I could, but I don't understand much about her either. She's an enigma that, somehow, I think is connected to the Riddle of the Sphinx. I don't think you should try to figure her out. Just like her for whatever it is that draws you to her. That's the best advice I can give to anyone."

"I know the riddle. It goes like this: In Greek legend, the Sphinx devoured all travelers passing by who could not answer the riddle it posed: What is the creature that walks on four legs in the morning, two legs at noon and three in the evening? The hero Oedipus gave the answer, a human being, causing the Sphinx to die. So, you're saying I should simply realize Electra's a most extraordinary human and not worry about figuring her out."

"Precisely. You'll rest much easier that way. And speaking of rest, it's time to go. You'll be up early to visit a drilling site. I've done it, and it's a lot of fun. Adom will be with you, and just watch how he takes care of Holy. I haven't pointed this out to Adom, but he exhibits all the signs of true commitment to the old gentleman. At Matt's age, if he can even talk about a committed relationship, you're very lucky."

The helicopter departed at sunrise for Holy's West Texas drilling site. The early morning shadows cast dimensional contours that gave Permian Basin oilfields a stark beauty that high noon brightness would obscure, so the early departure treated Robin to an unexpected panorama while preventing the sun from roasting everyone. And the two-hour flight would give Holy time to explain oil patch economics and operations that might help Robin understand better how to apply accounting principles to actual businesses. He would let Garth, his toolpusher, handle the drilling rig tour. Holy's down-home diction came through loud and clear over the chopper's drone.

"The oil patch is a great place to see econ in action. It shows how supply and demand meet where oil price says it should, and how damn speculators can trigger short-term booms or busts. It also shows that cartels don't last forever. You remember OPEC? People like me, along with our tech-smart service companies, finally broke its back. Adom, you tell Robin what you told me about them Arab oil producers."

"The guys running those state-owned oil companies are smart, having been trained at the best schools in the U.S. But their people back home never had to work for their wealth. It just came to them because they were sitting on huge oil reserves. As a result, they don't have the get-up and go like Holy and his kind of people. And only a couple of Middle East countries have diversified beyond oil and gas. That's bad because their reservoirs are running out, so if they don't push to join the modern world, they're going to dry up and blow away in a desert sandstorm." Holy had some insights here as well.

"Some of my joint venture partners are Arabs. Sure, they're Muslims, wearing robes and turbans, but under all that they think pretty much like I do. Lots of 'em pick and choose what they like from different religions, just like they do from different business practices. And they all say Isilabad is a bad hombre, forcing fundamentalism on its people. Too bad for the people stuck there. Hey, were approaching our drilling site, so buckle in for landing. And Robin, you greet Garth like I told you. He's a good ol' boy."

Garth hustled everyone into the trailer. *That's a real pretty young lady,* he said to himself. *But can she scoot up and down a drilling rig?*

Well, I'll give her a hand. Garth didn't realize he was in for a handful when Holy introduced her.

"I'd like you to meet Robin Setdarova. She handles the books for one of our partner companies, and I wanted to show her what it's like out here on a rig." Garth reached politely to shake Robin's hand. His startled expression dissolved into laughter.

"Young Lady, that's a mighty firm handshake. That sure ain't no velvet glove; that's a velvet vise."

"Hi, Mr. Garth. Mr. Holy thought my grip might convince you I can hold my own climbing up and down a drilling rig. Think I'll be OK?"

"You're better than OK. If a drill pipe gets stuck, we'll let you twist it loose. Come on people, let me run through the slide show."

Garth used it as part of roustabout training. Having worked twenty years for Holy, he knew what new hires needed to know so they could avoid accidents. Even today, with all the new technology, danger lurks for those who are careless or poorly trained, and Garth took pride in the company's safety record, giving much credit to Holy, who used only the best equipment and service companies. According to Garth, Holy built his business on wisdom and trust, and his protégé Adom would continue that tradition, adding his skills to make it even smarter and more focused.

Garth guided Robin's solo tour because Adom had persuaded Holy to remain in the comfort of the trailer, helping him read well logs for properties they might acquire and joking it would be a much better use of Holy's time, because his ninety years could do without ninety-plus temperatures.

The guide and guest came back ninety minutes later, smudged from the usual grit and grime, Garth perspiring and Robin glowing. The fellows didn't mention it, but the dark streaks on her cheeks added to her charm. A hard hat added to her roustabout look, complementing what she had seen.

"I never realized how complicated drilling an oil well is. It's a lot more than digging a hole. It takes muscle and brains. Garth says the equipment and computer monitoring are spinoffs from space exploration technology. And he told me all about MWD. Stands for measurement while drilling; it gives real-time downhole data. Makes for faster and more accurate drilling and completion." Garth chuckled, then complimented his pupil.

"You go, girl. You know what you're saying, so keep talking."

"And the ground level view is as impressive as the equipment. When I do a complete scan of the horizon, it's like I'm in the middle of a shallow plate. Everywhere I look the horizon is above me. And Garth, what do people in Midland-Odessa say about being on the second floor of a building?" He drawled the answer.

"You can see for two days."

"That's what it looked like from the drilling platform. Mr. Holy, I had a great time. Thank you all, especially my tour guide."

"Young Lady, you climb around real good, so you come back any time. But a pretty desert flower like you shouldn't bake in the sun. Here, let me dab the smudge from your cheeks." While Garth and Holy checked Robin, Adom checked the time.

"Let's unpack lunch from the coolers. Garth, please join us if you can. I brought extra grub for the crew, so I'll put it where they can grab what they want when they can..."

The excitement, exertion, and early morning flight caught up with Robin on the flight back. She dozed almost until they landed, and when refreshed from her nap she was radiant in the afterglow of the special day. She would have so much to tell Matt. The ladies departed mid-Sunday morning, and before leaving Robin gave Holy another poem Electra had selected.

"Mr. H, thank you for everything. You're such a special gentleman. I know you like poetry, so please let me give you a poem I think captures your outlook on life."

"Why thank you, but why don't you recite it. Then, whenever I read it I'll hear your voice." Robin controlled as best she could an emergent tremble.

"The poem is called "Bookends" because people at both ends of the time line have the same perspective. Here goes;

Young and old they look alike,
Calendars will report.
The lens they view their interests through,
The focal point is short.

The future for youth infinity,
A trillion years away.
Beyond their sight their spirit light,
They enjoy the now the day.

The days are shorter for the old,
No reason to fret or fear.
Joy is grand for what's at hand,
The glimmering golden year.

Alas for those wedged in-between,
Their focal point is long.
Can't struggle free from adversity,
Building future bright and strong.

But no matter what all will endure,
So try to realize.
The place to be is there for thee,
It's right before thine eyes.

I hope you like it."

"I do. It's touching. Just goes to show why you're my new best friend."

Robin hugged Holy, then dashed onto the plane before her emotions embarrassed her, but Holy knew how she felt and it gladdened his heart. There would always be a special place in it for the girl with the velvet grip.

CHAPTER 15

September 2119

"The Trojan Attack"

(Thread 3 Chapter 3)

ELECTRA'S GAMES WERE POPULAR with all players during the summer months that had just rolled by without incident, but only Electra knew all the rules or the score. She never burdened her people with more than they needed to know to keep ahead of the competition; instead, she challenged them, but avoided stressing anyone on her teams.

Electra enjoyed the "H&H Game" most of all because Hud knew how to take care of his people, how to play by Electra's rules, and how to swim with the sharks. He took care of Su and Adom, and he didn't ask questions about the neuro-device lab. And if the Chinese ever became suspicious or backtracked smart pill orders, the trail would stop at a vacant office building somewhere on the Cayman Islands. Hud was also politically astute. When "some guy" from the NIH contacted him about partnering on T-Plague vaccines, he called Electra immediately. The guy turned out to be Russell Conklin, and Electra said it's good to work with him, but she warned that Hud should give no background information that might connect to her, and he should avoid political debates. Just stick with vaccine development.

On her final Austin trip that summer, Electra helped Su develop additional line extensions for current vaccines, and then made pilot runs for additional drugs only she knew about. She would dedicate the morning of the last day to Tim by instructing him how to complete two new Brain Probe devices she would take with her, and the afternoon by walking him through her Virtual Reality White Paper.

At lunch after the morning session, Electra concluded Tim had his autism and obsessive-compulsive tendencies under control. *He looks lean but not gaunt, and his clothing and grooming are neat and tidy. He makes good eye contact, and though he talks rapidly, he's very articulate. And I like how he quotes one of my guiding directives: It is better to ask forgiveness than seek permission. No wonder he's making such great progress on my Brain Probes. Well, it's time to head back to the conference room and dive into virtual reality.*

Electra asked Tim an open-ended question to start the session.

"So, how do you like my White Paper?" Tim scratched his ear before picking up a copy and replying.

"I've read it a bunch of times, but I don't see where you're taking us. Maybe you can walk me through it so I know what you want."

"Fair enough, and I'll cut right to the chase. The oft-used quote that perception is reality applies to how you are combining AI and nano-technology. I need you to build virtual reality and augmented reality GUI's so users think they're part of or in the hardware or software we develop. You'll be coding Avatars into GUI's. I'm sure you know what Avatars do."

"I do. They're two or three-D figures that represent and are controlled by players in video games."

"How about augmented reality?"

"That's an overlay of 3-D space on a virtual space, and it gives a player an even richer visual experience."

"Right you are. It's sometimes called the 8th Mass Media, but until better apps come along, most of its uses will be for military and spillover to law enforcement, as well as entertainment. Look at the diagram in my paper. It shows how the military uses an array of on-station AI drones running in an augmented VR GUI for simulating short-term travel to past or future four-vector coordinates. There are many applications besides military, such as medicine, travel, or education. There are some questionable ones also, such as pornography, drugs, or gambling, but that's not our target.

"As we move forward, you will add VR GUI's for network security and medical device software. And we'll use helmets, goggles and glasses, whenever feasible, to replace computer screens. Longer-term, we'll connect directly into the brain, and doing so will usher in the Transhuman Age first, and then the Cyborg Age. Sounds sci-fi, but these applications have begun. Are you a sci-fi fan?"

"You bet. I like current as well as retro-series. And of all of them, StarTrek's Holodeck and Cyborgs are the most science-based analogs of VR and AI But let's face it. Most of sci-fi is too far out. I hope what you have in mind is actually doable for an engineer like me."

"As they still say in Minnesota, you betcha. So be ready. And I have an assignment for you. Please attend a network security seminar and report back what the competition is up to." Just then, Adom came in.

"I hope you're wrapping up, because my assignment is to drive you to the airport. Are you ready?" Tim answered before Electra.

"You betcha."

The flight back to DC gave Electra time to think about two other close friends, Robin and Matt. Robin hadn't accompanied her on this trip because accounting issues are being handled by Email or cell phone. She thought about Robin's growing assertiveness and willingness to deal with her sexuality. *Corresponding with Su and Holy must be helping, but probably not as much as her relationship with Matt. I'm happy for both of them and I hope their relationship will lessen Robin's emotional dependence on me. Time will tell how that game plays out…*

Electra used the "Guardian Party Game" to keep in touch with Zoe. She usually assisted when Zoe asked for help, but Electra had outgrown her erstwhile public relations mentor because Angus was now her Jared contact, and she thought they could rein in Jared if his programs became too aggressive. And working with Angus made Alice superfluous, but although Alice was on the sidelines because the Opposition Party had mothballed its covert operations, Electra kept in touch because she might be useful if additional resources were needed.

The nettlesome "Terrorist Game" posed her biggest challenge. Eavesdropping on network chatter locations she had coaxed out of Bijar, she was tantalizingly close to unraveling plans for the next attack. Although it might come soon, and in waves, she couldn't be more specific, but Angus would want to know, so she'd use what she knew to lead off their Saturday meeting.

Electra considered further how she was handling her new crop relationships as she drove on this warm and windy September morning to his home, a location they both liked for their bi-monthly weekend meetings. *Jared likes our meeting on weekends because it shows him how dedicated we are to him. And it lets us keep tabs on Jared, even though he's behaving himself. I like him better, now that I know what he's up to.*

I like Zoe, Alice, and Angus too. I'm using all three of them, but I don't think they know it. Besides, I'm not harming them. Without warning, an emotional ping jolted as Indira admonished from the shadows.

"You need to pay more attention to your emotional growth. Stop using friends as objects you manipulate. No matter how clever you think you are, they will walk away if your empathy languishes."

"Mother, you are right. I'm sorry. I still have to fight being too self-centered." Electra's inner voice softened.

"And you are winning. I simply sensed that this morning would be a good time to remind you. And I do like how you make a game for Angus of breakfast snack selections by bringing him a yogurt. So, carry on, my precious daughter." Electra did so by reviewing one more time what she wanted to cover. By the time she was sitting with Angus, she knew how to start the meeting.

"We're thinking alike today. I have blueberry yogurt for you, and you picked a blueberry muffin for me. That'll go nicely with my

Coke. Thank you." They bantered while snacking, then got down to business.

"Thanks for sending me an agenda. Let's go through it in the order you've listed, and if there's anything I think you left out I'll ask. So, tell me what you know about an imminent terrorist attack."

"I know a guy who's a pro at listening to terrorist chatter. He's telling me that some type of organized two-pronged attack is coming soon, somewhere in the U.S. I wish he had more details, but that's it. Does your CIA know about this?"

"We haven't intercepted anything like it, but that doesn't surprise me. Our counter-intelligence capabilities have slipped further since the beginning of the year. Your friend must spend most of his time listening, or just lucked into the right channels. I know it won't do any good because I know what your answer is, but I'll ask anyway. Why don't you give me your source?" Electra's smile showed they both know the answer.

"I prefer not to."

"I'll pass this info to my top counter-intelligence guy and let Jared know. At least we can report that we're coming up with something from intercepting terrorist chatter. Better to be on guard even if it's a false rumor." Other items covered routine activities, but Electra selected one that needed careful discussion.

"Let me give you my take on how Infra-Rebuild is sitting with the public. Zoe and I track public sentiment because we use it to spin news bulletins and speeches. People like Infra-Rebuild because it walks the walk for 'harsh times demand harsh measures,' and they don't much care about human rights violations or collateral damage, so you have some leeway when rolling it out. How is implementation going?"

"Better than expected in a couple of ways. The public is helping us find terrorist suspects, and tracking chips are inexpensive and easy to embed. And we're rolling up other types of bad guys besides terrorists. The public wants us to round up more criminals, whose numbers have grown with that of T-Plague victims. The hard part is assigning them to projects. Most of them don't have the skills needed for infrastructure projects, so we're coming up with low-tech work they can handle."

"As long as we're making some headway, I can spin the stories to our advantage. And so far, the media's comparison between Infra-Rebuild and World War II labor camps is being ignored. Have you and Jared considered a wider profiling net and putting those caught in some type of internment camp?" An incredulous look telegraphed his answer.

"I don't think even the most aggressive steering committee member would have thought of that. You must be asking simply to consider options. At least I hope so."

"Of course, I'm not pushing for harsher ones. But you and I have to stay ahead of Jared and his lieutenants by thinking through all possibilities, so I've listed them for us to discuss. And if or when they do come up, you need to guide Jared's decision on which ones are acceptable and which are beyond Guardian Party ethics. And that's where you need to be a clever negotiator, because Jared and his ethics are self-serving. Take a look at my list and add to if you can." Electra handed him a bullet point list, then quickly ticked off some of the items:

Potential Guardian Party Programs

- Establish labor camps and internment camps
- Deport "bad guys"
- Reinstate harsh interrogation techniques for terrorist suspects
- Reinstate harsher capital punishment for "serious crimes"
- No parole for any crime
- Convictions based on intent or dissention
- Guilty until proven innocent for "serious crimes"
- Reinstate medical procedures to neutralize suspects
- Curtail suspects' civil rights

- Exempt CIA from wearing videocams or from prosecution
- Use covert ops to destabilize rogue states
- Use T-Plague as a WMD against enemies
- Test everyone for T-Plague
- Assign all T-Plague survivors to "leper colonies"
- Remove terminally ill T-Plague victims from life support
- Suspend voting rights for "undesirables"

"Jesus, what did you do? Hold a brainstorming session for a police state?" She wanted to say *This is an ethics test for you and Jared. How far will you go to get what you want?* Instead she said,

"Forewarned is forearmed, so don't be angry with me. All these actions could be on the table if the country tumbles into the abyss. Who would you trust to make the call? If you and I don't work through these ethical dilemmas and advise Jared, who will? The T-Plague has dummied down so much of the population they can't think for themselves. And they don't want to. They want someone to make decisions for them. I know these are difficult issues, and I'm not expecting us to answer them today. But in future meetings, let's keep talking about how we might." Angus's tone softened.

"I see what you're getting at. I'm not going to share this with anyone until you and I have come to an understanding. For now, I'll tell my guys about a possible multi-pronged terrorist attack." Electra completed the thought which ended their meeting.

"And I'll prepare a news bulletin for Jared. If no attack comes, good. If it does come, your guys will need to do what they've been doing: terminate with extreme prejudice and do it quickly. The public will approve."

Terrorist attacks erupted before their meeting could take place. Three cities spanning the country—Orlando, Minneapolis, and Seattle—were the targets and the results were all the same. Hysteria and confusion. Lucky for Jared he had taken advice from Angus and used Electra's pre-and-post-attack bulletins when dealing with the media. That bought time with the public because at least the Guardian Party alerted people in advance, whereas the deposed administration couldn't do even that.

The attack galvanized Electra's hacking for more information, but yielded nada, so she changed tactics. She would hack into 3-D space instead of Cyberspace, and already knew who she would interrogate. They would meet tonight if he played her game. Social media surfing helped her set the rules of engagement, and she would call ahead to make sure her opponent was ready for her and vice versa.

Abdul had to stifle his joy. He was still basking in the thrill of victory a week after the attacks and would celebrate when talking tomorrow with his father and brother. But tonight, he and a trusted accomplice would celebrate discreetly at a popular "sensual pleasures" café where he would reward himself by tasting appetizers laced with recreational drugs and smoking aromatic tobaccos from a hookah. And if he was lucky, he might take home other tempting sweets. *Father would not approve, so whatever happens tonight will go no further. But Saint Augustine would forgive me for sampling Western-style decadence, for he beseeched his Lord to "Make me chaste, but not yet."*

Electra spotted Abdul when he exited the building. Earlier in the week she had hacked into his Emails, so she knew about this evening's socializing. She also knew where he worked and had called his office that afternoon to confirm he was in. As she watched from her car, she saw him waiting near the curb. *Good. His partner's picking him up*. She followed at a distance, hoping she would get lucky. If not, she would retrace her steps whenever his Emails suggested. And luck was with her. Her targets drove to a nearby trendy entertainment strip where she watched them enter a sensual pleasures café.

Electra knew all about sensual pleasures cafes, though she had never gone to one. When the government legalized marijuana a hundred years ago, it finally acknowledged that legalizing the safer recreational drugs would reduce gang-related drug traffic (no need to buy from street vendors) and raise revenues (tax new businesses). The cafes offered the younger crowd an escape from life's T-Plague induced grim realities, so they became an overnight success when they opened.

The evening crowd was starting to gather when Electra walked in. The pungent fragrance from smoke mixing with the aroma of fresh-baked goods made her mouth water. Subtle indirect lighting and muted new-century music added to the intimacy of filmy curtain-separated seating areas. Electra immersed herself in the experience before zeroing in on her opponent.

Electra, an expert body language communicator, had dressed appropriately for the game. No crutches tonight. She was subtly provocative, catching the attention of several males and females. She also made eye contact with her target, and she chatted nonchalantly with one fellow until Abdul cruised over, offering to buy her another drink. The person he came with was busy with another lady, so Electra and Abdul were in their own space, insulated by the surrounding white noise.

Abdul's body language announced he was interested. *Good. No reason to rush. I'm enjoying being here and I'll reel him in just slowly enough for his lower head to do most of the thinking.* As the crowd built, Electra made her move. Knowing what to say, she pressed her leg against his.

"It's a fun café, but a bit too crowded to get to know you better. Why don't we find another place?"

"I'd like that, but my friend drove."

"That's OK, I have my car. And I'll drive you home later. Maybe much later." That was an offer he didn't want to refuse. Dusk was upon them as they strolled to the car, and a different sort of poem flashed into the lightning brain:

"Will you walk me to my parlor?" said the spider to the fly;
"Tis the prettiest little parlor that ever you did spy.
The way into my parlor is up a winding stair,
And I have many pretty things to show when you are there."

Abdul came to in a place he didn't know, a glaring light bulb focused on him.

The last thing he remembered was sharing a drink with the woman now sitting in the shadows across the table. He was bound to a chair and wearing a cap that was connected to some sort of electronic device placed on the table. Beads of sweat were forming on his forehead.

"Abdul, I already know a lot about you, and I want you to tell me more. Please listen carefully to me before you speak. I know about your terrorist network run by your brothers and father. I'm going to ask you questions, and I want answers. Do not lie, because we will confirm the accuracy of your answers before you leave. You want to say torture won't get you to talk, so if you wish, I will demonstrate the Brain Probe that you're wearing. I can dial in many different sensations at different intensities. What do you prefer?"

"You can't make me talk! I have been trained to ignore pain."

"Very well. See how long you can resist drinking." Electra placed a bottle of water on the table, then dialed the knobs. A surging sensation of thirst overwhelmed him. He guzzled every drop.

"Are you convinced?"

"No! Allah will give me strength."

"Very well, let's see if you're strong enough to handle childbirth. Did you know that during the first few weeks, embryos are neither male nor female? That's when a small group of cells called the 'indifferent gonads' begins to form. They are capable of becoming ovaries or testicles. So, your brain can feel male and female sensations."

As Electra redialed the knobs, the pain in Abdul's groin became excruciating. She dialed back the intensity just after Abdul passed out. When he came to, all he could do was gasp and rasp.

"OK, OK. I'll tell you what you want to know. No more pain."

Electra confirmed that Abdul's answers were true, so it was time to end the meeting. She was about to terminate the conversation as she had done with Bijar when suddenly an emotional jolt broke through. She felt empathy and compassion for Abdul; she felt guilt and sorrow for herself. Then just as suddenly, her rational persona reasserted control. *Get with it soldier! Focus on the mission. Abdul must not remember this meeting.*

Electra numbed her emotions as she permanently erased Abdul's memory. She ended the evening by dumping him in a park where he'd be found tomorrow, another victim of the T-Plague. Electra could accept her decisions, but an emotional shiver jolted her once again. *What's going on with my emotional persona? The lightning brain must be making adjustments I do not yet understand, and I can't force the issue, so I'll have to wait, then follow when it's ready to lead me where I should go.* The shiver dissipated as quickly as it built.

Electra faked Abdul's place on the conference call, pretending the bad connection forced a listener's role only; no speaking on his part. Hassan and the other brother Cyrus would do the talking.

"Allah be praised for our success, my sons. Soon the first wave of our Trojan attack will sweep over the Great Satan, and we will watch him struggle in vain to understand. But he never will. We are too clever. You have earned a welcome rest while I prepare it. So, we do not need to talk until the end of October. Cyrus, please communicate with Abdul between now and when you arrange our next conversation. Allah be with us."

The call ended, marking the end of a watershed week. Electra had much to contemplate, much to add to the "Terrorist Game," much to tell Angus. But she could not tell him all she had learned about an unspeakably devious WMD, the Trojan Offense.

Hassan had initiated this secret project ten years ago when he and Chinese partners started a company to manufacture air and water filtration equipment. His three sons coordinated design; the Chinese handled manufacturing and marketing the equipment to municipalities and industrial parks in the Americas and Europe. Unbeknownst to all but father and sons, hidden inside each was a WMD: a reservoir of T-Plague virus that could be dispersed remotely into the environment by commands sent over the Internet. The virus would remain dormant for years until released, and the reservoir could be refilled if the Chinese-controlled company that serviced the equipment were instructed to do so. Of course, they would never know what they were really doing.

All the primitive suicide terrorist attacks that had come before were nothing more than a test or distraction. They tested how to disperse the virus and confirmed how it could terrorize, and it also tested Satan's counter-terrorist capabilities, but it was the Trojan Offense that would wreak a worldwide swath of devastation. Thousands of filtration units were silently waiting for instructions that would come from Hassan's control center. Only Cyrus and Hassan knew the commands for activating the release valves remotely.

Electra had much to do. *I have to hack into a directory containing locations and access codes for the Trojan filters. It's impossible to shut them down otherwise. What's a government supposed to do? How would it know which units to pick? How would it find hidden reservoirs welded deep inside? The economic impact of such efforts would be staggering.*

Electra shuddered when considering consequences once filters were activated. *Suppose a Trojan filter were installed at a bottled water filling location. Water coolers in buildings and bottled water at food stores would now contain the virus, making it virtually impossible to locate the source. The public would never know what caused an outbreak.*

There was much more to consider, so her lightning brain needed to think long and hard. But there was one thing she already knew. She would tell Angus at tomorrow's breakfast meeting what she needed him to know. It was time for the lightning brain to be left alone, so Electra went to bed. She knew that when she awakes, her brain would know what to do. There were no dreams that night.

Clarity greeted her as she awakened with the dawn, fully understanding how to engage the enemy. She had plenty of time for exercising while scribbling mental notes and practicing on the way what she'd say.

Angus scratched the back of his head before speaking.

"So, let me get this straight. Your guy says the latest attacks are controlled by Isilabad and are meant to divert our attention from the hidden ones about to occur. They've planted remote control devices in the United States and Western Europe that can release virus into the air or water, but he doesn't know where they're located. The only way we'll know is to look for sources when outbreaks occur. Jesus Electra, this is going to spook the public."

"Yes, but we have to issue some sort of warning so the public knows to look out for multiple outbreaks soon. Another wave is likely to follow, maybe a month later. This is part of a grand strategy to defeat the West by bringing 'the great Satan'—that's us—to our knees and then attacking Europe." Angus continued frowning when speaking.

"So, what are we supposed to do? We need to fight with more than harsh language."

"Find this guy—Cyrus Wassani—and interrogate him. He works in Silicon Valley. Have counter-intelligence trace him to a network of people or computers that control these machines. And don't tell the public his name until you catch him. If you do, he'll run for cover. Keep this to ourselves. And don't tell other countries because they're not targets and can't help us yet. While you're doing that, I'll write bulletins and speeches I can spin to make us look good because we're doing more than was ever done before. Tell Jared that Zoe's got to get them out immediately." Angus stood and stretched to relieve the tightness in his lower back.

"Let's stop here so I can go see Jared. And come back next Saturday so I can tell you what steps some of Jared's aggressive lieutenants want him to take."

Electra went for a run that afternoon to think more about Angus and the latest meeting. *Angus is what Moses Solstein had been: an intelligent, proactive and trustworthy patriot who places the nation's wellbeing ahead of everything else. If Moses had survived the crash, he and Angus might have joined forces. It's up to Angus to handle Jared and make sure power doesn't go to his head. But Angus isn't alone. I'm the brains behind the throne."*

Electra could have given Angus more information today but decided not to. She needed to protect both of them by withholding some of what she had extracted from Abdul to keep from drawing too much attention her way, something that must never happen. Angus had enough to keep his people busy, the public informed, and Jared under control.

That last thought brought her to a dead stop. *Here I am, helping to keep the public under control. But I have my reasons; my ethics are better than anyone's, and I know what's best. It's all part of these deadly games.*

That evening she considered next moves. Topping the list would be finding hidden Trojan filter locations, and this would depend mightily on what happens when the Trojans are unleashed.

Late the following week, media news reported scattered T-Plague outbreaks. *Good thing Zoe used my bulletins to get the warnings out. The Guardian Party was able to contain the public's fear, at least for the time being. The game is escalating, but it's still fun because I'm still in control. And I'll do all I can to keep it that way.*

CHAPTER 16

November 2119

"The Hunt for Electra"

(Thread 2 Chapter 5)

My sons! My sons! Cyrus murdered by the great Satan. Abdul and Bijar infected with T-Plague by some mysterious woman. I shall avenge my loss soon. I alone will carry out my plan, but this time on a larger scale. No one will know what's causing the attacks or who is controlling them. Hassan's bitter words would never be shared for there was no one left for whom he cared. There was no one left who needed to know.

Electra knew why there were no more conversations between Hassan and Cyrus. Securityguard agents, in their haste to roll up Cyrus, had rolled over him instead. A pursuit vehicle actually ran him down while he was fleeing on foot. The grisly chase went viral on social media but provoked little backlash because the public demanded harsh measures.

Too bad Cyrus was never interrogated. He might have told them locations and access codes for hidden filters. Now the CIA will have to hack into his computers for leads, and I don't think they're smart enough to get results. They couldn't even piece together a network containing Cyrus and his two brothers leading to Isilabad's Exalted Ruler. All this bungling is mute testimony to how far America's counter-intelligence capabilities have fallen. And if I tell them all the facts I know, they might treat me badly enough to stumble over my freakish genetic make-up, a secret that must never be revealed.

Electra could only guess what Hassan would do next. It's possible—but unlikely—that overwhelming grief would suspend his attacks. Or he might be galvanized to lash out mindlessly for revenge. That too is unlikely. She decided he would avenge his sons by methodically planning the next wave of Trojan attacks, this time needing no decoy, implementing it alone from his secret control center. She would give Angus an edited version of her predictions at their next meeting.

Electra received a disturbing call before then from Zoe, who breathlessly explained what she needed: a press release describing a revolutionary Guardian Party initiative to protect America's health and security. Zoe had just rushed from a Jared meeting where he outlined what some of his lieutenants wanted. He would act as soon as Angus flanged up the details, and Jared expected the Angus-Electra team to help make it bulletproof from attacks that might come from the media.

"I'm dashing off to another meeting, so please get all the details from Angus. But you've got enough to get started. Jared really depends on your press releases to sell his programs to the public."

Electra wasn't surprised by the initiative since it was near the top on the program list she had explained to Angus, but she was stunned by how early in Jared's reign it had surfaced. She immediately focused on what Jared wanted, and two word-spinning hours later had a suitable Newsflash and support document that would support a detailed speech.

She liked the invented program name, which is a play on the word repatriation: the process of returning a person to his or her place of origin or citizenship. She would call it the "Repatriot Progam," a euphemism for barefaced deportation. She read it again.

Newsflash! Guardian Party proposes New Repatriot Program

"The Guardian Party is preparing additional programs to help the country deal with crises previous administrations knew about but were afraid to confront. The next in line—the "Repatriot Program"—will allow people to choose the best place to live, based on their background, abilities, and health.

Many people who would be much better off relocating have been unable to do so because they lack resources. That's where "Repatriot" comes into play. It will provide counseling and financial aid so each person who participates can determine the best place to insure their health and safety, and to provide job opportunities that best utilize their talents.

The program is not only a win for participants, but for the country as well. It will streamline health and security procedures and cost, at the same time adding to economic growth by placing people in the jobs that fit them best.

The Guardian Party's Healthguard and Securityguard agencies will manage the program as soon as it is rolled out. Final approval and launch details are expected shortly. If you have additional questions, please contact Healthguard or Securityguard at your earliest convenience.

This initiative walks us into a political minefield, so Angus and I need to tread carefully. This will be our first topic for discussion. Electra sent Angus a copy plus an agenda for Saturday's meeting, and when she arrived she could tell by his expression he didn't like the sinister direction Jared wanted to steer.

"Your words make "Repatriot" sound about as good as we can make it, but some people might not like it if they understand the harsh reality: we're deporting a lot of people and some will be collateral damage. We may be getting rid of terrorists and criminals, or unskilled T-Plague victims that are draining healthcare or the economy, but we're trampling civil rights and moral issues."

"You're right, so that's why Jared has to go slowly and follow the spin I've put on the story. The only bulletin backlash will come from the target population—people fitting the profiles—and they won't get much sympathy. Some liberal groups might protest, but I don't think the public is going to disapprove because they don't know the details. They'll wait and see, and by the time the details are known they might like them, or they'll have lost interest in Repatriot." Angus nodded grudgingly.

"That's what I'll tell Jared when I see him Monday. Okay, what's your next topic?"

"It's too bad your agents couldn't interrogate Cyrus. Are they allowed to be so aggressive, or did they exceed your guidelines?"

"Jared doesn't want their hands tied, so they're now being held accountable to a lower standard. But I'm holding all section chiefs accountable to a higher one. They must balance field tactics against results. They didn't exceed guidelines chasing Cyrus and our guys did recover his computers. But they haven't been able to hack in. You think your guy could help?"

"No. Your people will never give it up to an unknown person, and I'm not telling you his name. But he did tell me some of the conversation sources he used to hack have gone silent. Has counter-intelligence been able to piece together a terrorist network from what they know about Cyrus?"

"No. But didn't your guy tell you the next attacks should come from Trojan filters, not from decoys. Have you spun a bulletin covering this?"

"Yes, and I've already given it to Zoe. Why don't you mention it to Jared. He'll give us high marks for thoroughness. Hey, I have to get to my lab. See you in two weeks…"

There was another Saturday meeting that Electra would have done anything to be a fly on the wall if she had known about it. It was a team leaders' meeting run by CIA section chief Peter Schmitzer. Elliot Spitzdieck, Project Death Shield team leader, attended and had been given the green light to resume playing a deadly game.

Elliot liked Peter's aggressive style and willingness to let his teams "upgrade" field tactics if doing so would get results. And he understood the implied meaning of Peter's statement: I only want to hear about blue sky, green trees and ducks swimming. Elliot could do whatever he wanted as long as he delivered. Peter did not want to know how, but if an operation "went south," the blame would stop with Elliot.

Elliot would run with this, especially since the "Cyrus Run-Over" was not even a bump in the road for government agents. And with increased pressure to roll up anyone or thing linked to T-Plague or terrorism, he knew he could get away with what he'd been wanting to do for a long time. Only he and one of his best agents would know his intentions, and soon both of them would know the outcome of a special interrogation.

Electra kept busy the following week, completing all documents so she would graduate at the end of the Fall Term. She had already breezed through on Monday her thesis defense; the review panel could muster only perfunctory questions. None of them understood much about her work, even though she had given them a dummied down thesis summary. But they were smart enough to realize this candidate had talent and approved her postdoctoral fellowship. This would be the next move in her "Education Game" because it would add to her official resume while providing cover for neuro-device development and related research areas. Professor Ravenhill called her mid-week.

"Kittner, Ravenhill here. Congratulations. Your thesis defense performance earned rave reviews."

"Good evening, Professor Ravenhill. Thank you so much. I couldn't have done it without all your help."

"Yes, yes. That's what the other committee members say, now that they finally understand a little. And I too must say that your experimental design and data analysis thoroughly demonstrate causation between a critical level of cranial neurons and the emergence of cognition. I particularly liked your reference to Popper's falsification epistemology. You have made an original contribution to cognitive neuroscience, and I didn't think you had it in you. But I have misjudged you. You are smarter than you let on." *I better watch what I say. I don't want to give too much away.*

"Perhaps, but serendipity played a role, as did you. Your recommendations kept me on track. That's why you are the coauthor on two of the published articles.

"I'm pleased you feel that way, because I do like seeing my name in print. However, let's talk about post-doc research. You could drill into quantum neuroscience, working on some of the conjectures regarding microtubules. Do you know what they are?" *Of course, I do. I'm way ahead of you. They take us away from science and into the realm of unobservable philosophic musing. But I won't say too much.*

"Yes, I have read some of the research papers. Microtubules are intra-neuron tunnels built from the protein tubulin, supposedly responsible for transporting information and charges that cause synapses to fire. Some researchers posit they are the building blocks of cognition, but I'm not so sure." *I have more to say, but let's follow Ravenhill's lead.*

"Hmm, so far so good. But what aren't you sure about?"

"Let me explain by analogy with the heroic age of high energy physics, which dates back to the early 20th century. The great physicists of that era could still make breakthroughs verified by experiments, but by the start of the 21st century they collided with asymptotic limits to what the human brain can comprehend. They ignored the Explosion Principle as well as Godel's incompleteness theorems, instead pushing ahead with fantastic mind experiments, taking high energy physics into the realm of philosophy. In their videos and papers, they sound like religious proselytizers. I don't want to go that route. Biotech and neuroscience are still in their heroic ages, and I can extend my thesis without disappearing into a quantum neuroscience black hole. What do you think?" Professor Ravenhill finally spoke after a pregnant pause.

"Hmm, I follow the outline of what you say, but not the details. But I'll make you a deal. I'll give you carte blanche to work on whatever you choose as long as you keep me in the loop so I know enough to assist and to get my name on published papers."

"I couldn't ask for more. Thank you."

After the call, Indira spoke from the shadows. "You are indeed clever. Not only did you recruit Professor Ravenhill into your game, but I sense your empathy is growing. You understand and respect him, making the game a win for him as well as for you. Carry on, my precious daughter."

Electra preferred not to march in the December Convocation because she didn't consider her PhD a major milestone. Graduation celebrations are family affairs, but she had neither family nor friends left to share the moment, so she would use the coming weekend to play other games. As cold and blustery Saturday wind gusts swayed the leafless branches on the big tree in front of the house, Electra watched from her favorite location, an ergonomically designed workstation, where this afternoon she was playing the "Terrorist Game," and it took a loud knock on the kitchen door to get her attention. She wasn't expecting visitors, but whoever was knocking needed to see she still used crutches, so she picked them up on her way to the door.

"Matt and I took a chance you'd be home this afternoon. Congratulations on getting your PhD! Invite us in, it's chilly out here." Robin and Matt bustled into the kitchen, exchanging hugs with the graduate.

"Thank you, and what a great surprise. I knew it would be better to be here today rather than go to the ceremony. I haven't seen you for a couple of weeks. Let's sit in the kitchen and catch up on the latest."

Robin and Matt were now Electra's closest friends, and she was happy to see their relationship growing, slower than Matt would like, but Robin was gradually sharing more. Robin's course work fit in nicely with her accounting work at H&H DNA, and Matt was considering working fulltime as an independent physical therapist so he could expand into fitness training. They were moving forward in spite of the harsh realities outside their control, one of which troubled Robin.

"My folks are concerned about the Repatriot Program. They're not citizens, but they've had had permanent residence status since I was born. They're worried they might be deported."

"Look, the program was just announced and the details are still being hatched. I'm sure that people like your parents aren't going to be affected. They've been here a long time and your dad has a good job." Matt agreed.

"That's what I've been telling Robin, but she's still worried, so I'm glad you see it like I do. We were going to take you out for dinner, but why don't I order pizza and we can eat in."

"Perfect. Robin and I will toss a salad, and I have plenty of drinks and desserts."

As they sat in the kitchen, happily chatting while setting the table, Electra was about to ask if they had ever gone to a sensory pleasures café when the font doorbell rang. Matt jumped to attention.

"That must be the pizza delivery guy. I'll get it." Robin went to the counter to retrieve the salad when suddenly Matt's muffled voice sounded an alarm. There was a commotion in the hallway, and Robin dashed to help. Electra's brain shifted into a higher gear. *That doesn't sound like pizza delivery. We've got a problem.*

As Electra ran towards the hallway clutching her crutches, she heard Robin screaming and Matt yelling, and then the hiss of a bullet fired from a silencer-equipped pistol...

"We're just about there, so tell me again why this Electra Kittner person will be a pushover?" Elliot smirked as he answered.

"She uses crutches and knee braces, so she can't move very fast. And I'm sure she's home because she doesn't go out much, especially when weather is bad. And it's good the storm clouds made it dark early."

Elliot had nothing other than hunches linking Electra to anything going on with terrorism or NIH R&D, but he was relentless once he started working on coincidences, and he had found so many they couldn't be ignored. No one believed his conspiracy theory, but now he would "dissect" the girl to get answers. And no one but Elliot and his partner knew what they were about to do.

"Here's the plan. You ring the doorbell and push in first. If it's not the girl, clobber whoever answers. I'll follow and have my pistol ready, just in case."

Matt was caught off guard when the two agents shoved into the hallway. Elliot watched anxiously as Matt and his partner crashed into the living room, wrestling on the floor. Matt tried to cover up, but the assailant on top kept punching. Just then Robin leaped into the fray, screaming and toppling the agent off Matt and onto herself. He pinned her to the floor, pummeling her savagely. Matt threw curses as he wrestled Robin out of the hailstorm of blows. Elliot's anxiety quickly turned to panic and he acted instinctively, clubbing Matt with his gun, accidently pulling the trigger. Matt collapsed in a heap; Robin screamed again.

"He's shot, he's shot! Elliot's accomplice kept slugging until her screams were silenced.

Electra stopped at the entryway, taking in the gruesome scene playing out before her: Matt bleeding from a bullet wound near the shoulder blade; Robin bleeding from nose and mouth. Both were unconscious; one assailant peered down at the mess while the other struggled to rise. Electra's brain shifted to an even higher gear. The Monster from the Id was about to strike.

It picked out the leader for its first target. Elliot never knew what hit him. Electra clubbed him twice with her cane, stunning him and twisting the gun away, knocking him unconscious to the floor. She did the same to his partner, then crisply snapped his neck. She was about to do the same to Elliot when her rational persona regained control. *Get with the plan, soldier! Kill him later. Patch Matt and Robin.*" Shoving him aside, Electra crouched next to Matt.

His gunshot wound was serious but not spurting blood; she charged to the bathroom, rushing back with bandages and medical tape to stem the bleeding. She checked Robin's wounds and saw they weren't life threatening, so she ran to her cell phone and called for help. When Clarence answered, she shouted out what had just happened.

"This is Electra. I'm at home. There's been an accidental shooting. One male shot in the back. Unconscious, but I've stopped the bleeding. We need your help." Clarence shot back, "I'm on the way."

The pizza arrived as Electra disconnected the call. She grabbed the boxes, shoved two twenty-dollar bills at the driver, and slammed the door. Then she rushed the pizzas to the kitchen. After that, she dragged the dead agent into a hallway closet and bound and gagged the other, dragging him into the kitchen. She used moistened wash cloths and towels to wipe the blood off Robin, then roused her.

"Come on, snap out of it! Listen to me. Matt's gunshot is serious and I've called Clarence. He'll be here ASAP. I've patched Matt best I can. You'll need to ride back to the clinic and stay with him. This is what I've told Clarence: the gunshot was an accident. Don't tell him anything else. If he asks for more info, tell him you didn't see what happened. We don't want this reported to the police. When Matt comes to, you tell him to say I accidently shot him when showing him a gun. Nothing else. Do you understand?" Robin nodded numbly, then stuttered.

"Who were those guys? Where'd they go?"

"I don't know, but they panicked when the pizza guy knocked. Look, you take care of Matt. When Clarence releases him, go home with Matt. I'll call you tomorrow. OK?" Robin nodded, then straightened her shoulders.

"I'll tell Clarence only what you say, and I'll stay with Matt."

Robin followed orders when the ambulance arrived. Clarence was too busy to ask questions, and Robin helped get Matt to the clinic. The lightning brain shifted to a lower gear; Electra calmed down enough to think things through at a less frenetic pace.

First priority was getting acquainted with the visitor in the kitchen, who was struggling to break free. She removed the gag, then hissed.

"I want you to answer three questions: what's your full name, where's your vehicle, and where's the key?" Out sputtered answers.

"Elliot Spitzdieck; parked down the block, but there's no key. It has fingerprint door locks, so you'll need me to get in." *I know that name. This guy is the Worldstars tormentor from the past. He's lying about the key, but I'll play along.*

"OK. Stay here while I get a hand saw."

"OK, OK. Key's in my right-hand pocket. The car's a four-door silver sedan." Electra found the key, then reinserted the gag. She ran out the kitchen door and down the driveway to the street. The rain came harder now, which gave her more cover because no one was out in the darkening storm. She drove the car close to the kitchen door and dodged back in.

"OK Elliot, I'm going to ask one question at a time, and I want the right answer. I'll encourage you if you don't cooperate. I have a device that is incredibly useful. If you refuse to answer, I'll be happy to demonstrate." Electra paused long enough to gauge Elliot would not need convincing. "First question: who do you work for?"

"The CIA."

"OK, next question. Who sent you?"

"I did. My section chief, Peter Schmitzer, doesn't know."

"Why are you after me?"

"I know about you because you worked on a Cognicom project team and I played a hunch. Too many coincidences for your team. You're the only one left. You must know something about T-Plague R&D or terrorist links." Electra's nightmare scenario had suddenly become reality. A last-ditch guess supported by nothing except Elliot's speculation had caught her, but she forced herself to be calm.

"No one can possibly believe you. I was only a retrieval clerk, and they fired me last year. I don't know a thing."

"They don't believe me now, but I know my hunch is right. They'll believe me when we get through with you. I radioed for backup just before we entered, and we're going to dissect you."

Electra knew he was bluffing because reinforcements would be her by now. *There's only one thing I can do: conclude with extreme prejudice. It's a matter of my life. My decision is final...*

What to do with the bodies? The lightning brain clicked into a different gear for an answer that flashed loud and clear. Electra needed every ounce of strength gained from fitness training to load the bodies into the trunk, and she was soaked with a mix of rain and sweat when she came back into the kitchen. Trembling with nervous excitement, she sat to steady herself after stripping naked. *It's time to change into evening wear: jet black running suit and shoes, black knit cap.*

It was eight-thirty and though not hungry, Electra forced herself to eat, gobbling a couple of pizza slices and washing it down with a Coke to boost energy for the trek ahead. After searching the Internet for a map to her destination, the lightning brain memorized it and Electra sped away into the windy, rain-swept darkness.

Murphy liked working nights at the industrial park recycling plant just beyond the northwest DC suburbs. The pace was slower than during the day, and hardly anyone dropped off scrap metal during his shift. And though he had contracted the T-Plague two years ago, his smart pills slowed the onset of dementia enough so he could still operate the equipment.

He particularly enjoyed operating the car compactor. He would drive—or push with a truck—a junk car into the jaws of the machine, then step back, watching the jaws crush the car into a dense metallic cube. Then he would activate the stacker, which would deposit the cube alongside or atop other crushed cars. Their power and precision awed him, and the sight, sound, and the gasoline-tinged aroma were strangely hypnotic. It was like watching a battle between an immovable object and an unstoppable force where the force always won.

Murphy had ten more wrecks to feed into his mechanical car crusher this evening. As he turned towards the storage lot, an unexpected silhouette, partially obscured by the slanting rain and frozen in the headlights of an idling car, spoke as he shuffled forward.

"Good evening. I have an offer you will not want to refuse because it's better than the other cash and crush deals you make. I no longer need the car and want you to take care of it. This envelope contains two thousand dollars. Do it next and the money is yours."

Murphy looked inside the envelope; he didn't bother to count because the stack of hundred-dollar bills was thick enough. Deals like this came his way occasionally, but never for this much. He was glad to get the business because the extra money helped him live on his own. And he never asked why. There was no need to know, and if the police ever snooped it would be impossible to connect him with any wrongdoing.

"It's a deal. You can watch, but just stay back and let me do my job." Twenty minutes later the car was atop the stack. Murphy turned to his customer, but the figure was gone with the rain-specked wind.

Electra had the wind at her back for most of the fifteen-mile run home. She settled into a pace she could handle, allowing her brain to freewheel away the stress. It was nearly three a.m. when she staggered into the kitchen. Though in superb condition, today's combination of physical and emotional exertion had drained her. She wolfed down three more slices of pizza while polishing off half a two-liter bottle of Coke, then peeled off all clothes and sat beneath a hot soaking shower that melted the chill, but then an empathy-laden emotional charge jolted her, much like the one she felt when dealing with Abdul. She sobbed uncontrollably.

Mother, please forgive me if I did wrong, but I did what I had to. My adversaries weren't evil. They were following different rules, obeying different commands that would have revealed my secret. Another sensation jolted her brain a minute later, stopping the flow of tears. As the water drained, Electra's mood changed to resolute certainty that the lightning brain had decided correctly. But she also realized the lightning brain was altering her emotional persona in ways that disturbed her cognitive self.

I must learn to balance better my cognitive and emotional selves. The lightning brain will teach me if I follow its commands. Electra emerged from the shower, toweled off and preparing for bed. She would plan next moves in her game when rested and reenergized, but now she needed to sleep so she didn't bother setting the alarm.

Electra felt surprisingly chipper when she awoke late Sunday morning. A quick set of stretching exercises helped remove some of the leg stiffness caused by her late-night run; she took another shower, washed and blow-dried her hair, then dressed in sweats. Her body craved carbohydrates so she devoured a stack of pancakes swimming in butter and syrup. The warm glow from recovering muscles and a satisfied appetite added to her upbeat mood as she powered on her computer and thought about yesterday.

There's no one left at the CIA to continue the hunt for Electra. That's all to the good. Now let's find out about Matt. Time to call Robin. She answered on the fifth ring.

"Hi, Electra. I'm staying with Matt until he can take care of himself, and Clarence says he'll recover quickly because the bullet missed his clavicle. And don't worry. Matt and I stuck to your story."

"Good. Well, this will be a different Christmas Holiday for both of you. Call me tomorrow evening. Love you both."

Electra had other calls to make, but she needed to proceed carefully. *So, what are my next steps? I'm going to ask Angus what he knows about Peter Schmitzer. And then, I'll call Alice. But before I do, I'll think things through.*

Angus didn't like what Peter had just blurted out, and his tone announced the depth of his displeasure.

"What do you mean you haven't heard from them since Friday? It's Wednesday and you should know what your people are working on. Find the car; maybe they're still close to it. You've got to control your people better, and remember what I said, the blame trail stops with you. Call me no later than Friday."

Angus thought more about Peter's report after the call ended. T*his is incredible. Two of Peter's agents missing, and he doesn't even* *know what they were chasing. And there's no tracking signal coming from their vehicle. It's like something swallowed them whole. Well, at least Peter is manning up, but I'm going to have to demote him as a lesson to everyone. I won't fire him, just get him reassigned as one of Jared's Secret Service guards. And I'll have to tell Jared some of our guys are becoming too aggressive. I'll add this to the list when I see him tomorrow. And I'll talk with Electra on Saturday. Maybe one of her contacts knows something.*

Electra kept busy the following week, juggling project activities and developing plans for the coming year. She always did so during the last weeks in December so she would launch full speed into the new year. It was now Saturday morning, and Electra hadn't Emailed Angus an agenda because she wanted to see if his choices matched hers. She shouldn't have worried, because their agendas matched. Peter was the first topic.

"I had disturbing news from one of my section chiefs, Peter Schmitzer. He's smart, seems committed and gets results, but last week two of his agents went missing. By any chance, has your contact stumbled over anything remotely related?"

"Why No. Just one name and generalities aren't enough. What are the details?"

"Here's all I know. Elliot Spitzdieck and another agent were chasing down some type of lead late last week, and they haven't been heard from since. Not a trace of them or their car. And they didn't tell anyone what they were doing, so Peter has nothing to go on. I had to demote him as a lesson to my other section chiefs. We can't have loose cannons rolling around." *That's good news. I'll pretend to be helpful.*

"Well, I'll ask my contact. Maybe someone can find something in Spitzdieck's files. I'm sure your people will check that out. OK if we switch subjects? What's the latest on Repatriot?"

"Jared liked the tone in your bulletin and agrees to go easy when we roll it out. Some of the lieutenants want to push hard right from the get-go, but I explained how easy it'll be to tighten the program if necessary. Initial targets will be recent terrorist profiling suspects." *More good news. That buys us more time to watch Jared.*

"We have to be careful with Repatriot. It could disrupt a lot of lives. A friend of mine is worried her parents might be deported, even though they've had permanent residence status for over twenty years." The smile from Angus added assurance to his words.

"I don't think our country can possibly fall that far. Tell your friend not to worry. What else is on your list?"

"I'll tell her. Now tell me, how's CIA. progressing with the 'Cyrus Affair?' Have they pieced together a terrorist network connection? Or detected chatter about another attack?"

"Not a thing. If Isilabad knew how blind we are, they'd run pell-mell across the borders. Maybe they're afraid of getting infected by T-Plague if they did. And to make spirits brighter, NIH is getting nowhere on outsourcing vaccine development. This isn't a very cheery yearend summary."

"No, but next year has to be better. And that reminds me, I heard on local media that Jared likes what you're doing and has bigger plans for you. And I wasn't asked to write the copy. Congratulations to you."

"No, it's congratulations to us. You're a bigger help than even he acknowledges. Let's postpone our next meeting until after the Holidays, when we know what he's up to. We can both use some R&R. But I'll send you a video of a confidential political briefing prepared by one of our think tanks. Make time over the Holidays to watch it, because next year we'll have to watch out as we navigate a political minefield."

R&R was the last thing on Electra's mind because game-playing provides high excitement that she thrives on, and after the last meeting with Angus she decided to engage a player who would pick up the CIA slack. Tonight's phone call would set up the game.

Though disappointed, Alice knew the Opposition Party's steering committee had run for cover because it couldn't offer anything better than what the Guardian Party was already doing. The public applauded the results and didn't care if harsh measures were used. If her London masters approved, she would explore opportunities for switching covert assignment from the Opposition to the Guardian Party, but she would wait to see what the new year might bring.

Alice recognized Electra's caller I.D. and answered promptly.

"How nice of you to call... Yes, it's too bad the Opposition Party went anchors, but I'm not giving up on the cause just yet. I should have given you a shout sooner, but let me invite you for dinner. Will next Saturday work?... Excellent. See you here at six. Cheerio."

Electra needed a convincing story that would explain what moves Alice should make in order to start the game. *Alice needs to ally Britain covertly with the Guardians, and she needs a network of well-connected people to assist her. I shall use my nightly endurance runs this week to come up with a plan. I think clearly when in the dark, and no one sees I don't need crutches.* Electra had assembled all she needed by mid-week and summarized it to herself while on the run.

Neither Alice nor her London masters know about Trojan filters controlled by Hassan. My three-pronged British covert operation will eliminate the threat. One prong will launch a T-Plague terrorist attack in Iran's capital, another will do the same in Isilabad's capital, and the third will hunt down Hassan, who'll be holed up in his hidden command center. That's where I'll interrogate him. And after the raids, Alice can use back channels to build an undercover network within the Guardian Party, using people I supply. This is a win-win-win-win game. Win for Britain and America because we shut down Trojan filters. Win for Angus and me because our undercover network can help control Jared.

I need Alice to set up and run the operation, and she needs me because only I have all the information. We'll be a great team. She's my cloak and shield when dealing with British Secret Service, and she can tell her boss that I'm her subject matter expert. This story will be a page-turner and then page-burner. It's for our eyes and ears only.

Alice spent most of Saturday preparing a hearty British supper: Shepherd's Pie paired with classic Fuller's London Porter. She would offer stilton cheese and biscuits for an appetizer and Manchester tarts for dessert. Her cooking and baking hobby provided a welcome weekend change of pace whenever she entertained a close circle of friends. *This should surprise my dear girl. I do look forward to a chatty evening.*

Electra arrived promptly at six, bringing with her a bottle of Bailey's Irish Cream.

"Well my dear, you certainly know what goes with our dinner." Electra smiled and returned a zinger.

"Mrs. T, I know a lot of things." Not even quick-witted Alice could handle that. She blinked in amazement.

"Well I'll be snookered. No one who knows me as Alice has ever called me Mrs. T. You are a most clever girl." Electra hurriedly explained.

"I don't think anyone else has ever figured out your other name, and I've told no one. And if you hadn't saved my life, I never would have connected the dots. Please believe me. We're on the same side."

"I knew you were extraordinary from the moment the chopper crashed. I thought I was managing everything, but it turns out you were. I can't wait to hear your story, but why not have dinner first. It will be my surprise for you."

Alice served a description of dinner along with the main course, even explaining the nuances of ales, porters and stouts, as well as Shepherd's Pie recipes. By the time Alice served the liqueurs, even the lightning brain was more relaxed than usual.

"Well my dear, I know you have an interesting story for me, so why don't you spin the tale." Electra spun slowly and thoroughly, drawing Alice into the game. Two hours later, Alice summarized what she understood.

"So, you uncovered an Isilabad-controlled terrorist network that can unleash T-Plague virus. The Great Satan is the first target, and when on its knees, Great Britain will be next. And you've been telling your Guardian Party contact just the right amount so America is prepared. And the CIA has been so degraded you want

British Secret Service to implement your plan. And when you and I complete this mission, you'll help me build a sympathetic Guardian Party network. Did I miss anything?"

"That's the gist of it, and I hope you'll play the game. And when you do, you're not allowed to reveal another secret. Please observe." Electra danced around the room without using crutches.

"My dear, now you are fast on your feet too. We'll make plans immediately to visit London. Do you have a passport?" Electra stopped prancing once she remembered she had never been out of the country, only to Cyberspace.

"No."

"Not to worry. I can arrange for yours. And I'll handle travel and accommodations. We'll leave early January and should be back by the start of February. I assume you've cleared your January calendar. We'll have a jolly good time."

Electra followed her post-Christmas week tradition, not cycling down or reminiscing but instead gearing up for the coming year's activities. Because they would include skirmishes in the political arena, she decided to watch the political briefing video Angus had sent. As soon as she heard the presenter's introduction, she knew the information would help her adjust plans for all her projects because he titled the talk "Terrorism, T-Plague, and the Political Climate, A Sobering Assessment."

He started by kidding that the government is getting its money's worth from this presentation because its two parts go far beyond sound bites. The first part explored the interrelationship among the three topics highlighted in the title, starting with Middle East terrorism that he compared to civilization's long-term viral infection pitting Islam against Christianity. He labeled each round of terrorism a subsequent Jihad—the current one employing T-Plague as a WMD—and saw only one solution: defeat radical Islam. And in order to do that, vaccines are needed to neutralize the T-Plague WMD. Though 20+ years of vaccine R&D have yielded paltry results, he projected confidence that a breakthrough would come.

He was much less optimistic when explaining the political climate because of the complex and interconnected post-modern world. Until the Guardian Party came to power, previous Washington Administrations refused to acknowledge that appeasement or coexistence with rogue states is doomed to fail. Boots on the Ground are needed to remove the bad actors, but that won't happen if the United States doesn't lead, and even though the United States is still the world leader, the T-Plague has lowered the nation's I.Q. and raised its fear and intolerance levels, making it vulnerable to tyranny. He even drew comparisons between the Caesars of ancient Rome and Jared Gardner's Guardian Party. He admitted the comparison was a bit of a stretch, but nevertheless warned of the possibility. And on that gloomy note the speaker introduced his female partner, who would deliver the second part of the talk, titled "America's Political Muddle." Her disarming smile and upbeat tempo lifted audience spirits, especially when she announced she would provide a way out of the muddle after describing how we got into it and what are its risks.

The muddle started with 911, when terrorism crashed New York's World Trade Center, and it became murkier when America lost the first Cyberwar—the 2016 Presidential Election—but America recovered quickly, making itself stronger and better equipped to lead the world. Among the steps she cited are revamped K-through-12 education, adjusted American Exceptionalism, hi-tech innovation, human rights protection, and strengthened Cybersecurity. But Washington subsequently became too complacent and the public took its eye off politicians. And then a perfect storm—Terrorism, T-Plague, and Hi-Tech Issues (DNA and AI)—swept in, elevating the Guardian Party, which though the public gives high marks, has yet to prove it can deliver longer-term what America needs. Though her bullet point slides contained a mind-numbing count of examples and disturbing parallels pointing to another Cyberwar, she concentrated on the top three and then launched into eight "must haves" in order for the United States to extricate itself from the muddle. *The top three are right in my wheelhouse: eliminating T-Plague, strengthening Cybersecurity, and controlling the Guardian Party. I'll learn more about the others while working with Angus.* The speaker's wrap-up invited the audience to watch the video several times in order to digest all it contained. *The lightning brain has already done that.*

Now I know how to adjust my plans and game preparations. And I'll use some of what I just found out when Angus and I meet again. Let the New Year begin.

This year like last, Robin asked Electra to join her at a New Year's Eve celebration. Electra noticed that Robin would accept Matt's invitation regardless of her decision because their relationship had grown. *I like how Matt's patience is wearing away Robin's ambivalence toward fellows. I think I'll tag along. And I'll bring my crutches to deflect any dance offers.*

While Matt and Robin danced, Electra chatted with a group of singles, one of them recognizing her from last year.

How nice to see you without a wheelchair. Matt told me you're almost ready to ditch the crutches. And no wonder. You look fitter than anyone on the dance floor. Congratulations." Electra recognized Christian, the fellow she met last year. *Two years in a row he's here without a partner. He's a nice looking and thoughtful guy, but I'm not going to pry. I don't want to send the wrong message.*

"Why, thank you. Yes, I'm planning to give them away next year. Who knows, maybe I'll be dancing up a storm next New Year's Eve."

"The way you look, you'd be in the eye of the storm. Your outfit is totally tony, and it complements your lightning bolt earrings."

"I can thank Robin for that. And speaking of Robin, here she comes, waltzing up with Matt." Christian spoke softly before the dancers arrived.

"I'm happy that Robin is paying more attention to him. He likes her more than he lets on. But please don't tell her." Matt pulled

Christian aside for a man-to-man greeting, leaving a glowing Robin talking to Electra.

"I'm feeling pretty good about the coming year. Matt says he'll tutor me when I take college algebra, and I know I'll do fine in accounting because you'll continue helping me, won't you?" *Uh-oh, Matt will have his hands full, but I'm not going to spoil tonight's party.*

"You know I will. And I know you'll master college algebra the second time around, especially with Matt's help. It's almost time to propose a toast for the New Year. Why don't you tell the fellows to get us champagne? Robin hugged her before doing so.

"And promise me you'll get rid of those crutches next year. I want you all the way back."

"You know me. I like numbers, so that's a 10-4…"

CHAPTER 17

January 2120

"The Intentional Tourist"

(Thread 1 Chapter 9)

IF ELECTRA HAD BEEN born in a kinder and gentler time she might have been a world traveler by now, perhaps visiting her mother's homeland India or studying abroad, but that was not to be. She had restricted travel only to Cyberspace, but that was far enough to know what London looked like. She even knew its history, dating to London's first century Roman founding, dryly noting how lengthy English history classes must be compared with American counterparts.

The drive to Alice's family home wove on narrow roads past quaint buildings, just like she pictured.

"It's so nice your brother is letting us stay at his house." Alice paused from looking about like a tourist.

"Well yes, it is. And he maintains it in Bristol fashion. We inherited it when Mum and Dad passed on, and I stay there whenever I come to London. Brandon's not back from Holiday, but he knows we're staying. No place like home, you know. Do you feel any jetlag, my dear?"

"No, I feel ready to go. I followed your advice and slept during the flight to counter jetlag people experience flying east across multiple time zones."

"Then you should do your sightseeing today while I sort through things at Agency Headquarters. You'll join me tomorrow to help convince my superiors why our operation will work. I'll even use your recommended codename: Holy Grail. Museums shouldn't be crowded today because it is Tuesday January second, so you'll have plenty of room. Which museums will you tour?"

"I'll go to the National Gallery, and if time permits to the Tate to see the Turner Impressionistic Collection. What time will you be back?"

"I should be home by seven. Please call my cell if you need anything. And do take ride-sharing rather than the Tube. London Januaries are damp and cold. No sense catching a chill walking about."

Electra had taken virtual tours of famous European art galleries, but she expected in-person viewing would trump Internet visits. Artists claim intimate contact engaging all senses is the fount of artistic creative inspiration, something which the lightning brain had never experienced for visual arts. The lightning bolt that had transformed Electra's brain had not endowed it with the soul of an artist. *I can't write poetry like Mother or feel music like Su or Robin, and I can't draw a decent stick figure. But if intellectual discovery is an art form, my brain, which is capable of self-directed growth, makes me a cognitive artist. Could I think myself into creating other art forms? Probably not, because drawing a picture, playing music, or writing a poem are crafts that can be taught, but the inspirational gift of creativity powered by emotions eludes logic. My rational abilities still exceed those of my emotional persona, but the gap may be closing. And, I appreciate rather than envy artistic geniuses. I should have plenty of them to applaud today.*

The National Gallery's collection has entire wings devoted to a single master, and its Renaissance to Romantic collections are among the best in the world. Electra wandered from gallery to gallery, absorbing the entire experience, confirming that in-person touring offers matchless richness and depth. She stood spellbound viewing of a wall of Rembrandts, struck by how the artist's dramatic lighting versus shadow spotlighted character and emotion. A genius for any age.

"Indira! My precious one. You have returned to me." A frail-sounding elderly voice pierced the vacant gallery, jolting Electra back to the present. She pivoted to locate the source, a wheelchair-bound woman in an electric blue saree waving at her.

"Mother please. Do not excite yourself. I will ask." A grandfatherly type with gentle eyes padded towards Electra. "Young lady, I am sorry if we are interrupting. My wife means no harm. It is just that you look remarkably like our daughter, who died nearly twenty-five years ago. Please, allow me to introduce myself. I am Satish Ramanujan, and my wife is Madhuri. And if I believed in reincarnation, you would be that of our daughter." The kindly gentleman paused, smiling and gazing steadily.

Even the lightning brain needed a moment to comprehend what serendipity had brought Electra's way. *My karma is crossing paths with Mother's parents!* She gasped, then spoke.

"My mother is Indira Jaswinder Ramanujan. I am your granddaughter, Electra Kittner."

The nearby pub's cozy ambiance provided an intimate setting for grandparents and granddaughter to chat for the very first time. Grandmother sat across the table holding Electra's hands, squeezing to the cadence of her emotions.

"My daughter, Indira. My granddaughter, Electra. You are as one. You are wearing the lightning bolt earrings. You are part of the eternal cycle." Satish explained Madhuri's words.

"Hinduism is not alone in contemplating reincarnation. Many great philosophers have expressed similar sentiments. Socrates said: 'The soul comes from without into the human body, as into a temporary abode, and it goes out of it anew. It passes into other habitations, for the soul is immortal.' Your grandmother is very intuitive and senses Indira's presence. And your mother possessed that same ability even as a child. I wish you could have met your grandmother before the T-Plague came. Today is one of her better days, so we are out and about."

"My father never told me about you. After mother died, did you keep in touch?" A look of concern dampened his smile as he looked at Madhuri who nodded, but Electra spoke first.

"Please! You must tell me everything about my background. I deserve to know." Madhuri's grip tightened.

"You are right. I am thinking clearly today so I will tell you. Your mother's death severed our communications with your father. We called several times, but he seemed emotionally detached and indifferent to us, as if he wanted to seal off the past."

"Father didn't handle emotions very well, but he and Grampa Kittner did a wonderful job taking care of me." Madhuri's eyes closed for a moment, then opened just before she spoke.

"I do not think you have ever heard what I am about to say. And you must promise never to tell. It must stay with only us, for your mother's honor. Will you honor our family's wish?" Electra nodded yes, saying nary a word.

"Your mother loved Jason, but she loved someone else more, a Su-Lin Song Chou. I still have Indira's last letter, which told she would not marry Jason but instead raise you in a same-sex household with Su. Jason never knew this. And she never told Jason what name she had selected for you, Alisha, which means protected by Allah."

Electra didn't know what to say. Her lips moved wordlessly, as if her brain were short-circuited. Satish came around the table and sat, putting his arm around her shoulder.

"Please, do not be upset. All this is in the past and cannot affect you. Your mother never dwelt on the past and was resilient. I am certain you are too." Electra snapped back into the present.

"Yes, you are right. I call Su Aunt Su, and she is still a source of strength for me. She has told me much about Mother, but not this. Did you know Mother wrote poetry? I need you and Grandmother to tell me more about what she was like as a child, before she went to America." A sad smile covered Madhuri's features.

"It cut like a knife when Indira left to study abroad. I didn't know if she would ever return home. She joked about this when she wrote, always telling me she would make up for lost time." Finally, the lighting brain switched into a quicker gear, finding words that would lessen Madhuri's sadness.

"Mother wrote two collections of poems, but she didn't bother publishing them. According to Su, Mother said she'd do that when she got older. But she must have thought of you often. Grandfather, if you have a piece of paper and pen, I'll write the poem Mother wrote for Grandmother."

Satish came back with what Electra needed. She scribbled furiously, then turned to her grandmother.

"Mother called this poem *Mother's Day Remembrance*. I'll read it slowly, and the two of you can discuss it sometime. Here it is:

'Abruptly we parted—and so unfair.
We both felt numb and cheated.
Nothing to do but sit and stare.
No sad farewells repeated.

'My wishes were always to care for you,
For all that you did for me.
But I caught you off guard—I ran away quickly,
Thinking it's time to be free.

'For you mostly pain-free, I left on good terms,
Your beautiful feelings intact.
'And you didn't have to listen to stories of yore,
You live in the present not oft looking back.

'To show my love I won't repeat,
The things you mean or have done.
I'll let it shine through in the things that I'll do,
As I greet each dawning Sun.'"

One tear trickled gently before Madhuri spoke again.

"Indira must dwell in you. I could hear her in your voice. Sometime, you must read more of her poems." It was now late afternoon and Madhuri was tiring; Satish needed to take her home.

"You must join us for dinner and spend the night as soon as you can. Perhaps you could spend an entire day, depending on what obligations you have."

"My gosh, it is late. Let's ride-share to where you live and I'll keep going to where I'm staying. I'll call you tomorrow to confirm, but how about I spend Saturday with you?

Satish looked at Madhuri, both nodding before he spoke.

"We will have several surprises for you…"

Electra cried softly on the ride back to Alice's as this most recent epiphany unleashed emotions breaking through from the other side. It filled her with joy that would be shared with only her Muse, and after that, perhaps with only one person, but not until she visited Texas again, and then only after she sorted through all her feelings.

Electra needed to prepare for tomorrow, so the lightning brain switched gears and by the time she reached Alice's, Electra had her agenda ready and waiting; likewise, Alice could say the same for the fish and chips carryout dinner she had carried in. As they chatted during supper about what tomorrow might bring, Electra's agenda and rehearsal occupied center stage.

"My dear, I know you are indeed clever, but now I see you are a convincing actress too. I think the museum tour allowed you to relax, so please tell me, what treasures did you see?" *Careful what I say. I don't want to get too emotional or reveal too much.*

"Serendipity kissed me on both cheeks today. I met my maternal grandparents for the very first time."

"Goodness, that is extraordinary. And you jolly well better visit them again. Getting to know one's family is priceless."

"If it's OK, I would like to do that on Saturday. Do you think that will work?"

"Of course. After all, you and I are putting on the show. And why don't we turn in early for a good night's sleep. We both want to be well rested."

Perhaps tea kept Alice awake, or perhaps anticipation for tomorrow, but more likely thoughts of Electra kept her tossing. *I am pleased for the dear girl, and I hope that getting to know her grandparents will help lower her emotional barrier. I would like to know her better, but I don't want to push in where I'm not welcome. Still, I think she is beginning to like me more. And that is jolly good. I shall sleep on that.*

CHAPTER 18

January 2120

"The Search for the Holy Grail"

(Thread 2 Chapter 6)

Alice awoke Wednesday without a worry about the day ahead because she had completed all preparations the day before when she outlined her plan to MI-X, aka the British Intelligence Agency, knowing her bosses wouldn't be ready for complete details but would demand them today. Supplying them would be easy: Alice would unleash Electra. Last night's rehearsal convinced her that she could sit back and enjoy the performance.

On the drive in, Alice primed Electra by repeating what to expect: the committee chairperson would start the meeting by summarizing what Alice had told them yesterday, and then ask Electra to explain the details for why and how the operation will work. The eight-person meeting started promptly at eight.

"Good morning everyone, and I want to thank Alice for her patience yesterday providing an overview to a most unexpected operation. Evidently, both the United States and Britain are in the crosshairs of Middle East terrorists, who can unleash T-Plague virus into air or water from a contraption. Sounds rather novel, so before we can decide how to proceed, we need complete details, and Alice wants her American associate—Electra Kittner—to do the honors. So Electra, the floor is yours." *Time to be assertive. I won't mince words.*

"Good morning everyone, and as you Brits know, we Americans get right to the point, so I'll say right up-front America needs your help dealing with T-Plague terrorism. And only you can make Operation Holy Grail work. And by helping us, you'll be helping Britain too. America's CIA is not up to the task. That's why Alice set up this meeting, and asked me to explain why I know what we should do." Electra paused for effect, then proceeded.

"And who am I? I'm the person who by chance happened to be in the right place at the right time to figure out a connection between Middle East terrorism and the T-Plague. And I managed to uncover critical information: Isilabad has placed equipment capable of releasing T-Plague virus in America and Western Europe in quantities that will cause pandemics. The bad guys call these air and water filtration units Trojan filters. A large number, all containing virus that can be released remotely, are already in place. America is the initial target; England's next.

"My contacts pieced together the terrorist network handling this and we need you to pinpoint exactly where in Isilabad the underground command and control center is located. Hassan Wassani, Isilabad's Exalter Ruler, is the mastermind behind the plan, and his three sons help him. All three have been neutralized, but Hassan can launch attacks by himself and will do so in the near future, although only he knows when and where.

"Operation Holy Grail will eliminate the threat. You need to get me into the center so I can interrogate Hassan, get filter locations, and shut them down. I'll also get names and locations of terrorist cells worldwide. And we'll bring him back for further interrogation.

"What I've just described is the third and final prong of the attack, which will be carried out by chopper and desert attack carriers. It will be preceded by two simultaneous decoy operations to confuse and destabilize Iran and Isilabad. These will be T-Plague attacks on their capitals, causing each country to accuse the other, giving us cover." As six sets of eyes drilled in, Electra paused, glancing at Alice, then continued.

"Washington knows nothing about the operation, and only after it's completed should you contact the Guardian Party through back channels. Alice knows best how to let the Guardian Party and British government share credit. Alice, please tell us operation code names."

"Of course. I shall be 'V2' and in charge; 'Lobber One' and 'Lobber Two' are decoy attack leaders; 'Charger One' and 'Charger Two' are the insertion chopper pilots; 'Teaser' is the attack carrier leader." Electra continued.

"I know you're wondering, 'Why bring me along?' You need me to hack into Hassan. I can do this because I have a Brain Probe device that will make him talk. And don't be concerned about my crutches. Simply load a pair and a wheelchair into the attack carrier. Once you give the OK to proceed, Alice will take it from there. And you're wondering how I can get him to talk, when you know he'd rather die than do so. I will be happy to demonstrate my Brain Probe, but I won't tell you how it works or where I obtained it. And only I know its password. Gentlemen, it's your move." All at the table paused uncomfortably, glancing at one another until Alice's boss broke the silence.

"I think we need a demonstration." Electra smiled politely.

"It's quite effective. Which one of you isn't thirsty?" Alice talked briefly fifteen minutes later.

"Jolly good you give us the OK. And I'll be frank. We may suffer casualties; Hassan might launch desperation attacks once he sees he's outfoxed. But I'll factor these into contingencies." The chairperson nodded, then ended the morning session.

"Very good. We'll reconvene after lunch."

Alice told Electra to go sightseeing that afternoon while she arranged for team training and logistics, including fly-in locations and dates plus coordination with British counter-intelligence. Electra could explore more of London, using her self-guided tours to compare England's T-Plague awareness with America's. What she saw confirmed what she already knew.

London seems to be running normally, but the same could be said most of the time during World War II. People are coming and going to work or running errands. And everyone's courteous. London commuters queue up in a civilized manner for boarding. New Yorkers should follow suit.

She stopped in a pub to eavesdrop. *I don't hear any T-Plague gossip or complaints about the city's infrastructure. And the tele-news isn't hyped like in America. I can't tell if the T-Plague has dummied down the population. British accents make everyone sound pretty smart.* That night at dinner, Alice agreed and added more.

"I think you'd see the same in most European capitals. They're coping because Europe's been lucky. America's the battlefield, and our little operation will keep it there. You're invited to our team training sessions so you see why."

Electra observed for the next two days, concluding the Brits are currently better than most of its American counterparts. Team members cross-trained to handle all equipment and duties, and no one complained about Electra's crutches or wheelchair. British determination added to overall confidence, so Alice ended training early Friday afternoon, reminding everyone to keep silent and report for deployment late Sunday night. At dinner that evening, Electra asked Alice if her Saturday outing should be considered a furlough.

"Officially, no. But please be back by noon Sunday so I don't have to report you A.W.O.L. unofficially. And of course, mum's the word to your grandparents. What time are you expected?"

"Nine a.m. Will you arrange for ride-sharing?"

"Of course. You've had a busy week, so why not trot off to bed so you are well rested?"

"Agreed, so I'll say 10-4 if that works in MI-X."

"Yes it does, my dear. We share the military ten-code with our American cousins, so off you go…"

"You must be Electra. Please come in. I am your Uncle Chandrajit. Friends call me Chandra, but call me Chandrajit until I decide what to make of you." *Another surprise. I didn't know Mother had a brother, and this one seems hostile.* The lightning brain connected immediately with Dickens. *Scrooge disliked his sister Fran's only child, blaming him for her death in childbirth. Uncle Chandrajit must feel the same way.*

Chandrajit ushered her into the living room where her grandparents were waiting. She hugged them both, then sat directly across from them while her uncle sat to their side.

"Welcome to our home, and please understand we did not tell you about Indira's brother for fear of overloading you with too many revelations. We moved to London fifteen years ago to be closer to Chandra and we bought this house. When Mother became ill, Chandra became her caregiver and now lives with us. Chandra, please tell your niece about yourself." *His body language says he doesn't think much of me or my visit.*

"Yes. Well, I have worked for Barclay's Bank since graduating with a doctorate in economics from the Indian Institute of Management. Unlike my sister, I attended schools in India, working first in Ahmedabad and then in London, where I have been for fifteen years." His sullen expression announced he would say no more. Satish broke an uncomfortable silence.

"Why don't you show your niece around our home? When we moved, Chandra chose Pimlico because of its subtle elegance, lovely townhomes, and central London location. I'm sure Electra would like to see your rug collection too."

"Very well. Come with me." Chandra conducted a cursory tour of both floors, ignoring period furniture his mother had collected as well as oriental rugs adorning floors and walls. Electra needed to clear the air before they went back to the living room.

"I think I'll call you Uncle Scrooge." Chandra stopped in his tracks.

"What did you call me?'

"I called you Scrooge. You're just like the *Christmas Carol* Scrooge. He didn't like his nephew Fred, blaming him for his sister Fran's death. You dislike me for the same reason, and I am sorry you feel that way. But I miss Indira more than you ever will. Please don't blame me for my mother's death. That was twenty-three years ago. You should have grown up by now." For the very first time Chandra displayed a glimmer of interest; his tone softened.

"It is indeed uncanny how much you look like your mother. And no one ever spoke to me like that except Indira. Mother and father have picture albums ready, so let's return to the living room."

The grandparents spent the rest of the morning showing pictures and telling stories; Electra felt that she was meeting her mother again, but for the very first time and from a new perspective. The lightning brain absorbed it all. Before stopping for lunch, Madhuri asked Chandra to bring her two wrapped items.

"These are gifts, still in original wrapping, I was going to send to your mother in celebration of your birth. One is a saree, and the other a Bombay black velvet neck choker holding a gold talisman clasp. They are yours. Please open them now." Electra carefully unwrapped a flowing red saree.

"It's beautiful. May I change into it?"

"Yes, please." Electra scurried to a bedroom, returning in splendor. Satish spoke for all.

"You are as beautiful as your mother. Now, please open your other present. Your grandmother has waited twenty-four years for it to be worn." Madhari placed the wide-band choker around Electra's neck.

"The clasp is the Hawa Ban Magic Talisman for protection against evil. Please look at yourself in the bedroom mirror."

Electra's reflection impressed even the lightning brain, for her striking features and darker tones made a stunning contrast. She hurried back to the living room, letting her smile speak for itself. The ice in Chandra's heart was beginning to thaw.

"My sister would be pleased with her daughter. Come, let us have lunch and talk more…" The food and beverages replenished everyone's emotional energy as the conversation continued.

"Uncle Chandra, what was it like growing up with Mother?" Chandra chuckled before answering.

"It was simultaneously fun and frustrating. Fun because Indira was so smart, so quick, so empathetic. Frustrating because I was the opposite. Sort of plodding and unemotional. Maybe that's why I became an economist. And your mother had a temper. She would call me out whenever she felt I needed an attitude adjustment, even though I was three years older. After she moved to America, we corresponded, but I didn't keep up my end of the bargain and we drifted apart."

"Mother must have thought about you because she wrote a poem called *For Brother One and Only*. If you bring me a pen and paper, I'll write it down and read it back." Chandra returned with what she needed. "Mother's poems reflect a depth of emotion and empathy that I haven't reached yet. I hope to get there some day. Anyway, I'll read the poem she wrote for you:

'Please have no doubt about me for you,
Snippy Brother oh so square.
No matter what fortune deals our way,
You'll find I'm always there.

Though we are very different,
Apparent from either side,
The love that binds remains through time,
It's buried deep inside.

Do not fret be too upset,
When we dicker or disagree.
We'll have our say won't walk away,
Tomorrow Gods referee.

Emotions are strictly a private affair,
So reluctant to put on display.
But if ever you doubt please hear verses out,
My feelings assuredly stay.'"

"I never knew Indira wrote poetry. Mother, what do you think?"

"I think Electra should visit us many times, and each time read more of your sister's poems to us."

"And each time I do, you will have to tell me more about Mother, things I never would know if we hadn't met at the museum…"

Time stood still into the evening as they shared more family history. Electra understood better why her father never talked about Indira—a combination of pain and tension between the families made him silent. And she understood even better why Indira was liked by everyone: she was practically perfect, even in her youth, possessing a rare blend of talent, personality, and humility.

All too soon Sunday morning came, bringing with it Electra's departure.

"I promise to return soon, and when I do I'll bring a special gift for Grandmother. I won't tell you what it is, but I know it will help." Smiles from all accompanied Mahdi's parting words.

"Always wear your talisman for protection from evil." Electra promised to obey her grandmother's command.

"I'm so pleased you enjoyed your stay with relatives. And you're back at a good time, so you can rest and prepare for tomorrow. We leave for our staging area at 2 a.m. I'm puttering in the kitchen. If you wish to work online, you can use whatever computer you like." Alice's guest-friendly style made Electra feel right at home, giving her run of the house and not prying into personal issues.

"Thanks. I think I'll take a nap, then help in the kitchen."

After dinner, Electra reviewed the operations plan one last time. All three prongs used one desert staging area comprised of tents and trailers large enough to conceal three choppers and support vehicles. The third prong would launch as soon as counter-intelligence identified the active command center and after the first two had been completed.

But before that, the first two prongs would insert Lobber teams at four-thirty, a half hour before sunset, discharging T-Plague aerosol canisters into crowded central marketplaces. Drone support, radar monitoring and the insertion choppers' firepower would suppress counter-attacks. Barring mechanical problems, all team members should return safely. Chargers One and Two would return to the staging area in case the third prong needs backup. The control chopper would monitor ground traffic and target activity. It might take up to an hour for Hasson to reveal his location, at which time the third prong would attack.

And that would be the Teaser ground attack personnel carrier, ferried in by the control chopper to an unobserved site located as close as possible to the targeted command center. Its mission-critical assignment: battle into the center to interrogate Hassan, collect filter and terrorist data, put Trojan filters and computer systems out of commission, kidnap or terminate Hassan. All Teaser team members are expendable except for one: Electra. This operation's success depends on her retrieving critical data and deactivating the filters.

The third prong would be the riskiest, because counter-intelligence had determined that the command centers have civilian staffs and permanent guard details that would be reinforced once decoy attacks are reported. Three Teaser team members would take Electra into the center, the three remaining would form a defensive perimeter guarding the personnel carrier. Electra would have no more than thirty minutes to complete her assignment or they could be overrun by reinforcements.

The lightning brain never experienced fear, converting it instead into the thrill of the chase or battle. Electra knew she would be ready for whatever might happen tomorrow.

It took Holy Grail teams ten hours to reach the staging area. Droning engines punctuated only by one aircraft change kept dialog to a minimum while everyone relaxed in personal space. There was no need for additional briefings; these professional soldiers were finely wound for what could be a deadly encounter. A world champion figure skater long ago told an interviewer he never left his performance on the practice ice, and like the skater, the teams were ready to skate in and out without falling.

All hands helped unload and prep equipment. Electra faded into the background, intently observing British covert ops MO. Even in better days the CIA would be hard pressed to match what she saw. She shadowed Alice unnoticed, marveling how her calm demeanor and appropriate small talk lowered collective stress.

By three o'clock all assets were primed and the teams suited up and stretching, just in case the operation would be launched today. Electra did not ask but could tell from body language that the teams wanted to go now. Alice was monitoring ground reports when a message crackled into the receiver: "Canary confirmed at Coal Mine Alpha."

"Roger that. We're good to go." Hassan was at the closer command center. Operation Holy Grail was about to commence; Alice calmly assembled her teams.

"We caught a break. We know where Hassan is holed up, so jolly good we launch now. Just follow your communications, and Bob's your uncle we're back in London tomorrow evening. You're invincible when you follow our plan and watch your partner's back. Bring back the Holy Grail."

Chargers One and Two deployed five minutes later; their next radio communications would be when they were ready to insert the Lobber teams. Alice positioned herself in front of the mobile communications center where she would remain for the duration. The Teaser team settled into a waiting mode, poised halfway between conserving energy and fidgeting about. Electra continued shadowing Alice.

Poor Alice reminded her of the Apollo 13 Flight Controller during the four-minute communications blackout as the space capsule plunged through the atmosphere to either a watery welcome or fiery funeral. There was nothing Alice could do but be the most intent bystander imaginable.

The minutes seemed frozen in a space-time continuum, but inexorably crept towards five-fifteen, the earliest time for Chargers to reach insertion locations. Five-fifteen came and went, then five-twenty, then five-twenty-five. Alice sat calmly drinking an iced tea. Suddenly, the receiver crackled to life.

"Charger One in position."

"Roger that…Hold for my command." Thirty seconds later, a second communication burst through.

"Charger Two in position."

"Roger that…Hold for my command." Alice was all business.

"Charger One, you're good to go. Do you copy?"

"Roger that. We are inserting now."

"Charge Two, you're good to go. Do you copy?"

"Roger that. We are inserting now."

All remaining personnel clustered about Alice.

"Right on schedule," was all she said. And if all unfolded according to plan, the next communication would report in ten minutes, the allotted completion time. The next message crackled through ten minutes later.

"Charger One extraction completed. All aboard. Returning to stable."

"Roger that."The next message crackled though 15 seconds later:

"Charger Two extraction completed. All aboard. Returning to stable."

"Roger that."

Cheers erupted all about Alice. She didn't smile but did offer a compliment.

"Perfect practice makes perfect." Then she contacted ground monitoring and air support in preparation for the third prong.

Electra had checked beforehand: January Middle East desert temperatures reach the fifties before the five o'clock sunset. The desert landscape had an enchanted beauty in a desolate sort of way, no vegetation and more undulation than what she knew about West Texas oilfields. Soon darkness would obscure everything unless she wore her night vision goggles, which would make everything glow in a greenish aura. She could feel excitement building as her lightning brain switched to a higher gear.

The remaining chopper was poised to ferry the attack carrier. It was six-fifteen and ground monitoring had not detected any enemy attack-related activity. Ten minutes later Chargers One and Two vectored in, guided by GPS and the homing beacon just switched on, executing flawless touch-downs. The teams hugged, then immediately clustered about Alice.

The atmosphere about her turned electric when the anticipated message sliced through the chilly night air. "Chatter reporting terrorist attack in Capitol marketplace. Traffic heading to Coal Mine Alpha."

"Roger that. We're good to go."

Alice turned to face her teams. "Time to go like billy-oh and make it so!" The Teaser team soared into the darkness a minute later.

The chopper pilot yelled out instructions. "Touch-down in five minutes and four clicks north of the road to the control center. Take the road eight clicks east and you're there. Make sure you help Electra into the carrier. Wheelchair and crutches already onboard. Be back in two hours. Communicate only with V2. She'll contact me if needed."

A random thought crossed Electra's brain. *What are the meanings behind the code names? Alice selected them for a reason. I'll make a guess, then compare it to her explanation. If I'm right she buys me a Coke.*

The chopper hovered, locating a level landing area for touching down. The rotors were still spinning when the attack carrier rolled out of the chopper, the Teaser team already on board and heading south. It was built for desert warfare and negotiated the terrain like a dune buggy, only much faster. The driver saw no headlights in the West as they pulled onto the road, which meant they were ahead of any reinforcement convoy. So far, so good.

The center looked just like what intelligence photos showed, so the team deployed as planned. It neutralized the security guards and Electra's group rushed her in, guided by a map counter-intelligence had stolen. Confusion from the market attack and Isilabad Military uniforms worn by the team helped clear the way to the computer center, where a locked door and "No Admittance" sign greeted them. Not a problem. The team used just enough plastic explosives to unhinge the door.

Electra and her team rolled into the network center, one large room lined with the latest hi-tech hardware and occupied by one person, Hassan Wassani, transfixed by the blast. One teamer rushed him, binding him to chair and dragging it to a nearby table. Electra rolled to the opposite side, setting her Brain Probe and attaching the helmet to Hassan. Her team stood guard outside the entrance while she prepared for a meeting of the minds.

"We know all about your network and your Trojan filters. Your sons told me a lot before they had to leave, and you will tell me the rest." Hassan was coming out of the initial shock, remembering stories about a shadowy female in a wheelchair. He swelled in anger.

"It is you who killed two of my sons! You will pay."

"No, you'll pay if you don't answer my questions. Your sons couldn't resist my Brain Probe. Neither will you." Electra placed a bottle of water on the table.

"Never! I am even stronger than they."

"Very well. See how long you can resist drinking." Electra dialed the knobs. Less than a minute later Hassan was guzzling every drop.

"If you don't answer my questions I will dial excruciating pain. Here's what kidney stones feel like." Hassan's screams were blood curdling.

"Stop!...Stop...I will tell you what you want to know."

Electra fired questions for fifteen minutes, then rolled to a computer station and logged in, transferring files to her home workstation, and then copying to a flash drive she would use for backup. Then she rolled back to the table.

"How do I decommission the filters?" Hassan sneered as he spoke.

"They can never be deactivated. They are always ready for my command."

"Very well. I will have to decommission you." As Electra dialed to full intensity, Hassan collapsed forward in his chair. Just then gunfire erupted outside the entrance. Security guard reinforcements were storming down the corridor in numbers that overpowered her team. Electra screamed warnings.

"I will kill Hassan if you don't stop your attack! All of you, come into the center."

As all trooped in, she counted only five guards remaining, but one of her team had been shot in the leg and limped badly.

"You see before you the Exalted Ruler. Only I can revive him. Here is what we will do. Two of you will stay with me to assist. The other three will wait in the corridor with my team. I will bring your Exalted Ruler partially back to life. Then you will escort us to our vehicle. And then I will restore Hassan. My terms are not negotiable. Decide now." The dumbfounded guards said nothing, so Electra made the call.

"You two, stay with me. Everyone else wait in the corridor. Do it now." The other guards took Electra's team into the corridor, while those remaining waited for further instructions.

"Lean next to Hassan, one on either side. Be ready to lift him when he awakens." The guards followed her instructions, awaiting one more. "Now watch him closely as I dial him back to life." Electra punched in the self-destruct code and dived under the table a split second before the Brain Probe blew up in their faces.

The sound and shrapnel startled everyone in the corridor and as Electra had counted on, her team overpowered the clueless guards. She triaged her victims, finding all dead, then joined her team in the corridor. The mission had become "take no prisoners," and as the lightning brain shifted to a higher gear, Electra took charge.

"One of you get my wheelchair so we can wheel out Simon. We have to dash for our carrier." Electra had memorized the route, so she led the escape to the exit, encountering no resistance. Her team loaded the carrier and escaped into the darkness before any of the reinforcements could react. The driver radioed Alice as soon as they were clear.

"Canary sang but stayed behind. All aboard and heading back."

"Roger that."

The team couldn't relax until airborne, because even though the attack carrier could outrun or outgun anything on the ground that got in its way, an air strike could be deadly. No one but the driver talked.

"We're at the turn-off. Four clicks left." Four minutes later, the radio crackled back a warning. Two aircraft approaching from the West at ground level. Calling in drone strikes."The driver's backup craned his neck trying to spot the enemy, but even with night vision goggles he spotted no planes approaching.

The attack carrier careened across the sand, now less than a kilometer from safety, when two planes zoomed overhead. The carrier had been spotted, even though it was running without headlights. The driver zigged and zagged crazily to confuse the attackers. Though he was too zoned in to cheer when one of the planes exploded, he knew a drone had taken care of half his problem. With only 800 meters remaining, the driver could see the helicopter preparing for liftoff. And just then, the remaining aircraft roared overhead, preparing for another strike. The driver swerved crazily but the aircraft zeroed in, then exploded a second after launching its missile, killed by another drone strike. Everyone could hear the missile homing in and the driver swerved madly to the right just in time to avoid a direct hit, but the ensuing explosion cartwheeled the carrier, coming to rest upside down and aflame only a hundred meters from the helicopter. All seven occupants crawled out just before the carrier exploded.

Alice watched in horror as the drone camera caught the carrier flipping and bursting into flames. She counted seven people scrambling out before the fuel tank exploded, knocking them down like duck pins hit by a ball of fire. Seconds later five were standing, then stooping to douse flames on the other two. One needed to be carried, the other was limping badly. The helicopter crew rushed to bring in the team. Alice heard nothing until it soared up and away. Then the pilot radioed, "All aboard. Returning to stable."

Alice's stomach knotted and she nearly heaved because she knew who needed to be carried; it could only be Electra. *What incredible déjà vu! What incredibly bad luck. Twice struck down by a bolt from the blue.* Alice was numb, unable to speak, barely able to think. *Don't go round the bend. Keep composed. No injury report, so it could be minor. Whatever it is, I'll handle it.*

The lightning brain was about to summon Electra back. It had determined there was no serious damage from the blow to her head, and the flames never reached the skin. Consciousness would no longer interfere with what the brain needed to do, so it reengaged the mind now that the immediate crisis was over.

Electra's eyes flickered open, greeted by five pair of worried eyes gazing down at her. It took a second to readjust, the droning blades adding to her confusion, but as the brain switched gears she knew exactly what had happened and, other than a jolt of pain when swallowing, felt fine.

"Don't try to sit up yet. Tell us how you feel. Can you move arms or legs?"

"Yes, I can flex them all. I get a pain in my throat when I try to swallow. Is there something wrong with it?"

"Let me check. Crikey, your throat's OK, but a jagged piece of shrapnel broke your medallion. If it hadn't been in the way, you'd have a bad cut." He held up the pieces, then said, "Maybe a jeweler can mend it. But you're still in one piece, and let's keep you that way." Alice's call crackled in.

"V2, requesting injury status."

"Simon's leg wound stabilized. No help needed."

"Roger that. ETA is fifteen minutes. Over."

For the first time in what seemed like an eternity, Alice could breathe without gasping. She didn't need to divert to an emergency medical site. The pounding in her chest subsided as the reality of total success grew.

Touchdown occurred twenty minutes later; the teams celebrated briefly and then loaded for departure. Alice watched while radioing flight plans for home. Outwardly she remained calm, but inwardly she sang joyously to the tune of her favorite English carol, for today had become her dancing day.

The raucous flight to London ranked with the best of Electra's childhood soccer celebrations. Laughter and singing tingled every spinal nerve as she shared an emotional bonding with her team, the depth of which could be forged only in life-or-death struggles. The men christened her "Crutches" because of her award winning "Tiny Tim" performance. Stream-of-consciousness comments bubbled out.

"You sure fooled us, hobbling about. You should be an actress…"

"I remember Bible stories about Jesus losing his sandals in the desert. You've added a new one: you ditched your wheelchair…"

"I was going to run for the exits when Hassan started screaming. What did you do, threaten to cut off his privates?" Electra couldn't resist responding.

"No, something worse. I simulated what it feels like to pass a kidney stone the size of a peach pit."

"How did you ever think to booby trap your Brain Probe?" She had a great answer.

"I get some of my best ideas watching retro sci-fi and action-adventure flicks. I stole it from *Mission Impossible*." Alice made a final announcement just before the final approach.

"Job well done. And everyone shares the credit when I debrief the committee Thursday morning. Please call in to your section supervisor Friday. And of course, as always, mum's the word."

Alice knew how to prepare for the debriefing session. She would let Electra prepare the agenda and script. Wednesday afternoon, Alice knew the drill. She would describe mission results; the committee would ask questions; Electra would give answers; Alice would summarize next steps.

After Electra answered all questions, the chairman concluded the meeting.

"Well young lady, you proved to be a resourceful ally. But I can't help thinking you know more than you're letting on. Why is that?" Electra knew how to keep the balance in her favor and had already prepared pithy answers.

"Leverage."

"Hmm. And you'll be able to decrypt the data files you obtained?"

"Yes."

"I see. And you'll share the data with us?"

"Yes, on a need to know basis."

"Hmm. And Alice will know more about what we should do once she has connected with the Guardian Party?"

"Yes."

"And what about those so-called smart pills. We'll need more because Hassan unleashed some—what do you call them—Trojan filters before you neutralized him."

"Yes. Alice knows who to talk with to get more."

"Would you be willing to loan us your, uh, Brain Probe?"

"No."

Frustration began to show in the chairman's tone.

"Well young lady, since we can't control you, I guess we better work with you." *This is just what I want to hear. I'll borrow a zinger I used years ago at a meeting in Austin.*

"How do you know I'm young, and what makes you think I'm a lady?" Alice chimed in as if on cue.

"Come come, my dear. Don't be so modest. I know you are a practically perfect young lady. Why don't I summarize our next steps. Electra will depart for Washington this evening and I'll return after spending more time with the Committee."

The lightning brain gave Electra the night off, letting her emotional persona sort through past and present. She had learned much about her family history. *Even as a kid, Mother was practically perfect. I might never reach her emotional maturity, but I can try.* And she had learned much about her current feelings. *I feel empathy toward Hassan. For those who believe in his cause, he's a martyr, not a ruthless terrorist. But his cause is not mine.*

Electra finally drifted asleep midway across the Atlantic, but while she rested the lightning brain continued working out next moves for all her games. *Games are ever so fun when I make up the rules and hold all the wildcards.* A verse from Indira whispered:

You can change the rules at will,
And when you take your playing field.
It's much more fun to call the tune,
Your marching band won't have to yield.

And the verse fits me to a T because I can change its second person reference to first person singular. Indira spoke from the shadows.

"Yes, my precious daughter, you are indeed singular. Now rest."

Electra obeyed.

CHAPTER 19

February 2120

"Panic in the Streets"

(Thread 2 Chapter 7)

JARED KNEW HIS PRIMETIME speech would cause panic. He was about to lob a bombshell into the public forum and couldn't be happier because it would solidify his grip on the Guardian Party, and the Party's grip on Washington, paving the way for sweeping victories in November elections. All this thanks to his Brain Trust—Angus and Electra.

Late last week they had alerted him to results and possible repercussions from a bold covert attack against Isilabad.

That Kittner girl has an uncanny ability to snoop; the info she digs up scoops the media and is weirdly accurate, and her spins on speeches and bulletins keep the public in my camp. And Angus has a sixth sense for tweaking my programs so I get few complaints.

Tonight Jared would go with what the Brain Trust had given him, adding a couple of his own twists he knew the public would endorse. He strode confidently to the podium, totally in command.

"Good evening Patriots.

I stand before you tonight with sobering news that your previous administrations could not possibly handle. They couldn't handle the truth! Their self-serving and smarmy policies pushed a kinder and gentler agenda that didn't work then, won't work now, and never will until we've turned out the lights on those who want to live in the Dark Ages. That's why you, the American people, installed me and the Guardian Party to guard our great nation. And you never believed the nay-sayers or backstabbers whose lies and innuendos accused me of a hidden agenda. In fact, what surfaced after all their digging was an agenda for you, the American people. And since you put me in command, I've stood tall and delivered. Tonight, I want to report just-breaking results for what we've just accomplished.

"Under my leadership and directed by Angus McTear—who I will nominate immediately for Secretary of Defense—we have built a 'Coalition of the Smart,' capable and like-minded countries able to battle terrorists on their home turf. We uncovered a devious network of machines—Isilabad codename Trojan Offense—hidden in America and major European countries, which can secretly poison our air and water by releasing T-Plague virus. We just completed a successful attack in Isilabad that defangs their evil intentions. But it is possible these cowardly terrorists, before we terminated them, might have pre-programmed their machines to poison us at unknown times or locations. So, if we start to see random T-Plague outbreaks, please do not panic. We are in control of the situation. Efforts are under way to turn off the machines.

"Also, you can rest assured knowing that our best and brightest minds at the National Institute of Health are working to come up with effective vaccines. And as I have previously said, I cannot promise overnight success. Your previous incompetent administrations mismanaged vaccine programs for decades, but we are beginning to turn their agony of defeat into a victory for you.

"Let me come back to the issue of terrorism. We continue rooting out terrorist cells. And we are discovering the terrorist profile is much broader than previous administrations thought. A wider range of nationalities and age groups, besides young, angry, Middle East males, exists for terrorists. How did we learn this? From rolling out our Repatriot Program. Based on this, we are ready to implement its next phase. I will direct Healthguard and Securityguard agencies to enroll a broader profile into Repatriot and within the next several months begin redeploying those registered.

"I urge all Americans to remain calm, knowing that the Guardian Party continues taking whatever measures are necessary to guard our health and our security. Much more needs to be accomplished, but our course is set and our future is bright.

"God bless you patriotic Americans, and God bless our great nation!"

As he strode from the podium, Jared knew from his staffers' "thumb's up" he had delivered a knockout punch to any remaining opposition. *The Opposition Party is now officially defunct; they have nothing to offer. Elected Republicans and Democrats better fall in line or they'll be crushed by my juggernaut.*

Jared toasted himself later that night, enjoying a scotch and soda in the privacy of his own thoughts. *The public loves me because they know I know what's best for them. Even if more of them could think for themselves, they'd feel the same way. And if I'm violating the rights of some of the people, so what? I'm doing more good than harm. And as for my hidden agenda, the real one is buried so deep no one will ever find it. And if they did, I can justify my actions, so just let 'em try.* Beeping on his private cell phone interrupted.

Damn, another call from Zoe. She worships the ground I walk on, and it's beginning to bother me. I would have kicked her out sooner had I known she's one of those women who love too much. I better change my bedside manner before she becomes a bigger nuisance.

"Why didn't you tell me? I'm so proud of you." Angus and his wife were listening to analyst recaps after Jared's speech. All the pundits applauded the nomination of CIA director Angus McTear to Secretary of Defense. If approved, he would become the first person ever to hold both cabinet posts simultaneously. Angus tried not to look too stunned.

"Dear, I found out when you did. Jared can be surprising."

"Yes, but it's no surprise the public loves him. He seems so genuine. You wouldn't be working for him if you didn't believe in him, would you?"

"No, dear. But one of the reasons I like working for him is to keep Guardians from pushing too hard in the wrong direction."

"But the world isn't a kinder and gentler place, is it? I think the public wants him to keep doing what he's doing." Angus was tired and didn't want to talk about the Repatriot escalation gambit, another surprise from Jared. Better to do that when he meets with the better half of Jared's Brain Trust.

The Conklins listened glumly to Jared's speech. Poor Russell. He was swimming with the sharks and had no safety cage now that the Opposition Party was permanently sidelined. His career was sidelined too because of suspicions about being an Opposition Party sympathizer. He hadn't been terminated because he was one of the few people who had any ideas for combatting the T-Plague, but his options were few; twenty years of NIH failure did not bode well. Russell considered his plight instead of the pundits' droning about Jared's speech.

If I knew then what I know now, I would have steered clear of the Opposition Party. I better get busy putting my career back together. I still have my home and wife. Maybe I can pick Electra's brain. She must have some ideas.

"Don't fret about the speech. I have an idea. Why don't you invite Electra and Robin for dinner? Electra always puts a positive spin on events."

"That's a good idea. I'll set it up for a weekend when we're all available."

Electra listened to Jared's speech while logged on to her computer. She knew what he'd say because she wrote the words, but he threw in three surprises that drew her attention. The first she liked: appoint Angus Secretary of defense. *He's as solid as the Washington Monument, and has more backbone and brains than Jared's lieutenants combined. He'd be a great president if ever called to duty.*

The second was troubling. *Terrorist profiling should be extended, but Jared might use it to justify harsher anti-terrorist programs. Angus better keep Jared from going too far.*

The third was even more nettlesome. *Enrolling more people in Repatriot means arrest or internment camps; redeployment means deportation. Either way, civil rights will be ignored and innocent people will become collateral damage. Jared better tread carefully or risk alienating larger segments of the public.*

Electra stretched, walked to the kitchen for a Coke, then sat in the living room to contemplate the Guardian Party's trajectory since taking control a year ago. It did seem better than recent administrations, which had lost their compass, ability, or will to protect America. They had lost their sense of history too, and as the 17th century English political theorist James Harrington summarized best: "No man can be a Politician, except he be first an Historian." Winston Churchill's October 1938 speech—nearly a year before the start of World War II—expanded that thought:

"…eager search for the line of least resistance, five years of uninterrupted retreat from British power, five years of neglect of our air defenses. These are the features I stand here to expose and which marked an improvident stewardship… We have sustained a defeat without a war…we will be weighed in the balance and found wanting."

Electra could trace the analogy better than most. The United States had been the staunch defender of democracy, taking the hard steps necessary to defend democracy, and was ultimately rewarded by the collapse of the Soviet Union. But then, as Churchill warned, American leadership lost its way, believing appeasement would protect the country from the wars against terrorism and T-Plague lurking in its future.

After twenty years of bungling administrations, the public wanted to pull the plug on the Washington Establishment, and when the Guardian Party started moving in the right direction, people flocked to it. Although Jared was not a deep thinker, at least he was reversing America's decline.

An odd thought came to Electra. *I'm turning twenty-three next week, and that's too young for anyone to believe I know what I'm doing, so I must continue working from the shadows. But when necessary, I can become "She, who must be obeyed." I'm mature enough emotionally and I can make my appearance be what's needed.* Another thought intruded.

I have no family or friends who'll bake me a birthday cake, but that's not a problem, for I stand alone. Not lonely, just alone. And I know the difference. Loneliness is a lack, a feeling that something is missing. But aloneness is a fullness, a joy of being, of being complete. And I always have my Inner Voice, calling to me from the shadows.

Electra snapped back to the present, ready to make moves for new political games that could be dangerous. *I don't know the outcome, but if I don't act, the wrong people will, so I'll follow advice given by Erasmus of Rotterdam, a 16th-century Dutch Renaissance philosopher: "In the land of the blind, the one-eyed man is king." And I can see better than mere mortals. My next move comes at Saturday's meeting with Angus.* Electra slept soundly.

"Well this is a surprise. You can walk without canes. I'm happy for you." Angus wrapped Electra in a bear hug, then hustled her into the house.

"We can celebrate that, along with your nomination. And in addition to your yogurt, I brought you a cranberry muffin. It's OK for you to splurge today. Jared will have you worn to a nub playing both offense and defense if you don't keep your strength up." The two traded small talk, then turned to the challenges Jared was lining up. Electra took the lead because she had prepared the agenda.

"It's good you'll soon be Secretary of Defense because you can better control all law enforcement agencies. Jared and the public will expect you to be aggressive when expanding the terrorist profile, but you'll have to soften it. What do you want to do?"

"We'll tell the troops to use the same level of force they're using now and not escalate further. And to keep them honest, we'll make sure they wear body cams so the public sees we mean business. And you can make sure Zoe uses them in her PR video releases." Electra nodded and then continued.

"When it comes to the Repatriot Program, we'll need to have Zoe spin how good it is to get rid of the bad people, but there'll be blowback if the public gets concerned about collateral damage. What's your take on this?" Angus scratched his head.

"I think the public is becoming mean-spirited because the T-Plague has put a big dent in our country's collective I.Q. and morals. Only a handful of political analysts will object, and they'll be ignored. But I think you and I can convince Jared to steer a moderate course."

"From what I know, Jared's not a deep thinker and has little historical perspective. A year ago, I suggested he read some books by Kahneman and Fukuyama or their successors to get a better handle on how and where he should be leading the nation. Did he ever mention that to you?"

"No, and I'm not sure how this fits in. Why don't you refresh my memory?" Electra was ready to do just that.

"I respect Jared because he's willing to act, to do what he thinks is right. The problem is he might not understand the complexities. Perhaps you remember Hegel's philosophical dictum: the rational alone is real. Based on late 18th century events, he predicted the end of history would be liberal democracy supported by capitalism. By fits and starts the world plodded in that direction, though the World Wars and Communism got in the way. After the Soviet Union collapsed, it appeared the world was finally headed in the right direction, but along came Huntington's *Clash of Civilizations* and Fukuyama's three volumes on political order and political decay, describing why the end of history is problematic. America was moving in the right direction until thirty years ago, when Middle East terrorism and the T-Plague dealt the United States crippling blows. I'm afraid Jared and the Guardian Party are too obtuse, so we need you to spoon feed Jared so he knows enough to keep the country on course. I don't think any of his other lieutenants would understand what we're talking about." Electra paused for Angus to catch up, then moved on.

"And here's why this is so important right now. My contacts tell me Isilabad is close to a political meltdown because most of its leaders have contracted the T-Plague. The same with China, but any meltdown there will be buffered short-term by its middle class. Very soon the United Nations—maybe led by the United States—might have to conduct Isilabad state building, and we better not make the mistakes we did a century ago in Iraq. The administration back then was so arrogant it never considered how embedded Islam's hostility towards liberal democracy or Modernity is. The war between Christianity and Islam is centuries old. You can't expect them to change to our worldview just because we can drop bombs on them."

"How can you possibly know Isilabad and Chinese governments are in meltdown?"

Of course I know. I made it so. Electra said that, and more, but only to herself. *I poisoned the Chinese "smart pill" pipeline that also supplies Isilabad leaders. That's what my Austin pilot runs were all about, and not even Hud knows. Only I control the shipments, and no one will ever be able to backtrack to Hud or to me.*

"I've picked up on rumors, so please trust me. We can spin this in a press release that gives Jared high marks for proactively dealing with world events. You'll need help from Britain carrying this out, so if it's OK, I'll put you in contact with someone who can assist from behind the scenes." Angus looked like he had heard enough, but Electra had more to say.

"Let's talk about T-Plague vaccines. You'll need a fresh approach, but an NIH Administrator who can help is under a cloud of suspicion because he might have been an Opposition Party person. That no longer matters because they're history. If it's OK, I'd like to put him in touch with you." Electra took a breath, then finished what she wanted to say.

"We both know that Jared must prove himself. You have to start building your own informal steering committee that can help rein in any extreme thinking. Start with two names I'll give you. And keep their identities unknown from each other until you're ready to trust them. And don't mention my name." Angus looked away, remaining silent until finally looking back.

"Isn't this, uh, sort of seditious?" Electra gave her favorite answer.

"Perhaps. But look at it this way. You're simply expanding the Brain Trust. And you don't have to do anything until you're ready." Angus nodded slowly in agreement.

"I see where this can go. OK, give me their names and numbers. And here's something I want you to do. Jared's programs will need economic justification, and I want to rely on you for that. Can you brush up on economics?"

"Studying a subject and then using it is always one of my favorite games, so I'll be happy to take on the role of Brain Trust Economist. And I won't have to take any time off to prepare. I think you'll be pleased."

Electra dived into an economics study program that evening after taking a late afternoon workout followed by a light dinner. She set herself in front of her home workstation, enjoying a dessert of Chocolate-covered Double Stuf Oreo cookies and a Coke while searching the Web for economics articles that caught her fancy. After skimming four, she compiled a summary, reciting it in her mind as the lightning brain devoured the words.

I like this definition of Economics: The study of how society chooses, with or without the use of money, to employ scarce productive resources to produce various products and services over time and distribute them for consumption, now and in the future, among various people and groups in society. It's never been a popular subject because people call it the "Dismal Science"(deals with scarcity and tradeoffs), but its two branches (Micro and Macroeconomics) touch many aspects of politics and social organization.

Econ is considered the hardest of the soft sciences because it constructs complex mathematical models to explain itself. Although its five key assumptions are intuitively obvious, econ models become so complex that computer software is needed to construct graphical output economists can understand. What a contrast to high energy physics, whose assumptions and complex models are understood by few, and whose results touch very little in the observable world.

After taking a Coke break, Electra returned to search for an online seminar that would extend what she had found in the articles, and she found precisely what she wanted: an entire online economics lecture series, compliments of MIT's Online University. Of all universities, MIT would be her first choice because of its powerhouse reputation in all areas of engineering as well as economics. MIT's Paul Samuelson (Nobel Prize 1970) started neoclassical economics in the 1950's, followed in 2010 by another prizewinner, Peter Diamond, for contributions in labor economics and taxation. Electra's father and godfather Adom had graduated from that famed institution.

Electra knew that engineering students often "disrespect" economics courses, considering economic theory and its models trivial in comparison to the "hard" sciences and engineering disciplines, often placing a pejorative label on B&E majors: Busted Engineers. *I want to see how well the Instructor defangs this crop of arrogant engineers.*

The instructor began his first lecture by giving a definition of economics that was identical to hers. After that, he gave a brief history of its founding and explained it consists of two major branches: microeconomics, dealing with the individual or the corporation, and macroeconomics, dealing with the overall economy.

Next, he explained the difference between positive economics (the way things are) and normative economics (the way things should be), then listed some of the major assumptions and mathematical tools, even using them to illustrate a practical example: a student's decision process for buying a new or used textbook, versus sharing one belonging to a study group. From the questions asked, Electra could tell the students felt confident the course would be a snap, but the instructor's subsequent slides deflated their egos.

He was diplomatic and accurate. Yes, it's true that economics uses only elementary calculus, but it applies it to a series of interrelated models whose solutions require constrained optimization coupled with "Big Data" computer modeling. Then he compared the state of economics to that of high energy physics. Most people can understand economic principles intuitively, and the results of economic analysis can be presented in a set of understandable graphs. Economic theory today incorporates behavioral economics, making conclusions and policy recommendations much more accurate than even fifty years ago. And then he stumped the students by showing how logical assumptions can lead to illogical backward-sloping supply curves or upward sloping demand curves, forcing the students to realize economics is harder than they thought. He even used a simple comparison of two telephone sales reps handling call-ins so he could illustrate Simpson's Paradox: comparisons can be reversed when lurking variables are taken into consideration. One representative might have a higher percentage of total correct calls for the month even though the other had a higher score each week. His comparison with high energy physics silenced all critics in the audience. High energy physics is unable to resolve conundrums posed by quantum mechanics. He concluded the first lecture by matter-of-factly ticking off bullet points that highlighted the superiority of economics to physics, concluding that economists consider themselves "Worldly Philosophers" whose policy recommendations can help guide what people or the government should do. Electra was delighted with the show.

I like our instructor. My summary touches most of the points he covered. I'm going to binge-watch more lectures. Not only will I add to my understanding, but I'll be entertained along the way. A sudden realization flashed into her brain. *No wonder online courses and open enrollment have reduced the cost and time to get a college degree. Universities offer these kinds of degree programs so students don't have to sit in classroom lectures at top tier schools to qualify for in-demand jobs. If they watch the lectures and work in study groups, they can master the material. And in my case, I don't need a study group because I'm auto-didactic. I can teach myself anything.* Electra came back with another Coke, then settled in to watch the next lecture.

Unlike Electra, whose lightning brain never needed downtime, Alice needed time off in London before flying back to Washington so she could deal with two reasons causing depression. The first was job-related; she was in a quandary for how to salvage the "America Strong" covert operation. She wasn't concerned about that because she could figure out what to do. Her boss wasn't concerned either and gave her as much time as needed to plan ahead. But the second would be harder for it was related to self-esteem. Alice was beginning to dislike her one-dimensional self.

Alice had put in twenty years of a foreign service nomad's existence and had little to show other than her career. No family or close friends. No church or civic ties. No hobbies other than cooking. She had a budding midlife crisis that only she could resolve, and she must resolve it quickly in order to regain her step.

Alice poked about London, realizing she had to return eventually to her London roots, where she'd pick church or community service organizations for volunteering. But all that was longer term, and right now she needed to resolve her relationship with Electra, for she had discovered, when Electra had been vulnerable and needed her care, the joy of giving fully to another. It was a glimmer of the unconditional love a parent gives to a child. *Maybe Electra will become the daughter I never had. Or, if not that deep a relationship, then maybe Electra will let me be a close friend. And in either case, we shall make a jolly game of it.*

Alice realized that no matter how clever she was or how carefully she covered her tracks, she would always see Electra's footprints ahead of her. *I'll pretend I'm in control and Electra will play along. And I'll hide my feelings too. I'll let my actions do the talking.*

The more she thought, the better she felt, so she told her boss she would soldier ahead, returning to Washington a day before Jared's speech. Perfect timing, for it provided an immediate reason to contact Electra.

Electra just stepped out of the shower early Sunday morning, the day after meeting with Angus, when her cell phone chimed. She recognized Alice's caller I.D. so she picked up rather than letting it go to answering

"Welcome back from London. How are you?"

"Ducky, my dear. I returned late Wednesday, and I thought you might like to chat over a late breakfast. Would today suit you?"

"Why, yes. What time?"

"I'll have the table ready by noon. Please bring your appetite."

Alice decided to serve a traditional English breakfast: scrambled eggs with mushrooms, bangers and fried tomatoes served with toast and orange marmalade; then she would make the opening move in a new game. Electra knocked as the clock struck twelve.

"How good to see you, my dear. Come sit down at the dining room table." Electra followed; soon after tucking into the meal, Alice redirected the conversation.

"After our London performance, my boss has asked me to consider how best to handle any follow-up, but Jared has given me pause. I know you always keep some things to yourself, so perhaps you might share your thoughts."

"It's possible Hassan launched a countdown attack that's still ticking. We're seeing random outbreaks in the States, and there may be more to come. Anything in Britain?"

"No, but you warned us so we're vigilant. What might you propose?"

"A return trip to Isilabad so I can hack deeper into Hassan's computers. I didn't find any encrypted countdown files or apps, and the terrorist location files are incomplete."

"We can't just walk in there again uninvited. How do you propose we get in?"

"Sources tell me Isilabad's government is nearing meltdown because many senior leaders have contracted the T-Plague. They'll let us in because they need our humanitarian aid. Tell your intelligence agencies to act on this as soon as they can. That's the first item. And here's the second.

"You know from Jared's speech that the Guardian Party is on a roll, and I've found two people you can join to form a Guardian

Party Insider's Group. Let Angus McTear take the lead. I told him about you. Let him make the first call."

"Goodness, you don't tiptoe to the top, do you? You barge right in. But I'll trust your judgement. Is there anything else?"

"Yes. I want to spend two days in London visiting my grandparents."

"Not to worry, my dear. I can arrange that. Is that all?"

"Almost. I think I figured out your code names for Operation Holy Grail. Charger refers to a crusader's warhorse, Lobber to a medieval catapult or trebuchet, Teaser for coaxing information out of Hassan. But what about V2? There are lots of possibilities. How about a clue?"

"My dear, you are a very clever girl. I will leave that for you to figure out. But please finish eating…"

Upon returning home, Electra reviewed a list from which she would select postdoc projects, convinced it would keep her challenged for as long as she wanted. Only for a moment did a twinge of remembrance cast a shadow over such a sunny forecast. *My dearly departed parents would have taken such joy helping Su and Adom build Worldstar Pharmaceuticals from such a list, but what should have been lives kissed by the sun turned into star-crossed tragedies.* Electra preferred not to linger in the past, so the twinge left as quickly as it came.

Electra met early that week with Professor Ravenhill and two of his GWU colleagues who would coordinate her postdoc appointment. They had participated in her thesis defense, after which they thought she might help them develop new biotech drugs or devices. But not even Ravenhill knew how far ahead she was, and that suited Electra. The labs would be her playground for advanced work, and she would give her advisors enough to keep them happy and out of the way. By week's end she gave them an outline of what she would pursue, keeping secret her separate work on T-Plague vaccines and extensions of her Brain Probe.

Electra decided to spend Friday evening at her home workstation, which hosted three computers displaying six monitors on three sides. *Ah, my fortress of solitude. Built by me and though Mother might not agree, it's my happiest place. When I'm here, I feel my lightning brain take flight as my thoughts soar, as if they're god-like, but controlled by me. Pilots must feel the same. I remember a friend who went to the Airforce Academy, telling me that cadets have to learn the poem "High Flight." They, like I, vanish into another world.* Electra's cell phone chimed, bringing her back to Earth.

"Hi, Robin. What's new with you and Matt?"

"We're doing fine. I'm sorry it's been so long since talking, but you must have been on a trip. Well, we can catch up on the latest if you'll let us take you out for a belated birthday celebration. We have a surprise location for you. Is Saturday about six good for you?"

"That would be perfect. And I have a surprise for you and Matt. Will you pick me up?"

"That's the plan. See you Saturday."

Robin sounds happy. I guess she's giving Matt a chance, and I hope she doesn't drain him emotionally, or use him as a punching bag for her anger. But that's for the two of them to work out. I'll stay out of the way.

Approaching headlights notified Electra that Matt's van was entering the driveway, so she donned her coat and out she went.

"Holy shit, Electra's running!" Matt rolled down the window to greet her.

"Hey, you've pitched the crutches. And you shocked Robin; she just spoke her favorite S-word." Robin leaned across Matt to shout a greeting.

"Parden my French, but, you're good as new. And you look so, too. I love the coat and scarf. Climb in and tell us more." Electra bounded in and the threesome drove away.

"Matt's therapy got me moving again, so we can thank him. And I've exercised enough to retire the crutches and throw away the wheelchair. And I decided the new me should have some new clothes."

"You can show them off at a new place Matt's taking us. Do you remember telling us about sensual pleasures cafés? We surfed the

Web for a popular one whose menu looked tasty, so that's where we're treating you."

Electra recognized the place. It was the café where she had drawn Abdul into her web but she made no mention of her previous visit. It was less crowded than before, which made the ambiance even more intimate for sharing stories. As they sat cross-legged on cushions, Robin reminisced.

"Who would have loved coming here?" Electra let Matt guess first.

"Your good friend Christi. From the pictures you've shown me, she was the prettiest of the Three Queens, which says a lot. Maybe Electra could tell us more."

"Glad to, but please, keep it confidential. Agreed?" Matt nodded, so Electra started in.

"Christi would like this place for one gigantic reason: she loved to experiment with drugs. When it came to drugs or sex Christi was fearless and bold. It almost got her into serious trouble when using them to improve her singing and dancing. I don't think Robin ever heard about the time we outran the drug dealer. She begged me to drive her to the exchange site, and when we got there the guy pulled a gun. All that did was make her mad. She kicked him in the privates and we ran for my car. I can still feel the thrill of the chase."

"You haven't told that story before. But I remember when she helped me the time two fellows drugged me at a Christmas party. I still can't imagine how I barfed up so much on that fellow." Electra turned the spotlight on Matt.

"Do you keep in touch with friends from high school?"

"I don't, because we've gone separate ways and have little in common. Seeing them is like living in the past, and even though conditions today are unsettled, I prefer the present because I can do things to make things better."

"Matt's right, and you've sure made your wardrobe better. I love the sweater and slacks. Christi would be pleased. She always criticized you for dressing down."

"Don't start thinking I'm a clothes horse. I just decided I need to look a bit more polished and professional. But enough talk; here comes the dinner sampler, and it's high time for indulging." Straight-laced Robin giggled at the double entendre.

Dinner included macaroni and cheese served with marijuana-laced "weed biscuits," topped off with "mile high brownies" for dessert. Even the lightning brain felt mellow and all were chatty, so they enjoyed fruit smoothies while Electra told another Christi story.

"Christi was smart as well as sexy, and she did a thorough study of psychoactive drugs. She told me that marijuana's been used as an appetite stimulant for medical use since the 1960's. And I didn't know that American Indians have used peyote for over five thousand years, but I found out the active ingredient is an alkaloid called mescaline. And marijuana, which comes from the cannabis plant, has been used for thousands of years in China and India. The Spaniards brought it to the New World in the 1500's." Matt said he knew that, so Electra added more.

"Christi told me about a couple of books that relate psychedelic drugs to sex, spirituality, and creativity. One of them is *The Doors of Perception* by Aldous Huxley. Did you ever hear of the late 60's rock group *The Doors*? They named themselves after his book, the title coming from a quote by the 19th century polymath William Blake: 'If the doors of perception were cleansed, everything would appear to man as it is, infinite.' Would you like to hear more?" The drinks were beginning to influence Robin. She slurred out her answer while leaning against Matt.

"I s'pose so. Just make sure Matt shows us the way home before I fall off the chair."

"OK, I'll make it quick. Here are Cliffs Notes summaries. She also told me about Timothy Leary, a leader of the 60's Hippie Movement who wrote *Tune In, Turn On, Drop Out*. He pushed the notion that LSD can expand the mind. And also Carlos Castaneda, who wrote *The Teachings of Don Juan*. These books contain no science. They're subjective ramblings, emphasizing a spiritual aspect that is now irrelevant. But they're nearly two hundred years old, and back then their ideas were mind-blowing. But by today's standards, their conclusions are hard to accept. Or to make a pun of it, hard to swallow, smoke, or digest—unlike our treats tonight. But here's an update regarding LSD and other psychedelics. Research during the last fifty years confirms users can't OD on them, and fMRI brain scans indicate they reduce activity in the brain's default mode network, which lessens depression, anxiety, addiction, or obsession. It looks as if Leary was right in one sense. LSD expands treatment options for mental illness. What a pleasant way to keep mental demons at bay."

"Thank you for the book reviews. And you finished just in time, because it's time to go after I get back from the little boy's room." Robin revived enough while Matt was gone to offer a suggestion.

"I have an idea. The Conklin's invited Matt and me for dinner tomorrow. Why don't you join us? I'll call Jennifer to let her know you're coming. We'll pick you up tomorrow at three. Deal?" As Electra nodded, Robin reached across the table.

"I've missed you. I like Matt, but you're my best friend. Next time you go on a trip, let me know so I won't worry." When Matt returned, Robin clued him in about tomorrow's dinner plans.

"That'll work, so let's go home. We should pace ourselves because tomorrow's another night out. But don't expect as high a time as tonight." *Nice pun,* thought Electra. *I became a punster long ago when the Worldstars were flying high.*

Jameel didn't like what he saw. *There, walking out with the man and his staggering date. Someone vaguely reminiscent of the shadowy woman who left with Abdul just before he contracted a terminal case of the T-Plague. She looks different, but a year has gone by, so she might be the one. I will find out and if she is, I will punish her in the name of Allah and Abdul. But first, I must follow and learn where she lives. I shall shadow them silently and then make plans, and I shall be patient...*

Russell was about to carve the rib roast when the doorbell rang, so Jennifer hurried to greet the guests. Having Robin and Electra visit would bring back memories, but Matt's presence would keep her from dwelling too much on the past. Christi's ghost was never far away, but after two years of working through grief she was getting better. She was still trim and as beautiful as her professionally decorated home. And when she opened the door, she came face to face with another ghost, the ghost of Indira. Jennifer hid her shock by hugging both girls, then shepherded them into the hallway.

"Matt, you're a fortunate fellow to be their escort. And I see that Electra's therapy sessions paid off. She looks even better without crutches." Russell joined them in the living room, announcing dinner would be served.

"I hope you're hungry because the roast is ready right now. The girls can help me put dinner on the table while Jennifer chats with Matt." All were seated fifteen minutes later, conversation flowing as freely as the Cabernet Sauvignon Matt had thoughtfully brought. As dinner turned into dessert, Jennifer turned the conversation to Matt and Robin.

"You two are a handsome couple. Don't you find it's good to make time for dating?"

"Yes. Matt helps me stay centered. I sometimes get stressed out by school and my part-time job. I'm glad the fall term just ended so I can catch my breath. And Matt says he'll coach me in college algebra."

"I'm pretty good at math, so I make a good tutor. And I know how to ease up so Robin doesn't get mad."

"Russell and I had always hoped that Christi would find a nice fellow like you. Now that Electra is fully recovered, perhaps you have a friend she might like to meet. Robin hid what she was thinking. *Holy Shit, Christi's parents never knew she and Electra were lovers. I must be the only person who knows, and the secret stays with me.* Electra steered the conversation to a safer subject.

"Why don't you tell Matt the story about how my mother treated my father when they were dating?" Jennifer's eyes sparkled with laughter.

"Your mother played the 'S-game,' collecting adjectives beginning with the letter S that fit. Smart, steady, stodgy, square, and so on. And she kept him at bay, often telling him that anything worth having is worth waiting for. Your father was her work in progress."

Did Mother have a temper? Did she ever yell or scream?"

"No. She was a genuinely nice person. Always looked for the best in others. Never criticized. I wish she would have given me her poetry."

"Aunt Su gave me some of them, and I can recall one that talked about you. It's called 'Jennifer's Gift.' If you'll bring me a pen and paper I'll write it down and you can read it.

Russell returned with the items, and five minutes later Jennifer read what Electra had written:

They can't be bought, they can't be sold,
They stretch beyond the years.
They grow in strength as you grow old,
Friendship through laughter and tears.

It's hard to explain its genesis,
A gift right from the start.
Resulting perhaps from synthesis,
Akin to till death do us part.

How many will Fate put in your way?
Small number that's unknown.
Stay alert invite them in,
Or else end up alone."

No one spoke until Electra broke the silence.

"Most of mother's poems are upbeat because she lived in the present, dealing with reality. She knew nothing's gained by looking back on things we've lost. Let me write down another poem you might like whenever you would like Indira to cheer you up. It's called *In the Now*." Electra scribbled for a couple of minutes, then Jennifer recited again.

"The past is but a memory,
The future a dream unknown.
But your present is a gift you see,
It's meant for you alone.

Past a melancholy view,
No more forever gone.
Future problematic too,
Outcomes may be wrong.

So busy yourself with what is now,
Focus on what's here.
Enjoy the most that fate allows,
Future memories will be dear."

Jennifer added more.

"How fitting for me, because I'm thinking about starting a nutrition and fitness counseling service. There's a growing customer base, thanks to the T-Plague." Robin's encouraging poke in Matt's ribs prompted him to speak.

I've been thinking about starting my own physical therapy practice, and what you're talking about would fit right in. Let's talk about combining forces when you're ready to start your business. And speaking of being ready, I think we're ready to go. Look at how late it is." Russell had the last words as everyone rose from the table.

"Jennifer and I thank you for a delightful conversation. I think all of us are ready for new directions this year. I may not be as quick on my feet as Electra, but I think I know where I'm headed." Electra commented only to herself. *Yes, you do, and I'll help you get there too.*

CHAPTER 20

April 2120

"Alice in Wonderland"

(Thread 2 Chapter 8)

The world's becoming a stranger place. Alice started ticking off the reasons why it seemed as if she had tumbled down the rabbit hole Lewis Carroll wrote about:

- Random T-Plague outbreaks occur in the United States and England
- Terrorist attacks start in France and Germany
- Iran and Isilabad declare war on each other and seek humanitarian aid from the United Nations to combat spreading T-Plague outbreaks.
- Isilabad's Exalter Ruler Steering Committee contracts T-Plague
- China's Leadership Committee contracts T-Plague
- America's smart pill pipeline empties.
- America's Guardian Party becomes even more assertive in its fight against terrorism.

There were more but she stopped for fear of getting her mind in a bigger muddle. She sighed, then bucked up because her partner and de facto planning expert, Electra, would explain why all this is happening and what they would do about it.

Alice, who knew political science better than most politicians, often wondered if they remembered the difference between a republic (a constitution or charter protects certain inalienable rights that can't be taken away) or a democracy (the majority is not restrained in this way and can impose its will on the minority). She would be pleased to give them a refresher course that the current political climate needed, so she rehearsed her lecture to an audience of one: herself.

It all started with those golden Greeks, the first civilization to jettison history's eternal cycle in favor of "linear" progress, and to build a political system anchored on duty to the state and an educational system for its citizenry that taught what was needed if the state were to survive. Duty and honor took precedence over trade and technique, and their systems worked well in their warring world. But they and their Roman conquerors lost their way as the populace became too soft.

It took a thousand years from the Fall of Rome late in the fifth century for the great minds of the Enlightenment to adapt politics from the "Ancient Regime" to the new realities of economics and the Industrial Revolution, allowing the framers of the U.S. Constitution to structure a brilliant political system balancing freedom and equality with human nature, and they realized it would take an informed, intelligent public to maintain it. They too believed in progress, and by fits and starts the world moved in the right direction. But the framers didn't expect a regress caused by the T-Plague. The world had dummied down, and America's kinder and gentler policy failed miserably when confronting Middle East rogue states.

Alice's partner would add to this refresher course highlights from political philosophy extensions attributed to Francis Fukuyama, Steven Pinker, and their acolytes, all warning that political systems can decay, and once a group seizes power, it can be difficult to dislodge. Electra was concerned that might be the case for the Guardian Party today, or if not now, then perhaps where the country may be heading.

Alice liked to play games as much as Electra, so she constructed one that would convert her current assignment into a metaphor, comparing it with Carroll's book *Alice in Wonderland.* Of course, she would play the role of Alice, and her partner would be an amalgam of the Cheshire Cat and the Caterpillar. Angus McTear would be the Mad Hatter and Russell Conklin, who would be added to the "Brain Trust" Angus was constructing, would be the March Hare. Jared Gardner plays the unpredictable Queen of Hearts; his steering committee fills out the Spade Gardeners that resemble animated playing cards. Alice smiled to herself. *We'll name my current assignment "Operation White Rabbit" and make it the centerpiece of a game. Let's see how long it takes for my dear girl to catch on. And I shall test her understanding of political philosophy as we move ahead. What a jolly time we'll have...*

All of Electra's games were advancing nicely, but "the Terrorism Game" demanded immediate attention because she needed to fill in data gaps remaining after pirating Hassan's files during the daring January raid, and thanks to Alice, she and Electra would visit London en route to Isilabad.

I'm pleased how adroitly Angus brought Alice and Russell into our Brain Trust—aka Guardian Party Insiders Group. And I can observe all from the catbird seat.

This afternoon Alice would visit her postdoc lab so Electra could go over the plan and agenda. Alice wanted to meet there for variety as well as for an opportunity to learn more about her enigmatic partner, and Electra was happy to comply. After the tour, Alice made a typically British observation patterned after the James Bond spy thrillers.

"Too bad Q is not able to join us. He would have appreciated it even better than I. And you do know what Q refers to, don't you?" Electra shook her head no.

"Goodness, I've stumped you again. Q stands for Quartermaster, or a reference to the decoy ships in WWII—heavily armed merchant ships. The Q Branch handles R&D for British Secret Service."

"Perhaps so, but you'll appreciate our plan and London meeting agenda even better than he would. I'll make you an iced tea while you read them." Electra sauntered to the kitchen area, giving Alice time to revise. When she returned, Alice was busily penning comments.

"If you had been at Churchill's side during WWII, the whole world might now be waving the Union Jack. Let me summarize what we have.

"We'll name our adventure 'Operation White Rabbit.' The objective this time is to get you back into both Isilabad control centers to sweep up additional data for locating Trojan filters and any remaining terrorist cells. Once that's done, some on our team will tour a couple of the hardest hit population centers to assess T-Plague damage. And as always, I will introduce my committee on Monday to our plan and then bring you into the discussion on Tuesday. The rest of the week will be for selecting and training the team. We'll deploy as soon as ground support is in place. And when we get back to London, we'll recommend next steps for my committee to approve. Included among them are further ties with the Guardian Party." Electra teased, using a favorite British expression.

"I'm chuffed to bits. When are we leaving?"

"Tomorrow, so you'll have all day Saturday and Sunday to visit your relatives. And as before, we'll stay at my parent's home. You can meet my brother Henry."

"I'm sure Operation White Rabbit has other code names that I'll try to figure out. And I think I've figured out codename V2. It stands for the German World War II rocket, because you're blasting into Hassan's command centers. Am I right?"

"I'm afraid you are incorrect, so you will have to try again. You may need to apply the full Monty if you want to crack them all."

"Goodness, you look so different wearing a saree. You didn't tell me your relatives are of Indian extraction. That's the largest ethno-national group in London. I'm certain you will have a pleasant visit, but please be back early tomorrow evening so we can go over one last time what I'll present on Monday,"

"I will, and thanks for arranging a ride share. I'm off to Pimlico, so cheerio."

Electra was on her way to learn more about her mother's childhood from the only people left to tell the tale. In return, Electra would bring something that might bring back her grandmother: the "R-Vac," a vaccine that could reverse the neural entanglement causing T-Plague dementia. She had tested it for safety, but not for efficacy. Her grandmother would be the very first clinical trial, which must never be revealed.

Chandra greeted her at the door, smiling and bowing the traditional Hindu namaste. Electra responded in kind.

"We are glad you are visiting London again. Father and I have much to tell you."

"I am happy to be here. We have much to share, and I hope Grandmother is able to be with us." Chandra's expression was one of disappointment.

"Mother had a bad day yesterday, and it continues today. Her dementia cycles, and the trend is downward. But she will sit and listen. I am sure your presence will help her. Come into the living room." When they entered, Satish rose to greet her.

"You are lovelier than I remember. Please forgive an old man's failing memory, but your visits will make it stronger." Electra greeted her grandmother next, again using a customary bow. Madhuri smiled but showed no recognition. After everyone was seated, Chandra started talking in the customarily polite Hindi way. As soon as she found an opening, Electra redirected the conversation.

"I have something for Grandmother. But you and Grandfather must never reveal what it is. May I continue?"

"Yes, by all means."

"I have advanced medications that might help reverse some of Grandmother's dementia. It is a closely guarded secret that few know about. You do not need to know how I obtained it. I will give you enough to treat Grandmother. If they work, give thanks to karma. If they don't you're no worse off." Electra gave several bottles to Chandra and waited for him to speak.

"It is for the son to care for his parents. How shall I treat Mother?"

"Give Grandmother two caplets three times a day. If they are going to work, you will see improvement in one week. If they are working, continue the dosing regimen until the supply runs out. I am giving you a two months' supply, which will reverse as much of her dementia as possible. They might not bring Grandmother all the way back, but they should help her think more clearly."

"Should we start now?"

"Yes. And in return, and as soon as Grandmother is better, she must tell me her stories about Indira before she went to America." Satish grinned impishly.

"As so many of your movie characters say, this is an offer we cannot refuse. Come, let us have our meal and talk." Chandra started Mahduri's dosing regimen while Satish served a traditional Indian meal: Chicken Tikka Masala with seasoned jasmine rice and vegetables, served with naan bread. As they dined, Chandra described the meal. Electra enjoyed everything.

"This is the most flavorful chicken I've ever tasted. And I never knew cumin seeds could lower blood sugar levels. Do the seeds make Jal-Jeera taste like lemonade?"

"Yes. I buy all the ingredients, and Father often does the cooking, like he did today."

"Chandra is also a good cook. He took over much of the cooking when Mother became ill. Unlike his sister, he took no interest in cooking until he had to help us, but that is normal because even today the Indian culture doesn't encourage men to do domestic chores."

"Please tell me more about Mother's childhood."

"She never disobeyed or argued. She did some house chores but would occasionally become restless because she would rather study. Until perhaps a hundred years ago, Indian girls were encouraged to emphasize domestic aspects of their personality, but that never interested your mother. We raised her to be a professional woman of

Modernity. Chandra often wondered why she wanted to marry, but your father must have had what she wanted in a man." Chandra's sour expression mirrored the words he spoke.

"Please don't take offense at what I'm about to say. I never met your father, and he must have been a nice person if Indira liked him, but from social media photos and postings, he was not that good looking, and he could be abrasive." Electra nodded.

"Yes, but as all children do, I loved Father unconditionally. And although he didn't follow sports, he and Grandfather encouraged me to play soccer. From what I know, the Indian culture has never emphasized athletics. Was Mother good in sports?"

"She was a fine soccer player, but deliberately held back to keep from being controversial. And she didn't mind, because she excelled in school. And she got along with schoolmates, except for her brother." Chandra smiled sheepishly and waited for Satish to finish a story, then added one of his own.

"I am going to tell a story not even Father has heard. Yes, Indira and I fought as children. I was three years older and teased her, but she never retaliated. Unlike your mother, I was not much of an athlete, which didn't bother me because my friends weren't interested in sports either, and we were good students, though not as good as your mother. My friends would sometimes join me in picking on her but she could outrun us, so we didn't have many opportunities to use her as our punching bag. But there was one time we did, and that was the last time I ever picked on her. Here's the story." Chandra shifted closer to Electra while pausing briefly.

"She was a high school freshman and I a senior. She was playing soccer on a gravel playground with school friends when I and two of my friends—Amil and Zabar—spotted her and thought this would be our chance to corner her. Well we did, and the two of them started pushing her around, just joking at first, but when she didn't get mad my two friends started to push harder. She warned them not to get her angry, but they kept pushing. By this time a crowd of boys had gathered to watch. All the girls had run away. When Indira tried to run away Amil tripped her and then Zabar jumped on top of her, ripping the top of her uniform off before I could stop him. Later, he said it was an accident, but Indian boys often disrespected girls. Anyway, he started slapping your mother and trying to kiss her, and that's when your mother became a different creature, as if his slapping unleashed something in her brain. To this day, I still can see the look of rage in her eyes.

"Her body writhed as she threw Zabar off. Then she jumped on top and pummeled him with her fists. Somewhere she had seen professional fighters throw punches and she landed haymakers, beating him to a bloody pulp. But she wasn't finished. She jumped up screaming, looking for another victim. All the boys started running, but she was faster. She tripped Amil and jumped on top of him, punching and gouging his face. I pulled her off and she turned on me, but when she recognized me her rage drained away. She didn't say another word but ran home like lightning. Her knees and knuckles were badly skinned; she told our parents she had fallen playing soccer.

"She never talked to me about the episode, and I never brought it up. I never picked on her after that, and that was the last time I spoke to those fellows. But the boys who were there never forgot, and they nicknamed your mother Shiva, the Hindu god that's the destroyer of worlds. Father, do you recall anything remotely like this?" Satish shook his head no. Electra screamed to herself, *I know how Mother felt! It's frightening and thrilling and at times I crave it. I am my Mother's daughter.* Then she matter-of-factly said to Chandra,

"Well, it's no wonder everyone got along with Mother. It was for their own safety. Are there any classmates I could meet? I'd love to hear their stories." Chandra knew the answer.

"None in London, but I know some of them still live where we grew up. Perhaps someday you will travel with me to India. I think you would enjoy seeing where we grew up."

"That will be something you and Electra can look forward to. And now, why don't you show Electra the neighborhood while I clean up the dishes and tend to Mother. The weather is so nice today. Let us make the most of it."

Chandra knew Pimlico's history, explaining while they walked why Pimlico is known for its garden squares and Regency architecture—it was renovated early in the 19th century when George IV was Prince Regent.

"It's central London location is situated in the city of Westminster. We're bounded on the north by Victoria Station, Thames on the south, Vauxhall Bridge Road to the east and the former Grosvener Canal to the west. So convenient for our purposes." Electra was happily absorbing the sights and sounds. A couple of minutes later Chandra changed the subject.

"I'm relieved I finally told the fight story. I've always felt guilty, even after all these years, for letting the situation get out of hand. Telling Father and you is like seeking redemption."

"Yes, human nature isn't always rational. There's no tangible benefit for sharing this secret, but we all need to confirm that what's been done is OK, or is all forgiven, or is just an event from the past without serious repercussions. Man is a social animal, and only by relating to others is he completely fulfilled." Chandra whimsical expression matched his words.

"You are indeed Indira's daughter. I hear her thoughts in your words."

Conversation continued through the evening, and Sunday morning Chandra took Electra to the Tate Gallery, serving once again as tour guide.

"There are actually four Tate Museums: Britain, Liverpool, St. Ives, and Modern. They house the U.K's national collection of British art, as well as its collection of international modern and contemporary art. I picked Tate Britain for today because it houses the Turner collection. Turner is Britain's preeminent landscapist of the Romantic Period, and he is generally regarded as the artist who elevated landscape painting to an eminence rivalling historical painting. He's noted for both oil and watercolor, and he is commonly referred to as the painter of light, whose Romantic paintings prefaced Impressionism. Let us wander through the galleries wherever you choose. I have said all that's needed, so ask me a question when you want me to continue."

Electra marveled at the artistic genius radiating from the paintings, coming face to face with the difference between cognitive and artistic creativity.

"Was Mother gifted in the arts?"

"Until you read me her poetry, I would say no. Neither of us liked practicing the piano, so lessons stopped after three years, but I had a better ear for music. And she couldn't draw a stick figure you'd recognize. My art teachers said I had ability, had a knack for landscapes, but I never pursued it. Maybe I will when I get older, just like your mother said she'd do with poetry." Electra frowned, feeling obligated to correct her uncle.

"No, Mother wrote poetry until the time of her death. What she said was she'd think about publishing when she got old. If you want to have painting as a hobby, you should start as soon as you can fit it in. If Grandmother responds to the drugs, you might have more time. And I hope she does, for all our sakes. She could tell me so much more about Indira. I never understood until meeting my grandparents and you why people are so interested in knowing their family history and relatives. It gives us a textured feeling for the fabric of our lives and ourselves."

"You really are the daughter of Indira. If I close my eyes, I can picture my sister talking. Come, let us have tea and biscuits at the Djanogly Café, located on the lower level. I shall treat, and you shall find the tea and cakes lovely. And I cannot begrudge the prices because the museum is free."

"I have been studying economics, and you really are an economist. Your last sentence fits you to a T. And I'll have the tea you recommend instead of a Coke."

"You are indeed quick-witted and pleasant. No wonder the time has ticked away. I must drive you to your friend's house after our pause. And please remember to call me when you return so I can report how Mother is doing…"

"Welcome back, my dear. You're right on time. We'll have a light supper as soon as you're ready."

"I'll change for supper, and I'm hungry. We must have walked a couple of miles at the Tate Gallery."

"Now you probably now know more about England's best-loved painter than most Americans ever will. And do you know who is our best-loved composer?"

"You've stumped me again. Who is it?"

"Why, it's Sir Edward Elgar. Now go freshen up."

Afterwards, the partners reviewed tomorrow's agenda and script. Alice insisted that Electra attend, even though she would be only an observer.

"A good negotiator always reconnoiters the terrain. I'll soften up the committee tomorrow, and you can close them on Tuesday."

"That sounds like a plan. I'll be ready…"

The committee's skepticism was less this time than last, but they did present what Alice termed later a "typically British indifferent air" during opening remarks, after which the chairperson turned the meeting over to Alice.

"Thank you for your kind welcome. I am here today to get your approval for Operation White Rabbit, which builds on the success of Operation Holy Grail. By the time I'm finished, I believe you'll understand why you must give it a go.

"My talk today has two parts. In the first, I'll outline the political background that supports our plan. In the second, I'll outline the plan. And tomorrow, my associate, Electra, will extend the political background and give plan details. Assuming you approve, the rest of the week will be for selecting and training our team, and for coordinating ground support so we can be inserted early next week and extracted no later than Friday.

"We often ignore political background issues when planning our operations because it seems so obvious. But in crisis situations like now, we must have a firm grip on what we're dealing with. So, I'll quickly take you through relevant background.

"I'll start at the beginning—the Golden Age of Greece. Aristotle identified six forms of government. Three he labeled good: Monarchy, Aristocracy, Republic. Three he labeled bad: Tyranny, Oligarchy, Democracy. This classification served well until modern times when a seventh form was added: Theocracy, which has no separation between Church and State. We must pay attention because Isilabad is an Islamic theocracy based on holy law as opposed to Christianity, which is faith based. As a result, Isilabad is dogmatic and inflexible, so it's no wonder they refuse to accept Modernity. Reasoning or appeasement has earned us nothing in return. "Kinder and Gentler" is not the way to deal with them. We must eliminate terrorism by aggressively confronting Islam. And Isilabad has helped us because many of their key leaders have contracted the T-Plague. Iran and Isilabad have unleashed T-Plague in each other's capitals. So, any operation we conduct in Isilabad should meet little resistance.

"The United States and Britain are experiencing random T-Plague outbreaks, which suggests Hassan Wassani started an 'Apocalypse Clock' before we could neutralize him. What does this mean? It means Trojan filters at pre-programmed locations and times will automatically spew undetected T-Plague virus into air or water. The data we found on our previous raid didn't tell us where the clock is ticking, or what its pre-programming is targeting. So, Operation White Rabbit will make an exhaustive search through both of Hassan's command center computer networks to find that data.

"For obvious reasons, attacks launched by terrorist cells are no longer coordinated by Hassan. We fear remaining cells will start operating in desperation on their own, so we will look for more terrorist cell location data when we search the network. It's possible none of the data we are looking for is stored electronically, which means searching manually through hard copy files will need to be done, but just where we do not know. We hope to find out when searching the command centers." Alice paused briefly, then continued.

"Let me turn to another tactic. Both Iran and Isilabad have asked the United Nations for humanitarian aid. They need smart pills to help their T-Plague victims. Operation White Rabbit will make a preliminary assessment of how far and fast the outbreak has spread in Isilabad's capital city, to get a better estimate of how many smart pills are needed. This becomes a sticky wicket because their pipeline is nearly empty, and who knows if the underground economy supply is safe, let alone effective. But we shall do our best.

"And that concludes my planned remarks, so what we should do next is hold a roundtable Q&A. I suggest a ten-minute break first. Grim faces agreed.

When reconvening, Electra gave the Committee high marks for perseverance as some asked for wide-ranging details.

"I understand where Isilabad fits in Aristotle's framework, but what about America and Britain?" Alice fielded that one effortlessly.

"Excellent question. Political systems in those countries modified Aristotle's Republic to account for the Rational Economic Man and the Industrial Revolution. Great minds, such as James Harrington and John Locke, Adom Ferguson and Montesque provided the insights that let the framers of the U.S. Constitution balance freedom and equality while providing incentives for the Colonies to pull together. It's an exceptional accomplishment, and Alexis de Tocqueville's *Democracy in America* chronicles from firsthand visits in the 1830's why it works for America."

"Why can't Isilabad figure out they're going against history's arrow? No one wants to go back to the Dark Ages."

"Another excellent question. And to answer that, we need to consider Islam's stated worldview. It is very difficult to understand their point of view unless we understand their culture. The people we label terrorists are often considered Isilabad's heroes or martyrs who are willing to die for the honor of upholding religious beliefs that permeate its government. Remember, Islam has no separation between Church and State. They accept the Koran as their holy law. Modernity has no place in it."

"Seems like an insoluble dilemma. What do you propose?" Alice laughed heartily.

"If I had the solution I'd be living at Ten Downing Street. Eventually we must convert the dilemma to a trilemma. We must find some acceptable middle ground. Short term that will mean America—and Britain too—must be more assertive, and as my remarks earlier concluded, we'll be able to push for what we want. Longer term is still a muddle." As the questions dwindled, Alice recommended they adjourn, reminding the committee that Electra's talk tomorrow would give more background supporting the plan. There was no talk as people filed out. Only Electra was smiling.

"You were spot on. Our script preparation paid off." A touch of fatigue showed through Alice's smile.

"Yes, but I'm a bit knackered. My people don't muck about. They get right to the point and keep going. Do you want me to help you rehearse more for tomorrow?"

"No, I'm as prepared as possible. Tomorrow, you can sit back and watch the show. And let's bring home fish and chips after you check your Email."

Dinner followed by a good night's sleep at home made Alice ready for day two. Her boss gave opening remarks, and then, peering over the top of his reading glasses, he directed his comments towards Electra.

"Young lady, you were helpful last time. The tutorial yesterday conducted by Alice has refreshed our understanding of civics, and she has promised you would tell us the details of White Rabbit. The floor is yours."

The audio-visual technician adjusted the lights and queued Electra's first slide.

Operation White Rabbit

- Needed to complete Operation Holy Grail
- Thwart the Apocalypse Clock
- Prepare for "smart pill" demand
- Interdict remaining terrorist cells
- Keep Guardian Party under control

"Good morning, and thank you for inviting me back. I realize how unusual it is for you to include me, but these are most unusual times and I'm glad your organization is up to the challenge.

"You know the results Holy Grail achieved. We made great strides identifying Trojan filters and terrorist cell locations, but there's more data we need if we want to eliminate them all. And we'll get if I can hack further into Hassan's command center networks.

"Hassan may have triggered an Apocalypse Clock, a pre-programmed computer app that activates selected filters at specified times. It's a retaliation for our putting him and his covert R&D out of action. We need to find the clock and turn it off. And since there's no central coordination for remaining terrorist cells, we have to roll them up before they roll out last-ditch attacks. All this should be clear and need no further explanation. But there's another issue: keeping the Guardian Party under control. It is the most problematic issue long-term. So, let me build on Alice's talk from yesterday." Electra advanced to the next slide.

Political Development Occurs Among these Interactions

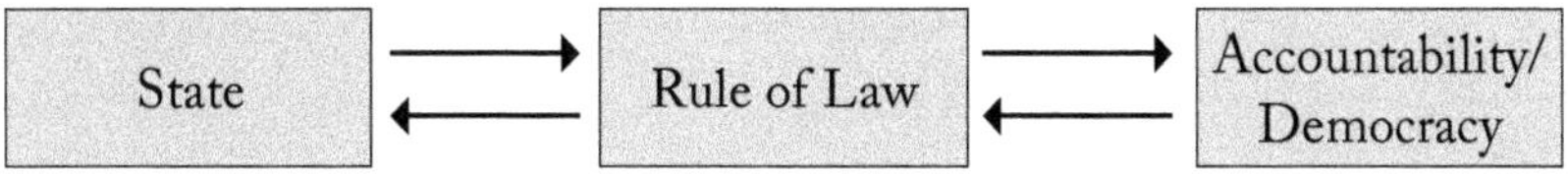

"I'm using a framework that illustrates how political order develops, but it also shows how political decay creeps in. It was developed by the political philosopher Francis Fukuyama, who extended Samuel Huntington's *Clash of Civilizations*, written just after the collapse of the Soviet Union in the late 1980's. What we have today is a centuries' long clash between Christianity and Islam. Early on—going back to Hegel in the 19th century—there was an optimistic belief that the end of history would be liberal democracy. But that's not necessarily the case because political development is the result of interactions among the boxes shown. Look at the next slide."

Dimensions of Development

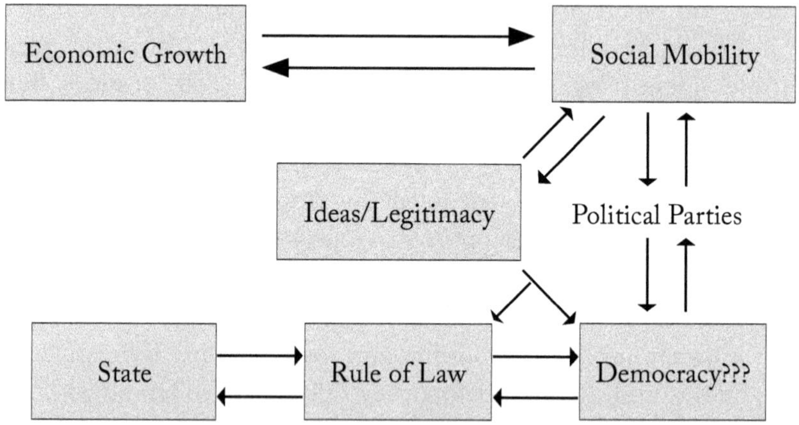

"Notice the question marks next to Democracy. Political development doesn't always trace a path to democracy. Witness how long it took for the Soviet Union to collapse. Consider how long North Korea has survived. Once a political party becomes entrenched, it can control the dimensions of development to stay in power. And a Theocracy like Isilabad can remain in power long after it no longer makes rational sense for it to rule. We can use this diagram to explain political decay. As conditions change in each of the boxes, the interactions among the dimensions change as well. What does this mean? A country must be ever watchful for changing conditions that disrupt desirable political organizations.

If the public gets fat, dumb, and lazy, you end up with a government not of the people, but a government controlling the people.

"In the short-term, we must be sensitive to what Isilabad needs in order to move towards democracy and Modernity. The U.S. government administrations were too obtuse, too arrogant during the Iraq wars in the late 20th century to understand the implications of their actions. They didn't even have contingency plans. We must be smarter today.

"And that brings me to the Guardian Party. They have tapped into a mean-spirited sentiment captured by one of their taglines: Harsh Times demand Harsh Measures. And so far, they have delivered results the American people demand. And the party doesn't appear to have a power grabbing hidden agenda. Before they came to power there were conspiracy theories, but what came out was an agenda pushing for what the public wanted, even if the Guardians had to stretch the truth. But let's never forget Lord Acton's quote:

> 'Power tends to corrupt, and absolute power corrupts absolutely.
>
> Great men are almost always bad men.'

"This innate human predisposition has been confirmed in numerous laboratory tests, and unfortunately the lab we're using to test the Guardian Party is Washington. Very dangerous. But it's too soon to tell how well the Guardian Party can resist temptation. And this is where the T-Plague figures in. The prerequisites for a liberal democracy include: a smart public willing to play an active role in government, a strong middle class that fosters opportunity for social mobility, a public that believes in capitalism and free enterprise, one that doesn't want the government meddling in their lives. The T-Plague has severely damaged America in all these areas. And if America falls further, the rest of the world will be dragged down. So far, the steps the Guardian Party are taking seem to be working. That's why the public loves Jared Gardner.

"I'm sure you've listened to his speeches. Excellent communicator; very charismatic. He's not a political rocket scientist, but so far his instincts have resisted some of the harsh recommendations made by his aggressive lieutenants. But we need to have an insider's view, and Alice has started assembling a group of Guardian Party influentials to help us do just that." *I'm losing them. Let's break.*

"So there you have it: a broad framework that supports Operation White Rabbit. And after a short break, I'll go into plan details. Any questions before then?"

"How did you come up with the name "Operation White Rabbit?" Electra grinned. "That is best answered by Miss Alice..."

Electra kept an upbeat tempo when the meeting resumed.

"Now you know how Miss Alice selected codenames from *Alice in Wonderland*, a wonderful choice because in some respects we are tumbling down a rabbit hole. But we're on our feet, moving in the right direction.

"Our first step is to assemble a team, and Alice will recruit from our previous mission. Once we're deployed, we go to the command center we penetrated last time. The objective: for me search for more data. If I can't find it there, we go to the mirror command center. Once I obtain the data, some of the team will do a triage of the cities suffering the worst T-Plague outbreaks. Then, we return to London.

"Alice will brief appropriate intelligence departments to implement the next steps: ferreting out remaining Trojan filters and terrorist cells, sharing information among allies, coordinating smart pill pipelines, and refilling them. And let Alice build a Guardian Party Insiders Group. Any questions before we open up a roundtable Q&A?" One of the members hesitantly raised his hand.

"Can you tell us more about the Apocalypse Clock?"

"No, I don't have enough information. But the name is an analogy to the Book of Revelation's Four Horsemen of the Apocalypse, which signify war, famine, death, and disease. I think it's time for Miss Alice to lead the way."

Alice handled the rest of the session, adding a warning.

"Our mission should pose fewer risks than before, but let's not think it will be a milk run. Even though we'll hope for the best, we shall plan for the worst. Rest assured that my associate and I will be most thorough."

Alice assembled next day the entire Holy Grail team, asking them to self-select a team of six to fill the roles of chopper pilot, driver, and four-man support team accompanying Electra. A contingency team consisting of pilot and four-man support would also be selected. That team would also assess how fast and far T-Plague had spread. Alice gave additional details after the teams had been determined.

"Jolly good to have you with us. Operation White Rabbit will take us back to Isilabad so Electra—I mean Crutches—can hack into both command centers for additional data we need. We are still covert, but this time we will wear our black commando gear. And the staging area will be the same as last time. We will plan for contingencies in case resistance is stiffer than our intelligence indicates. After we get the data, we'll do a T-Plague triage on the capital. You know your assignments, so plan, prepare, and practice between now and our Friday status meeting. We depart two a.m. Saturday. Please remember your codenames when communicating: I am Alice; Electra is Crutches; pilots are Pigeon 1 and Pigeon 2; team leaders are Dormouse 1 and Dormouse 2; team members are Mouse followed by the first letter of first name. And finally, please remember that we are playing a serious game, so make sure you have your game faces on when we land."

The rest of the week ticked by like clockwork, as did departure and insertion, so the entire operation bivouacked at their desert location by Sunday morning. Unlike last time, midday temperatures would be ninety-plus, and command centers would be oppressively hot if they had been abandoned. The team decided that late Sunday evening would be best for their visit to the first command center.

The drive this time was not déjà vu because there was no hint of resistance, and when they arrived there was only a skeleton guard assigned to prevent looting from the now deserted facility.

Dormouse 1 had no trouble convincing the guards to let them in; they told him electrical power was intermittent; temperature might exceed one hundred and fifteen degrees, so take plenty of water and backup lighting. Ten minutes later Electra perched in front of an array of computers and monitors, much like Hassan had done so many times before. *Lucky for me Hassan was so smug. He was certain his command centers were off limits to all but his people. That must be why network security is so simple.* His systems didn't use voice or optical recognition; she powered up and logged on using his Supervisor I.D. and password she had "teased" out of him on her previous visit, and now had complete access to all his networks and gateways into Cyberspace. There were too many directories and apps for even the lightning brain to sort through before the heat would force them to leave. *If I were Hassan, I would make the command centers mirror images as much as possible. Any differences would be my critical backup files, so let's look for them.* Electra logged on remotely to the other command center and ran file matching routines to identify unduplicated files. For the next two hours she scanned the local network. *Damn, nothing. I need to scan the other center.* But before she started, Mouse S—aka Simon—yanked her out of the room.

"It's too hot to keep working. We've got to get out of here." And then the lights went out. Simon flipped on his flashlight and led everyone out. Electra, soaked in sweat and beginning to feel lightheaded, had been so absorbed in her work she didn't notice a temperature approaching one hundred ten degrees. The team retreated to the desert personnel carrier, guzzling water and stripping off protective gear while joking.

"Now Crutches, don't be shocked by a naked male torso. Just think of people as naked apes who occasionally wear clothes."

"Not a problem for me. Just don't let your willy get the willies." After the kidding, Electra told them what they needed to do next.

"I struck out. Didn't get any data, so we need to go to the other center. Let's go back to base camp and have Alice confirm with our ground assets we're good to go tomorrow morning."

Back at base camp, Electra marveled at the fortitude of soldiers from previous generations. *Compared to WW1 and 2, modern warfare is a camping trip. Previous warrior generations had to survive at the front line for weeks on end* She and her team decompressed at a meal, then napped in preparation for tomorrow's early morning sortie, but while resting, the lightning brain considered the best search options. *I remember a telltale phrase Hassan blurted to his sons: And always remember: if Allah calls me you must return to the holy shrine to retrieve our IT Manifesto. The creation of the two Muhammads will reveal the secrets which you must always keep."*

Maybe the shrine is a physical location, not a place in Cyberspace. And perhaps the IT Manifesto is hard copy, not bits and bytes. Even I need hard copy backup. My temporary amnesia two years ago proved that. Maybe IT stands for Information Technology. I'll have to think like Hassan to decipher his phrase. Something will trigger in my brain when I continue the search tomorrow.

The team reached the second command center at first light; it too was lightly guarded and abandoned so the team gained access immediately. Command centers had identical layouts, and Electra was in action even faster because she had cooler temperatures and better lighting.

Electra knew all the nuances of SQL—standard query language—in addition to all Unix-based search extension languages. Even "Nth generation" computer languages shared much in common with techniques developed by its Unix founding fathers. She found the mother lode after two hours of intense searching: a promising directory containing ten files referencing all the keywords she was hunting for. She yelled to her partner,

"I've got what I need. Let's go back to base camp."

Electra spent the rest of the day picking through the encrypted files, refusing to give any hint of progress until she was certain of what she had. Alice instructed everyone to steer clear, knowing Electra's powers of concentration worked best in isolation. Late that afternoon she summarized to herself after rereading her report.

Hassan's sophistication and thoroughness are extraordinary. Now I know what he and his three sons were up to. "IT" stands for Islam Transformation, a metamorphosis that would take at least a generation or two to unfold. Hassan would be Mohammad's true successor, adapting Islam to Modernity. He didn't want his followers living in the Dark Ages.

And his IT Manifesto must contain the details to make it so. After turning technology and T-Plague against the West, he must have a series of social and religious programs to move away from Theocracy and achieve an alliance with Christianity and a secular world. He has to wean his followers from reliance on faith and holy law, and his sons are supposed to carry on. That's why he built a burial tomb. It's a holy shrine for ritualizing the process. I have to find the Manifesto. Hassan's phrase flashed in the lightning brain. *It has to be hidden in the tomb. Tomorrow, we shall be modern-day tomb raiders.* Electra ran to tell Alice the plan.

"We have to break into Hassan's burial tomb before sunrise. It contains the rest of the info I need. Have your support people tell us what we need, and then tell our team to get the gear."

"Dear me, I hope this doesn't get out of hand. Good thing we have backup. I shall contact support immediately."

A blazing rising sun in a cloudless sky greeted the team as they approached the shrine. And as Alice had predicted, there were no guards. The team made quick work of the door locks; soon Electra and Simon were standing at the vault area while the other teamers stood at the entrance. A three-day power outage made the place pitch black and suffocatingly hot. Already drenched in sweat, Simon asked for orders.

"Which vault do we search first?"

"Hassan's wife, because she's the connection between the Virgin Mary and the Holy Grail. Hassan intended his sons to carry on his work, so their mother's vault has to contain what they need. Drill out the lock and then stand back while I open it." Simon finished twenty minutes later.

"OK, now stand back. I know what to look for." Simon retreated to the vault entrance.

"Hold on to your butt." Electra beamed her flashlight on the vault door before delicately prying it open. Just before she screamed, she heard a click followed by a hissing sound and dull explosion that dropped a thick metal door, trapping her inside the vault.

"Crutches! Can you hear me?" Simon banged away but there was no answer. "I'm going for backup. We'll get you out." Simon ran for the exit.

"We've got a situation! The vault's booby trapped and Crutches is trapped inside." The team ran back, power lights piercing total darkness while they pounded again and again, hoping to stir a response, but none came. Simon spoke as they huddled after groping for some way to break through.

"All we have are plastic explosives, but we'll kill Crutches if we try to blast through. We need a laser cutter." They ran to their vehicle, yelling instructions to call Alice.

"This is Dormouse 1. Crutches trapped inside vault by a metal door. Condition unknown. Need a laser cutter. And it's bloody hot as hell. Copy that?"

"I copy. Will call Ground Support and report back laser ETA. Over." Then she radioed for help.

"Ground Support, this is Alice. We need laser cutter delivered to holy shrine ASAP to free team member trapped behind metal door. What is delivery ETA? Copy that?"

"This is Ground Support. We copy. Will locate closest laser cutter and report back ETA as soon as chopper on the way. Copy that?"

"Copy that. Over." Alice alerted the team, then slumped in her chair. There was nothing she could do except fight waves of panic and wait for Ground Support's call. Time ground to a halt for poor Alice.

Electra came to with a terrible headache but aware of the situation. She had spotted the countdown timer but couldn't disarm the knockout gas canister before it discharged, plunging her into oblivion for fifteen minutes. Her power light switch must have toggled off when she collapsed, and it took her a couple of minutes crawling in darkness to retrieve it. She wobbled to her feet and stood in place, trying to center herself as the lightning brain struggled to clear itself. Electra methodically paced the room.

My fate is sealed like the door. I'll die if my team can't get in soon. Damn, I didn't bring my water bottle, and I'm sweating like the proverbial pig. Well, let's see what the prize in the vault looks like. I hope it's worth the price of admission.

Electra peered into the vault, removing an oversized briefcase locked by two six position sets of rotary number locks. *No doubt booby trapped, so I'll play with it later. The temperature's rising and the oxygen's falling. I better get in a low energy state.* She stripped naked, forming a pillow out of her clothes, then lay on the floor. *It's time to take a nap.* A soothing calmness enveloped her as consciousness faded.

"This is Ground Support. ETA in thirty minutes. Do you copy?"

"Copy that. Over." Alice had been sitting in a trance-like state for two hours until the call jolted her, and the follow-up math she did caused another. *She'll be in that suffocating tomb for three hours before her team can begin cutting her out. There's nothing else we can do. Lord help her.* After relaying the report, Alice simply stared at the clock.

Finally, Electra's team had what they needed. Two teamers rushed the laser cutter into the shrine, accompanied by two more leading the dash, power lights blazing. They needed to cut an opening large enough for one person to crawl in and then drag out precious cargo. Simon crawled in fifteen minutes later and spotted what he wanted. He wrapped clothes around Electra's comatose body to prevent scraping, then shoved her through the opening. Words weren't needed; the team raced her out. Simon also found a briefcase, shoved it through the opening, then crawled through and dashed for the exit.

Those awaiting gaped as one of their team emerged, using a fireman's carry to secure Electra, whose arms and legs dangling like those of a rubber manikin, head bobbing like a short-amplitude pendulum. They placed her naked body on a blanket, then packed her in ice and poured water on the pile, hoping for a response. There was none. They hooked up an IV for rehydration and electrodes to measure vital signs. Her signs flat-lined the dials, and her body temperature pinned the thermometer at 110 degrees. Their only hope was that sweating had kept her body temperature below the death line. The team loaded the choppers and roared vertical before reporting.

"This is Dormouse 1. We're airborne. ETA to stable is fifteen minutes. Crutches and Holy grail extracted. Vitals flat-lined. Do you copy?"

"Copy that. Over." Alice had nothing left to say.

Only once—when terrorists nearly choked her to death—had Electra's lightning brain used its reptilian limbic system to enter suspended animation. The scientific term is brumation, a physical state that reptiles use to survive extreme conditions. The lightning brain had abilities far beyond those of reptiles, and it had used brumation to survive. And now that it had done so, it reawakened consciousness. Electra's eyes fluttered open and as she gasped for air, she saw a collection of wide-eyed teammates welcoming her back among the living.

"Christ on a crutch! Crutches just came to. Radio Alice."

"Crutches, can you talk? Say something." She did her best to rasp.

"You guys are the greatest. And I'll love you even more if you give me water."

Alice checked with Electra before lights out that evening. *My mentor warned never become emotionally attached to the troops you command, for it will compromise your ability to lead. I shall never place Electra in jeopardy again. She means too much to me, but no need to advertise my feelings.*

"Well my dear, you gave us a bit of a fright, but nice to see you up and about tonight. How do you feel?"

"Better, and a good night's sleep will put me back in the game."

"Yes, and your assignment tomorrow is to continue working through all the data and to crack into the briefcase. Meanwhile, we'll have a team conduct a T-Plague assessment. And at daybreak, day after tomorrow, we depart for London. So, get a good night's rest and get cracking when you get up." After she left, Electra listened to Alice's body language.

She's drained from the strain, and I'm to blame. Just like the hired guns in the epic "Magnificent Seven" movie, her emotions are getting in the way. She and I must be careful. I don't want attachments curtailing my actions. It's not a problem now, so I'll tuck it away for another day.

Next morning, after ferreting out all remaining data from the encrypted files, Electra sat back, trying to conjure the briefcase lock combinations. *Let's think like Hassan. Combos must be associated with something in his statement: If Allah calls me you must return to the holy shrine to retrieve our IT Manifesto. The creation of the two Muhammads will reveal the secrets which you must always keep. Hmm... Allah calls me might refer to Hassan's death. Holy shrine is the burial tomb. IT is Islam Transformation. That leaves only creation of the two Muhammads. What could that be?* The answer flashed into her consciousness. *It has to be related to their birth dates.*

Electra furiously searched the Internet for Muhammad's birth date: the year 570. Then for Hassan Wassani's: December 2077. *Maybe each set of six digits is some permutation of birth year and month. Hassan would have made them easy to remember, perhaps MMYYYY or YYYYMM". I'll try these numeric combinations first before including unknown day-of-month choices.*

Electra put on protective clothing, then hiked into the surrounding desert to find a secluded location before trying her luck. *Fool me once, shame on you; fool me twice, shame on me. It might be boobytrapped.* She found an unobservable spot that would also protect her from an accidental detonation, so she returned with the briefcase and methodically started dialing through all permutations.

Her twenty-fifth pick worked; the locks clicked open when she used 057012 for the left lock (Muhammad) and 207712 for the right. Electra rushed back inside to study the treasure.

The briefcase contained everything she wanted: Hassan's handwritten log of chronological changes, a printout of all Trojan filter locations, another for terrorist cells, instructions and locations for the Apocalypse Clock apps; a printed copy of the IT Manifesto. Operation White Rabbit had found its holy grail.

Electra silently screamed *"Eureka,"* fighting a natural urge to share her discovery. But she knew better. *Study thoroughly, draw conclusions, and then announce only what Alice needs.* She forced herself to take a break, walking outside under the shade of lattice-supported awnings. The desert shimmered in sun-drenched mirages, hot, dessicated winds stirring up sun devils and sand; its ambiance unexpectedly invigorating. Then she came in to the cool of the trailer for a Coke and snack to fortify herself for the remainder of the day as she immersed herself in the holy grail.

By early evening she had completed unraveled its contents, bringing with it a shudder of fear. *I'm like Jimmy Stewart in his 1956 classic, "The Man Who Knew Too Much," but in this game, I'm the girl who knows too much. And the biggest prize is knowing where and how the Apocalypse Clock works. It's worth a fortune, and if any organization finds out I know, I'll be a target. What's the quote by Francis Bacon? "Knowledge is power, " and I'm holding it. Hassan did too.*

He and Isilabad are much more advanced technologically than the West realizes. But he could let only his sons know because his followers are not prepared to march into Modernity. They would turn against him if they found out where he was taking them. A quiver of remorse jolted the lightning brain. *Hassan was brilliant. I must pay my respects to his accomplishments as I focus on his Apocalypse Clock.* Three hours later, Electra reported back to herself.

Hassan's Apocalypse Clock is brilliantly devious and subtle. It is not centralized on Hassan's computers. Instead, it is a redundantly distributed and mirrored application running covertly on multiple secured networks belonging to target governments, prominent among them are the United States, Britain, France and Germany. Why them? Because they are the leaders of the West, and clocks are hidden inside their systems. Electra thought back to 911 and Osama bin Laden. *Where was he hiding? Thirty miles from Islamabad in Pakistan, right in plain sight. And there's more.*

The clocks use encrypted, distributed files controlling where and when to unleash the thousands of Trojan filters now in place. Only Hassan—or his sons if they had the briefcase—would know how to reset the files. He could set all launch dates to any value he wished, then manually reset whichever filters he wanted to unleash at different times. As long as the launch dates are in the future, the world is safe. But now, for the devious twists.

If anyone tries hacking into any of the clocks, the launch dates will automatically reset to one month from whenever hacking is attempted. The same applies if any so-called computer guru tries to delete or deactivate just one of the clocks. The Apocalypse Clock is immortal. Even if you shut down and reboot all computer systems worldwide, the clocks will reboot when the systems are brought back up unless someone knows how to delete all Clock apps and files.

How ironic. I've spent my life keeping my freakish brain a secret. Today, no one will hunt me down because of what I am. No one knows about my extraordinary brain. But now they'll hunt me down for what I know if I tell anyone. So, what should I do?

I will relock the briefcase, putting inside blank papers and the booby trap. I will keep all the contents for myself. Suddenly, a tidal wave of empathy washed over her.

Hassan was not evil! To his people, his sons, and himself, he was a keeper of his faith. And by mere mortal standards, he was brilliant. A different time, a different place, we might have been friends. But I have done what I had to. Electra's pang of remorse receded as quickly as it had rushed in.

Alice checked with Electra as she made the rounds that evening.

"My dear, you have been quiet as a mouse all day. You look dejected."

"I've made some progress, but it's slow going. I've found so many files to sort through. And I can't touch the briefcase until I figure out its combination. I'll need to take it home and continue studying it."

"Well buck up, my dear. I'm sure you'll help me prepare a fine report and plan we can use going forward. I'll present an overview in the morning, and details in the afternoon. Electra smiled wearily. She knew Alice could be trusted, but she could never tell her much. Ever. Her life depended on it.

"Sounds like a plan. When do we leave?"

"Tomorrow at dawn. Our teams have completed a T-Plague assessment, and it is startling. Thirty percent of the population has been infected in some districts. It is a humanitarian crisis of biblical proportions. But, that will be taken care of by others, not us. Now come, please join us for a midnight meal. Then we'll finish packing…"

"Good work Alice, and if I may, I should like to summarize what you have told us. Operation White Rabbit came back with enough information so we can identify some of the remaining terrorist cells in America and Britain. And we now have a count of Trojan filters in several major cities, but not locations. Nothing indicates a Trojan attack is immanent, but we must monitor chatter via counter-intelligence. And no details yet on the Apocalypse Clock, other than it does exist in an unknown location. Finally, you told about an Islam Transformation Manifesto that suggests Isilabad might consider negotiating an end to Islam-Christianity hostilities. Am I on point so far?"

"Yes, spot-on."

"Well, proceeding to Middle East T-Plague outbreaks, it looks like a dire humanitarian crisis. We shall inform the United Nations. And now, we come to the most perplexing development. You retrieved a briefcase that might contain additional data to help us unravel even more of Hassan's scheme. But you've not been able to crack into it. More to follow regarding this when you present more details this afternoon. Well then, let's adjourn for lunch. Why don't the two of you join me?" Alice accepted.

The soft-lighted oak-paneled dining room added to a confidential ambiance conducive to sharing delicate subjects, and the conversation began on safe ground.

"Alice tells me you enjoy British cuisine. I think you'll find our fish and chips to your liking. As for me, I believe I'll have the pork pie. Alice, how do you rate our chef?"

"Top shelf, like the way we run all our activities. Our agencies have impressed Electra. We seem to be holding up better than our counterparts in America. What would you add, my dear?"

"Perhaps the Guardian Party can turn that around." The Chairman skillfully led the conversation into darker matters.

"Your working for us is most irregular, and if not for these—how does your Guardian party label them—harsh times it would never happen. Alice will have to determine when to use official channels rather than you and back doors. She has found contacts that will help mend fences. And that brings me to the briefcase. We have a better shot at cracking into it, so let me be perfectly frank. We must keep it, and we will share with Alice what we uncover." Electra had little to say.

"I understand your concern. I'm just a person thrust by odd circumstances into a situation I'm not really qualified to handle."

"Yes, how odd you know so much, but it's all coincidental. I'm glad it's settled. Alice can mention it this afternoon."

The Chairman summarized what Alice had presented so he could conclude the meeting.

"Now we know what's in store. Our chaps will crack into the briefcase and share what we find. And we can provide humanitarian aid as a carrot for Isilabad to negotiate. And Alice will be our liaison to the Guardian Party. So, as some from the older generation are fond of saying, that is a wrap." Electra added a postscript intended for her ears only.

If the Chairman knew what the briefcase contains, he would have borrowed Churchill's words to describe the surprise: It is a riddle, wrapped in a mystery, inside an enigma. As am I for Alice's London masters. I'm happy to say goodbye.

Electra had one more meeting to attend before flying home.

"My ride-share is here. I'll be back in time to pack up and leave for my flight back to Washington."

"Very good, my dear. I do hope you have a nice good-bye chat with your relatives. You can sleep on the flight home, and remember, it leaves at midnight."

As the car reached its destination, Electra sensed the importance of this visit. *I have no idea when I'll come back to London. I'll be surprised if it happens this year, but next year is a possibility. The story's not yet told.*

The best part of the trip greeted Electra when Chandra opened the door. Madhuri sat next to him in her wheelchair, eyes brighter and mind sharper. She reached for Electra's hand.

"You have completed the eternal circle. As I gave life to your Mother and she to you, so have you to me by bringing my mind back from darkness." Chandra ushered everyone into the living room for a long day's conversation into late afternoon.

"Satish and Chandra have told you stories, and now I shall do the same. What would you like to know?"

"Did Mother's girlfriends always consider her a leader? And did she like to dress up?"

"There was an event early in high school that propelled your mother into a leadership role, but she never discussed it. Indira was always modest, but afterwards she expressed her leadership instincts. And as for clothes, Indira liked to look good but not conspicuous; she wanted her appearance to be appropriate. And she could be feminine when she wanted. But she also had masculine traits; she could have excelled in sports if Indian culture then had allowed women to participate more."

Madhuri answered more questions until Electra sensed she was beginning to tire. Satish brought in refreshments, and Chandra kept track of time as the hours danced into late afternoon. All too soon Electra's ride-share arrived; Chandra handled farewells.

"Your visit has been good for all of us. It has put me in touch with feelings I should have explored long ago. I hope you return, and I would like to arrange for you to travel to India with me." Satish brought Madhuri to the front door for a final goodbye.

"I have another present for you, another neck bracelet amulet. The first one was for protection against evil, and we had it placed on a black neck choker. This one is for long life, and we chose red velvet. That color is so elegant and will highlight your features. You are mature beyond your years."

"I will treasure it always, and Chandra and I will correspond on the Internet. He will let me know if you need more medicine." Satish first, and then Chandra hugged their guest just before she hurried out to the awaiting ride. Two hours later Alice and Electra repeated the farewell.

"Have a safe flight back, my dear. I will call you when I return so we can continue our game."

"We accomplished our mission. Our next step is to keep the game going in our favor."

The eight-hour flight provided a restful cushion for the lightning brain to ponder all that had happened. The suffused cabin lighting and the serenely glowing mid-Atlantic moon complemented the muted sibilance of the engines, constructing an insulated space that suspended Electra in the moment. Having no immediate worries, she drifted to sleep, certain that when she awakens she would know where next to go because all the while the lightning brain was in control. Electra slept all the way home.

CHAPTER 21

May 2120

"Back to the Lone Star State"

(Thread 1 Chapter 10)

"YOU BET, LITTLE LADY. We'll have our plane at Dulles Airport tomorrow morning. And don't you worry about any travel snafus. Private terminals are the last to be affected."

"Thanks. The last time I flew, Dulles had long security check-in for domestic flights. I'm happy you're in control of my air travel."

"And I'm happy you're in control of the meeting. I've looked over the agenda and I know who to invite when. We'll be ready for you to tell us what to do. See you tomorrow afternoon."

The surprise agenda and phone call earlier in the week hadn't bothered Hud in the least because he knew Electra would supply all the particular pieces to his latest sales puzzle. From what she had told him, late-breaking events would generate more revenue for their joint venture if he moved quickly. Hud and his people knew how to hustle, so he was certain that Su, Adom, and Tim would run with her plans soon after the upcoming meeting.

Electra had been in perpetual motion since returning from London, creating three additional shell companies through which additional T-Plague vaccine sales soon would flow. She also rented three additional controlled substance warehouses in nearby Suitland, Maryland, only ten miles southeast of the Capitol, from which she would personally control targeted vaccine distribution.

The interlocking ownership among Electra's portfolio of virtual companies guaranteed anonymity and zero probability that sales would be traced to Hud.

How nice to be vertically integrated. I design, Su and Adom manufacture, Hud sells, and I distribute to special customers. Other countries don't care if we have FDA approval to support safety and efficacy claims. No one buying in the Cyberspace shadow economy cares, as long as what they buy works. And ours do. Hud's sales slogan, "Buy or die," might not rhyme in any Chinese dialect, but the words fit their predicament.

Electra had also made modifications for Tim to scale up for her next neuro-device: the Neuro-Knitter, a line extension of her Brain Probe, that would accelerate recovery from severe spinal cord injury. The technology could be adapted to other skeletal areas, but she chose the neck as redemption for how quickly she had recovered from a broken neck. Her new device could heal future accident victims.

This trip would be strictly business; no tours or weekend R&R, and Robin was not invited because she had her hands full doing coursework and accounting while letting Matt slowly weave his way through the Ice Queen's emotional defenses. As she drove past the main terminal, snarled traffic showed the sad state of disrepair for many pieces of the nation's infrastructure. And the news this week reported several automated interstate trucking lanes had to be shut down until programmers removed network viruses.

I need to brief Tim on my network security concepts. And I'll find out what he learned at the network security seminar he attended. Events are moving too fast for me to teach him all the details, so I'll give him just enough so he can implement what needs to be done. And the same for Adom and Su, but Su already knows what to do. And I'll review my meeting script as soon as the plane takes off.

Adom usually volunteered to greet Electra at the airport because it gave him an opportunity to talk one-on-one. And she always seemed different each time he saw her, more mature in different ways. He had heard she no longer needed a wheelchair, and he hoped she might be able to ditch the crutches. When he spotted the jet on the tarmac, he walked to greet the crew and its one passenger.

That can't be Electra. It's the reincarnation of someone I loved long, Indira. The figure waved, then ran to greet him.

"You look like you just saw a ghost. What is it?"

"You can run. And you look different. Your clothing, hairstyle, and make-up make you look elegantly mature. You could be Indira's twin."

"I'm the same underneath. I just have a new and improved external covering. And you look marvelous. Texas is the place for you." Adom regained his emotional footing as he drove them to the office, relating several oil patch stories before turning to the topic at hand.

"Hud sent us copies of the agenda, and we're looking forward to the meeting. I hope it's OK we don't stop for lunch. We'll have sandwiches at the meeting, and Su baked brownies. It's almost like the good ole Worldstar days." Hud and Su were sitting in the conference room when the receptionist buzzed that Electra and Adom had arrived. Hud walked to greet them but what he saw jolted him to a stop.

"Well I declare Little Lady, you sure look all grown up, nothing but sweetness and light. We'll have to get you a new nickname. Tarnation. You're prettier than stolen honey." Hud wrapped Electra in a bear hug.

"I told Adom it's still little ole me inside, just a different wrapping. It's good to be back, and we have lots of good things to talk about."

"Come on everyone. Grab a sandwich and soda, and then let's have our former Little Lady get us started." The light-hearted talk continued through a brownie or two, and then Electra turned more serious.

"I've learned from insider contacts that T-Plague outbreaks in Western Europe, China, and the Middle East might get worse. And that will mean S-Vac demand will skyrocket. So, we want to ramp up production and build inventory. And here's more news.

I have an improved formulation for S-Vac, and new I-Vac and R-Vac formulations. Su, please take my word that they're safe and effective. We aren't going to submit any clinical data to the FDA because we want to keep the patents and formulations secret. Hud, you should hire separate independent sales reps for each new shell company I've just set up. I've also set up a separate warehouse for handling shipments for each one. We don't want anyone tracing these vaccines back to us. So far, so good?" Hud scratched his head.

"Well now, how do we work with the FDA on the new vaccines?"

"We don't until they're ready to buy from us. Or else, they can buy from our shell companies in the underground market. And we'll keep brand names separate so no one connects the dots back to us. I've got it all set up where Robin enters the orders and I coordinate shipping from the new warehouses. Su and Adom will coordinate production so we build inventory." Hud was warming to the opportunity.

"Once the story gets out how good they work, we'll take a bigger chunk of the market. So that's why we you set up three shells; makes it look like there's competition when it's all controlled by us. This is better than black gold, and if that ain't a fact, God's a possum. But we better not be greedy on price. There'll be hard feelings if we charge too much."

"Right, so be diplomatic and emphasize the ethical angle. Set prices countries can live with and you can still make us money. And keep the existing sales people and pricing in place for existing customers.

"I've put a lot on the table, so let's take a break, then hold a roundtable discussion. Besides, I need another brownie." *And everyone looks like they need to come up for air.*

They spent the next hour confirming what needed to be done. By the time they adjourned, Hud had only one question remaining.

"What should we call Electra? I don't think 'Little Lady' fits anymore." No one but Hud had a suggestion.

"This is the first time I'm quicker with my wits than you people. I vote for 'Queen' or something like that. We can say 'Her Highness' or 'Her Majesty.' Long live the Queen." The Queen addressed her court.

"Yes, and let's live long and prosper. And tomorrow morning, Hud and I will meet right here with our Director of Neuro-Device Engineering."

As everyone chatted about dinner on the way out, Adom made the invitation.

"I'd like to take you out to dinner. We haven't had a one-on-one talk for what seems like years, and I'd like to share some things with you. I know a quiet Tex-Mex restaurant that'll be just right."

"I accept. I hope we leave soon. I'm ready for Tex-Mex."

"How about now?" Before they left, Su got in the last word.

"I'll let Hud call you Queen, but I prefer to call you Electra. And I've been to the restaurant you're going. The food's great, but it may not be as quiet as Adom hopes. But since it's the middle of the week, it might not be as noisy as it gets on Fridays. Whether or not you can hear Adom, you'll like the food."

Su's prediction proved to be accurate on all counts. The noise level was just enough to insulate them from the light crowd, and as Adom had kidded, even fast-food places are better in Texas. Adom skipped ordering dessert, instead getting another Dos Equis while Electra stayed with a Coke. *Hmm, Adom must have a private matter to discuss. Maybe he's found a rodeo queen to marry. Let's see where he leads us.*

"Dark Mexican beer is popular. Sure you won't try one? I don't think our server will card you."

"Thanks, but no thanks. I usually stick to my Coca Cola. We old folk get stuck in our ways."

"You're not old. You simply look like a subtly sexy adult lady. If some guy sitting at the bar wanted a hookup, he'd guess you might be maybe thirty. And he better have all the right stuff or he won't get within hailing distance."

"Sounds like you're talking from experience. Did you and Dad troll the bar scene much?" Adom leaned back and chuckled.

"Only the first year in grad school. I'd attract the ladies and one of them would sort of like your father, whose first impression even then was like a dull square. But then I stumbled across Indira and Su, and your Dad was a goner." Adom paused for a sip of beer, then led onward.

"Your mother was a genuinely nice person who, as Su would say, playfully reeled your father in slowly, reminding him that anything worth having is worth working for. No one ever figured out why your mother chose your father. She had it all—looks, killer anatomy, brains, personality, and an empathy that made people like her immediately. I'll bet you never knew your father was a gam's man, really liked a well-turned ankle. Anyway, whenever someone asked Indira why she likes your father she'd always reply that his best traits take time to appreciate."

"I knew some of this, but you tell it so much better. And I never knew Dad was a legs man. Dad always said you two were best friends." Adom's expression clouded as talked.

"Yes, we were. But I will always regret that one time I betrayed his trust. It's bothered me off and on for years. Did Su tell you about my carefree youth?"

"A little. You were the one who added humor to the Worldstars."

"And I was the Worldstar who never made commitments. I said I'd do that when I got older, when the time was right. And I let the others do most of the R&D heavy lifting. I sort of rode on their coattails. Su did the break-through grunt work, Indy added intuitive insight, and Jason pushed projects forward. I'm sorry only Su is left to see how I have changed. All the setbacks that started ten years ago have forced me to grow into a more responsible adult." Electra was about to talk, but Adom waved her off.

"Please let me finish. Anyway, there's an episode I've never told anyone. The only person who ever knew was your mother. Isn't human nature odd? There's no earthly reason why it should still bother me. It happened nearly twenty-four years ago, and no one got hurt. Maybe I should just leave it buried in the past." Adom seemed to waver, so Electra jumped in.

"I guess everyone wants redemption from whatever they think they've done to hurt others. Talking is the best way to deal with it.

I'm amazed how all of us can turn a trivial event into a crisis. You decide how much you want to tell me."

"There are only two people I'd tell, you and Su. I'll only tell one, and I think it's better I tell you, because it will help you understand your parents better, which will help you know yourself.

"I've known you since you were born, and I've watched you grow from a happy little girl who everyone knew had lots of ability into a more cautious and complex adolescent. Now you've become a talented young woman who's mature enough to understand. But don't rush to pass judgement. Don't yell at me until I'm finished."

"I'm a big girl now. I won't say anything until you want me to." Adom took a deep breath, then dived in to the deep end of his dilemma.

"Indira and I had an affair a year before you were born. When I first met your mother and Su, I was attracted to both. But your father was crazy about Indira, so I figured she'd get tired of him and then I could date her. I knew Indira was physically attracted to me more than to your dad. Look, I'm not bragging. I'm too old for that, but those are the facts. I was the guy the girls went for. Su will tell you that." Electra nodded but kept her word by saying nothing.

"But I gave up when Jason and Indira hooked up. They were together, from mid-way through grad school until the day you were born. Your father was rather blunt emotionally, like a lot of men. Indy could handle that and loved him for other reasons. Precisely what they were I never knew. Maybe Su does. But here's one thing I do know. Jason had to make a real effort to move beyond sex. Guys talk, just like the ladies. And he told me—now don't be shocked—that Indy was passionate in bed. Always active, always clever. But I don't think he really satisfied her. It was something I read in her body language whenever I was with them and joking about sex. Maybe Indy told Su, but I didn't ask and, anyway, Su wouldn't tell."

"A year before you were born I was kidding Indy about the clauses she had added to the marriage contract, and your mother became serious. She said she loved Jason, but had not yet experienced a wild, passionate orgasm. Our eyes met and I suddenly saw your mother's intentions. She needed an affair to test the trade-off between unchained sexual desire and the more subtle, nuanced feelings of love. So, in a manner of speaking, Indira seduced me." Adom glanced away, his thoughts journeying for an instant to a distant joy, then coming back to the present.

"We made love passionately and often. It was thrilling to watch her. Her head and eyes would roll and she would howl in ecstasy. It's a tremendous turn-on for a guy to see his partner satisfied. It's like the two of you become one. I've experienced it with other women, but never that fully.

"Our affair continued for about three months and no one ever found out. Indy was as discreet as Su. But even today, Su doesn't know when to show her feelings. Not so for Indy. She was completely honest with me because she knew it's the right thing to do. And she told me upfront when she decided to end our affair. Not because the passion had burned out, but because love won out over sex. You know how she ended it? After our last time in bed, she kissed me and started crying. I didn't know why, so I asked, and she thanked me for the best sex she ever had, but said she wanted love from Jason even more. That stunned me, and I didn't want her to leave, but she was in control. There could be no hard feelings, so we went back to being good friends. No one got hurt, and no one else knew." Electra rose quickly, then sat next to Adom, putting her arms around him, kissing him softly on his forehead.

"What a beautiful story. So many lessons of friendship and love are in it. Thank you for telling me. And you don't need redemption. If Mother were here she'd thank you again for one of life's great experiences." They sat until Adom broke the silence.

"Thanks for listening. I'm not really hungry, but let's go somewhere for a dessert. Indy liked Su's fruit tarts as much as you like her brownies."

Next morning's agenda spotlighted neuro-education so Tim would know how to scale up Electra's latest device. Hud stayed for fifteen minutes, happy to leave when business called him away. Tim gamely followed as Electra showed how the new device would electrify the world of spinal cord regeneration, and after two hours she paused so Tim could catch up.

"Now you understand how the Neuro-Knitter extends our Brain Probe. We use the same hardware, but adjust the software to focus and pulse the electromagnetic fields on the damaged area. And I'm counting on you to find a flexible wrap that covers the anatomy. You can embed the circuitry in its substrate."

"I think I get it. The picture's coming into focus. Just give me a couple of minutes to think it through." Electra went for a Coke so she wouldn't interrupt Tim's autistic-driven powers of concentration, stopping briefly to visit Hud.

"I'm sure glad Tim's catching on, because I didn't understand a thing you were saying. If dirt was dumb, I'd cover about an acre."

"You're smart in the ways of business, and if there weren't people like you taking risks and building businesses, people wouldn't have jobs. I better get back and give him his Coca Cola. We'll talk more later." Tim popped the top, taking a big gulp before talking.

It's amazing how the Knitter's software integrates separate electrical pulses sent from the brain and damaged vertebrae before outputting back. Now I understand why the device consists of the cranial helmet and flexible neck wrap. And its ingenious how it refocuses the radiation right on the damaged bone or nerve tissue. I can adapt the intensity dial from the Brain Probe to correlate injury depth or location with treatment duration. It shouldn't take me more than two months to have the first scalable prototype. I'll want you to recommend an online seminar I can watch to master more of the quantum biology concepts. What we're doing is way beyond cutting edge."

"You're the best person I could have hired. You learn concepts quickly and I know you'll tinker with the components until you have what we need. Let Hud know what additional resources you want. Do you have what you need to start?"

"Yep. I'll have it for you by September. Hud asked me if I want to take vacation, and I told him working here is better than that.

You just keep coming up with the concepts and I'll keep turning them into devices. And I bet you've already come up with a sales and marketing plan, so just let Hud and me know when you're ready to launch."

"We're not ready for launch just yet, but how about lunch?" Tim caught the play on words and responded accordingly.

"Su and Adom sometimes talk about the Worldstar days, and it must have been part of everyone's job description to enjoy playing with words. They tell me your mother was a great punster." Electra smiled, nodding in agreement as they headed out, saying nothing else to Tim, only to herself. *I love word games. And other games too, but I prefer not to explain some of the rules to you just yet, nor do I ever tell anyone the inner workings. These other games are getting dangerous, and I don't want to put you at risk. Better for you to be on the sidelines until I know how much you can handle.*

Electra changed topics after lunch.

"We're going to branch out into network security software development, and in preparation for that I want to go over my Cybersecurity Primer. What can you tell me about Cybersecurity."

"Lots. I went to a seminar and chatted afterwards with the presenter, Darla Tinabu, who's president of Cybergard. She's really impressive, and I got a chance to compare our work with hers. She really likes the stuff we're doing. She even Emailed me a copy of her presentation, and I'll upload it on your laptop so you can watch it."

"Good. Let me go through my primer, and you can compare it to hers. Here goes..."

For the next hour, Electra explained Cybersecurity history and how it makes networks available to users, while guaranteeing integrity and confidentiality. Security became a major problem in the early 2000's, when networked computers extending into the cloud became prevalent worldwide and Cybercrime became a big business. America's inferior Cybersecurity became the reason why America lost the first Political Cyberwar: Russia corrupted the 2016 Presidential Election.

America's hi-tech ingenuity quickly regained the upper hand. Silicon Valley upgraded security development lifecycle planning and implemented improved security protocols and standards maintained by the Computer Engineering Institute. And it developed next generation hardware and software reinforcing cloud-based virtual networks running on quantum computers.

"So, does this jibe with what you heard at the seminar?"

"I think so, but I need to go over it again. Are we done?"

"No. What I want to do is sketch the opportunities. We'll use existing quantum hardware, because it exceeds the needs of what Cybersecurity does today. Our approach will build and sell superior antivirus software, using my neural networked adaptive programming language and techniques to identify, kill, and remove viruses or bad apps. And, you'll put virtual reality-equipped GUI's on the front end to make using our software like playing a video game. Stay with me, and I'll take you beyond cutting edge."

Electra spent ten minutes more touching additional topics she would have Tim research, but she didn't tell him everything. *I can play Cyberwar offense and defense, but he's not ready for my suite of Cyberweapons that will destroy Cyberwar enemies. I'll tell him just enough to keep him engaged but not overloaded.*

Electra spent the rest of the afternoon with Su, who knew where the new formulations were leading and would help Adom work through the manufacturing procedures. At five o'clock Su led them to Hud's office so he could wish the Queen a fond farewell. He was the only one using Electra's new nickname, and his smiling sincerity touched her.

"Well, your Highness, come back and visit your Texas empire soon. We need you. And Su, you make sure Adom drives 'Texas friendly' to and from the airport." Su had volunteered to ride with Electra so they could catch up on some final matters that Electra brought up.

"Texas seems to be treating you almost as well as it's treating Adom. And when T-Plague and the political climate settle down, you can join Tim and me for joint pharmacological and neural device development. There'll be more than enough to keep you challenged for as long as you wish."

"I will always have more than enough to keep me challenged when I'm working with you. How pleasant it is to be with someone who looks like Indira, but you've inverted the relationship. When Indira and I worked together, she was the empathetic and intuitive sounding board that helped me hone my discoveries. Now I am the sounding board. Smart as I am, I can't keep pace with you. I don't think anyone can. And now, each time you visit, I sense your empathy growing, approaching the level of your mother's. How I wish your mother were still alive, for then my life would be complete. I would have Indira, the practically perfect person, and her daughter, even more perfect cognitively." *I don't want my visit to end on a downer. I better find something to buck Su up.*

"You and Mother have something I never will: artistic creativity, you in music and Mother in poetry. My brain isn't wired for it. And here is another of Mother's poems to help you deal with her loss. It's called *The Triple Crown*:

Are you where you want to be?
Engaged in what you meant to do?
With those who seem to care for you?
Joys of your maturity.

It's not like that past early years,
You search for meaning in your life.
The journey's often fraught with strife,
Some paths may lead to bitter tears.

This crown is worn by very few,
It's oft beyond the outstretched reach.
Try your best but Life will teach,
Be grateful for what's offered you.

You don't need me to interpret it. And I hope someday you will do what Mother would want; let go of kindred spirits from the past."

"Ladies, we're approaching the airport. Please put your conversation away until inside the terminal." Su patted Adom before answering.

"Thanks for reminding me. On your next trip, let's continue where we have to leave off. And I'll try to think of Indira-Jason stories you haven't heard yet." *I can't tell you mine, but please tell me yours next time.*

Adom carried one of Electra's cases as the threesome marched across the tarmac to the awaiting plane. Electra hugged them, then boarded. As Su watched the plane taxi down the runway and then whoosh skyward, arcing gracefully towards a deepening blue eastern horizon, a poignant emotion pinged. *You are more than Indira's daughter; you are an enigma I shall never fully understand. And I love you as completely as I shall ever love another. Someday I shall summon the courage to tell you.*

Electra powered up her laptop as soon as the plane reached cruising altitude so she could watch the security seminar Tim had attended, and as it started, she immediately understood why he had been so impressed. The presenter, Darla Tinabu—President of Cyberguard—commanded attention. Short, stocky, and in her late-forties, she spoke perfect English distinctively accented, reflecting African heritage. And her mastery and passion for her company's security software would convince anyone in the audience to buy what she's selling.

Darla used the presentation to educate and sell to network security users, such as financial institutions, social media companies, or military and government agencies. Darla summarized security history and the technological trends that are driving its trajectory, and she gave "geek only" technical insights that some in the audience actually understood, while the rest were impressed. She then gave a snapshot of security risks and how Cybergard software would deflect them. And she concluded by warning that hacker-and-cracker criminals will always be looking for an edge, but that Cybergard Network Security Software is one step ahead in quantum cryptography and security. So, defend yourself with cutting edge Cybergard tools. She asked for questions, but received none, only applause. Electra shut down her laptop and let the lightning brain free wheel.

Darla Tinibu is indeed impressive, but I detect sinister undertones. I hope Tim didn't tell her too much about what we're doing. We need to stay below her radar, but I've done that all my life, and I'll add Darla and Cybergard to my game of keep away. And that's a game I never lose.

CHAPTER 22

August 2120

"The Prolific Postdoc"

(Thread 2 Chapter 9)

Jared's approval rating continued climbing because he was the first president in over a generation that told the facts instead of cowering behind feckless policies that were not only "politically correct pablum" but toothless to boot. And though some actions were harsh, Jared's directives delivered results. And as long as there was some progress, the public gave him all the credit for repairing the damage caused by previous administrations' neglect for what had built and guarded America.

Even Electra considered him an improvement as long as Angus kept a lid on Jared's aggressive nature and moderated the harsher options attached to programs. The Infra-Rebuild Program was actually making inroads, at least for those fixes requiring lower-tech resources. The public noticed when driving on roads or across bridges, or when lights came on sooner after power outages. Abandoned buildings in marginalized neighborhoods were finally being razed, replaced by urban gardens. And some dilapidated public buildings were given a facelift that improved the government's image.

The Guardian Party activated several Repatriot program extensions designed to throw a wider net over targets needing "assistance," making them productive rather than a drag on society. Only those directly impacted dared to complain, but most remained silent for fear they might be among the first selected for "redeployment" to another country, a program extension held in reserve if Jared needed more undesirables to throw under the Guardian Party bus to keep it moving.

Securityguard's relentless rollup of suspected terrorist cells or gangs gave the public something to cheer about, and media snippets graphically displaying police removing the bad guys motivated the more aggressive citizens to buy guns. "Shoot First Read 'Em Rights Later" window signs grew in number as gun ownership restrictions dwindled; bumper stickers proclaiming "I'm a Gun-Tot'n Guardian" were displayed like a badge of honor. All told, Jared had put stronger teeth into public and private law enforcement.

Some of Jared's success was due to information Electra passed along to Angus, who distributed some directly to Jared, and some to Russell or Alice. Electra compared herself to a juggler keeping balls in the air. *But for me, the balls are my games, any one of which might become dangerous if it drops. Good thing I have fast reflexes. And I'll make sure my partners don't drop them either. Good that I'm meeting Angus this coming Saturday.*

"I'll be ready in a second; I'm just putting on finishing touches. I want to make a good impression on Angus." Russell shouted back,

"You don't need to fuss too much. You'd look great wearing a beat-up bathrobe." Jennifer and Russell Conklin were about to leave for a Friday evening dinner at Angus McTear's.

Though in her early fifties, Jennifer could pass for a thirty-something beauty. She was one of those rare individuals who maintained tone and fitness effortlessly. Russell had met her when she was working for a talent agency as a medical conference hostess. Russell kept her out of the clutches of a couple of "swordsmen surgeons," and their relationship grew from that first encounter. When he was about to marry, Russell's friends cautioned that Jennifer might be seeking a marriage of convenience. His friends warned he'd never be able to keep a woman that young and beautiful satisfied. How wrong they were. She was a devoted and loving wife, providing a lovely home and the emotional support Russell needed to balance his pressure-filled NIH senior executive position.

Russell had suffered even worse than Jennifer during the past two years. The death of their only child aged him physically. Then he was demoted because of whispered rumors that he had been aligned with the now defunct Opposition Party. But he stoically carried on, rebounding as best as a late sixties person could. The NIH could still use him because there were so few smart people left.

Then earlier this year, Russell had been referred to Angus McTear, the new Secretary of Defense, who needed someone at NIH to move the ball forward on T-Plague vaccines. The effect on Russell was immediate. His physical strength rebounded and he became once again a capable leader. And he liked Angus because they shared the same ethics. Russell recognized why Angus was Jared's favorite bureaucrat: the man was smart, thorough, and competent, a statesman who could get things done while respecting the limits of power.

Jennifer struggled after Christi's death but had worked through most of the grieving. And she liked keeping in touch with Electra and Robin because they brought back the best memories. Now she looked forward to extending her nursing credentials into nutrition as soon as she and Matt Fortier, Robin's "almost co-friend," start a holistic physical therapy and health counseling business.

Angus greeted his guests, bringing them into the living room just before his wife joined them.

"Mikita, why don't you show Jennifer how you're redecorating upstairs, and I'll take Russell to my study?" The ladies departed and Angus guided Russell while taking drink orders.

"I'm a scotch man myself. What's to your liking?"

"I'm partial to a dry martini with an olive. Any gin you have will do just fine. Do you have a favorite scotch?"

"I can give you Bombay or Beefeaters. It's your call."

"I'll take Beefeaters. What scotch do you prefer?"

"I go for Cutty Sark aged eight years. Soda and small cubes in the warm weather, straight over big cubes when it's cold. I've tried most, and I like the blended over single malt." The two traded stories about alcoholic spirits while they settled into the comfortable leather chairs in the study adjacent to the living room. The unhurried surroundings added to the drinks' pleasant effects; soon Angus steered the conversation towards his guest.

"I'm pleased how well you've picked up on T-Plague vaccines. And I like how you plan to have that Texas company supply more smart pills." Angus sipped his scotch before continuing.

"But I'd like you to tell me why you've been sidelined the past two years. I know all about the rumors, but why don't you level with me."

"Fair enough. You deserve the straight story because we see eye-to-eye on the big issues. I didn't like the previous administration, but I picked the wrong horse: the Opposition Party instead of the Guardian Party. I thought a more balanced approach would be better, but the public wanted harsh measures so it never gained traction and is now officially defunct. Angus sipped again before talking.

"When I contacted Jared, I had the same concerns you do and told him so. And I also realized he held the stronger hand so I signed on. After all, it's easier to know what's going on if you're on the inside. And so far, he's been able to keep most of my recommendations intact despite opposition from some assertive lieutenants." Both men sat in comfortable silence. Finally, Russell offered a suggestion.

"It might help if you form a Guardian Party Insider's Group, like a watchdog group. You could build it slowly." A careful smile emerged as Angus replied.

"Actually, I've already started building it: you and me, and a lady you don't know named Alice Bickerwith. There's another person who assists me on a part-time basis, but it's better if we keep that person anonymous. I want you to focus on vaccines and healthcare. Alice handles the international diplomacy issues, and from what she's uncovered, they'll come to a boil soon. We'll bring in others if and when the need arises, but we better be very careful. Jared can be very vindictive. It looks like you have a question, so ask away."

"I know our intelligence agencies aren't as good as they used to be. Have you been able to rebuild our capability?"

"No, but we've stopped the downward spiral. And I have contacts in the hacking community that I might be able to recruit. But I'm not there yet. We'll have to see how contingencies unfold. But enough shop talk. I'll set up a meeting soon for the three of us. And why don't we catch up with our wives after I make us both another drink..."

Jennifer didn't need to ask any questions on the drive home. She could tell from Russell's bearing that the evening had been a success, and that was good enough for her, for she knew he would make the most of whatever came his way. She touched his arm and when their eyes met, Russell could feel the warming glow of her lovely smile.

Angus must have had a hectic week because he pushed back our meeting from Saturday to Sunday. Fine with me. I need to have him rested and ready rather than wiped out. And he moved the time from eight to seven a.m. That's a sign he's prepared. Electra reviewed the agenda while driving to meet Angus. There was only one new issue: Zoe had recently begun revising some of Electra's PR copy. The changes weren't getting too aggressive yet, but Angus should let Jared know he might want to tone them down.

Electra liked how she tried to structure for each game the relationships among the players. In each game, she tried to recruit players who didn't know one another. Each thought none of the other anonymous players knew Electra, and each pledged to keep her identity unknown. *It's a practically perfect way to limit everyone's risk, especially mine, as well as to cross-check my players' intentions. "Trust but verify" are my watch-words.*

The lightning brain momentarily shifted gears to consider logic, just for the enjoyment of playing with a special mathematical concept: the Equivalence Relation. *For each of my games, if I stick to my recruiting rules, all the players in each game satisfy three laws described by logic. The first is the Reflexive Law: each element A is related to itself. The second is the Symmetric Law: if A is related to B then B is related to A. And the third is the Transitive Law: if A is related to B, and B is related to C, then A is related to C. If all three hold, our relationship is an Equivalence Relation, which divides the set of elements into distinct Equivalence Classes. And the way I've set up the rules, each player is in an Equivalence Class containing just one member: themselves. That limits everyone's risk. Tsk tsk to those who say math isn't fun or useful.* Indira chided from the shadows.

"Be careful. You are becoming too full of yourself, too smug regarding how good you are with numbers. You know that just about everyone—even so-called math geniuses—often struggle and tire when doing calculations because the human brain is designed to think fast and intuitively, not slow and logically. You are fortunate because you can switch gears and think either way, so be thankful and don't gloat. And I should point out that none of your sets of players satisfy your recruiting parameters, because in each set, several players know one another. And even if a set of players did satisfy your parameters, it would become difficult to recruit more players into the game without having them know some who are already in."

"I am sorry I disappoint you, but you are right. I was about to make a joke at my players' expense: they wouldn't understand what an Equivalence Class is and might confuse the term anti-symmetric with anti-Semitic. You have reminded me to be humble, not proud." Indira's tone softened.

"I know you were just playing, but everyone needs to be reminded from time to time. But I've said enough. It's time for you to shift back to the task at hand. Have fun today with Angus."

Angus was waiting outside, balancing a cup of coffee, a Coke, and a bag of muffins when Electra pulled into the driveway. His cheery greeting announced he was well rested.

"Good morning. I thought we'd hold a movable feast of a meeting to take advantage of the weather, so let's do this. I'll drive and listen while you talk. And I'll take a route I use whenever Mikita and I have out-of-town guests. There's so much to see in DC you might not know some of what I'll describe as we drive by."

"What a great idea. No wonder you wanted to start early. Traffic should be light. And I already have your coffee and yogurt, so we don't need to stop along the way." The meeting-tour combo began as soon as Electra and Angus climbed into his Mercedes.

"I'm driving because I know the route. Besides, your Ford Fiesta is too small for my dimensions. And my Mercedes is quiet. That car of yours makes too much noise. Why don't you fix it? *It is, to my liking, but I guess not to yours. But I know what to say.*

"Perhaps I need a new muffler. I'll have to get it checked."

Angus didn't need to check GPS because he knew all the short cuts. And he interjected historical commentary between Electra's chosen topics.

"We're driving past the Tidal Basin. It's partially manmade and originated in the 1880's to be a visual centerpiece as well as a means for flushing the Washington Channel. The Springtime National Cherry Blossom Festival held here is world renown, as are the memorials to Jefferson, Martin Luther King, and Franklin Delano Roosevelt that grace it. And the Jefferson Memorial is actually on an island; you have to cross a bridge to get there."

"I didn't know that, but now that you mention it, I do remember hiking across a bridge. Grandfather would take me to the Festival each year. He was a great sport. I must have tired him out, what with all the walking I made him do. He was a parent and grandparent all rolled into one. What great memories he gave me." Electra redirected the topic back to the present.

"Has Isilabad's government collapsed? If so, will the UN mediate a cease fire with Iran? And how will this affect the war on terrorism?" Angus had a ready reply.

"Thanks to Alice, we know Isilabad is imploding, but so far that hasn't stopped hostilities. Both countries have serious T-Plague outbreaks. And on the terrorist front, she's given us a credible list of sleeper cells in the U.S. Securityguard is rolling them up, so we're seeing fewer suicide attacks, but the undetected cells might keep launching last ditch attempts. A much bigger problem is posed by those damn Trojan filters whose locations are unknown."

"Are you aware of Hassan's rumored Apocalypse Clock?"

"Yes, but only through rumors. We have nothing tangible. Alice says the Brits are in the same boat, and between our two countries, I hope someone can figure out how to turn it off, or let it wind down gracefully. Otherwise, the public will be on edge forever." Angus was now driving past part of the Smithsonian Institute, so he again switched roles.

"The Smithsonian Institute is the largest museum complex and research institute in the world. Eleven of the nineteen museums are located in the area we're driving past. You could spend an entire summer vacation touring it. I confess, I haven't gone through all of them yet."

"Each summer, Grandfather would let me pick one of the museums to study. It became the topic of my back-to-school essay I had to write. Even though I was on the home-schooling track, Grandfather insisted I write it at the start of every grade school year. Thanks to Grandfather, I thoroughly walked through eight of them." Electra switched to another topic.

"You better tell Jared that Zoe is rewriting what I've been giving him, putting a more aggressive spin on it. It's not been a problem yet, but it might be, depending on how events play out. Especially when it comes to deportation." Angus grunted.

"Why don't you meet with Zoe and tell her. She's going four ways at once and lately seems a bit raggedy round the edges." Electra nodded that she would, so Angus switched back to his tour guide role.

"We're now driving by the "Newseum." It's an interactive museum of news and journalism displays, built in 2008. Since you write PR, you should go through it sometime. It has wonderful permanent exhibits for major national and international iconic events. Two of the most popular are retrospectives covering terrorism and biological pandemics. I sure hope they can close out some of our current events soon. I'll drive us past the International

Spy Museum. We're almost there. It's privately owned and is the brainchild of a Korean War code-cracker named Milton Maltz. I've been there, and I encourage all government agents to visit. It's very educational. You'd like it. It has retro-exhibits covering fictitious James Bond as well as factual Mata Hari, a Dutch exotic dancer executed by the French in World War I for being a German spy. Quite a story. Quite a brave woman. She refused to wear a blind fold and blew a kiss to her executioners just before the firing squad pulled the trigger." As Angus drove on, he asked a question.

"Does the year 2007 have any special meaning to you?" Electra said no.

"Well, let me provide some history that will help put today's economy into context. 2007 marked the start of America's 'Great Financial Meltdown' and the 'Great Recession'. Wall Street had to be bailed out, General Motors filed for bankruptcy, and GDP contracted by 5 percent. Unemployment rate spiked way past 10 percent in some parts of the country, and 8 million jobs were lost. Conditions did improve more quickly than in the Great Depression of the 1930's, but the so-called new normal afterwards was not encouraging. And the political environment for the next three elections was radioactive. Threats of government shutdowns and too much partisan politics led to Washington gridlock and ruder and cruder campaigns. But the country regained its footing when the public demanded more accountability and fairness, and the nation made progress addressing domestic economic, political and social issues, as well as cooperating better on the world stage. Things weren't perfect mind you, but the public was getting smarter and more involved in good governance.

"And then, thirty years ago, America fell victim to two plagues: Middle East Terrorism and the Techno-Plague. Both were insidious, and the Washington Establishment was asleep at the switch. Everything spiraled downhill from there until Jared and the Guardians stopped the free-fall. But you were born before then, so I don't need to say any more."

"Thanks for the history lesson. And let me add that we've a long way to go to get America back on track. Good government relies on an informed, intelligent public that's willing to think for itself. The T-Plague has dented the public I.Q. and has made too many people unwilling or unable to accept responsibility for themselves. They want Jared to tell them what to do or put things back together, and they don't care what he does to make it so. And I think you could make the same points regarding the war with Islam, but I'll leave that alone. Let's change the subject. When you refer to Jared and the Guardians, I can picture a New Wave rock group…"

And so, the movable meeting rolled on. By the time Angus rolled into his driveway, Electra had seen more Washington sites than most residents would ever visit. As she was about to leave, Angus brought up a final topic.

"I'm counting on you to be the brains for our Brain Trust, so I'm sending you a couple of videos I can't wrap my head around. They talk about artificial intelligence impacting a transhuman future and the American psyche. Frankly, I think the stuff is depressing and too futuristic, but I want to understand it better. And the speakers often connect a rosy outcome to getting rid of the T-Plague and Middle East Terrorism. So, you better teach me.

"I'll do that. And maybe that can be the topic of another meeting-tour combo. If we were to combine each meeting with a tour, how long would it take to cover all the tour-worthy places?"

"Why don't you ask me how high is up?"

As promised, Angus sent the videos, which Electra watched that evening. The first, titled "Our Transhuman Future," promised to give an "audience friendly" summary of how genetics, nanotechnology, and robotics will likely shape our future. The presenter touched on just enough scientific and cultural background to provide a foundation, then dived into artificial intelligence capabilities that pose ominous risks, even though there are plenty of shorter-term benefits if humans are "smart enough" to adapt. The presenter ended his talk problematically: "The jury's is still out on what AI can do in our transhuman future, but at least mankind should have enough warning to pull the plug on machines before the machines do that to us."

The second seminar, "Artificial Intelligence and the American Psyche," promised to provide an optimistic spin on what AI can do for America. The speaker highlighted that American youth, starting with the early 21st century iGen Generation, are world's best for embracing technology. She also described the steps taken by younger people to avoid spillover bad effects, such as withdrawing into Cyberspace or blindly following computer commands. But she did acknowledge that AI—empowered machines could clip the wings of mankind's "better angels" and bring back a more violent culture. Her solution:

- Find a cure for the T-Plague
- Resolve the violence-filled conflict between Islam and Christianity
- Have informed and intelligent citizens reclaim more control of Government

No wonder the videos depressed Angus. They'd depress me too if I couldn't be part of the solution. I'm satisfied where I'm going, and I'll bring Angus along.

One topic covered in her Angus meeting bothered Electra. *I like Zoe, but I've ignored her. I'll call her tomorrow.*

"Hi Electra. I've thought about calling you, but something always comes up… You'd like to meet this week? Let me check… How about Thursday at four over here? OK. I have another call to grab. See you then."

Good. The Zoe game is good for me because I keep her press releases on point. And it's good for her because I take some of the load off her shoulders. Maybe Jared's working her too hard. She doesn't have the pep or confidence that's always been her trademark. It's probably temporary. I better turn my attention to the Alice game next.

Alice had been busy enough after returning from Operation White Rabbit, catching or keeping up with cover and covert assignments, but thanks to her intuition, she sensed the Committee might want to sideline her. Chester Bowless, her covert operations boss, gave her fewer and fewer updates containing little she could pass on to the Guardian Party, so she did call Electra occasionally for business purposes. On a whim, she dialed the number, and this time connected.

"Electra my dear, this is Alice. How are you?... Good. I decided to ring you up on the chance you're free today. We could chat a bit about White Rabbit follow-up, but I thought you might enjoy taking in a concert with me, make a day of it… Yes, it is short notice and I understand… How about this; I'll pick you up in time to catch the concert, then we can have a bite afterwards… Good… I'll pick you up at four… Cheerio."

Alice was on time as always, and soon the ladies were on their way.

"My dear, you look stylish. Are those new clothes?"

"Yes, and thanks for noticing. I've made a conscious effort to upgrade my appearance."

"It appears you have. Since we first met, I've noticed changes. You conduct yourself more assertively and people notice you. Now, tell me all about how busy you've been."

"I've been making excellent progress on my postdoc projects. The world is poised to enter a brave new world controlled by genetic engineering and artificial intelligence if people are bold enough to step into it, but many are scared of its darker possibilities, so progress has been less than what's possible." *That's enough about me. Let's segue to the Brits.*

"And I've been able to meet occasionally with Angus, just to keep an eye on the Guardian Party. Has your Committee done much with Hassan's briefcase?" Alice clucked her disapproval.

"No. You must keep this confidential, but they might like to phase me out. But we can still be friends. I thought you might like today's concert. It's an all-British Composers concert playing two of my favorites: Elgar's *Enigma Variations* and Benjamin Britten's *London Symphony*. Have you ever been to DAR Constitution Hall? It was built in 1929 and is registered as a national historic landmark. It's still operated by the Daughters of the American Revolution."

"No, and what a fitting venue for an all-Brit concert. Even though the Colonies kicked out the King, they came back for the music. I've never listened to the Elgar piece, but from what I've read, each of the fourteen thematic variations represents a close friend, including his wife Alice, who was born in India. No wonder you like it."

"Well here we are, so let's pop in and give it a go..."

The hall and the music were as good as advertised. Electra saw how important public monuments and buildings are, providing symbols of a civilization's greatness, part of a legacy left for succeeding generations. *How sad that some Islamic radical factions destroy artifacts from the past.*

Electra insisted they stop for a dessert after the concert so she could treat.

"I like Elgar's piece even better than Britten's. And speaking of thematic names representing close friends, are you using any of the names from our recent adventure?"

"Why yes, but only when I talk to myself. McTear is the Mad Hatter and Conklin is the March Hare. But please, mum's the word. Goodness, it is getting late. I do enjoy chatting with you. We fall so freely into dialogue. I believe it shows that that we shall be ever the best of friends. Come, let us go..."

CHAPTER 23

November

"Free Fall"

(2120 Thread 1 Chapter 11)

DAMN THE WEATHER FOR snarling traffic this morning! I should have stayed longer on the expressway or left earlier. I didn't think the winds would pile up sleet and snow so quickly. These and other thoughts raced through Carter's mind as he tried to be patient, but in spite of much practice, it was difficult. He was not a very patient person.

Carter Quavah (his Hebrew-derived last name meaning to wait and be strong) had accumulated few serious character flaws other than impatience, a judgmental point of view and quick temper being the only other two. Now twenty-nine, he had learned how to control them by channeling his intensity towards his goals. Some associates considered them assets rather than liabilities, fitting words for the economist he is, while others said he would leave them behind as he continued climbing Washington's consulting career ladder. A California senator who took a liking to him became his mentor, connecting him with people who could advance his career, so he already served as an economic policy analyst for several prominent committees. Carter was one of the youngest staffers on the Federal Reserve Board's prestigious Economic and Financial Advisory Council, an accomplishment his modesty would not allow him to trumpet.

He came to Washington five years ago after earning a PhD in Economics and Finance from Stanford, becoming a CPA along the way. His trim musculature and coordination made him an outstanding athlete, almost good enough to earn collegiate All-American honors in tennis. And his quantitative thinking skills made him a standout in any cohort except physics, computer science, or mathematics majors. There he would be considered mediocre, but his singular combination of numeric and verbal skills placed him near the top in his field. He recognized his competitive advantage when winning a citywide grade school "sustainable business" competition, and ever since planned his academic and professional careers accordingly.

Carter grew up in northern California, where his Jewish parents provided all the support to make him and his older sister successful. His almost-close T-Plague encounter in first grade was deflected when his father paid for unapproved but effective medical services and smart pills available only in Cyberspace's underground economy, putting his son among the fortunate few who recovered completely. Carter's pragmatic problem-solving and people-handling skills, learned early at home and synagogue, made him popular among associates and senior staffers. His only extravagance was a late model Corvette (still America's premier sports car) on which he lavished the care and attention a devoted shelter pet owner would give to a four-legged foundling. All that, plus shortish light-brown hair and boyish good looks made him a great catch for female professionals, accentuated because the pool of counterpart males continued to shrink.

As the traffic inched forward, Carter saw the reason for the bottleneck. *Some fool dented a tire rim by driving too fast through a submerged pothole.* The car was being driven off to the side, clearing the right lane so he could crawl by as soon as the light turned green. Until then he would watch as the hapless driver struggled in the cold and damp. He would relieve his anger by glaring at the jerk and yelling silently, *Screw you for getting in my way!* But before the light changed, he had a change of attitude.

The driver, an attractive and stylishly dressed young women, appeared unruffled and ready to deal with what would be a messy job. Carter saw no signs of help on the way so he made a snap decision to be the Good Samaritan, parking around the corner then hustling back to minimize exposure to sleet and wind and cold.

"Let me give you a hand. I've had lots of practice changing tires." The young woman flashed a smile that would have cut through the fog of gloom anywhere. Carter involuntarily stared for a moment. *I know quality when I see it. The coat, the slacks, the boots are tailored and tony. And so is the lady wearing them.*

"Would you please? I'll pay for the dry-cleaning. Here, let me show you how to work the scissor jack. I've practiced, so I can help." Fifteen minutes later the ordeal was over.

"Let's swap cell numbers and names. I'm Electra Kittner, and you are?"

"Carter Quavah. Let's not talk now. We'll just get colder and damper."

"I'll call you tonight. You'll need to get your slacks and coat cleaned. Thank you again."

"Glad I could help." Carter turned without another word and dashed back to his car. Electra glanced momentarily at the receding figure, then ducked into her car, ready to finish driving to the lab.

Upon arrival, she examined her clothes for dirt stains. Though not a slave to fashion, she had acquired an appreciation for well-tailored clothing made from quality fabric and always took care of them.

Thanks to Carter, I'm spotless. I'll celebrate by having a blueberry muffin and Coke before plopping in front of my workstation. And I'll call him tonight. He seems presentable enough; perhaps I can arrange a double date to show Robin that fellows can be gentlemen. And if I date more, Robin might rely more on Matt instead of me. Matt will like that too.

Electra spent the rest of the day finishing a second revision of her "Cognitive Conjecture" white paper, a theory for how cognition and self-awareness emerge from the grand canonical ensemble of the brain's neural connections. It would guide her research into all related fields, but she would share only rudimentary pieces because she was far ahead of cutting edge, able to integrate quantum biology and genetic engineering using computer and nano-technology. *My groundbreaking confirmation that all mental and psychological phenomena result from matter interacting with matter will take years for other researchers to validate or overturn my results.*

I'm not worried because I know I'm right. And their role is to prove or disprove my work, because according to Karl Popper, the great 20th century philosopher of science, all claims must be tested in light of his theory of falsifiability. Every scientific statement is falsifiable if you can observe a single contradiction. Other researchers should thank me, because I've given them something to do. I'll even help them by explaining how my theory jibes with gravity and electromagnetism.

Electra had developed her theory by arguing from analogies. *Newton modeled the transmission of gravitational forces by constructing a gravitational force field, as did Maxwell when studying electromagnetism. When a critical mass of matter clumps together, gravity or electromagnetic fields simply emerge. It's useless to deconstruct these fields into finer-grained entities. Doing so only leads to a meaningless infinite regress from which you never escape. Newton accepted the fact that gravity simply is, and so did Maxwell, when they developed field equations.*

According to my model, when a brain has a critical mass of inter-neural connections, cognition emerges, similar to a force field. We can't measure it by weighing on a scale or counting neurons. Instead, we observe responses. I observed brain activity and correlated it with subjective emotional responses. I used my advanced Brain Probe to turn on a critical mass of targeted inter-neural connections, giving me precise mental states for which I measured physiological and mental phenomena.

And my model considers the brain a finite state machine because the number of inter-neural connections, though measured in the trillions, is still finite. I then used the latest computer circuitry and nanobot technology to control my Brain Probe.

Electra didn't worry about contradicting spiritual beliefs. *Religion's push for a spiritual dimension is unfounded, but my work doesn't concern the spirit world. Philosophers concluded a hundred years ago that it's impossible to prove or disprove God. But entrenched beliefs die hard. The Ancients believed in a "Cosmic Consciousness," and as recently as a hundred years ago, the Institute of Noetic Sciences pushed the same, but it was all subjective, had no theory or scientific foundation, and was dismissed as quackery.*

The lightning brain's creativity had raced far ahead of what Electra could actually accomplish unless she had people she could teach. Even the great Su and the industrious Tim struggled to keep up. Just for amusement, she occasionally fantasized a Fantastic Five Dream Team.

Even though my Dream Team is a pipe dream, I can have fun working with the people I do have. Only I will handle the Brain Probe because of its sinister undertones, but Tim can develop the Neuro-Knitter, and I'll tell Hud to hire a Director of Sales and Market Development to roll it out. And I'll show trusty Su how to attack Alzheimers. I've done enough for today. It's time to shift gears.

Electra made a mental note as she tidied up her workstation before leaving to get the dented tire rim replaced by the end of the week. And she planned to call Carter and Robin tonight.

Carter always answered his phone whether or not he recognized the caller's I.D. Unlike so many paranoid people for whom unknown callers cause more stress, he picked up as often as he could, treating each as an opportunity.

"Hello, this is Carter…Who?...Oh, the dented rim lady. Did you get home OK?...Good…Yes, I'll take my slacks and overcoat to the cleaners this week… You want me to join you and a couple of friends at a sensual pleasures café this Saturday?... No, I've never been to one of them… What are they like?... Hmm. Tell you what, I already have plans, but I'll go ahead and change them. Call me back to confirm the time and location. Thanks again, and yes, I'll bring the cleaning receipt. Bye." Carter thought for a moment about his apparent good fortune before returning to a stack of work he had brought home.

I'm surprised she called. Lots of ladies would have skipped it. This one is definitely not a giffen good, even though for my money she might have an upward-sloping demand curve. And since she's covering my dry-cleaning tab, I'll recover my opportunity cost."

Robin could point to two fellows causing her more stress. Matt finally convinced her to move in with him so she could get a better grip on her feelings as well as distance herself from her criticizing parents, while her father's predicament made her dislike him even more.

Years ago, her father had belonged to a Russian Emigres Group, whose radical members were clandestine terrorists. Securityguard shut it down a year ago and was now rolling up more than just the suspects. Her parents were "relocation candidates," courtesy of the Repatriot Program. Electra's call gave her an excuse to stop doing homework.

"I'm so glad you called. I'm all stressed out… I'll come over right now… Yes, I'd love to spend the night. I'll be over in about an hour. Bye." Matt overhead the end of the conversation.

"Why are you running off to see Electra? I want us to be co-friends, which means I should be the one you confide in. I like Electra, and I know the two of you go way back, but you need to rely less on her and more on me."

"Don't pressure me right now. Can't you see I'm upset enough as it is? I'm gonna fail college algebra if you can't teach me more about polynomials."

"I'm sorry. I didn't mean to upset you or make things harder. Look, spend the night with Electra and I'll see you tomorrow. Things will look better in the morning. They always seem to when you come back from her place." She hugged him, then threw some items into a gym bag and darted out, calming down as soon as Electra began talking.

"Even if your parents are deported, you still have a safety net of your good friends. Matt's your lifeline for just about any problem. And when you graduate next summer, you can work fulltime for Hud."

"I guess so, but please don't cut my umbilical cord. Even though I'm living with Matt, I still need you."

"I won't. You're my best friend. But remember, the only way you'll know if Matt's right for you is by living with him. Especially in today's unsettled times, people our age live together. It's the new normal and has been that way for years. I was born before my parents held a formal Vow-Cer. I'll bet your parents lived together before they got married. So, calm down."

"OK. But I won't calm down about school until Matt explains how trinomial factoring works, and he doesn't remember."

"I have an idea. Tell Matt to call me so I can explain it to him, and then he can teach you. OK?"

"I'll tell Matt." Robin had her emotions under control by the time Electra mentioned a possible Saturday double date.

"That'll be a lot of fun for Matt and me, a nice change of pace. And why don't we go shopping first? I'd like you to help me buy some new clothes. Matt will want to tag along. And when we're done, Matt will drive us to that trendy sensual pleasures café. Hey, have you been seeing this guy for very long?"

"No, but I owe him for helping change a tire. I'll tell you about it when he joins us. And I like the idea of going shopping. I don't have to worry about Carter picking me up. You and Matt can do that Saturday morning. I'll tell Carter to meet us at the café about six." Electra's stomach grumbled, telling her to change subjects.

"I'm hungry. I haven't had dinner yet. How about you? Have you eaten?"

"No, I was too upset."

"How about I make some cheese omelettes and toast? That's light enough for this time of night. And I want you to lighten up. You'll be fine tomorrow."

Robin wasn't the only one who felt better the next day. Matt did too because Electra had Emailed him an explanation of how trinomial factoring works. He called the very next evening in preparation for teaching it to Robin.

"Thanks for the write-up. I'll explain it to Robin as soon as you refresh my memory. Would you mind doing that now?"

"I'm happy to help. I know you have a good science background, so you'll have no trouble following. Here we go..." Electra ran through her write-up, explaining why the trinomial factoring algorithm is confusing; it uses an existence proof, which means problem solvers must rely on their wits for finding the right combination of integer factors. Fifteen minutes later, Matt knew enough to help Robin.

"I like your proof. My instructors never showed me one. They simply waved their hands when talking about 'FOIL,' you know: first, outer, inner, and last multiplication sequence. I never understood what they were doing, but thanks to you, now I do. I'll earn extra points when I show Robin how easy it is."

"Good, and just be patient. She isn't as quick with numbers as you are"

Matt decided after the call to hold an impromptu tutoring session. Thirty minutes later he proved conclusively that he needed more than patience. His fast reflexes let him dodge the book sailing over his head. Matt dutifully retrieved it from the hallway, then sat next to Robin at the kitchen table.

"Please don't get so upset. I think you're starting to catch on."

"Are you kidding? I haven't a clue about that existence proof stuff you're talking about. The only thing about factoring that exists is the headache I'm getting."

"I'm teaching you the best I can. And Electra said no one can teach you anything. She said that all I can do is facilitate your learning experience. She says you're supposed to meet me halfway by breaking an intellectual sweat."

"Are you kidding again? Of course, I'm sweating. I'll lose my scholarship if I fail the course."

"How about this. Let's stop here and have Electra tutor us Saturday afternoon when we stop for a snack at the mall." A hint of a smile lightened Robin's expression.

"That might work. She knows everything about math and is more patient than you are. She's my last best choice."

Robin wasn't the only one making choices. Ever since Securityguard had escalated its hunt for terrorist cells, Jameel and his lackeys had to keep a low profile. He became leader after Abdul succumbed to the T-Plague, and he pledged to avenge his death by punishing the woman who had infected him. He had been tracking her intermittently on weekends for the past nine months, looking for the right moment to confront her, but the woman proved elusive. As he cruised in his car, accompanied by three of his lackeys, he hoped today would be different.

"Allah be praised! There she is, and she is with the same couple. We shall follow. Let us be patient and observe at a distance." Jameel shadowed the van. Though the weather had turned gloomy and cold, mall traffic was heavy. Jameel parked as soon as he saw his targets walk to a nearby entrance.

"We have rehearsed the attack many times, but today will not be a drill, so let me repeat our plan. Take your attack gear and change, then stay hidden. I will shadow the woman so I know when to attack. Then I will call Anil, telling him my location so he can run towards me. I will point to the devil woman and he will attack her. Mirza and Roni, you run to opposite ends on the same level and spray virus. This is not a suicide mission. We need to carry out more attacks. We rendezvous at the car. I will wait, but no longer than five minutes. Are there questions?" There were none, so Jameel led the way...

"Where would you like to start?"

"I like your winter boots, so let's get them first. After that, let's look for a coat like yours. The high waist and extended length make it sexy. What do you think, Matt?" Matt, patiently in tow, agreed.

"It'll work on you too." And you ladies decide when to take a break so Electra can teach us factoring. I'll buy the refreshments."

After visits to three stores, the threesome acted on Matt's offer, and afterwards, since she often shopped at the mall, Electra led the way to a trendy coat store.

"They still have what I bought, but the color isn't right for you. We can always come back and ask them to order it, but let's check another store. It's on the second level; follow me."

Jameel, who had been tracking his quarry from the second level, was about to make the call. *Allah be praised! They are heading for the stairway close to where I am standing. It is time. And if she stays in the lead, Anil's knife will find its target.* He watched his accomplices jockey into position, the heavy mall traffic disguising their intentions. *My timing is blessed. Anil will meet her at the top of the stairs.*

Electra was about to step onto the second level when her warning system sounded an alarm. She saw an agitated person pointing at her just before coming face-to-face with a knife-wielding attacker who lunged at her chest, but she sidestepped the thrust, using his arm for leverage and swinging him three hundred and sixty degrees, then throwing him down the stairs into Matt. Matt staggered backwards, causing a chain reaction that piled shoppers in a heap on the lower landing. Robin grabbed for a railing but tripped, unable to stop from falling backwards down the stairs, gaining velocity with every stair. She was still vertical when reaching the landing but stepped on a pile of people that bounced her up and over the guardrail, plunging her headfirst towards the marble floor below, her screams lost in those of others. Matt staggered to his feet as the horror unfolded in slow motion.

"Robin!" he screamed, then rushed down the stairs. Electra saw everything but could do nothing until she dealt with the attacker, who had struggled to his feet and lunged again. She dodged the blade and grabbed his head, smashing it on her knee then pushing him down. People were rushing to help, so she grabbed the attacker's gun just before three men jumped on him, and then she jumped out of the way.

The attackers had miscalculated the public's anger; some were ready to fight instead of flee. A number of men at the mall joined the battle, pummeling the two who had started spraying. As she watched the melee and spotted the person who had been pointing, a sudden jolt surged through her brain, filling her with rage. She knew what he was, and she streaked on a collision course but reached the exit ten seconds too late, so she charged out and spotted him fleeing down a parking lot aisle. She ran just far enough to get a clear shot, then composed herself like a biathlete ready to shoot. She used a two-handed grip and took one breath before adjusting her aim. She exhaled slowly, then fired two quick rounds sprawling him face down, but he lurched to his feet so she fired again, taking him down for the count, then raced to her victim.

"I'm only going to ask you once: who sent you?" Electra knew from the gush of blood her adversary's words were a death rattle.

"Abdul, the one you infected… you have won. Allah will punish me…" His head rolled to the side and his eyes closed. Electra searched for his wallet and cell phone, then bolted away. No one was close enough to see what had just happened. She was free and clear. The lightning brain shifted gears again.

Electra shoved everything she was carrying into her pockets as she ran for a different entrance. Once in the mall, she was buffeted by a panic-driven stream of stragglers struggling to get out, but not far ahead she spotted a small crowd clustered in a ring at the base of a stairway. Matt was in the middle, along with an ambulance team that had just arrived. He had taken control until then; now he was helping as best as possible. Electra kept in the background, only watching because her help wasn't needed. Robin had landed on her head, coming to rest face down. A small pool of blood gathered next to her head, possibly from biting her tongue or cheek upon impact. There was no movement. The lead EMT barked out instructions.

"Keep her head and neck aligned just like they are. When we roll her onto the stretcher we'll use straps to immobilize head and shoulders. How are her vitals?" One of the crew snapped out the answer.

"Pulse 112. Labored breathing. I'll check for obstructions when we roll her over. Let's do it now." A minute later, the EMTs rolled a motionless Robin towards an exit. Electra slipped in next to Matt.

"You better ride in the ambulance. Give me your keys and I'll drive to wherever they're going." Matt nodded numbly, giving her his keys, never taking his eyes off Robin. Electra trotted to the ambulance by following the stretcher and asked the driver where they would go.

"Closest emergency center, and that's at Loudoun County Clinic." Electra ran to Matt's van as the ambulance gathered speed, its siren's mournful tone piercing the gloom. *They're taking her to Grandfather's clinic. I'm calling Clarence."*

Clarence was manning the reception station when his cell phone chimed, displaying a caller I.D. he recognized immediately. *Why is Electra calling? There must be an emergency.* He answered on the second chime.

"Clarence, it's Electra. Robin fell off a stairway landing and the ambulance is bringing her to you. Matt Fortier's with her. I think she has a broken neck. I'm coming too, so get ready."

Electra had been sitting patiently in the waiting area for three hours. There was no sign of Matt because he had insisted on staying at Robin's side. Finally, Clarence made his way to the waiting area.

"Robin's neck is broken in two places. Cervical fractures at the second and fifth vertebrae. Scans indicate complete but clean breaks. She's conscious and can talk, but she can't move arms or legs. Dr. Liefen-Liu is putting a neck brace on. By tomorrow he'll know if she needs to be in traction."

"Can I see her now?"

"No, the room's too crowded. You'd add to the confusion. Good thing Matt's with her. He's calmed her down. And he insists on taking her home as soon as the doctor says it's OK. Says he has all the equipment to handle her." Electra nodded in agreement.

"Yes, Matt's good. He took care of me when I broke my neck. You remember Christi? Well her mother, Jennifer Conklin, and Matt have started a caregiver business. They'll be able to take care of her."

"That'll be good for Robin. She's in good hands, and she'll get better care at home than anywhere else. Medical infrastructure is terrible. Overcrowded and understaffed. I have to get back, but I wanted to let you know how she is."

"Thanks. And please thank Dr. Liefen-Liu too." Clarence nodded, then marched back to his patient. Electra stared into space, trying to find a focal point but couldn't, so she sat down again. She absentmindedly fumbled through her pockets and pulled out the first object: her cellphone. It flashed 7:44.

Carter's waiting at the café. Damn, I forgot to call him. I'll do it right now. The phone flashed a warning message when she tried dialing: low signal—service unavailable—so she went to the reception desk phone and punched in Carter's number.

I haven't been stood up since my junior year in high school. And Miss Dented Rim didn't even call. Well, at least I know what a sensual pleasures café is like. And the waitress was understanding. She didn't charge for the coffee refill. Carter had waited impatiently for over an hour before storming back to his Vette; he was about to pull into his parking spot when his cellphone chimed. *Why is Loudoun Clinic calling me?* He answered on the third ring.

"Hello, this is Carter Quavah…Who? Sorry, I didn't catch the name. Must be a bad connection. I can't hear you over the exhaust rumble…Oh, it's Electra…You're calling from a clinic. Are you OK?...That's awful, and I'm sure you're upset. How about I call you tomorrow morning, about ten? …Thanks for letting me know." Carter replayed the call before parking. *I'm glad she phoned. I feel better about her now. I hope her friend bounces back.*

Electra hung up the phone just before a glowering Matt reached the reception area.

"Clarence gave me a report on Robin's condition. I'm so sorry. What can I do to help?"

"Let me drive you home. We'll talk on the way. Where'd you park my van?"

"In a Doctor's Only space because you have that Medical Staff sticker. Follow me." They walked on in awkward silence; Matt drove for five minutes before talking.

"I can think of only one thing you can do. I want you to stay away from Robin. Please leave her alone." Electra's eyes showed surprise but she didn't interrupt. "There's something about you. You're like a lightning rod. You're dangerous to your friends, but not to yourself. It's like you're Teflon-coated, like you have a protective shield that covers you but no one else."

"You're upset. How about we talk at the clinic tomorrow. I can help."

"No, I don't want you talking to me either, and I don't need your help. I'll take care of Robin. I'm taking her home as soon as I can."

"But she and I are best friends. We're good for each other. She'll want to see me."

"Didn't you hear what I just said? Your friends become collateral damage. It's time I sever the umbilical cord between the two of you." Electra said nothing as she was about to exit the van.

"Here we are, so it's time we say our final goodbye. Robin won't need me until tomorrow, so I'm going home to arrange the place." Electra got out and stared, leaving Matt's final words hanging in the air as he sped away.

Though she hadn't eaten since early afternoon and it was now after nine, she didn't feel hungry but knew she would feel better if she ate something, so she popped a Coke and made a peanut butter sandwich as she began sorting through Matt's hurtful words. Suddenly, a disturbing thought jolted her.

Am I dangerous to my friends? To the people I've loved, or love, or will love? A quote from the Hindu Bhagavad Gita flashed into her brain:

"Now I am become Death, the destroyer of worlds."

Am I the avatar of Shiva, the third god in the Hindu triumvirate? Those who know me well tell me I'm the reincarnation of Indira, my practically perfect mother. Is it possible that the things I do, though I try to help, turn out badly because I shouldn't meddle in other people's lives? I need to regroup and figure out what to do. Suddenly, an urgent feeling jolted.

I must see Robin now, tell her what Matt said, and seek forgiveness. Clarence has to let me in. She threw done the half-eaten sandwich and bolted to her car.

"Robin, it's Electra. Can you hear me?" Robin's eyes fluttered open. Nothing else but her lips moved.

"I'm so glad you're here. When you didn't come, I thought you were hurt, but Matt was too busy to talk about you." Electra knelt closer.

"I need to explain things, so listen carefully. I'm so sorry about what happened. Matt is terribly upset and he thinks I'm to blame, that I bring you bad luck. That's why he won't let me see you. But bad things happen to good people all the time for no reason. And I know I can help make you better. We'll make a game of it. I'll sneak in when Matt's at work. He's taking you home as soon as he can." Robin's lips quivered as she spoke.

"You always bring me good luck. If I could, I would kiss you for all you've given me." A new thought jolted Electra as the lightning brain shifted gears, telling her what to do.

"The next time I see you I'll tell you what we'll do to make you good as new. Now rest."

Electra awoke the next morning, brimming with energy and resolve to do what she must. She ran at sunrise through a cutting snow flurry, invigorated by the tingling sensation in her nostrils. Then she showered, and while eating breakfast, picked through Jameel's wallet and cellphone. When her phone rang at the stroke of ten, she spoke before the caller did.

"Good morning, Carter. You are a very punctual person, and I am too, so I apologize again for not calling you sooner last night.

"Good morning. I saw you on the news last night. The terrorist attack was big news, and the media used cellphone videos and eyewitnesses in their broadcasts. You were standing in the background. How's Robin?"

"Stabilized, but her neck's broken. I didn't watch the news last night. How did the media spin the attack?"

"They didn't need to spin anything; the facts spoke for themselves. People are beginning to fight back. All three of the terrorists were severely beaten, and the ringleader was shot dead in the parking lot. This is great material for Guardian Party PR because it fits their Gun-Tote'n slogan. Look, I'm sure you have lots to do today. I do too, and I have a busy week ahead. I would like to have dinner with you sometime, but I'm traveling this week in preparation for a seminar and panel discussion. Why don't you come to the seminar and we'll go out for dinner afterwards? It's the second Friday in December."

"I'd like that, but on two conditions only. First, I pay for the dry-cleaning and dinner. And second, you tell me the topic so I can be an informed listener. Deal?"

"That's a deal I can't refuse. But you might find the topic rather arcane, something only economists and government policy makers really understand. We'll be discussing socio-economic policy and inequality issues. Don't worry about it. I'll tell you more at dinner. How about if I call you ten a.m. Sunday after Thanksgiving to confirm?"

"I'll expect your call. Have a safe trip."

"I'll try. I'll call as planned."

Electra felt even better after the call. *Now I have another activity to plan for. And I'm always in a good mood when I know what to do. It's time to get started.*

CHAPTER 24

December 2120

"On the Mend"

(Thread 2 Chapter 10)

Robin's recovery occupied the top spot on Electra's priority list, and thanks to Jennifer it rolled out as planned. Matt handled Robin's physical therapy and Jennifer scheduled caregivers who stayed with Robin while Matt was at work. Matt never knew Electra stayed during the day, and no one knew what she did while there, not even Jennifer.

It's unfortunate that Matt is mad at Electra, but I'm not going to meddle. They have to settle things for themselves. And Electra is a good caregiver. She took care of Christi long ago.

But this time, there was more to do because Robin would be the Neuro-Knitter's first test patient. Each day she visited, Electra would affix its helmet and neck wrap, then dial the settings to optimize radio-stimulation for brain and affected vertebrae. And while being treated, Robin could chat or work on her laptop. She had regained limited use of arms and hands, and the more she used them, the better her fine motor skills became.

Robin was sworn to secrecy, and Electra refused to divulge progress, simply saying that that the healing process is similar to repairing a broken electrical circuit. Until the breaks knit, there would be little motion in arms or legs. But as soon as the Neuro-Knitter completed its job, motion would return fast and furiously, force multiplied by Matt's aggressive therapy. Robin might not be the first to notice because she lives in her body, but Electra certainly would.

Patients recovering from severe neck injuries often need four months to mend, but the conventional treatment was light years behind that of the Neuro-Knitter. Based on computer simulations, Robin's vertebrae could be knitted in six weeks, just in time for Christmas.

While treating Robin, Electra made time to monitor other games. Angus reported that Jared agreed to steer a moderate course; Alice disclosed that her boss was increasingly tight-lipped, essentially phasing her out. And at Thanksgiving dinner with the Conklin's, Russell said that NIH was planning to buy vaccines from a company in Texas.

She also made time for a chat with Chandra, who said Madhuri no longer needed smart pills because her mind had recovered to a level not far from where it had been prior to T-Plague. And this coming Friday would be the long-awaited date with Carter.

She had vetted "the guy with the Vette," learning he was indeed a talented fellow. Excellent resume, well connected, and level-headed. She found only one warning flag: his association with the Guardian Party. She would need to tread carefully until she knew more about that. The seminar-dinner date would be an opportunity to find out.

Electra decided to watch an online macroeconomics video while Robin worked on her laptop because that branch of economics covered the topics Carter had mentioned. She searched only among MIT's selection and came across *Policy Issues for Macroeconomics,* a symposium jointly sponsored by economics and political science departments, and as soon as the presenter began, Electra knew she had made the right choice.

She gave a practical definition of macroeconomics that highlighted the big issues it deals with: Growth, Wages, Unemployment, and Interest Rates, then launched into current issues facing the U.S. Topping the list is economic growth, historically shown to be driven by technology. Opportunities abound in the brave new world emerging from bio-tech and artificial intelligence, but many people fear its consequences. Job loss and income inequality are often cited. And she stressed how the T-Plague has exacerbated concerns. Survivors are cognitively impaired, no longer possessing hi-tech skills required on today's job market. But the problem is even bigger, because AI is taking over many white-collar professions. Her list of endangered occupations surprised many in the audience. It included lawyers, doctors, computer programmers, and teachers at all levels. And she warned that the educational system no longer should consider STEM a panacea for preparing youth for the job market. Pockets of personal service, experiential, and creative jobs may be the safest, and she hinted that even highly educated people should consider themselves robot assistants if they want to be employable in the coming AI Age.

At the end of the talk, the presenter broad-brushed government policies to consider. Until thirty years ago, the world community had been taking tentative steps in the right direction, but events since then caused a backward march that must be reversed. Anything to replenish dwindling Social Capital would help, as would efforts to bring economic and political realities into better balance, bolstering the Liberal Economic Order (open markets, multilateral institutions, liberal democracy, leadership by a "statesman nation"). And she emphasized that Globalization and Emigration need to be factored in. She tried to buck the audience up.

"Stay tuned. Come to the next symposium to explore options. There is plenty we can do. We aren't helpless victims. We can help shape the future. Be part of the solution." Electra agreed.

I like action, not indecision. And I'm ready for action at Carter's seminar. I shall find out more about "Mr. Vette."

Carter picked up Electra at noon, giving himself plenty of time to get her registered and then review his presentation slides already loaded on his laptop. He would be the first speaker, after which a moderator would call on others as he leads a panel discussion exploring both sides of each the issue.

"Thanks for being here on time. That, and the fact you called me when you left to get here tell me you're very thorough. Are all economists like that?"

"I can't speak for all of them, but it's my trademark, just like my Corvette, which is a hobby. And I economize my time when driving. I practiced my presentation while driving this morning. I hope you like it."

"I will, and I'm prepared. I studied up on the topics, and at dinner we can talk more about economics. I'm sure I'll learn a lot." Small talk filled the rest of the drive time, and as he ushered her into the hall, introducing her to fellow presenters, his desire to impress his guest grew.

Electra had attended many seminars, but never one covering what this one would. Glancing about, she noted that the audience had a mix of academic types (more faculty than grad students), government think tank staffers, and business professionals. *Looks like there are still some smart people who like macroeconomics.* At precisely one-thirty, the moderator welcomed the audience, summarized what would be covered, and then introduced the first speaker. Carter strode confidently to the podium.

Carter gave a brief overview, then explained his first slide: the Lorenz Curve:

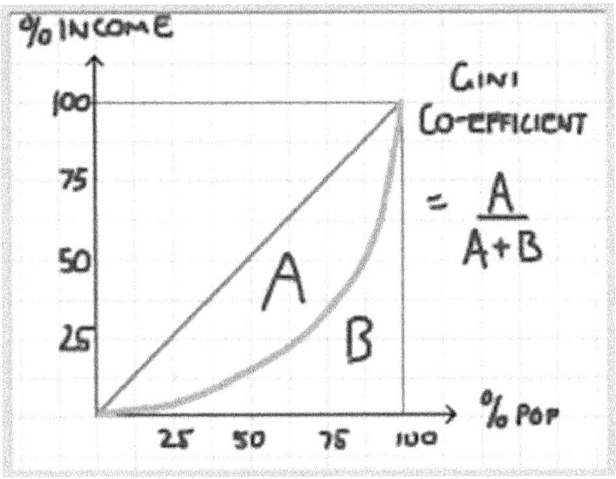

Electra's preparation would pay off.

I know this. It was developed by economist Max Lorenz in 1905. It shows graphically what income inequality looks like. Nice start. Carter first described how the Italian statistician and sociologist, Corrado Gini, in his celebrated 1912 publication *Variability and Mutability,* had developed the Gini Coefficient to quantify a definition of inequality. He then explained how Max Lorenz used it to form a convex graph: a greater coefficient means less inequality; the curve would be closer to the forty-five degree line.

His second slide highlighted some facts about the index:

- Index has cyclic time series for United States index values
- Index is greater in developed countries
- Correlations between index and economic growth depend on time lags and might not be statistically significant

Carter's explanation was clear and concise. Electra kidded to herself. *It shows that figures don't lie, but some liars can figure. But Carter's telling no lies. His slides look good.*

His next slide listed some of the misguided and simplistic reasons why economic inequality attracts so much attention:

- Inequality just seems "Morally Unfair"
- People are supposed to be equal
- Inequality harms people psychologically

I like his reasons, and why they make superficial sense. He's an excellent presenter too. He's connecting with the audience.

Now he explained why inequality requires more sophisticated reasoning:

- There is a trade-off between Freedom and Equality
- All people are not equal (Think of Athletic Ability and Sports Teams)

- Focus on Inequality diverts attention from what is really important
- Many examples where Ethical Decisions favor Equality lead to Disaster.
- Focus not on why some people have more, but on why people are poor

He's doing a great job connecting these points. This guy's sharp.
By now Carter was ready to address the key policy considerations:

- Must determine "How Much" is adequate to be above Poverty Level
- Must guarantee equal access to Key Resources (Education Job Opportunities)
- Must guarantee everyone treated with "Dignity and Respect"
- Must remove barriers to Social/Economic Mobility
- Must maintain large and thriving Middle Class

Extremely thorough. Carter, you've done your homework. Excellent presentation.

"So there you have it, my analysis for your consideration. We'll take a fifteen-minute break and come back for a panel discussion looking at the two sides of the debate: Is there or is there not an inequality problem in the United States? And if so, how should we deal with it? And we'll wrap up afterwards taking questions from the audience. See you back here in fifteen."

Electra walked to the entry area to get a soft drink and eavesdrop on conversations, many giving the speaker high marks; precisely fifteen minutes later the discussion started. Electra noted that panelists on both sides were qualified and prepared, citing examples supporting different points of view. They engaged the audience, many of whom asked incisive questions. Precisely at four, the moderator ended the discussion, thanking all in attendance and acknowledging that a complex issue like this requires careful consideration from smart people, especially since income inequality increases as the number of T-Plague victims grows.

Electra waited in the lobby for Carter; by the time he appeared most people had filed out. He looked tired but relieved. She knew from experience that public speaking is stressful, no matter how well prepared you are.

"Congratulations. I'm a good judge of presentations, and yours hit the mark: clear and concise. And you have excellent platform skills. I eavesdropped at the break, and I heard nothing but positive comments."

"Thanks, I'm glad you liked it. And please let me know if you find something I could have done better. I get better only by working on my weaknesses, not my strengths. I hope you're hungry, because I'm starved. Public speaking burns up lots of calories, and I've got us reservations at a nice Italian restaurant..."

Electra enjoyed the wine, lasagna, and tiramisu. But she enjoyed the conversation even more. She had been on few dates where her partner kept her interested. Not so with Carter, because he was quick-witted, knew his subject, and expressed himself well. When she asked about connections between cognitive psychology and behavioral economics, he didn't bat an eye.

"Those are great questions. Let me show you one of my presentations on the subject. It'll cover most of what you asked. As Carter busied himself, Electra smiled. *So, that's why he keeps his laptop with him. This guy is well prepared for whatever comes his way.*

"Let me scroll over the high points. Please note that behavioral economics is built on cognitive psychology, which substitutes the irrational emotional man for the rational economic man. We can thank Kahnemann and Tversky's foundational book—*Thinking, Fast and Slow*—for much of what we see today. But you won't find it in undergrad classes. Behaviorial Economics is the domain of graduate econ and finance courses.

"It's built on two major principles: Prospect Theory, and Weighting Functions. Take a look at the graphs. The mathematical models get rather complicated, so I won't try to teach it to you, but I'm sure you understand the major takeaways: people are overconfident and risk averse, and they don't know how to apply conditional probability."

Electra liked what she heard. *He'll never know how fast I can think, but that's OK. I'm impressed. Carter's smart, and I like his unassuming self-assurance. I'll toss him another question.*

"The moderator mentioned a connection between the T-Plague and income inequality. What do you think it is?"

"Here's what public policy economists are thinking. The T-Plague has damaged the I.Q.'s of a lot of people. Sure, they're still able to work, but no longer at the intellectual level that's needed. All they can get are low-tech jobs that don't pay much. So, the T-Plague has hollowed out the middle class, and that bows out the Lorenz Curve: too many people barely getting by, and too few able to achieve the American Dream. I hope some smart people can come up with vaccines that work. *I'm working on it, but that's not a topic for tonight. Time to switch subjects.*

What can you tell me about the economics of caring? Is Caring Economics an official branch?" Now it was Carter's turn to smile.

"I'm impressed. Not many people know about it. And to answer your question, it's an unofficial branch of economics that's gaining traction. It is often mentioned in the context of the Sharing Economy. Some of the earlier studies connect it with Adam Smith's classic, *the Wealth of Nations,* pointing to the emotional needs of people. Doing that might create whole new industries containing jobs immune to artificial intelligence, as well as build Social Capital. And that's all to the good as we move further into the AI Economy, for which platform companies are often cited. I won't go into the details because they might confuse you, but they're all about the algorithms that make the Internet more efficient. But there's a downside too, and I'm still working on it, and when I'm ready to stake a position I'll put in a position paper for a committee I'm on. And I can use it later at the Federal Reserve Board."

"Why don't you tell me about your work at the Fed. I know some of what goes on there, but I'd like to hear it from the inside."

"I'd be happy to. It's rather complicated how we create and control the supply of money, so I'll just cover only the basics, but you'll know more than most people by the time I'm done…" Carter talked for twenty minutes.

"I hope I didn't bore you. I know many professional women, but hardly any can discuss economics like you. I've enjoyed the day, and dinner with you has been the high point. I like exploring ideas. Would you like to get together again?"

"I think so. Please call me."

"I will, and I'll buy dinner the next time. And I think it's time I drive you home."

Electra thought more about Carter as she prepared for bed. *I like Carter's style. He's cerebral in a boyish, pleasant sort of way, and he doesn't force himself; didn't reach for a goodnight kiss. If he calls, we'll go out and I'll find out what he thinks about the Guardian Party. He's the best fellow I've ever dated.*

As the year wound down, Electra busily planned for the coming year, and when Carter called late the following week, she was so preoccupied she was almost curt.

"Hi, Carter. I hope you've had a good week. What's up?"

"Good evening. I'm wrapping up work for the Holidays, and that's why I'm calling. I would like to invite you to a New Year's Eve party. Did I call soon enough to reserve a place on your calendar?"

"Yes. Thanks for the invite and I accept. I'm busy right now and can't talk. I'll call you Sunday morning at ten for more details. Bye." Electra disconnected before Carter could get in another word, but he did talk to himself afterwards.

Now that was a bum's rush of the first magnitude. This is the first time a lady's been so cavalier with me. I'm the one who usually has to break off the call. Well, *maybe she does have a lot going on. And I'll be damned if I'm not intrigued by her. She doesn't reveal much; rather enigmatic; there's a lot hidden. I'll have to be patient.*

Carter wouldn't have been so miffed if he knew about Electra's current activities, especially the one for Robin. Tomorrow she would take her for another MRI.

Robin was a caregiver's joy. She never complained, tried to be cheerful, and was easy to lift in and out of the wheelchair. The light snow that Friday morning caused no problems, and by twelve-thirty Electra and her patient were waiting for Clarence to show the images that would be uploaded to her case file for the neurosurgeon—Henry Liefen-Liu—to study further. Clarence wasted neither time nor words.

"Matt's therapy is getting amazing results. After only five weeks, the first vertebra is completely knitted, while the second is almost at the fusion point. Robin should have feeling in legs by yearend. Tell me again why I shouldn't tell Matt?"

"Matt has a big emotional investment in our patient. So, we don't want to build up his hopes before we know." Clarence nodded.

"OK. And I'll tell Dr. Liefen-Liu mum's the word."

Robin had been housebound since her accident, so Electra decided they should celebrate the MRI results by stopping on the drive home for lunch. The change of pace proved to be an elixir; Robin sparkled as before.

"Matt will be surprised when I start moving my legs so soon. That'll be the time I'll tell him to let you visit. I'm sure that'll make things better between you two."

"I hope so. How are things with your parents?"

"Dad's still mad at me for moving in with Matt, but it's a case of displaced anger. He's worried being deported. And I hate him for putting the family in such a bad place. But if my folks are forced to go, at least they have family back in Russia and enough money to resettle. And I can stay here. But I'll feel better about the future once I can use my arms and legs."

"Don't worry. My Neuro-Knitter is working. You'll be walking by early next year or sooner, because Matt's therapy is keeping your muscle tone and strength."

"He's devoting all his spare time to me, but I feel like I'm being smothered. He treats me like an exotic orchid that needs constant attention, and it's too much. I haven't told him because I don't want to be ungrateful. But once I'm on my feet, I have to tell him it's killing our relationship. Do you think I'm being selfish?"

"No. Intimate relationships are tricky, even when everything is going well. Talk with Matt about the trade-offs among intimacy, commitment, and sex. Make sure you each give enough to keep the other happy.

"I thought I knew what I wanted when I moved in, but I've lost my way. I guess that's another reason I'm not pushing the issue until the accident's behind me. Do you want to give me some advice?"

"I thought I just did. You and Matt have to talk. Come on. I'll take you home for more neuro-knitting."

That evening, Electra thought about what Robin might do if she and Matt terminate their co-friendship. There were two options, so she called Jennifer.

"I just wanted to let you know Robin's broken neck is mending faster than the doctors thought, but please don't tell Matt. And I wanted your opinion on something that might help her. Is now a good time to talk?"

"Of course, it is. She's like a daughter. What are you thinking?"

"It might be good if she takes a break from living with Matt. She's beginning to feel smothered, and she doesn't want to move home because she's mad at her father. She could move in with me, or with you if you're willing, until she can be on her own."

"I'd love to have her. Just let me know when. And remember, we're there for you if you ever need us."

"You and Mr. Conklin are dear friends, and I thank you. And thanks again for inviting me for Christmas Eve dinner."

Between now and Christmas, Electra had only one more item on her to-do list, postdoc activity, which included T-Plague and neuro-devices. As she wrote year-end status reports for her advisors, they brought to mind a whimsical comparison. *Now here's an example where a quote from the early 20th century modern architect Mies Van der Rohe fits: less is more. The less they know the more I get done without their getting in the way.*

Postdoc activity also included scheduling a video conference to review vaccine production and Neuro-Knitter improvements. *Austin stays at the top of my partners' list. Hud's a shrewd negotiator and people motivator; Su and Tim know enough to get things done, and Adom is Su or Holy's go-to guy.*

An abrupt thought pinged before she placed the call. *There are more people in Austin I care about than in DC I have to live here today, but who knows what the future holds? Perhaps I can move it towards Austin, but it's too soon to know.* The ping disappeared as quickly as it came.

Hud's voice exuded confidence for the coming year as he added an exclamation point at meeting's end.

"Well now, your Highness, Happy Holidays. You can see that your loyal subjects are working hard so next year's results will please you. Do you have any final offers we can't refuse?"

"Not until next year when all us will be better than ever. And until then, you're all on Holiday break. We'll talk in January after you and Tim hold interviews for the Sales Development Manager. And I should be able to give you some updates that could accelerate timetables. So Happy Holidays, and thanks again for all you're doing." Hud asked one final question before ending the call.

"Holy asked about Robin. How's she doing?"

"Please thank your father for asking. Tell him she'll be walking soon. And she might be able to do more accounting work for you next year, but that will depend on how quickly goes back to school."

"You tell her we'll keep her chair warm. She's worth it..."

"I can't believe today is the start of winter. Everything's been a blur since my accident." Robin was propped up in her adjustable bed, using a lap desk to give her arms additional support while Electra sat in a nearby chair, working on her laptop. She glanced casually at Robin but kept one eye on what she was doing.

"Well, I can. Today's snow and cold feel like it, and I've checked everything off my yearend to-do list. You must be getting lots done too, judging by your Internet surfing. What topic catches your fancy?"

"The role of sex in co-friend relationships. Males and females have different orgasm clocks. Have you ever researched the biological explanation?"

"No, I haven't. You know more than I do, so please tell me what you've learned."

"I've scored a first. I've never been ahead of you on anything except the piano. I shall pat myself on the back." Robin continued talking after doing so, but Electra cut her off.

"Do it again."

"Do what?"

"Don't you realize what you just did?" You extended your arms." Electra walked towards the bed as Robin extended both arms over her head."

"Holy shit," is all she said as a look of surprise spread.

"Try moving your feet." Robin wiggled both of them as her expression morphed into a grin.

"Your Neuro-Knitter must have just finished its job. Electra knelt next to Robin and spoke while removing the cap and wrap.

"One step at a time. Let's check both arms, then legs." Robin pushed and pulled, then twisted and turned arms and legs for a half-hour while Electra increased the force of resistance.

"You're ready for the next step. I'll swing your legs over the side, and I'll help you stand as you hold on to your walker." As excitement built, Robin stood up less than a minute later.

"Matt's therapy has kept your muscle strength and tone. Now try to walk. I'm holding, so you won't fall." Robin shuffled hesitantly across the room.

"Excellent. Now, let's try it again." Robin's balance and footwork improved with each repetition, like a cyclist riding laps on a track after being off the bike for a month or two. Electra kept count, and fifteen minutes later gave a status report to the patient.

"I'm proud of you. Your pacing speed is getting faster the more reps you make, but let's break for lunch. You've earned it. And we'll do another set this afternoon, after you've rested. Electra helped her shuffle to the kitchen, then made peanut butter sandwiches while Robin chirped excitedly about walking further. After finishing a plate of cookies, Electra changed the subject.

"So, tell me what you learned about orgasms."

"According to one blogging site, we can throw out all those spiritual or psychological explanations. Sex and orgasms are physical processes. And a fertilized embryo isn't male or female until week six. That's when progenitor cells differentiate into either ovaries or testicles. So, the orgasm machinery for males and females is about the same."

"I knew about progenitor cells, but I never connected them to orgasms. Keep going."

"Another blogging site mentioned natural selection or evolutionary fitness theories might explain why female orgasms take longer. Men had to be fast in caveman days in order to be ready to defend themselves, and women had to be slow to increase the odds of fertilization. But one post disagreed, calling it a random mutation. Which do you pick?"

Electra kidded, "Neither. I have a better explanation. Suppose orgasms were fast and easy for both sexes. Cavemen and women might have become addicted to sex, causing the men to forget about survival skills, like hunting or building fires. The cavemen would waste away, like drug addicts today. Our ancestors would have screwed themselves to extinction." Robin kidded right back.

"I get it. Mankind would have gone out with a bang."

"You can post our explanations after you rest."

"No, I'd rather do more reps."

"OK. After your nap, we'll increase the distance gradually."

Robin was in motion an hour later, gaining speed and stability as well as confidence.

"Let me solo. Go stand by the front door, and I'll walk towards you from the hallway." The girls were in position, and Robin was about to glide away when Matt unexpectedly walked in and blew up.

"Jesus H Christ! Robin, are you crazy!? It's too soon to try walking!" He rushed to grab her, trampling Electra, who crashed awkwardly face-first onto an end table, then sprawled onto the carpet.

"Leave me alone! Can't you see I'm OK?" Robin's words froze Matt. Neither spoke, and the only sound came from Electra's groaning as she struggled to her knees, until Robin yelled again.

"Holy Shit! Look what you've done to Electra's nose!" When he turned, what he saw turned his stomach: Electra's nose jutting to the left, blood gushing onto her sweater. Matt knew instantly he was facing a badly broken nose.

"Oh Jesus, Jesus!" He stared mutely for a second at the damage, but then his medical training took charge. *I know what to do. I've done it plenty of times, but I better be quick.*

"I will fall on my sword tomorrow in front of you and Robin. I will grovel at your feet, begging forgiveness. But, I need to set your nose ASAP. I'm a pro at this, and I'll explain everything as we proceed. Robin, where's your wheelchair? I'll get it so you can sit and watch. Never mind, I see it in the hallway." Matt dashed for it, then parked Robin so she could observe.

"Please sit on the couch with your head tilted back. I'll get some towels and wash cloths." Matt came back in seconds, wiping away some of the blood that continued to trickle out. "I'm getting my supplies out of the van. Hold the wash cloth in place and apply pressure." Matt explained more after he dashed back.

"This is going to look worse than it really is, but squeamish people don't like watching. Maybe Robin should turn away."

"I ain't going anywhere." Matt knew better than to try changing her mind.

"Suit yourself." Matt devoted full attention to Electra, using another wash cloth and towel to clean her up, but when she tilted her head forward, blood continued to run.

"Keep your head tilted back. I need to set your broken nose before swelling sets in. There are two types of broken noses: displaced and non-displaced. Yours is displaced, which is harder to set because it's out of alignment, so I have to straighten it before I can push it back into place. But before I do that, I have to stop the bleeding by inserting medical swabs and packing into your nostrils. It will feel uncomfortable but it's not painful. Blow your nose into the towel to clear your nasal passages." Robin nearly gagged; the quantity of blood and the sight of swabs being twirled into nostrils looked awful, but Electra sat like a Stoic, ready for the pain that came her way.

"The medication will stop the bleeding in a minute. I'm out of topical anesthetics. Do you want me to go for Lidocaine?"

"No. Just get on with it."

"Let me check the ice supply and find an ice pack." Robin yelled he would find it in the bathroom cabinet. Matt hurried back.

"I'm going to remove the swabs in another minute. By then the silver nitrate will have stopped most of the bleeding. How are you feeling?" Electra's muffled reply was hard to hear.

"I can handle the pain. I think I've swallowed more blood than I blew out. It tastes like I'm drinking salt. I better add more to my eggs tomorrow. Eggs and dairy products help replenish blood supply. Ask Jennifer." Matt was too busy to reply; Robin just gaped at the spectacle. *How can she be so clinical about the ordeal? Maybe she's having an out- of-body experience.*

"I'm going to remove the swabs. Let me know if you need me to stop." Electra didn't make a peep, didn't move a muscle, but Robin flinched, feeling vicarious pain that made her woozy. *How can something so long be poked up her nose?*

"Now I'm going to straighten the nose by aligning cartilage and bone. The clicking you'll hear is normal. I'll place my thumbs on both sides of your nose and hold your cheeks while I push to your right." *This is going to hurt, so I better do it fast before she has too much time to think.* Matt did so before anyone could say a word. There was a loud SNAP. Matt stepped back to view his handiwork.

Damn, I've gone too far to the right, but we're closer to center.

"We're almost there. I need to make a final alignment by pushing to the left." This time there was an audible CLICK. Matt felt Electra shudder, but she uttered not a word; Robin cringed in utter horror, eyes transfixed on Electra's agony, bowels churning in anguish, queasiness congealing into a lump in her stomach, like a bad meal refusing to stay down. Giddiness instinctively forced her knees together until she could squeeze no harder.

Matt ignored Robin, focusing solely on Electra, calmly explaining the next step.

"The alignment is perfect; I'm ready to set your nose. We call it an adjustment. I will firmly but carefully grasp the back of your neck with both sets of fingers. I will then place my thumbs on either side of your nose and snap your nose back into place. You'll hear clicking or snapping. If I'm satisfied with the results, we're done. If not, I'll do another adjustment and repeat until alignment and adjustment are perfect." Robin refused to pay attention to her growing nausea but did ask a pertinent question.

"How many adjustments does it usually take?"

"Only one, sometimes, but usually two to get the alignment right. Are you ready for the first?"

"Yes."

"Close your eyes." Before positioning thumbs along each side of her nose, he explored the contours to locate the exact location of the break so he could force perfect alignment. *It's a clean break that will heal perfectly once the pieces snap into place.* Matt locked his eyes onto his thumbs, took a deep breath and pushed hard. There was another loud SNAP! Matt felt another involuntary shudder rattle his patient, but the head remained motionless. Although pain forced a flood of tears, Electra didn't squeak a syllable, but Robin mouthed the S-word as she squirmed.

"Keep your eyes closed. I'm studying the adjustment." *First adjustment looks good, but there's more distance to go.*

"We've closed the gap, and the alignment looks good. I'm going to do a second adjustment. Can you handle it?"

"Yes. Go ahead."

Matt repeated the adjustment, causing a loud CRACKLE! and another shudder. Robin nearly gagged.

"Keep your eyes closed. I'm checking alignment." *Alignment's perfect and the gap's almost closed. One more adjustment will do it.*

"The alignment is perfect. One more adjustment will close the gap completely. Your nose will heal without a trace of a break. Ready?"

"Yes."

The third adjustment was the charm. A loud POP signaled success as Matt's thumbs detected perfectly aligned closure. But this time poor Robin's stomach erupted as breakfast and lunch cascaded into her lap. Matt now had two patients to clean up.

Relief surged through Electra, bringing with it tears of gladness, as well as her wry sense of humor.

"I haven't seen Robin woof her cookies like that since freshman year in high school when she heaved on Liam."

"Oh, shut up. Matt doesn't want to hear." Matt paid no attention, sticking strictly to business.

"I'll clean you first so you can start holding the ice pack on your nose. If you stay overnight, I'll keep it there when you try to sleep. That'll take care of swelling or discoloration."

Though he had repaired the damage, Matt felt as bad as if he had just pitched his grandmother down the basement stairs, and he felt even worse when Electra explained why she was there. Matt called Jennifer after putting the room in order, reporting Robin's good news, and she arranged for an MRI, after which Robin would no longer need a neck brace. As he guided Robin to bed, she told him what else she no longer needed.

"Take me to the Conklin's when we leave the clinic. I don't need to stay with you any longer." Matt didn't argue since her mind was set as firmly as Electra's nose, so he retreated to the living room. Electra had heard Robin's parting shot because she was parked on the living room sofa.

"You heard what Robin said. What do you think I should do?"

"Talk to Robin. She'll feel differently in a day or two. Then find out what she wants and what you want."

"Would you help me talk to her?"

"I would if I could, but only the two of you can work things out. But here's something that might help. Have you ever heard the atta-boy story?" Matt shook his head no.

"It goes like this. Every time you do something Robin likes, you earn one atta-boy. But when you do something she doesn't, you earn a bunch of aw-shits. And it takes ten atta-boys to cancel one aw-shit. But keep doing good things, and she'll soften."

"I'll try, but didn't you tell me her nickname used to be the Ice Queen? Do you think she's returned?"

"I don't know. It's up to Robin and you to find out. Just do your best." Matt nodded, then straightened his shoulders as he walked to the kitchen to refill the ice pack. As she watched him go, a novel idea sparked in her lightning brain.

I know who can help. All I have to do is arrange a meeting, then watch what happens.

CHAPTER 25

December 2120

"The Holiday Gatherings"

(Thread 1 Chapter 12)

JENNIFER HADN'T FELT THIS good since the days when Christi decorated her life, and now that Robin had come to stay, she felt useful once again, helping Robin work through relationship issues. Christmas Eve dinner would be special.

"You can help me set the table when you finish dressing. Please let me know if you need help." *I'm so glad we kept Christi's bedroom intact. Robin's presence makes it feel almost like Christmas Past.* Robin glided into the dining room using the walker only as a precaution.

"I've put the settings and silverware on the table, and I'll let you arrange them. Russell will let us know when our guests arrive. And I'll be in the kitchen." Ten minutes later, Russell's voice boomed cheerily.

"Our guests are arriving. Here's comes Matt with Electra and her date. What's the fellow's name?" Jennifer sang out, "Carter Quavah." Russell added, "He must be a sports car enthusiast. He's driving a Corvette."

Patience is a virtue after all. Electra wasn't blowing me off. Not only did she accept my New Year's Eve invitation, but she invited me for Christmas Eve dinner with friends. And look at this. She's already outside waiting for me. That is one thoughtful lady. Better get out and get the door. Maybe I'll earn a good night kiss.

Electra was waiting in the late afternoon's frosty sunlit air. Carter would be her date at the Conklin's Christmas Eve dinner, which would give her another opportunity to learn more about him. And since Electra had convinced Jennifer to invite Matt, Carter's presence might help Matt soften Robin's heart of ice. Carter spoke first when he greeted Electra at the curb.

"Good evening. You look elegant. And your red velvet neck choker is a festive color. Here, let me get the door for you." Soon, they were in and on the way.

"I like guys who are punctual; it tells me they're thoughtful. I also like how patient you are. It's a sign of intelligence and maturity." Carter liked the conversation's direction.

"I have a confession to make. My friends tell me impatience is one of my flaws, and I'm sometimes judgmental. But at least I know about them and work to improve."

"If those are your worst flaws, your parents did a nice job. And yes, patience is a virtue. It's one of the Seven Heavenly or Contrary Virtues. The Seven Contrary Virtues are opposites to the Seven Deadly Sins: Humility against Pride, Kindness against Envy, Abstinence against Gluttony, Chastity against Lust, Patience against Anger or Wrath, Liberality against Greed, and Diligence against Sloth." Carter was impressed. He listened to himself for a moment as Electra kept talking.

How does she remember all this and rattle it off so quickly?

"You'll like Russell and Jennifer Conklin. They're lovely people, parents of my best friend Christi, who was killed a couple of years ago. Robin and Christi were my two best friends going all the way back to grade school. I'm so glad Robin's walking again. You'll meet her and her friend Matt at dinner tonight. Your GPS is working fine. We're almost there."

"I promise to be just as punctual New Year's Eve, and I know you'll enjoy the party. And I already know the way there. It'll be at the Palomar Hotel near Georgetown. The hostess has been my mentor since I came to DC She's the junior senator from California—Olivia Torres. Her husband's a full bird colonel from West Point, Ricardo Torres, who is currently on assignment at the Pentagon. I expect he'll be in uniform at the party. Dress code is black tie optional, so I'll wear a dark blue pinstripe and vest. I think you might prefer to wear a long dress or a cocktail number." Electra smiled as she nodded.

"Thanks for telling me about the dress code. I think I know what to wear." The two of them enjoyed a comfortable break in the conversation. As they approached the Conklin's, Electra outlined Matt's predicament.

"I see Matt's van pulling in. You need to know what's going on between him and Robin. They started living together just before Robin's accident. He's a physical therapist and gets credit for her rapid recovery. But Robin's been staying at the Conklin's for a week. She's angry because Matt broke my nose last week. It was an accident, but Robin thinks he shoved me too hard. He wouldn't let me see her because he thinks I'm bad luck, and when he caught me visiting he pushed me. But he set my nose right away."

"You mend quickly. It's healed without a trace of a break. And there's no discoloration or swelling. If he did the adjustments, he's got great hands."

"Don't let on what I've told you, but please find things to say that will put Matt in a good light. I'll do the same."

Jennifer and Russell greeted everyone at the door, Russell collecting coats as Jennifer guided them into the living room for drinks and appetizers before serving their family's traditional Christmas Eve dinner: beans and Swedish meatballs, cornbread, a selection of salads, and mince pie for dessert. Electra made introductions that segued into conversation that removed any remaining tension. Robin was of course the center of attention when she glided in five minutes later.

"Walking again is a wonderful Christmas present. I feel like I've risen from the dead, but that's an Easter metaphor, so I'll call it my Christmas epiphany. But let's talk about something else. Why doesn't Carter tell us how he met Electra." The conversation went from there through dinner, the soft lighting and glowing candles adding a warm intimacy. Talk slowed after dinner, giving Jennifer time to serve after-dinner drinks at the table and Electra an opportunity to steer the conversation.

"Mrs. Conklin, do you remember our "Three Queens Adventure" freshman year in high school when Robin took the wrong drink? We were going to tell Matt the story last week but couldn't find the right time."

"I will, but first I'll tell how "The Sisters" became "Three Queens." Christi and Electra were the stars of a grade school soccer team that won the league championship the last year they played. Christi's nickname was Goldi because of her good looks and valuable passes; Electra was Legs because of her speed and footwork. And the team's nickname became "The Sisters." Robin connected with the girls in grade school and the class nicknamed them the Three Queens.

"The wrong drink episode took place at a Christmas party hosted by a junior—Darlene Gustavson. Normally, freshman aren't invited to parties given by older cheerleaders, but Christi had connections because she was socially active. She had Darlene invite Electra and Robin. Robin was a center of attention because she played the piano for group singing, but two fellows decided to give her date drugs. Long story short, it backfired. Before they could do much mischief, Christi and Electra whisked Robin away. To this day, I still remember Electra's graphic description of the episode. I knew there was a cover-up when I retrieved them, but I didn't press the issue. I knew they would learn a good lesson without my scolding. I'm sure the girls can embellish the story. Electra, would you like to add anything?"

"Why, yes. Christi led us into a number of adventures that showed us how bad guys can be, as well as taught us what to look for in the good ones. I must have paid attention, because two of the best ones I've ever found are at the table. Thanks to Matt, I recovered from my accident, and thanks to Carter, not only did he change my tire, but he also changed my opinion about economists. You've been working with Matt. What have you learned about him?"

"Not only is he a skilled physical therapist, but he also knows how to handle business issues. He's helped me set up procedures for tracking invoices and scheduling patient visits. And female patients comment on how empathetic he is. They tell me he really understands their feelings." Matt decided he better say something because all eyes were looking at him.

"I give credit to my sister. I learned from her the full range of female emotions. Carter, do you have any sisters?"

"Yes, but she's three years older so we weren't terribly close. I learned from dating, and even more from the professional women I work with. They're as smart as fellows, and just as good in math. According to BLS employment statistics, women are taking more top spots in AI computer programming, ostensibly because they code better algorithms for processing neural inputs to output emotional responses. That's one of the few areas the Bureau forecasts double-digit job growth. Is your sister older or younger?"

"A year younger. I dated some of her friends, and she some of mine. She likes poetry and literature and often tells me what novels to read. Do you have a taste for the fine arts?"

"No. Like most economists, I stay on the practical side, and perhaps Electra can teach me poetry. But practical men often write better stories than literary types." Robin's ears perked up.

"I don't follow what you said. Literary types who write stories have much stronger empathy and deeper feelings than your so-called practical business or science types. And practical types write nonfiction, not stories. So, you're wrong."

"Let me give you an example. Assume that the better the story, the more people it impacts. Now, let's consider civilization. Civilization creates ideology-laden fictitious stories to develop religious, political, economic, and social order. The stories eventually become our beliefs about reality, so civilization transforms them into nonfiction stories. And no fictional novel ever written has impacted as many people as Marx's *Communist Manifesto.* So, that should prove my point." Electra noted that Carter's point proved to be a conversation stopper, so she scrambled to restart it.

"That was quite interesting, and I know you economists are smart when dealing with practical matters. But what about dealing with relationships? Perhaps you could enlighten us."

I could relate a story from economics, called the economist's commitment story, that explains how we choose our mates. Matt might want to hear it, but I don't want to monopolize the conversation, so maybe he and I can talk about it sometime."

"I certainly would. I'll call you so we can grab a beer and discuss further." Russell, who had been happy sitting on the conversation sidelines, came up with a question for Carter.

"You mentioned BLS labor statistics pointing to hi-tech job growth. I work at NIH, and we see the same trend in bio-pharmaceuticals. Do you expect that to continue?"

"Yes, and it will accelerate as we charge into the brave new Transhuman Economy. Transhuman technology holds great promise, but like all tech-driven paradigm shifts, it is highly disruptive. Fundamentalist societies, like Isilabad, are afraid of this future and want to turn back the clock by making the world read from an old storybook, but the old stories don't work today or in the future." Electra glanced at her cell phone before deciding what to say.

It's too late to talk about Jared. I'll ask Carter more questions next time, but now it's time to get up and go.

"Thanks for inviting Carter and me. I'd like to stay, but I have to say good night. Robin, I'll call you tomorrow." Matt also rose but sat down after Robin spoke.

"Call me tomorrow afternoon. Carter, I'm glad Electra brought you. You have a lot of interesting ideas. I don't like all of them, but you do have a lot of facts. And Matt, stay awhile so we can talk." Jennifer walked the departing couple to the door.

"You're a very handsome pair. Merry Christmas, and a Happy New Year."

Carter drove Electra home, puzzled by her sudden silence. *She's preoccupied, and I don't know why. Whatever it is must be important, but I won't push the issue. Besides, I'll see her New Year's Eve.*

They walked in silence to the front door, and as Electra opened it, a desire to kiss Carter passionately whelmed her. She spun, placed her hands behind his head and drew him to her, inhaling long and deep as her lips devoured his, taking his breath away as she suspended him in the moment. He recovered, trying to fold her in his arms, but she was too quick. She pushed away, wearing an inscrutable expression.

"This has been a wonderful Christmas Eve. Thank you for sharing it with me. I look forward to New Year's Eve. Now drive home safely." And without another word, she vanished behind the closing door. Carter stood motionless, drinking in every ounce of pleasure, finally turning, and then walking briskly to his Vette.

As soon as the door closed, Electra began preparing for her traditional midnight vigil held every Christmas Eve since the death of her grandfather seven years ago. It was a time to withdraw into her fortress of solitude, remembering the dearly departed, giving thanks for wisdom gained this year, and rededicating herself to her chosen path. From this synthesis would emerge a coherent reality for her three personas: the physical, the cognitive, and the emotional. And it would be in the context of this reality that Electra's actions would write her own story for the coming year.

Her preparations were always the same. She would sit beneath the shower head's cleansing cascade until the winter chill washed away, then soap away the remains of the day. Afterwards, after toweling off, she would wrap herself in a bathrobe and then take her keepsake box of remembrance notes and letters to the living room, where she would adjust the curtains and blinds to her liking. She always opened them so she could view the winter landscape gently aglow from traditional luminary candles spaced along the curb. Tonight, after reading again selected keepsakes and promising herself she would read the unopened letters perhaps next year, she would turn off all lights but keep the suffused softness of a multi-colored glow coming from an end table-mounted foot-high ceramic Christmas tree housing a small-wattage incandescent bulb. Then, wrapped in a blanket, she would nestle on the sofa, propping herself with several pillows, and let the lightning brain freewheel. Sometimes she would stay awake until dawn; sometimes she would dream. But sometimes her Muse would visit, an apparition so vivid it superseded reality. Tonight, as her eyes grew heavy, she drifted to sleep.

"Alisha? Alisha? I have come to pay you a visit. Awaken now and talk with me." Electra snapped to attention, instantly attuned to an enchanting voice, the voice that spoke only to her, the voice of her Muse—Indira. And as she gazed at a graceful apparition, haloed in a soft glow, sitting near, Indira's smiling, sparkling eyes mirrored her words.

"Alisha, that is the name I chose for you. And I am pleased that your empathy has grown. You are learning how to give what people you care for need from you. Do not withhold yourself; it is only by giving freely that you will receive what you want.

"And no longer are there adversaries threatening to reveal your secret. You have vanquished them, but you are now in danger not because of your lightning brain, but because you know too much. Be wary of those seeking your knowledge, for your life will depend on vanquishing them. Trust your lightning brain to make the right decisions, for its intentions are always for the greater good. And when bad things happen to good people, do not struggle to find causality in a Universe that is random, a Universe indifferent to man.

"How wonderful that serendipity brought you face-to-face with your only living relatives, my parents and brother, for now you understand the joy of family ties, and perhaps you will want to seek deeper meaning in friendship. Perhaps you are primed to experience the passion of love, but if so, remember that love shall remain forever inaccessible to rational explanation. You must follow your feelings, allowing yourself the joy of living in the moment. Balance it against your driving determination to reach for a better future.

"My precious daughter, it is time for my visit to end. And you are not allowed to ask questions regarding what you should do or what the future holds. Your lightning brain will know what to do, and your future is not yet written. That you will do as your tomorrows come into view.

"But I am allowed to ask one question for you, and then answer it. And I know your most urgent question: Is there more you can learn about me? If so, then you want to know, because the more you know about me, the more you know about who you are becoming. And you already know my answer. It is that of the Buddhist Monk.

"I shall leave you now, but I am always near. I will always dwell within. Now sleep until the dawn."

Electra blinked once, then bolted to an upright position as the glowing apparition receded to an indistinct horizon. A peaceful stillness enveloped Electra, watching over her as she descended into dreamless sleep.

Electra vaulted off the sofa at sunrise, energized by Indira's visit. She stretched, then suited up for her traditional Christmas morning run. As her effortless stride erased the miles, taking her further into a glorious sunrise, she vanished into the reality about her, body and mind becoming an extension of all that was immediate. Time disappeared. *Mother must have been a runner. How else could she have solved the conundrum of time? I can recall a poem of hers by that name:*

Is there time or just illusion?
Trying to answer will leave you behind.
Ponder no more and spare all confusion,
Take it for granted it's all in your mind.

Time is our relative measuring stick,
That ticks off the process twixt each life event.
When fully engaged there's not even a tick,
No trace or a clue to where the time went.

But when you encounter a trouble or two,
The ticking is loud streaming slowly ahead.
Minutes or seconds stretch way past your view,
The clock's in reverse or perhaps has stopped dead.

Maybe the atoms tell different tale,
Quantum pulse tracking trajectory of time.
But I cannot fathom its beyond human pale,
So I'll simply believe what is stated in rhyme.

Time, like reality, exists in our brain. Mother, I shall never be your equal in verse. My brain is not wired to write poetry, but I give thanks for having yours.

Invigorated by the breezeless cold air, Electra's pace quickened, and she reveled in her running's endorphins and primitive sensations. *What's that women runners' saying? Here it is: Men sweat; women perspire; ballerinas glow.*

As she glided down the street towards home, the lightning brain shifted to a normal state. Glancing at her cellphone, she was satisfied running ten miles before ten a.m. The soft crunching of snow underfoot was the only sound that stirred as Electra's eyes danced across the landscape. *Everything's the same as when I left. But no. That's Carter's Vette parked in front. And there he is, holding something. Why is he here? Hmm, this is good. He can answer my questions.*

Carter exited the Vette as soon as he spotted Electra, waving then calling to her.

"Merry Christmas! I thought I'd be up before you, but no. You are one fast lady." Electra slowed to a walk as she approached him.

"Good morning, and Merry Christmas to you. This is a surprise. Are these for me? Muffins are my favorite breakfast item. Thank you. Let's go in and have some right now." As they entered, Carter said he'd wait until she showered and changed.

"No, I like to eat first, then finish exercising before taking a shower. Oh, good. I see two of my favorites: blueberry and lemon poppy. Let's put them on the kitchen table. Would you like coffee?" He nodded yes, so Electra turned on the coffee maker, then set two places and put the muffins in a basket next to a butter dish. She found a Coke in the fridge and as soon as coffee was ready, Carter began munching as Electra gobbled hungrily.

"I get my caffeine from Coke, but I buy upscale coffee for my friends. How about you?"

"I don't do much entertaining at home, and I usually buy coffee on the drive to or from wherever I'm going. It's not cost-effective for me to make a whole pot for just one person, and I think the individual serving coffee makers are overpriced. *Hmm, That's Carter the Economist talking. But I like his pragmatic approach.*

"Which religious holidays do you observe this time of the year?"

"Hanukkah and Christmas. I follow both traditions, and I like the music and ceremony. The festivities offset darkness and gloomy weather. And my family gave gifts for both. Some of my happiest childhood memories come from December. How about you?"

"As a child, I preferred the magic of summer months. And now that I'm an adult, I've moved past all the Holiday hype. I go to Holiday concerts, but not to church services. Do you make time for them?"

"Yes, I go to synagogue and church often enough. Sometimes I listen to the service, and sometimes I let my mind wander. I know the traditions, and I usually come away refreshed. It's a nice break from weekdays."

"I thought our dinner table conversation last night did the same. It touched on many topics. Some of what you mentioned covered current events, and most of them have political undertones regarding the Guardian Party. What do you think of them?" Carter scrunched his nose.

"I've been warned never to discuss sex, religion or politics with most people because their minds are already made up and you end up arguing about opinions. But you're not like most people. Do you know much about political philosophy and constitutional law?

"I know some, but I'm sure you know more since you have political connections and do economic analysis. And I know enough to realize how interrelated economics and politics are."

"Let me start by explaining what swept the Guardian Party to power. It was the 'kinder and gentler' blunders of previous administrations and a complicit Washington Establishment that for too many years pushed a misguided progressive liberal agenda. They re-interpreted the Constitution. The Constitution is set up to be equal rights for all Americans and special privileges for none. They twisted it to become equal rights for no one and special privileges for the disadvantaged. And they applied it to policy decisions in all areas, and that led to disaster. They lost touch with Main Street America. Just before the Guardian Party took over, the Establishment hid behind their slogan 'That's not what we are' because they couldn't handle the truth. If it weren't for the Guardian Party, the Establishment would have tipped us over the edge. Terrorism and T-Plague exposed how clueless the Establishment had become. Together they created a perfect storm of terrorism out of control, of T-Plague unchecked, and of too few smart people left to keep the infrastructure and economy from spiraling downward. So, let's give Jared Gardner and his Guardian Party credit for making the tough decisions. He's pulled the country away from the brink. We're not in the clear yet, but his programs are gaining traction. We're seeing improvement. Is this making sense?"

"I think I follow what you're saying, but what about their slogan 'Harsh Times demand Harsh Measures?' What if the Guardian Party pushes too far in the harsher direction?"

"You've hit on a potential problem. Let's remember this: democracy requires an intelligent population that's willing to engage in debate to strike a balance between freedom and equality. And that balance is a swinging pendulum. The Establishment deposed themselves by letting it swing too far towards special privileges for the disadvantaged. The Guardian Party has it swinging back towards equality for all. And because the public's I.Q. has shrunk, courtesy of the T-Plague, we have to be careful the Guardian Party doesn't start making decisions they think are good for the people when they aren't. If Jared starts running amok we'll be in big trouble. Our hopes are he doesn't have a hidden agenda, that he steers a moderate course, and that he can figure out a way to defeat Terrorism and the T-Plague. So, we need to keep an eye on him and his party. What I should do now is segue into a discussion of political order and political decay, which addresses what happens when tyrants or dictators or rogue groups seize power and won't let go. But let's save that for another time."

"What are the economic implications of Jared's programs? I'm sure you've thought about that."

"He's a lot sharper than critics think, and he's tapped into sentiments of underserved segments of the population. Speaking strictly as an economist, I conditionally like the guy. On one hand, where I analyze issues using the prism of positive economics, I conclude many of his programs make economic sense. He's creating low-tech jobs for people left behind in the hi-tech race, and he's reducing budget deficits by exporting people who are a drain on healthcare or chew up law enforcement dollars. And he's reducing the pile of immigrants at the border demanding a ticket on America's gravy train. Those who complain he's ignoring the longer-term fail to realize you never get there if you don't survive the short-term. And some economists claim the long term doesn't exist, only a succession of short terms.

"On the other hand, where I use the lens of normative economics, I'm unwilling to make value judgements until I understand better what social issues are at stake. But let me give you a tentative opinion based on caring economics. Here again we have, on one hand, good outcomes if programs increase Social Capital or redefine jobs based on increases in happiness. But on the other, it ignores economic reality. You don't get paid for reading post-modern poetry or philosophy, nor can you make a buck singing kumbaya to your neighbors unless it becomes a reality TV contest, and I haven't found it on any media channel. Have you?"

"No, but let me ask you another question. I like your rational economic persona, but do you have more personal side?"

"I'm disappointed you ask. Don't you remember the origin of the word? 'Economics' is derived from the Greek word 'Oikonomia', which means 'household management'. What could be more personal than that? I can even use a solution to the Economics Commitment Problem to explain assortative mate selection. Would you like to hear?"

"Yes. You mentioned it last night. Go on."

"Here's a definition of assortative mate selection: it's a pattern and a form of sexual selection in which individuals with similar phenotypes mate with one another more frequently than would be expected under a random pattern. But from a rational economic position, we want the best possible partner, one that's better than ourselves instead of phenotypical. So, what does this do to our dating game?"

"I imagine people date as much as they can to find the best candidate."

"Precisely. But that means they never make a commitment, because if they did and a better candidate comes along, they'd have to pay for breaking up with a suboptimal partner. Do you see where that leaves us?"

"Yes. If we follow only our rational persona, we never commit to another person because we might miss out on a better opportunity. Instead, we hookup for short-term sex, disregarding longer-term social and moral imperatives. And I can see where this is heading. Homo sapiens choose partners for irrational, romantic reasons. Commitment and bonding are strengthened by cultural approval as well as sexual pleasure. What do you think?" Carter paused and blinked several times before answering.

"I think you have an excellent vocabulary, and unless you have already studied the Commitment Problem, your cognitive skills are quicker than mine. I don't think I can match you."

"Thanks for the compliment. You know your subjects. We can talk later, but now I want to finish my workout. You can watch what you want on the monitor or read some of the magazines you brought. By the way, why did you come over?"

"I was worried about you. You seemed so preoccupied when I left last night. I wanted to find out if anything was wrong. And I like hanging out with you. You articulate thoughts well. Mind if I watch while you finish your workout?"

"No. I'm going to change into shorts and a fitness top. I'll be right back." Carter smiled inwardly to himself.

The moment of truth is approaching, and it's a moment even fit women often want to skip. Designer clothes are made to disguise oversized body parts, but a scantily clothed body has nowhere to hide. I know from close encounters that even my prettiest dates look less appealing as more clothes peel off. Electra sashayed into the kitchen.

"I have my workout equipment in the basement, so follow me." Carter obeyed, talking only to himself.

Now that's a to-die for physique. I'll bet she deliberately hides it. If she wanted to, she could model. How did she get so toned? And those long limbs are incredible. She has the thighs and ankles of a figure skater.

"Watch your step. The stairs are a bit steep, so use the railing. Are you OK? You look flushed."

What should I say? She'll see right through me if I try to fake it.

"I apologize. I should have more hormonal control, but your physique is impressive. You must hear that all the time. I feel rather shallow."

"I live in my body, and as with anything you deal with every day, you take it for granted. In psychology, it's called the habituation effect. Perhaps economists give it a different name. I do take pride in being fit, but I don't train to be sexy. Some women obsess about thigh gaps or collarbone contests. And they do it because females want to look good when comparing themselves with other females, not because males appreciate it. When hooking up, most guys would just as soon put a bag over my head and turn out the lights when hopping in the sack." *Carter's flustered. Good.*

"I, uh, I didn't expect you to be so earthy."

"What do you mean?"

"You're usually so cosmopolitan, so upper class, not bawdy or crude." *Here's another zinger.*

"Oh, I get it. You mean Rabelaisian. Named after the French monk who wrote Gargantua." *He's flummoxed to the max. I better ease up.*

"I'm only teasing. I like you and want to know how you think."

Electra flipped on a widescreen monitor so Carter had something else to watch if he got bored following her exercise routine. He didn't.

This fitness center is equipped for a professional athlete. Damnation, she's so cut. I can read the labels on her six-pack. And she does sets of pull-ups. I can't match her."

"That's a wrap. I'm going to shower and change." Electra emerged thirty minutes later wearing oversize sweats.

"Well, now I look more presentable. Would you like more coffee and muffins? I'm going to have a Coke and a cornbread muffin." Carter took only coffee. Electra guided him into the living room so they could chat more comfortably.

"What do you think of my fitness center? I prefer to work out here rather than going to a health club."

"It's got everything you need. No wonder you're so fit." Electra smiled and waited for Carter to say more.

"I really like you, but I have to tell you how I feel. I'm not sure how my male ego is going to deal with you. After watching you work out, I'm intimidated. I thought I was in good shape, but not when compared to you. I can't compete with you. I think you'd beat me in an arm-wrestle too. You must have first pick in the dating pool. I don't think I can measure up."

"I'm disappointed. After what you said last night, I thought you were all for women being equal to men. And why do you want to compete with me? Aren't we supposed to help one another? If I were looking for males to compete with, I'd increase the intensity of my training and go play in the Co-NFL. And please answer me this:

why is it OK for a woman to appreciate a man's physical prowess, but not vice-versa?" *This is great! Now I'm learning about the real Carter.*

"I'm all for female equality, but in your case it's male inequality, and I've never experienced it before. Most of the ladies I date are in good shape, but they're the ones who rave about me, and I have to admit it's an ego boost. But you make me feel inferior."

"That's your problem to work through, not mine. I think you should figure out what you're looking for if our relationship is going to start. And you shouldn't worry about comparing yourself with other guys I might date. Worry instead about how the two of us relate. I was going to invite you to a Christmas Day dinner party, but from what you've just said, I prefer not to. And maybe I should make other plans for New Year's Eve." *He's squirming. Good.*

"I'm sorry what I said came out so poorly. I'm usually better with words. Please don't cancel New Year's Eve. Give me a chance to express my feelings better so I don't come across like a blunt fellow."

"Go home and think about it. I'll see you New Year's Eve. What time will you pick me up?"

"I'll be here at eight."

"Good. And talk with Matt. Compare notes about women. Ask him for a book on interpersonal communications and relationships. I don't think you did as well in that class as in Econ..."

Electra throttled back the week after Christmas to connect with friends, heeding a Biblical warning: Tomorrow is promised to no one. First call went to Alice the day after Christmas.

"Thanks again for inviting me to your Christmas Day dinner party. I enjoyed meeting your fellow Brits."

"Yes, they are solid sorts. And thank you for your gift. How easy it is to use a virtual assistant. I just plugged it in and it talked to me. And I even gave her a name and placed her in listening mode. What fun."

"So were the party favors and crowns."

"Why, yes. They are part of a traditional English Christmas Day dinner. As is the marzipan-iced Christmas cake laced with rum."

"And you aged the cake for nearly a year at room temperature so the rum would mellow the fruit bits?"

"Dear me, yes. That's one of my baking secrets. I have others I shall teach you. We shall have to make time for you to visit more often..."

Electra also took time to counsel Robin.

"I think it's good for Matt and Carter to chat over lunch. They can help each other get a better handle on building relationships with women. How did your Matt chat go after Carter and I left? Are you going to move back in?"

"I'm thinking about it. Listening to him and Carter made me realize how good they are. And here's more good news. I got incompletes rather than failing grades for last term because Student Services knows about my accident. My graduation date will have to be pushed back maybe two quarters, but I can live with that. And there's more. I'm going to do some of the bookkeeping for Matt and Mrs. Conklin's business. Between that and doing some for Hud, I'm getting a head start on my career..."

As New Year's Eve rolled in, Electra had all her January plans ready to roll out and might use the New Year's Eve party to determine where Carter might fit. At six-thirty she began to dress. *I'll be all black. I'm glad I swapped a couple of older outfits for a cocktail dress. The length is good and the bare shoulders will highlight my black choker.* At seven-thirty she looked at herself in the mirror hanging on the back of her closet door.

Mirror, mirror on the wall, who's the fairest of them all? No, it's not me. I'm not beautiful in the classic Hollywood sense. Christi was. High-cheeked willowy Robin is prettier too. My features are striking, but I have too much of a hard edge, especially when I'm not smiling. But my body matches my weight and running program. And I look mature; not old but I no longer have that naïve look. Depending on make-up and clothes, I might pass for early thirty-something. A startling thought jolted the lightning brain.

Grandfather's right. I can control my growth within the bounds of my DNA. I can will what my physical and cognitive personas become. But what about my emotional persona? No I can't, because it depends on what the people I care about think, or do, or feel, and that I can't control. Other thoughts began streaming in.

When I think about the future, is the lightning brain a crystal ball? No. Even though I have more power for self-directed growth than mere mortals, I cannot see into the future. Mother has told me it is not yet written, and all I can do is help write the story. An emotion never felt before sent shivers to her core.

This might be the last New Year's Eve I'll ever see. According to mythology, Achilles said the gods are jealous of man because he is mortal and understands how fleeting life is. And not only do I understand, but now I share the feeling, and so did Mother. When lightning struck, it wasn't her time to go. Like many other poets, she wrote her own epitaph. She named it 'Time to Go,' and I hear its verses:

I prefer to leave on my own terms,
And on a chosen day.
When interest in Life gives no returns,
And there's nothing left to say.

When all affairs are neatly done,
Still able to go my own way.
One lasting glance at setting Sun,
I prefer not to lengthen the stay.

When those once loved no longer living,
And remembrance a whisper of pain.
I still can wish with brief thanksgiving,
To see them once again.

Shed nary a tear this once promising woman,
Has come to the end of her run.
For those she has cared for to her last wish please listen,
Please pardon the wrongs she has done.

Mother died too young. But she lived life on her terms and so am I, so it makes no difference whether or not I ring in another new year besides tonight's. I better put these thoughts away so I cheer up. Otherwise, I'll be a poor party-goer.

Electra busied herself with final preparations as her mood lifted, and when Carter knocked she was ready to sparkle like champagne. She donned her red winter coat, then opened the door, launching herself into the evening. Carter's Vette whisked them away.

"I'm happy you and Matt had lunch. What did you talk about?"

"Romantic relationships were the main course, and I'm glad I skimmed one of the books you suggested. Matt's an expert. He even described the six types of love. I never thought romance required so much effort. I thought it just comes naturally, but psychologists warn that's not so. You have to work at love and relationships or they'll unravel before you know it. Matt says he's helping Robin figure out what she wants, and he's worried he might not be in the mix. But he knows it's her call, not his." Electra nodded, waiting for Carter to say more.

"I want to recommend a book you should read: *The Black Swan* by Taleb. You'll learn more about behavioral economics' impact on Wall Street. Let's make a New Year's resolution to discuss it soon."

"I will so I'm prepared for you to tell me more about it, but why don't you tell me about tonight's hostess."

"Olivia Torres is a second-term Guardian Party senator from California. You'll like her. She's a no-nonsense, social-minded politico, respected by all parties. Have you watched any of her interviews?"

"Yes. She looks to be mid-forties and comes across like a statesperson. And she disagrees with some of the Guardian positions. What about her husband?"

"That's Ricardo Torres. I think I told you he's a colonel assigned to the Pentagon. He works on DARPA projects dealing with UAV's. It's all classified, but he did tell me the future for unmanned aerial vehicles is all about AI command and control. That's why the military already has drones that take off, target, and land by themselves. And the Air Force is funding neuro-priming projects that connect through microchip implants pilot brains to a warplane's computer system. I'm sure the Army has similar programs to make even better 'Super-Soldiers' that are already wearing exoskeletons. Do you know about computers and artificial intelligence?"

"My current focus is DNA-related bio-drugs." Electra didn't have to sidestep more questions because Carter was entering the parking garage. He opened the door to help Electra unfold herself from the Vette.

"I forgot to mention how stunning you look. Your coat is so festive."

"Thanks for the compliment. I thought I should look my best for your friends. Will you know many of the people?"

"I think I might. I'm on several project committees for Senator Torres, and I'm sure some of the members will be here. I'll also introduce you to some of the politicos. And I might be able to do the same on the military side. One of my projects deals with Chinese demographic projections, which are a major interest at the Pentagon."

Carter placed coats in the check room, then steered a course to the reception area to meet Olivia and Ricardo Torres.

"Good evening Carter, and who is this lovely lady?"

"Good evening Senator Torres. I would like to introduce Electra Kittner. She is a bio-tech professor at GWU." The senator's smile was warm and genuine.

"Happy New Year, Electra. I'm happy you are here. And with the start of the new year comes the start of the new school term. I'm sure you're excited about that."

"Hello Senator. I'm afraid Carter has embellished my position just a tad. I'm not a professor yet. I am a postdoc, and if the school likes my work I may become tenure-tracked. But I'm taking it one step at a time. I've heard a lot about you, thanks to the media. You're well respected and come up with policy recommendations the people like."

"Thank you for the endorsement. And I depend on Carter to keep policy recommendations on target. He's very smart. Let me introduce you to my husband, Colonel Ricardo Torres." Colonel Torres had everything Electra expected: erect military bearing, athletic build, and short-cropped hair, all matching his crisp uniform.

"Hello Ms. Kittner. And the Senator is correct about Carter. He's spot-on for connecting demographics to socio-economic policy." The four chatted briefly, then Carter navigated among the groups gaily chatting, introducing Electra where appropriate. Her smile sparkled, and she touched on topics appropriate for New Year's Eve. Then she listened attentively to what others had to say. *Carter's sharp, pragmatic, and seems honest. I think I'll recruit him for one of my games, whether or not he's a quick study on relationships.* The two of them spun off from the crowd to enjoy champagne and a more personal conversation, the hum of people about them providing white noise insulation.

"Your associates are nice and know what they're talking about, and they say the same about you. How do you know so much about China? Do you really think they're about to collapse?"

"China has always fascinated me. It's the oldest continuing civilization. Did you know China developed the bureaucratic system during the Warring States Period in the Qin Dynasty? It supported the Legalism philosophy, where the state is supreme China's current predicament is caused by bad policy decisions made over a century ago by its Communist Party, and the problems are overwhelming. They have an aging population that will make America's baby boom entitlements seem like a senior citizens' bingo game. All this is caused by bad choices: one child policy, second class status for women, hostility towards immigrants, etc. China used to be called a paper tiger. That was right after World War II. Then they became a powerhouse as they pushed towards directed capitalism. But today we should call them a toothless tiger because they're old, and they never could innovate like our hi-tech companies can." Carter stopped for a moment as the crowd noise grew.

"But enough about the old. Let's ring in the new. Listen. They're starting the countdown: eight, seven, six, …"

At the stroke of Midnight, balloons descended and voices rose, singing the traditional Robert Burns poem *Auld Lang Syne* written three centuries ago. Carter clinked glasses and Electra brushed his cheek with a kiss, her eyes sparkling.

"Happy New Year Carter. I think the new year will hold fun and games for us…"

CHAPTER 26

February 2121

"London Bridges Falling"

(Thread 3 Chapter 4)

GOOD CHEER FOR THE new year lasted only until mid-January when a wave of terrorist attacks hit London and Paris, closely followed by a sensational story leaked to the media, stunning the world: Britain was holding back information on worldwide terrorist cell locations as well as on a doomsday "Apocalypse Clock." And two weeks' later, T-Plague outbreaks occurred in Germany, where no terrorists had struck. No one had a clue except Electra.

Remaining sleeper cells are striking on their own because the survivors in Hassan's inner circle are in disarray. And there must be another Apocalypse Clock launch file, because the one I have didn't include Germany. But the domestic locations I gave Alice must have covered them all because implausible outbreaks at home have stopped.

So, who leaked the story? It has to be Isilabad, hoping to delay a shooting war that might be launched by Jared's 'Coalition of the Smart.' I better tell Angus. Electra called him immediately on a secure line, and he spoke only after she finished her story.

"What you say fits what's happening. I'll tell Jared Isilabad is spreading bogus information, hoping he'll overreact and anger some of our allies. We want Jared to speak kinder words while Securityguard and our allies roll up all bad guys."

"And I'll write his primetime speech so he doesn't cause further public dissention. His worst critics label him the 'Polarizing President.' Though a near-majority back his harsher talk and like the Guardian programs, some of the so-called 'smart minority' are increasingly worried about longer-term repercussions. We'll have to watch the opinion polls after he talks."

The nation tuned to his early February speech, as did Electra. *If Jared sticks to my script, all is OK. But if he charts his own course, Angus and I will have to rein him in. Tonight will tell the tale.*

Jared strode to the podium, his expression projecting resolute confidence.

"Good evening fellow Patriots.

"I'm sure you have been watching in horror the tragedies that have struck many of our friends and partners in Europe. Our hearts go out to all those impacted. But those to blame be warned: our resolve to bring you to justice is strengthened. And tonight, I want to give you, the American people, the truth behind the stories. And with the truth comes both bad news as well as good. Unlike the previous Administrations, we know you can handle the truth, and you are giving me and the Guardian Party overwhelming support for carrying through on our pledge to make all our lives better.

"Let me begin with the truth based on facts Securityguard and supporting agencies have assembled: Middle East terrorists are making a last-ditch effort to infect the West. Remaining sleeper cells are acting on their own because our Coalition of the Smart sanctions have brought Isilabad to its knees. And they are the ones who have leaked lies to the media, feeding into hype intended to turn us against Britain. Britain has not been hoarding terrorist information, unwilling to share it with us. We have been working closely with them, and we know they can be trusted. They too have been targets, as have France and Germany. Why these targets? Because Isilabad is waging a War against the West. A War against Modernity. They are continuing the centuries' long war pitting Islam against Christianity.

"Though they will not win, I must report bad news first: we have not yet rolled up all remaining sleeper cells. They can still cause panic in the streets with their T-Plague aerosol attacks. And they have activated a devious 'Apocalypse Clock,' capable of unleashing into air or water T-Plague virus, silently infecting unsuspecting citizens. Our Coalition of the Smart, of which Britain is a major partner, is working hard to ferret out the remaining terrorist pockets, and to disable the Clock.

"But, I can report good news for America! We are no longer "ground zero" for attacks. And why not? Because of our unrelenting efforts to roll up all terrorist cells on American soil. We have terminated all known domestic terrorist cells. It is proof that harsh times demand harsh measures, and we will continue to implement all measures necessary to keep us safe. And thanks to the relentless efforts of our counter-intelligence agencies, we have turned off the Apocalypse Clock ticking in America. And we continue to strengthen our counter-intelligence measures so they are even better than before, so we will know in advance what the enemy is thinking before they carry out their treachery. And we will continue working with our Coalition of the Smart to help ferret out remaining terrorist cells abroad. And we will help our allies stop the ticking of the Clock in their countries.

"And here is more good news. Finally, this year, we expect the NIH, after years of getting nowhere, will be able to give us smart pills that work. Rest assured that we are using all means to protect all citizens.

"Our future is bright. Our Infra-Rebuild and Repatriot Programs are getting the results you want: roads and rail systems, air travel and power grids, and computer networks are better than several years ago. People are placed where they fit best. You have seen tangible improvements since you put us in charge. And our commitment to guarding what makes America great is stronger than ever. We will never stop pushing in the right direction for you."

"God bless you patriotic Americans, and God bless our great nation..."

Electra liked what she heard. *Excellent speech. Jared used my script. Content and delivery on point. I'll send an Email to Angus telling him we're copacetic. I don't need to set up a special meeting with him, but I'll remind him to contact Carter. Angus needs to recruit a Brain Trust economist.*

Follow-up opinion polls confirmed Jared's speech had hit the mark. Even the most outspoken critics found little to carp about, other than longer-term implications. But in Europe, street protests erupted, demanding their governments take action by forcing the United Nations to act before Britain or the Coalition of the Smart does. Some called for the United States to reclaim its mantle of American Exceptionalism. Electra decided that all this would provide opportunities for Jared and the Guardians, but only if handled diplomatically.

The next day, Electra considered sending Angus another Email to warn about the "Coalition of the Smart" as well as British intentions. On the last call, Alice had complained that her London masters could not be trusted, worrying they might phase her out too soon. *I'll talk with Alice before sending it, and I'll wait until the furor dies down.*

Deciding to devote full attention to postdoc activities now that those in the political arena were under control, Electra spent Friday morning looking into a topic Carter had touched on.

I'm going to hack into Ricardo Torres' network files. Not only will I test my network security software, but I'll compare my postdoc projects to some of DARPA's. If I can do it without triggering intrusion alarms, I'm beyond state-of-the-art security system detection and can penetrate anywhere.

Electra cruised in as if she were invisible, ferreting out links and passwords that took her to places that not even top security-cleared DOD personnel knew about. There she found a presentation whose title told her she had drilled to the bottom: *Beyond Dark—Into the Invisible.*

Two presenters from undisclosed military labs summarized high-priority projects. As they droned on, the lightning brain stored what it would add to its postdoc project list.

This is why the Government pours so much money into High Energy Physics R&D. It doesn't care if researchers find a Grand Unified Theory explaining all force fields, as long as its spillover finds more powerful algorithms for commanding air strikes and controlling robo-pilots. R&D gives us faster Quantum Computers. Without them, stealth fighters would be like Superstring Physics: pure fantasy.

It also gives us transhuman Super-Soldiers wearing Iron Man Suits and carrying precision-guided firearms. The Laser Bazooka is my favorite. With one of those I could command lightning. And Biotech R&D is creating better neuro-priming drugs, like the ones Jason Bourne took in the Bourne Identity movies. And now implanted computer chips are interfacing brains directly to computers for enhanced cognitive and psychological performance.

But my favorite is a Time-Travel Project. The Air Force is already using Time-Trapper Satellite Grids to downlink tagged-target Big Data that Quantum Computers can run forward or backward in time to track location and movement.

And I can improve on what DARPA has built. Now I know where to hack to get what I want when I'm ready to go. All I've seen is amazing. It's time for a Coke break.

Electra spent the rest of the day fitting what she had learned into a new projects list. *I'll let Su win the T-Plague war by manufacturing my latest generation of vaccines while I develop new neuro-drugs. And I'll let Tim scale up prototypes of next generation Neuro-Knitters while I extend the Brain Probe interface.*

Electra powered off her lab computer and tidied her workstation while ticking through a list of what she could accomplish. *Project possibilities are endless. Look what I can build by adapting the latest generation MRI, CAT, and PET neuro-technology:*

- *My next generation Neural Mapper for recording brain states. And I can turn it into a reader or writer to find out or tell a person what to think or do.*
- *My Brain Cloner for recording instantly all neural connections and potentiation states in a person's brain. I can use this to upload into Quantum Computers for Whole Brain Emulation.*

- *My next generation Brain Probe to control people.*

This is too much for even the lightning brain unless I build my Dream Team. Only they could understand my conjectures:

- *I can model the brain as a massively parallel finite state machine by computer-simulating trillions of neural connections. And by doing this, I can achieve what the great Renaissance and Enlightenment philosopher-scientists believed: man's brain is nothing more than a machine. If you know the state of every brain cell, you know what the man will do.*
- *This is the principle of materialism: the mind and brain are the same, dating back to the Golden Age of Greece. The spiritual world is a figment of our imagination. Everything in the Universe emerges from matter, which takes form in atoms and energy.*
- *Most scientists agree, but no technology available today can deal with the complexity of deconstructing the human brain's neural network. It has barely gone beyond mapping the ring worm's brain that consists of only 302 neurons.*
- *But my conjectures will take us beyond. I'll use swarms of organic nanobots to transmit location and potentiation levels, allowing 3-D brain mapping at individual neuron granularity. And my superior algorithms and ability to handle "Big Data" complexity can make breakthroughs using existing Quantum Computer technology.*

And I'll do the best I can with the best team I can recruit.

Electra stood for a moment to stretch, then ambled to the fridge for a Coke she would drink in the car while driving to Alice's for dinner. As she walked to her car, she checked her cell phone. *Six o'clock and all is well. The gusty snow shower won't make me late, and I know Alice expects me to be at her place on time for dinner. I'm glad I called her when I did, and I know I should visit her more often. I'll make a point of keeping this resolution.*

But Electra didn't know about the disturbing call Alice got from her boss late that afternoon. Alice dutifully repeated his instructions before she hung up.

"Very well. I understand your concerns. Have your people come by this evening after she and I have dinner. Good-bye." She said more to herself after disconnecting.

What a disturbing call. Debriefing sessions often end badly.

Three agents, inconspicuously parked where they could observe the entrance to Alice's building, reviewed for the final time their plan of action that the leader summarized.

"When we spot the girl going in, Jack and I will follow immediately. We'll tell Alice we need to talk to the girl alone, and then we'll bring her out. You stay in the car, and I'll call you on your cell if we need you, and if I don't call, or if we don't get back here in fifteen minutes, make sure you call me. Got that?" The driver nodded yes, so the leader said more.

"Section Control will take over as soon as we deliver her, and I didn't ask for any additional details. I think that's her. Hmm, looks older than I thought, but that's gotta be her. Let's check the time..."

Alice hurriedly opened the door when she heard a knock, but before she could speak Electra pushed into the apartment, locking the door.

"I spotted three men in a parked car watching the building entrance. Why are they here? Do you have a gun? We need to leave."

"They want to talk to us. Dear me, I don't have a weapon. Let's try the fire escape. It's through the bathroom window. Follow me." Alice hustled them into the bathroom; Electra glanced at the metal fire escape ledge and ladder that descended to the second floor. The buzzer sounded before Electra could say a word.

"These are my people, I'll be fine."

"You can't trust them. You better—" The buzzer sounded again. Alice pushed her towards the window.

"Go now." Electra pulled herself out; Alice closed the window and composed her thoughts as she strolled to greet her guests.

Electra reached street level in seconds as the lightning brain engaged. *I'll watch the building entrance and car until deciding what to do.*

There was no activity for fifteen minutes; then a man hurriedly exited the car and entered the building; Electra dashed to the car, climbing into the back seat when she saw no one in it.

There has to be a hidden gun. She found it tucked in a side compartment. *It's loaded and I know how to use it. I'm gonna attach the silencer. No matter what happens, I'm adding it to my weapons collection. And now, I'll make myself invisible and wait.* But before she did, she ran back to her car for something she needed.

The wait became long and cold as minutes turned to hours while the intermittent side street foot traffic faded away. Finally, at ten-thirty Electra spied one of the men coming to the car. Electra hunkered in the back, underneath a blanket that kept her invisible. He cautiously drove as close as possible to the entrance, then popped the trunk release. His two accomplices came out carrying what could only be Alice's sheet-wrapped body. Electra watched it all as the lightning brain shifted to an altered state.

While the second man dumped Alice's body into the trunk, the third hurriedly sat in the front passenger seat. *He's the leader. Wait for the third man before striking.*

The third man ducked into the back seat, using the door closest to Electra. She timed her first shot so he tumbled in but not on top or her. She leaped up, firing into the back of the leader, collapsing him into the side door. And then she pressed the barrel against the driver's head, hissing a warning.

"Don't say a word. Don't move until I tell you. I have plenty of bullets left, and at this range I won't miss. Keep looking straight ahead and keep both hands on the steering wheel. Nod your head slowly if you understand what I just said." He did; Electra closed the rear door while keeping the barrel in place.

"Now I'm going to ask you some questions. I won't ask you a second time. First question: is Alice dead?" A metallic voice answered.

"Yes."

"Where are you supposed to take us?"

"To our Section Chief. We're supposed to pick him up."

"What's his name?"

"Oscar Alden."

"Will he be alone?"

"Yes."

"Where does he live?"

"Reston." Electra had all the information needed, so questioning ended.

"Here's what you're going to do. I want you to slowly prop up your partner against the passenger door window. Do it now." The driver did so mechanically.

"Good. Now drive to Oscar's. If he calls, don't answer your cell phone. Any questions?" He nodded no.

"Good; start driving."

The drive to Oscar's upscale Reston neighborhood took less than twenty minutes, and the streets were ghostly quiet and deserted. As they approached the house Electra issued more orders.

"Park in the driveway; leave your headlights on. Wait for Oscar to appear."

A minute later Oscar came out the front door, carrying an overnight bag and stepping towards the car. Electra took the next step before he reached the car. She fired one bullet into the back of the driver, then leaped out of the car. Oscar froze in the headlights.

"Good evening, Oscar. Don't say one word until I tell you to. Keep both hands on your bag in front of you and don't move. First question: Is anyone in the house?"

"No. My wife is away."

"Second question: Is your car in the garage?"

"Yes."

"Here is what you're going to do. Park your car in the driveway. Then pull this one into the garage. I'll be sitting next to you all the while."

Neither Oscar nor Electra said a word. Five minutes later, Electra spoke.

"Before we go into the house, I want you to slowly remove wallets and cell phones from your people. If you make any sudden movement, I will shoot you. When we get inside, take me to the kitchen, where you will give them to me, along with yours and your car keys." Oscar followed orders, and when he regained consciousness, he was tied to a chair, wearing a helmet connected to a device set in the middle of the kitchen table. Electra sat on the opposite side.

"You need to answer more questions. "I know agents are trained to resist questioning, so what you're wearing will coax out answers if you remain silent. Let me give you a relatively painless demonstration." Electra placed a bottle of water in front of him, then tweaked the dials. Thirty seconds later, Oscar was begging for water. After pouring some of the bottle's contents down his throat, Electra said more.

"Now you understand. Please answer my questions..." After confessing all she needed to know, Electra dialed the Brain Probe to full power, completely erasing Oscar's memory. *If or when he regains consciousness, he'll be as mindless as a mushroom.* Electra untied him, leaving him slumped on the kitchen table. It was time to make a final phone call before vanishing. A yawning voice answered on the fourth ring.

"Angus, this is Electra. Please listen to me before you say anything. We have a situation you need to have your people clean up now. This can't wait and it must be kept top secret. And I need to brief you in person ASAP. Here's all you need to know to get your people started..." Electra ended the call, then packed her Brain Probe and all confiscated items, wiping the table for any fingerprints. And then she disappeared into the night, like a shadow into darkness.

Angus prided his ability to think clearly no matter the time, but at three in the morning he had difficulty wrapping his head around Electra's fantastic story that his agents had just confirmed after removing victims: three dead in a car and a body in the trunk, one unconscious in the kitchen, no identification. Angus scratched his head while collecting his thoughts, then growled slowly.

"Let's make sure I've got this straight. You were having dinner with Alice when some agents came to her apartment, so you ducked out the fire escape. And you watched the building entrance until the agents took her to their car, and you heard gunshots before they drove off, so you ran to help. And all four were dead. You think Alice shot a couple of them, or they were killed in the crossfire, before Alice was killed. How 'em I doing?

"Good."

"Then you got in the car and drove away, stopping to answer a cell call that came in on an agent's phone. And he told you to come to his place. And when you got there, he told you the dead guys are rogue Brit agents, and he had already called his superiors, telling them he would take care of the problem, and that everyone should play dumb. Am I still following the plot?" Electra nodded.

"And then you helped him put Alice's body in the trunk after swapping car locations. And when you got back into the house, he had a seizure and collapsed on the kitchen table. And that's when you called me."

"Yes. And then I drove here." Angus pushed back from the table.

"Jesus, do you expect me to believe this story?"

"Why not? Your people just corroborated it. Why don't you have them get Alice's virtual assistant that's in her living room. Listen to what it recorded." Angus grunted before changing subjects.

"Alice and you were friends. Did she say anything the last time you talked with her that might tie in?"

"Not in so many words, but when I saw her Christmas Day, she did make a cryptic remark about London Bridges falling. And earlier in December, she told me her boss had become tight-lipped, hinting she might be phased out. She wasn't sure she could trust him or British intentions. So, I might infer the Brits are withholding remaining terrorist cell and Apocalypse Clock information to upstage us and to take charge of the 'Coalition of the Smart.' If that's the case, Isilabad did us a favor by leaking the story."

"Then why did the rogue agents terminate her?"

"Perhaps she refused to join them. Or maybe she just pretended, but she couldn't kill them before they killed her. Either way, Jared can make take advantage of what happened."

"How?"

"Jared can tell the Brits he knows what they're up to, and he'll tell the world if they don't follow our lead. He can say America is about to reassert itself on the world stage. I'll tell my hacker guy to search for terrorist and Trojan data we can share with partners so we don't have to rely on London. And Jared can lead the Coalition of the Smart without waiting for UN approval. You know how he hates the United Nations. He can also turn the tables on China's drive to replace us as the top superpower. I can write a speech that will put everyone on notice while you coordinate what's needed to put teeth in his initiatives.

Angus nodded slowly.

"I see where this is heading. We won't need Alice's backdoor channel anymore. I better call a meeting of our reconstituted Insider's Group so they know the new order. Don't worry. All I'll say about Alice is that London called her home because backdoor channels are no longer needed. You can sit and listen while I update the Group and they update me. Looks like the new guy is coming onboard when we need him. You better come back Sunday."

Angus thought Electra would be pleased, but instead she looked like she was about to burst into tears. His tone and expression softened.

"Look, I know tonight is upsetting for you as well as for me. Alice was a good person." He didn't know what else to say so he paused, giving Electra enough time to bottle her emotions before speaking.

"Tonight's shock is wearing off. It's good we've put our game plan together. I need to go home so I can rest and be ready for Sunday."

"You might have left fingerprints or DNA in Oscar's car. Let my people dispose of it."

"I hadn't thought of that. Thanks for looking out for me."

"Come on, I'll drive you home."

"No. Please take me to my car that's parked near Alice's apartment. I'll drive home from there."

The lightning brain finally downshifted to a more normal gear by the time Electra reached the safety of home, shivering in the bitterly cold gloom. She stripped off her clothes, throwing them into a jumble, then soaked under the shower head until thawing out. Then she toweled off, wrapped into her warmest robe and trudged to the kitchen for a breakfast of cereal and muffins. Although she hadn't eaten in over twelve hours, she had no appetite but forced herself to eat, hoping food would fuel a better mood. Finally, she dragged herself to the living room sofa and collapsed into tear-filled grieving. It took a full ten minutes for the sharp pain to subside, after which her brain idled in neutral, letting random thoughts come to mind. When she closed her eyes all she saw was a blurred image of Alice's face wearing one of her typically amused expressions, accompanied by her throaty British accent.

Well my dear, we didn't expect our game to end quite like this, did we? But I know you'll carry on. I've done about all I can, and jolly well enjoyed our time together. I had hoped our friendship would grow, and we would become ever the best of friends, yes, ever the best. Well, tuck me away and think of me whenever it might help. Getting to know you has been marvelous. The voice faded as Electra finally escaped into a troubled sleep. She awoke five hours later, still depressed.

I have to shift into a better mood. I'll run after exercising, then have pancakes and bacon, which will boost my glucose level longer than pancakes alone. She took her own advice, then spent the rest of the day preparing for tomorrow's meeting. That evening, she held an Alice remembrance that let her move beyond grieving. A reenergized Electra greeted the dawn, ready for the meeting, even though she was the last to arrive.

"Carter, I think you already know Electra, and both of you know Russell Conklin. He's our link to NIH T-Plague drug development, and he'll tell us latest status. Russell, fill us in."

"NIH has terminated all Cognicom projects and is not actively doing drug development internally; I'm coordinating contract development and vaccine outsourcing. None of the contract development looks good, but that Austin company has drugs that work, and I've convinced our FDA regulatory committee to approve them without clinical trials or patent review. The Austin company isn't applying for patent protection. Instead, they're treating their formulations like the formula for Coca Cola. No one will ever crack it, and if they patented it, after the patent expires the generic drug companies could make them. So instead of twenty years' patent protection, they have a de facto unlimited number.

"I've also lined up a handful of underground economy suppliers of vaccines that seem to work. So, we're now filling the pipelines with what I would call the S-Vac drug that can suppress and suspend symptoms in T-Plague survivors. And the Austin company is ready to launch an I-Vac drug for inoculation. If it works, our worries about Trojan filters and T-Plague terrorist attacks are over. All we need to do is get everyone inoculated. It's possible that after thirty years of failure we are poised to win the war against the T-Plague. There's a third vaccine too—the R-Vac—which is supposed to dissolve the neural entanglements. If it works, the victim's cognition is restored. I'll monitor progress."

"You'll want to get the pipeline for I-Vac, or whatever you call it, filled ASAP. It'll be insurance or a lifeline against the Apocalypse Clock. Carter, why don't you tell us about socio-economic status. Start with Isilabad, then China, and then Europe."

Since this was his first meeting with the Insider's Group, he planned to show he knew his stuff.

"My job is to study the data our contacts get and then determine likely outcomes. Angus seems to have sources that are even better than most of the proprietary information databases I access. Here's my assessment. Isilabad is teetering economically because China is unable to provide as much financial support as it used to, and it's teetering politically because Hassan Wassani's regime has imploded. Most of his top people contracted the T-Plague. Their last-ditch effort to resurrect a terrorist network has no coordination. And finally, it's teetering militarily. If the UN hadn't intervened, the fighting with Iran might have toppled both countries. And then, the highly anticipated 'Coalition of the Smart' could have walked right in and over both." Carter gauged his listeners were with him, so he continued to another topic.

"Turning to China, its Communist Party is reaping the rewards of failed policies. Their aging population—and T-Plague survivor burden—add to a faltering economy. They're wobbling and can't stand up to America once Jared has our economy firing on all cylinders. That's a major reason we should stick with him. His 'America First' programs are reducing unemployment, rebuilding infrastructure, repairing corporate cash flow, and restocking the hi-tech pool of smart people."

"Turning to Europe, they'll be out for Britain's blood if it turns out the Brits have been withholding critical data, but they've probably released all they have. The statistics prove they've been hit harder by Trojan filter attacks and scattered terrorist attacks than other NATO countries. And it appears their infrastructure is in worse shape than they've officially been reporting. Power and communication network failures have become widespread since last year. Finally, many of our European allies are urging the United States to reassert its leadership position on the world stage." Carter had covered what Angus had asked for, but he had more to say.

"Let me give you my back-of-the-envelope assessment of the Guardian Party here at home. They've succeeded in righting the 'Ship of State.' There's still lots of repair work that will take years to fix, but at least the country has stabilized. Party popularity is soaring; they'll retain control of the Oval Office and could win House and Senate majorities in November elections. People like hearing the straight talk from Jared, and the more extreme supporters want more of the harsh measures as long as they get results. So, I expect him to roll out more of them, or extend the ones in place. And this will force him and the Guardian Party to walk the straight and narrow. If he can steer a middle course that can balance carrots and sticks, compassion and punishment, and actually break the cycle of conflict between the West and Islam, it'll get him a Nobel Peace Prize. And you'll share it for keeping him in line, whether or not you're officially recognized." Angus slapped his hand on the table.

"Atta-boy, Carter. You said exactly what I was hoping to hear. And I need to make sure Jared steers that middle course. We have a dummied-down population that has become mean-spirited and intolerant, and if Jared let's success go to his head, he might decide he knows what's best and ignore us, which in the long run is bad. Sometime I'd like you to talk to our group about the challenges we might face if Jared does get out of control. Build on the stuff you told me about political order and political decay, but that'll be for another day. Well, I think we have our plan well in hand, and before we adjourn I'd like Electra to tell us what's on her mind. Jared considers her and me his special Brain Trust."

"I think we're on target. I'll keep writing copy and speeches that will keep Jared and the Guardians in the public's good graces, and I hope more Apocalypse Clock clues come in. But I have a final question for Angus: are you planning to bring more people into your Insider's Group?

"Yes, I am, when the time is right. And I welcome any suggestions. Well, that does it. Breakfast Club meeting adjourned."

CHAPTER 27

March 2121

"The Farewells"

(Thread 3 Chapter 5)

ALICE'S DEATH TROUBLED ELECTRA all through the following week, causing another bout of depression. She knew that happiness and depression are at opposite ends of a mood scale, so she surfed for a video that might lift her spirits and found a Harvard cognitive psychology lecture whose title, *The Psychological and Philosophical Roots of Happiness*, sounded helpful, so she watched it that evening.

The professor's opening slides described how she would integrate conclusions drawn from a decades-long longitudinal study with insights gleaned from six philosophers. She mentioned that everyone experiences occasional sadness or depression because these moods have neurochemical roots, such as low levels of monoamines or other neurotransmitters, and she recommended using physical or mental pursuits rather than mood-elevating drugs for treating because the study had found four important activities that could help people feel better:

- Keeping busy physically and mentally.
- Staying socially connected. Loneliness is toxic. Have a close friends and family relationships/support group.
- Maintaining Hi-Quality Relationships. Better to break away than remain in high-conflict Co-Friendships.

- Volunteering to help others.

And she connected them with some of what six philosophers had to offer:

- Socrates: Seek the Truth even if it makes you unpopular.
- Epicurus: Balance the Simple Pleasures.
- Seneca: Be stoic when facing adversity.
- de Montaigne: Acknowledge your Body's Physical Needs.
- Schopenhauer: Expect Romantic Love to disappoint. Unconscious urges lead us astray.
- Nietzsche: Anticipate difficulties. Endure suffering if it leads to fulfillment.

She ended the lecture by warning that neither money nor fame can lead to happiness, then reminding that humans are responsible for finding their own happiness and recommending students read *The Consolations of Philosophy* by Alain de Botton, still relevant though written over a hundred years ago.

Mother already knew about happiness. Her poem, "The Triple Crown," distills its essence. And what I've learned about her tells me she put what she knew into practice. But was Father happy? No. He bottled up his emotions. What about Grandfather? Yes, he was because he gave to others. Someday I'll trace Father's family tree to learn more about his roots, but I don't need to do that for Mother because I can talk with her brother and parents. They've filled in a lot already.

Watching the video helps. I'll let the lightning brain replay it overnight so I'm in a good mood when leading Hud's conference call tomorrow afternoon.

"Yes, your Highness. I always take good notes, so let me summarize what we've got. Our new sales organizations are set up, and Su and Adom have ramped up production so we're filling the pipelines. And Tim is gonna talk more with the sales guy from Cybergard. He's real interested in being our Director of Sales and Market Development. And like you told me before, that Conklin guy got NIH to come around. They're placing orders without requiring clinicals or patent filings. And that recommendation you made for what our sales guys should say is working fine. How'd you come up with that sales pitch?" Hud paused for Electra to comment, then proceeded.

"Pushing I-Vac like an insurance policy or lifeline against Trojan filters really gets customers' attention. We're getting enough orders to keep us busier than a cat with two behinds. And, no one'll be able to trace sales back to us. Tracing our shell companies is harder than putting socks on a rooster. Well that does it, so we'll see ya here next summer, and maybe by then you'll give us the OK to launch R-Vac."

Hud sat back in his chair after Electra ended the video conference, thanking his lucky stars for all that was coming his way. But then he changed his mind. *Nope, I should thank Electra. I don't know how she pulled it all off, but after all these years we're getting close to pulling the plug on the T-Plague.*

Electra rewarded herself after the call by snacking on a brownie and Coke, pleased that Hud would reap the rewards from recent "free advertising" media reports hyping London T-Plague outbreaks and Trojan filter rumors. *I've done all that's needed to defeat the virus, and if Hud's team follows my instructions, that war is over. I can focus on my other games or add new ones.*

She was suiting up for a distance run when her cell phone chimed. Usually she let the call go to voice mail rather than stop a workout, but she picked up immediately when she recognized the caller I.D.

"Uncle Chandra, how are you and Grandmother?"

"We are well but your Grandfather is not, and it is my duty to report bad news. He awoke one day last week complaining of fever and headache, so I took him to our clinic. Tests were inconclusive, but the doctor thought he might have contracted the T-Plague. I'm certain your news reported outbreaks here."

"Yes. Is Grandfather better?"

"For several days, yes. The doctor had given me the latest smart pills and I administered them daily. Then, two days ago, he awoke feverish and confused. I called for the doctor to come. He did, but his examination was disheartening. Father's age and a new strain of virus have made death inevitable. He is at home resting as comfortably as possible, but if you wish to see him one last time, you must come immediately. I took the liberty of buying a ticket for tonight's United Airlines flight 924 departing Dulles at 10:15, confirmation number UADCL0315924505."

"I'm coming. I'll rideshare to your house as soon as I land. Goodbye." Electra printed the boarding pass, threw what she could think of into a carryon bag, then grabbed her laptop and bolted for the garage. She was about to drive off when an unexpected notion flickered in the lightning brain, forcing her to slam on the brakes. *I forgot to pack an item Alice might like me to use.* After dashing back to retrieve it, Electra raced away.

Luck was with her. Airport disruptions had delayed her flight just enough so she could scamper aboard alongside three other tardy passengers. She collapsed into her seat, relieved to have seven hours of solitude to collect her thoughts. As the flight arced over the Atlantic, Electra mapped out what she would do.

I made a pledge after Grandfather's funeral never to go to another unless it's for a family member. That was a safe bet until a year ago. I better surf the Net to find out what to expect if this is to be my final farewell to Indira's father. Uncle Chandra told me last time I visited that his parents had converted to Christianity for his and Indira's benefit but preferred their ancestral religion. I better research Hinduism. An hour later, she summarized the facts.

Thank you, Google, for morphing Project Ocean into Project Universe. Though not finished, your Web Crawlers and Spiders are working at Quantum Computer speed to digitize all knowledge. Look at what I bullet-pointed so quickly:

- Hinduism is third largest world religion, having nearly two billion Indian followers.

- Often considered the oldest religion, its holistic and cyclic themes continue to resonate in Modernity, sometimes able to complement secular or scientific philosophies.
- Unlike other religions, Hinduism has no founder, common creed, or doctrine. It teaches that God is within each being or object in the universe and is transcendent.
- It teaches that the essence of each soul is divine; the purpose of life is to become aware of that divine essence.
- The Hindu gods and goddesses can be called to help reach that goal: to transcend the world as it is ordinarily perceived and to help realize the divine presence.
- The many forms of Hindu worship, ritual, and meditation are intended to lead the soul toward direct experience with God, with Self.

Though I hope for the best, I'll plan for the worst, so I better know how Hinduism handles funeral rites. Electra knew enough after another hour of surfing.

- Death is not a mournful event. The soul does not perish but is instead reincarnated many times until it merges with the Supreme Soul and achieves moksha (liberation).
- The body remains at home until cremated the following day. Mourners wear simple white casual clothes. The oldest son or another family male presides at the service, which includes prayers and hymns.
- Cremation liberates the soul from the body.

Chandra will tell me more when I need to know. I better power off my laptop. It's time to prepare for landing.

Electra called from the airport to let him know she had landed. Two hours later he ushered her into the living room, where Grandmother spoke first.

"We are pleased you have come. Your presence will honor Grandfather. Satish died peacefully in sleep last night."

"I am so sorry. I so much wanted to talk with all of you many more times, but that was not to be."

"It is karma, so let us accept my father's death and move on. Funeral rites will be held tomorrow morning when you may view my father's open coffin, after which his body will be cremated. Father made a request that we sprinkle his ashes in the Ganges River near Kanpur, where he was born. I will fly the day after tomorrow to honor his wishes." Chandra smiled sadly, pausing for a moment, then continued.

"Father knew you wished to learn more about Indira, and he requested I invite you to join me so you can talk with Indira's closest childhood friend. Bhakti lives in New Delhi, close to where she and your mother grew up. I contacted her, and she agreed to meet with you. I have already made travel arrangements."

"Thank you. I'll come…"

Funeral rites the next day were as Chandra had described. There was no meal afterwards because custom calls for a life celebration feast twelve days later. Chandra was busy afterwards coordinating the cremation and making final arrangements for tomorrow's flight, a ten-hour trip that would give him time to show a travelogue that would make for a pleasant flight.

"Kanpur used to be called Cawnpore, which historians have made forever famous by linking it to the 1857 'Indian Mutiny,' an uprising caused by British rule through the East India Company. It took ninety more years, but India eventually gained independence. Did you know England's crown jewels still include the Kohinoor diamond, weighing in at one hundred and six carats? At one time, it was the largest diamond ever found. It comes from the storied lost Golconda mines in Southern India. Its name means 'Mountain of Light,' and legend has it that whoever possesses the gem will rule the world. India claims it was stolen centuries ago and Britain should return it. The bickering continues to this day."

"I didn't know. I'd like for you to tell me more about India's history when we travel to New Delhi from Kanpur. But would you tell me about the ceremony you have arranged?"

"Of course. We will hold the Asthi Visarjan Ceremony. Cremation is an important part of destiny, embracing a symbolic form of the human embryo, which began with the male seed developing into bones and the female blood resulting in flesh. At the end of one's life, a reversal takes place as the heat of the funeral pyre divides flesh from bones. The flames of the cremation fire are the means by which the human form, or body, is presented to the gods as a last sacrifice. Releasing the ashes into the Ganges starts the spiritual journey directed by the individual's good—or karma—that his or her actions accumulated while alive. You need do nothing but be a reverent observer. And day after tomorrow we will travel by train four hundred kilometers to Kanpur. Sightseeing by train is better than flying or driving. We will fly back to London from Kanpur."

"I am grateful for all you are doing. Thank you…"

There were several separate ceremonies taking place at the same time, each providing for family and friends an uplifting sense of the eternal cycle's renewal. As she watched, Electra commented to herself. *I see a unity of man's social nature and quest for emotional comfort. All civilizations, all religions share traits that must be rooted in DNA or memes through eons of evolution. Man is genetically predisposed to look for causality instead of randomness, for security in a God rather than the indifference of an endless void. No wonder people cling to religion, even though the observable world refutes most spiritual beliefs. But it is never my place to argue against faith. I can only offer contingent support for what science and reason have to offer. And if religion and ritual help the faithful find their way to a better day, so be it.*

Chandra took Electra back to their hotel afterwards.

"I could feel how important the ceremony is. I'm sure Indira would feel the same."

"Yes. Your mother had great empathy. And even though her faith was not as strong as mine, she understood how important ceremony and ritual are. You are indeed your mother's daughter. Now, please excuse me until tomorrow. I would like time for meditation. Tomorrow morning, we will walk to the Central Train Station."

"Fine. I'll busy myself on my laptop. Alvida until then."

Chandra was back to normal the next day, so he tour-guided as the train rolled through India's lush countryside and teeming towns.

Electra remarked, "India's population density dwarfs that of the United States', but seeing the flood of people walking through streets drives the point home."

"Yes, and we have so many young people. But that is a source of great strength. The quote 'Demographics is Destiny' from the French sociologist Auguste Comte is appropriate for my country. That is the reason India is dynamic while China is stagnating. Let me provide historical perspective." Electra settled back to listen, their private compartment insulating them from most of the din outside.

"Both India and China are among the oldest civilizations, dating back thousands of years. Trade routes connected them long before the great religions emerged. And both had historical periods called dynasties or empires. But the Europeans dominated India after the collapse of the Mogul Empire, starting around 1500. And it took over four hundred years after that to break free.

"The path forward has been difficult ever since India became world's largest democracy. The caste system, political corruption, and disrespect for women were roadblocks, but less so now. India has progressed over the last one hundred years. It has an intelligent, well-educated population, and it has had the good fortune not to be a target of T-Plague terrorism like Western Europe."

"What can you tell me about Bhakti and my mother?" Chandra paused for a moment to shift closer, then answered.

"Bhakti Nayak and your mother were best friends, starting in the early years of grade school. Both sets of parents wanted them to be professional women of Modernity, and both girls had the ability to succeed. Your mother wanted to study in the United States, but Bhakti preferred to stay in India. You will have to ask Bhakti if they corresponded after Indira left for America. It's odd, now that I think about it, but your mother never returned home. I think she had planned to visit on summer breaks, but that never happened. Maybe your grandmother knows why. I think you will enjoy meeting Bhakti. When I told her how much you look like your mother, only a bit more mature, she told me she has something to give you. Tomorrow, the two of you shall become acquainted."

Bhakti watched tentatively for the arrival of her guest, a young lady named Electra Kittner, the daughter of Indira. Indira, who had been her best friend, was inextricably linked to long-ago events she tried vainly to forget. Events that to this day cause humiliation and guilt. That is why she never tries to think about Indira. Only in troubled dreams does she appear.

Bhakti contemplated her reflection in the window, nice enough looking for a mid-fifties school teacher and casual poet of average height and build, with only a few strands of white against the lustrous sheen of long black hair. Never married, she lived alone in her father's ancestral home, leading a quiet lifestyle among friends from the present, never from the past. And it wasn't until last week that she talked with someone from the past, when Chandra Ramanujan called to ask if she would honor a last request of his just-deceased father: would she meet with his only granddaughter so she could learn more about her mother, Indira?

She was reluctant at first. Why deliberately resurrect painful feelings after all these years? No one alive knows; no one would ever know what causes her pain. But after thirty years of haunted dreams, might not this be an opportunity to confront the guilt that tortures her still, possibly offering redemption? *I must make the effort; if I don't do so now, I never will.*

Bhakti watched a car drive slowly down the street, its driver scanning for the right address. When it stopped, one passenger exited, glancing at the house, then stepping lightly towards her front door. Bhakti's heart skipped a beat, for the Indira from the past was stepping into her present. She calmed her emotions by recalling a Hindi proverb: *A Guilty Conscience is a Hidden Enemy. It is time to drive out the enemy within.*

Bhakti waited for Electra to knock, then opened the door and offered the traditional greeting to which her visitor replied in kind.

"I am Bhakti Nayak, and you must be Electra. You are most welcome in my home. Please, come sit with me in my living room." Once seated, Electra knew best how to break through any uncomfortable silence.

"Thank you for allowing me to visit. Last year my karma led me to my only surviving relatives, and now it leads me to you. I am the only daughter of Indira Ramanujan, who was a friend of yours." She paused, waiting for Bhakti to reply.

"Indira was more than a friend; she was my best friend. And if I believed in reincarnation, I would be talking to her now." Electra nodded, but said nothing. Bhakti had more on her mind.

"Chandra told me you seek to learn more about your mother. I did correspond with Indira, so before I tell you about her childhood, please tell me about her life since we were last together, the night she left to study in America." Electra was ready with an edited version.

"Mother earned a doctorate in virology at Harvard, where she met my father, Jason Kittner. The two of them and their two best friends all started their careers in Washington DC at the National Institute of Health. They fell in love and were planning to marry when Mother died in childbirth. This would have been thirteen years after you last saw her. I have learned all I can from people who knew her in America. They told me she was attractive, intelligent academically, socially, and emotionally, and very empathetic. Her closest friends say she knew who she was, which gave her confidence and respect for others. Her best friend in America is a lady named Su, who is my godmother, and I consider her my aunt. She tells me everyone instinctively liked Mother. She was a genuinely nice person. I wish there was more I could tell you, but she died too young." Bhakti sat in a contemplative silence for a minute before responding.

"Yes, I can picture all that, for your mother exhibited those traits in high school. I am sure they grew in America, but the seeds had germinated long before. Let me tell you how we met, and how our friendship grew..."

Electra sat spellbound for the next hour as Bhakti recounted how their parents introduced them while in grade school, recognizing that their complementary talents would make for a lasting friendship. Bhakti preferred literature and writing, and would seek a teaching profession, while Indira would follow her love for biology.

"Your mother was talented in everything she studied, and she was good in sports. Her poetry was better than mine, but she never entered contests. She would have won instead of me. I asked her why she didn't, and she said she was happy with what she had, preferring for me to win.

"Your mother grew tall and striking while in high school. She did not strive to be a leader, but the girls looked up to her. Indian male adolescents back then were much more disrespectful towards females than today. Your mother was very diplomatic, never embarrassing boys. But she would defend herself and her friends if they pushed too far, which they occasionally did. I have some something for you; I shall be right back." She returned a minute later.

"This is a copy for you to keep. It is the last picture I have of your mother and me and our close friend Premanand Thakkar. It was taken the week before your mother left for America." Electra glanced at the picture, waiting for Bhakti to say more.

"Our smiles reflect what we were like then. I'm sure you recognize your mother. Glowing and confident for the unbounded future that awaited us. I am the more reflective, more serious one. And Premanand was the adventuresome one, the one always looking for ways to enjoy life." *It's like pictures of me and Christi and Robin.*

"Are you and Premanand still friends?" Bhakti looked away wistfully.

"No, her karma took her away the following year. She died in a car crash." Bhakti abruptly changed subjects.

"You must be hungry. I have prepared a chicken curry you will like. Would you like to have lunch now?"

"Yes, thank you. I think curry is a wonderful spice. Chandra and his grandfather prepared a delicious Indian dinner when I visited last year, and I'm sure lunch will be just as tasty."

After escorting Electra to the kitchen, Bhakti poured each a glass of coconut water. She was about to serve lunch when she turned to Electra, a troubled look announcing a change of plan.

"I am glad you are here, but you must realize that talking like this is difficult. I have tried pushing the past far away and have severed all connections. But I continue to be troubled, so I need to tell you more. Before I do, I am unable to eat. I will serve you lunch, but I won't join you."

"I would rather listen. Please go on with your story."

"Very well, but please, sip on the coconut water while a talk." Bhakti sat down, pausing for a taste.

"Please look again at the picture. The boys nicknamed us the Three Shiva's because of our close friendship. Do you know about the Hindu god Shiva?"

"Yes. It is the Hindu god often shown in female form. From my study of Hinduism, I believe Shiva is sometimes called the Destroyer."

"You are correct. The boys chose the name Shiva because of a terrible playground fight freshman year. Several of the older boys started teasing the girls and it became ugly. They started beating Indira. All the girls—including myself—ran away. Chandra was there but didn't stop the fight. Indira became enraged, struggled to her feet and fought them off. From that day forward, the boys never picked on your mother or her circle of friends, and they nicknamed her Shiva because she actually beat up several of her attackers. I always felt bad about not helping your mother. I ran away instead." Electra was going to talk, but Bhakti spoke first.

"Please, I have much more to tell. Your mother and I never talked again about the fight. I could tell your mother had moved on, so I did the same, but I made a silent pledge that I would always be there for her. And I tried my best to do so. We shared many experiences, most of them happy, occasionally some were sad, the kind all adolescent girls have. But for the most disastrous episode of my life, I was not there for Indira. I have been ashamed of myself ever since. What I am about to tell you has never been told to anyone. Only your mother and I know, and I still silently carry the humiliation and guilt. One of the reasons I wanted you to visit is to help me seek redemption.

"I learned of your mother's death when Chandra called shortly after she died. He didn't know I had stopped corresponding, and he thought I would want to know because we had been such close friends. When I learned of this, my first reaction was one of relief. I was now the only person who knew the cause of my shame. I thought I could now leave the past behind, but I was wrong. My relief turned into stronger guilt; guilt for turning away from Indira; ashamed for not dealing with the past so I could move beyond.

"I feel as if I am talking to your mother, so I must tell you everything. The week before your mother left for America, she came to my house so we could say goodbye while chatting about the future. She would go to America to pursue her biology career. She knew America was where she belonged, and she would return to India, but only for visits. I, on the other hand, wanted to teach here. We promised to correspond, and she gave me a friendship bracelet as a keepsake. I called her a couple of days later and asked her to visit one last time before leaving, and we decided she would do so the night before her flight. I wanted to give her a remembrance bracelet too.

"Your mother drove here that evening. I was alone because my parents were visiting my brother, who had recently married. I thought Indira was knocking at the door, so I ran to greet her, but it was Kumar, one of the older troublemakers. He must have been watching and knew I was alone. He never liked any of the girls in your mother's circle, and he particularly disliked me because I won some of the writing contests. He was several years older and was not accepted into college because he scored poorly on entrance exams. He lived at home and had little ambition beyond manual labor.

"He pushed into the house and overpowered me, shoving a cloth into my mouth. Then he dragged me into the bedroom and raped me. He waited until I was conscious, then gloated that he would ruin my reputation by posting pictures, for he had used his cell phone to take pictures while on top of me. All this took place just before your mother arrived.

"The front door was unlocked, so Indira came into the house, and when she heard a commotion, came to my bedroom. Neither my attacker nor I was aware until your mother struck. She smashed Kumar's head from behind with a lamp. Its base had pointed edges that cracked his skull, killing him instantly. I was hysterical, and your mother had to slap me to bring me to my senses. We both saw he was dead, but there was no blood; just a deep pointed dent in his skill.

"Even today, a humiliation like this is difficult for a young Indian girl to overcome. My reputation, my life, and my family's honor would be ruined. So, your mother took control. She cleaned me up and got me dressed so I could help her carry the body to her car. Before she drove off, she told me never to tell anyone about what happened. It was our secret. She would dispose of the body. The last thing she did was hug me and tell me to Email her as soon as I calmed down. Then she would correspond to help me work through the shock. And then she drove away. I never saw her again, and I never Emailed her. She tried contacting me several times, but I refused to talk. My fear, my shame, were too great a strain; I wanted to forget the attack. I wanted to forget everything about the past.

"For the next week, I was terrified that the body would turn up and someone would link me to his murder. But to this day, I have never heard anything. Whatever Indira did, it was perfect, because the body stayed hidden.

"Over time, I learned to go on with my life, pretending nothing had happened, and I severed all connections with the past. But I am haunted in my dreams for twice running away from Indira, for not being there for her. I'm sure she was in shock too, and I could have helped her. Maybe she never returned for fear of being accused of murder." A trickle of tears marked the end of the story.

"You must help me. Please, tell me what Indira would say if we were meeting after all these years." Electra sat motionless, waiting for the lightning brain to find the right words.

"Mother left me her poems, which I treasure because they speak to me as if she were present. Long ago she wrote a poem called *Truth be Told* that speaks to you now. If you will give me a pen and paper, I will write it for you to read." Bhakti hurried back and Electra scribbled the poem.

Do you wish to hear the truth?
Are you ready to be shown?
It might not be what you will like,
The consequence is yours alone.

Often we are just pretending,
Things are good for you and me.
Afraid of some dark terror lurking,
Mirrored in reality.

But finally when the truth be told,
When all's stripped bare for all to see.
You cannot hide from what's left inside,
It is your karma that's meant to be.

Face the facts you cannot flee,
Till God or the Devil sets you free.

She handed it to Bhakti who read slowly to herself twice, then set it on the table and looked directly at Electra.

"I can hear your mother's voice urging me to tell you my story. Thank you."

"Indira's spirit sometimes visits me in dreams that seem real. In one of them she revealed to me that she would be my Muse, my inner voice, always there to help me understand. So, perhaps I am becoming her reincarnation." Bhakti nodded, waiting to hear more.

"And I think Indira would say that she is proud of you, pleased with the life you have made and understands why you could not talk about the past until this day. She would say she missed you terribly at first, but the passage of time revealed your karma and hers had taken different paths. And she would want you to put the episode behind and move on. The shame and the guilt are only in your head, in the past, and the past is but a memory that cannot hurt you unless you let it. So, just let go of it. Finally, she would thank you for meeting with me today, but then she would say we had to meet. It is our karma."

The two sat in the hushed stillness of an expanding moment. As a calmness enveloped Bhakti, a stunning revelation jolted the lightning brain. *I have reached another epiphany in my quest to know Indira. She killed out of wrath, and so have I. Indira must have felt the same as I when the lightning brain releases my Monster from the Id.*

"I will be right back." When Bhakti returned, she placed a gold bracelet on Electra's wrist.

"This is my friendship bracelet I never gave to Indira. But today, I am. Now please, have lunch. I am not yet ready to eat; I prefer to sit quietly with you. And when you are ready, would you do me the honor of telling me about your life as Electra?"

Chandra asked few questions when Electra returned, knowing she would tell him whatever was appropriate when she felt like talking. He noticed a gold bracelet on her wrist but didn't mention it. She looked happy, and that was all he needed to know. The return flight to London was rather quiet.

"Your rideshare is here. Chandra and I hope your karma brings you back to visit. Perhaps I can think of more to tell you, and you can tell us more about Jason and his father." As she bent forward to kiss her grandmother, Electra said one word meant for Chandra as well.

"Alvida."

"Do you have everything? You have plenty of time. Your flight is not until this evening."

"Yes, and I want extra time for a little more sightseeing. Thank you again for taking me to India."

"I have an envelope for you from Father. He told me to present it to you when you depart. I do not know what it contains. He prepared it soon after becoming ill, while his mind and body were still functioning. You might want to read it on your flight home."

"I'll do as you say." She tucked it into her shoulder bag, hugged Chandra one last time, and hurried for her rideshare.

Electra was telling only part of the truth. *Yes, I will do more sightseeing if time allows. But first, I want to pay someone a final visit, and at the same time erase certain tracks from the past.* The rideshare dropped her off at a London hotel.

"Director Bowless, you have an unscheduled visitor. An Indian lady wishes to see you. She says Alice Bickerwith wanted her to give you information about a clock."

Chester Bowless, sitting in his windowless office in a windowless building that housed several British Secret Service agencies, didn't know what to make of the interruption, so he checked his schedule before giving orders; he had an hour free before his next meeting.

"Did she go through security screening?

"Yes, sir. Everything checked out. Nothing but Kleenex and papers in her bag, as well as a bottle of water, a handheld computer, and Muslim headwear."

"Very well. Bring her to my office."

The name Alice Bickerwith was one that Chester preferred never to hear again. He had been her committee chairman just before giving orders to terminate, figuratively, not literally. Alice was no longer useful for keeping Britain and America's Guardian Party aligned. It was time to put her out to pasture. No more covert operations for Alice. All they needed to do was let her know she was being "retired," and then thoroughly interrogate her and her "helper" to make sure neither were withholding information. All that should have been simple enough, but the termination session had been botched miserably. Alice and the termination team vanished. *I'm certain she knows nothing about missing persons, but she might know about missing data. Hassan's briefcase came up empty when Q-Section finally unlocked it.*

Chester did not like loose ends that might reflect poorly on his reputation, so he had already destroyed files pertaining to covert projects Alice had touched. The only Alice facts he kept were safely locked in his head, where they would stay unless he needed to remind particular committee members who was the boss. *Too bad Alice has come to an unknown end, but such mysteries happen often in covert operations. I never really liked her; she was a bit too independent-minded, and her "helper" was hard to read.* Chester was sure Alice never knew his true feelings because his polished exterior hid from everyone his hard-hearted intentions.

Chester leaned back in his chair and smiled politely at the burqa-clad figure sitting across from him. "So please tell me, how do you know Alice?"

"Through my brother. He worked in one of Isilabad's computer labs and sent me encrypted files that British intelligence will pay for. He was told to send them to Alice and she would arrange for payment."

"Well now, that seems rather simplistic, doesn't it? Why would we pay you after you send them, or why would you send them after we pay you? And how much money are we talking about? And why are you here, instead of your brother?"

"My brother is infected with virus. He was promised five hundred thousand dollars. I will send you half of the files, then you will transfer half the money to a secure bank account. The next day, if you transfer the other half, I will send you the remaining files."

"I see. We will learn to trust one another. Well now, what is supposed to be on the files?"

"My brother said it contained Apocalypse Clock instructions and locations. I do not know anything else." Chester leaned forward, weighing his options before speaking. *The dollar amount is chump change and worth the gamble. If they contain what she says, we can use the info to keep partners in our camp.*

"I think we can do business. We should exchange information."

"Please give me pen and paper. I will write down my information for you, then I will write down your information for me." As Chester slid them across the desk, the lightning brain struck.

Electra seized Chester's head, pounding it on the desk until he could do nothing but moan. Then she strapped the Brain Probe cap to his head, plugged the cord into the Brain Probe, and was about to dial the intensity control to maximum power when the lights went out.

I've been in the dark before, and for the same reason: power outage. London's infrastructure has problems like ours. Alice and I have been in this office before, and she told me where he keeps emergency gear. She retrieved a pistol, cell phone and flash light, putting everything but the flash light in her bag. Then she switched the Brain Probe to battery source and dialed to maximum. Five minutes later she ran for the stairway, leaving Chester's memory-erased brain resting on the desk.

Electra spied no lights nor heard people groping in the dark because the outage was only ten minutes old, but she came across a younger woman stranded on a stairway landing. The lightning brain acted immediately.

Electra clubbed the woman senseless, then in the glare of the flash light changed clothes. By the time security guards were stumbling through the corridors, Electra was walking unnoticed on the streets of London, returning to her hotel room where she would change into her own clothes, dispose of what wouldn't pass security, and afterwards rideshare to the airport for her evening flight to Washington. She would decompress from the morning's excitement by strolling through the terminal or using her laptop.

Electra waited until the flight was midway over the Atlantic before looking at her grandfather's envelope. *I must open carefully to preserve it. I shall add it to my family notes and letters collection I tuck away in my keepsake box.* Inside was a handwritten letter and two pictures, which she studied closely. One must have been taken by her grandfather; it showed her grandmother, flanked by Indira and Chandra, ready for school, perhaps taken on her mother's first day of first grade. How excited, how happy she looks. The other showed the same people, but now Indira and her brother are adolescents, dressed as if going to a celebration. There was nothing written on the back, so Electra would let her imagination play with pictures and calendar.

She was finally ready to read the letter written in faltering penmanship, but as she read, the strength in her grandfather's words came through.

"Dearest Granddaughter,

Karma let us meet very late in my current life. I had hoped for you to visit often so you could learn more about us, and we about you, but that is not to be. My time is short, and I must do the best with what is left.

Today is one of my better days, and I am instructing Chandra to give this envelope to you after I have left this lifetime. And if you have studied the Bhagavad Gita, you will know this was meant to be and is part of the cycle. With this letter will be two childhood pictures of your mother. You should have them. I can think of nothing I have that you would treasure more.

I sense Indira's presence in you, but something more as well. I have studied the Gita my entire life, and my letter contains teachings that harken to your essence. Had we more time, I would tell you more, but karma granted us only two meetings. Still, they are ample for me to make a beginning.

I sense that you are able to reshape yourself through the power of your will and are following your dharma, your cosmic order, through which you will find happiness by casting aside doubt. You are striving to serve others, and no one who does good work for others will ever come to a bad end. Your efforts are pure because they come from mind and heart. Someday, you will electrify the world. You shall command the lightning found in your soul and use it in amazing ways.

Do not mourn my passing. Death happens only to the body, which is of no consequence, for the soul is eternal. You and I shall pass through many lifetimes. And we are each the beginning, the middle, and the end of creation. Always remember."

Electra read the letter again. *Grandfather sees Indira in me. And he sees me using my power for the greater good. Perhaps I am on the right path. Perhaps I shall pull lightning from the sky and command from on high…*

The flight attendant noticed a young woman sleeping. *She needs a pillow and blanket. I'll tuck her in, but I'll try not to wake her. She looks so peaceful.*

Electra rested securely for the remainder of the flight.

CHAPTER 28

May 2121

"The Biological Clock"

(Thread 1 Chapter 13)

Peter Schmitzer, a former covert operations section chief, had to marvel at his career path. And he had two people to thank: Angus McTear and Jared Gardner. Angus had softened his fall from grace by reassigning him to Jared's secret service squad instead of firing him when three of his direct reports went missing. And Jared had immediately recognized Peter's loyalty to the Party and to the person being guarded. Jared also liked his intelligence and assertive competence. In less than a year he had become the lead agent protecting the President. Sometimes he drove the limousine; sometimes he sat in the back seat next to the President. In either position, he knew his job: do whatever it takes to keep the President safe.

Tonight, after driving Jared to a Brain Trust session, he was standing guard just outside the conference room. The only other person he recognized when they entered was Angus McTear, so he knew the discussion must be important. It made him feel good to help guard the nation, for he believed in the Guardian Party's slogan: Guarding what makes America great.

Jared glanced around the table, making sure everyone was settled before starting the session.

"I want to compliment all of you, and especially Angus, for how useful our Brain Trust has become. Frankly, I was skeptical when he first proposed the idea of putting together a group that would do the—how did you say it—heavy thinking and then turn over the results for me to decide how I want my Inner Circle to do what we tell them. But Angus said it would become the power behind the throne, much like legendary Cardinal Richelieu. And it works. You're a counterbalance to my hard-charging Inner Circle. The public loves me and the Party, so let's keep the party going.

"Here's what I want today. We'll go around the table for summary updates, and I'll then have our public relations spin guru write my Memorial Day speech, using what she's heard from us and from news and social media. Let's start with Russell, since he is now handling T-Plague vaccine and will soon be promoted to a more senior NIH position as a reward for producing results. Russell, let's hear from you."

"I'll cover vaccines first. As you know, we discontinued in-house or co-development and are relying on that Austin company or underground economy suppliers because I convinced the FDA to waive clinical trials and patent disclosure. Frankly, there's no alternative so I can't claim much credit other than pointing out the obvious. So, we do have S-Vac for controlling or suppressing symptoms, and I-Vac for inoculating against the T-Plague, which means we're close to winning the war. And if that Austin company starts selling the R-Vac and it works, we can reverse neural entanglement and perhaps cure the victims. And here's the reason R-Vac is so important. We have too many mentally incompetent survivors. They're overloading our healthcare system and sucking up too much money. We don't have enough smart people in the workforce to fill the hi-tech positions. And too many victims can't think for themselves. They want the government to think for them, to take care of them. So, if we can cure them, it's win-win-win: system no longer overloaded; government expenditures shrink; workforce smarter." Jared nodded slowly and moved to the next person.

"I'm sure Carter will talk about how its ripple will affect economic growth. And I want him to comment on Infra-Rebuild and Repatriot programs. Carter, you have the floor."

"I'll start with Infra-Rebuild. The public likes to see tangible progress, and that's what our initial projects have done. Road, bridge, and rail projects have made transportation better. Somewhat the same for power systems, but the hi-tech computer and communications networks need more smart people. So, we need to exempt the highly skilled people we are deporting via Repatriot. And Russell is right on the money regarding mentally challenged survivors. If we can cure them, we'll have a larger pool of smart workers and a smaller budget deficit due to reduced healthcare costs. I haven't finished by socio-political analysis, and I want to recommend someone to join our Brain Trust to handle this area. I thought I could handle the socio-political and the economic analysis, but it's too much for one person. I'll give you the name offline." Jared nodded.

"Fair enough. One more won't get in the way. OK, Angus, why don't you summarize

our terrorist cell roll-ups and Coalition of the Smart status."

"Thanks to the additional information our contacts have provided on cell and Trojan filter locations, we have drastically reduced these kinds of attacks. And since Securityguard has been quick to terminate the bad guys, the public supports the harsher methods we're using. But please remember, we aren't being as aggressive as some of our more vocal supporters would like, and we need to walk a fine line between too gentle and too harsh.

"Now let me turn to the Coalition of the Smart, the international effort to contain rogue Middle East states. Britain had been angling to lead, and until we bolstered national defense and covert ops capability, they could make a good case for replacing us. But we've narrowed those gaps and widened our lead for finding hidden data. So, there are three reasons we want you to lead. First, our allies want us to reclaim our position as world leader. Second, we can no longer trust Britain. And third, the UN is too timid, too slow to act. We need to galvanize the world community to take action. It's time you wrestle control away." Jared's expression proclaimed satisfaction before he spoke.

"Good work. Now, let me tell the Brain Trust about two things the Inner Circle is pushing for. You'll see they tie in with all the above. The first is what I'm calling the 'Golden Years Program' in which we pay the family of terminally ill patients suffering from T-Plague, etc. for letting us pull the plug. This will reduce healthcare system overload and save money. The second is what I'm calling the 'Crime-Stoppers Program' where we let Securityguard roll up more criminals and terrorists, we reinstate a harsh death penalty, and we force judges and juries to use it. Look what this can do: reduce legal system and incarceration costs. It'll also increase the number of Infra-Rebuild workers." Jared paused to gauge reaction.

"Don't be so grim. Carter, I want you to run the numbers to show it makes economic sense. The crime rate will go down because we'll get more bad guys off the street. And the public will like it because they can watch media videos showing payoff from harsh methods. And we'll have Carter's addition to our Brain Trust measure the socio-political impact. And don't worry. Before we roll them out I'll make sure the Inner Circle follows Brain Trust suggestions. Will that make you happier?" There were grudging nods but no comments.

"I have only one more item. I want our spin guru to write my Memorial Day speech so the public likes what we're hatching. And that means Electra must explain to Zoe what we've talked about today. That way, any revisions I tell her to make will stay on point.

"I've thrown a lot on your plates, so you better think it through between now and our next session. I want you to keep the meeting going. Carter, make sure you give Angus the name of your candidate. Angus, think about what other additions we need. Electra, keep tabs on Zoe." As Jared strode from the conference room, Peter snapped to attention.

"Are you ready for me to take you to your next meeting, Mr. President?"

"You betcha. Every meeting energizes me because I see results. If I raise an eyebrow someone at the table reaches for a cell phone. You and I are alike in at least one respect. We both know where we should go. And I like how you follow orders: no questions asked."

"Yes, Mr. President. I know how to take care of you."

Angus and his people waited for Peter to close the door before reacting to Jared's parting shot. Russell spoke first.

"Did you notice how he's calling our recommendations suggestions? I'm worried he's going to stray outside the lines." Angus interrupted before Russell could say more.

"Listen up, people. There's a lot of good news here. Remember why we formed our Brain Trust: to make sure Jared builds programs that are moderate rather than harsh. We're doing just that, and he likes our work. So, what started out as a shadow insider's group is now officially recognized, which means we don't have to worry about causing suspicion, as long as we officially stick to the party line. Everyone, please buck up. There's a lot of work we need to do, but it's stuff we already have a handle on.

"Russell, there's nothing new for you. Just keep doing what you're doing. Carter, you need to crunch some numbers on programs you already know about: Infra-Rebuild and Repatriot. Then you'll do it for Golden Years and Crime-Stoppers, but don't do that until I develop the details. And I'll make them middle of the road. And we'll let your new recruit do the socio-political analysis. If we like the work, the person stays; if not we find someone else. I think you and Electra should vette ASAP whoever you're considering.

"Now, let's look at my part. I have a lot of diplomatic work to do with our allies and Britain on the Coalition of the Smart front, and then coordinate it with Securityguard and the CIA. Then I have to work out Golden Years and Crime-Stoppers. I'm going to recruit a like-minded and connected individual who can jump right in. And maybe I'll ask Electra or Carter to get that person up to speed.

"And for Electra, the only thing she has to do is come up with Jared's speech. You've got over a week, and I know you can handle it."

"I'll send it to you by the start of next week and then get with Zoe. Carter, please call me when you have that new recruit meeting set up."

"Will do. And I can tell you right now a lot of what Jared's proposing makes economic sense. We just have to make sure it's in our best socio-political interest as well. I'll call you soon to let you know the time and place." Angus was satisfied; his people could carry on.

"You've done well today, so let's do this before you go, I'll order you some snacks and drinks. Share your thoughts without Jared or me breathing down your necks. And let me know what else to get you."

Electra congratulated herself while on her evening run. *I've done it! T-Plague and terrorism are winding down. And if Jared gets out of control, the Brain Trust will figure out how to bring him back in line. Angus has the morals and backbone to handle him.*

Good that I have Angus and Zoe to keep Jared at a distance. He's beginning to make my skin crawl. I see right through his smarmy smile, pretending to like people when he's just using them. And that includes us.

Poor Zoe. He must be working her too hard. She seems frazzled. I like her. I'll try to be a better friend.

And I do like Carter. He's intelligent, professional, and considerate. Angus likes how he runs the numbers, and I like how he keeps our relationship private. I can't wait to meet his candidate.

All this good news makes for more postdoc progress. I see more AI and biotech in my future.

The miles sped by, and as she reached home, her thoughts and endorphins gave her a runner's high that would power her late into the night.

Carter called the following evening.

"I'm pleased how well the meeting went. We have lots to do, but that's all good. We're making progress, and that's why I'm calling. Let's vette my candidate Sunday. Her name is Mariah Robles. We met briefly when I was an undergrad, and we became friends, thanks to Senator Torres, when she came to Washington several years ago. She works for a think tank doing socio-political surveys and analysis, providing recommendations to government and private sector agencies. I think you'll find her sharp and like-minded."

"I think the timing's right. We want to add someone while we're still in Jared's good graces."

"Are you worried we might fall out of favor?"

"Look, I don't trust Jared. He's an opportunist, and if he finds an opening to go his own way, he'll ignore us, or worse. I don't see that happening this minute, but we're living in unsettled times, so let's bring her onboard while we can."

"I'll get Mariah, then pick you up Sunday at noon. Trust me, we'll all fit in the Vette. The model I bought has a jump seat that holds an extra person. And I'll pick a fun place to go." After the call, Carter reviewed how he would handle introductions.

I'm sure Electra and Mariah will like each other. And I didn't lie when I said I knew her briefly when in college. I don't think Mariah will talk much about our previous encounter. We have a different relationship now.

Mariah Robles always enjoyed Carter's company. He had become a good friend who looked out for her best interests, and she realized joining his Brain Trust would be good for her because it would benefit her career and feeling of self-worth.

Mariah had been born and raised in Los Angeles, the youngest daughter of hard-working Mexican immigrants who had become citizens, thanks to amnesty programs for illegal aliens. Her parents sacrificed for every opportunity to fulfill her dreams, while her older brothers shielded her from the harsher aspects of inner city life. Though not beautiful, she was cute, and her brothers made sure the wrong boys kept their distance. She was bright academically and socially; school counselors noted her determination to give back for all the help they gave her, so they told her parents that given the right guidance, their scrawny but fiery daughter would "go places."

And go places she did: from magnet schools to Latino community organizations, then to college and graduate work in socio-political studies. That was how she first met Carter. Both were sponsored by their congressmen to attend a DC summer workshop for politically-minded college students, she a junior and he a senior. Carter had attended the year before and knew his way around. He was attracted by her smart and outspoken ideas; she possessed an aura special to "women of color." Mariah noticed that the other girls who sought Carter had better looks and toned features, but she was happy he preferred talking with her late into the night. They became close and decided to start a relationship that would grow via the Internet and occasional visits since they both lived on the West Coast.

Eight weeks later Mariah discovered they had been too close; she was pregnant. Hiding her panic, she told no one. Some of her friends were married or single mothers at too early an age, and Mariah would not accept that future. She desired a career in Washington and was much too young to be encumbered with marriage and kids. And she refused to grow old before her time. She had seen too many haggard, shapeless women defeated by the demands of family because their segment of society disrespected women's rightful role. It took her a week to put the panic behind and the future ahead. She was old enough to need no one's consent but her own in order to schedule an abortion. By the time she told Carter, she was again in control of her future.

When Carter's shock wore off, he promised to assume his responsibilities. He offered to enter a committed co-friend relationship if she would have the child, and they could live together while going to school. She was genuinely touched by his sincerity, but she had already made up her mind. This turn of events would end their relationship, but she wanted to part friends, and they did.

That was the last of Carter until Mariah started her career. By chance, the two met at a Guardian Party meeting in Washington, where Mariah had just started working as a socio-political analyst for an established consulting firm. Both were young, upwardly mobile professionals working in a turbulent T-Plague climate that posed opportunity for those who were smart and adaptable. Though physical attraction remained, both had matured during the six-year separation, so they became good friends without the hormonal baggage of sex. And Carter helped her career blossom, providing economic coaching that added depth to her papers, as well as making introductions to the right people. She promised to do the same as she moved up the career ladder.

Mariah's cell call from Carter reported that he and his friend Electra would be at her apartment in five minutes, so she strolled out to meet them at the curb. Carter and Electra exited the car so he could make introductions. Since Carter and Mariah were already friends, Electra offered the passenger seat, but Mariah declined.

"Thanks, but I'm shorter than you so the jump seat is fine with me." And so began the initial conversation between Electra and Mariah. Carter, in an attempt to break the ice, gave thumbnail sketches—appropriately edited—of how he met each lady and where they'd be going today, but soon he decided to keep quiet. There was no ice to be broken; the ladies clicked so he was content to sit back and listen.

Carter was taking them to the DC area's "Corvette Sportscar Club Spring Rally," held each year two Sunday's before Memorial Day, a low-key event where owners could show off performance modifications they had made to their cars and swap stories of driving exploits, some of which might actually be true. This year's rally was being held near Little Bennett Regional Park, a pleasant drive northwest of the Capitol. Carter knew many of the owners and had fun introducing the ladies to the world of automobile enthusiasts, explaining America's hi-performance car history. They walked and talked for about an hour until he thought it was time to switch from cars to politics, so he parked them at a sun-shaded picnic bench and would soon bring back soft drinks. Mariah wanted to know how Electra fit in with the Brain Trust.

"How did a bio-tech professor get involved in politics?" *I've heard this before and have an answer in store.*

"The more research I do, the more I realize how far-reaching bio-tech is, which means the government is going to regulate issues that arise. I'd like to be a participant in the solution, not a clueless victim, so I decided to be a Guardian Party volunteer. They liked what I did and I moved into a part-time public relations role. That's how I met Angus McTear." Carter came back with the drinks and listened to the conversation until finding a place to join in.

"Maria touched on a problem that has no easy political solution. Once a political group has established a power base, history has shown how difficult it is to dislodge them. Currently, the Guardian Party, which Electra and I contingently support, is solidifying its base, and we've not seen yet where they're abusing power. Perhaps the T-Plague has reduced the nation's collective I.Q. to a level where the Party knows best, but that's a dangerous assumption. Remember the quote: power tends to corrupt, and absolute power corrupts, absolutely. Because Mariah is critical of Jared and the Guardian Party, she'll be a useful addition to the Brain Trust. We'll be following Lincoln's 'team of rivals' approach."

"From what you've said about the Brain Trust, maybe it can rein him in or at least sound a warning if he takes a wrong turn. And I can be the one to handle the socio-political tracking. So, Angus will bring me onboard if I do good work on my first assignment?"

"You always do good work, so change the if to when and you're in. And you told me you have something to show us. What is it?"

"A presentation, but I forgot my laptop. Sorry."

"That's not a problem. I have a spare in the car. I'll be right back." Mariah spoke before Carter returned.

"I can always count on Carter to be prepared. I'll logon and retrieve my presentation. Let me know if I'm too progressive. Since you're a politico novice, the first part of my presentation will help you understand enough about Liberalism to follow my recommendations." Carter overheard the last remark as he returned.

"Electra usually knows more than she lets on, so be ready for questions." Mariah powered on the laptop and launched her presentation.

"I prepared this to orient prospective clients about one positioning our agency can model, but my boss says it's too divisive, so I'll have to tone it down. But it says what I think, so you be the judge." Electra sat silent as a stone, letting Carter take the lead.

"You call your presentation *The Second Coming*, subtitled *Guardian Party Slouching Towards Washington.* Do you think people watching will catch your allusion to Yeats's poem, and if they do, what the connection to the Guardians is?"

"I think so. Our clients are smart and should know Yeats didn't like Modernity's direction." Carter nodded for Mariah to start.

"Look at the facts. America is in danger of foundering. 22nd century liberalism is in jeopardy because the T-Plague has dummied down too many people and has made them intolerant and afraid of Middle East Terrorism. People are helpless as technology threatens their jobs and their genetic makeup. All this comprises a perfect storm that catapulted Jared to prominence.

"Let me give you a brief civics lesson on Liberalism. It's a sociopolitical philosophy that's supposed to advance civilization beyond corrupt governance and outmoded beliefs by promoting Liberty and Equality built on Democratic principles supporting Rights and Human Dignity. The framers of the Constitution knew all this, so they built in checks and balances limiting government's growth while limiting excesses of human nature and emphasizing local activism. And it worked. Liberalism defeated Fascism and Communism. But most people have forgotten that Liberalism supports both Republicans—they're supporters of classical Liberalism—and Democrats—they're supporters of progressive Liberalism. And they don't realize both ends of the spectrum expand in tandem because Liberalism's success sows the seeds for its failure.

"The issue came to a head right after the 2016 Presidential election. A number of books came out, explaining why Democracies die, and why Liberalism fails. They were too pessimistic, but did highlight problems, such as income inequality, environmental degradation, and declining educational standards. And America responded. It took the right steps to put the nation back on course.

"But a perfect storm started building about twenty years ago, and if we're not careful, Jared and the Guardians are going to backslide further. Now do you see why I allude to Yeats?"

Electra deferred to Carter.

"I do. And you and I are poles apart. I like free markets and individualism, whereas you like progressive big government welfare states. This is not the time for my rebuttal. Let's ask Electra what she thinks."

"I think that between Mariah and Carter, Angus will have a balanced team of rivals that can chart a middle course Angus can implement so we keep Jared under control while keeping the best of Liberalism. But remember what Jefferson said: The price of freedom is eternal vigilance. He also said: 'I hold it that a little rebellion now and then is a good thing, and as necessary in the political world as storms in the physical.' Let's move on. Carter brought some items for you." Carter handed out papers.

"Here's an issue for Mariah to analyze, including an outline for your write-up. Let me explain it…" Carter wrapped up the discussion half an hour later.

"So, I'll invite you to our next meeting. And you don't need to give a slide show presentation. I'll distribute copies of your analysis the day before. At the meeting, all you need to do is walk us through your analysis. Electra, is there anything you wish to add?"

"No. Your details-oriented thoroughness is surpassed only by your punctuality. I imagine Mariah would agree."

"I would also add Carter's ethics. He always tries to do the right thing, especially when looking out for others." Carter nodded, smiling self-consciously at Mariah.

"Ladies, I think we've done our homework. How about we visit the Vette Accessories display, then stop for dinner on the way home?" Complete agreement; the trio went on its merry way.

Great weather and lively chatter contributed to a pleasant drive home, which Carter extended by taking local roads winding through smaller towns instead of the Interstate, giving a better choice of restaurants. He let the ladies choose a cozy diner just outside Gaithersburg. Judging from the half-filled parking lot, he concluded there would be plenty of empty tables because it was too early for most Sunday drivers to stop for dinner. Carter approved because he never liked waiting for service.

The ladies picked a booth towards the rear, and as soon as they were settled the waitress took beverage orders. Electra teased that the designated driver shouldn't order a beer, but Mariah kidded he could handle a bottle, even if it weren't a twist-off.

"I'll stick to my Coca Cola," was Electra's order, and the waitress soon came back with the drinks. Carter proposed a toast that the Brain Trust be strong and smart, and then talked about current assignments. Electra glanced at the groups in the diner, commenting to herself that they are a cross section of America's diversity. *Young and old, a variety of ethnic groups, all enjoying America. I like that Middle East family. The mother's wearing a hajib, while her kids look like they just came from Disneyworld. Goes to show that emigres want what America has to offer.*

The comfortable atmosphere changed abruptly when two unkempt thirty-something fellows clumped into the diner, staking out territory at the bar. Electra recognized the type: low I.Q. brutes who disrespected those they could pick on. Soon they were making comments about Islam.

"All those damn Muslims are covering for their terrorist relatives. I say we should deport 'em all!" Then the larger ambled towards the Middle East family.

Like everyone in the diner, Carter and company couldn't avoid noticing an impending confrontation. The lightning brain switched to a higher gear just in case action was needed, but Electra decided to be quiet until then. She had learned from childhood adventures never to enter a contest unless wearing a game face. She could tell from Carter's expression he didn't like where things were heading, but before she could caution him, he got up, talking softly while still holding his half-empty bottle of beer.

"That's not the way to treat people. Maybe I can defuse the situation." Carter smiled as he approached the other booth.

"I couldn't help overhearing. Is there a problem here?"

"Yeah, buddy. You're the problem. Butt out."

"This family means no harm. Why don't you leave them alone?"

"Why don't you get back to your booth, or I'll turn you into a bleeding Muslim lover." As the thug pulled out a pushbutton stiletto, Electra screamed to herself, *Carter, you're in way over your head! Back off.*" But he startled everyone watching. He escalated the awkward scene by smashing the bottle, spraying beer and glass. His opponent's lizard-like eyes registered surprise, forcing him to back-peddle as his buddy stepped forward.

"I got your back, man. Keep going." Electra had seen enough. It was time for the lightning brain to act.

"Wait here. We'll be right back." Electra picked up her shoulder bag and calmly strode next to Carter, then spoke quietly.

"I think there's too much testosterone in the air. Let me give you money to clear the place. Will twenty dollars do it?" The thugs looked confused as she reached into her bag and removed what was needed, a Traser. The bigger thug went stiff as Electra unloaded a jolt into his chest, toppling him forward. Carter pushed him backward into his partner, crashing them to the floor in a heap of arms and legs. Electra got in the last words as she picked up the stiletto.

"I prefer to wear rather than stab with them, but if I ever see your buddy again I'll be happy to return it. I'm sure he'll get the point." Then she hissed to Carter, "Let's go before anyone wakes up." Carter retrieved a still-stunned Mariah and the three hurried to the Vette. By the time people at the diner snapped to their senses, helping the family first and then reviving the stiff, the Vette had disappeared. No one spoke until the lightning brain shifted to a lower gear.

"I don't think we paid for our drinks. Well, Carter's beer came in a defective bottle. It shattered to bits. The bar is lucky we're not suing."

Mariah added, "You did a great job handling the bottle as well as the situation. I'm proud of how you stood up for what's right."

"Thank you for your compliments, but I'm glad it didn't come to a fight. I know how to handle myself, but you never know what's going to happen. Thank you, Electra." Electra simply nodded, leaving the last comment for to Mariah.

"If Jared's Crime-Stoppers Program gets those kinds of guys off the street, maybe there's something to it."

Mariah was too keyed up from the day's adventure to fall asleep, so instead of lying in bed she sat in the living room jotting notes in a diary. Today had convinced her that she should join the Brain Trust while reaffirming how much she admired Carter. But what affected her the most was an uncharacteristically strong attraction to the lady she had just met. *Young according to the calendar, elegantly mature in appearance, and sharp even by Carter's standards. And beneath that charming exterior lies a decisive, fearless creature. I need to know her better. I'd like to become friends."* Mariah finally fell asleep on the couch.

Electra awoke before dawn, possessed by an overwhelming desire to have sex with Carter. Only when Christi was her partner had she felt such an intense urge. But then the craving was for making love, for its prolonged foreplay and intimacy. Now she lusted for uninhibited sex, not knowing why. *Something unsettling, something thrilling is happening inside the lightning brain. I better understand what before being hijacked by my emotions.* Forcing herself into a less agitated state by stretching and preparing for an early morning run, Electra began to think clearly.

I've been physically attracted to Carter ever since we met, more so than to the guys I've dated. Maybe my desire is linked to the way he handled yesterday's situation. He showed real strength of character. I can't say I love him. I don't know him well enough. I don't know what makes him tick, or what he wants to give or take in a relationship. Maybe I should take it to the next level. Maybe it'll help me decide my own sexuality. Do I seek exclusive intimacy with a male or a female, or shall I always be bisexual, seeking new partners? My practically perfect mother had been bisexual before choosing Su. How different life would be if not for the lightning bolt of my creation. But it does no good looking backward."

Electra stepped into the exhilarating cool fragrant breeze now pregnant with possibility. Each quickening stride took her towards a horizon layered with hues spanning darkest blue to brightest pink. She could feel her body shift gears as the endorphin rush enveloped her. And suddenly, she was jolted by the reason why her hormones had come alive. *I want to have children! They will be extraordinary like me and I shall mold them into my Dream Team! I shall have a family of peers that will understand me and I them. My biological clock is ticking. Now I understand why women are driven by this primal urge.*

As she ran, her cognitive persona warned that her children might not be as exceptional as she, for "regression to the mean" would come into play. *Statistics teaches what regression to the mean is all about: if a variable is extreme on its first measurement, it will tend to be closer to the average on its second and subsequent measurements. I can live with that because I'll make my children smarter than the brightest of mere mortals. Now I have another game to play. I won't tell the details, but Carter should find it a most enjoyable game.* Electra's plan began taking shape as she raced towards the rising sun.

CHAPTER 29

July 2121

"Run for the Exit"

(Thread 1 Chapter 14)

I'M GETTING BORED. ZOE still puts out, trying to gimme that old time sex, but it's no longer good enough. I gotta find a way to get something different or get her outta my bed. As she hurried back from the bathroom, Zoe could see Jared's dissatisfaction.

"Would you like more? Do you have enough time?"

"No, and those aren't the problems. You are. You don't seem to have the same passion that you used to. Are you still committed to me and the party? I want you to scream 'Oh Jesus,' like they do at revival meetings. Why don't you go to some and find that spirit again?" A knock at the door gave Jared a reason to get off the sofa and away.

"Mr. President, it's time I drive you to your next meeting."

"Gimme five. We're wrapping up our PR session…"

Zoe left before Jared, worried she would lose Jared if she didn't heed his warning. Though she didn't know what to do, she knew someone who could give her good advice. *Electra's meeting with me today, but we'll be too busy working on the Fourth of July speech. I'll have to find a better time.*

Zoe waved Electra into her office while ending a phone call, then reached across the desk to greet her and, after a quick smile, breathlessly came to the point.

"I didn't have time to read your Email. Please walk me through the speech."

"Glad to. Most of the points will be controversial if we don't spin them correctly. That's why I touch on just the highlights, and I've chosen the best euphemisms I could think of to make them seem less harsh. The tone is soft enough for critics on the left and hard enough for those on the right when Jared punches out the words." Zoe scanned one more time.

"This is good enough as is. Let's go with it. And I've been thinking about how to stage it. The weather forecast looks good, so I thought Jared would deliver his speech from the White House lawn. The South Portico pillars will provide a classic backdrop. And we'll invite a select audience to add gravitas. Afterwards they can mingle and share cheese and fruit and the standard beverage selection. What do you think?"

"My only suggestion would be to have tents, just in case the weather turns. And at eight p.m. you could use some lighting. Other than that, you're set. And I'll be listening at home."

"Thanks. I can always count on you. And sometime I'd like to talk with you about other matters, but not now. I'm off to another meeting…"

Although postdoc projects and plans for snaring Carter kept Electra busy for the rest of the week, she and the nation tuned in to the President's Thursday evening address. Promptly at eight, cameras followed Jared stepping from the White House to the podium, where bracketing flags spaced to frame columns added to his stateman-like bearing. Lighting added just the right amount of brightness to the glow from the setting sun. Electra liked what she saw.

Perfect staging. Jared looks more and more presidential. His demeanor exudes confidence and purpose, but no hubris. I have to give him credit for being a great actor, but his ratings will plummet if people ever see the man behind the masquerade. And I have to keep pretending I like the guy if I want to stay close enough to know what he's up to. It's good that I can act too.

"Good evening fellow Patriots.

"As I stand before you on the eve of our most glorious national holiday, I am whelmed with emotions shared with all that have led our great country.

- I am in awe of the strength and resilience of you, the American people, who rise to whatever level is needed to vanquish our foes.
- I am humbled by the responsibilities and trust you have bestowed upon me, ever vigilant to guard what makes us great.
- And I pay tribute to those who gave so much to the founding of our country, so that we, the inheritors of what their great vision built, never forget our debt to those who came before, nor lose sight of what is needed to keep us great."

"Let us bow our heads for a minute of silent prayer, to whatever God or belief you choose, to honor those who have led us forward—whether in the uniform of a soldier or in the dress of a private citizen—and to keep their deeds and ideals alive always in our minds and in our hearts."

Great work, Zoe. God Bless America playing softly and the camera panning the audience, the White House, and Capitol is a moving picture.

"And now, let me summarize tonight some of the reasons that add to our Fourth of July Celebration tomorrow. I am privileged to report to you the victories we are achieving and the progress we are making in our war with the twin terrors of our generation: Terrorism and T-Plague. And I am also here to report how we will build on our successes as we move towards our bright future:

- The war against terrorism is fast drawing to victory for us. Thanks to our counter-intelligence and Securityguard agencies, we continue to roll up the last vestiges of domestic terrorist cells. And we continue to defang the silent, deadly Trojan filters.
- The major battles in the war against T-Plague are winding down. Healthguard has taken great strides to rebuild our healthcare infrastructure so we can deal swiftly and surely should any outbreak occur. And after decades of effort, we are on the verge of having vaccines capable of dealing with all aspects of this deadly disease.

"All this took sacrifice and toil, because we had to overcome years of incompetence from previous misguided administrations. But we are beginning to see the fruits of our labor:

- Thanks to our Infra-Rebuild Program, our nation's roads and bridges, networks and terminals are being restored.
- Thanks to our Repatriot Program we are giving people the choice to be where it is best for them.
- Thanks to our Securityguard and law enforcement agencies, and to the proactive assistance from fellow citizens, we are terminating terrorists and other villains as soon as the show their cowardly faces.

"The work here is not done, and these efforts will continue. The times are still harsh, though not as harsh as a couple of years ago. We cannot let our guard down. We must continue pursuing harsh measures until our adversaries are eliminated. So tonight, I want to introduce you to new initiatives that will further the cause:

- We will bolster Repatriot to increase the exit of the undesirables so they are no longer drain our economy. Better to err on the side of too many relocated than too many left behind.

- We will launch a "Golden Years" program that will allow the relatives of terminally senile or terminally ill T-Plague or other victims to gracefully conclude their loved one's journey. They will be rewarded for helping us lower the burden on our healthcare system.
- We will launch a "Crime-Stoppers" program that will aggressively remove more bad people from our streets. Too many criminals are preying on fellow citizens. We must terminate these bad people. Our new program will help stop the downward spiral of our nation's morality, and it will reduce legal, law enforcement and incarceration costs. It will also include harsher death penalty punishment to a broader range of crimes.
- We will develop a "Go Get-em" Program to ferret out those two-faced citizens working against what we know is right.
- And we will regain world leadership because we are an exceptional nation. Soon our Coalition of the Smart will offer Islam a choice. No doubt the United Nations will want to take part in the process, and we will let them so long as we get the results that you, the American people want.

You will hear much more about program details in the coming weeks. So, let me end by wishing all of you all the best for a happy and safe Fourth of July. It is but a prelude to America's glorious days to come."

"God bless you patriotic Americans, and God bless our great nation..."

Cameras slowly panned the venue and a spirited rendition of the National Anthem played. Jared walked from the podium towards the audience to greet invited guests, chosen for a balanced ethnic and socioeconomic mix. Most of the talking head commentary gave the speech high marks, but Electra disagreed.

Uh-oh, where did Jared get "Go get-em?" Jared might be stepping outside the lines. Just then her cell phone chimed. She answered, too distracted to notice the caller I.D.

"Hello, this is Electra Kittner."

"Good evening, Carter here. I'm calling to congratulate you. "You wrote a great speech. And my congrats to Zoe for an impressive staging."

"Thanks, but what's your takeaway on Go Get-em?"

"Nothing. I didn't give it a second thought. Is there something wrong with it?"

"I never heard of it until tonight, but I can follow up on it next week."

"Yes, I'm sure you will. And before you do that, I would like us to celebrate if you are free this Saturday."

"I am, but please remember, it's the day after the Fourth, so places are going to be crowded, and I know you don't like waiting."

"I won't mind. It'll be an opportunity for us to talk more. We'll take in a late afternoon movie and then have dinner."

"You are so sweet. I accept. Will you pick me up?

"Of course. My Vette and I will whisk you away at one p.m. Bye for now."

Electra sat back, smiling inwardly. *I'll deal with Jared after I know more about his intentions. And Carter just kick-started my newest game. I'll make sure we enjoy more than just a good movie.*

Carter would always remember the Christmas Eve good night kiss that took his breath away, delivered unexpectedly and with a passion he couldn't understand. Until Electra delivered "the Kiss that could launch a thousand ships"—his Helen of Troy analogy—he felt she was indifferent towards him. And it bothered him that he still didn't know her intentions. *I should try to be more like Matt. Be patient and enjoy letting the lady reveal what she wants. And I've dated enough to know Electra is special. She might be the one for me. So, while I'm being patient, I'm thinking through what I'd like in a long-term relationship: Vow-Cer and marriage contract, dual careers, plenty of space for each of us, and as many children as she wants. And at least one must be a boy. What I want is reasonable, and I hope it fits with what she wants.*

Carter's cerebral side wrote the summary; his emotional side would add more. *I'm addicted to her. I've never met anyone like her. She takes my breath away, suspending me in the timeless presence of her being. It's magical, and I have to fight my hormones so my cerebral side defers to her. Maybe tonight she'll grant more than a goodnight kiss.*

Electra was outside when the Vette pulled up on that sunny early-afternoon Saturday, so she moved with feline grace towards the curb, toting a festive shopping bag. She was wearing a short red skater dress, form-fitting at the waist and flaired below to accent her killer legs, bare-shouldered to display her sexy clavicles, while her hair was adorned with stylish sunglasses and her feet with strapped black heels. Carter's eyes weren't the only part of his anatomy to notice. *I could watch her walk to Walla Walla and back and want to watch some more.* She folded herself into the front seat and smiled, waiting for Carter to say something. Finally, his power of speech returned.

"You look too good to be bottled up in a theater. How about we walk the Alexandria Summer Festival of the Arts? Will that be comfortable for you? And how I wish my Vette were a convertible."

"That's a nice change of plan. I've never been to it, but I have been to most of the others in the area. And it is a lovely day to enjoy being out and about."

"I noticed your shopping bag. Do you want to return something you bought?"

"Oh no, it's for later. You've been so generous taking me out, I thought I'd fix us a light dinner at your place. I've never been to your apartment and I'd like to see if you are a better housekeeper than most fellows. And don't worry. I've packed dinner in an insulated container so it will keep cold."

"Good. And you be the judge of how well I keep my place, but I think it'll pass inspection. Mother raised me and my sister right. And, I deliberately keep minimal furniture until I take the next step and buy a place, but what I have is quality stuff. You'll see after the art fair. Well, let's go…"

The two chatted comfortably on the short drive, and Carter found one of the last parking spaces. Electra commented that maybe the large crowd was an indication people were finally overcoming their fear of contracting the T-Plague.

Carter replied, "Maybe so, and maybe Jared's speech bucked everyone up. But let's forget about him and enjoy the day."

As they walked and talked, stopping at booths and strolling to mingle in the crowd, Electra offered a silent comment. *How different now than not too many years ago. I no longer have to worry about being noticed, about attracting attention. As long as I follow my instincts and don't flaunt, I'll be OK. There are still talented people in spite of the damage done by the T-Plague. I just need to blend in with the best.*

Carter thought Electra had walked enough, so he suggested they stop for a drink.

"Thank you for complimenting my footwear. And this pair is actually more comfortable than you think, as long as I stay on hard surfaces. But I am ready to sit and talk." Carter found a shaded table, then returned with soft drinks. Electra let him lead the conversation. *I like how he doesn't dwell on himself so much. And having an older sister perhaps accelerated his learning to deal with females. Well, I have a question that will turn the topic back to him.*

"How did you learn so much about art?"

"I remember my parents taking my sister and me to art museums. I didn't understand much then, but I guess it piqued my interest. I even took an art appreciation class, then followed it up with another on art history. And I buy reproductions of paintings I particularly like. I have a collection of framed posters from art museums I have visited. *Thanks for the segue, Carter. Let's see if you catch on to this old-time chat-up line.*

"Do you ask all your lady-friends if they want to come up to your place and see your etchings? If so, perhaps you should ask me."

"Well now, if you're ready for dinner, we can head back to my place. But I thought you might like to look a bit further. Maybe you'd like to buy a framed photo or painting you could take home and mount." *I can't tell from his expression, but his words say he caught my message. Whether or not, here we go.*

"I've seen enough, so let's go to your place. Maybe we can come again." As he led her through the crowd, Electra concluded Carter hadn't caught her latest double entendre. *He's definitely a cerebral type of guy, but he'll catch on soon enough.*

"Welcome to my humble abode. I've lived here ever since coming to DC I didn't want a bigger place. No sense paying extra for space I didn't need. And it has covered parking, which my Vette likes."

"And you do keep the place neat as a pin, just like your Vette. Tell you what; show me the kitchen and dining area and I'll take care of the rest."

"Can I watch you in action?"

"Sure, but it's nothing special. I didn't do the cooking, just the buying. I thought we'd start with some cheese and crackers and a Cabernet Sauvignon. For dinner, I have some egg rolls and chicken fried rice, and for dessert I have some gourmet brownies. I also brought a selection of Chinese herbal teas we can compare. I know you were raised in a Jewish household, but do you eat pork? I like pork fried rice even more than chicken."

They continued chatting as Electra set the table after Carter set out the dishware. She placed candles on opposite ends and would light them when dusk settled. She noted again how comfortable she felt, an experience not often shared with males, and she liked how he handled himself. The conversation and wine flowed effortlessly as they nibbled on cheese and crackers, then advanced to the main course, the soft glow from the lighted candles adding to the intimacy.

"Where has the evening gone? It's late, and I know you always take an early Sunday morning run, so I better run you home."

Carter was about to move to the front door but stopped when he saw Electra saunter towards the bedroom. She turned, waited for Carter to catch up and said coyly, "Perhaps, but dawn is hours away."

She kissed him lightly on the lips, eyes wide open. His joined hers, first in surprise, then in pleasure. This time when he put his arms around her, she didn't pull away. Instead, she pulled him close and entwined both arms around his neck. Carter's arms wrapped around the small of her back and his lips opened to hers, hands becoming bolder. He felt her pelvic spasm as she inhaled sharply, and then his pent-up desires broke through. He kissed her deeply, passionately and Electra responded in kind. She went soft in his arms and he swept her up and into his bedroom…

Where did she go? Carter felt panic rising until he saw a note on the pillow: "Good morning! I'm on my morning run, heading east towards sunrise on your usual trail. Catch me if you can. I took your key and locked the door. I'm sure you have a couple more."

The words melted his worry; he rolled over to check the time; it was only six-thirty but he was wide awake and ready to run to meet Electra in the glorious early morning light. He set a personal best suiting up and hitting the trail.

Carter felt the runner's high right from the get-go because it was a continuation of last night's passion. *What a fantastic lover she is. That's the best sex I've ever had. She's so active in bed, and it's thrilling the way she shows her enjoyment. I hope she feels the same way.*

Electra had reached her turnaround on the trail, appreciating the freshness of the morning while savoring last night. *Best sex ever with a guy. It's way too soon to tell where our relationship is heading, but after last night I know the time's right for us to be lovers. No amount of talking or thinking can take the place of primal emotion.*

Carter spotted her first and sprinted to the spot where she stopped. All too often the morning after is awkward and tinged with regret, but not for them. They shared laughter as he gently cupped her glowing face in his hands and said he'd do all he can to keep up with this fast woman.

"We can go further if you like. It'll give us more time together on the run."

"Good idea. It'll help burn off my excess hormones." Off they went, chatting gaily about the lighter side of life, effortlessly erasing the miles on the run back.

"I'll shower first, so I can cook breakfast. Just show me where you keep the pancake mix and syrup." By the time he joined her, she had breakfast on the table and a Carter shirt on herself. *Damn, she is so sexy, and she's not even aware of it. Come on, don't let your emotions get too far ahead of your thinking. I can tell she wants to talk, so let's be ready.* And talk they did, as Electra chose the starting topic.

"Thank you for last night. That was great sex. *It's too soon to talk about Christi. I'll get into that if our intimacy escalates.* Carter reached across for her hand.

"You are extraordinary in so many ways. I'm not as clever with words as you are, and even though I've given a lot of thought to relationships, you need to teach me more about what you're looking for. As for me, please don't think I'm overreacting to last night, but you've got what I want. And I mean long term. I can see getting married, having careers, having lots of kids— Oh Jesus!" Carter stopped mid-sentence, then rushed to explain.

"We didn't have protected sex last night. In the heat of passion, I forgot. I want kids but maybe you don't. I hope I didn't get you pregnant." *I hope you did. I need to start building my Dream Team.*

"I'm touched by your concern, but please don't worry. I keep track of my menstrual cycles and there was no possibility of that last night." Carter still looked perplexed, but she waited for him to continue.

"I need to tell you more, so you know more about me. Years ago, while still in college, I got a girl pregnant. When she told me I figured hey, I really like her and we could be Co-Friends while finishing up college by going to the same grad school. After that, we'd go the Vow-Cer route if it fit. We could balance all that and a baby, before having more. And I want to have kids. It's very important to me, especially having a son. But she wasn't ready to start a family. She wanted a career first. I said I'd pay for an abortion, even be there for her, but she said no, she was in control of the situation. She thanked me for being concerned and we parted ways. Ever since then, I've been very careful."

"I trust your instincts. I know you're a great guy. Otherwise I wouldn't be here. And let's not make the mistake of talking or analyzing things too much too soon. It'll be better just to let our relationship flow. Every now and then we can talk about what you want or what I want, and how we're doing, but it's way too soon. I would like us to be discreet until we know how to get to the next level, which could be either escalating or deescalating our intimacy. We'll make a game of it. We'll pretend at work and with friends that we have only a casual relationship. Believe me, it's much better that way."

"I like that, but I have one big concern right now. Guys usually want more sex than their partner. You'll have to let me know if I'm pushing beyond what you want." Electra's coy smile jolted Carter in a most pleasing way.

"Why Carter, by now you should know I'm no pushover. I'll let you know..."

And so, Electra's most joyous summer since that of magical childhood began. *I know I can't compare childhood summers' past, conjured by wide-eyed innocence, unsullied by the external world and protected by unconditional love given by Father and Grandfather, to summers' present, for as Thomas Wolfe proclaims, you can never go home again. But I'm ready for the joys of intimacy. The world's pulling back from the brink. I can feel my emotional persona blossoming. I shall risk madness and the most.*

The two lovers engaged one other fully, passionately, all summer through, keeping their love affair invisible while it energized everything that touched them. Carter was eager to learn, eager to please; he followed Electra's lead, giving his complex and forever enigmatic lover private time and space, never taking her for granted. In return, she always found surprising, exciting ways to sparkle when making love, or when simply making small talk. As August drifted towards September, Carter thought he had found his dream.

The love affair began softening some of Electra's hard edges. At first, she was caught off guard by how emotional she was becoming. She felt more deeply, more intimately. *The lightning brain is adjusting my feelings and empathy. Going forward, the combination will be even stronger when it synchronizes rational and emotional personas. And my physical persona is always on guard, whether it be fight or flight. It's thrilling and frightening. Whenever my Creature from the Id breaks on through, it will be deadlier than before. But I can't control it; only the lightning brain can, so I'll consider no further.*

Only two people—a close friend of each separately—had an inkling that Electra and Carter had become lovers, and each was conflicted by the thought. *I like Carter and Matt being friends, but I don't want to share Electra. I'm her best friend. I'll keep quiet, but when I get a chance I have to talk to her.*

Mariah also guessed. *I'm happy for Carter, and I like her too, but she's too busy for me to barge in. Carter might or might not stick, but either way, I'll get to know her when their relationship stabilizes.*

It wasn't that Mariah lacked intimacy. Fellows found her attractive, though most were looking for more because she was flat chested and scrawny, but if they looked closer they would find a toned body that included well-proportioned legs. She had the alluring facial features of Hispanic women, but her eyes could be a touch too intense, especially when focused on passionate interests.

Although she realized males today are kinder and gentler, more attuned to females than generations ago, she also knew most fellows spend little effort on the first couple of dates looking beneath the surface. If they did, they would find a bright and caring lady, eager to share with the right person. But she found few fellows she wanted to share much, other than perfunctory sex when she needed to relieve Nature's relentless instincts. The short-lived Carter affair had been an outlier due his innate qualities and her inexperience, and though it fizzled after she became pregnant, he remained her gold standard. *I can be very happy even if the right guy never comes along. I can do just fine having my career, outside interests, and a handful of close friends. Maybe Electra will be one.*

There was only one thing bothering Electra, but unfortunately it was a very big thing. *I can't get pregnant, even though I've done all I can for three months to make it so. Now it's the Labor Day weekend, and it's time to face the truth: I'm infertile.*

Her rational persona had studied the predicament. She knew each ovary is equipped at birth with two to three million eggs, though the number declines to about three hundred thousand at puberty. Infertility may be caused by hormonal imbalances, damage to fallopian tubes, or injury to other female structures. Research estimates that half the time the problem is male-related, and the other half female. But the lightning brain knew what's causing the problem.

I'm the problem. The lightning bolt changed my DNA, making conception impossible, as if Nature said my DNA is off limits, no more genetic trespassing. And I refuse pregnancy counseling. Testing and fertility therapy are also off limits. No one shall ever probe my DNA.

Upsetting news indeed, leaving Electra depressed and tearful, causing feelings unknown until now. *Infertility might deliver a fatal blow to our affair. Carter wants to build his family centered around at least one son. I want to build my Dream Team centered on my DNA. We have a problem I can't ignore any longer.*

I have to tell Carter I can't give him children, so why not use his Labor Day weekend dinner party to break the news, and deescalate our intimacy too? Good thing only Robin, Mariah, and their dates will join us, and I'll do it as quietly and as pain-free as possible before they join us.

Carter's Saturday evening party plan was unfolding nicely. It would be his way of showing friends how much Electra meant by staging a surprise "Co-Friend Commitment" Celebration at his boss's country club, and no one would know the theme until arriving. He had arranged a light dinner at the club for his and Electra's respective best friends and dates before guests would arrive, planning to give her his proposal—complete with marriage contract and family heirloom engagement ring—before dinner.

At five-thirty, Carter and Phil, the club events manager, were sitting in the bar, making final arrangements. *Electra should be here by now. I hope the rain hasn't caused traffic problems. I don't know why she wanted to drive alone. Well, I'm sure she has a good reason.*

Not much had gone right for Electra today. The heavy rainstorm forced her to shorten her morning run, after which she managed to overcook oatmeal and burn breakfast toast. Then it took her nearly an hour to reprogram her computer's gateway after a power outage, and by the time she finished updating a postdoc project status report she had to rush getting ready for the party. The easy part was showering and dressing; the hard part would be preparing what to say and putting herself in the proper frame of mind.

Since it was not yet Labor Day, she would wear a new all white pants suit, a tight black-and-white-patterned blouse underneath, and a gorgeous paisley red scarf around her neck. She remembered Christi telling her long ago that "black and white and a color accent" is a classic eye-catching fashion statement. With it she would wear skin-tone dress sandals and only one piece of jewelry: the friendship bracelet from Bhakti. Dressing slowly steadied her nerves (they had never bothered her before the love affair) and gave her courage she'd need to tell Carter right away she could not give him children.

It was raining steadily by the time Electra reached the country club. When she made a final clothing check before dashing to the entrance, a sudden pang pierced her heart. She was wearing the Gucci paisley scarf Carter had given her for her birthday. She remembered his smile and his words: "I love shopping for you because I enjoy looking at the results". *Come on! Don't get all choked up. Do what you know you have to.* She took a deep breath and ran to the entrance, but a gust of wind pushed her off balance; she fell forward into a puddle located in front of the entrance awning. The parking lot had been freshly paved so the water was clean, but there were now garish semi-circular black stains on her spanking white slacks, making her knees look like frowns. Only one word came to mind: Robin's favorite S-word.

She stopped inside the entrance to regroup, standing next to the Saturday evening directory prominently displayed in the corridor, and to her horror she read: Quavah-Kittner Co-Friend Commitment Party—Eagle Room Number 1. Now two words came to mind:

"Holy Shit."

She hurriedly apologized to a middle-aged couple standing nearby. *I am so rattled. This isn't like me.* She took a couple of deep breaths to center herself, then trudged toward the bar where Carter should be.

"Here comes Electra. You and I finished up right on time."

"Right you are. Tell you what, I'll get each of you a drink. You say your fiancée likes Coca Cola? I'll bring her a Rum and Coke, and a beer for you." Carter's smile cut Electra to the bone; she was beginning to feel like running for the exit. His smile turned into a look of concern as she approached the table, and he stood up to reach for her hands.

"I'm glad you're here. I was beginning to worry. You look upset. What happened to your knees? You're not injured, are you?" By now, Electra was so frazzled all she could do was blurt out the worst.

"I have bad news for you; I'm not pregnant." That turned eyes from a couple of nearby tables.

At first the now wide-eyed Carter was speechless. Then a grin emerged as he snickered while seating her at the table.

"Your sense of humor and timing always surprise me. You've just inverted the classic line a girl might give to a bum boyfriend so he does the right thing." Electra cracked a weak smile but yelled only at herself.

Oh no! He doesn't understand, and it's not his fault. I screwed up what I wanted to say. Just then, Phil came back, carrying the drinks.

"You must be Electra. Carter has told me what an extraordinary young lady you are. I am pleased to meet you."

"I have to tell you the joke Electra just pulled on me." Electra kicked Carter's shin before he could say more. Phil noticed; Carter covered.

"Sorry Electra. I forgot it's a private joke. Anyway, Electra has a wonderful sense of humor, and we both thank you for the drinks." Phil prepared to beat a hasty retreat.

"Well, I'll leave you two alone." Electra swallowed her embarrassment and after Phil left whispered what she meant.

"Carter, please listen. I've been trying to get pregnant for three months and I just can't get there." Carter's look changed to genuine concern as he replied in a hushed voice.

"I didn't know. I didn't think you wanted to get pregnant. What gives?"

"I know a family and children, especially a son, are important to you. It is for me also, and I wanted to start now so I know I can deliver what you want. But I can't."

"It's only been three months. I've researched family stuff too, and sometimes it takes a year, or longer. And I look at it this way, what a pleasant year that would be."

"We could try until we land a man on Mars, and the results will be the same."

"Is there something I'm doing wrong?" Carter looked so crestfallen tears welled in her eyes.

"Carter, Carter. I'm the problem. I'm just not built to get pregnant. I'm sorry. We better cool our relationship."

"But we can go to pregnancy counseling. They have all sorts of tests and techniques."

"That's not for me! I refuse to be treated like an experiment." Just then, the servers who would work the party came to the table, bringing an announcement from their boss.

"Phil wants to add to the entertainment by having us perform one of our clapping verses. We'd like to audition it for you." Rhythmic clapping preceded their chant.

Lovely Lady expectant Groom,
Now we know why his heart went Boom!
Come what may this day September,
Tonight's event we will remember!

Electra smiled as bravely as she could, but Carter could tell she wished a trap door would swallow her. He graciously told the servers he liked what they had concocted, but tonight might not be the best time for singing. As soon as they were out of earshot, he demanded Electra tell him what she wants to do about the party.

"This is going to be really awkward. What do you want me to say to the guests? Oh Jesus, here come Mariah and Robin."The two ladies and their dates waved. Today's cumulative embarrassment was more than Electra could handle.

"Please tell them anything but the truth. It's too personal. Tell them I'm not ready to make a commitment. Invent something. I have to go right now." Electra abruptly ran toward another exit, which fortunately was away from her approaching friends. Matt tried his best to soften an awkward scene.

"Maybe she left something in her car. Maybe she prefers to make a late arrival."

Electra needed to get away, period. It was raining harder and getting darker, perfectly complementing her situation, and she needed something to take her away from a totally disastrous day. She jumped into her car, speeding into the gathering gloom. The rural roads leading to the Interstate had little traffic, so she released some of her frustration by pushing the accelerator, pushing the car over the speed limit. And to make the day complete, a state trooper pulled her over. As the trooper walked to greet her, she thought back to childhood days when she would pretend to cry so her father would give in. This time her streaming tears were genuine. The trooper took one look and realized the young lady was terribly upset, so he asked in a consoling tone what was the matter. Electra steadied her voice as best she could.

"Officer, I just ran out on my engagement party. All I want to do is go home and crawl under the bed." The officer sized up the situation and decided a ticket was not in order, but fatherly advice might be.

"Young lady, I have two daughters about your age, and I know how the T-Plague has impacted your generation. It's forced many to put their lives on hold. I'm sure you have a good reason for running out, but you need to remember this: no matter how dark the situation, it will be brighter in the light of a new day. I won't give you a ticket if you will do this for me. Stay parked on the shoulder until you calm down and then drive home. Will you do that for me?" Electra wiped away her tears before replying.

"Yes officer, and thank you." He smiled and patted her head. "You have your life ahead of you. Make the most of it by listening to your inner voice. It knows what's right." *That's exactly what I shall do.*

Electra awoke early Sunday. The cool winds had chased away the rain, bringing a sparkling sunrise, so she started a dialogue with her inner voice as soon as she started running. The further she ran, the clearer the next step became as sunlight chased away the morning mist. As her mood rose, so did her cognitive persona, which tucked away her summer romance. *Labor Day marks the unofficial end of summer. Will Carter be part of my autumn? Not even the lightning brain can control that…*

CHAPTER 30

September 2121

"The TKO"

(Thread 3 Chapter 6)

Jared Gardner had many reasons to be happy. The public loved him and his programs, clamoring for him to do even more on national and world stages. Opinion polls showed that many people—especially T-Plague victims or those afraid of the future—wanted him to make their decisions as long as their lives improved.

His imprimatur was everywhere, seen when the media featured Securityguard apprehending bad people, even more so when "Gun Tote'n Guardians"—vigilantes armed to seek out suspects—took the initiative. And people didn't care much if surveillance nets were cast so wide that innocent citizens were snared. What mattered more was loading them into Infra-Rebuild, Repatriot, or Crimestoppers programs where they could be put to use, behind bars, or out of the country. And the initial response to the "Golden Years" program showed that economics took precedence over family ties. The public preferred cost-effectively paying relatives rather than prolonging the inevitable. Tolerance was waning, religious or cultural xenophobia was waxing, and attacks on minorities drew more praise than condemnation.

No wonder Angus worried that adulation could corrupt Jared. It hadn't happened blatantly yet, but Angus could see that possibility because of Jared's burgeoning hubris, which Angus counterbalanced as best he could. He had recently been nominated for Secretary of State, which if confirmed would make him the first person ever to hold SecDef and SecState posts simultaneously.

Jared's relentless push for a shooting war between the Coalition of the Smart and Islam set off warning alarms, so Angus called a Brain Trust emergency meeting to sort through options, gathering at his home on a mid-September Thursday evening to avoid prying eyes of Jared's lieutenants, who were envious of the Brain Trust's influence and wanted action now. Angus came to the point as soon as everyone had settled around the dining room table.

"Please, no more pats on the back for being nominated Secretary of State. It'll be more work for us all, but it puts us in touch with just about all the key policy issues being brought to the table that are relevant for us merry little band of patriots. I'm going to ask our newest member to summarize." All eyes turned to Mariah.

"All of us signed on with Angus to make sure Guardian programs don't go too far. History shows the pendulum swings back and forth between too harsh and too gentle. And we want to be the early warning system for a swing too far towards repression and intolerance. I'm concerned that Jared's popularity will go to his head and he'll lose sight that "kinder and gentler" compromises are needed. Look at what's starting to happen or might happen." Mariah handed out a bullet point list of grievances before elaborating.

- Collateral damage in all of Jared's programs could increase. Civil rights of innocent citizens are being trampled. Here's an example right in our midst: the parents of Electra's best friend were deported.
- Tyranny of the majority could become oppressive. We could have too many people trusting Jared and intimidating those who protest.
- Once a regime has too much power, it is hard to dislodge. Think Iran. Think North Korea.

- World opinion might turn against America if we become too aggressive and xenophobic.
- If all this goes too far and becomes ingrained in the system, the prevailing public disposition might harden. Think Nazi Germany."

"I love America and would support Jared if he were abiding by the Constitution, but he's perverting what makes us great. I know my concern is stronger than others in this room, but Angus brought me into the Brain Trust to forge a team of rivals, where differences of opinion become strengths." Angus didn't wait for comments.

"Thank you for your passionate, articulate summary. Carter, what would you like to add?" Carter nodded thoughtfully, glanced around the table, and then replied.

"Yes, Mariah states what might unfold. But to date, none of it has, and let's take a look at how the programs have helped the country. Economic growth has returned, or at least the decline has slowed. Infra-Rebuild has created jobs and will make us more productive. Repatriot has removed a lot of dead wood from the welfare rolls. Crime-stoppers has terminated a lot of 'bad guys' so law enforcement and incarceration costs are lower. And pulling the plug on terminally ill—whether from T-Plague or whatever—eliminates a chunk of the healthcare deficit. So much of healthcare costs are sucked up in the last year or two of a person's life. The Golden Years Program eliminates that." Carter continued before Mariah could complain.

"Look, don't be mad at me. I'm stating the economic facts, and the public sees them in their pocket books. People are more interested in money rather than morals." Angus pointed to Russell, who talked next.

"We can't dispute what Carter just said; he knows the economics piece, and it counters what Mariah said about the socio-political piece. And I can see how some of this is affecting Guardian Party emphasis on vaccines. Jared pushes I-Vac to prevent new cases, and S-Vac to provide symptomatic relief and keep people working as long as they can. But there's little interest R-Vac, which is supposed to cure victims. These could be the reasons why: it costs too much and when victims are able to think again, they won't support Jared's harsh measures." Again, Angus didn't wait for comments.

"I hadn't thought of your second reason. Let's file that away. Electra, you're up."

"Let me first compliment everyone for their efforts. And let's always remember where we are. It's better having a seat at the table than on the outside looking in. We have first class seating, so let's use it to our advantage. Here's how.

"Angus has already convinced Jared that he's harnessing Brain Trust and Inner Circle to form a team of rivals that critics believe give balance. I'll keep peppering his speeches and press releases with references to how good the balance is working. The media has already picked up on it, and a couple of us have been quoted or interviewed. That's all to the good but remember, it's OK for us to argue among ourselves, but we must present a united, supportive front in public. Please remember to support Jared and the Party whenever the media come calling."

"And let's give the devil his due. Jared has actually hit a public sweet spot, and for the short-term we can let him push a bit further on the harsh side because people want it after so many years of weak government. This will cut back on some of the Inner Circle's sniping at us and keep Jared from suspecting we might oppose him longer term. I know we'll be able to reel him in if he goes too far. And I think we should add to the Brain Trust two additional people that Carter recommends. Please tell us who they are."

"That's California Senator Olivia Torres and her husband, an Army Colonel currently assigned to the Pentagon. Both are well known and respected Guardian Party advocates, but they share our concern about harsh measures. And both have extensive contacts. They'll add to our credibility." Angus nodded his approval, ready to adjourn as soon as Electra concluded her commentary.

"And finally, pay close attention to what Jared says at the UN debate. He will speak for the Coalition of the Smart versus the

Islam-China axis. I'll send you copies of the introductory remarks I wrote for him. They're pretty much what he'll say in his prime time address this coming Friday, which is the day before the debate starts."

"Excellent work, people. I want you to stick with what we covered tonight. When I meet with Jared tomorrow, I'll make him realize what we like and support. That'll stroke his ego and his confidence. We'll reconvene next week."

Electra waited for everyone to leave before cornering Angus.

"I'm relieved you share my concern that Jared's beginning to hoist himself on his own petard. And I think he's becoming insufferable. He's going to start turning more people against him if he doesn't act better. You spend more time with him than anyone. Doesn't he get under your skin?"

"I guess my skin's thicker than yours, but you're right. But let's shelve the discussion until after the debate..."

Jared awoke Saturday, confident that he was ready for battle. *Soon I can push harsh measures harder. I know I'm right and the people do too. And after last night's "under-the-covers"session, I can push harder there too. It's exciting how far Zoe goes to keep me interested. But I deserve it. She owes me for all I've done for her.*

And when I'm ready to replace her, maybe I can get her former protégé to take her place. She's a clever word-spinner. That girl sure has grown up in the past couple of years. Looks older and more confident, and she's a sharp dresser. And if she won't play along, I can trust Peter's selection of ladies to keep me satisfied.

Jared's preparation for the weekend UN debate made his primetime address one of the easiest in his tenure as President. *I like how Zoe staged the speech. I'll be speaking from my desk in the Oval Office. It'll make me look hard working and thoughtful. Well, that's the truth too.* Jared's talk began promptly at eight Friday night.

"Good evening Patriots!"

"It my distinct honor to speak to you tonight on the eve of our United Nations debate, where I will present our case for defanging

Isilabad and its Middle East allies. In my previous chats, I have highlighted the results of our actions. And I have also explained how my actions are well thought through, thanks to my team of rivals approach drawing from my Brain Trust and my Inner Circle, giving you the best possible programs and policies. I know what is best for you and how to get it.

"The rest of my talk will lay our cards on the table for the world to see what makes sense right now. Thanks largely to our nation's sacrifices, we have defeated Terrorism at home and are helping mop up the rest abroad. And we think we now have the vaccines to eradicate the T-Plague. So, it is time to focus on what me must do once and for all. We must conclude a centuries' long war between Islam and Christianity. Your previous gutless administrations did not have the courage to do that. As the great President Harry S. Truman said: If you can't stand the heat, get out of the kitchen. Well not only can I stand the heat, but I can turn up the burners, and that's what I plan to do.

"I have assembled a Coalition of the Smart, comprised of allies that are ready, willing, and able to bring Isilabad and its Middle East Allies to their knees. And believe me when I say I can do this quickly and with minimal risk to our men and women in uniform. We will offer Isilabad one last chance to accept our terms: abandon all terrorist activities; eliminate your extremist factions; live in peace with the West; join the 22nd century.

"The great Winston Churchill said: To Jaw-Jaw is better than to War-War. But there finally comes time to shit or get off the pot.

"We have talked till our jaws are dropping off and listened till our ears are wearing out, and all we get are the same old stale replies and rebuttals. From now on, there will be no more lines drawn in the sand that our adversaries can cross with impunity. Now we take a stand. The world wants us to take command; to reclaim our exceptional status. And that's what I will do starting tomorrow for you, the greatest people on the planet. It is in your best interests, and in the best interests of the civilized world. "God bless you patriotic Americans, and God bless our great nation…"

Electra's cell phone chimed not more than a minute after Jared's speech ended.

"It's Carter, and I must congratulate your speech. I think the public will love it. But tell me this: did you put in the S-word?"

"Hi Carter, and thanks for the compliment. And no, the S-word must have come from Jared or Zoe. But it certainly is an attention grabber."

"I agree. With or without it, I think his speech serves notice for action at the weekend UN debate. We'll have to stay tuned. And why don't I treat you to dinner next week. We can talk about work and other things without being pressed for time."

"I'd like that. What do you suggest?"

"I'll pick you up at your lab next Friday at six if that's convenient."

"It is. I look forward to seeing you. Good night."

Although Carter's party plan had surrealistically blown up only a couple of weeks ago, he never missed a beat after Electra bailed out. Guests thought he handled the bizarre turn of events as diplomatically as possible, and most stayed to help salvage the evening. They praised his resilience and sense of humor, sharing a bit of fun when he joked that tonight was just a rehearsal for the surprise party, so next time all guests must remember to act surprised. And then he poked more fun at himself by saying that next time, he was sure he wouldn't have to act surprised because he wouldn't know ahead of time what would actually happen.

Although depressed for a day or two, Carter perked up when he realized Electra had done the right thing. He was still in love, but he needed to reconsider what he wanted. *She can't give me a son, but maybe that isn't the end. I know she enjoys our relationship, but she needs to reevaluate too. We need a time out, but not a complete break. I've suffered a knock-down, but not a TKO yet. We'll talk about it over dinner.*

By the time Sunday afternoon rolled around, Jared had heard enough. Too many garbled words had rattled around in his head yesterday; right now the other speaker was droning on and on, and Jared was primed for action. And action he would soon deliver.

The satellite-televised debate had started well enough Saturday morning. The Secretary General introduced the debate topic; Jared staked his position; Isilabad's Exalted Ruler did the same. But as speakers came and went, Jared fumed because he could never remember Middle East names or terms. *Too many syllables and vowels in all the wrong places.*

Juried researchers for each side appointed by the UN Security Council presented historical background and recent developments, all meant to set the stage for a Sunday afternoon conclusion. And to dramatize the importance of the event, a three-foot high dais had been assembled in the middle of the UN Chamber. There was a podium in the center for the moderator and one on either side for respective speakers. Two tables flanked each side of the dais, with chairs tucked behind for handlers or substitute speakers.

At dinner Saturday night, Jared's handlers congratulated him for a winning day.

"Please remember tomorrow to keep your temper under control. And tell the Assembly you won't make the arrogant mistakes made in previous Gulf wars, where our side tried to push through democratic nation building in the face of centuries' old beliefs. Tell them you realize that terrorists on one side look like patriots for the other. You don't have to believe it, but just lie so you look like you'll compromise and be reasonable." Jared said he'd do his best.

The moderator reconvened the debate Sunday at 1 p.m. He was a distinguished looking diplomat from Sweden, who looked ready to hand out a Nobel Peace Prize. At the moment, he was looking leftward toward the Isilabad speaker, the Exalted Ruler. The moderator detected movement to his right and stepped back, smiling to greet Jared, who he thought was going to ask a question. That was the last thing on Jared's mind. He gruffly pushed past, heading toward the other podium. The moderator lost his balance and fell backward thudding loudly, his momentum sliding him off the stage. When he came to rest, all that was visible were the soles of his shoes dangling above the edge.

Jared rushed the other speaker, grabbing him by the beard and yanking him toward the far table where he proceeded to bash the turbaned head twice. Then he dragged his foe to the front of the stage where he summarily booted him off. The assembly watched spellbound at what was becoming a parody of UN diplomacy.

And Jared was not done. The alternate speakers at the opposition table finally rose from their seats. The one from China, closest to Jared, turned just in time to catch a solid right to the jaw, sending him crashing into his partner from Iran; both tumbled noisily backward and slid off the stage in slow motion, grabbing onto one another as if clinging to a raft about to go over the falls. Jared's handlers rushed to restrain him from doing further damage. Jared was not out of control; he was in complete control of the situation. He walked to the central podium and in a commanding voice said what he had prepared last night.

"I win by a technical knockout. And my actions speak louder than all the words you've heard. So, get behind me or get out of the way." Jared strode off the stage, handlers in his wake, as pandemonium erupted among the delegates.

Electra was first to make the call to Angus.

"I'm sure you've been watching. You'll have your hands full tomorrow."

"Jesus, Electra. Did you plan any his performance?"

"No, but it might rally more support. And I'm glad his handlers jumped in when they did. I was deathly afraid he was going to jump up on the table and start pounding his chest, like King Kong."

"He must have planned it all out, and here's what I think: the public will love it, the media will make fun of it, and the world leaders will be scratching their heads."

"And the Middle East will get Jared's blunt intent. I think you have a big job this week keeping Jared from gloating too much. Don't let this go to his head. Tell us at the next meeting what luck you have..."

Media pundits trumpeted for several days the debate debacle, blaring headlines such as "President KO's the Middle East" and "UN renamed Unleashed Knuckles as U.S. Strikes Back." One of the more clever analysts suggested—only half joking—that future conflicts should be decided by returning to a method from antiquity: a "winner take all brawl" between only the rulers of each side. Main Street rallied in Jared's corner, and Wall Street soared because the smart money knew that when push comes to shove, always bet on the U.S.

Angus warned Jared when meeting Monday afternoon that public sentiment is fickle.

"You won the battle yesterday, but we're in a war. People don't like a prolonged conflict, so you need us to help you throttle back. Let's keep some of the harsher measures in reserve in case we need them later."

Although Angus wasn't sure when the meeting ended if Jared would follow his advice, nothing new came up so the Brain Trust needed only to watch Jared closely.

Electra kept busy at the lab all week, working on postdoc projects and scheduling an October trip to Austin for which she Emailed an agenda to Hud. Only one item remained on the week's schedule, dinner with Carter. Thoughts of him brought bittersweet memories as she prepared to leave.

Thanks to Carter, I've grown emotionally since we became lovers, but choosing a co-friend is a tricky proposition. Indira lived with Jason for five years, balancing her thoughts, feelings, and partner. Carter excites me, and I don't want to hurt him or throw away what might work. Where we go after tonight depends as much on him as on me. We'll have to decide what the tradeoffs will be.

True to his practical nature, Carter called as he was about to arrive, eliminating the rigamarole of parking. Electra was at the curb when he pulled up, and she quickly folded into the Vette, getting out of the gentle rain that had just begun. She could read happiness in his expression, which added to a warming flutter that enveloped her when he spoke.

"Good evening, Electra. Even the rain can't dampen your radiance. I'm happy to see you tonight." She stroked his cheek before answering.

"I'm glad you invited me to dinner. How has your week been?"

"It's been good. I'm developing regional economic forecasts, and I should be able to forecast growth next year. I'll tell you more at dinner. Do you have a particular restaurant in mind?"

"No. Instead, let's pick up a pizza and have dinner at your place. I think that's a better place to get to know each other again—for the very first time."

"I'd like that. I've missed you more than you know. You bowled me over when you ran out, but I managed to get up and keep moving, so it wasn't a TKO. But it did hurt."

"I'm so sorry; I didn't mean to, but I couldn't go on misleading you. We need to decide where we want our relationship to go. I'm not expecting us to make a final decision tonight, but we can make a start." Carter's smile showed his sense of humor had never left.

"I was afraid you were going to flush me down the toilet of your heart, but at least for tonight, my fate is much better than that. I don't want to push my luck, but maybe I can push for a kiss or two."

"I think that can be arranged, and I'll let you decide if you'd like that before or after dinner. Maybe both, depending on how hungry you are. How's your appetite?"

"I'm famished."

"Me too, so drive on but don't get a speeding ticket. And speaking of tickets, let me tell you about one I nearly got…"

CHAPTER 31

September 2121

"The Mystery and Melancholy of Love"

(Thread 2 Chapter 11)

Robin had an additional reason to be upset. Her parents, now living among relatives in St. Petersburg, Russia, had been deported two months ago after exhausting the appeals process and spending too much money prolonging the unavoidable.

Such a blow would have knocked high-strung Robin into a full-fledged nervous breakdown had it occurred two years ago, but during that period she had toughened up from handling setbacks, while Matt and Electra provided a safety net.

Matt also had reasons to be upset. Robin's ambivalence towards males put him through an emotional wringer even though she trusted him more than any fellow she had ever dated. She also put him through a financial press, forcing him to buy her parent's house, then resell it for another because she wanted to rid herself of all memories.

But Matt knew how to handle life's challenges. He was an even better person than Robin realized, always patient because he understood how to handle her high-maintenance emotional problems caused by disastrous dating experiences, conflicted sexuality, and parent-directed anger. And Matt's generosity matched his patience. He named Robin co-owner when she consented to live with him again, though she warned against it because she was still grappling with issues that might push them apart. He did it anyway, saying he trusted her to do right by him. He believed her morals were as strong as her walnut-cracking grip.

The couple made the last Saturday in September moving day, and as customary for the younger crowd, their friends would help make a party of what otherwise would be a back-breaking chore. Robin expected Electra and Carter, and Carter's good friend Mariah, to arrive shortly. She hadn't seen Electra since Carter's bizarre party and hoped they could have some private time to talk about her troubling issues. She also wanted to get to know Mariah better.

Carter brought Mariah while Electra drove herself, planning to use her grandfather's van for hauling boxes. Having seen Carter and Electra recently, Mariah was relieved that both had rebounded but would not pry into personal affairs unless Electra wanted to chat. She felt a peculiar attraction that needed to be explored, so talking to Electra would release her feelings from solitary confinement.

All helpers arrived a little after nine, so the party started in the kitchen where coffee, fruit juice, Coca Cola, and muffins awaited. After Carter defused momentary embarrassment—he kidded that Electra can run out today as often as she likes as long as she keeps loading her van—everyone shared stories about previous moves. When the ladies let the men take charge, Carter kidded again.

"I'm glad the movers Matt hired already carted away most of the furniture. There's nothing very heavy left. He and I can handle the light stuff and leave any additional heavy lifting to the ladies. After all, aren't women supposed to be stronger than men?"

Matt said, "I'm not sure about the other ladies, but Robin can crush steel cans in either hand." The ladies smiled, thinking of a comeback; Mariah was the first to let one fly.

"Yes, women are stronger but we need to recover on the weekends from all we had to do during the week to cover for the men. So, we're counting on the guys to handle most of the load. We'll supervise."

The group divided into teams: Electra and Mariah in one, Robin, Carter, and Matt in the other, convoying the first load at eleven and the last at four-thirty. Everything was unloaded by seven and enough unpacked for Matt and Robin to spend a comfortable first night in their new house. There were no sore muscles, but even the guys were tired enough to call it a day. Before adjourning, Electra asked the ladies to join her tomorrow.

"Tomorrow's weather is supposed to be sunny and warm, so I have a suggestion. I'll pick up Robin and Mariah at ten, and we'll have an outing at the National Zoo, followed by lunch. And I think I know a good starting subject, so I'll lead the discussion and we'll go from there. The ladies agreed; now it was Carter's turn.

"How about we play tennis, then grab a hamburger and beer? I'll pick you up at one." Matt was happy to oblige.

"You're on…"

Mariah was in a good mood when Carter dropped her off, but as she entered her apartment her mood clouded abruptly, like a boat gliding from sunlit waters into a fog bank. She sat in the gloom of her unlit living room, trying to understand what had come over her. *The five of us had a fine time today, but I'm a fifth wheel. Robin and Matt are a pair; so are Electra and Carter, even though their relationship is changing. And Electra and Robin go way back; they'd probably like to talk by themselves about private matters. I'm sure they don't want me to be there. They'll think I'm a voyeur if I push in. I better call Electra to bow out gracefully.*

Electra was about to surf the Internet when her cell phone chimed. She didn't recognize the caller I.D. so she answered matter-of-factly.

"Good evening, this is Electra Kittner… Hi Mariah! You were a big hit with Robin and me today. The three of us make a great team…What?...No, please don't feel that way…Look, I have an idea. Why don't I drive over and tell you a little more about Robin and myself. It'll make you feel a lot more comfortable…Yes, I know how to get there…I'll see you in about forty-five minutes."

Electra used the drivetime to Mariah's apartment in McLean, Virginia to think through why Mariah thought she'd be intruding. *Mariah's bold and assertive professionally, but introspective and unassuming personally, sensitive to people's feelings, reluctant to show hers. But why? Maybe she doesn't want to risk revealing how she really feels. I've been there, so maybe I can help. And I know what to tell her about Robin and myself.*

Though it was dark when she arrived, there was enough streetlight to appreciate the upscale neighborhood of the McLean Gardens apartment building, nicely situated for Mariah's daily commute to her DC office. *It's hard to believe there are still so many slums in the Capitol. When T-Plague goes, I hope urban renewal comes back.* Mariah had been watching from the front window, so she opened the door before Electra knocked. Mariah gave her a tight but shy hug.

"Come on into the kitchen so I can get you a Coke. Or would you prefer the sparkling Chardonnay I'm having?"

"I'll join you in the Chardonnay. I like how you've decorated. It looks trendy. Have you lived here long?"

"It's the only place I've lived in since I came to Washington. Carter helped me settle in when I relocated from the West Coast…" The two of them chatted comfortably as Mariah took them into the living room, Electra sat on the sofa and Mariah in the chair on her left.

"I'm glad you came over, because I want to go out with you and Robin tomorrow. I'm sorry for being so skittish." Electra folded her legs underneath.

"I understand how you feel. We've become casual friends and I think we'd like our relationship to grow, but you don't know much about me and Robin. Am I on the right track?"

"Yes. I know I'm a couple of years older than you, but you're very mature. And you're comfortable with who you are. I'll bet your parents were that way. It must be in your DNA." *You'll never know how close to the truth you just came, but I have a good cover story.*

"Maybe so, but I've worked at it too. And let me start by telling you Robin's story. Here's a picture of Robin and me and a person you might hear us mention from time to time, Christi Conklin. Mariah studied it carefully while commenting.

"I recognize Robin. You too, but you look sort of embryonic, like you're just starting to emerge. And I recognize the name Conklin. Is the stunning blonde Russell Conklin's daughter?"

"Yes, that's Christi. I'll tell you more about her when I tell you my story. But I want to sketch Robin for you, because she'll be our focal point tomorrow. The three of us were best friends going way back to grade school. Robin is musically gifted, and as you must have picked up, is also high strung and emotionally fragile. She's complex and is working through her relationship with Matt while coming to terms with her sexuality. She's had bad luck with fellows. She needs to loosen up and enjoy sex. Poor thing hasn't had a good orgasm. We'll continue her story tomorrow." Electra paused to sip her wine, shifting into another comfortable position.

"There was a time not too long ago when I was reluctant to tell anyone much about myself, but I've grown past that. I feel comfortable telling you enough about who I am so you can determine if you want to take our relationship further. Depending on what happens, we'll both learn more about one another. Now, let me get back to Christi.

"She and I were best friends since first grade, and her mother, Jennifer, helped fill in for what I never had: my mother died in childbirth. Christi and I had a great time growing up, and we grew to love one another in all ways. We became lovers and hid it from everyone except Robin, who guessed it and shared it from afar. Christi and I had good sex with guys, but we both chose one another. Christi was killed in a car crash three years ago; I was injured but recovered, thanks to Matt and Robin taking care of me. Matt's a physical therapist who met Robin while handling my case.

"After Christi, I didn't think I would want to commit again. Sex would be to scratch hormonal itches. But I've grown emotionally and have decided to risk failure for the rewards of committed love. And I'm still bisexual. You already know how Carter and I met. Carter's a great guy, and for a variety of reasons we became lovers. He gives me great sex. But we ran into a big stumbling block and we need to reconsider what we want. I can't give him what he wants, what's very important to him. I can't give him children. I tried for over three months and couldn't get pregnant. And I made him promise not to tell anyone." Mariah snapped to attention.

"What a bizarre twist of fate. I broke up with Carter because he got me pregnant, and you're breaking up because he couldn't." Electra cocked her head to one side, a quizzical smile on her lips, waiting for Mariah to tell more, which she did immediately.

"I was a college junior when we met at a summer political seminar, and one thing led to another. After I got pregnant, he offered to marry me or help in any way I wanted, but I was too embarrassed and had other plans, so I took care of everything on my own. To this day, my parents don't know I had an abortion. You are the only person other than Carter who knows." Electra slid closer to Mariah before talking.

"Let me wrap up my story so you can decide where you'd like to take our relationship. I'm not actively on the prowl for sex partners. I prefer love to sex, and I'm sure you know the difference. And getting close to someone doesn't have to include sex. I don't know your sexual orientation, and I don't know what you're looking for, but I hope you've had good sex with males. I like you, and I would like to know you better. I hope I haven't talked too long or embarrassed or scared you off. Whenever you're ready, we can talk more. But for tomorrow, it's better we don't talk with Robin about anything other than her issues. She'll be our 'Queen for a Day.' I'm tired of talking. I'm going home, and I don't want to hear a peep out of you until you've thought things through." Electra stood up, preparing to go.

"Well if you won't let me say good night, at least let me hug you goodbye." This time, the hug was anything but shy.

"What a glorious day to drive to the zoo, but why did you pick this location?" Electra answered from behind the steering wheel, looking straight ahead rather than glancing at Robin, who was sitting in the passenger seat.

"Today we're going to talk about subjects near and dear to you: sex and relationships. And what better place than the zoo, where we can see up close and in person examples of intimate relationships among our closest ancestors. Apes don't seem to struggle with them as much as you do. Mariah, what do you think? Mariah giggled from the back seat.

"I've never thought about interpersonal relationships quite that way, but I guess animals have mastered it. Those that didn't are extinct. I think you told us you took an animal behavior course, so please tell us more."

"When it comes to pairing and sex, apes display even more diversity than what's found in humans. They rape and practice homosexuality. And the females advertise when they're fertile, engaging in public sex. And they even have sex just for pleasure. But we humans, complex psychological creatures that we are, can make a muddle of it. We should learn from the apes: sex and orgasms are primarily biological tools for efficient mate selection and reproduction, and only secondarily for long-term bonding or offspring care."

Robin said, "I'm glad the apes didn't learn about sex from black widow spiders or praying mantises. Don't those females eat the males after sex?"

"Yes, and there's a biological reason. Once the male insect has fertilized the eggs, he's useful only as a source of food." Mariah grimaced before replying.

"Guys are more useful than that. If you won't tell us why, I will."

"We're here, so we can walk and talk after I park. And let's have Mariah lead our 'Robin Relationship Day' discussion.

Foot traffic matched the weather on this last September Sunday. Sunlight and temperature still spoke summer, but brightly colored leaves tumbling gently from the trees heralded autumn. As the trio walked and talked, Electra felt a tingling remembrance for the Three Queens of long ago, but let the feeling slip away, perhaps to return another day. It was noon when Robin declared time out to sit and talk, so the ladies found a suitable table. Electra concluded her part of the lecture.

"So, we must always remember that the physiological differences between men and women will always impact relationships. Even though human emotion is much more complex than what animals experience, sex, survival, and safety are always lurking near the surface. It takes thousands of years for evolution to encode in our DNA how and why we behave the way we do. And ever since the Renaissance, the rapidity of change, fueled by science and technology, has exacerbated the mismatch between how people should act when thinking rationally, compared to how they do when reacting emotionally."

"Robin's not the only one who has problems with relationships. I struggle too. Have you ever seen Giorgio de Chirico's painting, 'Mystery and Melancholy of a Street?' It's in New York's Museum of Modern Art." Neither Electra nor Robin had, so Mariah's words painted it for them.

"It's a mesmerizing though unsettling surrealistic painting of a girl's silhouette rolling a hoop along an alleyway adjacent to a huge coliseum that is lined with darkened archways. In the distance is a threatening shadow of a large man. This painting is a metaphor for how I feel about relationships. I need relationships, but I don't know what they'll hold, and I'm uncertain how I want a male to fit in."

"Holy shit, uh, pardon my French, but I feel the same way."

Electra snickered then said, "Please excuse Robin's favorite S-word. And your painting metaphor is perfect. Robin's not alone, but by this time she should realize Matt's not like the other guys. They need to talk about what they want. And that includes sex. If the apes could talk, they'd tell her not to overthink sex. Just dive in. Mariah, what would you like to add?"

"We've talked enough. Let's move on and have lunch…"

"That's game, set, and match." Carter walked towards the net as Matt did likewise to retrieve the ball he had just hit into it.

"I'll buy the hamburgers, but I was planning to do that anyway. You were such a brick helping us move."

"Do you want to grab a bite here, or stop on the drive home?"

"It's too nice to be indoors. Let's find someplace with outdoor seating."

"You're right. We might not get another day like this. If you like onion ring towers, I know just the place."

The two traded stories about favorite hamburger toppings as Carter's Vette rumbled into a sports-themed restaurant parking lot. Then they grabbed an umbrella table in the sunlight, talking about micro-beers until the server took their order. When she returned with the beers, Matt took a long swallow before talking.

"Mariah fits in nicely with Electra and Robin. Though she's not as pretty, a fellow who's looking for a thin female would go for her, but is she always so quiet?"

"Only in social settings. She can be very outspoken in the workplace. And I find her combination of body and brain attractive. What attracts you to Robin?"

"There's a hormonal-related physical attraction, but all our senses pick up signals. Robin might not be as smart as Electra or Mariah, but she has morals and character second to none. What about you and Electra? I don't mean to pry, but it might help if you talk to me." Carter set his glass down and leaned in.

"I find intelligent women sexy. And when I got to know her better, I found her appealing in other ways. Look, I'm sure Electra will tell Robin the reason she ran out at the party. I promised not to tell, but since you and I are connected through them, you should know."

"We're friends in our own right, so I'll tell you about Robin after you tell me about Electra. We can help each other."

"I agree, so here's my story. Electra and I have been in an intimate relationship for four months, and it's been the best four months of my life. But we ran into a big problem. She can't get pregnant. She never told me she was trying. And I believe her when she says I'm not the problem. She knows I want kids, so when I sprung the surprise party, the timing couldn't have been worse. That's when she told me. She couldn't face her friends, so she bolted, putting our relationship on hold. We're sort of back together, but she's lowered the intimacy level so we each have some space to consider what we want. And that's where we're at. Any ideas?"

"You and Electra are the smartest couple I know. My only suggestion would be to follow her lead. Don't push her. She'll figure out what's best for both of you. Maybe it'll hurt short term. If it does, the pain will go away over time. And never forget that you have legitimate needs also. You want to give a lot, but you must at least get what you need."

"You're right on both counts. I like your advice, and I like talking with you. Thanks."

"Now, it's your turn to listen. Here's the scoop on Robin. My neuro-sensors are attuned to her, but although she likes me, hers don't pick up on sex the way mine do. I hate to say it, but I don't think she's ever climaxed when in bed with me, and I know other women have, so my technique isn't lacking. Jesus, don't you dare mention this to Electra." Carter leaned in even closer.

"You fool, what do you think they're talking about today? And in much more colorful terms. But don't worry, I won't say anything. But I will offer advice.

"You've got a bigger relationship problem than I do, but in your case the problem isn't yours. It's Robin's. You're a patient and understanding guy, but there'll come a time when you might have to walk away. You can't live your life kowtowing to a drama queen. And remember this: we're young. If Electra or Robin can't cut it, we have plenty of time to find other partners, and I don't mean settling for a consolation prize. Settling is for old farts, not for young bucks like us. And I'll be brutally frank; we're prime targets for younger professional women."

"I like what you say, and I think each of us knows how to handle our current relationship."

"Yes, but it's good that you're dealing with Robin. I don't think I could deal with all her baggage. You're much better than I when it comes to understanding females and relationships. How did you get to know so much?"

"Give yourself some credit too. You know more than a lot of fellows, and in general, males today are much better than a couple of generations ago. Part of the reason I know a lot is from working with women. And I might be a bit more practical, more empathetic than cerebral types like yourself. I've always been interested in female psychology, and I even took college courses covering interpersonal communications, gender theory, and the role of women in society as told in literature. I could give you a summary, but you've probably heard enough."

"No, please, go ahead. I always enjoy conversations that cover what I don't know."

"OK, but I'll make it quick because I need to go home and help Robin. Women have been scapegoats, going all the way back to Greek mythology. Helen of Troy causing the Trojan War. Amazon women stirring up trouble. Women on Lesbos dissing men by refusing to have sex, instead becoming lesbians. The Greeks didn't mind men hooking up with men, but not women doing likewise.

"Religious writings demonize women. Eve corrupted Adam. Women can't be trusted, have to submit to husbands who own them. And until a hundred years ago, women couldn't serve as priests or ministers. Pretty shabby treatment, wouldn't you say?"

"Seems so. Keep going." Matt glanced at the time.

"OK. Medieval literature is no better. Mythical witches and female ghosts treat men badly. Elizabethan, Renaissance, and Victorian literature consider women inferior. Read Defoe's *The Amorous Adventures of Moll Flanders*, Flaubert's *Madame Bovary*, or Lawrence's *Lady Chatterly's Lover*. They paved the way for the Women's Rights Movement. And some 21st century novels have taken cognitive psychology into the micro-politics of gender equality."

"I'm impressed. You must do a lot of reading. Do you ever discuss it with Robin?"

"No, but if she gets less hyper, I'll try."

"I can add some socio-economic points to what you've said. Do you have time for a summary?" Matt checked his cell phone.

"OK, but please talk fast."

"Will do. It's taken several hundred years, but America is closer to gender equality now than ever. Now we have many acclaimed female artists, business leaders, composers, and scientists. And look at the progress made in women's athletics. The Co-NFL and Co-NBA are wildly popular. You'd think there'd be a similar coed soccer league, but that hasn't happened because soccer is more popular internationally, and the rest of the world is behind when it comes to the gender equality curve. And men didn't have to pay much attention to women's rights until technology replaced brawn with brain. From an economic standpoint, women don't need a man to support them, nor to give them children. They don't have to trade sex for resources. But, have you ever considered the issue from the male point of view?"

"No, but I'm sure you have. But please, speed up your pitch."

"Will do. The Industrial Revolution and technological changes put a double whammy, first on working class men in the mid-1960's, and then on professional males by the early 21st century. Globalization, job outsourcing, and competent women in the workplace aggravated the problem: males who couldn't adjust to the hi-tech, service-based economy became downwardly mobile. Most males adjusted or compensated, but a backlash Men's Rights Movement surfaced. An MGTOW online social media community emerged, pointing out that social conditions were becoming biased in favor of women. By the way, the acronym means Man Going Their Own Way. Some of the more extreme proponents shunned the idea of romantic relationships, becoming openly hostile towards women. But 'Migtow,' that's how you pronounce the acronym, gained little traction. Next generations of males learned the skills to get good jobs and to get along with the opposite sex. And when T-Plague goes away, everyone will be happy. By the way, MGTOW is analogous to the more extreme factions of Third Wave Feminism. And that's the end of my summary, but I could extend our discussion into society's comfort versus carrying capacity. Calhoun's mice studies confirm the emergence of MGTOW and third wave feminism appropriate for the species." Matt hustled Carter to his feet.

"Thanks for educating me. You talk just like a professor, and if you ever become one, just make sure you know when time's up. We gotta go…"

Dusk had just descended, casting the first floor into semi-darkness by the time Matt entered. *She's gonna be upset I'm not home sooner to help unpack more stuff. Well, I'll pitch in pronto.*

"I'm home." There was no reply but, hearing soft footsteps upstairs, he headed for the second floor. There were no lights on, only a soft glow flowing past a partly opened bedroom door. When he reached the top of the stairs, Robin emerged from the bedroom, neither smiling nor frowning, wearing only a thong bikini bottom and tank top. Matt was about to apologize for being late, but Robin's actions were quicker. She wrapped her arms around his neck and drew him to her open lips. Matt's saucer-sized eyes took in all he saw; Robin had already turned down the bed and had turned unpacked boxes into night stands adorned with lighted candles and iced tumblers of white wine. Then his emotions took control. He drew her into his arms and tasted her lips, stopping just long enough for Robin to take the next step. She dragged him into the bedroom where she started removing his shirt. Matt caught on and stripped naked. Then, she tumbled him into the bed and made the next move. She was not to be disappointed. She was not to be denied…

Robin glowed deep into the night, unleashing pent-up passion that took Matt to levels he had never been to before. And Matt gave as good as he got. He could tell by her sharp gasps and moans that accompanied her pelvic thrusts that Robin had finally received what he had been dying to give her, joyous ecstasy rewarding primal desire. Her body finally went limp as she collapsed into his arms, sobbing softly.

No words needed to be spoken as he cradled her, softly stroking her hair while his lips gently removed her tears. He kissed her lips, then helped her sit up. Handing her a tumbler of wine, Matt proposed a toast, his emotionally charged words surprising both of them.

"No matter tomorrow whatever's in store,
Tonight is ours forevermore…"

Tears of happiness returned as she kissed him again.

Much later that night, after showering together and whispering her to sleep, Matt mulled over the future as he watched over his fragile sleeping beauty.

What's the saying? One swallow doesn't a summer make. Well, one night of passion doesn't cement our relationship either. Robin still has to sort out what she wants, and she's still dragging a lot of emotional baggage. But I'll do all I can to help her break free. This is as good as it gets for me.

The following week, a mid-evening cell call interrupted Electra while at her lab making changes to a postdoc research report. Though it took three chimes to tear her away, she was happy to answer once she recognized the caller I.D.

"Hi, Mariah. What a pleasant surprise. How are you?"

"Working late at the office. I'm about to call it an evening and thought you might join me for a cappuccino."

"I'm at my GWU lab, which isn't far from where you are. I'll pick you up. Is your building still open?"

"Yes. If you'd like to see my office, just sign in at the security desk. Our offices are on the twenty-fifth floor."

"I should be there in about a half hour. See you then."

As she hurried to her car, Electra could feel a cold front blowing in faster than forecast, threatening to trigger a band of late evening thunder storms. The few stragglers still outside were hustling to seek shelter. Traffic was light and she knew the way; her immediate concern was finding the nearest parking space in case the rains came before she was inside the building. The day had been too warm to wear a jacket, but she had armed herself with a spear-like oversize golf umbrella—Carter played golf and gave her a colorful one for good luck in bad weather—to keep the rains off just in case the blow started too soon. She spotted the security desk when she entered, but the guard was somewhere else so she went directly to the elevator bank and pushed the button.

The two "enforcers" were thoroughly professional, knowing how to handle any job requiring persuasive muscle. Their assignment tonight should be easy; convince someone complaining too loudly about the Guardian Party to lighten up, or the next visit would be harsher. Neither knew the identity of their client and vice versa, which at their level was standard operating procedure, but they had his phone number and would call as soon as the job is done. He had called them a half hour ago, giving orders to proceed because the target would be the only one at the office. "Enforcer" number one gloated to his partner.

"This is gonna be easy. The security guard's nowhere in sight and you picked up his key ring, so we'll just walk right in."

As she waited for the elevator, Electra thought about what Mariah might like to do. *I could drive us to one of those pleasure cafes if the weather's OK. Or stop at a diner for a dessert if I drive her home. We'll figure it out when I know what's on her mind.*

Electra noticed how well the older building had been maintained. The elevator didn't rush from floor to floor but moved in a stately manner, delivering her nonstop to the twenty-fifth floor. *Hardly anyone's in the building, and the floor sounds deserted.*

The lightning brain's warning system triggered an alarm as Electra approached the glass doors to a suite of offices. *Why is there a key ring still in the lock? And why is there an overturned chair in the reception area?* Her brain switched to a higher gear as she slipped inside, listening for clues. She heard a muted commotion from an office down the corridor, so she followed her ears to what could only be Mariah's office. The door was closed but enough sound came through for Electra to piece together the situation.

Electra's response happened with a speed and finality controlled by the lightning brain, a sudden coherence jolting as cognitive and emotional personas fused, entire body tingling yet a strangely calm. She didn't know if her Monster from the Id would be unloosed, nor did she care. She wanted to leap into action and let her lightning brain decide.

She placed her umbrella and shoulder bag on a nearby desk, then silently opened the door. The sight appalled her. Two thugs were beating Mariah; one held her while the other pummeled with gloved fists.

"Stop! You'll kill her," she screamed, then slammed the door.

"Don't let her get away! Grab her."

Electra greeted the gloved thug as charged through the doorway. She rammed the umbrella nine inches into his gut, stopping him dead in his tracks. He doubled up in pain and collapsed to his knees. She left the umbrella embedded in his stomach and grabbed his head, violently wrenching it sideways until she heard a crisp SNAP. Then she pushed him out of the way as she grabbed her Traser and bolted into Mariah's office. Her attack had been so quick thug number two hadn't moved, able only to shove Mariah to the floor.

"Stay where you are. Bend down and tell me how badly injured she is. Do it now; I won't ask you again." Her adversary had a stocky, slow-moving build.

"Not too bad. We just punched her up a bit. Her nose ain't broken and the split lip will mend."

"Good. Here's what I want you to do. Take off your belt and tie her hands. Then we'll get your partner's belt and tie her feet. Then gag her and put her in that closet. Do it now and don't say a word." The bad guy looked confused but did as commanded.

Electra supervised, keeping enough distance to stay in command no matter what he tried. He looked at her stonily as soon as Mariah was out of the way. "Let's go visit your partner again. I want you to sit in a nearby chair so I can ask you some questions. I will ask one time only. He's dead, and you will be too if you don't give me good answers. Do you understand?" Naked fear replaced his look of confusion. He nodded numbly.

"Who sent you?"

"I don't know. Everything's anonymous. I don't know them and they don't know me."

"Why were you sent?"

"To shut her mouth about the Guardian Party. That's all I was told."

"What are you supposed to do next?"

"Call the client when the job's done."

"Write down the number, then call him on the speaker phone so I can hear. There's a pen and paper on the desk. Do it now."

The thug wanted to stall for as long as he could, but even his dim wits figured there was no way out. He was so dumb Electra had to activate the speaker.

"Yeah, the job's done... The target's unconscious but won't show too much damage. She knows to shut up or we'll come again... Yep, that's the account number to wire the money... OK, we're done." He hung up and spoke in a dull tone.

"What's next?"

What happened next surprised them both. The lights went out, plunging the entire building into total darkness. The thug stumbled for the door, instead colliding with the wall, but Electra was already in position, on hands and knees at the office entrance, ready to play a deadly game of cat and mouse. She would be the cat, waiting silently until she spotted the mouse. The cat was nimble and quick, the mouse heavy and slow, but the darkness added uncertainty. Electra had her Traser at the ready.

All her senses adjusted to near-total darkness, and she spotted him crawling, clutching a knife. She was about to strike when a second surprise hit. The power came back on, giving her adversary an advantage because his dull eyes adjusted faster.

He rose to his knees before hurling the knife, but Electra instinctively dived away so the knife whizzed by her cheek. Then he lunged forward, grabbing for her Traser, ripping it away. Electra spun out of his clutches and kicked him in the side of his head, then leaped to her feet after diving for the weapon. The thug made a last-ditch dive to save himself, tackling her backwards onto the floor, but she hung on to the Traser. He threw wild haymakers, connecting with her nose and mouth, but she pushed him to the left and rolled to her right, jumping into the clear. He got to his knees, gasping as Electra prepared to end the battle. And then a third surprise hit. The Traser wouldn't fire; its charge had leaked away. The fight had now taken a deadly turn away from Electra, and that's when the Monster from the Id crashed through.

Electra grabbed the nearest chair and smashed it over her opponent's head. The first blow stunned and the second put him down. A desk phone was the nearest object; she grabbed it and clubbed him until it broke. She was wrapping the cord around his neck when a voice yelled out inside her head.

"Get with the plan, soldier! This is not a drill. Wrap up quickly and vanish." Her rational persona had regained control. The Monster submerged into the subconscious, snapping the thug's neck before disappearing.

Electra jumped to her feet and surveyed the damage, ignoring the blood flowing from her nose and mouth, simply wiping it on her blouse. But there was more. The knife had sliced a two-inch gash on her right cheek. She tore a piece of cloth from her adversary's shirt and wiped away the dripping blood. Her plan had become a shambles, but a better one sparked to life.

She ran to the office door and found what she was looking for: the security guard's key ring. *It's gotta be on it, and I'll know it when I see it.* It was; she found the magic key and ran to make sure it fit. It did, so she ran back to take penultimate steps.

She stripped the bodies of all keys, wallets, and cell phones, shoving them into her shoulder bag. Dead bodies are heavy, but the smooth carpet made it easy to drag them out, positioning them for the final push. Then she used the magic key to open doors. She would drop the bodies down elevator shafts.

Electra knew every elevator door has a small round opening for a key that unlocks the outer door. The first elevator door slid open and she pushed the first body into the shaft, not caring if the car was above or below. Either way the first thug was out of sight. She disposed of the second down another shaft, the reverberations in each telling they were at the bottom. *Not their final resting places, but by the time they're found, any trail of clues will be stone cold dead.*

Electra rushed to put the office back together and then untie Mariah.

Poor Mariah! But I had to get her out of the way for her own good, and for mine. She can't know the full story. She might not cover for me.

Mariah was just coming to, terrified and confused, because the action had taken place so quickly. She clung for support as Electra pulled her off the floor. She was in shock, so Electra shook her to explain.

"You're OK. And I got away from your attackers when the lights went out. Come on, let's get you cleaned up. Where's the ladies room?"

"It's down the corridor. My God, Electra. You're bleeding worse than I am. Your blouse is a mess. I need to take care of you first." Mariah led her into the ladies' room where she set her on a couch, returning with moist wash cloths and towels, and gently began wiping the blood away. Electra closed her eyes.

How calming, how sensually pleasant to be cared for. I've changed; I've matured; I want intimacy.

Mariah wiped blood from Electra's cheek and chin, then Electra did the same for Mariah, cautioning her about keeping quiet.

"Your comments about the Guardian Party rub some people the wrong way. Those guys were sent to shut you up. I don't know of anyone else who's been threatened. Do you?"

"No. Angus hasn't said anything. What do you think we should do?"

"Don't tell anyone what happened here, and please tone down your rhetoric. That will make whoever sent them think you got the message. In a week or so when we know more, we'll tell Angus.

And in the meantime, be watchful. Keep people around you. Don't get caught alone."

"Gad, the cut on your cheek needs stitches. Let's take you to an emergency clinic. I know the closest one. Come on, let's go."

Electra was stitched up three hours later, thanks to the E.R. doctor.

"The stitches will dissolve by themselves, so you don't need to come back unless the cut becomes infected, and that shouldn't happen if you use my topical antibiotic prescription. And I'm good at subcuticular stitching, so you shouldn't have much of a scar, but if it's more pronounced than you like, you should seek the services of a plastic surgeon. Do you ladies have any more questions?"

"No, and thanks for all you've done. I'll make sure the patient gets home. We're ready to go."

The storm had blown through but the winds were still gusty and turning colder, so the two hugged onto one another as they stepped quickly to Electra's car. Electra detected Mariah's tremble, and as she steadied her, Mariah asked a question that had been on her mind for several days.

"Would you spend the night with me? I really want to know you better." Electra's smile was as good as her answer.

"I was about to ask you the same..."

The two would talk the night away, and for the very first time Mariah would experience the tenderness that comes from sharing her bed with another lady. Come the morning, she would want to know even more about this remarkable creature that had entered her life.

Electra drove Mariah to work, then decided to work from home. She wanted to release excess energy so when she arrived, she suited up to run.

I picked up a new dueling scar last night. And perhaps a new relationship that could leave emotional scars. But I'll risk it. I'm ready to welcome madness and the most.

CHAPTER 32

October 2121

"Grasping for Faith and Friends"

(Thread 2 Chapter 12)

ZOE NEEDED HELP. SHE was unraveling like a worn piece of yarn, and if someone didn't intervene, the threads of her life would be hard to knit back together. The Zoe that people thought they knew might never be seen again.

How sad that such a talented young lady who started with such great expectations should be in this predicament; it never should have come to this. She had been perky and popular in school, where her enthusiasm and passion for social causes ignited her academic achievements that fast-tracked her career to the Guardian Party. And before coming to Washington from her roots in Cincinnati, she always had a diverse circle of friends who kept her grounded regarding life in general and relationships in particular, warning her whenever she was about to sacrifice more than she should for whatever cause she championed.

But Zoe unwittingly lost her way once in Washington. She left her friends behind and when she constructed a new set, the replacements were surface rather than substance because all of them focused, just like she, on a socio-political career.

Problems lay dormant because her socially active but one-dimensional crowd pretended they were pleased how quickly her Guardian Party career had blossomed. She had few satisfying relationships because fellows often took advantage of her idealistic nature, but she ended all of them once Jared Gardner, an obsession she hid, started using her public relations talent.

Jared had no degenerate intentions when Zoe dragged him to bed. He treated her well enough at first because he liked her work, but as he became indifferent, he became more demanding, taking more liberties as Zoe's codependence grew and she kept stoking his ego.

Jared's lieutenants did likewise because he was scoring in the political arena. And as his political power grew, he felt he deserved more from the people he used, especially women. *Zoe's too predictable, too clinging. I have to find a clever way to dump her. Maybe she'll decide to leave if she doesn't like the mind games I'll start playing.*

Poor Zoe hadn't a clue. She was too close to the problems she had brought on herself, and she had no close friends to help her break free. To observers, Zoe looked rosy because she hid behind a fake image. But a true friend would have seen the real Zoe, a once confident lady filled with self-doubt and loneliness, desperately in need of codependency counseling that would end Jared's tyrannical games before Zoe lost too much more of body and soul.

Electra was working at home on a mid-October Wednesday when a call from Zoe came. She responded to Electra's cheerful greeting.

"I'm fine. You haven't called me in a while, and I need your advice, so I thought I'd give you a shout. I'm not interrupting, am I? I know how busy you get."

"Of course not. I apologize for not calling you. What advice would you like?"

"Religious advice. I recently joined the Church of the New Age Fundamental Faith and would like to invite you to a new believer's workshop. Could you come next Sunday? I'll tell you more in person."

"I'll make time. What time should I pick you up?"

"Would nine a.m. be OK? We can talk before the workshop."

"That works for me, so I'll see you then. Bye." *Something's going on in Zoe's life, but I've been too busy to notice. Benign neglect is a bad way to treat her. She's been a better friend to me than vice versa. Let's see how I can help. I'll start by researching New Age Fundamentalism.* Three hours later knew the basics.

I can see why certain types are attracted to this recent offshoot of the more popular fundamental Christian movements. It still keeps at its core the faith-based beliefs in the Holy Trinity, but it scales back most of the dogma and paraphernalia that clutter the older, stagnating branches. And Its holistic approach plus a "God and Nature" combination seems inviting and inclusive, as does its belief in human potential and alternative medicine empowering us to take control of our lives. But I don't buy in to channeling. It's fantasy to think that divine authority can be communicated to believers through a handful of chosen human demi-gods and spiritual masters. That's blindly following what you're told to think and do. And how do the masters get picked? What a dangerous game if you're on the receiving end.

I'm glad I've done my homework for Sunday. I know enough to help Zoe.

Electra wrapped up all work and household chores by Saturday lunchtime, so she rewarded herself by taking an afternoon run on neighborhood sidewalks and streets leading to a popular biking trail. It was too cold for shorts, so she wore form-fitting navy-blue tights and a matching long-sleeve half-zip top color-coordinated with her new Nike running flats, letting her brain focus on whatever it picked out on the route. Red and yellow autumn leaves meandered in the light breeze, decorating the sidewalks.

I've been running this route for many years, but seldom have I paid attention to houses or occupants. Each one contains a family sheltered warm and safe inside. I'm sure each has a story that its owner could provide. Suddenly her path crossed that of a small gray puff of an Angora cat crouched in a patch of sunlight. An emotional pang brought her to a stop. Electra came to a halt next to the tiny creature that gazed at her with wide somber eyes. Electra knelt to offer an index finger and as the cat's nose sniffed, her heart reached for the cat. *It looks so gentle, so sad. I wonder if it's lost. I don't want any harm coming its way. I have to take it home.* Unbeknownst to Electra, the owner was perched on the front steps.

"Her name is Kitten. I rescued her 18 years ago when she was seeking shelter from a cold November night rainstorm." The voice startled Electra; she had been so focused on the cat she didn't spot the elderly lady watching over what must be her pet. Electra arose to respond.

"Oh, hi. I've run past your house many times, but this is the first I've seen your cat. It's so tiny, I thought it was a kitten." The woman ambled towards Electra.

"No, she was small when I found her, and she never grew very much. She gets plenty to eat and the veterinarian says she's healthy, but as she gets older she's shrinking, becoming just skin and bones." As they talked, Kitten strolled to Electra's feet, it's fluffy tail swishing to and fro.

"May I pick her up?"

"Go right ahead; she won't scratch." Electra scooped with one hand; Kitten nestled for warmth in the crook of her neck.

"Kitten must like you; she's purring." Electra continued petting, then scratched under the chin before handing back.

"I don't know your name, but my husband used to call you the runner girl. For years, we've seen you run past the house. He used to run in local races and sometimes looked for you, but he never saw you there. And that surprised him, because he said you were built for the sport. Said you were a toe runner; light frame and light on your feet, like a dancer. And he sometimes commented on your running attire, which used to be much like his. He never wore fancy running outfits; stuck to sweat pants and sweat shirts."

"Does your husband still run?"

"No, he's been in a nursing home for a year. He has T-Plague dementia. I used to take care of him, but I'm not strong enough to get him up, then bathe and dress him. But I visit him every day. Now it's just me and Kitten taking care of the place."

"I'm so sorry. I wish I had met you sooner."

"On good days, my husband recognizes me. But I don't think he'd recognize you. You've matured. You don't have that gaunt look anymore, like someone should be forcing you to eat. You're still very thin, but you've filled out in all the right places. And you could model running clothes. You look like you just stepped out of an upscale women's fitness store. By the way, my name is Diane Whooten. What's yours, if I may ask?"

"I'm Electra Kittner, and when I was a kid my friends called me Kit."

"Well Electra, I'd be pleased if you'd stop by any time for lunch. I'm sure Kitten would like to see you again too. And you better get on with your run. I've detained you long enough." Electra said her goodbyes to Kitten and then ran on, the cadence of her stride putting her mind at ease as she considered the cat.

My brain is changing. I've never felt such an emotional tug for a pet. The only pets I've had are the houseplants. Why did Kitten grab me so? An answer came as she approached home.

I know why. Kitten reminds me of the joy I had when taking care of Grandfather. How good it felt to be needed. I miss that. I bet if I walked a pet, I'd meet fellow pet owners, and they're some of the nicest people. They give their animal unconditional love, and from what I see, it gives what it gets. I'm a social animal too, and the lightning brain is telling me to reach out, so I'll start tomorrow.

Zoe, waiting outside for Electra, waved pertly as she pulled to the curb, then hopped into the car and greeted Electra in her breathless manner.

"Thanks for picking me up. You look great. You really know how to pick stylish clothes."

"You look good too, better rested. And I have you to thank. I learned a lot about business styles from you, and I've spruced up my casual wear too."

"Maybe we can go shopping sometime. It's more fun hunting in pairs. Do you do much online shopping? If so, I can give you links to some great online shoe stores."

"I do most clothes shopping online using virtual fitting room apps. All you do is upload a photo of yourself in the buff. The app computes correct sizes and overlays on your virtual image how the clothes you pick look. And the upscale stores have apps that utilize 'four-pi holography' that creates a 3-D rotating virtual. What do you do to get correct shoe sizes?"

"That's easy. I scan an outline of my foot into the computer and upload it to the shoestore's app. It works fine. Try it sometime."

"I shall. Online shopping saves time, especially the drone delivery part. Automated delivery vans have a good safety record and are better for heavier stuff than heli-drones."

Zoe didn't completely agree.

"I like to save time, but I still like shopping at stores because of the social interaction. Let's do this sometime; we can pick and order online, pickup in person, have lunch, and walk the mall."

"I'd like that. And I imagine you like the social interaction at church rather than viewing the online televangelists."

"I do. Being there is the best way to get the message. What church do you go to?"

"None regularly. But I surfed to learn more about New Age Fundamentalism, and it sounds pretty interesting. How did you get interested?" Zoe's smile faded.

"I'll tell you, but you must promise to keep it confidential. Jared's a believer, but he doesn't advertise it. It's not good for his presidential image because the public trusts more traditional branches better."

"Do you know why he likes it?"

"Sort of. He tells me he's always had strong faith in fundamentals, but for the past year he's been struck by the idea of channeling. I'm not sure what that is, but he told me to put my faith in him. He says he knows what's best for me and for others."

"We can talk more about it later. We're here, so let's park and go in…"

Many of the newer fundamental churches are rehabs of those from the more traditional religions whose congregations have been withering away, and the one they were attending fit that description. Electra liked that; it was much warmer and welcoming than the impersonal monoliths often seen online. And she listened attentively to the service. The lay minister and her associates seemed genuine and caring, as did the midsize congregation. After the service, there was a fifteen minute "say hi" session at the entrance, where all were invited to attend a workshop that would discuss the Bible as well as enroll new members.

Electra had learned years ago never to speak up at meetings like this. She had selected her religious philosophy early on, leaning far towards reason rather than faith, but she also knew human nature wants to believe in a higher power, a belief that is rooted in DNA or social memes, and she respected each person's choice. She honored all religions that give its followers dignity and respect, and she liked much that she heard. From time to time she glanced at Zoe, who kept fidgeting and seemed to have trouble concentrating. *Something's really bothering Zoe. I need to find out what's the matter.*

Electra spoke first as they walked to the car afterwards.

"How about we stop for lunch? And I'll treat. I owe you a lot more than lunch for all you've done for me."

"I prepared a chicken salad. I was hoping you'd come back to my place so we could talk."

"I like that. It'll be more private, more comfortable."

Electra set the kitchen table while Zoe dished up the plates and heated rolls in the oven. Zoe even served a chilled Chablis and an herb butter bought from her favorite gourmet shop. Electra always had a good appetite for well-prepared dishes, and the chicken salad passed her taste test.

"This chicken salad is delicious. It's seasoned just right, and it's just the right consistency." Zoe smiled, but only picked at what was on her plate. *She's embarrassed and afraid to tell me what's bothering her. I have to take the initiative.* She put down her fork, smiled at Zoe and offered an overdue apology.

"Getting to know you better has been on my to-do list, but I've let other things get in the way. I'm ashamed of myself for not making the effort sooner. I've known you for over three years, and by this time I can read your body language. Something's bothering you, so please tell me what's on your mind. We can make a game of it. You tell me only what's comfortable for you to say, and I'll fill in the gaps. Fair enough?" Zoe took a deep breath to steady her nerves then spoke hesitantly.

"It's hard for me to tell anyone, but if I don't do it now I don't know how I'll go on. I'm in a relationship I know is bad but I just can't break away. And it's my fault. I trapped myself." As Electra studied Zoe's face, she noticed bruises that her neck scarf didn't completely hide.

"I started it about two years ago. I was—and still am—infatuated with the person. And he treated me well at first. It was my dream come true. But then it all changed. He started losing interest in me, started being mean, and then started playing mind games." Electra grabbed for Zoe's hands to stop her from saying another word. *Zoe, now I know. the President of the United States is abusing you.*

"You're in an abusive codependent relationship, and I know who's hurting you. I'm going to take you to a codependency counselor as soon as I can." Zoe covered her eyes.

"I can't go! I can't tell them Jared's abusing me. They'll never believe me."

"We won't tell them it's Jared. The advice and steps you'll take would be the same no matter who the pervert is. This stays just between you and me."

"There's more to it. Jared's most trusted secret service agent—a guy named Peter Schmitzer—sometimes brings in prostitutes. I haven't been part of that yet, thank God. I think one of the prostitutes died of a heart attack, or maybe something worse.

"And Jared's been using me as a mental punching bag when he talks about religion and channeling. I'm sorry, but I lied to you. I know all about channeling and Jared thinks he's been chosen to lead the country. He even consults with a spiritual advisor. I'm sure you've noticed he's becoming more extreme in dealing with the bad guys. Well, sometimes he doesn't know who the bad guys really are. And now he's thinking up all on his own new programs that are even harsher than the ones already in place."

"Do you know what they're all about?"

"No. He hasn't talked about it with me because he's not ready for press releases. I just heard him mention it to Peter. But here's something I do know about: Jared's hidden agenda. He's been funneling service contracts to companies he controls."

"Can you prove any of this?"

"I can't, but maybe you can because you're good at digging up dirt. I can give you the name of the escort agency Peter gets kick-backs from, and I overheard the name of two of Jared's service companies. But please, please don't tell anyone. Jared doesn't know I've overheard, but he might think I'm blackmailing him if rumors leak out."

"I promise I won't, but please scribble down the names for me just in case we need them later. Better yet, why don't you spend the night at my place. We can talk about other things, and I'll drive you to work tomorrow. And I'll give you a personal cell phone we can use to keep in touch. It'll be our private hotline. Only you and I will know the number."

"Would you? And we can stop at the mall so I can buy a dessert for later and get flowers for your place. I always keep a fresh arrangement in my apartment. It reminds me of springtime."

Zoe perked up after spending the night at Electra's. She looked less stressed on the drive to work as she twittered about another action-packed week. Traffic flowed smoothly all the way to her office building.

"Thanks for the ride. Will you call me tonight?"

"Yes, on our hotline. Just make sure you always keep it with you." Zoe gave Electra a tentative hug, then flitted into her busy day.

Perhaps it was good that traffic dragged after that. It gave Electra time to confront a gigantic failing that made her sick.

I can't hide from it; there's no place to run. I must deal with it now. I've failed to treat Zoe like the friend she is. I let her down and have disgraced what I'm supposed to be. I'm no better than Jared. I just use people, even people who are my friends. I'm nothing more than what Richard Dawkins' book says: a selfish creature controlled by primal instincts.

Electra knew she was extraordinary, thanks to her grandfather's training that taught how to focus her lightning brain. Her physical and cognitive personas made her superior physically and cognitively to mere mortals, and from an early age knew how to direct them without additional guidance. But emotions and ethics were harder and more nuanced, developing later as adultlike complexity intruded. She had learned from her grandfather that she could be superior here as well if she paid attention to others, but his death ended these counseling sessions, which had been mirrors for measuring herself. Recent events revealed glaring chinks.

I'm manipulating Angus and Carter; Robin makes me angry, and I use Hud and the Austin crew to serve my purposes. And now I see how badly I've treated Zoe.

But hold on. I've had my hands full and couldn't take time for Zoe, and she seemed to be doing OK. And we were helping each other. But Electra couldn't buy her own rationalization.

I can accept no excuses. I failed her. I'm not so good after all. I'm just a pretender. If I want to reclaim the mantle of superiority, I must start now.

By the time she reached the lab she knew what she must do. First order of business is to schedule an appointment to take Zoe for codependence counseling. An empathetic social worker told her when to come in.

Next, she called Carter to warn him that Jared is becoming dangerous. She wouldn't tell him the details over the phone but instead would arrange a time and place to meet. The call transferred to his voice mail, so she left a message for him to call back ASAP.

Electra's final call went to Hud, explaining she would visit first week in November to brief his team on late-breaking developments. She would come alone and send an agenda so his people could prepare.

This morning's self-evaluation and flurry of phone calls had drained her emotional energy, so she let her brain freewheel while taking a cookie and Coke break. Her mood elevated as the lightning brain shifted to a better state, allowing her to focus on postdoc projects, disappearing into that cerebral world ruled by science and logic, free of emotion and under her control. By the end of the day Electra's enthusiasm had returned. She was ready for action.

Though the weather had turned gloomy, Electra hardly noticed as she continued ticking items off her to-do list. Dinner with Carter now sat at the top. When returning her call early last week, he invited her for dinner tonight, the last Friday before Halloween.

Electra was first to arrive at the restaurant. The cold rain made for a dismal late afternoon drive. Carter, who would be driving back to Washington after a two-day economics seminar hosted by Philadelphia's Federal Reserve Bank, had selected one located near an I-95 exit south of Baltimore. She could tell by scanning the half-empty parking lot that she was the first to arrive, so she picked a booth where she could watch the entrance, reminding herself to pay attention to Carter's feelings as well as words while letting his body language fill in between the lines. He waved when he spotted her, then kissed her lightly before sliding in across from her, a puzzled look on his face. When Carter asked what had caused the scar on her cheek, Electra gave a well-rehearsed answer.

"I got careless. The bar slipped off its support bracket when I was doing bench presses, and the bolt on the retaining collar slit my cheek. It didn't hurt, and the cut healed quickly."

"It's actually rather sexy, like a European dueling scar, and it adds to your mystique. But try not to add any more. Speaking as an economist, let me explain why by drawing an analogy. De Beers deliberately limits the quantity of diamonds to increase the value of those on the market."

"I hadn't looked at it quite that way, but I can always count on you for an explanation that makes economic sense. I'm glad you're here."

"I'm not too late, am I? Traffic going through Baltimore was slow."

"No, you're fine. Mine was a bit heavy too, but it'll be better driving back if the rain doesn't get worse."

"I hope the weather clears for Halloween. I always had clear skies and mild temps for trick or treating when I was a kid. That was a fringe benefit of growing up on the West Coast. But I had college friends from Chicago who told about trick or treating in near-freezing rainstorms. Must have been tough on the parents who had to hold umbrellas. Perhaps having kids isn't such a good idea after all." Electra smiled, then changed the subject.

"How was your seminar?"

"Good. But before I tell you about it, I need your advice regarding something Matt told me a month ago. He says I often talk like a professor and dump too much information on the listener. Is he right?"

"It depends on the setting. If you're teaching or giving a lecture, that's good. But cerebral types like you often do it in casual settings too. Most people get bored listening to too many words that are stuck on the same topic, but actually, that's one of your traits that attracts me." Now it was Carter's turn to smile.

"Thanks for your assessment. I'll have to use Occam's razor when I talk with friends. Do you want me to use it tonight?"

"No, just talk like you usually do when we're together."

"Fair enough, but I'll stick to the highlights. The speakers are projecting a better regional economy next year. The decline has stopped, and there are signs for job growth. And I could tell the audience feels better than they did last year. There seems to be general acceptance of Jared's programs, and many attendees think T-Plague damages have run their course. But recovery will take time."

"Speaking of attendees, did you notice anyone watching you, or following you on the drive tonight?"

"No. Is there a reason I might be followed?"

"Possibly, and it's up for discussion. Here comes our waiter. Let's order first, then I'll explain." A beer and Coke came shortly, and after a few sips Electra continued.

"I've learned some things about Jared that raise big red warning flags. Did you know he's a closet member of the New Age Fundamental Church?"

"No. I thought the only religion he pays attention to is the Gospel according to Jared. Why's that a problem?"

"An insider told me Jared believes in channeling. You know what that is"?

"Sort of. That's where a divine spirit selects people to do its bidding."

"Yes, and Jared is starting to act like he knows what's best for the country. Have you noticed how he's putting a harsher spin on what our Brain Trust recommends? And he's starting to think up his own programs without getting our input."

"Now that you mention it, yes. Uh-oh. We'll be able to see if he does the same with his latest idea. Angus just told me about it, and he doesn't know who dreamed it up. According to him, the Brain Trust has to flesh out a 'Guardian Pillars' program. It has two parts. The first is a 'Citizen's Guard' program, controlled by Securityguard. Think of it as local vigilantes. The second is a 'Health Watch' program, run by Healthguard. It's a group of neighborhood snoopers poking into people's private lives. These could get real harsh real quick."

"That's ominous. And let me add some additional news. Another insider tipped me off about what might be the tip of Jared's hidden agenda. Did you know he has controlling interests in security services companies?"

"No, but come to think of it, I'm not surprised. I've heard rumors that a lot of manpower contracts are awarded without bidding, and that's against the law, even if you can show it's providing the lowest cost available. I hope you don't have any more news."

"I'm afraid I do. It might not be against the law, but it certainly violates ethics. Jared's abusing one of his staffers and bringing in prostitutes."

"Can you prove any of this? We could use it as leverage to slow him down or to leak to the media if he won't listen."

"I can't prove it, but my sources might. I'll find out just in case the loose cannon rolls faster in the wrong direction."

"Why don't we do this. Since I talk with Angus more often than you do, let me brief him, and then he'll lead a Brain Trust edited version discussion. But I won't mention Jared's abusing staff or using prostitutes."

"Good idea. And here's another. Let's change the subject to something happier or I won't have any appetite for dessert."

Try as they might, neither could find much that was cheery. Neither ordered dessert. Carter paid the waiter, and while they waited for him to return with the receipt, Electra brought up the final reason for having dinner tonight.

"Please do me and everyone in Brain Trust a favor. Tell them not to criticize Jared or the Guardians anywhere except at our meetings, and please tell everyone to be watchful at all times. Someone might be shadowing us."

"Why would anyone shadow you or me. You haven't been interviewed by the media, and mine have been bland. I'm always the diplomatic economist, giving pros and cons covering both sides. But I'll caution Mariah. She did blast Competitive Capitalism in a Democrat-sponsored media spot. Are you aware of her position?" Electra nodded no, so Carter proceeded to enlighten her.

"She thinks caring economics, non-competing companies, and sharable resources will lead the nation's GDP out of the doldrums. I could show her cognitive psychology studies that confirm people want to compete, not live in Utopia. She worries about the state of the nation's happiness, when most people worry about keeping their jobs. By the way, measures of happiness are still too subjective to be of much use analytically." Carter emptied his glass before saying more.

"Here's another reason why Mariah is against the Guardian Party. Her position on justice is politically naïve. She pushes for social justice meeting her definition of fairness or needs, instead of realizing that realpolitik justice answers to power. Would you like to hear more comparisons?"

"No thanks. Let's table that for another time, but let's pretend we're being shadowed. I'll leave first, and you can follow a minute later if all's well. Try to walk out with other people. I see a couple getting ready to go, so I'll leave when they do. That'll distract anyone who's been watching outside. And I've been paying attention to comings and goings. I don't think anyone's observing us inside. Did you park close to me?"

"I'm in the same row but further towards the exit. You're being overly dramatic. I can't believe Jared or Guardian supporters would be that devious, but your wish is my command." He kissed her on the unscarred cheek before she slipped out.

Though steady rain made visibility poor, entrance lighting would show who's coming or going so Electra circled to the far end of the lot where she watched, engine idling and headlights off. She wasn't the only one.

"There he is by himself. Bring him back quick." Two enforcers had been shadowing Carter at the Philly seminar, waiting for the right time to convince him that all Brain Trust personnel should keep their mouths shut. Although they worked for the same organization that had sent messengers to visit Mariah, their contact never mentioned how poorly that visit had ended. One of them intercepted Carter a couple of car lengths from the Vette.

"Mr. Quavah, we need to talk. Let's go to my car for a spin. Don't make me poke a hole in you." Carter froze, not knowing what to say or do. The fellow reached for Carter and that was his last action.

Electra blasted towards Carter, headlights blazing; she picked off his would-be assailant like a sitting duck in a shooting gallery, pinning him underneath, then screamed through the door she had shoved open.

"Get in!" He clambered in, still in a daze. Electra backed up, leaped out to grab the gun, and patted her victim for wallet or cell phone. She jumped back in and took careful aim as she drove forward, crushing the victim's neck, then raced out of the parking lot and into the rain-filled darkness.

"Watch for another car coming out of the lot." The command jolted Carter out of his mental fog. He swiveled to look behind.

"Jesus, who was that? Oh Jesus, a car just pulled out." Electra said nothing but punched dashboard buttons to activate all performance systems; the lightning brain had already shifted to a higher state, filling Electra with the thrill of a chase.

"Buckle up. We'll outrun them." She punched the accelerator and the little beast roared to life. According to the GPS screen, there were enough twisty rural roads to turn into an escape route, but she would not toy with her pursuer; she would put as much distance between them as fast as she could.

The rain-slick road was deserted as she raced on tree-lined rolling asphalt. The little beast handled the curves better than its pursuer; his headlights faded. But just as she roared out of a right-hand turn, two deer appeared in the headlights. Electra swerved hard to the right to avoid a direct hit, scoring only a glancing blow, but that was enough to launch the little beast into an uncontrollable spin. It twirled twice before flipping and pitching down the embankment, coming to rest against a tree.

Electra screamed, "Get out, get out! She took her own advice but Carter couldn't. He was dazed from colliding with the windshield. She dashed to drag him out, and as he sat up the sound of gravel crunching told her the pursuit car had arrived Electra darted away from the wreck. A bulky silhouette soon staggered down the embankment, trying to keep from falling. Electra fired twice, sending him tumbling on top of Carter.

"Get up, get up!" Carter struggled to his feet as she searched the dead man.

"Help me drag him into the driver's seat." Carter was still moving in slow motion, so she shoved him away from the car and made a final inspection. She reached inside to remove all clues, packing them in a gym bag that she always kept in the back seat. The trunk couldn't be opened but it contained nothing valuable, and if anyone tracked the VIN or license plate, it would lead to a rural cemetery far away and long ago. The time had come to say goodbye to her stealth street racer. She fired two bullets into the gas tank and waited until the leaking gas ignited. Then she pulled Carter up the embankment and into the dead man's car.

"Don't touch anything. We can't leave any evidence." Carter stared at her mutely. After checking the bruise on his forehead, she announced it wasn't serious. As the gas tank exploded, lighting a funeral pyre for the car and occupant, Electra drove on in silence. Carter sat like a stone, finally mumbling after a minute.

"What are we gonna do?" The lightning brain knew the answer.

"I'm driving back to the restaurant. If no one's found the body, we're gonna load it into the trunk, and you'll drive me home in the Vette. But if cops are there, we won't stop. We'll have to come back later to get your car."

Luck was with them. They swapped cars and drove off after stuffing the dead man into the trunk. Electra let Carter drive because that would help break him out of a stupor. They were twenty miles away by the time Carter asked his question again.

"What are we gonna do now?"

"You're gonna drive me home, and both of us will keep our mouths shut about the whole evening. And we aren't going to report this to the police. Whoever sent those guys aren't going to call them either. We're in the clear. And don't tell Angus about this either. Just tell him what we discussed at dinner. OK?" Carter nodded.

"What about you? What about your car?"

"No problem. I'll use my grandfather's van. And I'll just keep doing what I've been doing and act naturally. Make sure you do the same." Carter nodded again and said no more. Electra tried to get a handle on her unsettling emotions.

I'm really keyed up. I have this urge for sex right now. World War II stories about the Battle of Britain flashed in her brain: stories of couples make passionate love on rooftops during the height of nightly bombings. *Deadly events can trigger primal passion, and that's what I'm feeling.* But one glance at Carter showed he would not be in the mood. Instead, he was lost in his thoughts.

I thought I could handle anything thrown at me, but I'm wrong. Electra did things I didn't think possible. How can she suddenly transform into a coldblooded killer? It's like she has it all planned. This isn't the Electra I fell in love with. I don't know what I'm dealing with. I'm glad she ran out at the party. I have to figure out what she really is.

They drove in silence to Electra's where Carter awkwardly kissed her goodnight, not knowing if this could be the last time. She reminded him to do as told and to talk with her regularly so they could keep Angus ahead of Jared. He said he would, then drove on.

Electra went in, stripped off all clothes, and sat under the shower head, letting the stream of hot water wash away the chill and help her shift to a better state. Then she toweled off and went to the kitchen. *I'm still wired. Maybe the tryptophan in peanut butter and milk will help me go to sleep.*

As she lay in bed recapping the week, Electra added one more task to her to-do list. *I better call Angus before I go to Austin. He needs to hear the complete story from me. And if Jared gets too far out of line, I'll change the rules of engagement. Good that only I know the rules of the game.*

CHAPTER 33

November 2121

"Last Worldstar Standing"

(Thread 3 Chapter 7)

"WHY CAN'T YOU HACK into Godfrey's directories? Our infiltration tools are beyond state-of-the-art." Sitting across the desk from Cyberguard president Darla Tinibu, Brian Ritz shifted uncomfortably in his chair.

"I don't know, and our best people have been trying for three days, but his network firewall is neutralizing our malware before it can penetrate. And its network security app is blocking malware transmissions. My people are stumped."

"That's not an option. He's working on software we need, so you have to get in there or you're out. I'm sure you get my message."

"I do, and I have a backup plan ready to go. One way or another, we'll be in and out and will have decompiled what we need by February, which gives us time to adjust some of next year's second quarter app updates." Though not delighted, Darla settled back in her chair.

"Make it so, and tell me when it's ready to go..."

Electra delayed the Austin trip for a couple of days so she could troubleshoot why her prototype network security software she had installed on Hud's company network had begun sending intrusion warnings. She concluded it wasn't a glitch; someone was trying to hack in to Tim's Emails.

Somebody's radar is tracking Tim, but whoever it is can't get in. I won't tell Tim until I locate the hacker. And when I do, I might make a game of testing my new security apps on them.

Electra gave Angus all the details related to Jared's hubris before she left so he knew more than Carter and was as ready as possible to handle Jared one-on-one. As Hud's chartered jet whisked her away early Wednesday, she was able to devote full attention to the Austin agenda.

I'll meet with people individually, Hud being first. I'll brief him on Washington intrigue and its potential sales impact. Su's next. I'll give her next generation formulations that'll keep her busy for two years. Then I'll give Tim modifications for current and prototype devices that should occupy him for a couple of years also. Austin can work on these while I work on my advanced projects. And in all the meetings, I'll pay attention to other people's feelings besides mine.

Adom waved as soon as he spotted Electra, getting ready to take pictures. He still filled the "Official Worldstar Photographer" role, and Su always wanted photos chronicling every visit. As she approached, Adom saw once again a fresh picture.

Every visit since college graduation brings a different Electra, more mature, more confident. She's grown cognitively and emotionally too. And now, she's becoming more assertive, in control of all situations. I'm glad I'm part of her world. Electra hugged him, then spoke.

"You're looking good. Life must be treating you well."

"Well, I can say the same about you. And I'll tell you the latest on the drive, but first I need to take pictures, so please pose for the smartphone." Electra did as instructed, then asked the attendant to snap several that included Adom, after which Adom loaded her carry-ons into the van, talking all the time.

"Our schedule is just as you planned, but we've added two events. Tomorrow, Su wants to have dinner with you, and we'll all spend Friday on the cattle ranch Holy and I started. It's a new business that he's mentoring me to manage, just like he did for oil and gas. Coming to Austin has been the best possible career change for me.

I like my Texas businesses better than biotech, and Su needs me only part-time."

"How is Su? She's such a private person it's hard to know how she really feels."

"You're right about that. Oriental reserve's her trademark. I do know she's happier in Austin than at NIH in DC, but I think she's disappointed that she's not as smart as she used to be. She gets frustrated it takes her so long to understand the changes you make. I tell her you're smarter than all of us combined, but she gets upset anyway. Don't tell her I mentioned it, but you need to say something to her."

"I will. After all, she's the brightest of the Worldstars, and though its numbers have been cut in half, those remaining are the best to be found. I'm glad you're still with her."

"And that's where I plan to stay until something unexpected takes me away, but I don't foresee that happening. I'm having too much fun. Maybe someday, you can join us."

"I'll give my favorite answer: perhaps."

Adom took Electra to Hud's office as soon as they arrived, then left to pick up Holy.

"Howdy, your Highness. Your visits always make us dollars and sense, so come on in." She and Hud sat at a small conference table, snacking on tacos and tamales while trading personal stories. Afterwards, Electra dived into her agenda.

"A lot has happened recently in Washington that's going to impact our sales. Let me go over what you need so you can adjust next year's plans. But first, let me congratulate you for managing sales generated by our shell companies." Hud beamed proudly.

"Them shell companies you set up really work. They keep us hidden, and no one knows we control them all. Everyone thinks they're competing with one another. And according to Su, we're way ahead of the pack, so customers have to buy from us because nothing else works as good."

"That's all to the good for us, but here's what next year might hold. The U.S. and its Coalition of the Smart might start a shooting war in the Middle East. You'll see a big spike in orders for I-Vac and S-Vac if that happens because of fear it'll cause a new wave of T-Plague attacks. And you should see a gradual ramp-up of R-Vac sales. I hope America is the first to realize the need to cure T-Plague victims, and that's what R-Vac will do. It'll dissolve neural entanglement, making victims smarter.

"Tomorrow when I meet with Su, I'll give her the details, but I want you to know where she's heading. I'm giving her improved formulations that'll keep her busy for the next two years. And I'm also giving her starting formulations for your next blockbuster: an Alzheimers vaccine. It won't be ready to market for a couple of years, but until then you'll be busy getting your customers to buy our better smart pills."

"Yes, and we'll be ready to handle it. So far, you've been Miss Sunshine, but I'm smart enough to know that sunshine can throw shadows. What else do you see?"

"Here's one darker issue. Washington might try to nationalize H&H DNA Partners for reasons of national security. I need you to think about it, and you and I will talk further early next year. I don't see it happening tomorrow, but possibly later next year."

"Them's sobering words, even for a Texan."

"Don't worry yet. Just develop contingencies. I will too, and when the time comes we'll be ready to deal. Now let's talk about neuro-devices. Have you hired a neuro-device Sales and Marketing Director yet?"

"No, but we plan to have one onboard early next year. Tim's in charge of hiring, so we'll be ready when you OK device launch."

"Good. Tomorrow I'll meet with just Tim to give him the latest modifications for the Neuro-Knitter and the Brain Probe. He'll launch the Neuro-Knitter first. Then he'll launch a generic Brain Probe, but we have to control distribution carefully. Lots of downsides and ethical issues come with it. Tim will have enough work for two years. And while your people are launching these devices, I'll be coming up with new ones. That covers what I wanted to go over. Do you have anything to add?"

"Only that your wish is our command. And I have something new for you, but I'll tell you about it at dinner tonight. How 'bout I take you to a great barbecue joint?"

"Now that's an offer I can't refuse. Meeting adjourned."

Electra busied herself on the computer until Hud finished business for the day. Then he drove them to Big-O's Barbecue, bragging that Texans takes pride in down-home recipes; Big-O's lived up to its reputation, its casual comfort and tangy aroma showing Texans know how to combine great food and comfortable surroundings.

"I love the selection of barbecue sauces. Sweet to sharp, hot to mild, smoky to tangy onion. And the homemade lemon meringue pie is best ever. Thanks for taking me."

"You're welcome. And I wanna thank you again for sending Su and Adom my way. It's been great all the way around. And that's what I wanted to tell you. Adom and Holy are a real Texas two-some. Dad's pushing past ninety, but thanks to Adom, he's probably good to a hundred. Let me tell you about their latest business. It's Dad's idea, but Adom is the guy that set it up and can run it. Here's the deal.

"You're too young to remember, but lots of meats used to taste much better than they do today. All this concern for lean, low-fat, grass-fed, range-free, and all-natural stuff has taken the taste out of food. Can you believe it? Kids today are supposed to munch on carrots instead of chocolate chip cookies. Anyway, there was a time when you got a lot of tasty fat in cuts of beef or pork. Not anymore, so Dad's building a fat-stock ranch, where he and Adom raise cattle and hogs that have lots of tasty fat marbled into the meat. He's got a deal with some livestock processors to handle it special and target restaurants or gourmet food stores lookin fer great tasting cuts.

"Last year spring, they bought a ranch that's a couple hours' drive from here, and on Friday they want to show us how it works. They're about ready to load trailers, and it'll be nice fer you to see the spread in action."

"Adom mentioned it but didn't give any details. I'm looking forward to the tour. And thanks to you and Holy, Adom is having the time of his life. We could chat more, but I think it's time we call it a night. I have a full day tomorrow and want to be fresh."

Poor Su. She had pored over the white papers Electra had sent before visiting, so she was able to follow the two-year drug development timeline Electra mapped out during their Thursday morning meeting, but she still had questions.

"I think I understand what you're recommending. We can improve efficacy by hooking onto the receptor sites you've identified. But how did you find them?"

"I applied atomic force microscopy to cell structures and molecular segments I thought might contain them. Computer simulation shows it'll work, and I need you to confirm it as you extend my work and begin testing."

"I can handle that, but what about the Alzheimers vaccine? How did you come up with its formula?"

"I used the I-Vac formulation as an analogy because both T-Plague and Alzheimers cause neural entanglement. What do you think of the timeline?"

"It has challenging milestones, but if I can use you as a consultant when I get stuck I should be OK. I wish I were smarter. I wish I had another you."

"Please don't be so hard on yourself. I follow the research literature, and no one is close to where we are. Give yourself credit for what we're doing." Su wistfully shook her head.

"Change the we to you. All this is your creation. Your mother and I working together couldn't match you. You're in a class by yourself; your intuition and creativity are superior to Indira's, and you integrate logic and mathematical precision far better than I ever did."

"Please don't compare me to Indira, or you to me. It's not fair to any of us. Mother was superior to me in some ways, just as you are. I just happen to have a knack for finding effective formulations. And take my word for it; there's no one better than you for working with me."

"I'll keep trying to convince myself you're right."

"I'll come back to set up an experimental pilot run after I meet with Tim. And Adom says you're taking me out to dinner. I hope it's for more Tex-Mex."

Tim's meeting was easier for Electra to conduct because he didn't worry about understanding all the theory; he just wanted to make the neuro-devices work. By mid-afternoon she asked Tim to summarize what they had covered.

"I see how my two-year timeline matches rollouts for our first two devices: the Neuro-Knitter and the Brain Probe. And the Knitter line extensions for other bones and joints are achievable. I'm good at tweaking until everything works. But I can do more for you if you teach me how you come up with your designs."

You'll be ready for that next year, after going to additional training seminars. Working together, our neuro-devices will electrify the world. And from what Hud told me, you'll have a sales and marketing director onboard early next year."

"Yes. I've lined up three excellent candidates. Will you want to make the final selection?"

"No. That's up to you and Hud. I trust your judgement. We're finished here, so I'm going to make a pilot run. And tomorrow, we're taking a ranch tour. Have you been there before?"

"No, but Adom's says it'll be a surprise."

"I imagine it will be. But I hope there are no surprises on my pilot run. Wish me luck."

"You never need luck. You're always in control."

Electra completed the pilot run just before Su threatened to kick them so they'd be on time for a dinner reservation. Electra asked about the restaurant as they walked to car.

"This must be a really upscale Tex-Mex place if we need reservations."

"Actually, I've chosen something different for tonight, and we're going home to change. I bought some early Christmas presents I want you to wear, a stylized black wrap dress and color-matched strapped heels. I want us to dress up because we're going to the

Capital Grill, which is noted for its outstanding seafood and wine list. It's considered the destination restaurant in Austin's Warehouse District, and its elegant ambiance is better suited for a more intimate conversation. I hope you like the menu, and I hope you like our topic. We need to talk about three people: you, Indira, and myself." Electra simply nodded, saying nothing because Su had just parked. As they entered Su's townhome, she talked to herself instead.

I'll stay where it's safe when talking about Indira. I know more about Mother than Su does. She doesn't know about my grandparents or Uncle Chandra. She doesn't know about the last letter Mother wrote to Grandmother. And she doesn't know about Bhakti and the murder.

If Su mentions how much I've changed, I'll tell her an edited version of the truth: my emotional persona is maturing, taking me into new relationships where I care for people more and use them less.

I hope Su tells me more about herself. There's much I don't know, but even in the most intimate relationships you never know your partner completely. You always keep learning as relationships grow, and you never should tell all. That's the way it's supposed to be.

"So, do the dress and heels meet with your approval?" Su studied Electra from top to toe before answering.

"Yes. Very elegant and eye-catching. Diane von Furstenberg's iconic design is made for your proportions. And your black neck choker accents the dress. Where did you get it?"

"From my grandmother." Su's expression changed ever so slightly.

"You mean from Indy's mother?"

"Yes." Su wanted to ask more, but Electra's brief answers told her not to go further, so she didn't.

"We can talk about that another time."

Music rather than words accompanied them on the drive to the restaurant. Su listened exclusively to two radio stations: KMFA for classical music or KVRX for the latest chatter about University of Texas. Both ladies preferred listening to Pachelbel's Canon instead of a report on UT's won-loss record against Oklahoma, their number one rival that UT would play in Norman next Saturday. The Canon set a better tone for the dinner discussion each was contemplating.

"You picked an elegant restaurant, and we're dressed for it. Linen table cloths, napkins, and muted lighting for the wall hangings make for a sophisticated and intimate ambiance. So do the well-dressed servers, candlelight, and classical music. What would you recommend we order?"

Su selected a Pinot Grigio when the waitress took her Red Snapper order; Electra did likewise when she ordered Su's recommendation, Chilean Sea Bass. They sat in the pleasant comfort of their private space, insulated from other parties by ample table spacing. It was now time for Su to give Electra another Christmas present.

"I want to give this to you in person so I can tell you why I treasure it so. It's special, just like you. It's a photo album I've built over the years. No one except me has ever seen it. And now you'll have your own copy. It's a photo album centered on Indira. Once a year I read again your mother's final letter, then go through the album. I'm sure you know the date: it's February eleventh, the day you were born and the day your mother died. Every year I hold my vigil in her honor. I need to tell you more before you can appreciate its full meaning, so please let me continue. These are things I've waited to tell only you. I love you dearly and I've waited until you're mature enough to handle knowing more about your mother and father, so you understand better your own emotions.

"I know how much you loved Christi. And I loved your mother in the much the same way, but I never told her until it was too late. Your mother loved your father; that's one of the reasons she became pregnant before a Vow-Cer marriage celebration. But the main reason was to have a child. I told her several months before you were born how I felt, asking her to consider a permanent co-friend relationship with me. She never gave me an answer, but she wrote a letter for Jason to give me if something happened during childbirth. Your father gave me the letter a day after Indy's funeral. In it, she told me she loved me more than Jason; the two of us would bond;

we would raise you. She would tell Jason after you were born, but she died before she could. No one else ever knew." Su paused for a sip of wine, then handed the album to Electra.

"Please let me finish my story before you glance at the pictures. I was attracted to Indira right from the start, even though we dated fellows. When Jason and Adom came along, we formed the Worldstars, and Indy thought we should start a Worldstars photo album because she knew we would stay together going forward. Everyone but Jason liked the idea. Jason was always unsentimental and had little use for memories captured in pictures. Adom volunteered to be our official photographer and he continues taking the photos I place in the album. Your mother is in most of the early pictures because she was the driving force, the glue binding us.

"In her last letter, Indira asked me to be your Godmother and to help raise you, and I decided to continue placing pictures of you in the album. Adom did a great job taking pictures from your earliest years until he fled to Austin." The waitress came to the table, announcing she would serve dinner shortly, but Su asked her to wait.

"When you view the pictures—they're arranged in chronological order—you will see what I sensed as you developed. You became more and more like your mother. I don't believe in reincarnation, but if I did you would be it. The resemblance is striking, though you are a tad taller, and physically stronger. But if Indira were alive and we dressed her as stylishly as you now dress, people would mistake you for twins. And from what I have seen, you are superior mentally, and growing to match her empathy. The more I am with you, the more I feel I'm with her.

"I would like us to spend more time together, work together. Perhaps you would consider relocating to Austin. You would have no trouble becoming an associate professor at University of Texas, and you could help accelerate my progress on vaccines. Together, you and I will resurrect the Worldstars and command the biotech world; you and Tim will electrify the world with your neuro-devices. But please, do not give me an answer tonight. You need to think about all I've said. Perhaps early in the new year you will let me know if this would fit your plans." Electra finally replied.

"I, uh, I don't know what to say." Su returned an inscrutable smile.

"Tell me next year. And I see our waitress is bringing dinner, so I'll want you to tell me how you like your Chilean Sea Bass, and please don't wait until next year to do so…"

Su went to bed soon after returning home, but Electra sat in the living room. *I'm not as good as Su thinks I am. I have to be better. Mother handled feelings and empathy effortlessly. I struggle, and I lose control when my Creature from the Id rages. I have much to learn.*

I'm getting depressed. I better go to bed so I'm cheery for the fat-stock tour. The lightning brain will keep thinking while I'm asleep. It'll know what to do.

Austin is located in the heart of the Texas Hill Country, rugged forested terrain that flattens into meadows and grasslands as the land stretches toward West Texas. That was the direction Hud drove his tour group, which included Su, Electra and Tim. Holy and Adom were already at the ranch; since Hud knew all about Texas, he provided colorful background commentary.

"Betcha didn't know Texas can divide into three states whenever it wants. Only reason it doesn't is to avoid fighting over who keeps the Hill Country. Landscape's so pretty it could make you plow through a stump. And come springtime the meadows glow with Indian Paint wildflowers."

Electra asked, "The ranch is over two hundred miles from Austin. Is that still the Hill Country?"

"Nope. Ranch land is flat and sparse, but the cattle like it, and if they do, the cattlemen do too. Has Adom told you much about what they've done?"

"No. Just that they're ready to ship cattle. I guess Holy's fat-stock business has a market."

"Sure does. And wait till you see the holding pens and chutes they use to load the cattle carriers. It's real efficient. Today's ranching isn't like what you see in the movies. The hands don't live on the ranch anymore, and sometimes they ride off-road vehicles instead of horses; it's exciting. You'll see…"

Hud was right. Adom's demonstration impressed everyone.

"Some of the tools we keep in the holding pen shed keep the cattle moving. Tim, you might like this one. It's an electric cattle prod. First, we open the gate into the chute, then we jolt a couple in the herd, and the others charge ahead with them. Let me show you how it works…" Tim asked all the follow-up questions.

"You've got lots of equipment. I see lighters, lanterns, flash lights, and emergency medical supplies. But do you carry guns? And how long does it take help to get here if you run into trouble?" Adom chuckled, then replied.

"Good questions. The shift foreman usually carries a gun and has a cell phone, but often we use two-way radios because cell phone reception is pretty spotty out here. And we've never called for help; we're pretty self-sufficient. We'll come back here tonight so we can sit around the campfire. It'll be pitch dark so you'll see the Milky Way in all its glory. But let's hop in the jeeps so I can show you more."

The tour ended late afternoon back at the ranch house where Holy greeted the group. They would rest before having dinner, then the group—minus Holy—would talk around the campfire when the stars come out.

The five Wu brothers were clever men; that's why their Shangahi-based Chinese private security agency rose to the top. The oldest two started it fifteen years ago, bringing in the younger three as its reputation grew. They built it on ruthless and relentless resolution of every case; failure was not an option. And the current assignment that the younger two were about to conclude for Sino Bio-Drug would be no exception. They were about to uncover the source of the bad smart pills that had poisoned many high-ranking government officials.

Sino Bio-Drug, a publicly traded Chinese drug company, years ago abandoned its T-Plague vaccine program, instead searching for suppliers. There were only a handful that had drugs that worked, and the companies that pushed them deliberately stayed in the shadows of the underground economy, where networks of shell companies and phantom locations kept them invisible for good reasons. The vaccine market was caveat emptor—buyer beware. It was cash before delivery, no questions asked, no returns. Suppliers had to watch their backs to avoid customer blowback.

It had taken a year of Internet and on-the-ground tracking to locate a company in Austin that might be the source: H&H DNA Partners. Bo and Chi had been in the area for five days, waiting for an opportunity to interrogate a Mr. Hudson Haller, and the opportunity had just arrived. Their interrogation skills and surveillance gear, including night vision goggles, matched those of the Chinese military; soon they would use whatever they needed when joining their victims at the campfire.

"We stay together when we jump the leader. Then one stays with him and the other rounds up the rest. And we don't shoot until we get the info we need..."

I never went to camp or looked into a star-filled pitch-black sky. I'm only twenty-four, so I have plenty of time to take care of my bucket list. I just need to start checking items off. Suddenly, a jolt similar to the one felt last New Year's Eve interrupted that happy thought. *This could be my last chance to see the Milky Way. Why is Father's warning coming into my thoughts so often? I remember something I read in Greek mythology: the gods are jealous of man because he is mortal and understands how fleeting life is. I better put these thoughts away. Tonight's not the time to think that way.* Something more immediate came to mind.

"Where's the Port-a-John?"

"It's back by the chute gate. Careful where you walk. It's dark. Do you want a flash light?"

"No, I'll be fine." Her night vision was acute, just like her hearing, so she steered herself in the right direction. *It's dark. Maybe I should've taken Hud's offer. Well, I can handle being in the dark. I've been there before.*

It was easier finding her way back; the campfire became a beacon. As she stopped to gaze into the sky, her ears picked up yelling and cursing. The lightning brain shifted gears as she picked her way back; then the crack of a gunshot brought Electra to a state of even higher readiness. Nervous energy surged through every neural fiber.

"All of you, shut up and listen! I will shoot anyone else who comes at me. You, you must be Hud. You come with me."

Electra watched from the cover of darkness, the glare of the campfire outlining what was becoming a deadly confrontation. Two men were pointing guns at Hud's people; whoever had been shot lay motionless. Electra had seen all she needed. She ran close enough for the assailants to see her—they had removed their goggles because of the campfire's glow—then screamed.

"You guys are in big trouble! I'm running for help!" Then she fled into the darkness.

"Get her, Bo! Don't let her get away." Bo ran pell-mell towards Electra's last sighting, falling once in the darkness, then scrambling to his feet and following the noise. He spotted a shadow leaping a fence and charged ahead.

Electra unleashed her attack just as Bo stumbled into the chute. She had already opened the pen gates and was prodding cattle with lightning-like bolts. The bellowing dull roar of the stampede grew to a crescendo as a hundred head trampled over everything in the chute. Bo froze in his tracks, unable to see much but heard trouble fast approaching. He started running blindly, crashing into the chute fence, then fell backwards. He scrambled to his feet as the ground rumbled, but he had no clue which way to run; he tripped again, sprawling face down as the first steer thundered past. He rolled over and tried to stand, but the herd was on top of him. Countless hooves crushed him into the dirt. By the time Electra got to the body, the stampede was over, the flash light she had grabbed in the shed illuminating the twisted remains. She took the gun still clutched in a mangled hand.

All the noise caught Chi by surprise, but he was too clever to panic. He herded everyone to the gunshot victim and guarded them at a distance, waiting for Bo to return with another prisoner. Then he would pick up where he left off. And he would be kind. He would let the Chinese woman tend to the black gunshot victim. He waved the gun as he spat out words.

"You, see how he is." Chi was about to belittle Hud again, but words never came. Two bullets cut him down, followed by Electra's screaming run to the campfire.

"Hud, what's going on?" Hud yelled an answer.

"We got ourselves a problem! Su, how's Adom?" Tim knew first aid and took over. Hud yelled again.

"Electra, run for the medical kit in the shed." As Tim rolled Adom onto his back, Su cradled his head in her arms.

Adom choked out, "Su, Su, I'm sorry. Just when I'm becoming what you want me to be." Su clenched him in her blood-drenched arms.

"Adom, Adom! You can't go like this. It's not your time."

"I, I loved you best I could." Adom's eyes flickered shut as his head rolled toward Su.

Racing back with the medical supplies, Electra screamed.

"Tim, do something!" Hud grabbed Electra but said nothing. Tim stood next to her as they mutely stared at the tragedy lying on the ground. Su finally stuttered.

"I, I can't believe he's gone. They're all gone. First Indy; then Jason; now Adom. I, I'm the last of the Worldstars." Electra tried putting her arms around Su, but she pushed them off.

"Long ago Jason said we are kissed by the sun. Then later, he said we are cursed by the devil." Su would say no more that night. She sat on the ground, holding Adom until Hud returned with a blanket, using it for Adom's shroud. Tim helped carry him to the jeep. When they returned, Electra summoned an emergency meeting.

"What happened tonight better stay right here. Hud, why are we targets?"

"Sino-Bio hired Wu Brothers Security Agency to find the source of poisoned smart pills that infected Chinese Communist Party leaders. But that can't be us. Our Q.C. checks every batch." Electra kept the deception alive.

"You're right. They screwed up somewhere tracking bad pills, but no matter, we have to keep police out of the picture. Which brothers did we kill?"

"Bo got himself trampled and Chi got shot."

"There's a good chance they haven't reported back to their handler, so we're still invisible, and we need to stay that way. Let's bury the bodies out here and report Adom's death as an accidental gunshot. I'll collect their guns, cell phones and wallets. You get rid of their rental car, or whatever they're driving if you can find it, and then backtrack to wherever they're staying. I'll give you the motel key I found. Do this ASAP." Hud's glum expression matched his tone.

"I can't think of anything better. Let's head back to give Holy the bad news after we hide the bodies. Tim and I will dump them down an abandoned shaft tomorrow when we can see what we're doing."

Hud sat everyone at the dining room table before retelling the story. A deathlike silence followed, broken finally by Holy's resolute voice.

"I loved Adom like a son. He and I had big plans for takin care of me as well as operations. I got a big hole to fill, bigger than most I fell into before. But I got no choice; I gotta go on."

Electra kept to the sidelines while Hud and Tim decided what to do. An hour later, Hud gave everyone marching orders.

"So Electra, you drive Holy and Su back to Austin tonight. Then fly back commercial to DC as soon as you can. Tim and I will clean up here as soon as the sun comes up, and then we'll get Adom to our family mortician. He'll run interference for me with the Austin police. Any questions?" Electra's inner voice warned her. *Su's done nothing but stare into space. Say something.*

"All of us need to push ahead as we decided yesterday. How about I call Su next week to help her get started?" Su nodded but said nothing. Hud broke the awkward silence.

"And make sure you call me and Tim between now and yearend."

There was nothing left to say, so Electra loaded Su and Holy for the drive back, which turned into a grim wake. No music; no voices. Nothing but the sound of Su and Holy staring into the darkness. Electra would be alone because her inner voice had gone silent. She could do nothing but stare numbly, dumbly at the white lines on the road ahead, knowing only for certain that Adom was dead.

Electra took a cab to the airport early next afternoon, relieved to get away. She had enough space to lie down in her unoccupied row, and the flight attendant let her do so. Though weary to the bone, she was unable to sleep, tossing fitfully, struggling to reconcile Adom's death. Then without warning, she bolted upright.

Adom told me Indira's pregnancy upset him, and when I was an infant, I overheard Father say the same to Su, saying that Indira said Adom was afraid Father wouldn't have time to pal around like he used to. But when I asked Su, her reply didn't jibe. There's a disconnect I don't understand. A pang of disbelief shook her violently.

Oh my God! Adom must have thought he got Indira pregnant. Adom could be my father. Indira spoke from the shadows.

"Yes, my precious daughter. That is indeed a possibility. I did have a test to confirm you would be female, but none for paternity."

"Mother, I have witnessed three deaths in which each could have been that of my father. Once when Jason blew himself up, then again when I failed to resurrect him from a suspension pod, and last night when Adom was killed. And if Adom is my father, I broke my pledge because I won't attend his funeral."

"Do not be upset about missing funerals. They are merely for the living. Those who have died do not care, nor does a funeral help them. It helps only those seeking solace, and you are beyond that. But would knowing who's your father be useful? Jason and your grandfather stored DNA samples. Perhaps you wish to test Adom's." The answer flashed instantly.

"No. It would serve no purpose. I know what I am. I am your daughter, transformed by the bolt of my creation, and cared for by Jason and Grandfather. They helped form me into what I am. I shall always love Adom, but Jason is first among equals."

"Rest, my precious daughter. Prepare for another day."

"I shall, but I need to ask two remaining questions. I have tried running to ground all clues about you. Have I missed any? Where else should I look?" Electra could hear good humor in the reply.

"You already know the answer to your first question. And it would be no fun for me to tell you the second. That is a game you must continue playing. Now go to sleep."

Electra obeyed.

CHAPTER 34

November 2121

"The Last of the Guardian Lovers"

(Thread 2 Chapter 13)

THOUGH SHE HAD LAID Adom's death to rest, the entire episode rekindled Electra's concern about ethical dilemmas. *Would I ever choose death over life if it would end suffering? After all, that is at the core of Jared's Golden Years Program. My answer is yes in all cases: for strangers, for loved ones, and for myself, but only if I were unable to turn the dilemma into a trilemma where I find a better alternative. And if I did choose death for a loved one, I know that my grieving will ultimately transition into reaffirmation of life's promise.*

But what about murder? I know all variations of the philosopher's trolley problem in which you deliberately kill one person to save one you love, or to save many innocent lives. If the one person is evil, or if the utility of the many exceeds the utility of the one, then yes, I would throw the switch and kill the one. But would I look for a redemptive alternative if the one is evil? And what if the utility of the many exceeds the utility of the one, but the one is a person I love? Philosophers love to construct a solution, but no one knows what they will decide until they confront the moment of truth. I've been there and I know I must trust the lightning brain. And I know that no matter my choice, afterwards I must move on and keep busy.

Electra followed her own advice, burying herself in work after returning from Austin. She recorded pilot run results in notebook logs, updated journals, and stored the experimental drugs where only she could find them. They could be deadly in the wrong hands, even in hers, but she needed them at the ready in case her worst "Jared contingency" were to occur. She also prepared for the next Brain Trust meeting that would be held Thursday at the private conference room adjoining Angus's office in the Pentagon.

Electra went there twice since he had become Secretary of Defense, and each time she came away more impressed. Construction of the Pentagon, a symbol for the U.S. military and a metonym for the Department of Defense, took two years, starting in 1941. It is the 17th largest square footage building in the world, covering 6.5 million square feet stretching 17.5 corridor-miles consisting of five above-ground floors, each containing five ring corridors housing 23,000 military and civilian employees along with 3,000 support personnel. The Pentagon is the original ground zero, a nickname bestowed during the Cold War on the presumption it would be targeted by the Soviet Union at the outbreak of a nuclear war. As she passed through security clearance, Electra's inner voice kidded that not even the lightning brain would want to deal with a blackout in building this large and convoluted. She arrived just before Angus, who wasted no time setting the tone.

"Good morning, people. We have a lot on our plate, so let's get right to it. I'm ready for your assessment of what Carter and I provided you. And I'll give you a quick update. You heard the press releases last week regarding the Pillars programs. Jared tasked me to develop the details, and I'll turn that over to you. And I'm observing firsthand Jared's growing hubris. He's started scribbling press releases and speeches that ignore our recommendations. But worse than that, he's demanding we implement harsher programs we haven't been given a chance to dial down. I'm still able to rein him in for the most part, but it's getting harder, taking a lot of cajoling to do so. We'll come back to this when we wrap up. OK Carter, you lead off."

"My focus is economic impact, and on that basis all of Jared's programs get high marks. They reduce government costs and boost productivity by taking people off the welfare role and putting them to work. The PR news bulletins spin them in Jared's favor and the public approves. Angus, back to you."

"O.K. Let's look at healthcare impact. Russell, give us your assessment."

"The programs work economically, but you might question their ethics. Take the Repatriot Program, which is a thinly disguised deportation program. We've kicked out people sucking up a lot of healthcare dollars which is good, but their life expectancy plummets. And the Golden Years Program euthanizes the terminally ill who consume a lot of healthcare resources. Currently, the family determines who gets unplugged, but that could become a government mandate in the future. And I certainly don't like the Party's reluctance to use the R-Vac drug, which can cure T-Plague suffers, making them smarter. Sure, it costs time and money to nurse them back to a smarter mental state, but long term it's worth it. Maybe Jared wants to keep them dumb so they'll support him and let him do their thinking. That's bad. Angus, you should agree with me on that."

"I do, and it's one of the items I keep pushing. Mariah, it's your turn."

"I've got big problems with Jared, the Guardians, and their programs. They don't want to play by the rules of the Constitution. Let's look first at international policy and security. Declaring war on the Middle East could be justified, and I might agree that previous administrations gave away our American exceptionalism, but I think his foreign policy is simplistic. He's unwilling to compromise, so unless he kills off everyone in the Middle East, there will always be different views on politics and religion. But I do agree with his military and counter-intelligence build-up. The previous admins let them slip way too far. Now let's look at domestic policy.

"This is where the warning flags are flying. He's close to becoming the worst kind of imperial president: deciding on his own what is best for the nation and pushing through programs that implement his will, even though they violate the Constitution and individual rights. And here's why he might be able to get away with it. The T-Plague has sapped the intelligence of too many people. Russell's right; we need to make victims smart again by treating them with R-Vac. That way, the public can vote him and his kind out of office. But let's not kid ourselves. Once a tyrant like Jared comes to power, it's hard to dislodge him and his cronies. And let me make a final observation. You and Carter told us about Jared's sudden interest in the New Age Fundamental Church because he believes in channeling. Watch out if Jared thinks he's been chosen to speak for divine authority. Now I'd like Carter to comment on what he's found out about Jared's hidden agenda."

"What we know so far is that a growing number of government service contracts have been funneled without bidding to companies controlled by Jared and some of his key supporters. But, I could write a press release defending him if it ever gets leaked. Here's what I'd have him say: my companies are better than the competition; we charge less and deliver more; I save time and money by cutting through the red tape and awarding contracts without getting bids. I think the public would buy it, especially since they love the guy. Mariah, let me ask you about the Pillars Program."

"It's terrible; it's a throwback to George Orwell's book "1984," where the government watches and persecutes everyone. It would start by building a network of local vigilantes and neighborhood snoops. And who knows where this could lead? Angus, you need to be really careful with that one."

"Right. OK, next up is Olivia Torres, our newest Brain Trust member. Olivia, what would Capitol Hill say about all this?"

"It's generally supportive because so many are Guardian Party members. Even the more thoughtful ones have a wait-and-see attitude. They want to give Jared time to show his true colors, and a lot of them like the harsher approach. Even those that are looking for compromise say he's implementing what the public wants.

And this raises an ethical dilemma I don't think we want to touch just yet: if your job is to enact the will of the people but they're wrongheaded, what should you do? Maybe we should just keep doing what we're doing: recommend moderation and see where it leads."

"Well, we've heard from everyone and I'll task Electra to give me a forward-looking position paper that builds on what we've discussed. Do you think you can finish it before Thanksgiving?"

"I'll do my best."

Electra did her best to leave as soon as the meeting ended. There was no need for additional Brain Trust small talk; she had work to do at home as well as prepare for Zoe's second codependency meeting late that afternoon. She called her soon after getting home to confirm when and where to pick her up. Then she reviewed all the articles given by Eileen, the assigned counselor who completes Zoe's three-person support team.

Zoe waved as Electra drove up in the van, then quickly hopped in.

"Thanks for driving. You navigate the traffic much better than I do." Zoe seemed less nervous, less confused than last time, but Electra winced when her inner eye compared her to a fragile bird with an injured wing struggling to fly.

"You look good. More like the Zoe of old. And the support group meetings will describe how others put the articles into practice. Did you read the one Eileen assigned?"

"I did. I liked the seven steps article the best. I realize it's up to me to get out of the relationship, and it'll take time, but I have to practice saying no. And that's where my support team can help me follow through on what I know I must do."

"I liked that one too, and I also liked the article that talked about regaining control of your life. No one can control you unless you give them permission. It's time you stop giving Jared permission. Are you holding him at a distance now?"

"I'm trying, but sometimes I have an urge to call him on his personal cell number, just to hear his voice. I want Eileen to give me more advice for keeping myself at a distance but still keeping my job."

"I'm sure Eileen will give us some pointers. I'll drop you off, then park. I'll join you and Eileen in a couple of minutes."

Eileen and Zoe waited for Electra before launching into a review of the assigned articles. Eileen gave Zoe high marks for asking the right questions.

"I can tell you've given a lot of thought to your problem. Keeping your distance will help diminish this person's impact. Here are four steps to take. First, face the truth that you're being abused. Second, accept the fact your partner won't change. Third, take responsibility for your safety and sanity. And fourth, give up your dreams about being with the other person. Electra, please google supporting articles.

"The hour's nearly over, so let me give you the names of the three women in your support group. I'll have the leader Email to you the date and location for its next meeting."

The ladies compared notes as they drove toward Zoe's.

"The more we talk, the better I feel. So much of what Eileen says is common sense, but I guess that's the hardest kind to understand."

"You're not alone. No one exercises common sense when feelings get in the way, and even the best relationships create emotional stumbling blocks. I'll go with you to first support group meeting. Hey, let's stop for dinner. I'll treat."

"I'd like that. You're the most thoughtful person I know. I'm lucky to have you for a friend." Electra hoped that Zoe hadn't noticed her momentary grimace. *I'm so sorry I haven't been a better friend, but I'll make it up.*

"I know a good place for pizza, and it's on the way."

New clothes became the main dinnertime topic.

"I noticed your eye for fashion when I became a Guardian party volunteer. Have you always been interested in clothes?"

"Yes. It's a requirement in my profession. Women working for PR firms or ad agencies have to look tony. And the men do too, because image is everything. But that doesn't hold at my client accounts. The women still dress well, but men's standards have slipped. When did you get interested in clothes?"

"A couple of years ago, when I started socializing more. I even took an online fashion design course to learn about styles and color coordination."

"You're the most organized and disciplined person I know. Those traits must be in your DNA. Would you like to go shopping on Saturday? I'll take you to a couple of my favorite stores. And I'll buy lunch if you drive."

"Deal. Not only do I like to shop, but I also like to drive."

"You drive like a guy, and I say that as a compliment. But I have to ask, why are you driving this van instead of your hatchback. The van doesn't match your style." *Zoe's the first to ask, and she's right. I better come up with a good excuse.*

"I sold it because I'm getting a new car next year when I trade in this van. I don't need two vehicles anymore. Come on, I'll take you home."

Pre-Thanksgiving mall traffic on Saturday's shopping expedition added to a festive feeling as the duo hiked from store to store, window shopping along the way. After returning home, Electra took a late afternoon run, then puttered about while planning for Thanksgiving, aware of a growing attraction to Zoe, which was deeper than Mariah's in a sheltering way.

My emotional persona is changing. In the past year I've added Carter, then Mariah, and now Zoe to the list of people I care about. No longer is my cognitive persona warning me off. I'll invite them for Thanksgiving. It's over a week away, so they might not have made plans yet. Mariah and Zoe can stay the night before, and Carter can invite two guy friends if he wishes. Three's a crowd, but not three couples.

Electra called the ladies Sunday morning to make arrangements and luck was with her. Thanksgiving calendars were still open. Then she called Carter, who accepted immediately and promised to bring two of his tennis partners.

"And the guys will bring wine. Would you like red or white?"

"How about some of each? Beaujolais and Pinot Grigio would go well. And don't be late; we'll start serving at four. See you then."

Electra spent the rest of Sunday outlining next year's plans. *I normally do this over the Christmas Holidays, but I have an unsettled feeling this year will be different, so I'll plan ahead.* Three hours later, she made a final pass through the documents.

Terrorism and T-Plague are over for me, so next year I focus on postdoc projects where I can make the most progress. I pick network security and AI software. I can add virtual reality too if I had a Dream Team, but I'll do the best I can with my grad students.

I'll scale back my Brain Trust and PR work because Angus has added the right people, and he should be able to keep Jared in line. And if he can't, I have a contingency plan ready if Jared goes rogue.

After powering off her computers, Electra strolled to the kitchen for a bowl of cereal before going to bed but changed her mind before adding milk. *I won't fall asleep until I let the lightning brain freewheel. Instead, I'll have peanut butter on crackers and a glass of milk, then listen to music in the living room. Maybe I'll fall asleep on the sofa.*

She brought a blanket and pillow, then turned off the lights and curled up after selecting one of her favorite pieces, Copland's third and final symphony, which contains his inspiring *Fanfare for the Common Man.* Electra's thoughts roamed as the music cast its transformative spell, then they abruptly pivoted to what she didn't have.

I know what I'm missing and its connected to my reaching out. I have no close relatives, and people without emotional attachments suffer acutely during holidays because that is the time for family gatherings. My emotional persona is attempting to weave a network of lasting relationships. And I have heard counselors claim that enduring friendships can be as good as kin. In fact, the strongest morph into love. Dearly departed Christi taught me the Greek words describing the four kinds of love: Agape for the love of duty and doing what's right,

Phileo for the love of friends, Storge for the love of family, and Eros for erotic love.

So, who's in my network? Su and the Austin crew. Robin too. Maybe Jennifer, Russell, and Matt. And now Mariah, Zoe, and Carter. And possibly Angus. I think I'll invite Su to visit for the Holidays. And I'll sleep on all this before making further plans, but I'm certain Christmas this year will be special.

Electra awoke the next day, brimming with enthusiasm. *I'm happy as a clam at high water, and I even know that simile's genesis. Open clams look like they're smiling, and at high tide clams are free from the attention of predators, surely the happiest of times in the bivalve mollusk world. New Englanders started using it early in 19th century, 1833 to be precise. I'm beginning to sound like Carter. I'm probably the only person immune to my penchant for details. I'll make a New Year's resolution to be more concise in personal conversations.*

But she was not a happy camper the next morning when hearing a news bulletin rumoring that President Gardner might be getting contract kickbacks or secretly practicing a cult religion that abuses women sexually. *Someone finally dug deep enough to uncover Jared's secrets. Could Jared suspect Zoe's a leaker? I hope not, but you never know what Jared's thinking.*

Electra dismissed the notion as she finished her drive to the lab, but the premonition returned, bothering her enough to leave early. She suited up to run as soon as she got home, hoping exercise would lift her mood, but the miles added to a foreboding image in her head, accentuated by cold and blustery winds scudding wintry clouds across a moonlit sky that silhouetted leafless branches swaying to and fro on the trees she ran past. She connected it to a poem first heard in seventh grade, and again third year in high school, the legendary Alfred Noyes 1903 British ballad *The Highwayman,* and for some quirky reason the lightning brain incessantly repeated the entire poem, intent on forcing Electra to feel its pain and see its drama mirrored in the sky.

The wind was a torrent of darkness upon the gusty trees,
The moon was a ghostly galleon tossed upon cloudy seas,
The road was a ribbon of moonlight looping the purple moor,
And the highwayman came riding—
Riding—riding—
The highwayman came riding, up to the old inn door.

He'd a French cocked hat on his forehead,
and a bunch of lace at his chin;
He'd a coat of the claret velvet, and breeches of fine doe-skin.
They fitted with never a wrinkle; his boots were up to his thigh!
And he rode with a jeweled twinkle—
His rapier hilt a-twinkle—
His pistol butts a-twinkle, under the jeweled sky.

Over the cobbles he clattered and clashed in the dark inn-yard,
He tapped with his whip on the shutters,
but all was locked and barred,
He whistled a tune to the window, and
who should be waiting there
But the landlord's black-eyed daughter—
Bess, the landlord's daughter—
Plaiting a dark red love-knot into her long black hair.

Dark in the dark old inn-yard a stable-wicket creaked
Where Tim, the ostler listened—his face was white and peaked—
His eyes were hollows of madness, his hair like mouldy hay,
But he loved the landlord's daughter—
The landlord's black-eyed daughter;
Dumb as a dog he listened, and he heard the robber say:

"One kiss, my bonny sweetheart; I'm after a prize tonight,
But I shall be back with the yellow gold before the morning light.
Yet if they press me sharply, and harry me through the day,
Then look for me by moonlight,
Watch for me by moonlight,
I'll come to thee by moonlight, though hell should bar the way."

He stood upright in the stirrups; he scarce could reach her hand,
But she loosened her hair in the casement!
His face burnt like a brand
As the sweet black waves of perfume
came tumbling o'er his breast,
Then he kissed its waves in the moonlight
(O sweet black waves in the moonlight!),
And he tugged at his reins in the moonlight,
and galloped away to the west.

He did not come in the dawning; he did not come at noon.
And out of the tawny sunset, before the rise of the moon,
When the road was a gypsy's ribbon over the purple moor,
The redcoat troops came marching—
Marching—marching—
King George's men came marching, up to the old inn-door.

They said no word to the landlord; they drank his ale instead,
But they gagged his daughter and bound
her to the foot of her narrow bed.
Two of them knelt at her casement, with muskets by their side;
There was Death at every window,
And Hell at one dark window,
For Bess could see, through her casement,
the road that he would ride.

They had bound her up at attention, with many a sniggering jest!
They had tied a rifle beside her, with the barrel beneath her breast!
"Now keep good watch!" and they kissed
her. She heard the dead man say,
"Look for me by moonlight,
Watch for me by moonlight,
I'll come to thee by moonlight, though Hell should bar the way."

She twisted her hands behind her, but all the knots held good!
She writhed her hands till her fingers
were wet with sweat or blood!
They stretched and strained in the darkness,
and the hours crawled by like years,
Till, on the stroke of midnight,
Cold on the stroke of midnight,
The tip of one finger touched it! The trigger at least was hers!

The tip of one finger touched it, she strove no more for the rest;
Up, she stood up at attention, with the barrel beneath her breast.
She would not risk their hearing, she would not strive again,
For the road lay bare in the moonlight,
Blank and bare in the moonlight,
And the blood in her veins, in the moonlight,
throbbed to her love's refrain.

Tlot tlot, tlot tlot! Had they heard it?
The horse-hooves, ringing clear;
Tlot tlot, tlot tlot, in the distance! Were
they deaf that they did not hear?
Down the ribbon of moonlight, over the brow of the hill,
The highwayman came riding—
Riding—riding—
The redcoats looked to their priming!
She stood up straight and still.

Tlot tlot, in the frosty silence! Tlot tlot, in the echoing night!
Nearer he came and nearer! Her face was like a light!
Her eyes grew wide for a moment, she drew one last deep breath,
Then her finger moved in the moonlight—
Her musket shattered the moonlight—
Shattered her breast in the moonlight and
warned him—with her death.

He turned, he spurred to the West; he did not know who stood
Bowed, with her head o'er the casement,
drenched in her own red blood!
Not till the dawn did he hear it, and his face grew grey to hear
How Bess, the landlord's daughter,
The landlord's black-eyed daughter,
Had watched for her love in the moonlight,
and died in the darkness there.

Back, he spurred like a madman, shrieking a curse to the sky,
With the white road smoking behind him
and his rapier brandished high!
Blood-red were his spurs in the golden
noon, wine-red was his velvet coat
When they shot him down in the highway,
Down like a dog in the highway,
And he lay in his blood in the highway, with
the bunch of lace at his throat.

And still on a winter's night, they say,
when the wind is in the trees,
When the moon is a ghostly galleon tossed upon cloudy seas,
When the road is a gypsy's ribbon looping the purple moor,
The highwayman comes riding—
Riding—riding—
The highwayman comes riding, up to the old inn-door.

Over the cobbles he clatters and clangs in the dark inn-yard,
He taps with his whip on the shutters, but all is locked and barred,
He whistles a tune to the window, and
who should be waiting there
But the landlord's black-eyed daughter—
Bess, the landlord's daughter—
Plaiting a dark red love-knot into her long black hair.

Neurons snapped in the lightning brain as it shifted to a higher gear. *Zoe was supposed to call and she hasn't. Something's wrong.* Electra halted to call the number of the hotline cell she had given her but there was no answer, so she displayed its location on the screen. *Why is she driving northwest? She's already gone past my neighborhood. Something bad's going to happen if I don't get to her.* Electra raced home then sped away in the van.

Jared had concealed his rage when a staffer told him about the bulletin, but he let loose when Peter drove him to the next meeting.

"This has got to be an inside job. Someone close leaked, and now they'll start telling lies to make it sound worse. We've got to plug the leak and do it quick. Who knows? Anyone at the escort service? Any of your partners? Who have you been talking to?"

"Mr. President, I never tell anyone anything. You know I can be trusted. Haven't I proved myself enough times already? And I'll clean this up if you tell me who's to blame." When Jared composed himself enough to think, one name sprang into his head.

So that's why Zoe called last night! She said I'd be sorry if I didn't help, but I didn't think she'd go this far. And they'll connect more dots if she spouts off again.

"Peter, I have an assignment for you and someone you can trust. You've handled it before, so do it again."

Peter watched for Zoe to leave her office building. She sounded flustered when he called, but she calmed down when he said Jared would see her.

"What's the name of the target?"

"You don't need to know. Just know she's a security risk that's leaking too much. Do it quick when we get out of the city. And be neat, no blood stains. Roll her down the slope when we get to the dump site, then use your gun. There she is, the lady in the red coat. Go bring her back."

Electra closed the gap between vehicles without being noticed. The target vehicle slowed abruptly, then turned onto a side road. *We're in the middle of a rural nowhere, but they're driving slower so I can douse the headlights. When they stop I'll go into action.* As the van coasted to a stop, Electra's vision sharpened and her pulse pounded as she focused on what she would have to do. And suddenly, a calming clarity broke through as the Monster from the Id emerged.

Peter peered into the back seat as soon as he stopped. "Man, you sure messed her up. No wonder she hasn't made a peep. Good thing she doesn't weigh much. You don't need me to help."

His partner nodded but said nothing. He dragged the body out, then hurled it down the slope, uncertain moonlight strobing its trajectory, revealing lifeless limbs as they unfurled on a downward arc. It landed noiselessly then tumbled on a steep grassy slope slick from rain to the riverbank twenty feet below. He staggered toward the body, drawing his pistol, then stared for a second at the victim now trying to crawl on the muddy trail along the river's edge. And that was his final second.

Electra kicked the legs out from underneath her target, crashing him backwards, then kicked him twice in the head and grabbed his gun, shooting twice, then pushed him into the river. She knelt beside poor Zoe, who was trying to push herself up, only partially clothed, shivering from shock and cold.

"Zoe, it's Electra! I'll take care of you. I'll be right back."

Peter felt better after hearing two gunshots. He expected his partner would appear soon. Then they could drive away from the dump site and give Jared the good news. But instead of his partner, a fantastic creature loomed out of the darkness. He ducked just before a bullet shattered the passenger side window.

Peter's survival instincts took over as he squealed away. Another bullet shattered the rear window and another whizzed past his head, smashing into the windshield, causing him to jerk the car into a fishtail, but he regained enough control to speed out of the line of fire. By the time he reached the main road he had calmed enough to call Jared, who answered on the second ring. "Mr. President, this is Peter. We have a bigger problem..."

Electra ran down the slope after driving the van closer, bringing a thermal blanket.

"Stay with me! Fight to stay conscious." Electra's adrenaline-charged strength was enough to get them up the slope and into the van. She propped Zoe in the passenger seat then made the call. "Clarence, it's Electra. I need your help..."

Electra had been glumly waiting in the clinic's reception area for two hours. Finally, Clarence paced towards her.

"Your friend is out of danger. The head wounds didn't need stitches but you'll need to treat them with an anti-bacterial cream I'm prescribing. This looks like a rape, and I'm supposed to report all cases. What happened?"

"You can't report this. Believe me, if you do, all of us will be in danger. Look, it's late and we're the only ones here. Please do what I say."

"I always have. And I'll do it again. But there's more to tell. Your friend miscarried. You need to watch for hemorrhaging. Take her to an ob-gyn as soon as you can."

"Clarence, thank you. When can I take her home?"

"You can take her home now. She'll need looking after for a day or two. It depends on how quickly she gets over the shock. Let's talk to her now."

Even though she smiled, Zoe looked so fragile it made Electra shiver.

"I'm sorry you have to be here." Raw emotion crackled in Electra's reply.

"Don't ever say that to me again. I'm here to be your friend. I'm the one that's sorry, but I'll make it up to you. You're coming home with me." Clarence watched from the background.

It was four in the morning by the time Electra finished bathing, feeding and putting Zoe to bed, but she was not tired; instead she was energized. *I shall be Zoe's caregiver. It will become part of my redemption. I'll take a shower, then sit here until she awakens.*

As she sat, the sad refrain of a long bygone folksong looped through her brain, lulling her to sleep:

"Are you going away with no word of farewell,
Will there be not a trace left behind?
I could have loved you better didn't mean to be unkind,
You know that was the last thing on my mind."

Electra snapped awake as soon as Zoe stirred at noon.

"How do you feel?"

"I used to wonder what a mugging would feel like, and now I know. I hurt all over."

"Let's get you in a hot shower to loosen you up, then we'll get you dressed in sweatshirt and pants." Electra got Zoe up and eventually to the kitchen for oat meal and muffins, after which she described the starting point for putting Zoe back together.

"Today's the first day of a game you and I will play. Let's call it the 'Zoe Redux Game' because last night we brought you back from the edge. And we'll play the game from here until you're ready to move back to your apartment. And on Friday, we'll schedule a doctor's visit for you. The clinic thinks you're OK, but let's make sure. We'll also pick up whatever you want to bring here. Now let's make sure we have the facts straight. I'll start and you fill in where needed.

"Jared sent Peter and his partner to get rid of you, and they aren't gonna tell a soul. And neither will we; not even the police. You can't go back to work, so you'll have to tell your boss that you're taking vacation until January. Make up a story about Holiday family issues. And you'll stay out of sight by staying with me until its safe. In January, we'll know if you should go back to the Guardian Party or work somewhere else. So far so good?"

"I guess so. I can Email my boss as soon as I logon. But what about your Thanksgiving party?"

"It stays on, but I'll disinvite Carter and his friends. Then I'll call Mariah to let her know about the change. It'll be good for the three of us to be together. We'll have fun preparing dinner while planning how to get you back in action."

"So far so good, but what about Jared?"

"There are two immediate steps I can take to keep Jared in line. I'm going to leak all the info you have to one of my media contacts. And I'll call Jared to cover for us. I'll work it so he'll want me to take your place writing speech copy, and I'll start by writing one for damage control he'll need ASAP. Other steps will follow, but it's too soon to talk about them."

"I can't think of anything else. If you'll log me on, I'll send the Email."

While Zoe busied herself on the computer, Electra contacted Carter. He didn't answer, so she left a voice message, then called Mariah, who picked up right away.

"Mariah, it's Electra…I'm OK but there's a change in plans for tomorrow. Zoe and I want to make our Thanksgiving dinner party an all-ladies affair. Will that be OK with you?...Good…I already left a message for Carter…Why don't you come over as early as you like…We'll have fun cooking and chatting…See you tomorrow morning."

Two down, and the big one to go. Time to call Jared. Electra knew his personal cell number, which Jared answered right away.

"Hello, it's Electra Kittner…Thank you, and Happy Thanksgiving to you also…I heard the news bulletin yesterday and want to make a recommendation. We need to counter it by having you give a primetime speech ASAP. I've already prepared a draft that'll minimize damage. When and where do you want me to send it?... You need it by six tonight because you're speaking prime time at nine. I'll Email it to you in the next couple of hours…No, I haven't heard from Zoe. I've lost touch with her the past month…I'm sorry to hear that, but it would be a privilege for me to work more closely with you and your staff…I'll do my best for you…Thank you, Mr. President." Electra's inner voice was cheering as she ended the call.

This is as good as it gets. Jared wants me to take over for Zoe's PR work immediately. I'll write the speech he'll give tonight, and that'll bring me in close. Two hours later she Emailed the speech and then talked with Zoe.

"I sent my Email and even scheduled a doctor's appointment for next week Tuesday. What have you been up to?"

"I made my calls and we're set for tomorrow. I'll tell you more this evening. And I think we should watch the news while we have dinner."

The two of them were settled on the living room sofa just before Jared's address to the nation. Though hastily scheduled, it had been the only story for the past nine hours. Televisions everywhere tuned in as Jason strode purposefully to the podium.

"Good evening, my fellow Patriots.

"On this Thanksgiving Eve I stand before you giving thanks for what you have given me: the honor of being your chosen leader in these harsh times. And thanks to my vision and the heroic efforts of your Guardian Party, we have delivered the measures you have demanded. Our record speaks louder than rhetoric. The T-Plague War is nearly over; Terrorism is crushed. And we are poised to bring all Middle East rogue states to their knees.

"Included in our string of victories is our battle with the mendacious media. They know I win when they stick to the facts, so in desperation they have turned to their only weapon remaining, their WMD, their Weapon of My Destruction. And what is that? Today's news bulletin is their latest salvo: rumors and lies about me, supported only by terrible tongues and poisoned pens.

"How dare they accuse me of mistreating my staff or holding orgies in the Oval Office. I invite them to meet my staff and see for themselves that my ethics are unassailable.

"How dare they attack my religious beliefs. We are a nation built on religious tolerance that separates Church and State. Do I ask the Fourth Estate where they spend Sundays? Of course not, and they should extend me the same privacy.

"How dare they accuse me of a hidden agenda. What they say distorts the truth. Yes, some government service contracts have gone to companies I have interests in, but these companies have demonstrated time and time again they give superior service at cost below that of the competition. And I save you time and money by doing away with useless bidding that would only show again that my companies are the people's choice. But I humbly seek your forgiveness if I have erred. Going forward, all contracts will be awarded through bids.

"My future rests in your capable hands and sound minds, just like our country's future rests in mine and my Party's. Please allow me to continue doing what I've been chosen for: to guard our nation's health and security, and to keep us the leader of the civilized world.

"Happy Thanksgiving. May God bless all patriotic Americans, and may God bless our great nation."

The camera panned out as Jason marched away, his charismatic command of the situation on display. Zoe scooped the commentators.

"That speech will raise his approval ratings higher than ever. You've got the gift of speechwriting gab."

"Maybe so. I'm happy as long as it makes my next steps that much the easier. We'll have to wait and see…"

Next day's news trumpeted Jared's victory; headlines such as "President blows away Media Lies" and public opinion polls agreed. It appeared that Jared was alive and well and ready to roll on.

But Jared was not the topic of conversation for the ladies at Electra's. Instead they talked about Thanksgiving recipes, friendship, and first steps to get Zoe back on track. Electra spoke first as they sat down for dinner.

"When I was a child I had two best friends. We shared much excitement and were nicknamed the Three Queens. But that was then. Today I propose a toast to the three of us. All of us have overcome adversity and, like the Phoenix, have risen from the ashes. I christen us the Phoenix Trio. May our friendship be strong and last long."

Electra helped Zoe adjust to her new lifestyle, which by mid-December was comfortable for both. Recovery might take several more weeks, but Zoe's natural resilience was bringing her back sooner rather than later.

Electra had all Jared and Guardian Party plans completed by mid-December. Jared had promoted her into his Inner Circle, allowing her to use whatever support people she needed to get jobs done. And she used them to help arrange for a pre-Holiday surprise party to celebrate Jared's victory over the media rumor mill. It would be held on December 21st, the winter solstice, immediately after the last Inner Circle meeting for the year. Electra would deliver all invitations in person and take responsibility for ordering food and beverages as well as setting up the refreshments table.

Electra had her world under control as the party approached, so she worked for several days before at her university lab, putting notes and procedures in her logs, journals and diaries. The first day of winter dawned cold and clear, and as she finished her morning run Indira's "Winter Solstice" poem echoed in her inner ear:

We've reached the Winter Solstice,
Shortest day of the year.
Though longest night the stars shine bright,
Aglow with hope and cheer.

Dwindling days are over,
Brightness emerging instead.
Soon the weather getting better,
Good tidings ring out in my head.

Life too holds many a Solstice,
Turning points march into view.
At steadfast pace then turn about face,
Take heart joy's waiting for you.

Mother sure could paint with words. If I'm ever invited back for another life, maybe I'll develop other talents besides my extraordinary cognition. Mother had her poetry, Su and Robin music. Alice was a gourmet chef and Adom a champion runner. And my dear Christi was almost good enough to be a professional entertainer. I'm not talented in the arts, but I'm only twenty-five and time's still on my side. Maybe I'll blossom later.

Zoe was stirring, so Electra teased her to do warmup exercises while she cooled down, then showered and after breakfast made final party preparations. Then she loaded her shoulder bag and alerted the charter Brain Trust members for a possible meeting later tonight, details to follow. After a light lunch, she changed into the holiday slacks and blouse she had purchased when shopping with Zoe and asked for an opinion.

"You look very professional, yet Holiday party-ready. And the neck choker is eye-catching no matter what outfit you wear. You'll knock 'em dead. When will you be back?"

"Probably late, depending on how much people talk afterwards. I'll call you if it runs past ten. Zoe gave her a quick hug as she headed for the van.

"You're always prepared, but please be careful. I want you to stay out of Jared's clutches. Make him play your game, not his."

Anticipation built as she drove to the hotel that her support staffers had picked. As she parked, the lightning brain shifted to another gear that simultaneously elevated her mood and warning system. *Time to wear my "life of the party" game face.* She pranced into the lobby, asking the concierge for directions and he pointed to the security screening area. One of agents recognized her, so she breezed through to the meeting room forty-five minutes early. *Time for one last walk-through. Perfect practice makes perfect.*

She wouldn't have to give a PR status report because Jared's last speech had done that, but she would give a brief kick-off welcome, then observe Jared's key people, listen to upcoming program plans and afterwards serve refreshments, making sure Angus leaves when he must. As the attendees started filing in, game-time excitement started flowing through the lightning brain. Electra was ready.

Jared, accompanied by Angus, was the last to arrive. *Excellent to see them sitting together, talking so earnestly. Angus has his full confidence.* And before Jared could start the meeting, one of his staffers announced there would be a surprise party afterwards and asked their party planner to give a brief welcome. Electra rose to speak.

"Good afternoon, and welcome to the last Inner Circle meeting of the year. We're holding a party afterwards in celebration of Jared's recent victory over the vicious media attacks. And we're also celebrating your contributions to what we've achieved this year. I'm sure Jared wants to build on our successes by rolling out new programs next year. But tonight, I believe he wants us to enjoy the moment for jobs well done. And I personally want to thank him for promoting me into higher PR positions, and to thank all of you in advance for welcoming me into the Inner Circle. And now, let's hear from the President." Jared nixed the scattered applause, but his magnanimous smile showed how much he enjoyed the spotlight. He remained seated at the head of the table, but his ego didn't need to be propped up on legs to command attention.

"Why thank you, Electra. You've earned all I've given you, and next year I know you'll deliver even more, just like everyone here, and after we get updates from my lieutenants seated around the table, I want to focus on a timetable for declaring war on Islam. I've tasked Angus to flesh out the details so we attack by mid-year, with or without our Coalition of the Smart. I know this is the first you've heard I'm pushing harder for the war, but we're in the driver's seat and the public is with us. But let's get the updates first."

Electra could tell by the buzz that Jared's warmongering was welcome news. She learned nothing new from the updates, and as Jared led the timetable discussion she learned that neither Jared nor his lieutenants knew much about military planning. Angus diplomatically tabled further discussion until after the Holidays. The staffer who introduced Electra made a final announcement.

"OK everyone, work's over and it's time for fun. Electra will wheel in refreshments, so please mix and mingle. Other guests will be arriving, so let's party-hearty. And don't worry about driving if you drink. Peter Schmitzer will handle that."

Electra had three refreshment carts set up. She rolled in the first that contained cheese and fruit. Then she scooted back to the nearby service room where she sliced the cake before calling Russell Conklin.

"It's Electra. The meeting with Angus is a go. Call everyone except Olivia and Ricardo Torres and tell them to get to his house by eight. I'll join as soon as I can. I gotta go."

Now she placed the call to Angus, but he didn't pick up, so she hustled to the conference room and discreetly separated him from the group surrounding Jared.

"I just got a call from Russell Conklin. Something's come up and he needs you to hold an emergency Brain Trust meeting at your home. He's contacting charter members only and asked me to tell you. He needs you there ASAP. I'll get there as soon as I can get away. Believe me, you have to go now."

"Jesus, the timing is terrible, and—" Angus stopped mid-sentence. Electra's look told him he had to follow her orders, so he lowered his voice.

"OK. But whatever's going down better come up sevens."

"I'll explain later. Just tell Jared you've got a meeting you can't miss. I've got to get the other refreshments ready, so please leave now."

Electra pretended to straighten up the first refreshment cart while watching Angus act out his part; he left a couple of minutes later, so she hurried back to the service room.

The punch she was about to prepare is a Holiday favorite: rainbow sherbet mixed with chilled fruit juices, ginger ale, and spiked with vodka. But she would add a final ingredient: enough A-Vac to poison everyone. It was concealed in a "Holiday Party Punch Mix" bottle that she stirred in thoroughly. She put plates and a dessert slicer next to the cake, then arranged stacks of plastic cups next to the punch bowl. She made one final check as the lightning brain bolted through would happen next.

My A-Vac accelerator vaccine completes the set, turning them into the perfect WMD, better than a neutron bomb. It gives my enemies the T-Plague, for as long as I say. And I can bring them back if I want. After tonight, Jared's key lieutenants and everyone ahead of Angus on the succession chart are gone. I'm playing god, but so what? If I don't put Jared out of action, he'll take us where we don't want to go. If I can pull this off, I go to a new phase in my life. And if I can't, I go to my next contingency plan.

Electra turned the cart towards the door but stopped before taking a step. Peter Schmitzer was standing in the doorway, arms folded, just watching. The lightning brain shifted into a higher gear, ready for whatever action it chose.

"Hi Peter. I was so busy getting the cake ready I didn't notice you."

"But I've noticed you. What did you say to Angus that made him leave? And what did you just put in the punch?"

"I got a call that there's a Brain Trust meeting he has to attend, so I told him he needed to go now."

"OK. What about the punch"

"It's a Holiday Punch recipe. And I put in some extra punch mix for added flavor. Here, I'll pour you a glass." Peter approached warily, stopping on the other side of the cart, never glancing away.

"Why don't you drink it?" Electra smiled before taking a big gulp.

"The floating sherbet keeps it cold and creamy. I'll pour you a glass." Peter's expression never changed.

"Why don't you finish your glass first?"

"OK. I'm thirsty after the meeting." Electra drained her cup.

"I really need to serve the others, so if you don't want any I'll get going." She started pushing the cart, but Peter pushed in the opposite direction.

"Tell you what, have another glass while I tell you what I think. I think you've spiked the punch, and I think you and that damn Brain Trust are out to get Jared."

Electra sipped another glass, listening patiently and carefully slicing more cake while Peter vented his anger, the number of accusations growing.

"My job is to protect the President, and I'm going to blow the whistle. I don't trust you. You've done something to the punch."

"The only things I've done are mix the punch and cut the cake. Lean forward and sniff the punch's fragrance. It's fruity and festive." And the cake is delicious."

As he leaned in, Electra thrust the cake slicer deep into his neck, just below the Adam's apple, then pushed backwards to keep him from plunging into the punch bowl. He sprawled onto the carpet, gargling blood and muffled words, eyes wide with terror and the slicer jutting out. Electra calmly walked around the cart and knelt to finish the job. She plunged the slicer in once more, then wrapped his neck with a towel to stem the flow of blood. Peter died silently, but the job was not yet finished. She wiped the blood off the slicer, then dragged the body into a closet. After tidying the cart, she rolled it into conference room and began serving punch to everyone on her target list, especially Jared.

"You've been talking a lot. Why don't you have another glass to quench your thirst?"

"Thanks. It's a really tasty recipe, better than any I can remember. Make sure you save a glass for my number one secret service guy. Have you seen him?"

"No, but I'll take a glass to him right away."

"You're a very nice person. Both of us are. And that's why you'll enjoy working closely with me next year, even better than Zoe did."

"I'm looking forward to it, but now I'll look for Peter. If I don't see you again this evening, let me wish you a Merry Christmas."

Peter was not what the lightning brain was looking for. Electra needed to fabricate a cover for Peter's dead body and did so on the way out. She ran down a service stairway leading past a circuit breaker box that she smashed open using a fire ax mounted next to a fire extinguisher. Two strokes of the ax severed enough connections to plunge part of the building into darkness. Then she fled through the emergency door at the bottom, still carrying the ax. The resulting scramble would provide cover for whatever story the lightning brain would invent, and by the time Electra arrived at the meeting it was ready for publication.

Angus sat at the head of his dining room table, Russell Conklin flanking him on one side, Carter and Mariah on the other. Angus had placed an ice-filled glass and a twenty-ounce bottle of Coke at the opposite end. No one wanted to speak much until Electra arrived. When she did, she sat down, poured a glass and drank half before launching into her monologue.

"I have two stories to tell. First, I'll tell the real deal, and then the cover. I'll be as concise as possible and tell you more when you need to know.

"Here's reality. I gave poison punch to Jared and his key lieutenants, as well as everyone on the Presidential succession chain ahead of Angus. They're not dead, but they'll be mental vegetables in a day. Peter Schmitzer caught me so I killed him.

"Here's the cover story the media gets. China tried to decapitate our government by poisoning as many people in the succession chain as they could. Peter Schmitzer turned traitor and helped carry out the attack, and the Chinese killed him to cover their tracks. And it was only by the grace of God that Angus was spared. Jared's a hero who had the country's best interests at heart, and Angus is Jared's chosen successor." No one spoke, instead shifting blank stares back and forth from Angus to Electra until Angus asked incredulously.

"But why?"

"I had to stop him before he took us too far down the wrong path, ending in a Middle East war and other disasters." Electra waited for another question.

"Now what?"

"You'll become president. You'll have your hands full, but you can appoint people you want. You'll need to unwind harsh measures gradually. Otherwise, you'll lose support from Capitol Hill and a sizeable segment of the population. And you've got to rally a Coalition of the Smart behind you, which means you have to come up with sensible long-term goals that dovetail with domestic ones."

"When are people gonna know?"

"Except for the people in this room, only the cover story will ever be known. It'll come out as soon as I leak it and poisoned people get the T-Plague. I'll hand-deliver a speech you'll give as soon as the story hits. It'll be like Pericles' Funeral Oration. You'll look like a statesman and the country will rally behind you." Finally, Carter's question showed that someone besides Angus was beginning to recover from Electra's jolt.

"How many people did you kill?"

"Only one, but there was no choice."

"You're playing God, and that's a dangerous game. Lots of ethical issues. Do you really believe you can make the calls?"

"I wouldn't have acted if I didn't." Russell was the next to revive.

"You're trying to sign all of us up for your scheme, but you could be signing our death warrants. What makes you think all of us will go along?"

"Here's another story. Do you remember the espionage thriller, *The Hunt for Red October?* A Russian submarine captain sends a letter to his superior, announcing his intention to defect after it's too late to stop him. He tells his fellow conspirators what he has done, adding that Cortez burned his ships when his troops landed in the New World. Fear motivates the men. All of us agreed when we signed on that if Jared becomes too harsh and gets out of control, we'd work to remove him. He did and tonight I set in motion the end game. If we don't stick together and complete the job, our conspiracy will be exposed, and we'll be tried for treason. The CIA will uncover Emails and document directories that will convict us all." As Angus glanced around the table, he decided no one had anything left to say, but Mariah spoke before he could end the session.

"Maybe we should have given Jared more time. I mean, he did push back some of the mistakes made by previous administrations and—"

"Shut up! I told you early on that some of his programs made economic sense and—" Angus boomed over Carter.

"Quiet, people! We're all stressed out and tired. Go home and over the Holidays think things through but keep your mouths shut. I'm the only one that needs to do something. Electra, get me the speech immediately. For everyone else, take a break until January. Go home, people. A good night's sleep always helps." Nothing moved but four pairs of eyes following Electra as she stalked out.

Zoe was asleep by the time Electra reached home, so she crept around quietly, logging onto her computers to draft a speech for Angus. Then she used her network security software to plant bogus evidence linking Peter and the Chinese to the poisoning. Three hours later, she leaked the story to a reliable contact who would run it immediately on social media and then give it to traditional channels. Exhausted, she sat under the shower head, letting the lightning brain roam at will. Tomorrow she'd discover her new world and what she would do.

Electra's boundless energy returned as she awoke early the next morning, certain that she and the Brain Trust could finish the job she had started last night. Although the day had dawned cold and overcast, a morning run boosted her mood, and as the miles sped by, she made a final review of all plans.

Last night's actions cause no change to any of them. And when they finish, I no longer need to seek shelter from all the storms that have come before. The storms are ending.

As she finished her run by jogging the last mile, Electra recalled verses from Indira. *Mother wrote a poem called Shelter from the Storm. How fitting for me:*

Each of us since we were born,
Is seeking shelter from the storm.
Some thing or place or calming pause,
That grants a purpose to because.

Hard to find still harder to last,
All to soon it rushes past.
Some odd unknown or misplaced should,
And the love of your life is gone for good.

And though alone the remaining while,
There remains for you an inward smile.
A trace of what can't be compared,
The longed-for joy that once was shared.

The poem stirred other thoughts that emerged while taking a shower. *Now I'll have more time to spend on the personal side of life. I can make my relationships deeper, and I think I'll bring Angus into my network of friends. But I must pay attention. I must do all I can to protect what I've gained. I must stay in control. And I'll start right now.*

Electra delivered the speech to Angus after breakfast, then drove on to her lab, ready to record more information in her assortment of notebooks she uses to keep track of all activities. Even though the lightning brain could remember most of what was needed, having hard copy backup is the ultimate protection from hacking. Her temporary amnesia, caused by the helicopter crash nearly four years ago, proved that not even the lightning brain is infallible, so ever since then Electra kept detailed notes in case the unthinkable might happen. She was busily writing when a sudden wave of nausea, accompanied by a stabbing headache, brought her to a complete stop. Five minutes later it vanished, so she kept working, ignoring what could only have been an anomaly. But nausea and headache reoccurred late-afternoon, lasting longer. *My brain is telling me I've done enough. Time to go home and start enjoying the Holiday break. And I'll start by listening to Angus on prime time.*

"Angus is about to give his speech. Come watch." Zoe settled next to Electra on the living room sofa just in time for the anchorwoman to recap the bizarre events leading up to tonight's talk.

"News of a Chinese Attack broke late on the 22nd, sending waves of panic racing around the globe. But by mid-day Wednesday calm had been restored when it was announced that Angus McTear would take over the White House reins. McTear, the first person to hold Secretary of State and Secretary of Defense positions conjointly, is a respected figure at home, and tonight the world will meet him. We expect him momentarily." A marine opened a door to the Oval Office, from which Angus strode resolutely to a nearby podium.

"Good evening to all Americans and to our friends around the globe."

"By now you've heard about events that took place in our Capitol last Sunday. An unknown group tried unsuccessfully to destabilize our government. We're still piecing the puzzle together, but let me assure you, the American people, that you were never at risk. And let me announce to the world that America is open for business and ready to lead. As you have seen, the sun came up today and you continued on the path you were walking the day before. There were and will be no disruptions.

"The cowardly attack poisoned a number of our leaders and support staff. They are receiving the best medical treatment possible, and we pray for a speedy and complete recovery. Please join me for a minute of silence as we bow our heads in tribute to those who were struck down...

"Yes, we will hope for the best, but must plan for the worst. And that is why we have to put new faces in place. I am now the acting President of the United States, and I am putting in place capable people who will carry out what's already in motion. Some of you know me, but many of you don't. And I pledge to you to fulfill the presidential role to the best of my ability. And let's always remember this: our great nation and democratic government are not dependent on one person or a handful of leaders. Indeed not. We have many who are ready to serve when called to action, and we are calling some of the best right now.

"You know that Jared Gardner was a true patriot who every day did his best to guard the health and security of our nation. I had the privilege of serving him, and he trusted me to carry through on many of his programs. He and I recently talked about how he wanted to change some of the existing programs and add new ones in order to continue leading us in the right direction. Tonight is not the time to explain the details, but I will do that in the coming weeks. You will be pleased with what we plan to do next year.

"At times like this there is always an urge to rush to judgement, but I will avoid that trap. You have heard the rumors and unsubstantiated stories that China was behind the attack. And if that's the case, there will be consequences. And let me assure you, there will be consequences for whoever is responsible. But we need to investigate thoroughly and then respond. I pledge to keep you informed as we move forward.

"So please, take comfort this Holiday Season, knowing we are safe and have a bright future. Merry Christmas to all no matter your religion."

"God's blessings on our people and on America."

Angus took no questions, pivoting instead and marching into the Oval Office. Zoe liked what she heard.

"Did you write that? If you did, you get an A+."

"I plead guilty as charged. Let's listen to what analysts have to say."

Opinions all agreed. At times like this, Americans always support the new leader, especially when as qualified as Angus. Content and delivery of the speech built confidence and trust, implying Angus would be a thoughtful yet forceful Commander in Chief, starting where Jared ended but would be his own man when deciding where to lead.

"They love what you wrote. I hope Angus can carry through."

"I think he'll be great." Zoe sat for a moment, then changed the subject.

"Tomorrow is Christmas Eve. Tell me again who's arriving when."

"Mariah will call in the morning to let us know when she'll get here. And Su's flight gets here at noon. She'll call when she lands and will ride share or grab a cab to get here. And we'll call Robin to wish her and her co-friend Matt a Merry Christmas. You haven't met Matt, but I know you'll like him when you do."

"From what you've told me, I'm sure I'll get along with all your friends. And I'm sure glad we did all our shopping earlier. The pantry's full so we can stay in tomorrow. I hope the storm holds off until Mariah and Su get here. Why do you think there've been so many freak thunder storms lately? Is it because of climate change?" Electra gave her favorite one-word answer: "Perhaps."

CHAPTER 35

December 2121

"Fade to Black"

(Thread 1 Chapter 15)

A SUDDEN GUST OF wind rattled ice pellets against Zoe's bedroom window, ending her recurring nightmare of being chased down a deserted hallway lined with locked doors. Sometimes she reached the stairway at the end and sometimes she didn't, but she always awoke feeling awful. This was the first time the dream haunted her since staying with Electra, and the dreadful feeling dissipated once she realized Electra was near. Electra always came in to wake her if she forgot to set the alarm. A glance at the clock showed it was almost eight, which was an hour past the alarm setting. She had forgotten to activate it.

Where's Electra? I hope she didn't try running. The storm already blew in and from the sound of it, the footing's bad. Maybe she's sleeping in. Zoe stretched herself awake, then put on her robe and tiptoed to Electra's bedroom, where she found her asleep face down on her pillow. *I know she likes to get up early, so I'll shake her awake.*

Zoe tried rousing her, but there was no response, so she shook harder. Still no response, so she rubbed her hair and called her name. The result was the same. There was no movement. Electra was sleeping as if she were dead to the world. Zoe pulled the covers off, rolled her over and shook even harder. And then Zoe's feeling of dread crashed back, caused not by a dream but by a sudden realization that something was terribly wrong. Electra would not wake up.

As panic and confusion rose in tandem, Zoe did nothing other than stare at Electra's lifeless body until an idea finally broke through. *I'll call the clinic that treated me. Someone there must know her.* She found the prescription and called the number on the container.

Clarence was sitting at the reception desk, watching through the entrance doors the snow swirl randomly about. He had rotated to the day shift for Christmas week so he could attend Christmas Eve services he had been going to since childhood, a celebration filled with lighted candles and carols that always brought him cheer. And he would attend tonight, no matter how bad the weather. A phone call snapped him back to the present from his thoughts about the past or future.

"Loudoun County Clinic. This is Clarence…Who?…Yes, I know Electra Kittner…She won't wake up?…It might be sleep paralysis. Do this, then call me back…"

Zoe finally roused Electra. Though slapping and yelling didn't work, a cold-water treatment did. But Electra couldn't move and could barely whisper distorted syllables. Zoe knelt beside the bed and grabbed her by the shoulders.

"Electra, Electra! What's wrong?"

"C-can't t-talk."

"Has this ever happened before?"

"Nuh-Noo."

"I'm getting Clarence."

Zoe's second call to Clarence was disheartening. He couldn't leave until his partner arrives. She should take temperature and pulse readings and call him only if Electra's condition deteriorates. That was the best he could do, but Zoe thought she might do better if only she could understand Electra.

"I called Clarence. He'll be here as soon as he can. Until then, he wants me to check your temperature and pulse. Can you tell me where your thermometer is?"

"Ba-ba-room ca-cab-net."

"Do you have a blood pressure-pulse meter?"

"Nooo."

"Are you thirsty?"

"Wa-wa-ter."

Zoe used a forehead digital thermometer and her fingers and digital clock to get readings.

"Your temperature is 104 and pulse is 115. Let's prop you up bed so it's easier to drink. Are you hungry?"

"Nuh-noo."

"OK. I'll be right back."

Although she had lost body strength and the ability to talk, the lightning brain was feverishly working to diagnose the problem. *I've been this helpless only once—that was after the helicopter crash. I don't know what's causing it now. It's gotta be something recent; something different.* Suddenly the answer flashed. *I poisoned myself! I'm not immune to the T-Plague mutation. It'll kill me if the lightning brain can't kill it first.*

The A-Vac caused rapid onset of dementia because it used a mutated T-Plague strain. Electra had assumed that her immunity would not be impacted because the mutation was so similar to the original, but she was wrong. The symptoms—dizziness, fever and nausea—were worsening, and everything except basal life support systems was shutting down. Her cognition would remain active for as long as possible, but even that would be sacrificed if death becomes imminent. Until then, her thoughts and feelings were imprisoned in a lifeless body that worked one way. Electra sensed what was spinning about her but could not communicate. All she could do was lie there and think.

I drank two glasses thanks to Peter, but maybe I accidentally poisoned myself before. I developed and packaged my samples in white room labs, so I didn't do it there. What about the contact poison I used on a couple of Jared's people? I thought I kept my gloves on, but maybe I splashed some on my skin. How I got it doesn't matter. What matters is how I get rid of it.

Electra's sense of humor remained intact, which helped her deal with the quandary she was lying in. *I remember an "Alfred Hitchcock Presents" mystery about a critically injured driver lying on an emergency room table. He couldn't move, not even open his eyes, and although still alive and brain fully functioning, had a pulse too weak to be detected. As he listened to the doctors planning an autopsy, his body gave him one last chance to save himself: he could wiggle his little finger. He would use that to signal he was alive inside, but when the orderlies rolled him onto the stretcher, his hand was pinned underneath. He couldn't signal, so the autopsy would kill him for sure. But as the attendants wheeled him away, one of them noticed something odd: a couple of tears rolling down the man's cheeks. So, tears saved the driver. I can do better than that. I can blink.*

Zoe held a runner's bottle equipped with a flexible straw while Electra sucked.

"I can't understand a single thing you say, and we've got to talk. Can you blink yes or no answers to my questions?" Just then she noticed Electra's eyes blinking rapidly, then slowly. *Fast-fast-fast… Slow-slow-slow…Fast-fast fast.*

"You're blinking Morse Code. I'll ask you questions and you blink me your answer. One for yes, two for no." One blink and a whisper of a smile.

"Do you need to pee?" One blink.

"OK. I know you have a wheelchair somewhere. Is it in a second floor closet?" Two blinks.

"Is it in a first-floor closet?" One blink. "Good. I'll look till I find it." It was folded in the third closet searched and light enough for Zoe to lug upstairs.

"I'm not as strong as you, so you gotta help as much as you can when I lift and pull." Zoe's adrenaline and Electra's light frame made the job easier than she thought. Zoe made all the moves a caregiver would, supporting Electra in all the right places, and Electra's look of gratitude warmed Zoe to the core. She wheeled her back into the bedroom just as Electra's cell chimed.

"Hello, this is Zoe for Electra…Hi Mariah. Listen, we've got an emergency. Electra is sick and I don't know what she has. She might be contagious, so you better not come…You're coming anyway?… You're sure?…OK and thanks, and drive carefully."

"Mariah's coming to help. You're the expert on this next question. Are you contagious?" One blink, then two blinks.

"I got it; you don't know." One blink. "That's OK, we'll take our chances." Another phone call came, answering Zoe's prayer.

"Clarence is coming! He says he'll be here in about forty-five minutes. Let's put you back in bed. Do you need anything else?" Two blinks.

Zoe sat in a chair next to the bed, gathering her thoughts for what next to expect. *It's almost one; Su should call soon if her flight got through. And I'm going to call Robin.*

The lighting brain was thinking too. *I've got to tell Zoe to get the samples of all improved vaccines I brought back from Austin. The new I-Vac and R-Vac might kill what I've got if my brain can't get my immune system to do it. Damn. They're at my university lab, next to my letters and notebooks.*

Electra's cell phone rang again. "Hello, this is Zoe for Electra… Hello Su. I'm a friend of Electra's…Yes, I know you're visiting for Christmas…We've got an emergency. Electra is sick. I don't know if she's contagious so you might want to stay away…Yes, I could really use your help…You know her better than anyone? OK and thanks. Bye."

"That's Su. She's on her way. I'm calling Robin. Could you blink me her number?"

Robin had postponed all Christmas activities until finals week ended; she was wrapping presents when her cell phone beeped, flashing a caller I.D. she knew well.

"Hi Electra. I'm sorry I haven't called you yet, but final exams put me way behind…" Robin's smile turned to a look of surprise.

"Who are you?…Zoe?…Oh, you're the friend from Guardian Party public relations…You're calling because she's sick?…And you don't know what it is?…Holy Shit…Yes, I was her caregiver a couple of years ago…No, I'm not worried about getting infected.

I'll be there as soon as I can." Zoe relayed all the news to Electra after disconnecting.

"Lots of help is on the way. Just knowing that should make you feel better. Let me take your temperature and pulse again, and then I'll get you more water."

Electra knew before Zoe stuttered the numbers that her condition was deteriorating: temperature 106 and pulse 128. When Zoe asked if she needed anything else, she blinked twice. *All I want to do is lie here and conserve energy. I'm having trouble thinking, and my heart and head are about to explode. I feel hotter than when I was trapped in Hassan's tomb.*

Clarence was the first to arrive, and he wasted no time recording telltale vital signs. They were dangerously high, but he needed more information before diagnosing or prescribing what to do next.

"All readings—temperature, pulse, blood pressure and respiratory rate are elevated. Does she know what's causing this?"

"I already asked her and she said no, but let's ask her again." Zoe explained how they communicated but before she could ask, the doorbell rang. Zoe dashed to answer and brought Mariah to the bedside, introducing her to Clarence, who led the conversation.

"We've got to find out what she's caught, and she's unable to talk. Zoe communicates by asking questions and having Electra blink—" Mariah interrupted in mid-sentence.

"I know what it is. She's got T-Plague. Ask her to see if that's what she says."

"You've caught the T-Plague. Is that correct?" One blink. The doorbell rang again; Zoe hurried back, this time bringing Robin and Su. After making rushed introductions, she picked up where she left off.

"Do you have any drugs at home that might help?" Two blinks, which were Clarence's queue to talk.

"We need to get vaccine in her ASAP. I have some at the clinic that'll—" Su interrupted this time.

"She brought advanced vaccines back from Austin. Ask her where she put them." There were now five people hovering over

Electra, all talking at once, so Clarence organized what had become a cacophony of jumbled sentences.

"Hold on now. I'll run the discussion and Zoe will ask Electra the questions. Zoe can ask only yes or no questions, so let's think through how to find out what we need to know. It'll work best if we let a volunteer pose the question for Zoe to ask. If they run out of questions, we'll switch to the next volunteer. Who wants to be first?" Su did.

"Let me be first and take over for Zoe. I'll think for a minute to collect my questions. And why don't we take our coats off and get chairs. Zoe, could we please have something to drink?" Mariah helped Zoe bring items while Su prepared questions and Robin placed a call to Matt.

While Electra listened, a whimsical thought came to her. *My dear friends are doing their best, but it sounds like they're holding a wake. They're standing and jabbering above me and I can't reply. So, let's replay Joyce's "Finnegan's Wake." They can splash vaccine rather than whiskey on me and I'll come back to life.*

Su had her questions ready when the group reassembled.

"Did you bring back the right vaccines?" One blink.

"Do you know where they are?" Once more, one blink. Su turned to her audience.

"Now the game begins: Twenty Questions."

"Are they here at home?" Two blinks.

"Are they stored in the garage?" Two blinks.

"Did you leave them in the car?" Two blinks.

"Did you leave them with someone other than yourself?" Two blinks.

"Are they at your university lab?" One blink.

"Now we have to figure out how to get in and find them. I don't think it's open at four thirty on Christmas Eve, but I'll ask.

"Is your lab open?" Two blinks. Su turned back to her audience.

"Clarence, you should have the pull to get University Security to take us to her lab." She didn't wait for his reply before asking another question.

"If the guards let Clarence and me into your lab, can you tell us where to look?" One blink.

"Are they in plain sight?" Two blinks.

"Are they locked in your workstation desk?" One blink.

"Is there anything else in the desk we should bring back, like your notes or logs?" One blink.

"I'll bring back everything in the desk." One blink and as big a smile as Electra could muster. Clarence took over once again.

"Sherlock Holmes would be proud. I'll make some calls and then I'll drive us in the ambulance. No matter how much snow we're getting, I've got sirens and flashing lights and the right of way. And before we leave, let's take vitals to see if she's stabilizing."

Clarence made the calls, took vitals, and reported the facts.

"We're all adults, so I'll tell you the truth. Her condition is bad, and she'll go into convulsions and coma in a matter of hours if her temperature doesn't come down. After Su and I go, you three must watch her closely. Keep her hydrated and get her to the bathroom if she feels nauseous or has to pee. Then let her rest. And gather up snow and start packing it around her. I'll call to report where we are, and you call me if her condition dives. Let's swap cell numbers." Clarence collected what he needed then marched away, taking Su with him.

Electra now had three caregivers at her side: Robin, Mariah and Zoe. They followed the instructions Clarence had given, then sat next to her. Although they weren't hungry, Zoe forced them to eat. Afterwards, they tried unsuccessfully to find something to talk about, so Robin found a Christmas concert broadcast that diverted their attention until the doorbell rang. Robin leaped to her feet.

"That's gotta be Matt." She returned with Matt and Carter in tow. Robin made the introductions while Zoe prepared more food. Matt took one look at Electra and knew her condition was critical.

"I'm getting my medical bag from the van. Carter, get more snow and be ready to pack it around her when I say." After hurrying back, he checked Electra's vitals and reported to his partners.

"Every reading's in the danger zone, and I'm hoping the snow brings them down. Look, we all want to help, but there are too many people in the room. Please take the chairs and sit somewhere else. I'll yell if I need you." Everyone did as told.

Electra was aware of all that was being done but knew it wasn't enough because time had become her worst enemy. *It's eight o'clock and no news from Clarence. I'll be dead by morning unless Clarence gets back with the new vaccines, or unless my brain figures out how to kill the virus. I'm burning up; I'm starting to hallucinate. And all I can do is lie here and think, but I'm having trouble doing even that.*

Finally, the phone rang, but when Zoe answered it was not what she expected.

"Yes, this is Zoe Vargas for Electra... Who are you?... What?... Where are they?... Yes, let me check. I'll be right with you." All eyes were on Zoe when she stammered out what she had just heard.

"Clarence never got to the lab. He crashed the ambulance. The police need us to explain what Clarence said just before he died. And Su's in critical condition. What are we going to do?" Carter shot to his feet and grabbed the phone.

"Hello officer. My name is Carter Quavah. I can explain what Clarence was after, but it's complicated..." Five minutes later, he summarized what he and the police would do.

"So, your people will go to the lab and start looking, and I'll get there as fast as I can. Let's swap phone numbers. Call me if you find what we need before I get there. And I'll call you if I get stuck in the snow. Bye." Carter disconnected the call, then gathered everyone around Matt.

"Here's the plan. I'm gonna help look for the vaccines. Robin, why don't you come with me? Matt, let's swap cell numbers so we stay in touch in case more stuff hits the fan."

"I've got yours and you've got mine. Good luck driving, and better luck finding what we need." Robin had already grabbed her coat and was waiting at the front door.

Electra's home team had dwindled to three. Matt told Mariah and Zoe he would call for them if he needed help. Zoe stared at Electra before the ladies filed out.

"How can someone so strong and smart be brought so low by something so small? She's my best friend, and I can't lose her. If only I could clone her and keep her with me."

Electra heard every word. *I should have been your best friend sooner. I'm so sorry. I need to make it up to you, but how I don't know.* Her cognition began to fade as breathing turned to panting, tunneling her vision.

Suddenly, the lightning brain's brilliance flashed again. *I understand! Now I see how my work is converging. I can control matter by manipulating atoms, brains by manipulating neurons, spacetime by manipulating quantum physics. I see the Universe in its wholeness and unity. The Universe and God are one. I am reaching out to touch His face. I can become godlike if only I were immortal.*

That's it! I will clone myself. Su will help me. Immortality is within reach. I will make things better because I will know what to do. I shall electrify the world! I shall command the lightning brain to make it so!

Then abruptly, a wave of doubt-filled fatigue swept in, clouding her vision; her brilliance dimmed as energy drained away. Neurons flickered off as the lightning brain struggled to survive. Electra felt a heaviness, as if death were creeping closer, now resting on her chest, waiting.

But I don't know what to do. My loved ones are dead because of me: first father, then grandfather, then Mo and Christi, then Alice, then Adom and Clarence. Perhaps as prophesied, I am become death the destroyer. Perhaps no creature should be immortal, as Swinberg's poem warns:

From too much love of living,
From hope and fear set free,
We thank with brief thanksgiving,
Whatever gods may be.
That no life lives forever;
That dead men rise up never;
That even the weariest river,
Winds somewhere safe to sea.

Electra's hallucinations became more vivid, more real than what she was now living through. She heard the roar of waves surging onto sand and stones, followed by a sibilant hiss as they receded. She saw those dearly departed, standing on a windswept beach facing an infinite ocean, illuminated by the glow of a rising though waning moon, their faces expressionless, neither joyous nor sorrowful. Just waiting patiently. Waiting for what?

Waiting for Electra, for Electra to emerge from the waves, to walk towards them. For Electra to join them in an endless sleep. She saw her father, her grandfather. She saw Mo between them, and then Christi. Alice marched slowly to join. She saw Adom too, and then Clarence. They joined hands to form a closing circle. Two open arms extending from each end reached towards her, for her to join them, to close the circle. But she did not see Indira.

"Mother!" she screamed. "Where are you? I need you. Tell me what to do. Is it time to leave? Should I stay or should I go?"

A radiant white image danced like mirage. It was Indira, whose melancholy smile accompanied her final words.

"I am with you, my precious daughter, but I cannot tell you what to do, for you already know the answer. Think back to the Buddhist monk."

Electra's arms jerked as the muscles in her limbs convulsed. Matt yelled when he saw her thrashing.

"Mariah! Zoe! I need you!" The ladies rushed to his side, the three of them now standing next to Electra. They saw her eyes flutter as she choked out a moan while her body stiffened. And then it suddenly relaxed as a soothing calmness enveloped her. A tender smile emerged and she looked one last time at those hovering above. She felt their love and it brought one joyous tear. She felt the power of her lightning brain take flight, rising to the challenge of its prime directive: to survive, to go on living.

Electra concentrated by exhaling slowly, closing her eyes while searching for the answer. She found what she was looking for but Indira had gone, replaced by a final reality now fading to black, a sound of silence closing in. One final word remains to be heard as its echo dies softly away.

Perhaps...Perhaps...Perhaps...

Glossary

Every book in the Lightning Brain Series introduces abbreviations or terms collected here for convenient reference.

Actual Scientific or Sociopolitical Terms

Atomic Force Microscopy—An atomic force microscope includes a tip mounted on a micromachined cantilever. As the tip scans a surface to be investigated, interatomic forces between the tip and the surface induce displacement of the tip. A laser beam is transmitted to and reflected from the cantilever for measuring the cantilever orientation

CAGE—Conjugative assembly genome engineering (CAGE) is a precise method of genome assembly using conjugation to hierarchically combine distinct genotypes from multiple *Escherichia coli* strains into a single chimeric genome. It permits large-scale transfer of specified genomic regions between strains without constraints imposed by *in vitro* manipulations.

CDC—The Centers for Disease Control and Prevention is the leading national public health institute of the United States. The CDC is a United States federal agency under the Department of Health and Human Services, headquartered near Atlanta, Georgia

Caring/Sharing/Platform Economics—21st century business trends fueled by the Internet and career adjustments caused by Artificial Intelligence.

Caring Economy: Focus on personal/societal needs rather than consumption.

Sharing Economy: Focus on peer-to-peer renting/subscribing possessions rather than buying from large companies. The supply side partner is the Collaborative Economy.

Platform Economics: A digital platform economy emerged in the 21st century. Companies such as Amazon, Facebook, Google, Salesforce, and Uber are creating online structures that enable a wide range of human activities. This opens the way for radical changes in how we work, socialize, create value in the economy, and compete for the resulting profits.

Cognition and Self-Awareness—Neuroscientists conjecture that cognition and self-awareness are emergent phenomena coming from billions of neurons forming trillions of interconnected associative patterns in the brain. They draw parallels with force fields (gravitational, electromagnetic, weak and strong nuclear, etc.) that emerge from incomprehensible numbers of interacting atoms. Current research indicates the cognitive part of the brain may be able to self-direct organic development.

Collaborative Consumption—A cultural and economic force that emerged during the "Great Recession" of 2007-2008. People began to share, barter, lend, or swap online for goods and services. The phenomenon launched businesses that transformed the economy by focusing on resource allocation and distribution rather than consumption intersection of supply and demand.

Crowdsourcing—The practice of obtaining information or input into a task or project by enlisting the services of a large number of people, either paid or unpaid, typically via the Internet.

DARPA—Defense Advanced Research Projects Agency is an agency of the United States Department of Defense responsible for the development of emerging technologies for use by the military. It created the first computer network (ARPANET) in the 1960's

Intelligent Design versus Self-Directed Design—Intelligent Design asserts God, a Universal Life Force, hovers just outside man's cognition, controlling man and nature. Most contemporary theologians or philosophers agree the answer to the question Does God exist? is inaccessible. Each person chooses what to believe. Self-Directed Design focuses only on humans, conjecturing a person's cognition affects brain states controlling how the brain and body develop. Buddhist monks' brain scans show how mind control affects brain waves and cognitive states, altering physiological processes like heart rate or blood pressure. Might not prayer or holistic medicine help alter a patient's brain state so the body "heals itself?" Neuroscience research continues to study the phenomena.

Internet of Things—The interconnection via the Internet of computing devices embedded in everyday objects, enabling them to send and receive data.

If one thing can prevent the Internet of things from transforming the way we live and work, it will be a breakdown in security.

MAGE—Multiplex Automated Genome Engineering rapidly introduces changes across a genome.

MGTOW—Men Going Their Own Way. An online social media community resulting from 21st century Men's Rights Movement, analogous to the extreme factions of Third Wave Feminism.

Microaggression—a statement, action, or incident regarded as an instance of indirect, subtle, or unintentional discrimination against members of a marginalized group such as a racial or ethnic minority.

NIH—The National Institutes of Health is the primary agency of the United States government responsible for biomedical and public health, founded in the late 1870s. It is part of the United States Department of Health and Human Services with facilities mainly located in Bethesda, Maryland. It conducts its own scientific research through its Intramural Research Program (IRP) and provides major biomedical research funding to non-NIH research facilities through its Extramural Research Program.

SWAT—SWAT (Special Weapons and Tactics), a paramilitary unit of law-enforcement agencies.

WMD—Weapon of Mass Destruction

Terms created by projecting Current Trends

America Strong—British covert operation established to help the United States deal with Middle East Terrorism and the Techno-Plague

Apocalypse Clock—Hidden software controlling Trojan Filters.

Brain Probe—Biomedical device using software-controlled electromagnetic radiation to simulate sensory perception in human brain.

Brain Trust—Advisor group, reporting to the President of the United States, that develops policy recommendations and implementation.

Co-Friendship—Term coined by the Gay Community in the 21st century, referring to an intimate relationship between two people of either sex. Signifies a serious longer-term relationship.

Co-NFL—Professional football league offshoot created by the National Football League and Cross-fit Training Association. Teams comprised of elite male and female athletes. Rules and physical requirements set to allow exciting, fast-paced competition between offensive and defensive teams comprised of both males and females. League formed in late 21st century because women in the United States had achieved parity with men in most careers. There is a similar Co-NBA for basketball. Professional sports are considered the ideal combination of physicality and entertainment.

Cognicom Project—Codename for CDC project responsible for developing vaccines against the Techno-Plague. Divided into three sub-projects:

- I-Vac Project: Develops inoculation vaccine that protects
- R-Vac Project: Develops reversal vaccine that cures
- S-Vac Project: Develops symptomatic suppression vaccine that alleviates pain

Guardian Party—National political party surging to prominence in the early 22nd century after a string of incompetent government administrations and complicit Washington Establishment were unable to protect America from twin pandemics: Worldwide Islamic Terrorism, Global Techno-Plague.

The Guardian Party has its own "Guardian Agency", complete with its own covert ops group, to spy on other agencies, political parties, or governments.

Guardian Party Programs—Harsh programs designed to guard America's health and safety while cutting budget deficits.

Crime-Stoppers: Aggressive hunt for terrorists or criminals

Infra-Rebuild: Put people to work rebuilding roads, communications systems, power systems, etc.

Repatriot: Deport useless or dangerous people.

Golden Years: Euthanasia for the senile or terminally ill

Pillars: Consists of two sub-programs: Private Citizens' Vigilantes to fight local criminals and terrorists, Health Watch Local groups poking into neighbors' private lives to uncover community health risks.

H&H DNA Partners—Biotech Pharmaceutical Company started by Hudson (Hud) Haller and funded by his father Hollis (Holy) Haller

Healthguard—Intrusive national government agency established to guard private citizens against health risks. Championed by the Guardian Party.

Home-Track Schooling—American grade and high school educational systems are more flexible in the 22nd century, allowing customized education for gifted children or those with physical or mental handicaps. Home-Track Schooling allows a child to study at home using computerized learning and tutoring programs. The program is monitored by Healthguard, the agency which tests, accepts, and monitors children in the program.

Insiders Group—Clandestine group created to spy on the Guardian Party.

Isilabad—Rogue Middle East State created midway through the 21st century to reestablish Islamic Caliphate and catapult Islam to its rightful place on the world stage.

Mega-Media—Umbrella term describing a worldwide computer network linking all types of communications networks and media. Includes smart cellphones and computer tablets when connected to "Worldwide Internet Grid".

New-Wave—Generic term referring to early 22nd century younger generation tastes and lifestyles.

Neuro-Knitter—Biomedical device using software-controlled electromagnetic radiation to accelerate neural healing required after broken neck or back.

Opposition Party—Concerned Washington politicians and insiders opposed to Guardian Party's harsh measures for dealing with opponents. It has a clandestine steering committee that controls a covert operations team.

Project Death Shield—Covert operation run by CIA (Central Intelligence Agency) to monitor how Techno-Plague impacts U.S. government stability.

Securityguard—Intrusive national government agency established to guard private citizens against domestic or international threats. Championed by the Guardian Party.

Sensual Pleasures Café—many recreational drugs were legalized in the 21st century. A Sensual Pleasures café is a restaurant featuring foods, drinks or tobacco products containing legalized recreational drugs.

Techno-Plague—Also called T-Plague. Infection from a mutant manmade virus causing neural entanglement similar to Alzheimers, leading to rapid cognitive impairment and senility. It Spread gradually but inexorably, becoming a global pandemic early in the 22nd century.

Traser—State-of-the-art law enforcement weapon: dual tranquilizer and electric stun gun.

Trojan Filters—Hidden devices that can release T-Plague virus into air or water.

Vow-Cer—The institution of marriage remains in the 22nd century a cornerstone of society, but adjusts to the needs of people. Vow-Cer is a Marriage Vow Contract Certification Ceremony. Two people affirm their commitment to each other, agreeing to honor their written marriage contract. Couples usually become Co-Friends before celebrating a Vow-Cer.

Worldstars—Name given by Indira Ramanujan to herself and three other talented biotech researchers: Su-Lin Song Chou, Adom Ola, and Jason Kittner.

Appendix

The scientific or guiding principles presented in this book are factual, as are technological applications. For readers who might enjoy reading more of the details, this appendix contains charts or diagrams referenced in the book's narrative or dialogue, identified by page number.

Page 81—Isilabad Manifesto

The evolutionary trajectories of all Societies are dictated by Universal Myths, Legends, and Beliefs.

Evolutionary Arc of Societies
Traditional Societies

Modern Societies

Bands Tribes Chiefdoms Developing States
Developed States Small/Primitive Large/Sophisticated
Isilabad The West

Societies' Concerns:

- Establish Physical Boundaries Protect Itself
  Guard Resources Organize Itself Maintain Stability
- Three types of People: Friends Enemies Strangers

Characteristics that distinguish types of Societies

- Population Size Acquisition of Food/Resources
  Political Organization Social Stratification

Societies contribute to how People:

- Care for the Young Care for the Old
  Care for Health Wage War Treat One
  Another (Moral Code) Express Themselves

Isilabad Superior to the West for:

- Family Values   Care for the Old   Care for Health Social Richness   Restorative Justice

West Superior to Isilabad for:

- Material Richness/Technology   Avoiding War Tolerance   Self-Actualization   Impartial Justice

Religion plays fundamental role in Societies

- Man is genetically predisposed to believe in a God
- Religion emerges from Man's quest for understanding the Universe

Definition of Religion: Unified system of beliefs and practices relative to sacred things set apart by symbols and rituals that people follow and use to put order and understanding in their lives and the world they observe.

Attributes of Religion:

- Belief in Supernatural   Shared Membership in Social Movement   Proof of Commitment Practical Morality   Rules God is in our Lives

What Religion gives its People and its Priests:

- Supernatural Explanation   Reduction in Anxiety Comfort Organization for Obedience and Belonging Pulpit for preaching Political Obedience Moral Code towards Outsiders and Enemies   Justification for War

Religion is Isilabad's Major Stumbling Block (inward focus and denial of Modernity or Science)

My Mission

- To eliminate the worst of Isilabad and add the best of the West as I build a major player on the World Stage
- To control my Minions using Islamic Religious beliefs (though most are obsolete)
- To: Preach Political Obedience Strengthen Solidarity and Hatred of the Great Satan Sow Fear and Intolerance of the Outsider Justify War against Christianity
- To turn the West's Technology into WMD's directed at the Great Satan

Page 45—Relationships Among Scientific Disciplines

Older Disciplines (Math, Physics, Quantum Physics) reaching asymptotic limits of Human Intelligence. Breakthroughs still await Younger Disciplines (Computer Science, Molecular Biology, Neuroscience) and their descendants.

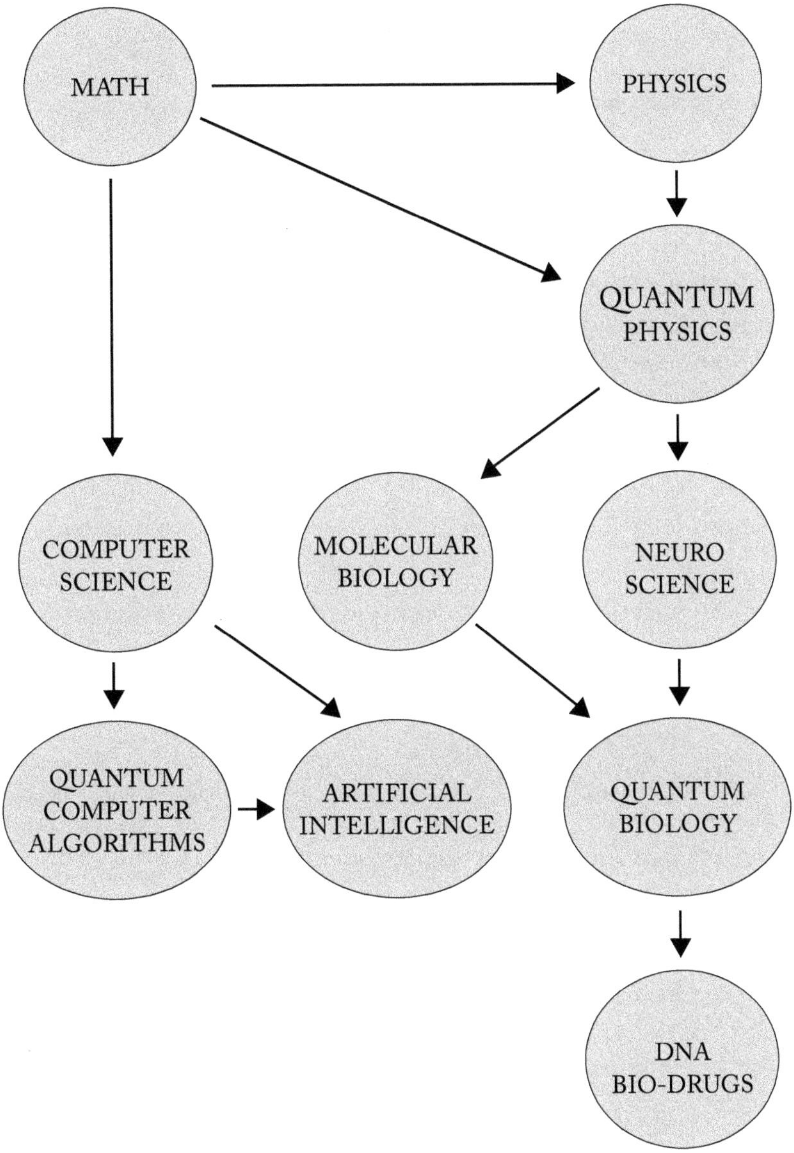
MATH
PHYSICS
QUANTUM PHYSICS
COMPUTER SCIENCE
MOLECULAR BIOLOGY
NEURO SCIENCE
QUANTUM COMPUTER ALGORITHMS
ARTIFICIAL INTELLIGENCE
QUANTUM BIOLOGY
DNA BIO-DRUGS

Electra's Philosophy, Religion and Science Summary Synthesis

CUT TO THE CHASE: Contingent Conclusions

Philosophy useful if we stay at the shallow end of the Discipline!

Religion plays a useful role in Modernity!

Math and Physics approaching Asymptotic Limit of Man's Cognitive Ability!

- Purpose of the Universe: To construct increasingly complex aggregates of matter
- Purpose of Life: To survive and to go on living
- Purpose of Civilization: To extend Rational Progress
- Purpose of Philosophy: Contribute to Civilization's Progress by integrating Contingent Knowledge found in Multiple Disciplines
- There are Five Levels of Complexity (lowest to highest): Atomic Chemical Biological Mental Cultural Each Succeeding Level Emerges from Preceding Level and cannot be "explained" by Reductionism (Whole greater than Sum of Parts)
- Human Beings are designed to seek answers to Metaphysical Questions (Reality and Existence Matter and Time) There are only Contingent Answers
- Higher brain functions (Consciousness, Emotions, Intelligence, Self-Awareness) are Emergent Phenomena
- Consciousness is the tip of the iceberg

- Truth, Ethics, and Knowledge are "Mystical" (inaccessible to rational analysis) Questions about God's Existence are meaningless.
- There's room for all Three: Religion, Agnosticism, and Atheism
- Darwin's Theory validated once and for all (21st century Oceanic Exploration)
- Time exists only as a Construct of the Brain (Mind and Brain are the same)
- Free Will exists but Cognition is aware only after the Will has acted
- Society needs an intelligent, educated public able to "understand" the above, then optimistically and pragmatically proceed to an everyday way of living
- Man has reached the limits of High Energy Physics, but can make progress in Neuroscience and Artificial Intelligence

Tracing the Intertwined Threads

- Genesis: Self-Aware Prehistoric Man
- Sought answers to explain their World (Metaphysics and Ontology)
- Rudimentary Philosophy is the First Thread
- Primitive Religion (Second Thread) emerged from Myth, Legend, and Superstition
- Written Language allowed for Civilizations to transmit learning to succeeding generations
- Golden Age of Greece set the standards for Philosophy (Idealism versus Materialism)
- Philosophy coopted by Religion and Scholastics to reconcile Faith versus Reason (St. Augustine reconciled

Greek Philosophy with Christianity St. Aquinas reconciled St. Augustine with Reason)

- Science (Third Thread) emerged in the Renaissance and challenged Religious Authority; Since then the Threads have intertwined
- The Enlightenment (17th century) marks the start of Modernity (Science dethrones Religion)

Modernity complicates the Tale of the Thread

- Focus of Philosophy shifts from Contemplation to Action based on Reason, Liberalism, Freedom, Democracy. Progress in Ascendance
- Science powers: Industrial Revolution Materialism Reason Rationality (Descartes, Leibnitz) triumph over competing approaches (Humanism/Romanticism (Rousseau)

Start of the 20th century: Apply methods of Science to perfecting Philosophy

- Phenomenology (Husserl and Heidegger) attempts to make Philosophy like Math or Science
- Positivism (Frege, Russell) refines Phenomenological Rigor

But contradictions arise:

- Physics (Relativity/Einstein and Quantum Mechanics/ Heisenberg) reveals paradoxes
- Mathematics (Incompleteness/Godel) reveals Mathematics is Inconsistent
- Social Sciences (Psychology/Freud and Sociology/Weber) inject "Irrational Man"

Attempts to fix:

- Vienna Circle and Pragmatism (Dewey) integrate Man into Positivism
- Analytic Philosophy (Wittgenstein) concentrates on Language/Meaning
- Emergence Theory (Can't explain the whole from the parts) formulated
- Philosophy fragments into study of distinct disciplines (Physics, Biology, Psychology, etc.)

Along come the World Wars

Entire train of Modern Philosophical Thinking derailed. How could Civilization unleash the Holocaust? New Post-Modern Schools of Philosophy abandon the Enlightenment and Tradition

Post-Modernism associated with the European Continental Philosophers

Emphasizes Individual's Personal Experience Refutes logical approaches to Philosophy

- Existentialism (Sarte, Camus) focuses on Man's alienation Man is free to construct his own reality (Relativism) but is responsible for his actions. Freedom causes fear and anxiety
- Deconstructionism (Derrida) and Structuralism (Levi-Strauss) turn Reductionism against Physical and Social Sciences
- Post-World War II Malaise: Rational Progress abandoned Philosophy is "Dead" (Killed by Science) Pessimism rules Ethical Relativism triumphs
- Culture and Language (Hermeneutics) considered Source of Self/Meaning

Philosophy rescues Itself from Post-Modernism in Late 20th century

- Michael Rorty: Traditional Philosophy not "Dead" but at an "End" (Can never evaluate Truth or Philosophical Foundations objectively)
- Positivism scaled back and incorporates Psychology and Emergence
- Theory of Falsification (Popper) allows Science to be accepted contingently
- Anthropocentrism abandoned (man is not at the center)
- Relativism replaces Absolutism
- Ultimate truth and meaning inaccessible to Man (Metaphysics/Reality and Ontology/Being might always elude Man's Grasp)
- Progress neither linear nor circular, but instead an outwardly expanding spiral
- The role of Philosophy in the 21st Century: Contribute to Civilization's Progress by integrating Knowledge found in Multiple Disciplines
- Rational elements of Kant/Enlightenment using Neuroscience, Physics, and Emergence but scaled back to accommodate the limits of Experiential Data/Observation
- Leads to a Consilience of 21st century Philosophical Approaches: Neuroscience Emergence Naturalism/Science dialogue with Humanism/Arts Pragmatism Hermeneutics
- 21st century philosophers extended Alain de Botton's useful application of selected famous philosophers' principles.

Page 47—Survival of the Fittest Redux

PURPOSE OF LECTURE: PROVIDE graduating Science and Engineering Majors a current perspective on Evolution.

Thomas Hobbes was correct when observing Nature: "Life is solitary, poor, nasty, brutal, and short". Tennyson agrees: "Nature red in tooth and claw…"

But Darwin was correct also: Theory of Evolution supports Animal Adaptation and Behavior as well as the latest findings in Human Neuroscience and Psychology.

Snapshot of Animal Adaptation:

- Darwin's Bark Spider spinning webs spanning 25 meters across Madagascar rivers.
- Egyptian locusts sprouting wings and swarming only when rainfall supports bountiful plant growth.
- Chameleons' swiveling eyes and tongues twice as long as body.
- Crocodiles eating only once a year when animal migration brings prey to water.
- Ibex leaping on soft-cloven hooves navigating precipitous rock cliffs

Snapshot of Animal Behavior:

- African wild dogs hunting in cooperative packs
- Wildebeest herds clustering to defend against predators

- South African Meerkat burrow communities exhibiting group cooperation
- Antarctic Emperor male penguins huddling to keep eggs warm
- Flocks of birds exhibiting Emergence: Lower Level Organisms/Intelligences interact to create a Higher Order Organism/Intelligence
- Schools of killer whales and dolphins joining forces to feed on swarms of smaller fish
- Snow leopards in the High Himalayas signaling their presence to mates by rubbing or spraying scent on sheer rock walls
- Andean flamingos parading in a mating dance

21st Century Exploration

- As robust as that conducted in the 18th and 19th centuries
- 21st century Target: The Oceans
- New technology allowed Marine and Evolutionary Biologists to probe ocean depths: advanced computer-controlled submersible vessels, underwater cameras, and microphones
- The Deep Ocean is still largely unexplored. It is the realm in which man can observe and confirm that evolution has driven the trajectory of all living organisms.

Key Findings:

- Diversity of deep sea creatures remarkably well adapted to thrive thousands of feet deep where pressures are enormous, light never penetrates, and temperatures barely above freezing. Marianas Trench 7 miles deep. Few mammals (whales) journey so deep.
- Some examples: fish that are all mouth and teeth, trailing eel-like long bodies. Fish with enormous eyes able to detect light reflected from their bioluminescent eyes. Fish discharging chemicals that stun their enemies.
- Some creatures display: Perfectly transparent bodies. Bioluminescence for hunting or avoidance systems. Body surface organs to generate or detect electric currents or motion in the water, allowing them to see. Predator and prey evolution for offense or defense.

- Deep Sea fossil records more complete than those on land because of less turbulent environment.
- Deep Sea fossil records confirm Punctuated Evolution Theory.
- Punctuated Evolution: Theory that after extended periods of little change (stasis), speciation and organ emergence occur rapidly.
- Thermal nutrient columns supporting bacteria. Origin of Life conjecture.

Darwin's Theory of Evolution has been irrefutably confirmed.

Note Richard Dawkins Quote: "If God doesn't believe in Evolution, He's missing a great tool for accomplishing Life's mission: not just to go on living, but to thrive."

Note the analogous human behavior!

- Communication, Cooperation, Cognition and Memory are products of Nature and Nurture
- Homo Sapiens not qualitatively different
- Ecological balance achievable with or without man's intervention
- Animal cognition and awareness of Time dictated by the flow of real world recurring events. Only Man has constructed an arbitrary measure of time (which is a purely cognitive creation.)

Page 99—PHILOSOPHY TIMELINE

Antiquity & Golden Age　　　　Renaissance Enlightenment

	Pre-Modern		Modern	Post-Mod	Post Post-Mod
400 BCE	400 AD	1100 AD	1700—1800	1900 2000	2100+
Plato Aristotle	St. Augustine	St. Thomas Averroes	Descartes Kant Locke Hume Berkeley	Kierkegaard Derrida Sarte Camus Wittgenstein	???
Timeless World Of Ideals	The Mind of God Explains Everything	Reconcile Christianity With Aristotle	Atomic View Of Nature Man can Know The World The Rise of Science Cause and Effect	Uncertainty Ambiguity Contradictions	Balance Mod with Post-Mod

EVOLUTIONARY TRAJECTORY OF PHILOSOPHY

BRANCH	PRE-MODERN	MODERN	POST-MODERN	POST POST-MODERN
Metaphysics/ Ontol. (Reality and Being)	Religion Supernatural	Interest in the Natural World	Skepticism of Natural World Anti-Realism	Science & Tech within Limits

Epistemology (Theory of Knowledge)	Mysticism Faith	Reason Empiricism Science	Use of Narrative Limits to what is Knowable	Hard-Wired Brain Plasticity for Adaptation/ Learning
Human Nature Psychology & Economics (How People Act)	Man born in Sin Man is Fixed	Tabula Rasa Individ. Efforts Learning	Group over Indiv Nurture Psychological Complexity	Social Animal Neuroscience Nature & Nurture Individ. Dignity Diversity
Ethics (What is the Good Life)	Duties & Service	Pursuit of Happiness	Conflict Opposition Corruption Relativism	Balance Relativism with Biological Needs and Wants
Politics (How to Organize Society)	Feudal Hierarchical Authoritarian	Rule of Law Liberty Equality Republic/ Democ.	Socialism Egalitarianism Power Struggle	Republic/ Democ. Safety Nets Diversity Inclusion

SOCRATIC DEBATE / DIALECTIC FOR PHILOSOPHY RESOLUTION

Thesis (Modernity)	Antithesis (Post-Modern)	Synthesis (Post Post-Modern)
• Objective Truth • Reason • Universals • Individual over Group • Pro Science &Tech • Progress • Unbounded Optimism • Capitalism	• Subjective Truth • Relativism • Group over Individual • Anti-Science & Tech • Language is Problem • Spirit of Socialism • Cynicism/ Pessimism	• Neuroscience explains how the brain functions • Objective Truth (within Limits) • Pro Science and Tech (within Limits: Gen. Rel. Quantum Mech. Uncertainty) • General Agreement on Meanings in Language • Causality (within Limits) • Republics & Capitalism • Guarded Optimism

Page 105—Electra's Post-PhD R&D

High Energy Physics a Dead End

- Super-Strings, Multi-Verses and Black Holes exist only in sci-fi
- Grand Unified Field Theory unable to control Gravity Waves
- We must obey the well-established laws of Classical Physics, Relativity, and basic Quantum Mechanics
- Atoms and Second Law of Thermodynamics (Entropy) set Scientific Limits on What is Possible

"Merely human" scientists aren't smart enough. Bring in Electra's discussion of math and explain she can think fast and slow. But she won't waste her time here because there is lots of breakthroughs to make in Genetic Engineering and AI

Areas to Pursue-Biotech

- Nano-Technology, Molecular Machines and Artificial Intelligence will power future R&D
- Plenty of Room for Asymptotic Growth in Genetic Engineering and Artificial Intelligence
- Designer Drugs to improve Quality of Life
- DNA Modification using Molecular Machines found in Bacteria, Viruses and T-Cells leading to "Improved Humans"

- Artificial Intelligence extending Quantum Computing Breakthroughs leading to Transhumanism
- Note: Advanced Computers pave the way for Molecular Machines, Designer Drugs, DNA Modification, Transhumanism

Areas to Pursue-Advanced Computers

- Advanced Computers are extensions of "Neural Networks" that self-learn and self-modify
- They are needed to handle calculations too complex for "merely human" scientists, who are not "smart enough" to utilize today's hardware (Software not "smart enough")
- "Neural Network Computers" were called "Deep Learning" when first developed
- Neural Network Computer contains Multi-Layers of interconnected Microprocessors that accept Input Signals, process them with Feedback Loops, and emit Output Signals.
- "Learning" occurs when the Software self-modifies or brings in additional Hardware Components

NEURAL NETWORK DIAGRAM

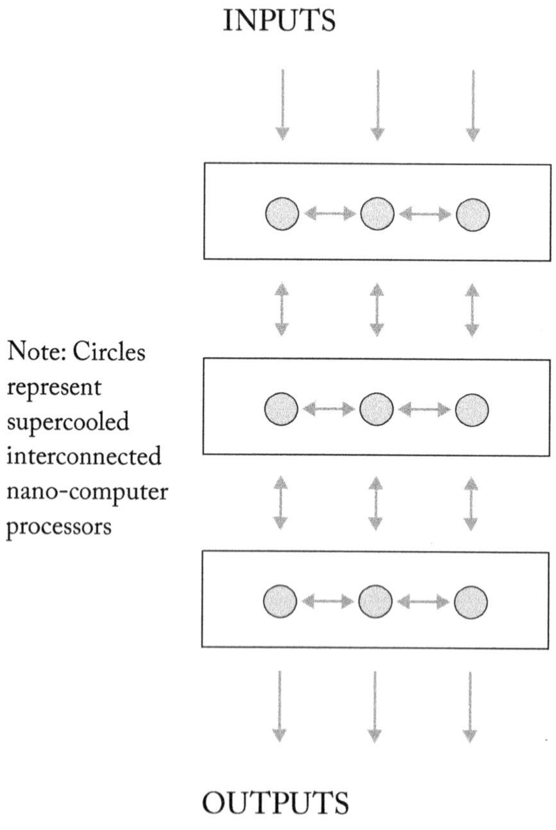

Today's Quantum Computers employ Super-Cooled Neural Networks

- Microchips constructed by "Nano-Machines" (manipulate individual atoms)

- Supercooling needed to stop atomic vibrations and take advantage of Quantum Effects
- Qubits store 0's and 1's simultaneously in Individual Electron Spin values
- Quantum Phenomenon: Superpositioning stores 0's and 1's simultaneously in multiple states (highest memory density possible)
- Quantum Phenomenon: Entanglement allows for simultaneous interaction among 0'1 and 1's in parallel calculations
- Quantum Phenmenon: Coherence keeps Qubit values in phase
- Quantum Phenomenon: Tunneling reduces energy consumption

Why I Can Do What the Others Can't

- Lightning Brain smarter (can think fast and slow)
- Lightning Brain can apply Extended Real Number System to handle "Complexity"
- My adaptively extended object-oriented programming language built on massively parallel, autoregressive, multithreaded recursive programming that exceeds what Others can do
- I can achieve breakthroughs using current technologies and computer hardware!

What I Shall Do in DNA/Genetic Engineering Short-Term

- Use current Organic Molecular Machines and DNA Modification Technology to manipulate Bacteria and Viruses and T-Cells in order to develop the "ultimate" suite of T-Plague vaccines

- Use current Nano-Technology and Quantum Computers to map Human Brain's Neural Structure
- Build Brain Probe Device

What I shall do in Artificial Intelligence Short-Term

- Develop my own programming language and use it to write AI operating systems and software apps
- Develop better software for Cyber-Theater
- Develop better software for Computer Network Security
- Develop better software for Computer Graphical User Interfaces
- Develop AI links between Brain and Computer Hardware

Page 117—The Great Quantum Conundrum

Quantum Mechanics: A Major Factor in Quantum Biology and Quantum Computing

Note Einstein's quote regarding Quantum Mechanics: "Its Mathematics is elegant but its physics is Dismal."

Mere Mortals haven't been able to extend it to the next level.

- "It is safe to say that nobody understands quantum mechanics."—Richard Feynman
- "The most incomprehensible thing about the Universe is that it is comprehensible."—Albert Einstein

The Challenge: Biological and Computational Systems Enormously Complex! Both use sophisticated definitions of Entropy to define Information Storage and Transfer

Biological Reference Points:

- Brain contains 10**11 Neurons 10**15 Synapses Uses 25% of Body's Energy (25 Watts) Processes 10**19 bits/sec (Remarkably energy efficient compared with the best Supercomputers)

Our best guess today: Cognition is an Emergent Phenomena attributed to the interactions of trillions of Synapses that each comprise Memory and each encapsulate a Quantum Computer.

Biological and Brain Processes too complex and too fast if it weren't for Quantum Processes. Some Examples: Photosynthesis Mitochondrial Metabolism Vision Olfactory Sense Consciousness

Quantum Biology Systems use these Quantum Mechanical Phenomena:

- Quantization of Energy and Entropy for DNA and enzyme activity
- Tunneling for transporting Hydrogen atoms and Electrons through Energy Barriers
- Superposition and Coherence for combining many bio-molecular states
- Entanglement for Action-at-a-Distance and Instantaneous Communication to explain enzyme 3-D folding and reaction rates
- Electron Spin for living organisms to detect magnetic fields

What's Next:

- Quantum Biology still in its infancy. Practical applications await those who integrate Biotechnology, Nanotechnology, Genetic Engineering, and Artificial Intelligence.
- Don't worry about Man's Asymptotic Limits! There's much we can do when applying the basics.

The challenges are almost as daunting in the field of Quantum Computing

Most "interesting problems" cannot be solved in Polynomial Time

- They are classified NP which means Non-deterministic Polynomial Time

- Most "interesting problems" are at least EXP or hard (beyond NP) Possible to solve in a finite amount of time but we don't know how.
- Beyond that is the R class of problems. Can't be solved in a finite amount of time (Turing's Halting Problem)
- And beyond the R class are insoluble problems.

Quantum Computing Systems use these Quantum Mechanical Phenomena:

- Supercooled computer chips to store 3-D densely packed 0's or 1's (Q-bits) in the spin states of individual Electrons.
- Superpositioning and Entanglement to model algorithmic programming output linked by Neural Networked computer chips in order to speed up parallel processing calculations

Model the Brain as a Massively Parallel Deeply Recursive Neural Network capable of learning

Electra's Lecture Notes

Quantum Mechanics now plays a big role in Biology and Computers

Note Einstein's quote regarding Quantum Mechanics: "Its Mathematics is elegant but its physics is Dismal."

Mere Mortals haven't been able to extend it to the next level.

- It is safe to say that nobody understands quantum mechanics —Richard Feynman
- The most incomprehensible thing about the Universe is that it is comprehensible—Albert Einstein

The Challenge:

- Biological Systems Complex Quantum Mechanical Systems Deep

Now is not the time for me to study the complexity or depth because:

- I don't have a Dream Team
- I don't want to be noticed

What I will do:

- Pirate/apply cutting-edge technology so I can use my superior cognitive ability to solve practical problems
- Apply my Quantum Mechanics insight into Drug Development DNA Research Computer Network Security and AI Software

Quantum Mechanical Principles I use:

- Wave Equation explains probabilistically how objects behave
- Quantization of Light and Energy explains how systems use Energy
- Quantum Mechanical definition of Entropy explains information transmission and coherence/decoherence in DNA (C A T G alphabet) or Computers (0 1 alphabet)

Quantum Biology Systems use these Quantum Mechanical Phenomena:

- Quantization of Energy and Entropy for DNA and enzyme activity
- Tunneling for transporting Hydrogen atoms and Electrons through Energy Barriers

- Superposition for combining many bio-molecular states
- Entanglement for Action-at-a-Distance and Instantaneous Communication to explain enzyme 3-D folding and reaction rates
- Electron Spin for living organisms to detect magnetic fields

Quantum Computing Systems use these Quantum Mechanical Phenomena:

- Supercooled computer chips to store 3-D densely packed 0's or 1's (Q-bits)
- Superpositioning and Entanglement algorithmic output linked by Neural Networked computer chips to speed up parallel processing calculations

My Approach to Continued Biotech Research

I know the Biological underpinnings:
Fundamental Biological Concepts: Cell DNA Evolution
Biology has evolved from purely descriptive to a "Principle-Based" Science

Guiding Principles:

- Energy Optimization: Cells use energy efficiently
- Entropy Reduction: Living Organisms highly ordered

Biological Process Categories:

- Growth/Division Reproduction Death
  Ingestion/Metabolism Excretion Motility

I focus on Biotechnology: The application of engineering to Biological Systems Engineering: All about Measuring Manipulating Modeling Making

Biology revolutionized by the discovery of DNA. Modern Biology is in its Infancy primed for rapid breakthroughs (Compare to High Energy Physics)

The "Hot" Research Areas:

- Biopharmaceuticals Genetic Engineering Neuroscience

Though Public apprehensive and Government is "Go Slow," China and Japan pushing ahead and U.S. must remain the leader of the Biotech revolution

I already know:

- Atomic Force or Cryo-Electron Microscopy Nano-Chromatography PCR CAGE MAGE Scanning CRISPR genetic engineering techniques to identify and slice and dice and splice and modify genes into DNA.
- Computer DNA Programming (I developed it from pirated/modified Genetic Programming) for Neural Networked evolution/simulation and effectiveness evaluation of new biopharmaceuticals or modified gene sequences.
- DNA and Molecular Programming for developing bioactive molecules

I will use these techniques as follows:

- Biopharmaceuticals: Build on my Techno-Plague development to eradicate T-Plague Apply results to "cure" Alzheimers Additional R&D Focus is TBD
- Neuroscience: Develop "Brain Probe" line extensions Map the Brain Unravel Cognition AI/Nano Technology Enhancements for Humans

Summary of My AI Approach

- Two components: Hardware and Software
- I won't build new Hardware. I'll use existing Quantum Computers because their computing speed, power, and memory exceed what current Software can handle.
- Quantum Computers: Supercooled collection of Deep (multi-level) Neural Networked computer processors able to store 0's or 1's in the spin states of individual electrons. Computers able to add virtual hardware components while running because they learn by reading "Big Data"
- Quantum Computers use "Entanglement" and "Superposition" to speed up calculations, and Qubits increase data storage density by storing 0's and 1's in spin states of individual electrons.

Page 150—My Approach to AI Software

Some Background:

- Software is all about thinking computationally for dealing with Knowledge
- Two Types of Knowledge: Declarative (statement of what is) Imperative (statement of how to derive)
- Need a Programming Language for Modeling computations

Dimensions of Programming Languages:

- High Level versus Low Level
- General versus Targeted
- Interpreted versus Compiled

The best current languages for AI Programming are extensions of Python (named for 70's Monty Python show).

Python is an interpreted, object-oriented, high-level programming language with dynamic semantics. Python's simple, easy to learn syntax emphasizes readability and therefore reduces the cost of program maintenance. Python supports modules and packages, which encourages program modularity and code reuse.

Here is what I can do to make them better:

- Incorporate Modal Logic
- Write massively parallel deep neural network-learning object-orientation apps extended with relational database, multi-threaded, and recursive algorithms.

- I can go where other AI developers have never gone because my brain can handle complexity better than Mere Mortals. (But I don't know if my programs lead to "Emergence." And I haven't tried to extend digital to analog data representation for taste, touch or spatial orientation.)
- I can deconstruct programs into finer-grained apps, and I can handle complexity (many components) better than Mere Mortals.

Here is what I plan to do:

- Use AI to build my Brain Probe and Brain Mapping devices
- Use AI to build a suite of Network Security software tools
- Use the current state of Augmented or Virtual Reality to build the front end for Users of my software tools

But here are the limitations of General Artificial Intelligence that we must obey:

Limits to Artificial Intelligence

- AI Scientists and Engineers have been in the "Imagination Age" for the past 100 years. They are unable to move into General Artificial Intelligence because they don't know how to build "Emergent Computers" or "Emergent Programs" that can accept inputs from all senses (taste, touch, sight, sound, smell, spatial orientation)
- The best we can do is model the brain using Input—Process—Output Model
- Dendrites—Neuronal Cell Body—Axon is what is in the brain.
- Deep (multi-level) Neural Networks model how Neurons interact.

- But the brain dynamically brings in more inputs (learns) and subdivides the Problem into sub-problems that run in parallel.
- The Brain ultimately constructs "Emergence"—a higher order intelligence when enough neurons and interconnections allow Cognition and Emotion phenomena.
- To create a "Terminator" we would need to build a General AI model for each Persona (Physical, Cognitive, Emotional) from which emerges a higher order program AND then integrate them together.
- Achieving this will frustrate Man until the human brain evolves to a higher level of intelligence, and even then it may remain beyond Man's grasp.
- Until then, we must be satisfied with Expert Systems and rudimentary Artificial Intelligence. In the future, AI scientists and engineers will incorporate more Neuroscience findings that may improve how well computer hardware and software model the brain.
- Hoped-for Quantum Computing breakthroughs so far have run into unavoidable limits dictated by the laws of Quantum Physics. It is impossible to scale up from second generation Quantum Computers. Quantum programming breakthroughs heralded by Shor's algorithm for speeding up execution time of "Big O" polynomial and beyond complexity are unattainable. Quantum Cryptography unable to improve on RSA public key encryption. RSA provides network security if keys are "long enough").

The Future of Genetic Engineering

- Combine Genetic Engineering, Artificial Intelligence and Nanotechnology

- Eliminate disease, make people and life better
- Leads to the Trans-Human Age: Organically + Enhanced People
- Can Man's Human Nature handle it?

Civilization might benefit, but people might be reluctant to proceed as fast as the breakthroughs, even though the story is compelling:

The Genetic Engineering Story

- DNA is like Computer Tape containing a Person's Owner's Manual
- Today's Technology (CRISPR/Cas-9 extensions) allow targeted Genome Editing
- Safe and Effective Track Record eliminating Diseases (Genetically Modified Foods, Sickle Cell Anemia, some Cancers, etc)

Many research areas whose proven techniques are waiting to be commercialized

Applications for a Better World

- Each Person "can read" their DNA
- Genetic Screening for Possible Diseases
- Designer Babies (Germ-Line editing)
- Grow Spare Body Parts
- Slow down Aging Process

But according to the professor, many people are uncomfortable. Some oppose genetic engineering for ethical, religious, or political reasons:

Public Backlash

- Too much change too soon for Human Nature to handle
- Risk of leaking too much personal Genetic Information
- Dark Side to Genetic Screening (Eugenics could run amok)
- Could lead to Inequality (Race of Superhumans)
- Impossible to control

Ethical Issues

- Some applications seem Unnatural or Counter to Religion
- Cloning and Growing Body Parts frighten People
- Quality of Life may be more important than Quantity of Life (Living Longer)
- Risk blurring Humanity's Red Line and Human Dignity

The Future of AI and Nanotechnology

- AI and Nano-T make Yesterday's Sci-Fi today's Reality
- Powered by Smaller, Faster, Energy-Efficient Chips and Devices
- Today's Hardware more advanced than Current Software
- As with Genetic Engineering, Public is Scared

AI Story

- Brain is not a Computer but AI utilizes Neural Networks
- Neural Network: Layers of Interconnected Computer Chips
- Neural Network "learns" how to solve problem instead of relying on Algorithms
- "Deep Learning": Many Layers of Computer Chips
- Quantum Physics allows for Uncertainty and Network Evolution

Neuron Cell Body

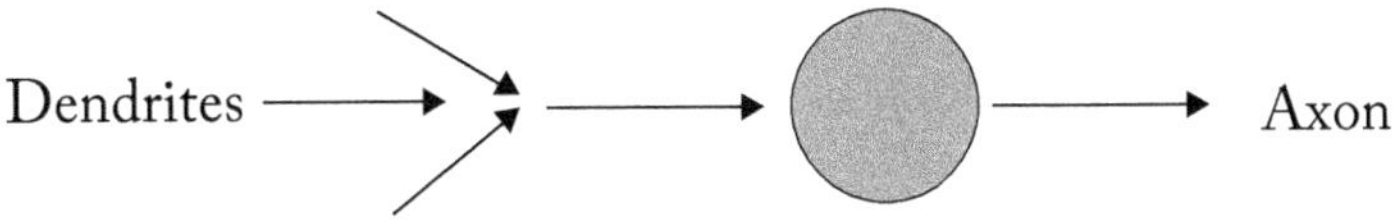

Computer Chip

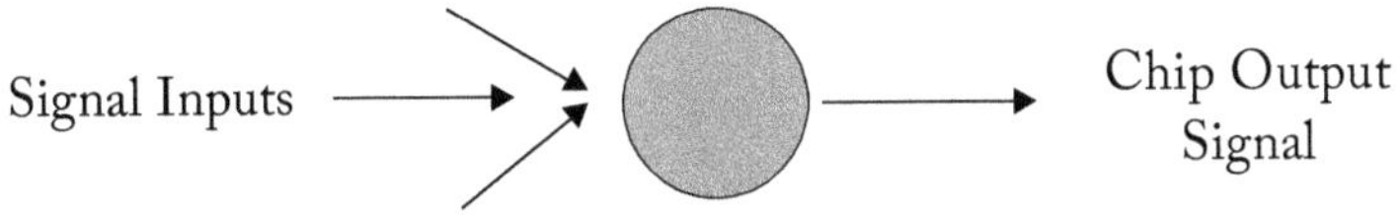

Applications that make Life Easier

- "Internet of Things" Digital Houses/Factories/Office Complexes
- "Smart Weapons" (Autonomous—Decides When to activate/Who to Target)
- "Augmented Reality" (Implanted Chips interfacing with Brain)
- "3-D Printers" (Think of Star Trek Replicators)
- Industrial Robots replacing Hi-Tech and Service Jobs
- "Robot Teachers" replace human teachers
- "Robot" Caregivers for Elderly
- Androids (Human-appearing Robots)
- Socio-Psychological Android Partners

Public Backlash

- Loss of Jobs and Loss of Human dignity
- People becoming Obsolete
- Fear of Trans-Human Capabilities

- Fear of Artificial Emotional Intelligence (Robots that have Feelings and Emotions)
- Fear of the "Singularity" (Machines become Self-Aware / Man is "Threat")
- Fear of Androids (Robots that look and act human)

Page 150—Tim Godfrey's Notes on Autism

Some facts:

- Autism more accurately called ASD (Autism Spectrum Disorder) for it covers a range of aberrant brain disorders.
- Sometimes misdiagnosed as ADHD (Attention Deficit/Hyperactivity Disorder).
- Symptoms include: Eye Contact and Verbal Communication Avoidance Inability to Sleep Poor Appetite Repetitive/Obsessive Behavior
- Awareness, not incidence has increased.

Who gets it?

- Can be diagnosed at 2 years of age.
- Males four times as likely as Females to manifest condition
- 1.2% of population has autism.

Causes:

- 70% Genetic-Related (Y-Chromosome sequences/interactions)
- 50% Environmental Factors (Pesticides Metals)
- Virus affecting Mitochondrial Metabolic or Cellular Defense Pathways
- Anti-Depressants taken at pregnancy
- Older Parents

Treatment:

- Drug Intervention (Serotonin Uptake Inhibitors)
- Childhood Education Strategies / Brain Training
- Socialization Practice
- What worked for Me:
- Studying Computers
- Social Skills drills
- Exercise and Eating Regularly

Page 153 and 199—Virtual Reality White Paper Summary

Perception is Reality. Whatever our Brain perceives is our reality. Note the distinctions: Virtual Reality is completely computer generated; Augmented Reality superimposes a computer-generated layer over 3-D reality. It will become the 8th Mass Media.

- First Seven (in Chronological Order): Print Radio Cinema Radio TV Internet Mobile

And it may be possible to link it directly to the brain by implanting computer chips, thus eliminating the need for helmets, goggles, glasses, or contact lenses.

Sci-Fi series StarTrek—The Next Generation created a plot device—the Holodeck 3-D virtual reality. Farfetched implementation, but conceptually believable. Here is the current state of Virtual Reality.

1. Computer Software creates a holographic world in which actual environments are scanned in and the User can modify or interact with through a Graphical User Interface (GUI).
2. Software allows the User to embed Avatars (one or more for the User) that simulate the User. The Avatar interacts with a game, script, movie or actual 3-D reality. The interactions are not pre-programmed, but instead are event-driven.
3. Virtual Reality Helmets or Goggles or Glasses or Contact Lenses, Haptic Gloves and Clothing (Wearable Technology) provide sensory input. (Smell-O-Vision

developed fifty years ago by neuroscientists and food chemists who decomposed all tastes and fragrances into Sweet, Sour, Bitter, Salty, and Umami (corresponds to taste of glutamates) and discovered how to recreate any by taste or fragrance by combining an appropriate proportion of each. Computer engineers devised digital encoding/decoding, allowing for a Smell Track (S-Track) that can inject aromas into the User's environment when the track is played. This track is analogous to audio and video tracks. Two additional tracks are being developed: a Spatial Orientation Track (O-Track) to simulate interaction with the environment (temperature directional motion intensity frequency), and a Touch Track (T-Track) for physical contact. The O-Track is used in Military Simulators and is being used more and more in commercial movies. A Brain Track (B-Track) for direct connection between the brain and device is in beta-testing and is not currently available in the public domain.

There are many beneficial applications:

- Medicine/Surgery News Sports Travel History Education Entertainment

There are also negative ones:

- Pornography Gambling Drinking/Drugs

Overarching negative implication: People withdrawing into Virtual Reality

The following diagram depicts a Military or Law Enforcement application already deployed: 24/7 Surveillance (Virtual Time Travel.) Cover geographic area with Drones or Satellites. Record high resolution data. Select ID's of Targets (People, Vehicles, etc.) to track. Use the data to construct Target Movement. Project backwards from "Crime Scene" to locate combatant Source Location. Project forwards to predict Battle Locations and Outcomes.

My idea: Deploy 24/7 Surveillance in Cyberspace to track, defend, or launch Cyberattacks.

24/7 Surveillance—Virtual Time Travel

On Station Drones / Satellites Recording High-Resolution Data

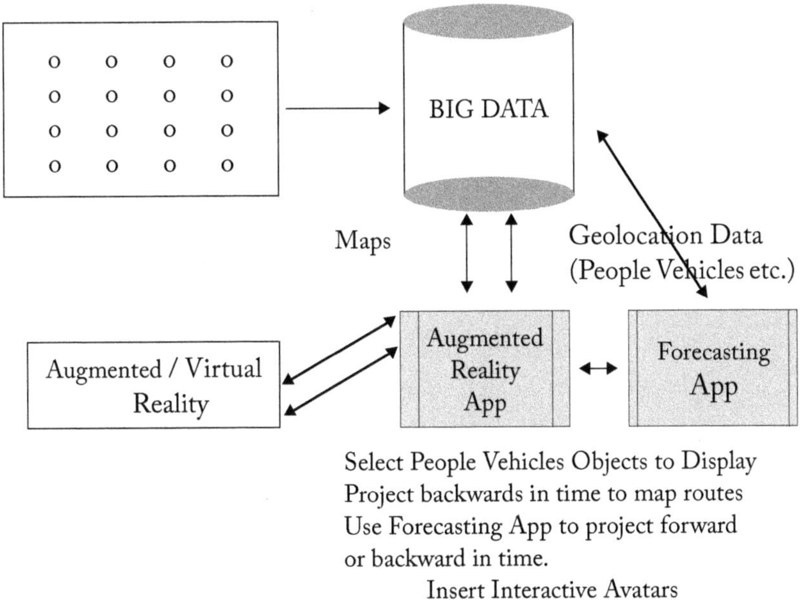

Virtual Reality ushers in a new age, the Virtual Age, which transcends distance and time, connecting us experientially with people and places. A chronology of mankind's ages includes: Stone Age, Agrarian Age, Industrial Age, Information Age, Knowledge Age, Virtual Age. Many people fear it, for it could lead to:

- Transhuman Age: Technology allows man to evolve beyond physical and mental limitations by embedding biotechnology and artificial intelligence in humans.
- Cyborg Age: Androids and artificially enhanced humans rule.

Pessimistic pundits predict those kinds of dystopias. The optimists, however, project the Wisdom Age. Just as Knowledge is the integration of information with experience, Wisdom is the integration of Extended Knowledge with Compassion and Empathy. Brave new ages await.

Users access virtual reality through a User Interface (UI). Doug Englebart, who extended Vannevar Bush's Memex concept, built the first GUI in the 1960's. His PhD thesis addressed how computers could augment human intelligence. He and Bill English, working at Xerox Palo Alto Research Center (PARC), invented the Mouse. PARC attracted the brightest minds and had many visitors, among them Bill Gates and Steve Jobs who saw the commercial potential. GUI's evolved rapidly:

- Command Line Interface (CLI) Mouse-Enabled Graphical User Interface (GUI) Tactile User Interface (TUI) Verbal User Interface (VUI) Bionic User Interface (BUI) Neural User Interface (NUI)

Users choose whatever UI works best for them. The Military uses Bionic and Neural User Interfaces, but only adventurous geeks and gamers go much beyond the conservative GUI.

UI computer graphics software is incredibly complex because it must project three dimensions onto only two. Color, shading, orientation, and texture must make the computer screen image (pixels) look three-dimensionally real. Dedicated graphics chips, computers, and projective algorithms push the limits of processing speed and complexity. Computer scientists admit there are asymptotic limits to what they can achieve, but are confident significant breakthroughs await.

Page 185—Soft Sciences Summary for Scientists and Engineers

Why Important to study:

- Advances in Computer Science and Genetic Engineering are driving changes in all areas of Society
- You need to add Soft Sciences to your Knowledge Base

Hard Sciences:

- Physics Chemistry Mathematics
- Biology Neuroscience Psychology

Soft Sciences:

Political Science Economics Sociology Anthropology

Designated as Sciences because they use Scientific Method

Starting Point: Sociology, because all other Soft Sciences fit underneath.

Definition of Sociology: Scientific study of Social Behavior that is embedded in a Culture. Identifies Problems and the Behaviors/ Actions taken to solve.

Comte, Spencer, Durkheim, Weber, and Marx developed Sociology in response to Darwin and Industrial Revolution.

Concerned with Group Relationships that determine: Status Income Power

Groups segmented by: Social Roles Ethnic/Racial/Gender Education Wealth/Power

Definition of Society: Large Social Group sharing Geography, Political Authority and Cultural Expectations

Types of Model Societies:

- Utopia Dystopia Cyberia Cybertopia

Definition of Culture: What a Society makes: Beliefs, Norms, Values

Culture shares products Groups make: Material Products Non-Material Products

Dimensions of Culture: Technology Symbols Language Values Norms

Social Change caused by: Disruptive Technology Integration of Outsiders Unrest

Types of Cultural Diversity: Extra-Societal Intra-Societal

• Sub-Cultures	Share important traits
• Counter-Cultures	Reject important traits
• Ethnocentrism	Exaggerated superiority of Own Group
• Reverse Ethnocentrism	Disrespecting certain Groups

Cultural Universals Exist: Family, Marriage, Society, Religion, Values

Cultural Variations:

- Peaceful versus Warlike
- Spiritual versus Material
- Faith versus Reason

Pay attention to:

- Diversity
- Watch out for Cultural Bias
- Balance Cultural Bias with Cultural Relativism

Frontline Issues today:

- Microaggression Gender/Sexual Discrimination Islam versus the West

Political Philosophy

- Oldest Soft Science dating back to Golden Age of Greece
- Very Stable because only a handful of Political Regimes/ Systems are viable: (Rule of the One Rule of the Few Rule of the Many)
- Progression of Great Thinkers: Socrates/Plato/Aristotle Machiavelli Hobbes Locke Hamilton/Madison/Jay Marx Tocqueville
- Addresses: Rights Liberty Freedom Equality Government Structure Law
- What is the "Best" form of Government? What is the "Best" Citizen?
- Courses in Politics would cover all the above in great detail

Definitions to Know

- Politics: The process by which Individual Interests are reconciled with Collective Action and the Provision of Public Goods.
- Regime: Political State/Government accorded monopoly power to enforce the Law.
- Democracy: Government ruled directly by the People.
- Republic: Form of government in which power is explicitly vested in the people, who in turn exercise their power through elected representatives. Today, the terms republic and democracy are virtually interchangeable, but historically the two differed.

- Monarchy: A country that is ruled by a monarch, and a monarchy is this system or form of government. A monarch, such as a king or queen, rules a kingdom or empire. In a constitutional monarchy, the monarch's power is limited by a constitution. But in an absolute monarchy, the monarch has unlimited power.
- Oligarchy: A form of rule in which power rests a small number of people.
- Feudalism: Feudalism was a combination of legal and military customs in medieval Europe that flourished between the 9th and 15th centuries. Broadly defined, it was a way of structuring society around relationships among Peasants, Knights, and Royalty, and derived from the holding of land in exchange for service or labor.
- Communism: Political theory derived from Karl Marx, advocating class war and leading to a society in which all property is publicly owned and each person works and is paid according to their abilities and needs.
- Socialism: A political and economic theory of social organization that advocates that the means of production, distribution, and exchange should be owned or regulated by the community as a whole.
- Totalitarianism: System of government that is centralized and dictatorial and requires complete subservience to the state.
- Fascism: Form of radical authoritarian nationalism, characterized by dictatorial power, forcible suppression of opposition and control of industry and commerce that came to prominence in early 20th-century Europe.
- Natzism: National Socialism more commonly known as Nazism is the ideology and set of practices associated with the 20th-century German Nazi Party in Nazi Germany and of other far-right groups. Usually characterized as

a form of fascism that incorporates scientific racism and antisemitism.

- Theocracy: A government in which Church and State are one and the same.
- Kleptocracy: A government with corrupt leaders (kleptocrats) that use their power to exploit the people and natural resources of their own territory in order to extend their personal wealth and power.

"Well-Known" Facts about Politics

No one likes Politics because:

- It is a fight over Scarce Public Resources
- Those unfamiliar with Democracy are startled by the arguing
- There are winners and losers
- Compromise guarantees everyone is "unhappy" they didn't get everything wanted

U.S. Political System makes it hard to make changes quickly. (Per Kahneman, this is good!)

Current Trajectory of Politics

Purpose: To summarize Political Dynamics that shape direction and project where current trends lead.

Politics as old as Civilization but the philosophical underpinnings for Political Dynamics are "new."

- Hegel's World View: His philosophical system, supported by Enlightenment, predicted Civilization would move by "force of will" dialectics (thesis antithesis synthesis) towards Liberal Democracy.

- Kogeve: Extended Hegel to conclude "End of History" at the French Revolution (Socialist-Capitalist synthesis)
- Francis Fukuyama: Concluded in the 1980's "an end of History" culminating in Liberal Capitalism

Collapse of the Soviet Union (1989) confounded "End of History". Samuel Huntington's book "The Clash of Civilizations" (1996) presents a better explanation.

- Collapse ends World Polarization into Free World and Communism camps.
- Clashes will develop at the fault lines between major Civilizations: The West (America, Great Britain, Australia), Europe, China, India, Japan, Russia, Islam, Africa, Latin America
- Clashes caused not by Ideology or Economics, but by Culture.
- Early 21st century events confirm validity.
- Warnings for America: Scale back Democratic State-Building Avoid War

Fukuyama responds by writing two landmark books: The Origins of Political Order Political Order and Political Decay

Findings:

- State-Building is driven by Modernization and Technology
- Liberal Democracy is not the guaranteed "End of History"
- Must have three collections of Institutions: State (Power and Administration) Rule of Law (stems from Religion) Accountability (stems from Interest Groups)
- Not all roads lead to "Denmark" (Denmark considered desirable "End")

- Interplay among Economic Growth Social Mobility Ideas/ Legitimacy determine path to an End-State
- Revolution sometimes necessary to dislodge corrupt government.
- Once Denmark is achieved, State must be ever-watchful to maintain supporting Institutions (avoid political decay)

New generation of Political Scientists include Network Theory

- Historical Tools: Printing Press Railroads Interstate Highways Internet
- Networks empower Social Animal Man and limit Hierarchical Government
- Cyberspace: the Next Battlefield
- Futuristic Network: Collective Consciousness

Current Landscape:

China's march to world dominance ended by:

- Aging Population: Too many Retirees Too few Young Workers
- Economic Stagnation: Directed Capitalism Inefficiency Crony Capitalism Corruption Middle Class Frustration
- Disrespect of Immigrants and Women
- Bureaucracy and Educational System Inadequacies for Creativity or Innovation

Russia marginalized itself on the World Stage:

- Rule of Law still inadequate
- Government still a Kleptocracy
- Economy still Resource-Based
- Population still imploding

Islam remains Problematic:

- Economy still dominated by Oil and Gas (ineffective diversification)
- Islamist Theocracy rejects Modernity
- War against Christianity continues
- Entrenched Intolerance towards Westerners and Women

The rest of the World still has problems but is moving forward:

- Europe halts population decline by absorbing Middle East Immigrants
- India endorses Democracy and Human Rights
- Democracy and Capitalism spur African Development
- Latin America moderates "Boom/Bust" Economic Cycles and Political Instability
- America remains the World's Economic Engine but must cope with Terrorism and Techno-Plague while relearning the Politics of Compromise, reducing International Free-Riders, while avoiding the rise of Populist Nationalism.

America's Internal Issues:

- Job Loss and Income Inequality due to Automation
- Infrastructure Decay (Transportation, Energy, Communications)
- Political and Population Polarization
- Public's growing reluctance to embrace new technology (AI Genetic Engineering)
- Vetocracy leading to Gridlock
- Declining Public Participation
- Washington "Disconnect" with Main Street
- T-Plague ramifications

The Current World Order not amenable to "Kinder and Gentler"

- Realpolitik practices necessary
- State Sovereignty impacted by Culture and Geography
- Friendly Autocracies might be better partners than Unruly Democracies
- Prudent Projection of Power required
- Humility required instead of Hubris

Page 216—A Bullet Point Critique of My Thesis

WHAT MY THESIS ACCOMPLISHES:

- Designing my Neural Probe device that potentiates neurons associated with cognition and emotional states
- Developing drugs that target selected brain cells
- Using my Neural Probe to activate a "critical number" of neurons
- Measuring neural responses that confirm cognitive and emotional states
- Empirically demonstrating that consciousness is an emergent phenomenon caused by a critical number of interacting neurons and synapses.

My work demonstrates that cognitive neuroscience can be studied "scientifically" according to Karl Popper's falsification epistemology because it is measuring observable phenomena. It builds on the four foundational principles of Cognitive Neuroscience

- Cognition emerges from complex inter-neuronal interactions
- Synaptic signal strength mediates learning and memory
- "Information processing" done at the cell membrane, not inside the cell
- Bayesian statistics (prior probabilities updated by results to yield posterior probabilities) models neuronal outputs

I can extend my thesis into many practical areas, such as genetic therapy, genetic modification, neural stimulation, brain emulation

I do not need to drill down into the microtubule level to make practical contributions. Microtubules are neural structures made of tubulin protein that conduct charges along nerve axons and dendrites. Quantum Neuroscience theorizes that consciousness is embedded in nerve signal firing mediated by microtubules. Consciousness is quantized into nerve signal firing analogous to light quantized into photons.

- Protein/enzyme reactions as charge carriers travel along a microtubule mediate information transfer that embodies awareness/cognition.
- Quantum mechanics needed to "explain how it works" (are living organisms too warm, wet, and noisy for quantum mechanics?)
- Quantum mechanical principles needed: Wave Function Uncertainty Principle Tunneling Superpositioning Entanglement Coherence

Quantum Neuroscience today is similar to "the Heroic Age" of High Energy Physics for which new theories could be tested experimentally. The heroic age ended almost 200 years ago when "Mere Humanity" collided with reality:

- Asymptotic Limits. There are concepts/phenomena that are inaccessible to the human brain (carbon-based cognition)
- Complexity. The human brain cannot handle complexity much beyond "billions and billions," even with the aid of quantum computers
- Computability. The human brain cannot handle computational algorithms beyond "polynomial time." Even with quantum-enhanced neural network computers, "Mere

Mortals" can't solve NP problems. Turing Computability remains an impenetrable barrier.

- Godel's Incompleteness Theorems. Mathematics and mathematical logic, as structured by the human brain, is contradictory. Their formal systems contain true statements that cannot be proved, and provable statements that are not true.
- High Energy Physics degenerated from science to a "religious philosophy" because it can no longer test its theories experimentally. Its thought experiments are fanciful constructs.
- The Explosion Principle. A theorem in logic proving that anything can be proved from two contradictory assumptions. Legendary 20th century physicist Richard Feynman used it to blow up many scientific or philosophic conjectures, often labeling their contents "Baloney."

Page 230—Terrorism, T-Plague, and the Political Climate

A Sobering Assessment

PART ONE: "BEYOND THE Soundbite" Summary of Three Interrelated Issues

Terrorism:

- A Virus infecting Humanity
- Long-term Issue
- Ideology-Based: Islam versus Christianity
- Each Terrorism Round another Jihad
- Current Round uses T-Plague as WMD
- T-Plague eventually (?) controlled, but another Terrorist WMD (TBD) will be Unleashed
- The Cure: Defeat Radical Islam Ideology

T-Plague:

- Incredibly difficult to control
- 20+ Years of R&D have produced little
- "What doesn't kill me will make me strong?"
- Must be realistically "Optimistic"

Political Climate:

- Post-Modern World requires Global/International Outlook
- Policy of Appeasement/Coexistence doomed to fail
- Confront the illegitimate Regimes
- Partner with those who desire Modernity
- Support Revolution from Within
- "Boots on the Ground" may be unavoidable

"America Strong" Required for Success but there are disturbing trends here:

- National I.Q. lower
- Intolerance higher
- Fear Factor higher
- Self-Reliance lower (Let the Government take care of everything)

Blame it on the T-Plague! Liberal Democracy demands an Intelligent, Informed, and Involved Public

Disturbing Parallels between Today and Roman Caesars:

- Rising Inequality
- Dislocations of Traditional Ways of Life
- Increasing Political Polarization
- Breakdown of Unspoken Rules of Political Conduct
- A set of "Elites" obsessed with Own Privileges

Could Tyranny rule in America?

- Unable to balance the Politics of Inevitability (End of History is Liberal Democracy) versus Politics of Eternity (Vicious Cycle)

Lessons on Tyranny

What to look for:

- One-Party State (Support multiple parties)
- Paramilitary Groups (Beware the Vigilantes)
- Abandonment of Political Ethics
- Lies replacing facts
- Politicians hiding behind Patriotic Slogans
- Politicians turning Crises into Exceptional Moments that become Permanent Emergencies
- Government prying into Private Lives
- Governments combining forces to Control People

How to Combat:

- Don't obey in Advance (Civil Disobedience)
- Defend/Support Conservative Institutions
- Dig into the Details (Go beyond Soundbites)
- Get involved in Local Politics
- Be Calm if/when the Unthinkable happens
- Be as Courageous a Patriot as You can be
- Don't surrender Freedom for Safety

"If no one is willing to die for Freedom, then all of us will die under Tyranny."

U.S. fortunate to know all the above! "Those who do not learn from History are destined to repeat it!"

Part Two: America's Political Muddle

Purpose: Explain how we got to Now. Now and its Current Risks. The Way Forward.

The path to Now:

- Started with 911 (America awakened to Terrorism in an interconnected World)
- Exacerbated when America lost its "First Political Cyberwar" (2016 Presidential Election: Russia violated America's political sovereignty by using the Internet, Political Climate, and Inequality to divide voters and get their preferred candidate elected)

America learned what it needs to "keep America strong"

- Democracy, Capital, and Innovation mutually support a strong America
- A smart, self-reliant and politically engaged people are fundamental
- Embrace four convergent technologies: Nanotech, Biotech, Infotech, Artificial Intelligence

And it took the right steps that would lead to a prosperous and sustainable future

- Upgraded it K-16 educational system to tailor programs to each student and make universal education affordable. The result: America's Youth equipped for the future job market.
- Protected human rights, privacy, and dignity for the individual

- Embraced globalization, world trade, and interconnected politics
- Adjusted "American Exceptionalism" to be a smarter Superpower
- Allowed capital markets to embrace technological development
- Addressed Economic and Social Inequality
- Strengthened Political Cyberwar Defenses (Better Internet Security Hardware/Software, heightened protection for News and Identity)
- Returned to civil political debates for Compromise towards the Middle

What Went Wrong?

- Public took its eye off the politicians
- Administrations became too "Kind and Gentle" dealing with international issues
- Administrations became too lax on terrorism and security
- Administrations lost sight of what made America great
- Public became fearful of Biotech and AI Trends

Then Came the Techno-Plague

- Insidious damage to public I.Q. and Psyche (dumber, frightened, intolerant, shun personal responsibility for controlling Government)
- Frayed infrastructures (Transportation, Energy, Communications

Creating a "Perfect Storm" (T-Plague, Terrorism, and Hi-tech Issues) allowing the Guardian Party to emerge.

- Jury is still out on the Guardians
- Ideally, their policies can find the golden mean between "Kinder and Gentler" and "Harsh Times demand Harsh Measures"
- Hidden agenda may be overblown

Political/Guardian Party Climate Today

- Backward rather than forward-looking
- Might curtail individual rights and freedoms
- Turning away from immigration and an interconnected World
- Curtailing technological progress to preserve suboptimal jobs
- Short-term policies not in longer-term public interest
- More Populist than all-inclusive

Disturbing Parallels for a Second Political Cyberwar

- China replaces Russia (China is faltering because of an aging population, a closed society, and backward-looking Communist Party, but wants more Power on the World Stage)
- T-Plague replaces the Internet Crisis and contributes to Polarized Politics
- Artificial Intelligence contributes to Inequality and loss of meaningful jobs

The Way Forward

- Must repair T-Plague damage
- Must repair infrastructures and prepare for the next field of battle (Cyber-space)

- Must work with the International Community
- Must balance Hi-tech with Economic and Ethical considerations
- Must guard against Second Political Cyberwar
- Must balance shorter-term Realpolitik national interests versus longer-term state-building values
- Must protect Multi-Party Dialogue and deescalate Populism
- Must balance "Politics of Distinction/Local Circumstances" against "Ends-Based Vanguardism/Elitism"

Page 270—My Introduction to Economics

ECONOMICS: THE STUDY OF how society chooses, with or without the use of money, to employ scarce productive resources to produce various products and services over time and distribute them for consumption, now and in the future, among various people and groups in society.

Economics labeled the "Dismal Science" because it deals with Scarcity and Tradeoffs. Economics founded by Adam Smith in the 1770's, and Paul Samuelson launched Neoclassical Economics in the 1950's. (See his classic text *Economics an Introductory Analysis.*) Robert Heilbroner's book, "The Worldly Philosophers," trumpeting the founders of Economics, gives a good introduction to how "The Dismal Science" started.

- Two Branches: Microeconomics studies the Individual and the Corporation Macroeconomics studies the overall Economy

The following topics support both branches:

- Positive Economics analyzes the way things are. Normative Economics discusses the way things should be. (Note the connection to Ethics).
- Fundamental questions to answer: What Goods and Services to Produce? How to produce them? Who gets them? (Note the connection to Philosophy)

Modern Economics constructs complex Mathematical Models to explain itself.

- Constrained Optimization Theory must often approximated, leading to Opacity and Imprecision.
- Consumers optimize "Utility" (note connection to Philosophy) and Corporations optimize Profits (note connection to Ethics)
- The most important State Variable is PRICE
- Today we have a system of "General Equilibrium Models", but as with High Energy Physics, the models are only approximate

Economics built on Five Key Assumptions

1. Unlimited Wants and Scarce Resources
2. Trade-offs due to Scarcity
3. Individuals and Corporations respond to "incentives" according to Self-Interest
4. Decisions made according to Rational Marginal Cost Marginal Benefit Analysis
5. Output of General Equilibrium Models best explained by a set of Graphs approximating Real Life

Note: Number 3 and 5 confounded by Behavioral Economics! Try to adjust the models for the Irrational Economic Man.

Illustrative Example: A student deciding how to get the textbook for a course. Should the student buy a new text ($140) or a used text ($70) or work with a team that gets only one book? You think about it!

Macroeconomics deals with "Big Issues" at the National level:

- Growth Income and Inequality Wages Unemployment Inflation International Trade Interest Rates

Facts to Consider

Applying Economics relies on:

- Common Sense explanations
- Intuitive Graphical representation of Economic Theory and Equations
- Sophisticated software that presents graphical "constrained optimization" solutions
- Big Data and Empirical Testing of Theory and Policy
- Substitution and Income Effects, though easy to understand, can confound Conventional Wisdom. Here are some examples of how Psychology impacts observed results via Behavioral Economics: Backward-Sloping Supply Curve for Labor (Raise the Wage rate and people work less). Downward-Sloping Demand Curve violation (Demand increases if you raise Price)
- Economic Analysis very useful assessing Government Policies

Contrast this with High Energy Physics

- No Common Sense explanations
- No intuitive graphical representation of Theory or Equations
- No graphical "constrained optimization" solutions
- No Empirical Testing of Theory
- Quantum Mechanical Effects not easy to understand AND confound conventional wisdom. Some examples: Supercooled Helium climbs out of a container. Particles being in two places simultaneously.
- Usefulness of High Energy Physics is problematic.

Page 274—High Flight

(Flying Officer John Gillespie Magee, an Anglo-American RAF Fighter Pilot and Poet, died in an accidental mid-air collision over England on December 11, 1941)

Oh, I have slipped the surly bonds of earth
And danced the sky on laughter-silvered wings.
Sun-wards I've climbed, and joined the tumbling mirth
Of sun-split clouds—and done a thousand
things You have not dreamed of.
Wheeled and soared;
And swung high in sunlit silence; hovering there.

I've chased the shouting winds along,
and Flung my eager craft through footless halls of air.
Up, up the long, delirious, burning blue air.

I've topped the windswept heights with easy grace
Where lark, or even eagle flew.
And while with silent, lifting mind I trod
The high un-trespassed sanctity of space;
Put out my hand and touched the face of God.

Page 312—Cybersecurity Primer

- Purpose of Cybersecurity: Make networks available to User while guaranteeing Integrity and Confidentiality
- Security became a problem only when computers became prevalent and networked.
- Industry recognized the problem around 2000 when Cybercrime became a "big business" (Perfect Storm caused by Proliferation of Networked PC's Collapse of Soviet Union Computer Industry "asleep")
- Darknet's Silk Road surfaced in 2013 America lost first Political Cyberwar in the 2016 Presidential election

Steps Taken on Corporate/Political Front

- Computer Industry placed Security Development Lifecycle in its Hardware/Software Development Lifecycle
- Developed security protocols and standards maintained by Computer Engineering Institute
- Added "Vulnerability Management" to its suite of Customer Services
- Government acted quickly to confront a new enemy: Cybercriminals (Established laws and international alliances Built Cybersecurity Agencies ultimately reporting in to Securityguard

Steps Taken on Technological Front

- Recognized areas of vulnerability: Social Networking/ People Network Snooping Password Protection Software Virus Attacks Hardware/Firewall/Network Surface Attack Points

Solutions

- Make users aware of Cybersecurity risks (Works for Governents and Corporations but not well for individuals)
- Develop better private key/public key encryption algorithms
- Build Biometric Authentication (Voice Recognition Fingerprinting Visual Recognition DNA Identification)
- Combine for Multi-Factor Authentication
- Develop antivirus software to identify/kill/remove malware
- Build malware protection into firewalls
- Place Client Virtual Computer/Network in Server Cloud Hardware
- Reinforce Cloud Surface Attack Points to thwart Attack Vectors

Caveats

- Quantum Computing poses threat for simplistic encryption algorithms
- Cybercriminals always looking to exploit security flaws

Opportunities for Our Company

- No need for us to build better hardware. Current hardware exceeds the needs of competitive cybersecurity software.
- Our approach: Sell our superior antivirus software

Why Our Software is Better
(This Slide is Just for Me)

- Competitors are "mere mortals" who don't have the programing skills I do
- My antivirus software incorporates neural network techniques that allow it to learn/identify/kill/remove viruses and malware

For the Future

- Develop my suite of Cyberweapons to destroy my enemies in a Cyberwar

Page 325—Network Security Seminar

(Presented by Darla Tinabu, President of Cybergard)
Network Security in the Brave New World of Artificial Intelligence

RUSSIA DEFEATED THE UNITED STATES IN 2016 CYBERWAR I !!!

- Russia hacked into Media Sites and Email Accounts, planting bogus information that swayed voters so Donald Trump elected.
- Ever since, the United States has upgraded Network Security to avoid a Cyber 9/11 and guard against more Cyberwars.
- But threats are still lurking. Even Air-Gapped Networks protected by Firewalls can be penetrated.

Some of the Risks Network Security guards against:

- Identity Theft Data Theft Misinformation Substitution
- Power, Transportation, Communications, Banking Network shutdown
- Computer Hijacking Malware/Virus Intrusion
- Rogue Operating System or App launch to take over the Internet of Things

All threats launched by:

- Intercepting Encrypted Data, Decrypting and Altering/Embedding, then Encrypting and Re-Transmitting the Data

- Planting Apps controlled by "the Enemy"

Note the convergent technology-driven trajectory of Computing. It went from Mainframes to Personal Computers to Laptops to Tablets to Mobile Computing to Distributed Device Computing (factory machines, military weapons, home appliances, wearable devices, body implants). Today, all devices connect to a Network that interconnects with the Internet. All are subject to the security threats previously described.

Cybergard's proprietary network security hardware and software can neutralize attacks from all the above-identified risks (even for Air-Gapped Networks defended by Firewalls) by using:

- Randomly generated passwords and biometric authorization methods
- Verification or encryption/decryption techniques
- Virus Detection/Removal supplied by propriety software.

If you are concerned about the data on your air-gapped machine, I highly recommend that you:

- secure that machine either offsite in a safeguarded room;
- make sure all cables to the machine are properly shielded (don't cut corners on cables here);
- plug unused USB slots with the USB port blockers;
- turn the machine off when it is not in use (and unplug from power);
- replace standard drives with SSD;
- encrypt your data.

Ultimately, air-gapped machines should be considered a viable solution for sensitive data that doesn't need to be accessed over a network. With a few simple precautions, you can avoid that data getting into the wrong hands.

Two Components to Network Security:

- Social Engineering—Manipulate people to divulge information
- Network Engineering—Computer Hardware and Software automatically send information or run apps without human intervention.

Today's talk covers Network Engineering Security you can buy from Cybergard.

Quick History:

- DARPA (Defense Advanced Research Projects Agency) created first computer network (ARPANET) in the 1960's. The Goal: Defense Department computer capability survive nuclear attack.
- Personal Computer Revolution in the 1980's spurred growth of the Public Domain Internet.
- Worldwide Web explosion created new uses for sending data over the Internet.
- Internet Security became "big issue" when Government and Industry realized "big threat" from hacking by Criminals or Companies or Foreign Countries.

Computer Networks Today

Computer Network: An interconnected collection of computers, each one controlling information or devices, that exchange data and compute results of value to the end user.

Most computers exist as "virtual computers" created in Cyberspace (Cloud Computing) and controlled by physical hardware owned by an Internet Service Provider.

Network Security needed to protect the user from criminal intent. The list of threats grows and grows. Some examples:

• Identity theft	Hacking into Private Accounts	Hijacking the Computer
• Planting Malware or Viruses	Stealing Data	Planting False Data

Network Security has these basic components:

User Verification Firewalls Data Encryption/Decryption

Virus Detection Virus Removal

User Verification includes Passwords Q&A Handwriting Biometrics (Facial Recognition Retinal Scans Fingerprint Voice Recognition DNA Matching)

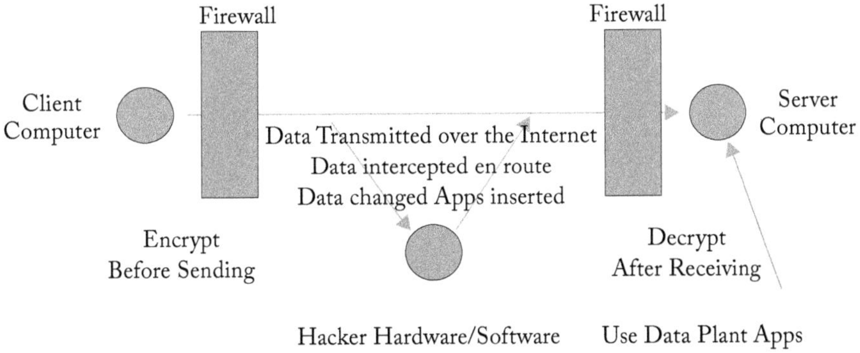

Encryption/Decryption and Malware/Virus recognition techniques are used for Data as well as for apps transmitted to Client or Server Computers.

Historical Encryption/Decryption Techniques:

- Caesar Cypher: Shift the alphabet
- Engma Machine: WWII German device encrypt and decrypt messages

Today, all techniques for stealing Data or inserting Apps are an extension of the "Grand Daddy" encryption methodology: RSA Public/Private Key Encryption (Roberts-Shamir-Ableman)

Simple Idea: Encrypt with Public Key and Decrypt with Private Key

For Geeks Only

Godel's Completeness Theorems: Propositional and Predicate Logics are consistent and complete: if a statement is true, it can be proved, and if it can be proved, it is true. Important because much of Artificial Intelligence programming relies on it.

However, as we advance to Modal Logic and more inclusive mathematical systems, we encounter unsolvable problems described in other Godel theorems.

Godel's Incompleteness Theorems: Two theorems of logic that demonstrate the inherent limitations of every formal axiomatic system containing basic arithmetic. Very dense, difficult theorems that conclude not every true statement can be proved, nor is every proof correct.

Why important: Alan Turing and John Nash used them to guide "Universal Computer" and "Algorithmic Game Theory Program Design."

Big Issue today for Network Security: NP computer problems that can't be solved in "Polynomial Time", and can't be verified in Polynomial Time.

What it means: Even Quantum Computers to not have enough Memory or Processing Speed (cycles per second) to verify a solution. Major stumbling block for AI.

Data Encryption for Network Security is critical example where the stumbling block helps. RSA and its extended encryption algorithms are built on Abstract Algebra theorems for relative prime number factoring. Encryption based on Public and Private "keys" that are relative prime numbers. Security demands it be an NP problem so the Private Key can't be cracked.

Graphic Analogy: You can tie a multiply-tangled knot quickly, but it takes a long time to untangle it.

The longer the keys, the safer the algorithm. (Safety measured in the length of time to crack the private key and decrypt a message.)

Note: State-of-the-Art Quantum Computing and programs require "Years" to decrypt 1024 bit-length keys.

Network Security is Top Priority Today

- Cryptographic attacks signal the start of Cyber-Warfare
- Shadow-Cyberspace and the Darknet use TOR Browser (The Onion Routing Browser) to circumvent detection
- Risks are greater than ever for Personal, Corporate, and National Security

Government, Industry, and International Law Enforcement have cooperated. Today, if state-of-the-art techniques are used, data can be exchanged confidentially and accurately.

Even the best hackers and crackers, using the latest Quantum Computers and Quantum Programming techniques, can't achieve data storage and processing speed requirements needed to "break in" if you use Cybergard Security Systems. Our systems are equivalent to Quantum Cryptography. We're as good as it gets.

THE BOTTOM LINE: YOU CAN DEFEND YOURSELF WITH CUTTING EDGE CYBERGARD TOOLS.

ANY QUESTIONS?

Page 346—Why Trinomial Factoring Works

TRINOMIAL FACTORING IS A "rite of passage" for just about all high school or college students when taking a College Algebra course. It is perhaps the first time in their mathematical studies when the connection between an algorithm they are using (what they do to factor the trinomial) and the desired result (expressing the trinomial as the product of two linear factors) is not very apparent. After some amount of practice, students are able to factor trinomials and become quite good at "experimenting" until they find the right combination. However, they often feel they are missing some "trick" that would make the process obvious.

If you have ever encountered the above situation, you might find the approach described in this paper to be more to your (and your student's) liking. And along the way, your students will learn a bit more about algorithms (a very important topic in computer programming) and proof theory (constructive versus existence proofs).

We start by stating what an integer coefficient trinomial is, and what we wish to accomplish:

A trinomial with integer coefficients is a polynomial containing terms of the zero, first and second degree. Here is an example:

6X**2 + 13X + 6

What we want to do is express the trinomial as the product of two linear factors each having integer coefficients. In this example, it is:

(3X + 2) x (2X + 3)

In general, the trinomial is expressed as:

AX**2 + BX + C

where A, B and C are integers.

What we want to do is express it as follows:

AX**2 + BX + C = (MX + N) x (PX + Q)

where M, N, P and Q are also integers.

Next we state what our procedure, or algorithm is for solving the problem:

"Our procedure is first to find two integers (call them r and s) such that their product equals A*C and their sum equals B. We might not be able to do this, in which case we cannot factor this particular trinomial into integer coefficient components."

"After we find these two integers, we then write the original trinomial as:

AX**2 + (r + s)X + C = AX**2 + rX + sX + C

At this point we must experiment (using trial and error with the commutative and associative laws by grouping one of the linear terms with AX**2 and the other with C) to remove common factors. Once we do this, we will be able, by inspection (i.e. by looking at what we have), to identify a common factor between the two groupings. Pulling out this common factor gives us the factored trinomial."

We need to illustrate how our algorithm works using a simple example for which A = 1. This will help our students understand how to use the algorithm.

X**2 + 7X + 12 (A = 1 B = 7 C = 12)

According to our algorithm, we must find two integers whose product is 12 and whose sum is 7. We start by tabulating all combinations of 2 numbers whose product is 12. (Tell your students that this is an application of the Fundamental Theorem of Arithmetic!). The combinations are : 1,12 2,6 3,4 -1,-12 -2,-6 -3,-4.

Put their sum in a table:

Combinations whose product is 12 1,12 2,6 3,4 -1,-12 -2,-6 -3,-4

Sum of the integers 13 8 7 -13 -8 -7

We see that the 3,4 combination sum equals 7, so we have found our 2 integers.

Now we write our trinomial as:

X**2 + (3 + 4)X + 12

Now we group (by experimentation or trial and error!) either the 3X or 4X with X**2 and the other term with 12 to get:

(X**2 + 3X) + (4X + 12)

And now pull out the common factor in each to get:

X(X + 3) + 4(X + 3)

And now (by inspection) we see the common factor of (X + 3). We can use this common factor to arrive at our final answer:

(X + 3)(X + 4)

Students will need to see or work additional simple examples to become more comfortable with the procedure. It takes practice!

We now should illustrate the algorithm when the coefficient of the second degree term is different from 1. This is harder for students to see the connection between what they do and what they want. (We will explain why this is so later.)

Let's apply our algorithm to this example:

8X**2 + 2X-15 (A = 8 B = 2 C = -15)

We want to find two integers whose product is -120 and whose sum is 2. Here is the "combinations table":

Combinations whose product is -120 -1,120 -4,30 -6,20 -8,15 -10,12

Sum of the integers 119 26 14 7 2

We see that the -10,12 combination sum equals 2, so we have found our two integers.

We write our trinomial as:

8X**2 + (12-10)X-15

And group the terms (by trial and error or experimentation or inspection!):

(8X**2 + 12X)-(10X + 15)

Remove common factors to get:

4X(2X + 3)-5(2X + 3)

which can be written as:

(4X-5)(2X + 3) which is our final answer.

By this time, the students should have seen and worked enough examples and problems to feel pretty comfortable applying the algorithm. It is now appropriate to explain a bit more about algorithms in general, and the "trinomial factoring algorithm" in particular. You might try the following:

"An algorithm is a step-by-step procedure (list of instructions) that tells you what to do to accomplish something. (For example, your Mother has an algorithm for baking a cake!) Algorithms are very important in computer programming, because when you write a program you are actually writing an algorithm your program will execute. ALL the steps must be specified completely when you write a program, because the computer cannot fill in any missing or "vague" steps."

"Take another look at our trinomial factoring algorithm. It mentions in several places that you must figure something out by experimenting, or by trial-and-error, or by inspection. What this means is that you must "play with the expression," using the basic laws of algebra to arrive at term groupings that let you pull out common factors. There are so many combinations to try that it is impractical to write all of them down step-by-step! This is the main reason why students feel a bit uncomfortable at first with the algorithm. The algorithm tells them in a step-by-step fashion what to do up to the point where the students must now "fill in the rest of the steps" by themselves. THINKING is now required!"

So now your students are able to apply the trinomial factoring algorithm, and understand why they initially felt a bit uncomfortable with it. And some of them should be thinking or asking the question, "Why does the algorithm work?" The answer takes us into the basics of proof theory. You might try the following explanation:

- There are basically two types of mathematical proofs: constructive and existence. In a constructive proof, the thing you are looking for is actually derived (constructed) in the proof. An existence proof, on the other hand, simply shows that the thing you are looking for exists, but it does not derive the actual result.

From what we have learned about the trinomial factoring algorithm, we might suspect that we can establish and existence proof. (There are too many possible factoring combinations to incorporate into a constructive proof.) So, here is an existence proof:

Suppose we can factor an integer coefficient trinomial into two linear factors each having linear coefficients (i.e. rational roots). Then we can write our trinomial as follows:

$$AX**2 + BX + C = (MX + N)x(PX + Q) =$$
$$MPX**2 + (MQ + NP)xX + NQ$$

where A, B, C, M, N, Q, and Q are all integers.

Because this expression is an identity, we can equate coefficients to obtain:

1. A = MxP
2. B = MxQ + NxP
3. C = NxQ

Combining 1) and 3) by multiplying and keeping 2), we get these two equations:

1. AxC = MxPxNxQ = MxQxNxP
2. B = MxQ + NxP

But MxQ and NxP are simply integers. Call them R and S. Our equations become:

1. AxC = RxS
2. B = R + S

In other words, integers R and S exist such that their product equals A and their sum equals B. This is precisely what the Trinomial Factoring Theorem says.

We have just proved that if an integer coefficient trinomial can be factored into integer coefficient components, we can find two integers whose product equals A times C and sum equals B. And because the proof is done with inequalities, it also proves that if we can find two integers whose product equals A times C and sum equals B, we can factor the trinomial.

Let's summarize. We have noticed that the trinomial factoring algorithm is at first often puzzling for students because a proof is often omitted in textbooks, and even if it were, it is only loosely connected with the step-by-step factoring procedure because it is an existence proof. In this paper, we have illustrated how the factoring algorithm works and have given an existence proof.

Best wishes to you and your students…

Page 336—Our Transhuman Future

(Post-Biological Age dominated by Self-
Improving Thinking Machines)

Purpose of this Seminar: Provide an "audience friendly" summary of a Transhuman Future debate between the Two Cultures (Arts versus Sciences) guided by believable principles:

- The Singularity emerges in a Distant Dawn (the Singularity is "Not Near")
- Assumes current trajectory of Genetics, Nanotechnology, and Robotics (GNR)
- Must stay within the lines drawn by Falsifiable Physics (Matter and Energy Equivalence Entropy and Quantum Mechanics set Asymptotic Limits)
- Must stay within Neuroscience principles (Mind and Brain are one, Cultural Memes become embedded in DNA)
- "Mere Humanity's" Physical, Cognititive, and Emotional Personas experience no short-term "Punctuated Evolution"
- Avoid long-term projections that are the realm of Science Fiction (Emergence of "Thinking Universe" that avoids "Heat Death" caused by Entropy Grand Unified Field Theory reveals Multi-verse)
- Focus on short-term because that's where we live

Where Man Came From

- 100 million years ago—Favored gene lines stumbled onto "Learning"
- 10 million years ago—Primates learned to use tools
- 1 million years ago—Homo Sapiens' tribes emerged
- 100 thousand years ago—Cultures emerged
- 10 thousand years ago—Snowballing advances in culture dominate favored changes in Gene Pool

Where Man is Going
Six Epochs of Man

- Epoch One—Physics and Chemistry rule (using Math, Matter/Energy, Time)
- Epoch Two—Biology and DNA (Utilize Biotech to harness DNA power)
- Epoch Three—Human Brain at the top of the "Food Chain"
- Epoch Four—Artificial Intelligence-based Technologies (Man and Machine cooperate)
- Epoch Five—Transhumanism (Merger of Artificial Intelligence-based Technologies and Biological Organisms)
- Epoch Six—Transhumanism awakens the Universe (Life spreads/found "Out There")

We are in Epoch Four

Five Stages of Civilization

- Stage 0—Dead Planet: Fossil Fuels Minimal Recycling
- Stage 1—Planet Power: Harness Earth's Energy (Wind Tides Solar) Recycle
- Stage 2—Star Power: Sci-Fi Conjectures (Think Star-Trek)

- Stage 3—Galaxy Power: Far-Out Sci-Fi (Think Star Wars)
- Stage 4—Power of the Continuum: ??? Universe Awakens (The Q-Civilization)

We are on the Cusp of Stage 1

Artificial Intelligence Status

- Narrow/Weak AI—Non-Sentient Computers good at focused tasks (Medical Diagnosis, Chess) Exhibit Intelligence and Learning
- Strong/General AI—Computers master Cognitive Skills and Learning beyond Homo Sapiens Capabilities (This is the Singularity!)

We are well into Narrow AI

- Quantum Computer storage capacity and speed spearheads Hardware Development and Solutions of "hard problems—Non-Deterministic Polynomial time (NP Problems)
- Needed: Better Software!

Impediments to Progress

- We aren't "smart enough" to take physics to the next level
- We aren't "smart enough" to close the gap between hardware and software
- Society ambivalent about what AI offers
- People are afraid of what they don't understand
- Government attempts to control development (Impossible to put Genie back in the bottle!)
- Humanity contains a spiritual component that cannot be measured
- Man is genetically predisposed to conservatism and to seek God

Risks

- Exponential Growth leads to runaway General AI
- Unforeseen Side Effects damage Societies
- Software Viruses "cripple" Worldwide Web
- Cyborg "Terminators" eliminate Man

Note: Creating a "Terminator" requires integrating General AI among Physical, Cognitive, and Emotional Neural Networks. Look for them only in Sci-Fi Movies!

- Silicon-based Emergence characteristics unknown

Short-Term Benefits

- Human potential increased
- Scarcity eliminated (Robots drive production costs to "zero")
- Daily life made easier (Internet of Things, driverless vehicles, Caregivers)
- International Relations smoothed

Short-Term Drawbacks

- Machines replace Man (most job categories dominated by AI machines)
- Gap between Rich and Poor widens
- People become bored and withdraw into Virtual Reality
- Arms Race escalates to Robotics and Nanotechnology
- Tyranny replaces Liberal Democracies because people "give up"

The Jury is Still Out
(But Science makes a Stronger Case than the Arts)

- Empower R&D but establish "guidelines"
- Stay within Falsifiable Physics and Neuroscience principles
- Tipping point not on the Horizon and there should be advance warning
- Man is the Handiwork of a Blind Watchmaker

Artificial Intelligence and the American Psyche
(Reasons for Optimism)

Purpose of Video: Provide a summary of how AI impacts our American Culture. The interaction unfolds within the context of Neuroscience!

Start at the Source: the early 21st century "iGen Generation" (the first A.I-digital Generation)

The Good:

- Digital Natives (grew up with AI tools)
- Broad Context Social Awareness
- Independent Thinkers (access to unlimited data)
- Relationship Oriented (Social Networking)
- Tolerant of all Groups (Ethnic, Racial, Sexual Diversity welcomed)

The Bad:

- Reduced Attention Span (want immediate access/feedback)
- Less Physical Contact (withdraw into Cyberspace)
- Less Entrepreneurial (less confident, predisposed to alienation or depression, want security)

- Less engaged in political process
- Predisposed to "following" computer orders

How American Culture handled (redefined American Parenting Paradigm)

- Hover-parenting linked with accelerated/innovative schooling tracks
- Experimental Space for Relationships
- Increased independence at earlier age
- Male/Female Equality gap narrowed

The Outcome:

- America has the best equipped society for dealing with AI

AI Impact on "The Better Angels of our Nature"
(Measure by tracking "Violence")

Cruelty and Violence have been stains on human nature since prehistoric times. But until recently, they have trended downwards.

Observed Trends:

- Every transition to a new age brings conditions making cooperation "win-win"
- Sanctified forms of violence abolished (despotism, sacrifice, slavery)
- Countries stopped waging "many" wars
- Economic linkage assigns large penalties to violence
- As countries develop, emphasis on Human Rights and Dignity increases

Humanity's Inner Demons
(Embedded in our DNA)

- Predatory/Instrumental Violence (take what you want)
- Dominance (control the weak)
- Revenge (eye for an eye)
- Sadism (enjoyment inflicting pain)
- Ideological Vision of Utopia (kill those that won't convert)

Our Better Angels

- Empathy (people care about others)
- Self-Control (man is able to defer immediate gratification for the greater good)
- Moral Sense (people share a common code of conduct)
- Reason (rational thinking can often overcome emotional outbursts)

Historical Forces that Shaped Trends
(The Past is always less innocent and the present less Sinister)

- Leviathon: Creation of a state granted judicial monopoly of violence
- Commerce: Trade reduces violence
- Feminization: As the women's role expands, it tempers male predisposition to violence
- Escalation of Reason: Common sense always weighs in against violence

Is AI contributing to Increasing Violence?

- Could the Milgram Experiment come true? (People blindly following harmful orders)

- Possibly, but Human Nature is Robust and Conservative by Nature
- People equipped to deal with AI threats
- Humanity wants to preserve "what it means to be Human"

Possible Causes

- Escalating War between Islam and Christianity
- Techno-Plague "dummying down" Society's I.Q. (people afraid, intolerant, unwilling to stand up for themselves, readily follows orders)
- Government oversteps its bounds

Solutions

- Find a cure for the T-Plague
- Resolve the conflict between Islam and Christianity
- Informed and Intelligent Citizens reclaim more control of Governments

Page 357—Policy Issues for Macroeconomics

MACROECONOMICS: THE STUDY OF a National Economy. Economy built up of Individuals and Corporations for which Microeconomics applies.

Macroeconomics deals with "Big Issues"

- Economic Growth (A rising tide lifts all ships)
- Wages and Income Inequality (Must have a thriving Middle Class)
- Unemployment (People must have jobs in order to be Consumers)
- Interest Rates (Too high is bad domestically (stunts Borrowing or Investment) but good Internationally (stimulates Foreign Investment)
- Inflation (Erodes Purchasing Power Good for Borrowers Bad for Lenders)
- Foreign Trade and Foreign Exchange (Deals with Law of Comparative Advantage)
- Stability (Moderate "Boom and Bust" Cycles)
- Savings Rate
- Welfare Costs
- Government Regulation (Longer-term impact of Healthguard and Securityguard policies unknown)

Current Issues facing United States:

- Innovation/Technology drive Economic Growth.
- Genetic Engineering and Artificial Intelligence driving Innovation/Technology but Public fears them. China and Japan pushing ahead.
- T-Plague reducing Worker Productivity.
- Unemployment growing (AI replacing Workers T-Plague reducing pool of Smart People)
- Administration's Foreign Policy stance damaging International Relations
- Administration's short-term policies might damage economy longer-term (Punitive Immigration policies Restricting the use of Biotech and AI)
- Infrastructures (Power, Transportation, Communications) must be modernized.

Case in Point: Technology and the T-Plague

- Healthcare costs skyrocketing because of T-Plague Victims
- Genetic Engineering battles T-Plague
- People "afraid of Genetic Engineering" (Aldous Huxley's *Brave New World)*
- AI provides more Products and Services People want
- People losing jobs because they can't compete with Automation or because they aren't "smart enough"
- Low-Skilled and High-Skill jobs impacted. Low-Skill jobs at risk: Cashiers/Tellers Fast Food/Store Clerks Delivery/ Mail Carriers Order Pickers…
- High-Skill jobs at risk: Lawyers Accountants Truckers Foot Soldiers Police Firemen Pilots Financial Advisers Computer Programmers

- Teachers (all levels) Tutors Doctors Engineers Lab Techs Caregivers Fitness Trainers

In the Past, New Technology created more jobs than it destroyed. Will that still hold?

Jobs that appear to be immune from Technological Replacement:

- Personal Service Jobs: Salespersons Plumbers Barbers/Hair Stylists Cosmeticians Electricians Bar Tenders Mental Health/Substance-Abuse Counselors
- Clergy Negotiators Home Repair Persons
- Experiential Jobs: Actors/Entertainers Amusement Park/ Cruise Ship Workers
- Creative Jobs: Scientists Mathematicians Virtual Reality Developers Innovators Entrepreneurs Writers Politicians

"Stay tuned. Come to the next symposium to explore options. There is plenty we can do. We aren't helpless victims. We can help shape the future. Be part of the solution."

Page 362—A Summary of Behavioral Economics

- Behavioral Economics, based on Neuroscience/Cognitive Psychology, replaces Rational Economic Man with the Irrational Man. Supports current findings in Finance, Business, and Sales/Marketing.
- People have "Bounded Rationality" (We behave rationally only some of the time)
- Emerged in the late 1990's thanks to the work of Daniel Kahneman and Amos Tversky.
- Subject covered in higher-level courses. It adds to the mathematical techniques found in Neoclassical Economics elements of Man's Irrational Behavior.
- Adam Smith, the Founder of Economics, incorporated basic opposing psychological principles (Selfishness and Altruism). Read "The Theory of Moral Sentiments" or "Wealth of Nations".
- Its findings can be used to "manipulate" (for good or bad) People's economic, financial, or market behavior.

Built on Two Major Principles

- Prospect Theory: People are Risk Averse and view it asymmetrically.

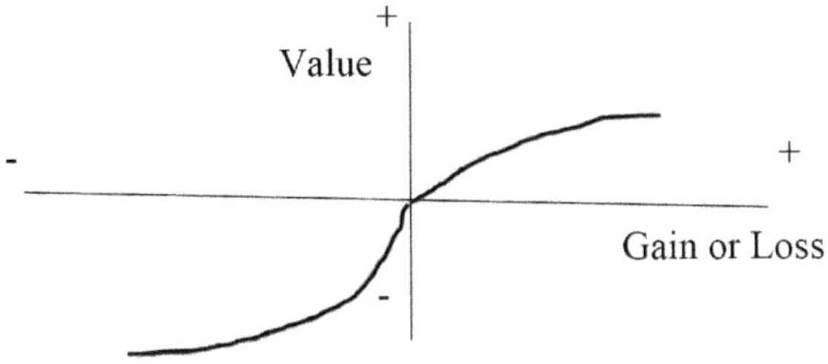

- Weighting Function: People aware of only small changes in wealth and underweight its probability of occurring (underestimate when probability low and overestimate when probability high).

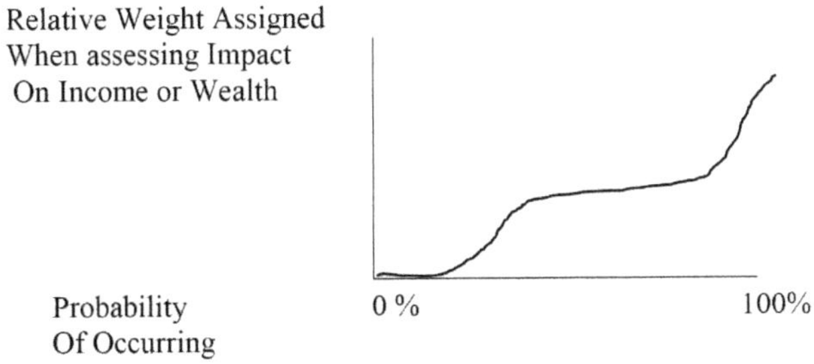

Some Major Findings

- No one is "good" at dealing with numbers (Thinking Slow).
- Thinking "fast"/intuitively can trip us up.
- We don't learn from our mistakes unless we make a big effort.
- People are "Overconfident" (Illusion of Understanding)
- People cling to what they believe even when they know it's wrong (Cognitive Dissonance)

- People give too much weight to what they know (WYSIATI What You See Is All There Is)
- People are influenced by their Subconscious or the Actions of Others (Anchoring and Framing and Herd Instinct)

Illustrative Applications

- "Nudging" People to do what is "good" for them or society (Organ Donor programs)
- Helping People's short-term behaviors consistent with long-term Values. (Stay on a Diet)
- Getting People to pay more than they should (Designer label Brands)
- Exploiting People's Weaknesses like : Gambling Drinking Drug Addiction (Overconfidence)
- 1630's Dutch Tulip Mania and 2008 Financial Meltdown (Herd Instinct).
- People buying Appliance, Automobile, or Funeral Insurance (Framing).

Presenter's Personal Takeaways

- People crave Social Interaction
- People are Risk Averse: Hate short-term losses even when long-term insignificant
- People's Actions always constrained because of unwanted consequences for Loved Ones
- Behavior drives Attitudes and Values, not Vice-Versa

Additional Observations

Think of Economics as the Politics of Free Market System (Who What Why Where When How)

Definition: The study of how men and society choose, with or without the use of money, to employ scarce productive resources to produce various commodities and services over time and to distribute them for consumption, now and in the future, among various people and groups in society. Divided into Microeconomics (Study of the Firm) and Macroeconomics (Study of National Economy)

Great Economists: Thomas Malthus ("Dismal" theory of Population Growth) John Stuart Mill (Utilitarianism) Adam Smith (Founder of Modern Economics) David Ricardo (Comparative Advantage)

Ludwig von Mises and disciple Friedrich von Hayak (Classical Liberalism and Rigorous Methodology) Peter Schumpeter (Creative Destruction) John Maynard Keynes (Fiscal Policy) Milton Friedman (Monetary Policy) Paul Samuelson (Neoclassical Economics) Daniel Kahneman and Amos Tversky (Behavioral Economics) Robert Schiller (Asset Pricing)

Economics came to prominence in the Enlightenment / Industrial Revolution

- Capitalism and Free Market Economies have withstood the test of time
- Directed or Controlled Capitalism attempts to "smooth" Boom and Bust Cycles

Page 401—Beyond Dark—Into the Invisible Top Secret++

"We own Land-Sea-Space because
We're Masters of Command and Control"

WEAPONS PROJECTS FOR COMMAND & Control:

Definitions: Command for integrating Multi-Vehicle Tactics

Control for piloting Individual Vehicle

C&C Projects:

- AI enhancements for UAV's and UMV's
- Networked Attack
- Surveillance & Fire Control (24/7 On-Station AWACS Drone Grid)

UAV and UMV Projects:

- Avionics Systems for Enemy Detection and Vehicle Cloaking/Stealth
- Super-cruise and Thrust Vectoring

Time-Travel Project:

- Time-Trapper Satellite Grid

Super-Soldier Projects:

- Modular Advanced Robotic Systems: Bomb Removal Weaponry
- Smart-Guns: Precision-Guided Firearms
- Active Denial Systems: Microwave Barriers
- Iron Man Exo-Skeletons for enhanced physical performance
- Plasma forcefields to neutralize "Incoming"
- EMP's to cancel Electromagnetic Field
- EMP Rail Guns
- Vehicle/Hand-Held Laser Guns

Bio-Tech Projects:

- Neuro-Priming Drugs for enhanced physical/psychological performance
- Computer chips interfacing Brain to Computer/Exo-Suits
- Cybernetic Implants for Sensory Enhancement

Page 414—The Psychological and Philosophical Roots of Happiness

- Happiness and Depression polar opposites
- Low levels of Neurotransmitters affect both feelings

We will report Major Findings from Longitudinal Study investigating Why People are Happy and integrate findings with teachings of Six Philosophers.

Major Findings:

- Money or Fame will not lead to happiness. Happiness found in Relationships with the People or Ideas
- Keep active physically and mentally
- Stay socially connected. Loneliness is toxic. Have close friends and family relationships/support group
- Maintain Hi-Quality Relationships. Better to break away than remain in high-conflict Co-Friendships
- Good Relationships protect Brain and Body

What the Philosophers Say (Recommended reading: *The Consolations of Philosophy* by Alain de Botton)

- Happiness comes from following simple advice
- Socrates: Seek the Truth even if it makes you unpopular
- Epicurus: Balance the Simple Pleasures
- Seneca: Be stoic when facing Adversity

- de Montaigne: Acknowledge your Body
- Schopenhauer: Do not count on Romantic Love. Unconscious urges lead us astray.
- Nietzsche: Life is difficult. Endure suffering if it leads to fulfillment.

EACH OF US IS RESPONSIBLE FOR OUR OWN HAPPINESS!

Page 445—"The Second Coming" Guardian Party Slouching Towards Washington

American Experiment in danger of Foundering. 21st century Liberalism in Jeopardy:

- Public's I.Q. damaged (T-Plague)
- Public's Tolerance diminished (Terrorism)
- Public's Primacy endangered (Technology)

"Perfect Storm" catapulted Guardian Party to Prominence

Primer on Liberalism. A Sociopolitical Philosophy that:

- Advances Mankind beyond corrupt governance and outmoded beliefs
- Promotes Liberty and Equality based on Democratic Principles supporting Rights and Human Dignity.
- Defeated 20th century Fascism and Communism
- Took 500 Years to reach 21st century American Apex

Liberalism's Success insidiously sows the seeds of its Failure

- Divides into Conservative Liberalism (Individualism and Free/Global Markets) versus Progressive Liberalism (Statism and Conformity)
- Political Polarization and Economic Inequality

- Both grow inexorably/symbiotically
- Institutional Damage (Impersonal Leviathon)
- Economic Damage (Ruthless Zero-Sum competition)
- Educational Damage (STEM emphasized Liberal Arts devalued)
- Technological Damage (Conquest of Nature)
- Societal Damage (Culture and Customs devalued Alienation, Frustration, and Helplessness grow)

Early 21st Century Political Philosophers/Scientists proactively addressed the Causes after America lost First Cyberwar (2016 Presidential Election Battleground) and offered Solutions

- Educated and Smart Public demanded Politocos become Statesmen
- "Better Angels of Our Nature" spotlighted
- Liberalism's destabilizing factors reined in
- State and Local involvement emphasized

But a "Perfect Storm" derailed improvements!

Steps to take NOW

- Guard against Unilateral Guardian Party Policies
- Guard against Demagoguery
- Guard against Short-Term Focus at the Expense of Longer-Term Cultural Inheritance
- Eliminate T-Plague and Middle East Terrorism

CPSIA information can be obtained
at www.ICGtesting.com
Printed in the USA
BVHW031653191118
533073BV00001BA/1/P

9 781949 362817